JOURNEY
to the
WEST

JOURNEY
to the
WEST

by Wu Cheng'en

Translated by W. J. F. Jenner

Volume I

FOREIGN LANGUAGES PRESS   BEIJING

First Edition 1982
Second Edition 1990
Second Printing 1995

TRANSLATOR'S ACKNOWLEDGEMENTS

I am deeply grateful to Li Rongxi for giving generously of his broad, profound and many-sided scholarship in removing errors from this version and resolving problems. I am also greatly indebted to the staff of the Foreign Languages Press, and especially to Huang Jingying for the infinite patience and care with which she has checked and improved typescript and proofs. Responsibility for the many remaining mistakes is mine.

W. J. F. J.

ISBN 7-119-00653-3
English Translation © by W.J.F.Jenner

Published by Foreign Languages Press
24 Baiwanzhuang Road, Beijing 100037, China

Printed by Beijing Foreign Languages Printing House
19 Chegongzhuang Xilu, Beijing 100044, China

Distributed by China International Book Trading Corporation
35 Chegongzhuang Xilu, Beijing 100044, China
P.O. Box 399, Beijing, China

Printed in the People's Republic of China

PUBLISHER'S NOTE

This is a complete three-volume translation of the Chinese edition of *Journey to the West* in 100 chapters published in 1955 by the Beijing People's Literature Publishing House.

A well-known mythological novel based on folk tales, *Journey to the West* was probably put into its present form in the 1570s by Wu Cheng'en (1500-82).

Many different editions of the novel have appeared over the past 400 years. The Chinese edition of 1955 was based on the earliest known edition, the Shidetang woodblock edition printed in Nanjing in the 20th year of Wanli reign (1592) in the Ming Dynasty, and was further checked against six different editions from the Qing Dynasty.

The illustrations were selected from a lithographic edition (New Edition of Pictures for *"Journey to the West"*) published in the 14th year (1888) of the Emperor Guangxu of the Qing Dynasty.

A "Translator's Afterword" will be found at the end of Volume 3.

The Lord Buddha

二郎神

The God Erlang

唐太宗

The Tang Emperor Taizong

唐僧

Sanzang, the Tang Priest

孫行者

Monkey (Sun Wukong)

猪八戒

Pig (Zhu Bajie)

沙僧

Friar Sand (Sha Wujing)

鐵扇公主

Princess Iron Fan

蜘蛛精

The Spider Spirit

獅子精

The Lion Spirit

CONTENTS

猴王出世
流水性
大修
生持
道山源

The Divine Root conceives and the spring
breaks forth;
As the mind's nature is cultivated,
the Great Way arises.

Before Chaos was divided, Heaven and Earth were one;
All was a shapeless blur, and no men had appeared.
Once Pan Gu destroyed the Enormous Vagueness
The separation of clear and impure began.

Living things have always tended towards humanity;
From their creation all beings improve.
If you want to know about Creation and Time,
Read Difficulties Resolved on the Journey to the West.

In the arithmetic of the universe, 129,600 years make one cycle.
Each cycle can be divided into twelve phases: I, II, III, IV, V,
VI, VII, VIII, IX, X, XI and XII, the twelve branches.* Each
phase lasts 10,800 years.

Now within a single day, the positive begins at the time
I; at II the cock crows; at III it is not quite light; at IV the
sun rises; V is after breakfast; and at VI one does business.
VII is when the sun reaches noon; at VIII it is slipping towards
the west; IX is late afternoon; the sun sets at X; XI is dusk;
and at XII people settle down for the night.

If you compare this with the big numbers, then at the end
of Phase XI Heaven and Earth became blurred and everything
was in an inauspicious state. 5,400 years later came the beginning of Phase XII, when all was darkness and both human

---

* Represented also by twelve animals: mouse, bull, tiger, hare, dragon,
serpent, horse, goat, monkey, cock, dog, and pig.

beings and inanimate things vanished from the world, for this reason it was called Chaos. Another 5,400 years later Phase XII was drawing to a close and a new cycle was about to begin. As Phase I of the new era approached, gradually there was light. As Shao Yong said,

> "When the winter solstice is at the mid-point of Phase I
> The heart of Heaven does not move.
> Where the Positive first appears
> Nothing has yet come to life."

At this time, Heaven first had a foundation. 5,400 years later, in the middle of Phase I, the light and pure rose upwards, and sun, moon, stars, and constellations were created. These were called the Four Images. Hence the saying that heaven began in I.

Another 5,400 years later, when Phase I was nearing its end and Phase II was imminent, things gradually solidified. As the *Book of Changes* says, "Great is the Positive; far-reaching is the Negative! All things are endowed and born in accordance with Heaven." This was when the earth began to congeal. After 5,400 more years came the height of Phase II, when the heavy and impure solidified, and water, fire, mountains, stone, and Earth came into being. These five were called the Five Movers. Therefore it is said that the Earth was created in Phase II.

After a further 5,400 years, at the end of Phase II and the beginning of the Phase III, living beings were created. In the words of the *Book of the Calendar*: "The essence of the sky came down and the essence of earth went up. Heaven and Earth intermingled, and all creatures were born." Then Heaven was bright and Earth was fresh, and the Positive intermingled with the Negative. 5,400 years later, when Phase III was at its height, men, birds and beasts were created. Thus the Three Primaries — Heaven, Earth and Man — now had their set places. Therefore it is said that man was created in Phase III.

Moved by Pan Gu's creation, the Three Emperors put the world in order and the Five Rulers laid down the moral code.

The world was then divided into four great continents: The Eastern Continent of Superior Body, the Western Continent of Cattle-gift, the Southern Continent of Jambu and the Northern Continent of Kuru. This book deals only with the Eastern Continent of Superior Body. Beyond the seas there is a country called Aolai. This country is next to an ocean, and in the middle of the ocean is a famous island called the Mountain of Flowers and Fruit. This mountain is the ancestral chain of the Ten Continents, the origin of the Three Islands; it was formed when the clear and impure were separated and the Enormous Vagueness was divided. It is a really splendid mountain and there are some verses to prove it:

It stills the ocean with its might,
It awes the jade sea into calm.
It stills the ocean with its might:
Tides wash its silver slopes and fish swim into its caves.
It awes the jade sea into calm:
Amid the snowy breakers the sea-serpent rises from the
    deep.

It rises high in the corner of the world where Fire and
    Wood meet;
Its summit towers above the Eastern Sea.
Red cliffs and strange rocks;
Beetling crags and jagged peaks.
On the red cliffs phoenixes sing in pairs;
Lone unicorns lie before the beetling crags.
The cry of pheasants is heard upon the peaks;
In caves the dragons come and go.

There are flowers of jade and strange plants that wither
Miraculous birds and black cranes in the trees.
There are flowers of jade and strange plants that wither
    not;
Green pine and bluish cypress ever in leaf,
Magic peaches always in fruit.
Clouds gather round the tall bamboo.
The wisteria grows thick around the mountain brook.

And the banks around are newly-coloured with flowers.
It is the Heaven-supporting pillar where all the rivers
*   meet,*
The Earth's root, unchanged through a myriad aeons.

There was once a magic stone on the top of this mountain
which was thirty-six feet five inches high and twenty-four feet
round. It was thirty-six feet five inches high to correspond
with the 365 degrees of the heavens, and twenty-four feet round
to match the twenty-four divisions of the solar calendar. On
top of it were nine apertures and eight holes, for the Nine
Palaces and the Eight Trigrams. There were no trees around
it to give shade, but magic fungus and orchids clung to its sides.
Ever since Creation began it had been receiving the truth of
Heaven, the beauty of Earth, the essence of the Sun and the
splendour of the Moon; and as it had been influenced by them
for so long it had miraculous powers. It developed a magic
womb, which burst open one day to produce a stone egg about
the size of a ball.

When the wind blew on this egg it turned into a stone
monkey, complete with the five senses and four limbs. When
the stone monkey had learnt to crawl and walk, he bowed to
each of the four quarters. As his eyes moved, two beams of
golden light shot towards the Pole Star Palace and startled the
Supreme Heavenly · Sage, the Greatly Compassionate Jade
Emperor of the Azure Vault of Heaven, who was sitting surrounded by his immortal ministers on his throne in the Hall
of Miraculous Mist in the Golden-gated Cloud Palace. When
he saw the dazzling golden light he ordered Thousand-mile
Eye and Wind-accompanying Ear to open the Southern Gate
of Heaven and take a look. The two officers went out through
the gate in obedience to the imperial command, and while one
observed what was going on the other listened carefully. Soon
afterwards they reported back:

"In obedience to the Imperial Mandate your subjects
observed and listened to the source of the golden light. We
found that at the edge of the country of Aolai, which is east

of the ocean belonging to the Eastern Continent of Superior Body, there is an island called the Mountain of Flowers and Fruit. A magic stone on the top of this mountain produced a magic egg, and when the wind blew on this egg it turned into a stone monkey which bowed to each of the four quarters. When he moved his eyes, golden light shot towards the Pole Star Palace; but now that he is eating and drinking, the golden light is gradually dying."

In his benevolence and mercy the Jade Emperor said, "Creatures down below are born of the essence of heaven and earth: there is nothing remarkable about him."

On his mountain the monkey was soon able to run and jump, feed from plants and trees, drink from brooks and springs, pick mountain flowers and look for fruit. He made friends with the wolves, went around with the tigers and leopards, was on good terms with the deer, and had the other monkeys and apes for relations. At night he slept under the rockfaces, and he roamed around the peaks and caves by day. As the saying so rightly goes, "There is no calendar in the mountains, and when winter's over you don't know the time of year." On hot mornings he and all the other monkeys would play under the shade of some pines to avoid the heat. Just look at them all:

Climbing trees, picking flowers, looking for fruit;
Throwing pellets, playing knucklebones;
Running round sandy hollows, building stone pagodas;
Chasing dragonflies and catching locusts;
Worshipping the sky and visiting Bodhisattvas;
Tearing off creepers and weaving straw hats;
Catching fleas then popping them with their teeth and
    fingers;
Grooming their coats and sharpening their nails;
Beating, scratching, pushing, squashing, tearing and
    tugging;
Playing all over the place under the pine trees;
Washing themselves beside the green stream.

After playing, the monkeys would go and bathe in the stream, a mountain torrent that tumbled along like rolling melons. There is an old saying, "Birds have bird language and animals have animal talk." All the monkeys said to each other, "I wonder where that water comes from. We've got nothing else to do today, so wouldn't it be fun to go upstream and find its source?" With a shout they all ran off, leading their children and calling to their brothers. They climbed up the mountain beside the stream until they reached its source, where a waterfall cascaded from a spring.
They saw

> One white rainbow arching,
> A thousand strands of flying snow,
> Unbroken by the sea winds,
> Still there under the moon.
>
> Cold air divides the greeny crags,
> Splashes moisten the mountainside;
> A noble waterfall cascades,
> Hanging like a curtain.

The monkeys clapped their hands and exclaimed with delight, "What lovely water. It must go all the way to the bottom of the mountain and join the waves of the sea."

Then one monkey made a suggestion: "If anyone is clever enough to go through the fall, find the source, and come out in one piece, let's make him our king." When this challenge had been shouted three times, the stone monkey leapt out from the crowd and answered at the top of his voice, "I'll go, I'll go." Splendid monkey! Indeed,

> Today he will make his name;
> Tomorrow his destiny shall triumph.
> He is fated to live here;
> As a King he will enter the Immortals' palace.

Watch him as he shuts his eyes, crouches, and springs, leaping straight into the waterfall. When he opened his eyes and raised his head to look round, he saw neither water nor waves. A bridge stood in front of him, as large as life. He stopped, calmed himself, took a closer look, and saw that the bridge was made of iron. The water that rushed under it poured out through a fissure in the rocks, screening the gateway to the bridge. He started walking towards the bridge, and as he looked he made out what seemed to be a house. It was a really good place. He saw:

> *Emerald moss piled up in heaps of blue,*
> *White clouds like drifting jade,*
> *While the light flickered among wisps of coloured mist.*
>
> *A quiet house with peaceful windows,*
> *Flowers growing on the smooth bench;*
> *Dragon pearls hanging in niches,*
> *Exotic blooms all around.*
> *Traces of fire beside the stove,*
> *Scraps of food in the vessels by the table.*
> *Adorable stone chairs and beds,*
> *Even better stone plates and bowls.*
>
> *One or two tall bamboos,*
> *Three or four springs of plum blossom,*
> *A few pines that always attract rain,*
> *All just like a real home.*

He took a good, long look and then scampered to the middle of the bridge, from where he noticed a stone tablet. On the tablet had been carved in big square letters:

HAPPY LAND OF THE MOUNTAIN OF FLOWERS
    AND FRUIT
CAVE HEAVEN OF THE WATER CURTAIN.

The stone monkey was beside himself with glee. He rushed away, shut his eyes, crouched, and leapt back through the waterfall. "We're in luck, we're in luck," he said with a chuckle. All the other monkeys crowded round him asking, "What's it like in there? How deep is the water?" "There's no water, none at all," replied the stone monkey. "There's an iron bridge,

and on the other side of the bridge there's a house that must
have been made by Heaven and Earth." "How ever could you
see a house there?" the other monkeys asked. The stone
monkey chuckled again. "The water here comes under the
bridge and through the rocks, and it hides the gateway to the
bridge from view. There are flowers and trees by the bridge,
and a stone house too. Inside the house are stone rooms, a
stone stove, stone bowls, stone plates, stone beds, and even
stone benches. In the middle of it all is a tablet which says
'Happy Land of the Mountain of Flowers and Fruit, Cave
Heaven of the Water Curtain'. It's just the place for us to settle
down in — there's room there for thousands. Let's all move in,
then we won't have to put up with any more nonsense from heav-
en. In there

> *We can hide there from the wind,*
> *And shelter from the rain,*
> *With nothing to fear from frost and snow,*
> *And never a rumble of thunder.*
>
> *The coloured mists glow bright*
> *And the place smells lucky.*
> *The pine and bamboo will always be beautiful,*
> *And rare flowers blossom every day."*

The other monkeys were all so delighted to hear this that
they said, "You go first and take us with you." The stone monkey shut his eyes, crouched, and leapt in again, shouting, "Follow me in, follow me in." The braver monkeys all jumped
through. The more timid ones peered forward, shrank back,
rubbed their ears, scratched their cheeks, shouted, and yelled at
the top of their voices, before going in, all clinging to each other.
After rushing across the bridge they all grabbed plates and
snatched bowls, bagged stoves and fought over beds, and moved
everything around. Monkeys are born naughty and they could
not keep quiet for a single moment until they had worn themselves out moving things around.

The stone monkey sat himself in the main seat and said,
"Gentlemen, 'A man who breaks his word is worthless.' Just

now you said that if anyone was clever enough to come in here and get out again in one piece, you'd make him king. Well, then. I've come in and gone out, and gone out and come in. I've found you gentlemen a cave heaven where you can sleep in peace and all settle down to live in bliss. Why haven't you made me king?" On hearing this all the monkeys bowed and prostrated themselves, not daring to disobey. They lined up in groups in order of age and paid their homage as at court, all acclaiming him as the "Great King of a Thousand Years". The stone monkey then took the throne, made the word "stone" taboo, and called himself Handsome Monkey King. There is a poem to prove it that goes:

> All things are born from the Three Positives;
> The magic stone was quick with the essence of sun and
>   moon.
> An egg was turned into a monkey to complete the Great
>   Way;
> He was lent a name so that the elixir would be complete.
> Looking inside he perceives nothing because it has no
>   form,
> Outside he uses his intelligence to create visible things.
> Men have always been like this:
> Those who are called kings and sages do just as they
>   wish.

Taking control of his host of monkeys, apes, gibbons and others, the Handsome Monkey King divided them into rulers and subjects, assistants and officers. In the morning they roamed the Mountain of Flowers and Fruit and in the evening they settled down for the night in the Water Curtain Cave. They made a compact that they would not join the ranks of the birds or go with the running beasts. They had their own king, and they thoroughly enjoyed themselves.

> In spring they picked flowers for food and drink,
> In summer they lived off fruit.
> In autumn they gathered taros and chestnuts;
> They got through the winter on Solomon's-seal.

The Handsome Monkey King's innocent high spirits could not, of course, last three or four hundred years. One day he suddenly felt depressed during a banquet with his monkey host, and he started to weep. The startled monkeys crowded round, bowed to him and asked, "What's the matter, Your Majesty?" "Although I'm happy now," the Monkey King replied, "I'm worried about the future. That's what's getting me down." The other monkeys laughed and said, "Your Majesty is being greedy. We have parties every day; we live in a mountain paradise, in an ancient cave in a divine continent. We are spared the rule of unicorns, the domination of phoenixes, and the restraints of human kings. We are free to do just as we like — we are infinitely lucky. Why make yourself miserable worrying about the future?" To this the Monkey King replied, "Yes, we don't have to submit to the laws and regulations of human kings, and we don't live in terror of the power of birds and beasts. But the time will come when we are old and weak, and the underworld is controlled by the King of Hell. When the time comes for us to die, we won't be able to go on living among the Blessed, and our lives will have been in vain." All the monkeys covered their faces and wept as everyone of them thought about death.

Suddenly a gibbon jumped out from their ranks and shrieked in a piercing voice, "If Your Majesty is thinking so far ahead, this is the beginning of enlightenment. Now of the Five Creatures, there are only three that do not come under the jurisdiction of the King of Hell." "Do you know which they are?" asked the Monkey King. "Yes," the ape replied. "They are the Buddhas, the Immortals and the Sages. They are free from the Wheel of Reincarnation. They are not born and they do not die. They are as eternal as Heaven and Earth, as the mountains and the rivers." "Where do they live?" the Monkey King asked. "Only in the human world," the ape replied, "in ancient caves on magic mountains." The Monkey King was delighted to hear this. "I shall leave you all tomorrow," he said, "and go down the mountain. If I have to, I'll roam the corners of the oceans and go to the edge of the sky to find these

three kinds of beings and discover the secret of eternal youth
that will keep us out of the clutches of the King of Hell for
ever." Goodness! Because of these words he was to learn
how to be free from the Wheel of Reincarnation and become
the Great Sage Equalling Heaven. All the monkeys clapped
with approval and said, "Great! Great! Tomorrow we'll
climb all over the mountain and get lots of fruit to give Your
Majesty a really big banquet to send you off."

The next day the monkeys set out to pick magic peaches,
gather rare fruits, dig out yams, and cut Solomon's-seal. Magic
fungus and fragrant orchid were collected, and everything was
set on the stone benches and the stone tables, with fairy wine
and dishes. You could see

> Golden pills and pearl pellets,
> Bursting red and plump yellow.
> The golden pills and pearl pellets were winter cherries,
>   beautiful and sweet;
> The bursting red and plump yellow were ripe plums,
>   tasty and sharp.
> Fresh, sweet-fleshed longans with thin skins,
> Fiery lichees with tiny stones in a red sack.
> Branch after branch of crab-apples,
> Yellow-skinned loquats with their leaves on.
> Rabbit-head pears and chicken-heart jujubes
> To quench your thirst, remove your cares, and sober you
>   up.
> Fragrant peaches and tender apricots,
> As sweet and luscious as jade wine.
>
> Crisp plums and arbutus,
> As sharp as glistening yoghurt.
> Ripe melons with red coats and black seeds,
> Big, four-sectioned persimmons with yellow skins.
> Bursting pomegranates:
> Cinnabar pips shining like fire-crystal pearls.
> Opened water-chestnuts
> With firm round flesh like golden agate.

Walnuts and gingko fruits to eat with tea;
Coconuts and grapes to make into wine.
Dishes loaded with pine cones, yew-nuts, filberts, and
   crab-apples;
Tangerines, sugar-cane and oranges covering the table.
Hot roast yams,
Tender boiled Solomon's-seal.
Pounded china-root and Job's tears.
Simmered in broth in a pot of stone.
Although we humans have rare delicacies to eat,
We are no happier than those monkeys in the mountains.

The host of monkeys ushered the Handsome Monkey King to the seat of honour and sat down below him according to age. Each of them took it in turns to bring him wine, flowers, and fruit, and they drank hard for a whole day. The next morning the Handsome Monkey King got up early and ordered, "Children, tear down some old pines and make me a raft. Find a bamboo pole to punt with and load it up with fruit. I'm going." He went aboard the raft all by himself, pushed off with all his might, and floated off towards the waves of the ocean. He intended to sail with the wind and cross over to the Southern Jambu Continent.

The heaven-born monkey, whose conduct was so noble,
Left his island to drift with heaven's winds.
He sailed oceans and seas to find the Way of Im-
   mortality,
Deeply determined to do a great deed.
The predestined one should not have vulgar longings;
He can attain the primal truth without care or worry.
He is bound to find a kindred spirit,
To explain the origins and the laws of nature.

He had chosen just the right time for his journey. After he boarded his raft the southeasterly wind blew hard for days on end and bore him to the northwestern shore of the Southern Continent. Testing the depth of the water with his pole he found that it was shallow, so he abandoned the raft and jumped ashore. He saw humans by the coast, fishing, hunting geese, gathering clams, and extracting salt. He went up to them, leaping around and making faces, which so scared them that they dropped their baskets and nets and fled in all directions as fast as they could. The Monkey King grabbed one of them who was a poor runner, stripped him of his clothes, and dressed himself in them like a human. He swaggered through the provinces and prefectures, learning human behaviour and human speech in the market places. Whether he was eating his breakfast or going to bed at night he was always asking about Buddhas, Immortals and Sages, and seeking the secret of eternal youth. He observed that the people of the world were too concerned with fame and fortune to be interested in their fates.

> When will the struggle for fame and fortune end?
> Toiling from morning till night, never pleasing yourself.
> Those who ride donkeys long for stallions,
> The Prime Minister always wants to be a prince.
> For food and clothing they endure great hardship;
> They never worry that the King of Hell will come to get them.
> When trying to ensure their sons and grandsons inherit their wealth and power,
> Not one will ever turn back and repent.

Although he asked about the way of the Immortals, the Monkey King was unable to meet one. He spent eight or nine years in the Southern Jambu Continent, going through its great walls and visiting its little counties. When he found that he had reached the Great Western Ocean he thought that there must be sages and immortals on the other side of it, so he made himself another raft like the last one, and floated across the Western Ocean until he came to the Western Continent of Cattle-gift. He went ashore and made extensive and lengthy enquiries until one day he came upon a high and beautiful mountain, thickly forested on its lower slopes. Not fearing wolves, and undaunted by tigers or leopards, he climbed to the summit to see the view. It was indeed a fine mountain:

A thousand peaks brandishing halberds,
Screens ten thousand measures tall.
In the sunlight the mountain haze is lightly touched with
*   blue;*
After the rain the black rocks look coldly green.
Withered creepers coil round ancient trees,
And the old ford marks the bounds of the mysterious.
Rare flowers and precious plants,
Tall bamboos and lofty pines.
Tall bamboos and lofty pines,
Green for ever and matching the land of the blessed;
Rare flowers and precious plants,
Flourishing in all four seasons, rivalling fairyland.
The nearby cry of a hidden bird,
The clear running of a spring.
Valley upon valley of magic mushroom and orchid,
Lichen growing all over the cliffs.
The range rises and dips in dragon-like majesty.
Surely there must be lofty hermits here.

As he was looking at the view the Monkey King heard a
human voice coming from the depths of the forest. He rushed
into the trees, and when he cocked his ear to listen he heard
a song:

"Watching the chess game I cut through the rotten,
Felling trees, chop, chop.
Strolling at the edge of the cloud and the mouth of the
*   valley,*
I sell firewood to buy wine,
Cackling with laughter and perfectly happy.

By a green path in autumn,
I pillow myself on a pine root, looking up at the moon.
When I wake up it is light.
Recognizing the old forest
I scale cliffs and cross ridges,
Cutting down withered creepers with my axe.

When I've gathered enough to make a load
I walk down to the market with a song,
And trade it for three pints of rice.
Nobody else competes with me,
So prices are stable.
I don't speculate or try sharp practice,
Couldn't care less what people think of me,
Calmly lengthening my days.
The people I meet
Either Taoists or Immortals,
Quietly sitting to expound the Yellow Court."

The Monkey King was overjoyed to hear this, and he said
with glee, "So this is where the immortals have been hiding."
He bounded deeper into the woods for a closer look and saw
that the singer was a woodcutter cutting firewood.   He was
wearing the most unusual clothes:

On his head he wore a hat
Woven from the first skin shed by new bamboo shoots.
The clothes on his body
Were made of yarn from the wild cotton-tree.
The belt round his waist
Was of silk from an old silkworm.
The straw sandals under his feet
Had straps torn from rotten sago trees.
In his hand he held a steel axe
On his back he carried a hempen rope
At climbing pines and felling dead trees,
Who was a match for this woodcutter?

The Monkey King went closer and called to him, "Old Immortal, your disciple greets you." The woodcutter dropped his
axe in astonishment and turned round to say, "No, no. I don't
even have enough to eat or drink, so how can I possibly let you
call me an Immortal?"   "If you're not an Immortal," the
Monkey King said, "why do you talk like one?"   "I don't talk
like an Immortal." the woodcutter said.   "At the edge of the

wood just now," the Monkey King replied, "I heard you say,
'The people I meet are Taoist or immortals, quietly sitting
to expound the *Yellow Court*.' It contains the truth about
the Way, so if you're not an Immortal, what are you?" The
woodcutter laughed. "It's quite true that the song is called
*Mantingfang,** and an immortal who lives near my hut
taught me it. He said he saw how hard I had to work and
how I was always worried, so he made me sing this song when
things were getting me down. It lightens my cares and makes
me forget my weariness. I was singing it just now because
I had some problems on my mind, and I never imagined that
you would be listening." "If you've got an immortal for a
neighbour, you ought to learn from him how to cultivate your
conduct and get him to teach you a recipe for eternal youth."
"I've had a hard life," the woodcutter replied. "My mother
and father brought me up till I was about eight, and just when
I was beginning to know about life my father died. My mother
remained a widow, and I had no brothers or sisters. As I
was the only child I had to look after my mother morning
and night. Now she is old that I can't possibly leave her.
Our land is so overgrown that I can't grow enough to feed and
clothe both or us, so I have to cut a couple of bundles of firewood to sell in the market for a handful of coppers to buy the
few pints of rice that I cook for myself and for my mother.
That's why I can't cultivate my conduct."

"From what you say," the Monkey King replied, "you're a
filial son and a gentleman — you're bound to be rewarded for it
one day. But I'd be grateful if you could show me where that
immortal lives, so that I can go and pay him my respects." The
woodcutter said, "It's not far from here. This mountain is the
Spirit Tower Heart Mountain, and in it there is the Cave of
the Setting Moon and the Three Stars. In that cave lives an
Immortal called the Patriarch Subhuti. I don't know how many
disciples he has trained — there are thirty or forty of them cul-

---

* The name of the song he was singing.

tivating their conduct with him at the moment. If you take that path south for two or three miles you'll reach his home." The Monkey King tugged at the woodcutter and said, "Take me there, Elder Brother. If I get anything out of this, I won't forget your kindness." "You idiot," the woodcutter replied, "didn't you understand what I told you just now? If I went with you I wouldn't be able to earn my living, and who would look after my poor old mother then? I've got to get on with my woodcutting. Go by yourself."

After hearing this the Monkey King had to take his leave. He came out of the forest and found the path, which led up a mountain slope for two or three miles, when he saw the cave. He pulled himself up to his full height to take a look, and it was a really magnificent place:

> Misty clouds scattered colours,
> Sun and moon shimmered bright.
> A thousand ancient cypresses,
> Ten thousand lofty bamboos.
> A thousand ancient cypresses,
> A soft green drawing the rain from the sky.
> Ten thouand lofty bamboos,
> And a misty valley is azure blue.
> Outside the gate rare flowers spread brocade;
> Beside the bridge wafts the scent of jade blooms.
> Rocky crags jut, glossy with green moss;
> On overhanging cliffs blue lichen grows.
> Sometimes the call of the crane is heard,
> And often you see the phoenix soar.
> The call of the crane
> Echoes beyond the Ninth Heaven and the Milky Way.
> When the phoenix soars,
> The brilliance of its wings colours the clouds.
> Black apes and white deer can be just made out;
> Golden lions and jade elephants prefer to keep hidden.
> If you look closely at this happy land,
> You will see that it rivals paradise.

He saw that the doors of the cave were shut fast, and that everything was still, with no signs of any people. He turned round and noticed that there was a stone tablet about thirty feet high and eight feet wide at the top of the cliff. On it was carved in enormous letters:

SPIRIT-TOWER HEART MOUNTAIN, CAVE OF THE SETTING MOON AND THE THREE STARS.

The Monkey King exclaimed with delight, "The people here really are honest. The mountain and the cave do exist." He took a good long look, but did not dare to knock on the door. He climbed to the end of a pine branch and ate some pine seeds to amuse himself.

Before long the doors of the cave opened with a creak, and an immortal boy came out. In the nobility of his bearing and the exceptional purity of his features he was completely different from an ordinary boy.

> *His hair was bound with a pair of silken bands,*
> *His flowing gown had two capacious sleeves.*
> *His face and body were naturally distinguished;*
> *His mind and appearance were both detached.*
>
> *For many years a guest beyond the world of things,*
> *An eternal child amid the mountains,*
> *Untouched by any speck of dust,*
> *He let the years go tumbling by.*

When this boy had come out he shouted, "Who's making that row out here?" The Monkey King scampered down the tree, went up to him, and said with a bow, "Immortal child, I am a disciple who has come to ask about the Way and study under the Immortal. The last thing I'd do would be to make a row here." The boy laughed. "So you've come to ask about the Way, have you?" "Yes," the Monkey King replied. "Our master has just got up," the boy said, "and has now mounted the dais to expound the Way. Before he had started to explain about origins he told me to open the door. He said, 'There is

someone outside who wants to cultivate his conduct. Go and
welcome him.' I suppose he must have meant you." "Yes, he
meant me," the Monkey King said with a smile. "Come with
me," the boy said.

The Monkey King straightened his clothes and followed the
boy deep into the depths of the cave. He saw majestic pavilions
and towers of red jade, pearl palaces and gateways of cowrie,
and countless rooms of silence and secluded cells leading all
the way to a jasper dais. He saw the Patriarch Subhuti sitting
on the dais and thirty minor immortals standing below it.

> *A golden immortal of great enlightenment, free from
> filth,*
> *Subhuti, the marvel of the Western World.*
> *Neither dying nor born, he practises the triple medita-*
> *tion,*
> *His spirit and soul entirely benevolent.*
>
> *In empty detachment he follows the changes;*
> *Having found his true nature he lets it run free.*
> *As eternal as Heaven, and majestic in body,*
> *The great teacher of the Law is enlightened through*
> *aeons.*

As soon as the Handsome Monkey King saw him he bowed
low and knocked his head on the ground before him many
times, saying, "Master, master, your disciple pays his deepest
respects." "Where are you from?" the Patriarch asked. "You
must tell me your name and address before you can become my
pupil." "I come from the Water Curtain Cave in the Flowers
and Fruit Mountain in the land of Aolai in the Eastern Continent of Superior Body," replied the Monkey King. "Throw
him out," the Patriarch roared. "He's a liar and a cheat, and
even if he tried cultivating his conduct he would get nowhere."
The Monkey King desperately kept hitting his head on the
ground and said, "Your disciple spoke the truth. I promise I
wasn't lying." The Patriarch asked, "If you were speaking the
truth, why did you say that you came from the Eastern Con-

tinent of Superior Body? Between here and the Eastern Continent there are two seas and the Southern Jambu Continent, so how could you possibly have come here from there?" The Monkey King, still kowtowing, replied, "I sailed across seas and oceans, crossed frontiers and wandered through many countries for over ten years before I arrived here."

"So you came here by stages," the Patriarch remarked. "What is your surname?" "I'm not surely," the Monkey King replied. "If people call me names it doesn't bother me, and if they hit me I don't get angry. I'm just polite to them and that's that. I've never been surely." "I didn't ask if you were surely. I wanted to know the surname you inherited from your parents." "I didn't have any parents," the Monkey King replied. "If you had no parents, did you grow on a tree?" "I grew not on a tree but in a stone," the Monkey King replied. "All I remember is that there was a magic stone on the top of the Flowers and Fruit Mountain, and that one year the stone split open and I was born." Concealing his delight at hearing this, the Patriarch remarked, "In other words, you were born of Heaven and Earth. Walk around for a moment and let me have a look at you." The Monkey King leapt to his feet and shambled round a couple of times. The Patriarch smiled and said, "Though you have rather a base sort of body, you look like one of the rhesus monkeys that eat pine seeds, and I ought to give you a surname that fits your appearance and call you Hu ('Macaque'). The elements that make up the character Hu are 'animal', 'old' and 'moon'. What is old is ancient, and the moon embodies the Negative principle; and what is ancient and Negative cannot be transformed. But I think I would do much better to call you Sun ('Monkey'). Apart from the 'animal' element, the character Sun has one part implying male and one part suggesting a baby, which fits in with my basic theories about children. Your surname will be Sun."

When the Monkey King heard this he kowtowed with delight and said, "Great! Great! Now I have a surname. I am eternally grateful to you for your mercy and compassion, master. I beg you to give me a personal name to go with my

new surname, then it will be much easier to address me."
"There are twelve words within my sect," said the Patriarch,
"which I give as names. You belong to the tenth generation
of my disciples." "What are these twelve words?" asked the
Monkey King. "Broad, great, wisdom, intelligence, true,
likeness, nature, sea, bright, awakened, complete and enlightenment. If we work out the generations of disciples, then you
should have a name with Wu ('Awakened') in it. So we can
give you the Dharma-name Sun Wukong, which means 'Monkey Awakened to Emptiness'. Will that do?" "Marvellous,
marvellous," said the smiling Monkey King. "From now on my
name will be Sun Wukong." Indeed,

> When the Great Vagueness was separated there were
> no surnames;
> To smash foolish emptiness he had to be awakened to
> emptiness.

If you want to know what success he had in cultivating his
conduct, you must listen to the explanation in the next instalment.

CHAPTER TWO

He becomes aware of the wonderful truth
of enlightenment;
By killing the demon he realizes
his spirit-nature.

The story goes on to tell how after being given a name the Handsome Monkey King jumped for joy and bowed to Subhuti to express his thanks. The Patriarch then ordered the others to take Sun Wukong out through the double doors and teach him how to sprinkle and sweep the floor, answer orders, and deport himself properly. All the immortals went out in obedience to this command. When Sun Wukong was outside the doors he bowed to all his spiritual elder brothers and laid out his bed on the verandah. The next morning and every following day he studied language and deportment under his spiritual elder brothers, expounded the scriptures, discussed the Way, practised calligraphy, and burnt incense. When he had any spare time he would sweep the grounds, dig the vegetable patch, grow flowers, tend trees, look for kindling, light the fire, carry water, and fetch soy. Everything he needed was provided. Thus six or seven years slipped by in the cave without his noticing them. One day the Patriarch took his seat on the dais, called all the immortals together, and began to explain the Great Way.

> *Heavenly flowers fell in profusion,*
> *While golden lotuses burst forth from the earth.*
> *Brilliantly he expounded the doctrine of the Three*
> *   Vehicles,*
> *Setting forth ten thousand Dharmas in all their details.*

*As he slowly waved his whisk, jewels fell from his
     mouth,
Echoing like thunder and shaking the Nine Heavens.
Now preaching the Way,
Now teaching meditation,
He showed that the Three Beliefs are basically the same.
In explaining a single word he brought one back to the
     truth,
And taught the secrets of avoiding birth and understand-
     ing one's nature.*

As Monkey sat at the side listening to the exposition he was
so delighted that he tugged at his ear, scratched his cheek and
smiled. He could not help waving his hands and stamping.
When the Patriarch noticed this he said to Monkey, "Why are
you leaping around like a madman in class instead of listening
to the lesson?" "Your disciple is listening to the exposition
with all his attention," Monkey replied, "but your marvellous
words made me so happy that I started jumping around without
realizing what I was doing. Please forgive me." To this the
Patriarch replied, "If you really understand my marvellous
words, then answer this question. How long have you been
in my cave?" "You disciple was born stupid," Monkey replied, "so I've no idea how long I've been here. All I know
is that whenever the fire in the stove goes out I go to the other
side of the mountain to collect firewood and there I see a hill
covered with fine peach trees. I've had seven good feeds of
peaches there." "That hill is called Tender Peach Hill. If you
have eaten there seven times you must have been here seven
years. What sort of Way do you want to learn from me?"
"That depends what you teach me, master. As long as there's
a whiff of Way to it, your disciple will learn it."

"There are three hundred and sixty side-entrances to the
Way, and they all lead to a True Result," the Patriarch said.
"Which branch would you like to study?" "I will do whatever
you think best, master," replied Monkey. "What about teaching
you the Way of Magic Arts?" "What does 'the Way of Magic

Arts' mean?" "Magic arts," the Patriarch replied, "include summoning immortals, using the magic sandboard, and divining by milfoil. With them one can learn how to bring on good fortune and avert disaster." "Can you become immortal this way?" asked Monkey. "No, certainly not," replied the Patriarch. "No. Shan't learn it."

"Shall I teach you the Way of Sects?" the Patriarch asked. "What are the principles of the Sects?" said Monkey. "Within the branch of Sects, there is Confucianism, Buddhism, Taoism, the study of the Negative and Positive, Mohism, medicine, reading scriptures and chanting the name of a Buddha. You can also summon immortals and sages with this branch." "Can you attain immortality that way?" asked Monkey. "To try and attain immortality that way," the Patriarch replied, "is like 'putting a pillar in the wall'." "Master," Monkey said, "I'm a simple chap and I can't understand your technical jargon. What do you mean by 'putting a pillar in the wall'?" "When a man builds a house and wants to make it strong he puts a pillar in the wall. But when the day comes for his mansion to collapse the pillar is bound to rot." "From what you say," Monkey observed, "it's not eternal. No. Shan't learn it."

"Shall I teach you the Way of Silence?" the Patriarch then asked. "What True Result can be got from Silence?" said Monkey. "It involves abstaining from grain, preserving one's essence, silence, inaction, meditation, abstaining from speech, eating vegetarian food, performing certain exercises when lying down or standing up, going into trances, and being walled up in total isolation." "Is this a way of becoming immortal?" Monkey asked. "It's like building the top of a kiln with sun-dried bricks," the Patriarch replied. "You do go on, master," said Sun Wukong. "I've already told you that I can't understand your technical jargon. What does 'building the top of a kiln with sun-dried bricks' mean?" "If you build the top of a kiln with sun-dried bricks they may make it look all right, but if they have not been hardened with fire and water, then they will crumble away in the first heavy rainstorm." "There's nothing eternal about that either, then," replied Monkey. "No. Shan't learn that."

"Shall I teach you the Way of Action then?" the Patriarch asked. "What's that like?" Monkey asked. "It involves acting and doing, extracting the Negative and building up the Positive, drawing the bow and loading the crossbow, rubbing the navel to make the pneuma flow, refining elixirs according to formulae, lighting fires under cauldrons, consuming 'Red lead', purifying 'Autumn Stone', and drinking women's milk." "Can doing things like that make me live for ever?" Monkey asked. "To try and attain immortality that way is like 'lifting the moon out of water'." "What does 'lifting the moon out of water' mean?" "The moon is in the sky," the Patriarch replied, "and only its reflection is in the water. Although you can see it there, you will try in vain to lift it out." "No. Shan't learn that," Monkey exclaimed.

When the Patriarch heard this he gasped and climbed down from his dais. Pointing at Sun Wukong with his cane he said, "You won't study this and you won't study that, so what do you want, you monkey?" He went up to Monkey and hit him three times on the head, then went inside with his hands behind his back and shut the main door, abandoning them all. The class was shocked, and they all blamed Sun Wukong. "You cheeky ape, you've no idea how to behave. The master was teaching you the Way, so why did you have to argue with him instead of learning from him? Now you've offended him we don't know when he'll come out again." They were all very angry with him and regarded him with loathing and contempt. But Sun Wukong was not bothered in the least, and his face was covered with smiles. The Monkey King had understood the riddle, and had the answer hidden away in his mind. So he did not argue with the others but bore it all without a word. When the Patriarch hit him three times he had been telling him to pay attention at the third watch; and when he went inside with his hands behind his back and shut the main door he had told the Monkey King to go in through the back door and be taught the Way in secret.

The delighted Sun Wukong spent the rest of that day with the others in front of the Three Stars Cave, looking at the sky and impatient for night to come. At dusk he went to bed like all the others, pretended to close his eyes, controlled his breathing, and calmed himself down. Nobody beats the watches or calls out the hour in the mountains, so he had no way of knowing the time except by regulating the breath going in and out of his nose. When he reckoned that it was about the third watch he got up very quietly, dressed, and slipped out through the front door away from the others. When he was outside he looked up and saw

> *The moon was bright and clear and cold,*
> *The vast space of the eight points was free from dust.*
> *Deep in the trees a bird slept hidden,*
> *While the water flowed from the spring.*
>
> *Fireflies scattered their lights*
> *And a line of geese was stretched across the clouds.*
> *It was exactly the third watch,*
> *The right time to ask about the Way.*

Watch the Monkey King as he follows the old path to the back door, which he found to be ajar. "The Patriarch has left the door open, so he really intends to teach me the Way," he exclaimed in delight. He tiptoed forward, went in sideways through the door, and walked over to the Patriarch's bed, where he saw the Patriarch sleeping curled up, facing the inside of the room. Not daring to disturb him, Sun Wukong knelt in front of the bed. Before long the Patriarch woke up, stretched out both his legs, and mumbled to himself:

> *"It's hard, hard, hard. The Way is very obscure.*
> *Don't make light of the Gold and the Cinnabar.*
> *To teach miraculous spells to all but the Perfect Man,*
> *Tires the voice and dries the tongue in vain."*

Sun Wukong said in reply, "Master, your disciple has been kneeling here for a long time." When the Patriarch heard that it was Sun Wukong who was speaking he pulled some clothes

on, sat up cross-legged, and shouted, "It's that monkey. Why
have you come into my room instead of sleeping out in front?"
"Master, you told me publicly in front of the altar yesterday
that your disciple was to come in here through the back gate
at the third watch as you were going to teach me the Way. That
is why I made so bold as to come to pay my respects beside my
master's bed." The Patriarch was very pleased to hear this
and said to himself, "This wretch was indeed born of Heaven
and Earth. Otherwise he wouldn't have been able to understand my cryptic message." Sun Wukong said, "There is
no third pair of ears in this room; your disciple is the only
other person here. I hope, master, that in your great mercy
you will teach me the Way of Immortality. If you do, I'll
always be grateful to you." "You are predestined," the
Patriarch said, "so I shall be happy to tell you. Since you understood my cryptic message, come over here and listen carefully while I teach you the miraculous Way of Immortality." Sun
Wukong kowtowed with gratitude and knelt before the bed,
listening with all his attention. The Patriarch said:

> *"The esoteric and exoteric are perfect true spells,*
> *The only sure way of protecting one's life.*
> *They all come from essence, vapour, and spirit,*
> *Must be stored away securely, and never be divulged.*
>
> *Must never be divulged, and be stored in the body,*
> *Then the Way I teach you will flourish of itself.*
> *Many are the benefits of learning spells:*
> *They give protection from evil desires and make one*
>   *pure.*
> *Make one pure with a dazzling radiance*
> *Like a bright moon shining on a cinnabar tower.*
> *The moon contains a Jade Rabbit, the sun a Golden*
>   *Crow,*
> *The Tortoise and the Snake are always intertwined.*
>
> *Always intertwined, then life is firm,*
> *And one can plant golden lotuses in fire.*

> *Grasp all the Five Elements and turn them upside down,*
> *And when you are successful you can become a Buddha,*
> *or an Immortal."*

The Patriarch's explanation went to the root of things, and Sun Wukong's heart was filled with bliss as he committed the spells to memory. He bowed to the Patriarch to express his deep gratitude and went out of the back door to look. He saw that there was a trace of white in the east, while the golden light of the moon was shining in the west. He went to the front door by the old path, pushed it open gently, and went in. He sat down where he had been sleeping earlier, shook his bedding and said loudly, "It's dawn, it's dawn. Get up." The others were all asleep, unaware of Sun Wukong's good fortune. At daybreak he got up and muddled through the day, while secretly keeping to what he had been told. In the afternoon and evening he regulated his breathing.

After three years had passed in this way the Patriarch once more sat on his lecturing throne and expounded the Dharma to the students. He recounted famous sayings and parables, and discussed external phenomena and external appearances Without warning he asked, "Where is Sun Wukong?" Sun Wukong went forward, knelt down and replied, "Your disciple is present." "What Way have you cultivated since coming here?" "Your disciple is now fairly well conversant with the Dharma," Sun Wukong replied, "and my Source is getting gradually stronger." "If you are conversant with the Dharma and you know about the Source," the Patriarch replied, "and if the spirit has already flowed into you, then you must beware of the Three Disasters." Sun Wukong thought for a long time, then he said, "Patriarch, you're talking rubbish. I have often heard that the Way is lofty and its power mighty, that it is as eternal as Heaven, that it can overcome fire and water, and prevent all illnesses from arising, so how could there be Three Disasters?" To this the Patriarch replied, "This is not the ordinary Way: it involves seizing the very creation of Heaven and Earth, and encroaching on the hidden workings of the sun and moon. Once the elixir is made, devils and spirits cannot tolerate it. Although it will preserve the youthfulness of your face and prolong your life, in five hundred years' time Heaven will strike you with a thunderbolt. You must be clear-sighted in nature and mind, so that you can hide from it before it comes. If you succeed in avoiding it you will live as long as Heaven; and if you don't, it will kill you. Another five hundred years later Heaven will burn you with fire. This fire will be not heavenly fire or ordinary fire but 'hidden fire'. It will burn you from the soles of your feet to the crown of your head; your five viscera will be reduced to ashes, your four limbs will be destroyed, and a thousand years of asceticism will have been so much wasted time. Yet another five hundred years later a wind will blow at you. It will not be the north, south, east, or west wind, nor will it be a warm, fragrant wind from the northwest; nor will it be the kind of wind that blows among flowers, willows, pine, and bamboo. It will be what is called a 'monster wind'. It will blow through the crown of your head down into your six entrails. It will go through the Cinnabar Field below your navel and penetrate your nine orifices. Your flesh and your bones will be destroyed and your body will disintegrate. So you must avoid all three of these disasters."

When he heard this Sun Wukong's hair stood on end, and he kowtowed with the words, "I implore you, my lord, to show pity and teach me how to avoid these three disasters. If you do I will be grateful to you for ever." "That would be easy," the Patriarch replied, "but for the fact that you are different from other people — which means that I can't." "I have a head that faces the sky and feet standing on earth," said Sun Wukong. "I have nine orifices and four limbs, five viscera and six entrails. How am I different from anyone else?" "Although you are quite like other people, your cheeks are too small." Now that monkey had a funny face, with cheeks that caved inwards and a sharp chin. Sun Wukong felt it with his hand and replied with a laugh, "Master, you didn't take everything into account. Although I'm a bit short of jaw, I've got more dewlap

than other people to make up for it." "Very well then," the
Patriarch said, "which would you prefer to learn: the thirty-
six heavenly transformations or the seventy-two earthly ones?"
"Your disciple wants to get as much out of it as he can, so I
would like to learn the seventy-two earthly ones." "If that's
what you want," the Patriarch replied, "come here and I'll
teach you the spells." Thereupon he whispered into Sun Wukong's ear, and who knows what miraculous spells he taught
him? The Monkey King was the sort of person who understands
the whole of something once he is told a tiny part, and he learnt
the spells on the spot. He practised and trained until he had
mastered all seventy-two transformations.

One day the Patriarch and all his disciples were enjoying
the sunset outside the Three Stars Cave. The Patriarch asked
Sun Wukong, "Have you succeeded yet?" Sun Wukong replied, "Thanks to your infinite mercy, master, your disciple's
results have been perfect, and I can now rise on the clouds and
fly." "Let me see you try a flight," the Patriarch said. Sun
Wukong used his skill to perform a series of somersaults that
carried him fifty or sixty feet into the air, then walked around
on the clouds for about as long as it takes to eat a meal. He
covered about a mile altogether before landing in front of the
Patriarch, folding his arms across his chest, and saying, "Master,
that's flying and soaring in the clouds." The Patriarch laughed.
"That's not soaring on the clouds — it's just climbing up them.
There is an old saying that 'an immortal visits the Northern
Sea in the morning and Cangwu in the evening'. But to take as
long as you did just to go a mile doesn't count as climbing on
the clouds." "How can it be possible to visit the Northern Sea
in the morning and Cangwu in the evening?" Sun Wukong
asked. "All cloud-soarers start off from the Northern Sea early
in the morning, visit the Eastern, Western and Southern Seas,
and then come back to Cangwu. Cangwu is what the Northern
Sea is called in the Lingling language. When you can go beyond all four seas in a single day you can regard yourself as a
cloud-soarer." "But that must be very difficult," Sun Wukong
observed. "Where there's a will there's a way," the Patriarch

replied. "Nothing by halves, Master," replied Sun Wukong with bows and kowtows, "I beg of you in your great mercy to teach me the art of cloud-soaring. I promise that I will always be grateful." "Immortals take off with a stamp of their feet," said the Patriarch, "but you do it differently — just now I saw you pull yourself up. As that is the way you do it, I'll show you how to do it your own way and teach you the 'somersault cloud'." Sun Wukong bowed again, imploring him to do so, and the Patriarch taught him the spell. "For this kind of cloud," the Patriarch said, "you make the magic by clasping your hands in the special way, recite the words of the spell, clench your fist, shake yourself, and jump. With one somersault you can go sixty thousand miles." When the others heard this they all exclaimed with a laugh. "Lucky old Sun Wukong. With magic like this he could be an express messenger delivering official letters and reports, and he'd never go short of a meal." When it was dark the Patriarch and his pupils returned to the cave. That night Sun Wukong moved his spirit, practised the technique, and mastered the cloud somersault. From then on he was free from all restraint and he enjoyed the delights of immortality, drifting around as he pleased.

On a day when spring was giving way to summer, and all the students had been sitting under some pine trees listening to lectures for a long time, they said, "Sun Wukong, in what life did you earn your present destiny? The other day our teacher whispered to you how to do the transformations to avoid the Three Disasters. Can you do them all yet?" "It's true, brothers," said Sun Wukong with a grin, "I can do them all. In the first place, it's because our master taught me; and in the second place, it's because I practised them hard day and night." "This would be a good time for you to give us a demonstration." At this suggestion Sun Wukong braced his spirit to show off his skill. "What's it to be, brothers? Tell me what you'd like me to turn myself into." "Turn into a pine tree," they all said. Sun Wukong clenched his fist, said the magic words, shook himself, and changed into a pine tree. It was truly

Green and misty throughout the four seasons,
Raising its upright beauty to the clouds.
Not in the least like a demon monkey,
Every inch a tree that withstands frost and snow.

When the students saw it they clapped their hands and chuckled aloud, saying, "Good old monkey, good old monkey." They did not realize that the row they were making had disturbed the Patriarch, who rushed out through the door, dragging his stick behind him. "Who's making a row out here?" he asked. The students hurriedly pulled themselves together, straightened their clothes and went over to him. Sun Wukong, who had now resumed his real appearance, said from the forest, "Master, we were holding a discussion here, and there were no outsiders making a din." "Yelling and shouting like that," the Patriarch angrily roared, "is no way for those cultivating their conduct to behave. If you are cultivating your conduct, the subtle vapours escape when you open your mouth, and when you wag your tongue, trouble starts. What was all the laughing and shouting about?" "Just now Sun Wukong did a transformation for fun. We told him to turn himself into a pine tree, and he did. We all praised and applauded him, which was why we disturbed you with the noise, master. We beg you to forgive us."

The Patriarch sent them all away except for Sun Wukong, to whom he said, "Come here. Is that a way to use your spirit? To change into a pine tree? Is this a skill you should be showing off in front of people? If you saw somebody else doing that, wouldn't you ask him to teach you? If other people see you doing it, they're bound to ask you to teach them, and if you want to keep out of trouble you'll have to do so; otherwise they may do you harm, and then your life will be in danger." Sun Wukong kowtowed and said, "Please forgive me, master." "I shan't punish you," the Patriarch replied, "but you'll have to go." Sun Wukong's eyes filled with tears. "Master, where am I to go?" "Go back to where you came from." Sun Wukong had a sudden awakening, and he said, "I came from the Water Curtain Cave on the Mountain of Flowers and Fruit in the country of Aolai in the Eastern Continent of Superior Body." "If you hurry back there," the Patriarch replied, "you will be able to preserve your life. If you stay here it will be absolutely impossible to do so." Sun Wukong accepted his punishment. "Yes, master," he said. "I've been away from home for twenty years and I do miss the old days and my children and grandchildren. But when I remember that I have not yet repaid your enormous generosity to me, I can't bring myself to go." "What sort of kindness would you be doing me if you stayed? I'll be happy enough if you keep me out of any disasters you cause."

Seeing that there was nothing else for it, Sun Wukong bowed and took leave of him, saying goodbye to all the other students. "Now that you're going," the Patriarch said, "I'm sure that your life will not be a good one. Whatever disasters you cause and crimes you commit, I forbid you under any circumstances to call yourself my disciple. If you so much as hint at it I'll know at once, and I'll tear off your monkey skin, chop up your bones, and banish your soul to the Ninth Darkness. I won't let you out for ten thousand aeons." "I promise never to give away a single letter of your name," said Sun Wukong. "I'll just say that I taught myself."

Sun Wukong took his leave and went away. Making the spell by clasping his fist he jumped head over heels, summoned a somersault cloud, and went back to the Eastern Continent Within two hours he saw the Water Curtain Cave on the Mountain of Flowers and Fruit. The Handsome Monkey King was so pleased that he said to himself:

> "When I left here my mortal flesh and bones were heavy,
> But now I have the Way my body's light.
> No one in the world has real determination,
> To the firm will, the hidden becomes clear.
>
> When I last crossed the seas the waves got in my way,
> But now on my return the journey's easy.
> While the parting words still echo in my ears;
> The Eastern Ocean is in sight again."

Sun Wukong put away his cloud and headed straight to the Mountain of Flowers and Fruit. As he followed the path there he heard the call of the cranes and the cries of the apes. The crane calls echoed beyond the Milky Way, and the ape cries were pathetically sad. Sun Wukong shouted, "Children, I'm back."

Big monkeys and little monkeys came bounding in their thousands and tens of thousands from caves in the cliffs, from the grass and flowers, and down from the trees. They all crowded round the Handsome Monkey King, kowtowed and said, "Your Majesty, you're a cool one. How could you stay away for so long and abandon us all here? We've been desperate for you to come back. A demon has been mistreating us terribly. He's occupied our Water Curtain Cave, and we've been fighting for our lives with him. Recently he's been stealing our things and carrying off many of our youngsters. We've had to stay awake all night to guard our families. Thank goodness you've come back! Another year without you, Your Majesty, and every one of us would be under his control, cave and all." Sun Wukong was furious. "Who is this demon? What an outrage! Tell me everything about him, and then I'll go and give him what's coming to him." The monkey host kowtowed again and said, "Your Majesty, the wretch calls himself the Demon King of Confusion. He lives north of here." "How far away is his place?" Sun Wukong asked. "He comes and goes in cloud and mist with wind and rain, or thunder and lightning, so we don't know how far it is." "If that's how it is," Sun Wukong replied, "then don't worry. Just keep yourselves amused while I go and find him."

The splendid Monkey King jumped up into the air, and as he somersaulted towards the north he saw a high and precipitous mountain. It was a fine sight:

> Perpendicular peaks jutting straight up,
> Deep-sunk winding streams.
> The perpendicular peaks jutting straight up pierced the
>   sky;

The deep-sunk winding streams led to the underworld.
On pairs of cliffs the plants compete in strangeness;
Elsewhere pine vies in greenness with bamboo.
To the left are docile dragons,
To the right are tame tigers.
Iron oxen ploughing are a common sight,
Golden coins are always sown as seeds.
Hidden birds sing beautifully,
Red phoenixes stand facing the sun.
Racing over stones, the clear waves
Twist and bend in a vicious torrent.
Many are the famous mountains in the world,
And many the flowers that bloom and wither on them.
But this scenery is eternal,
Unchanging through the four seasons.
It is truly the mountain from which the Three Worlds
  spring,
The Cave in the Belly of the Water that nourishes the
  Five Elements.

As the Handsome Monkey King stood gazing in silence at
this view, he heard voices. When he went down the mountainside to look he found the Cave in the Belly of the Water
facing the cliff. Several minor demons were dancing around
in front of the cave doors, and they ran away as soon as they
saw Sun Wukong. "Wait a moment," Sun Wukong said. "I
want you to take a message for me. I am the King of the
Water Curtain Cave in the Mountain of Flowers and Fruit that
lies due south of here. I've come to find that Demon of Confusion of yours, or whatever he's called, the one who's been
mistreating my children and grandchildren, and have it out
with him."

The minor demons scuttled into the cave and reported, "A
disaster, Your Majesty." "What do you mean, disaster?" the
demon king asked. "There's a monkey outside the cave," the
minor demons reported, "who says that he's the King of the
Water Curtain Cave on the Mountain of Flowers and Fruit. He

says that you have been bullying his children and grandchildren, and that he's come specially to find you to have it out with you." The demon king laughed. "Those monkey devils are always going on about a king of theirs who renounced the world to cultivate his conduct; I suppose it must be him who's here now. Did you see how he was dressed or what weapons he was carrying?" "He hasn't got any weapons. He's bare-headed, and he's wearing a red gown belted with a yellow silk sash, and a pair of black boots. He isn't dressed like a monk, or a layman, or an immortal. He's bare-handed and empty-fisted, and he's standing outside the doors yelling." "Bring me my armour and weapons," said the demon king when he heard this. The minor demons produced them at once, and when he had donned his armour he went out of the door with all the demons, his sword in his hand. "Who is the King of the Water Curtain Cave?" he roared. Sun Wukong took a quick look at him and saw that

> On his head he wore a dark golden helmet,
> Glistening in the sun.
> On his body he wore a black silk gown,
> Flapping in the breeze.
> Below that he wore black metal armour,
> Girt with a leather belt.
> On his feet he wore patterned boots,
> As splendid as a field-marshal's.
> His waist was ten feet round,
> And his height was thirty cubits.
> In his hand he held a sword,
> With gleaming point and edge.
> He called himself the Demon King of Confusion
> And his appearance was truly dazzling.

"You insolent demon," shouted the Monkey King. "Your eyes may be big but you can't see who I am." The demon king laughed at him. "You don't even stand four feet from the ground, you're still in your twenties, and you've got no weapon in your hand. What sort of mad courage makes you challenge me to a fight?" "You insolent demon," retorted Sun Wukong, "how blind you are. You may think I'm small, but I can grow easily enough. You may think I'm unarmed, but I could pull the moon down from the sky with my two hands. Don't worry, old Sun Wukong will sock you one." Sun Wukong gave a jump and leapt into the air, taking a swing at his face. The demon king put out his hand to stop him and said, "Look how big I am, you dwarf. If you use your fists, I'll use my sword. But I'd only make myself look ridiculous if I killed you with a sword. Wait till I've put my sword down and then I'll give you a display of boxing." "Well said," exclaimed Sun Wukong, "spoken like a man. Come on then." The demon king dropped his guard to throw a punch, and Sun Wukong rushed in towards him, punching and kicking. When he spread out his hand it was enormous, and when he clenched his fist it was very hard. Sun Wukong hit the demon king in the ribs, kicked his backside, and smashed several of his joints. The demon king seized his steel sword that was as big as a plank, and swung it at Sun Wukong's skull. Sun Wukong dodged the blow, and the sword only split air. Seeing how ugly the demon king had turned, Sun Wukong used his magic art of getting extra bodies. He pulled out one of his hairs, popped it in his mouth, chewed it up, and blew it out into the air, shouting, "Change!" It turned into two or three hundred little monkeys, who all crowded round him.

Sun Wukong now had an immortal body, and there was no magic transformation of which he was not capable. Since he had followed the Way he could change each of the eighty-four thousand hairs on his body into anything he wanted. The little monkeys were too quick and nimble for sword or spear. Look at them, leaping forwards and jumping backwards, rushing up and surrounding the demon king, grabbing him, seizing him, poking him in the backside, pulling at his feet, punching him, kicking him, tearing his hair out, scratching at his eyes, twisting his nose, all picking him up together and throwing him to the ground. They went on until they had beaten him to a pulp. Sun Wukong snatched his sword from him, told the little monkeys to get out of the way, and brought it down on the crown of his head, splitting it into two. Then he led his force charging into the cave, where they exterminated all the demons, big and small. He shook his hair and put it back on his body. The monkeys who did not go back on his body were the little monkeys the demon king had carried off from the Water Curtain Cave. Sun Wukong asked them how they had got there. There were thirty or forty of them, and they replied with tears in their eyes, "It was after Your Majesty went off to become an immortal. He has been fighting with us for the last two years. He brought us all here by force. All the things here — the stone bowls and plates — were stolen from our cave by the beast." "If it's our stuff, take it all out," said Sun Wukong. He then set fire to the Cave in the Belly of the Water and burnt it to a cinder. "Come back with me," he ordered the monkeys. "Your Majesty," they replied, "when we came here all we could hear was the wind howling in our ears as it blew us here, so we don't know the way. How are we ever going to get back?" "There's nothing at all to that spell he used," said Sun Wukong. "I can do it too, as now I only have to know the smallest bit about something to understand it completely. Shut your eyes and don't worry."

Splendid Monkey King. He recited a spell, took them riding on a hurricane, then brought the cloud down to the ground. "Open your eyes and look, children," he shouted. As soon as the monkeys' feet touched the ground they recognized their home. In their delight they all ran along the familiar path to the cave, and the monkeys who had stayed in the cave all crowded in as well. They divided themselves into age-groups and bowed in homage to the Monkey King. Wine and food was laid out to celebrate, and they asked him how he had defeated the demon king and saved their children. When Sun Wukong had told them the whole story the monkeys were full of admiration. "Where did you learn such arts, Your Majesty?" they asked insistently, "When I left you," Sun Wukong replied, "I followed the waves and the currents, and drifted across the Eastern Ocean to the Southern Jambu Continent. Here I taught myself to take human form and to wear these clothes and boots. I swaggered around for eight or nine years, but I never found the Way, so I sailed across the Western Ocean to the Western Continent of Cattle-gift. After long enquiries I was luck enough to meet a venerable Immortal, who taught me the True Result, which makes me as immortal as heaven, and the great Dharma Gate to eternal youth." The monkeys all congratulated him and exclaimed that his like could not be found in a billion years. Sun Wukong laughed and said, "Children, we should congratulate ourselves on having a surname." "What is Your Majesty's surname?" the monkey masses asked. "My surname is now Sun, and my Buddhist name is Wukong." The monkeys all clapped their hands with joy and said, "Your Majesty is Old Sun, and we are Second Sun, Third Sun, Thin Sun, Little Sun — a family of Suns, a nation of Suns, a den of Suns." They all offered Old Sun their respects, with big plates and small bowls of coconut toddy, grape wine, magic flowers, and magic fruit. The whole household was happy. My word!

> *By uniting themselves with a single surname*
> *They are waiting to be transferred to the Register of*
> *Immortals.*

If you don't know how this ended and want to know about the rest of their lives there, then listen to the explanation in the next instalment.

CHAPTER THREE

The Four Seas and Thousand Mountains
all submit;
In the Ninth Hell the Tenth Category
is struck off the register.

We have related how the Handsome Monkey King returned home in glory, bringing a large sword he had captured when he killed the Demon King of Confusion. From then on they practised the military arts every day. He asked the little monkeys to cut down bamboo to make spears, carve swords out of wood, and learn to use banners and whistles. They learnt to advance and retreat, and build a camp with a stockade round it. They spent a lot of time playing at this. Once Sun Wukong was sitting in his seat of meditation when he wondered: "What would happen to us if our games were taken for the real thing? What if it alarmed some human monarch or gave offence to some king of birds or beasts? They might say that we were having military training for a rebellion, and attack us with their armies. You would be no match for them with your bamboo spears and wooden swords. We must have really sharp swords and halberds. What are we to do about it?" When the monkeys heard this they all said with alarm, "Your Majesty has great foresight, but there's nowhere we can get them." When it was the turn of four older monkeys to speak — two bare-bottomed apes and two gibbons — they came forward and said, "Your Majesty, if you want sharp weapons they can be very easily obtained." "How could it be easy?" asked Sun Wukong. "To the east of our mountain," they replied, "there is a lake some seventy miles wide that is the boundary of the country of Aolai. That country has a princely capital, and huge numbers of soldiers and civilians live in the city. It must have workshops for gold, silver, bronze and iron. If you went there, Your Majesty, you could either buy arms or get them made; then you could train us to use them in the defence of our mountain. This would give us long-term security." Sun Wukong was delighted with the suggestion. "Wait here while I go there," he said.

Splendid Monkey King! He leapt on to his somersault cloud, crossed the seventy miles of lake, and saw that on the other side there was indeed a city wall, a moat, streets, markets, ten thousand houses, a thousand gates, and people coming and going in the sunlight. "There must be ready-made weapons here," Sun Wukong thought, "and getting a few by magic would be much better than buying them." So he made a magic with his fist and said the words of the spell, sucked in some air from the southeast, and blew it hard out again. It turned into a terrifying gale carrying sand and stones with it.

> *Where the thunderclouds rise the elements are in chaos;*
> *Black fogs thick with dust cloak the earth in darkness.*
> *Boiling rivers and seas terrify the crabs and fish;*
> *As trees are snapped off in mountain forests tigers and*
>   *wolves flee.*
> *No business is done in any branch of commerce;*
> *And no one is working at any kind of trade.*
> *In the palace the king has gone to his inner quarters;*
> *And the officials in front of the steps have returned to*
>   *their homes.*
> *The thrones of princes are all blown over;*
> *Towers of five phoenixes are shaken to their foundations.*

Where the storm blew, the prince of Aolai fled in terror, and gates and doors were shut in the streets and markets. Nobody dared to move outside. Sun Wukong landed his cloud and rushed straight through the gates of the palace to the arsenal and the military stores, opened the doors, and saw countless weapons: swords, pikes, sabres, halberds, battleaxes, bills, scimitars, maces, tridents, clubs, bows, crossbows, forks, and spears were all there. At the sight of them he said happily,

"How many of these could I carry by myself? I'd better use the magic for dividing up my body." Splendid Monkey King. He plucked a hair from his body, chewed it up, spat it out, made the magic with his fist, said the words of the spell, and shouted "Change!" It turned into hundreds and thousands of little monkeys, who rushed about wildly, grabbing weapons. The strong ones took six or seven each and the weaker ones two or three, and between them they removed the lot. He climbed back up on the clouds, called up a gale by magic, and took all the little monkeys home with him.

The monkeys big and small of the Mountain of Flowers and Fruit were playing outside the gates of the cave when they heard the wind. At the sight of countless monkey spirits flying through the air they fled and hid. A moment later the Handsome Monkey King landed his cloud, put away his mists, shook himself, replaced his hair, and threw all the weapons into a pile beside the mountain. "Children," he shouted, "come and get your weapons." When the monkey masses looked they saw Sun Wukong standing by himself on some level ground, and they all rushed over to him to kowtow and asked what had happened. Sun Wukong told them the whole story of how he had raised the gale and taken the weapons. After all the monkeys had thanked him they snatched sabres, grabbed swords, seized battleaxes, fought for pikes, drew bows, stretched crossbows, shouted, yelled, and so amused themselves for the rest of the day.

The next day they paraded as usual. Sun Wukong assembled all the monkey host, and they numbered over forty-seven thousand. This had alarmed all the strange beasts of the mountain — wolves, monsters, tigers, leopards, deer, muntjacs, river-deer, foxes, wild cats, badgers, raccoons, lions, elephants, orang-utans, bears, stags, wild boar, mountain cattle, antelopes, rhinoceroses, little dogs, and huge dogs. The kings of various kinds of monsters from seventy-two caves all came to pay homage to the Monkey King. They offered tribute every year and attended court in each of the four seasons. They also took part in drill and paid their seasonal grain levies. Everything was so orderly that the Mountain of Flowers and Fruit was as secure as an iron bucket or a wall of bronze. The kings of the monsters sent gongs, drums, coloured flags, helmets, and armour in great abundance, and every day there were military exercises.

One day, amid all this success, the Handsome Monkey King suddenly said to the other monkeys, "You are now expert in the bow and crossbow, and highly skilled in other weapons; but this sword of mine is too clumsy for my liking. What shall I do about it?" The four veteran monkeys came forward and submitted a suggestion: "Your Majesty is an Immortal, so mortals' weapons are not good enough for you. We wonder if Your Majesty is able to travel underwater." "Since hearing the Way," Sun Wukong replied, "I have mastered the seventy-two earthly transformations. My somersault cloud has outstanding magical powers. I know how to conceal myself and vanish. I can make spells and end them. I can reach the sky and find my way into the earth. I can travel under the sun or moon without leaving a shadow or go through metal or stone freely. I can't be drowned by water or burned by fire. There's nowhere I cannot go." "If Your Majesty has these magical powers, the stream under our iron bridge leads to the Dragon Palace of the Eastern Sea. If you are willing to go down there, go and find the Dragon King and ask him for whatever weapon it is you want. Wouldn't that suit you?" "Wait till I get back," was Sun Wukong's delighted reply.

Splendid Monkey King. He leapt to the end of the bridge and made a spell with his fist to ward off the water. Then he dived into the waves and split the waters to make way for himself till he reached the bed of the Eastern Sea. On his journey he saw a yaksha demon who was patrolling the sea. The yaksha barred his way and asked, "What sage or divinity are you, pushing the waters aside like that? Please tell me so that I can make a report and have you properly received." "I am the Heaven-born Sage Sun Wukong from the Mountain of Flowers and Fruit, and your old Dragon King's close neighbour. How is it you don't know me?" When the yaksha heard this he hurried back to the crystal palace and reported, "Your Majesty, Sun Wukong, the Heaven-born Sage from the Mountain of Flowers and Fruit who says he is your neighbour, is coming to your palace." Ao Guang, the Old Dragon King of the Eastern Sea, leapt to his feet and went out to meet Sun Wukong with his dragon sons and grandsons, his prawn soldiers, and his crab generals. "Come in, exalted Immortal," he said, taking Sun Wukong into the palace where they introduced themselves, seated him in the place of honour, and offered him tea. Then the Dragon King asked him, "Exalted Immortal, when did you find the Way, and what magic arts did you acquire?" "After my birth," said Sun Wukong, "I renounced the world and cultivated my conduct, and thus obtained an immortal and indestructible body. Recently I have trained my sons and grandsons to guard our cave, but unfortunately I have not yet found myself a weapon. I have long heard that my illustrious neighbour enjoys the delights of a jade palace with gate-towers of cowrie, and I was sure that you must have some magic weapons to spare, so I have come especially to beg one of you."

Not wishing to refuse this request, the Dragon King sent Commander Perch to fetch a large sword and offer it to Sun Wukong. "I don't know how to use a sword," said Sun Wukong, "so could I ask you to give me something else?" The Old Dragon King then sent Colonel Mackerel and Guard Commander Eel to fetch a nine-pronged spear. Sun Wukong leapt down from his seat, took it, tried it out, then flung it down, saying, "It's too light, far too light; and it doesn't suit me. I beg you to give me another." The Dragon King smiled as he said, "Exalted Immortal, don't you see that this weighs three thousand six hundred pounds?" "It doesn't suit me, it doesn't suit me at all," protested Sun Wukong. The Dragon King, feeling frightened now, ordered Provincial Commander Bream and Garrison Commander Carp to bring out a patterned heavenly halberd for warding off spells that weighed seven thousand two hundred pounds. As soon as he saw it Sun Wukong bounded forward to take it. He tried a few postures and thrusts with it then stuck it in the ground between them. "Still too light, far too light." The Dragon King, now really terrified, said, "Exalted Immortal, that halberd is the heaviest weapon in my palace." "As the old saying goes," said Sun Wukong with a grin, " 'Never think the dragon king has no treasures.' Have another look, and if you find anything satisfying I'll give you a good price for it." "I really have nothing else," the Dragon King replied.

As he was speaking, his dragon wife and dragon daughters came in from the back of the palace and said, "Your Majesty, by the look of him this sage must be really somebody. The piece of miraculous iron that anchors the Milky Way in place has been shining with a lovely rosy glow for the last few days, and creating a most auspicious atmosphere. Perhaps it has started to shine to greet this sage." "That piece of miraculous iron is one of the nails that Yu the Great used to fix the depths of rivers and seas when he brought the waters under control," said the Dragon King. "What use could it be?" "Never mind whether it's useful or not," his wife replied. "Just give it to him and let him do with it as he pleases. At least you'll get him out of the palace." The Dragon King did as she suggested and described the piece of iron to Sun Wukong, who said. "Bring it out and let me see." "It can't be moved. You will have to go and look at it yourself, exalted Immortal." "Where is it? Take me there," said Sun Wukong. The Dragon King took him into the middle of the sea treasury, where all of a sudden they could see ten thousand rays of golden light. Pointing at it, the Dragon King said, "That's it, where all the light is coming from." Sun Wukong hitched up his clothes and went to give it a feel. He found that it was an iron pillar about as thick as a measure for a peck of grain and some twenty feet long. Seizing it with both hands he said, "It's too thick and too long. If it were a bit shorter and thinner it would do." As soon as these words were out of his mouth this precious piece of iron became several feet shorter and a few inches thinner. Sun Wukong tossed it in his hands, remarking that it would be even better if it were thinner still. The precious iron thereupon became even thinner. Sun Wukong was taking it out of the sea treasury to have a look at it when he saw that it had two gold bands round it, while the middle part was made of black iron. There was a line of inlaid writing near the bands which said that it was the AS-YOU-WILL GOLD-BANDED CUDGEL: WEIGHT 13,500 POUNDS. Sun Wukong was delighted, though he did not show it. "I think that this little darling will do whatever I want." As he walked along he weighed it in his hand and said reflectively, "If it were even smaller still it would be perfect." By the time he had taken it outside it was twenty feet long and as thick as a rice bowl.

Watch him as he uses his magical powers to try a few routines with it, whirling all round the crystal palace. The Old Dragon King was trembling with fright, and the little dragons were scared out of their wits. Terrapins, freshwater turtles, seawater turtles and alligators drew in their heads, while fish, shrimps, lobsters and giant turtles hid their faces. Holding his treasure in his hands, Sun Wukong sat down in the main hall of the palace of crystal and said with a smile to the Dragon King, "Many thanks, worthy neighbour, for your great generosity." The Old Dragon King humbly acknowledged his thanks, and Sun Wukong went on, "This piece of iron will be very useful, but there is one more thing I want to ask." "What might that be, exalted Immortal?" asked the Dragon King. "If I hadn't got this cudgel, that would be the end of the matter, but as I have got it the problem is that I don't have the clothes to go with it. What are we to do about it? If you have any armour here, I'd be most obliged if you gave me a suit." The Dragon King said he had not any. " 'A guest should not have to trouble two hosts,' " said Sun Wukong. "I won't leave without one." "Please try some other sea, exalted Immortal — you may find one there." " 'It's better to stay in one house than to visit three.' I beg and implore you to give me a suit." "I really don't have one," replied the Dragon King. "If I had I would present it to you." "If you really haven't, then I'll try this cudgel out on you." "Don't hit me, exalted Immortal, don't hit me," pleaded the Dragon King in terror. "Let me see whether my brothers have one that they could give you."

"Where do your brothers live?" "They are Ao Qin, the Dragon King of the Southern Sea, Ao Shun, the Dragon King of the Northern Sea, and Ao Run, the Dragon King of the Southern Sea." "I'm damned if I'm going there: as the saying goes, 'Two in the pocket is better than three owing.' So be a good chap and give me one." "There is no need for you to go, lofty Immortal," the Dragon King replied, "I have an iron drum and a bronze bell. In an emergency we strike them to bring my brothers here in an instant." "In that case," said Sun Wukong, "hurry up and sound them." And indeed an alligator general struck the bell while a terrapin marshal beat the drum.

The sound of the bell and the drum startled the other three dragon kings, who had arrived and were waiting together outside within the instant. One of them, Ao Qin, said, "Elder Brother, what's up? Why the drum and the bell?" "It hurts me to tell you, brother," the Old Dragon King replied. "There's this so-called heaven-born sage from the Mountain of Flowers and Fruit who came here this morning saying that I was his neighbour, then demanded a weapon. I offered him a steel-pronged spear but he said it was too small, and a patterned halberd that he said was too light. Then he picked up the miraculous iron that fastens the Milky Way and tried a few movements with it. Now he's sitting in the palace and demand-ing a suit of armour, but we haven't got one. That's why I used the bell and the drum to call you here. You three must have some armour. Please give him a suit, then we can get rid of him." When Ao Qin heard this he said in a fury, "To arms, brothers. Arrest the criminal." "No! No! It's out of the ques-tion," said the Old Dragon King. "If that iron cudgel of his gets you you're done for, if it hits you you die, if it comes close your skin is broken, and if it so much as brushes against you your sinews are smashed." Ao Run, the Dragon King of the Western Sea, said, "Second brother, you must not attack him. Instead we should put a suit of armour together for him, then send him away. We can send a memorial about it to Heaven, then Heaven will of course punish him." "You're right," said Ao Shun, the Dragon King of the Northern Sea. "I have a

pair of lotus-root cloud-walking shoes." "I've brought a suit
of golden chain mail," said Ao Run, the Dragon King of the
Western Sea. "And I have a phoenix-winged purple gold
helmet," added Ao Qin, the Dragon King of the Southern Sea.
The Old Dragon King was very pleased, and he brought them
into the palace to meet Sun Wukong and present the equipment
to him. Sun Wukong put on the golden helmet and the armour
and the cloud-walking shoes, then charged out, waving his
cudgel and saying to the dragons, "My apologies for disturbing
you. The four Dragon Kings were most indignant, but we
will not go into their discussions on the protest they sent to
Heaven.

Watch the Monkey King as he parts the waters and goes
straight back to the iron bridge, where the four senior apes can
be seen waiting for him at the head of the monkey host. Sun
Wukong suddenly leapt out of the waves without a drop of
water on him and gleaming with gold. As he came across the
bridge the monkeys were so astonished that they fell to their
knees and said, "How splendid you look, Your Majesty, how
splendid." Sun Wukong, his face lit up with youthful vigour,
climbed up to his throne, thrust his cudgel into the ground in
their midst. The foolish monkeys all tried to grab this treasure,
but it was as futile as a dragonfly trying to shake an iron tree:
they were unable to move it in the slightest. Biting their fingers
and sticking out their tongues they said, "Grandpa, it's so heavy,
how can you possibly lift it?" Sun Wukong went over, lifted it
with one hand, and laughed as he said to them, "Everything
has its rightful owner. This little treasure has been lying in the
sea treasury for goodness knows how many thousands of years,
but it just happened to start shining this year. The Dragon
King thought it was just a piece of ordinary iron, and said it
was the miraculous treasure that holds the bed of the Milky
Way in place. None of his men could move it, so he had to
ask me to go and fetch it myself. It was more than twenty feet
long then, and as thick as a peck-measure. When I picked it up
I felt that it was too big, and it shrank till it was several times

as small. I told it to get even smaller, and it did that too; then I told it to get smaller still, and it got many times smaller again. I hurried out into the light of day to look at it, and I saw that there was an inscription on it that read 'AS-YOU-WILL GOLD-BANDED CUDGEL: WEIGHT 13,500 POUNDS'. Stand aside, and I'll make it change again." Holding his treasure in his hand he said, "Shrink, shrink, shrink," and it became as small as an embroidery needle, tiny enough to be hidden in his ear. "Your Majesty," the monkeys cried out in astonishment, "bring it out and play with it again." So the Monkey King brought it out of his ear again, laid it on the palm of his hand, and said, "Grow, grow, grow." It became as thick as a peck again and twenty feet long. Now that he was really enjoying himself he bounded over the bridge and went out of the cave. Clasping his treasure he used some of his heaven and earth magic, bowed, and shouted, "Grow." He became a hundred thousand feet tall; his head was as big as a mountain, his waist like a range of hills, his eyes flashed like lightning, his mouth seemed to be a bowl of blood, and his teeth were as swords and halberds; the cudgel in his hands reached up to the Thirty-third Heaven and down to the Eighteenth Hell. The tigers, leopards and wolves, the beasts of the mountain, and the seventy-two monster kings all kowtowed and bowed in terror, trembling so much that they went out of their minds. A moment later he reverted to his proper size, turned his treasure into an embroidery needle, hid it in his ear, and went back to the cave. The panic-stricken kings of the monsters all came to offer their congratulations.

There was a great display of banners and drums, and the air resounded to the sound of gongs and bells. Rare delicacies were set out in great quantities, cups brimmed with coconut toddy and the wine of the grape, and the Monkey King feasted and drank with his people for a long time. Then training went on as before. The Monkey King named the four senior apes as his four Stalwart Generals: he named the two bare-bottomed apes Marshal Ma and Marshal Liu, and called the two gibbons General Beng and General Ba. He entrusted the stockade, questions of discipline and rewards to these four. Thus freed from cares, he mounted the clouds and rode the mists, wandering round the four seas and enjoying the thousand mountains. He practised his martial arts, visited many a hero, used his magical powers, and made a wide and distinguished circle of friends. He met with six sworn brothers of his: the Bull Demon King, the Salamander Demon King, the Roc Demon King, the Camel King, the Macaque King, and the Lion King. With him included as the Handsome Monkey King, they made seven. For days on end they talked about politics and war, passed round the goblet, strummed, sang, piped, danced, went off on days out together, and enjoyed themselves in every possible way. A journey of thousands of miles seemed to them to be no more than a walk in the courtyard. It could be said that they travelled a thousand miles in the time it takes to nod one's head, and covered three hundred with a twist of the waist.

One day he instructed his four Stalwart Generals to arrange a feast for the six other kings. Oxen and horses were slaughtered, sacrifices were made to Heaven and Earth, and the assembled monsters danced, sang, and drank themselves blotto. When he had seen the six kings out and tipped his senior and junior officials Sun Wukong lay himself down under the shade of the pines beside the bridge and was asleep in an instant. The four Stalwart Generals made the others stand round and guard him, and they all kept their voices down.

In his sleep the Handsome Monkey King saw two men approach him with a piece of paper in their hands on which was written "Sun Wukong". Without allowing any explanations they tied up his soul and dragged it staggering along till they reached a city wall. The Monkey King, who was gradually recovering from his drunken stupor, looked up and saw an iron plate on the wall on which was inscribed WORLD OF DARKNESS in large letters. In a flash of realization he said, "The World of Darkness is where King Yama lives. Why have I come here?" "Your life in the world above is due to end now," his escorts said, "and we were ordered to fetch you." To this the Monkey King replied, "I have gone beyond the Three Worlds, and I am no longer subject to the Five Elements.* I don't come under King Yama's jurisdiction. How dare you grab me, you idiots?" But the fetchers of the dead just went on tugging at him, determined to drag him inside. The Monkey King lost his temper, pulled his treasure out of his ear, and gave it a shake. It became as thick as a rice bowl. It only took a slight movement of his arm to smash the two fetchers of the dead to pulp. He untied his bonds, loosed his hands, and charged into the city whirling his cudgel, so terrifying the ox-headed and horse-faced devils that they fled in all directions for cover. All the devil soldiers rushed to the Senluo Palace and reported, "Your Majesty, disaster, disaster! A hairy-faced thunder-god** is attacking us out there."

Stricken by panic, the Ten Kings who sit in the ten palaces, judging the criminal cases of the dead, hurriedly straightened their clothing and went out to look. When they saw his ferocious expression they lined up in order and shouted at the tops of their voices, "Please tell us your name, exalted Immortal." "If you don't know who I am," replied the Monkey King, "then why did you send men to bring me here?" "We wouldn't dare do such a thing. The messengers must have made a mistake." "I am Sun Wukong, the Heaven-born sage of the Water Curtain Cave on the Mountain of Flowers and Fruit. What are your posts?" "We are the ten kings." "Tell me your names at once if you don't want a bashing." To this the ten kings replied, "We are the King of Qinguang, the King of Chujiang, King Songdi, King Wuguan, King Yama, King Impartial, the King of Mount Tai, the Metropolitan King, the King of Biancheng, and the King of the Ever-turning Wheel." To this Sun Wukong replied, "You are all kings, and have esoteric understanding, so why don't you know any better? I, Sun Wu-

---

* According to Buddhism, all beings in the Three Worlds are subject to births and deaths. The Five Elements, according to the Chinese classics, are Metal, Wood, Water, Fire and Earth.

** In Chinese mythology, the thunder-god looks like a monkey with a pointed chin.

kong, have cultivated the Way of Immortality and will live as
long as Heaven. I've soared beyond the Three Worlds and leapt
outside the Five Elements, so why did you send your men to
get me?" "Please don't be angry, lofty Immortal," the ten
kings said. "Many people in the world share the same name,
so perhaps the fetchers of the dead went to the wrong place."
"Nonsense, nonsense. As the saying goes, 'The magistrate may
be wrong and the sergeant may be wrong, but the man who
comes to get you is never wrong.' Go and get the Register of
Life and Death for me to see." The Ten Kings invited him to
come into the palace and look through it.

Sun Wukong went into the Senluo Palace with his club in
his hand, and sat down in the middle of the hall facing south.
The Ten Kings then ordered the presiding judge to fetch the
register, and the judge hastened to his office and brought out
five or six documents and ten registers. He looked through
them all one by one, but could not find Sun Wukong's name in
the sections devoted to hairless creatures, hairy creatures, feath-
ered creatures, insects, or scaly creatures. Then he looked
through the monkey section. Now although monkeys looked
like men, they were not entered under the humans; although
they were like the hairless creatures, they did not live within
their boundaries; although they were like running animals, they
were not under the jurisdiction of the unicorn; and although
they were like birds, they were not ruled by the phoenix. There
was another register, and Sun Wukong looked through this one
himself. Under "Soul No. 1350" was the name of Sun Wukong,
the Heaven-born stone monkey, who was destined to live to the
age of 342 and die a good death. "I won't write down any
number of years," said Sun Wukong. "I'll just erase my name
and be done with it. Bring me a brush." The judge hastily
handed him a brush and thick, black ink. Sun Wukong took
the register, crossed out all the names in the monkey section,
and threw it on the floor with the words, "The account's closed.
That's an end of it. We won't come under your control any
longer." Then he cudgelled his way out of the World of Darkness. The Ten Kings dared not go near him, and they all went

to the Azure Cloud Palace to bow in homage to the Bodhisattva Ksitigarbha and discuss the report they would send up to Heaven. But we will not go into this.

After charging out through the city wall the Monkey King tripped over a clump of grass, tried to regain his balance, and woke up with a start. It had all been a dream. As he stretched himself he heard his four Stalwart Generals and the other monkeys saying, "Your Majesty, time to wake up. You drank too much and slept all night." "Never mind about my sleeping. I dreamt that two men came for me. They dragged me to the city-wall of the World of Darkness, where I came round. I showed them my magic powers and went yelling all the way to the Senluo Palace, where I had an argument with those Ten Kings and looked through the Register of Life and Death of us. Wherever there was mention of your names in the register, I crossed them out. We won't come under the jurisdiction of those idiots any more." All the monkeys kowtowed to him in gratitude. The reason why from that time on so many mountain monkeys have never grown old is that their names are not on the books of the officials of the Underworld. When the Handsome Monkey King had finished telling his story, the four Stalwart Generals informed the other monster kings, who all came to offer their felicitations. A few days later his six sworn brothers also came to congratulate him, and all were delighted to hear how he had struck the names off the books. We will not describe the daily feasts that followed.

Instead we will describe how one day the Supreme Heavenly Sage, the Greatly Compassionate Jade Emperor of the Azure Vault of Heaven, was sitting on his throne in the Hall of Miraculous Mist in the Golden-gated Cloud Palace, surrounded by his immortal civil and military officials at morning court, when the Immortal Qiu Hongji reported, "Your Majesty, Ao Guang, the Dragon King of the Eastern Sea, has presented a memorial outside the Hall of Universal Brightness, and is awaiting a summons from your Imperial Majesty." The Jade Emperor ordered that he be called in, and the Dragon King came to the Hall of Miraculous Mist. When he had done obeisance an immortal page came from the side to take his memorial. The Jade Emperor read it through. It ran:

Your Subject Ao Guang, the Humble Dragon
of the Eastern Sea of the Eastern Continent of Superior Body in the Nether Watery Regions Reports to the Jade Emperor of the Azure Vault of Heaven

Recently one Sun Wukong, an immortal fiend born on the Mountain of Flowers and Fruit now living in the Water Curtain Cave, bullied this humble dragon and occupied my watery house by force. He demanded a weapon by displaying magical prowess; he insisted on having armour by showing off his evil powers. He terrified the watery tribe and made the tortoises and alligators flee in terror. The dragon of the Southern Sea trembled, the dragon of the Western Sea was made miserable, the dragon of the Northern Sea had to hang his head and come in submission, and I, your subject Ao Guang, humbled myself before him. We had to present him with a miraculous iron cudgel, a golden phoenix-winged helmet, a suit of chain mail, and a pair of cloud-walking shoes; and we escorted him out politely. He continued to show off his martial arts and magic powers, and all he had to say for himself was, "My apologies for disturbing you." There is truly no match for him, and he is uncontrollable. Your subject now presents this memorial, and respectfully awaits your sage decision. I humbly beg that heavenly soldiers be sent to arrest this evil demon, so that the sea and the mountains may be at peace, and the ocean may enjoy tranquillity.

When the Jade Emperor had read this through he ordered, "Let the Dragon God return to the Sea; we shall send generals to arrest the demon." The Old Dragon King bowed till his head touched the floor and took his leave. Then the Venerable Immortal Ge, a heavenly teacher, reported, "Your Majesty, the

King of Qinguang, one of the ministers of the Underworld, has come with a memorial from the Bodhisattva Ksitigarbha." A jade girl messenger took the memorial, which the Jade Emperor read through. It ran:

> The regions of darkness are the negative part of the Earth. Heaven contains gods while the Earth has devils; Positive and Negative are in a constant cycle. Birds and beasts are born and die; male and female alternate. Life is created and change takes place; male and female are conceived and born; this is the order of nature, and it cannot be changed. Now the evil spirit, the Heaven-born monkey of the Water Curtain Cave on the Mountain of Flowers and Fruit, is presently giving full rein to his wicked nature, committing murders, and refusing to submit to discipline. He killed the devil messengers of the Ninth Hell with his magic, and he terrified the Ten Benevolent Kings of the Underworld with his power. He made an uproar in the Senluo Palace and crossed some names out by force. He has made the race of monkeys completely uncontrollable, and given eternal life to the macaques. He has annulled the law of transmigration and brought them beyond birth and death. I, humble monk that I am, risk offending the might of Heaven by presenting this memorial. I prostrate myself to beg that Heavenly soldiers be despatched to subdue this fiend, bring the Positive and Negative back into order, and give lasting security to the Underworld.

When the Jade Emperor had read this through he ordered, "Let the Lord of Darkness return to the Underworld. We shall send generals to arrest the demon." The King of Qinguang then bowed till his head touched the floor and took his leave.

His Celestial Majesty then asked all his civil and military officials, "When was this monkey demon born? What is his origin, that he should have such powers?" Before he had finished speaking, Thousand-mile Eye and Wind-accompanying Ear came forward from the ranks of officials and said, "This

demon monkey is the stone monkey who was born of heaven
three hundred years ago. At the time nobody paid any attention
to him, and we do not know where he refined himself and became an Immortal in recent years, so that he has been able to
make the tigers and dragons submit to him and to strike his
name off the register of the dead." "Which divine general shall
be sent down to capture him?" asked the Jade Emperor, and
before he had finished speaking the Great White Planet* stepped
forward, bowed down, and submitted, "All beings in the upper
worlds that have nine apertures can become Immortals. This
monkey has a body that was created by Heaven and Earth and
conceived by the sun and moon. His head points to the sky and
his feet stand on the earth; he drinks the dew and eats the mist.
How does he differ from humans, if he has succeeded in cultivating the way of immortality and can subdue dragons and tigers?
I beg Your Majesty to remember your life-giving mercy and
hand down a sage edict of amnesty and enlistment, summoning
him to this upper world and inscribing his name on the list of
office-holders, thus keeping him here under control. If he obeys
Your Majesty's heavenly commands, he can later be promoted;
and if he disobeys, he can be arrested. This will both avoid
military operations and be a way of winning over an Immortal."
The Jade Emperor, delighted with the suggestion, ordered that
it should be put into effect. He told the Wenqu Star Officer to
compose the edict, and commanded the Great White Planet to
persuade the monkey to accept the amnesty.

The Great White Planet left Heaven by the Southern Gate,
and brought his propitious cloud down by the Water Curtain
Cave, where he said to the little monkeys, "I am an envoy from
Heaven, and I am carrying a divine edict inviting your great
king to the upper world. Go and tell him at once." The little
monkeys outside conveyed the message by relays into the depths
of the cave: "Your Majesty, there's an old man outside carrying a document on his back. He says he's an envoy from Heav-
en with an invitation for you." The Handsome Monkey King

---

* A name for the planet Venus.

was delighted. He said, "I'd been thinking of going up to Heaven to have a look round for the past couple of days, and now a heavenly envoy has come to invite me." "Ask him in at once," he shouted, hastily straightening his clothes and going out to meet the envoy. The Planet came straight in, stood facing the south, and said, "I am the Great White Planet of the west, and I have come down to earth with an Edict of Amnesty and Enlistment from the Jade Emperor to invite you to Heaven to be given office as an immortal." "I am very grateful to you, venerable Planet, for condescending to come here," replied Sun Wukong with a smile; then he told his subjects to prepare a feast to entertain the visitor. "I'm afraid I can't delay," replied the Planet, "as I am carrying a divine edict, so may I ask Your Majesty to come back with me now? We can talk at leisure after your glorious elevation." "Thank you for coming," said Sun Wukong. "I'm sorry you couldn't take some refreshments before leaving." Then he called for his four Stalwart Generals and ordered them, "Give my sons and grandsons a thorough training. When I've had a look round in Heaven, I'll take you all to live with me up there." The four Stalwart Generals accepted their orders, and the Monkey King made his cloud carry him up above the clouds. He was

> Raised to a high-ranking heavenly office,
> Listed among the courtiers in the clouds.

If you don't know what office he was given, listen to the explanation in the next instalment.

CHAPTER FOUR

Dissatisfied at being appointed Protector of
the Horses;
Not content with the title of Equal
of Heaven.

The Great White Planet left the depths of the cave with the
Handsome Monkey King, and they ascended together on their
clouds. As Sun Wukong's somersault cloud was exceptionally
fast he reached the Southern Gate of Heaven first, leaving the
Great White Planet far behind. Just as he was putting away his
cloud to go in, his way was barred by the Heavenly King
Virudhaka and his powerful heavenly soldiers Liu, Gou, Bi,
Deng, Xin, Zhang, and Tao, who blocked the gate of Heaven
with their spears and swords and refused to let him in. "This
old Great White Planet is a trickster," said Sun Wukong. "He
invited me here, so he has no business to have me kept out with
spears and swords." Just as he was kicking up a row the Planet
suddenly arrived. Sun Wukong flung his accusation at him:
"Why did you play this trick on me, you old fogy? You told
me you came with an Edict of Amnesty from the Jade Emperor
to invite me here, so why did you arrange for these people not
to let me in through the gate of Heaven?" The Great White
Planet laughed. "Don't be angry, Your Majesty. You've never
been here before, your name is not on the books here, and the
heavenly soldiers have never met you. Of course they could
not let me in just for the asking. But when you've seen His
Celestial Majesty and been given office among the immortals,
you will be able to come and go as you wish, and nobody will
try to stop you." "Be that as it may," said Sun Wukong, "I'm.

not going in." The Great White Planet weuld not let him go and asked him to go in with him in spite of it all.

As they approached the gate, the Planet shouted, "Heavenly officers of the fates of Heaven, sergeants and soldiers, let us in. This is an immortal from the lower world, and I am carrying an edict from the Jade Emperor summoning him here." Only then did the Heavenly King Virudhaka and his soldiers withdraw their arms and stand back. Now the Monkey King began to trust the Great White Planet. He walked slowly in with him and looked at the view. Truly it was his

> *First ascent to the upper world,*
> *Sudden entry into paradise.*
> *Ten thousand beams of golden light shone with a reddish*
>   *glow;*
> *A thousand strands of propitious vapour puffed out pur-*
>   *ple mist.*
> *See the Southern Gate of Heaven,*
> *Deep green,*
> *Crystalline,*
> *Shimmering bright,*
> *Studded with jewels.*
> *On either side stood scores of heavenly marshals,*
> *Tall as the roofbeams, next to the pillars,*
> *Holding metal-tipped bows and banners.*
> *All around stood gods in golden armour,*
> *Brandishing their clubs and halberds,*
> *Wielding their cutlasses and swords.*
> *The outside was remarkable enough,*
> *But the inside astonished him.*
> *Here were several mighty pillars,*
> *Round which coiled tawny-bearded dragons, their gold*
>   *scales gleaming in the sun.*
> *There were long bridges,*
> *Where strutted phoenixes, brilliant of plumage and with*
>   *bright red crests.*
> *A rosy glow shone with heavenly light;*

Thick green mists obscured the Pole Star.
In this heaven there are thirty-three heavenly palaces:
The Palace of Clouds Dispersed, the Vaisravana Palace,
*   the Palace of Five Lores, the Sun Palace, the Palace*
*   of Delight in Transformations.*
Every palace had golden animals on its roof.
Then there were seventy-two precious halls:
The Hall of Morning Audience, the Hall of Rising into
*   Space, the Precious Light Hall, the Hall of the*
*   Heavenly Kings, the Hall of the Master of Miracles,*
Jade unicorns on every column.
On the Terrace of the Star of Longevity
Grew flowers that never wither.
Beside the Stove for Decocting Elixir,
Were herbs that stay green for ever.
In front of the Facing the Sage Pavilion
Crimson gauze clothes
Glittered like stars;
Lotus hats
Shone with golden brilliance.
Jade hairpins and pearl-sewn shoes,
Golden seals on purple cords.
As the golden bell tolled,
The three classes of divinities approached the steps and
*   submitted memorials.*
As the heavenly drum was beaten,
Ten thousand sage kings attended the Jade Emperor.
Then they entered the Hall of Miraculous Mist,
Where jade doors were studded with gold,
And phoenixes danced before the crimson gates.
Winding arcades,
Everywhere carved in openwork;
Layer on layer of eaves,
With dragons and phoenixes soaring.
On top was a majestically purple,
Bright,
Perfectly round,

And dazzling
Golden gourd-shaped finial;
Below, fans hung from the hands of heavenly consorts,
While jade maidens proffered magic clothes.
Ferocious
The heavenly generals guarding the court;
Majestic
The immortal officials protecting the throne.
In the middle were set
Crystal dishes
Filled to overflowing with Great Monad Pills;
Agate jars
In which stood twisted coral trees.
All the wonderful things in Heaven were there,
None of which are seen on Earth:
Golden gates, silver chariots, and a purple palace;
Precious plants, jade flowers, and jasper petals.
The jade hares paying respects to the king ran past the
* altar;*
The golden rooks worshipping the sages flew down low.
The Monkey King was fated to come to Heaven,
Rather than be sullied by the mortal world.

The Great White Planet led the Handsome Monkey King
to the outside of the Hall of Miraculous Mist. He went straight
in to the imperial presence without waiting to be summoned,
and did obeisance to the throne. Sun Wukong stood bolt
upright beside him, not bothering with any court etiquette, but
just concentrating on listening to the Great White Planet make
his report to the Jade Emperor: "In obedience to the Divine
Edict, your subject has brought the demon Immortal here."
The Jade Emperor lowered his curtain and asked, "And which
of you is the demon immortal?" "Me," replied Sun Wukong,
only now making a slight bow. The faces of the officials went
white with horror as they exclaimed, "What a savage monkey!
He has the impudence to answer 'Me', and without even prostrating himself first! He must die!" In reply to this the Jade

Emperor announced, "Sun Wukong is a demon immortal of the lower world who has only just obtained human form, so he is not acquainted with court procedure. We shall forgive him this time." "We thank you for your mercy," said the immortal ministers. Only then did Sun Wukong express his respect by bowing low and chanting "re-e-er" at the top of his voice. The Jade Emperor ordered his immortal civil and military officials to find a vacancy in some department for Sun Wukong. The Star Lord Wuqu stepped forward from the side and reported, "There are no vacancies in any of the palaces, halls, and departments of Heaven except for a superintendent in the Imperial Stables." "Then make him Protector of the Horses," ordered the Jade Emperor. All the ministers thanked him for his mercy, apart from Sun Wukong, who just expressed his respect with another loud "re-e-er". The Jade Emperor then told the Wood Planet to take him to the Imperial Stables.

The Wood Planet accompanied the delighted Monkey King to his post and then went back to the palace. The Monkey King then called together the deputy and the assistant superintendent, the book-keeper, the grooms, and all the other officials, high and low, to find out about the duties of his department. He found that he had to look after a thousand heavenly horses:

> Chestnuts and stallions,
> Coursers and chargers:
> Dragon and Purple Swallow,
> Pegasus and Sushun,
> Jueti and Silver,
> Yaoniao and Flying Yellow,
> Taotu and Feathers,
> Red Hare and Faster Than Light,
> Dazzler and Horizon,
> Mist-soarer and Victory,
> Wind-chaser and Matchless,
> Flying Wing and Galloping Mist,
> Lazy Whirlwind and Red Lightning,
> Bronze Cup and Drifting Cloud,

Skewbald and Tiger-Stripe,
Dustfree and Purple Scales,
The Four Ferghana Steeds,
The Eight Chargers and Nine Gallopers,
Coursers that can cover three hundred miles —
All these fine horses were
Neighing in the wind, chasing the lightning, mighty in
* spirit;*
Pawing the mist, climbing the clouds, great in their
* strength.*

The Monkey King looked through the register and counted the horses. In the stables the book-keeper was responsible for ordering the fodder, the head groom was in charge of currying the horses, chopping up and cooking the fodder, and giving them water; the deputy superintendent and his assistant helped to oversee the work. The Protector of the Horses looked after his charges, sleeping neither by day nor by night. It is true that he busied himself with them by day, at night he looked after the animals with great diligence, waking them up and making them eat whenever they fell asleep, and leading those still on their feet to the trough. At the sight of him the heavenly horses would prick up their ears and paw the ground, and they became fat and plump. Thus more than a fortnight slipped by. On one morning that was a holiday all the officials of the stables held a feast both to welcome and congratulate the Protector of the Horses.

In the middle of the party the Monkey King suddenly put down his cup and asked, "What sort of office is this 'Protector of the Horses'?" "What the name suggests, that's all." "Which official grading does it carry?" "Unclassified." "What does 'unclassified' mean?" "Bottom grade," the others replied, going on to explain, "it is a very low and unimportant office and all you can do in it is look after the horses. Even someone who works as conscientiously as Your Honour and gets the horses so fat will get no more reward than someone saying 'good'; and if anything goes at all wrong you will be held re-

sponsible, and if the losses are serious you will be fined and
punished." The Monkey King flared up on hearing this,
gnashed his teeth, and said in a great rage, "How dare they
treat me with such contempt? On the Mountain of Flowers
and Fruit I am a king and a patriarch. How dare he trick me
into coming here to feed his horses for him? It's a low job
for youngsters, not for me. I won't do it, I won't. I'm going
back." ·He pushed the table over with a crash, took his treasure
out of his ear, and shook it. It became as thick as a rice bowl,
and he brandished it as he charged out of the Imperial Stables
to the Southern Gate of Heaven. As the celestial guards knew
that his name was on the register of immortal officials they
did not dare to block his path, but let him out through the gate.

He descended by cloud and was back on the Mountain of
Flowers and Fruit in an instant. Seeing the four Stalwart
Generals and all the kings of the monsters drilling their troops
there he shouted in a shrill voice, "Children, I'm back." The
monkeys all bowed to him, took him into the heart of the cave,
and asked him to sit on his throne, while they prepared
a banquet to welcome him back. "Congratulations, Your
Majesty," they all said. "After over a dozen years up there
you must be coming back in. glory and triumph." "What do
you mean, over a dozen years?" asked the Monkey King. "I've
only been away for a fortnight or so." "Your Majesty can't
have noticed the time passing in heaven. A day in heaven lasts
as long as a year on earth. May we ask what office you held?"
"It hurts me to tell you," replied the Monkey King with a wave
of his hand. "I feel thoroughly humiliated. That Jade Emperor
doesn't know how to use a good man. A man like me 'Protector of the Horses'! That meant I had to feed his animals
for him and wasn't even given an official grading. I didn't
know this at first, so I fooled around in the Imperial Stables
until today, when I found out from my colleagues how low the
job was. I was so angry that I pushed the table over and quit
the job. That's why I've come back." "Quite right too," the
other monkeys said. "Your Majesty can be king in our cave
paradise and enjoy as much honour and pleasure as you like,

so why go and be his groom?" Then they gave orders for wine to be brought at once to cheer their king up.

As they were drinking someone came in to report, "Your Majesty, there are two Single-horned Devil Kings outside who want to see you." "Ask them in," said the Monkey King, and the two formally-dressed devil kings hurried into the cave and prostrated themselves. "Why have you come to see me?" asked the Handsome Monkey King, and they replied, "We have long heard that Your Majesty is looking for men of talent, but we were unable to see you before. Now that Your Majesty has been given heavenly office and come back in triumph, we would like to offer you this yellow robe as a token of our congratulations. We also hope that you will not reject us although we are low and worthless, but will accept our humble services." An exultant Monkey King put on the yellow robe and his happy subjects bowed to him in order of precedence. The two devil kings were appointed Commanders of the Van, and when they had thanked the Monkey King for this they asked, "What office did Your Majesty hold while you were all that time in Heaven?" "The Jade Emperor has no respect for talent," replied the Monkey King. "He made me something called 'Protector of the Horses'." "Your Majesty has such miraculous powers: you should never have been feeding his horses for him. You should have been made a 'Great Sage Equalling Heaven', shouldn't you?" The Monkey King was beside himself with delight at this suggestion, and he kept saying how splendid it was. "Get me a banner made at once with the words 'Great Sage Equalling Heaven' in big letters on it, and put up a pole to hang it from," he ordered his four Stalwart Generals. "From now on I am to be called 'Great Sage Equalling Heaven', not 'Your Majesty' or 'King'. Pass this order on to all the other kings of the monsters." We will leave him at this point.

When the Jade Emperor held his morning court the next day the Heavenly Teacher Zhang led the deputy and assistant superintendents of the Imperial Stables to the vermilion steps, bowed low, and reported, "Your Majesty, Sun Wukong, the new Protector of the Horses, left Heaven yesterday because he thought his office was too humble." Just as he was speaking the Heavenly King Virudhaka came from the Southern Gate of Heaven with his heavenly soldiers and reported, "The Protector of the Horses has gone out through the gate. We do not know why." On hearing this the Jade Emperor commanded, "Let the two divine officials return to their posts; we shall send heavenly soldiers to capture this devil." The Pagoda-bearing Heavenly King Li Jing and Prince Nezha stepped forward from the ranks of those attending the audience, and they memorialized, "Your Imperial Majesty, we beg you to command us, your incompetent servants, to subdue this fiend." The Emperor was delighted with this suggestion, and he appointed the Pagoda-bearing Heavenly King as Demon-quelling High Marshal, and Prince Nezha as God of the Three Mass Altars. He told them to take their forces down to the lower world at once.

Heavenly King Li and Nezha kowtowed, took their leave, went straight back to their own palace, and assembled their troops, commanders and officers. They put the Mighty Miracle God in charge of the vanguard, and General Fishbelly in command of the rear, while General Yaksa was made adjutant. Within an instant they were outside the Southern Gate of Heaven, and they went straight to the Mountain of Flowers and Fruit. They chose a piece of level and open ground on which to construct a fortified camp, and ordered the Mighty Miracle God to issue the challenge to battle. On receiving this order the Mighty Miracle God tied on his armour firmly and went to the Water Curtain Cave, holding his flower-spreading battle-axe. When he got there he saw huge numbers of devils — wolves, tigers and leopards — wielding spears, brandishing swords, leaping around, fighting each other, and making a great noise outside the little entrance to the cave. "Accursed beasts," shouted the Mighty Miracle God, "tell the Protector of the Horses at once that I am a heavenly general come on the orders of the Jade Emperor to subdue him. If you make him come out and surrender immediately it will save the lot of you from being wiped out." The devils went rushing into the cave and reported, "Disaster, disaster." "What disaster?" the Monkey King asked. "There's a heavenly general outside who says he's come on the orders of the Jade Emperor to subdue you. If you go out and surrender immediately, he says he'll spare our lives." "Fetch me my armour," said the Monkey King. He then donned his golden helmet, tied on his golden armour, put on his cloud-walking shoes, and took his as-you-will gold-banded cudgel in his hand. He led his troops out of the cave and drew them up in battle array. The Mighty Miracle God gazed wide-eyed at the excellent Monkey King:

> On his body was gleaming golden armour,
> On his head a dazzling golden helmet,
> In his hand a gold-banded club,
> On his feet a pair of cloud-walking shoes to match.
> His devil eyes shone like stars,
> His ears were long and hard.
> His sturdy frame could be transformed at will,
> His voice rang clearly as a bell.
> The sharp-mouthed Horse Protector with protruding teeth
> Wanted to become a Sage Equalling Heaven.

The Mighty Miracle God shouted in a harsh voice, "Insolent ape! Don't you recognize me?" The Great Sage Sun Wukong replied at once, "I've never met you before. How should I know which wretched little deity you are? Tell me your name at once." "I'll get you, you conceited baboon. So you don't know who I am? I am the Heavenly General Mighty Miracle, the commander of the vanguard for Heavenly King Li, the Pagoda-bearer. I have come here on the orders of the Jade Emperor to accept your surrender. Take off your armour at once and submit to the mercy of Heaven, or I'll wipe out every animal on the mountain. And if you so much as hint at a refusal, I'll smash you to powder." "Stop talking so big, you lousy god," retorted the furious Monkey King, "and give that long tongue of yours a rest. I'd just love to kill you with this cudgel of mine, but if I did there'd be no one to deliver my message for me, so I'll spare your life. Hurry back to Heaven and tell that Jade Emperor that he doesn't know how to use a good man. Why did he make me waste my infinite powers on feeding his horses for him? Take a look at what's written on my standard. If he's willing to give me this title officially, I'll call off my troops and let Heaven and Earth continue in peace; but if he refuses I'm coming up to the Hall of Miraculous Mist to knock him off his dragon throne." When the Mighty Miracle God heard this he looked hard and saw that a tall pole had been planted outside the entrance to the cave, on which hung a banner reading GREAT SAGE EQUALLING HEAVEN. "Heh, heh, heh," he mocked, "you ignorant ape. What shameless effrontery, to want to be a 'Great Sage Equalling Heaven'! Take that!" He swung with his battle-axe at the Monkey King who, quite unflustered, parried with his gold-banded cudgel. It was a fine battle:

> The cudgel was called As-You-Will,
> The axe was named Flower Spreader.
> As soon as the two met,
> You could not tell which was better:
> Axe and club
> Locked together.
> One was concealing his magic powers,
> One was a big-mouthed boaster.
> They used their magic
> To breathe out cloud and mist;
> When they opened their hands
> They scattered sand and dust.
> The heavenly general was a master of magic;
> Endless were the changes the Monkey King could make.
> When the cudgel was raised it was like a dragon playing
>   in the water;
> As the axe came down it was a phoenix among the
>   flowers.

Although the fame of Miracle was known throughout
*   the world,*
His skill was no match for his enemy.
If the Great Sage lightly twirled his club,
A mere touch on the head would paralyze you.

The Mighty Miracle God was no match for his opponent.
He hastened to block the Monkey King's first blow with his
axe, which broke in two with a crunch. He fled for his life as
fast as he could, and the Monkey King said mockingly, "You
bag of pus, I'll spare you this time. Hurry back with my message, and look sharp about it."

The Mighty Miracle God returned to his camp, went straight
to the Pagoda-bearing Heavenly King Li Jing, knelt before him,
and said with an awkward laugh, "The Protector of the Horses
has really tremendous magic powers. I was no match for him.
He beat me, and now I have come to take my punishment."
"This fool has ruined our morale," exploded the Heavenly King
Li in a fury. "Take him away, and off with his head." Prince
Nezha, who was standing to one side, stepped forward, bowed,
and said, "Do not be angry, Your Majesty. Forgive the Mighty
Miracle God, and let me go and do battle; then we'll see who's
boss." The heavenly king accepted his advice, and told Mighty
Miracle God to go back and look after the camp while he await-
ed his punishment.

When he had put on his armour and helmet, Prince Nezha
charged straight out of the camp to the Water Curtain Cave.
Sun Wukong, who was just going to pull back his troops, saw
the ferocity of his onslaught. What a fine prince he was:

His hair in tufts barely covers his scalp,
His cloak not over his shoulders.
How striking his intelligence,
How elegant his air.
Indeed he is the scion of a unicorn in Heaven;
In truth he is a phoenix Immortal from the clouds.
The seed of dragons is different from the common herd;
This fine youth is not at all like mortals.

With him he carries six divine weapons;
Endless his transformations as he soars through the air.
Now he has received an edict from the Jade Emperor's
*   mouth,*
Making him God of the Three Altars of the Masses.

Sun Wukong went up to him and asked, "Whose little boy are you then? What do you mean, charging up to my door?" "Stinking monkey fiend," shouted Prince Nezha, "don't you know who I am? I am Nezha, the third son of the Pagoda-bearing Heavenly King, and I have been commanded by the Jade Emperor to come here and arrest you." "You do talk big, don't you, little prince," said Sun Wukong, laughing at him. "But as you've still got all your milk teeth and are still wet behind the ears I'll spare your life and I won't hit you. Do you see what it says on my standard? Go and tell the Jade Emperor that if he gives me that title I'll call off my armies and submit to him once more. But if he doesn't do what I want him to, I'll surely attack the Hall of Miraculous Mist." Nezha looked up and saw the words "Great Sage Equalling Heaven". "You wicked monkey! How dare you give yourself a title like that, whatever your magic powers may be! Don't worry, all you're getting is my sword." "I'll take a few swipes, then," replied Sun Wukong, "I won't move." "Change," yelled Nezha in a passion, and at once he had three heads and six arms, which made him look most ferocious. In his hands he held six weapons, a demon-beheading sword, a demon-hacking cutlass, a demon-binding rope, a demon-quelling pestle, an embroidered ball, and a fire-wheel — and wielding all these he rushed straight at Sun Wukong. At the sight of him Sun Wukong exclaimed with astonishment, "Well, my boy, you certainly know a trick or two. But just behave yourself and watch what I can do." Our dear Great Sage shouted "Change", and he too had three heads and six arms. He shook his gold-banded cudgel, and it turned into three cudgels, which he gripped with his six hands to ward off Nezha's blows. It was a great fight, and it made the earth shake and the mountains tremble:

Six-armed Prince Nezha
Heaven-born Monkey King:
Well-matched opponents,
Both in the same class.
One sent down to the lower world on a mission,
The other priding himself on fighting against Heaven.
Sharp is the point of the demon-beheading sword,
And evil spirits fear the demon-hacking cutlass,
The demon-binding rope like a flying snake,
While the demon-quelling pestle has the head of a wolf,
The fire-wheel flashes with lightning,
Rolling everywhere like an embroidered ball.
The Great Sage's three as-you-will cudgels
Block and parry with consummate skill.
Though many hard-fought rounds prove inconclusive,
The prince refuses to call the battle off;
Making his six weapons multiply in number,
He throws them in their millions at the Monkey King's
*   head,*
But the fearless Monkey King roars with laughter
As his iron clubs whirl and think for themselves.
One becomes a thousand; one thousand, ten;
Their wild dance fills the sky as if with dragons.
All the demon kings shut their gates in terror;
Every goblin on the mountain finds some place to hide.
Cloud-black, the anger of the heavenly troops;
Whistling like the wind, the gold-banded cudgels.
On the one side,
The blood-curdling war-cries of the heavenly host.
On the other,
The spine-chilling banners of the monkey fiends.
Both parties are equal in fighting courage;
Neither could be said to be the winner.

Prince Nezha and Sun Wukong both used their divine powers to the full as they fought thirty rounds. When the six weapons of the Prince turned into thousands and tens of thousands, so did Sun Wukong's gold-banded cudgel. The air was filled as if with drops of rain or shooting stars, and there was no way of telling who was winning. As Sun Wukong was deft of hand and quick of eye, he plucked one of the hairs from his body in the midst of the fray and shouted "Change!" It changed into his own double to mislead Nezha while his real self leapt round till he was behind Nezha and struck at his left shoulder. Nezha was in the middle of performing a spell when he heard the whistle of the cudgel through the air and twisted away as fast as he could. But he was unable to avoid the blow and had to flee wounded. He brought his magic to an end, put his six weapons away, reverted to his true appearance, and abandoned the field of battle in defeat.

This had all been observed by Heavenly King Li, who was on the point of sending reinforcements when his son appeared before him and reported in fear and trembling, "Father, the Protector of the Horses is very powerful. My magic was outclassed and he has wounded me in the shoulder." The colour drained from the face of the horror-struck Heavenly King as he said, "If the creature has magic powers like that, how are we going to defeat him?" "Outside the gates of the cave," the prince went on to report, "there is a banner on a pole that reads 'Great Sage Equalling Heaven'. He bragged that if the Jade Emperor gave him this title he would call everything off; otherwise he said he would attack the Hall of Miraculous Mist." "In that case," said the Heavenly King, "we'll disengage now, go back to Heaven, and request that more heavenly troops be sent to capture this wretch. There is plenty of time." The prince, in pain and unable to go on fighting, went back to Heaven with the Heavenly King and put in this request, but of that no more for the moment.

Watch as the Monkey King returns to the mountain in triumph to receive the congratulations of the seventy-two kings of the monsters and his six sworn brothers. There was great drinking and singing in the cave paradise. Sun Wukong said to his six sworn brothers, "As I've called myself Great Sage

Equalling Heaven, you can all call yourselves great sages too."
"Honourable brother, you're right," roared the Bull Demon
King. "I shall call myself the Great Sage Matching Heaven."
"I'll be the Great Sage Overturning the Sea," said the Salamander Demon King. "I'll be the Great Sage Throwing
Heaven into Confusion," said the Roc Demon King. "I'll be
the Great Sage Who Moves Mountains," said the Camel Demon King. "I'll be the Great Sage Who Travels with the
Wind," said the Macaque King. "And I'll be the Great Sage
Who Drives Away Gods," said the Lion King. The seven
great sages then did just as they pleased and gave themselves
the titles they chose, and after enjoying themselves all day they
went home.

Heavenly King Li and Prince Nezha led their forces straight
to the Palace of Miraculous Mist and made this request: "We,
your subjects, took our forces down to the lower world, under
your Divine Edict, to subdue the immortal fiend Sun Wukong.
But to our surprise we found that his magical powers were too
far-reaching for us to be able to defeat him. We therefore hope
that Your Imperial Majesty will send more troops to exterminate
him." "How could a mere monkey goblin have such great
powers that you actually need more troops?" asked the Jade
Emperor. Prince Nezha then came forward and memorialized,
"We beg Your Majesty to spare us the deaths we deserve. That
monkey fiend has an iron cudgel that he used to defeat the
Mighty Miracle God and wounded me on the shoulder. He has
set a banner up outside the entrance to his cave that reads Great
Sage Equalling Heaven', and he says that if you give him this
office he will stop fighting and submit; otherwise he will attack
the Hall of Miraculous Mist." When the Jade Emperor heard
this he asked in horror, "How dare that monkey fiend talk so
wildly? Send all the generals to execute him at once."

As he spoke the Great White Planet stepped forward from
the ranks of officials. "That monkey fiend knows how to talk,"
he suggested, "but he has no idea about real power. If more
soldiers were sent to fight him, they might not be able to overcome him at once and their energies would be wasted. But if

Your Imperial Majesty were to show your great mercy, you could send down a pacificatory amnesty and let him be a Great Sage Equalling Heaven. It would only be an empty title that he was given, just an honorary appointment." "What do you mean by an honorary appointment?" asked the Jade Emperor. "He would be called a Great Sage Equalling Heaven, but he would not be given any responsibility or paid any salary. He would be kept between Heaven and Earth, where his evil nature would be under control and he would be kept from wickedness. Thus Heaven and Earth can be at peace, while sea and sky enjoy tranquility." The Jade Emperor approved this suggestion and ordered that a new edict should be issued for the Great White Planet to deliver.

The Great White Planet left once more through the Southern Gate of Heaven and went straight to have a look at the Water Curtain Cave on the Mountain of Flowers and Fruit. It was quite different from before. There was an awe-inspiring and spine-chilling atmosphere, and every kind of fiend was present. They were roaring and leaping around with their swords, spears, cutlasses and staves. As soon as they saw the Great White Planet they all went for him. "Will your commander please come forward," said the Planet. "I would trouble you to inform your Great Sage that I am a heavenly envoy sent by the Jade Emperor, and I am carrying a divine edict with an invitation for him." The fiends rushed in to report, "There's an old man outside who says he's come from Heaven with an edict of invitation for you." When Sun Wukong heard this he said, "I'm glad he's come. I expect he's that Great White Planet who came before. Although I wasn't given a decent job last time I went to Heaven, I did get up there and learn my way around. If it's him again, his intentions must be good." He told his commanders to put on a big display of banners and drums and to turn out a guard of honour to welcome him. Then the Great Sage, wearing his helmet, his yellow robe over his armour, and his cloud-walking shoes, hurried out of the cave at the head of his monkey host, bowed in greeting, and shouted in a loud voice, "Please come in, venerable Planet. Forgive me for not being here to welcome you."

The Planet walked straight into the cave, stood facing the south and said, "Great Sage, when you left the Imperial Stables because you found the post too humble, the officials of that department naturally reported the matter to the Jade Emperor. The Jade Emperor decreed that all officials have to work their way up from the bottom, and asked why you objected to its being humble. After this Heavenly King Li took Nezha down to the lower world to do battle with you. Your divine powers, Great Sage, were more than they expected, and they suffered defeat. On their return to Heaven they reported that you had set up a banner and wanted to be a 'Great Sage Equalling Heaven'. All the generals wanted to punish you; but I, Great Sage, ran the risk of punishment by suggesting that the armies should not be called out, and that Your Majesty should be given a post instead. The Jade Emperor approved my memorial, and that is why I have come here to invite you." "I am most grateful for this honour after the trouble I caused you earlier," replied Sun Wukong, "but I am not sure whether there is such a title as 'Great Sage Equalling Heaven' in the upper world." "After obtaining imperial approval for this title," said the Planet, "I came down bearing a decree. If anything goes wrong, I'll bear the responsibility."

A highly delighted Sun Wukong tried his hardest to persuade the Planet to stay to a banquet, but without success, so he went with him by propitious cloud to the Southern Gate of Heaven. The heavenly generals and soldiers all greeted them with respectfully folded arms, and they went straight to the Hall of Miraculous Mist. The Great White Planet did obeisance and said, "In obedience to the imperial edict your subject has summoned Sun Wukong, the Protector of the Horses, and he is present." "Let Sun Wukong come forward," said the Jade Emperor. "We do now proclaim you Great Sage Equalling Heaven. Your rank is now very high. Let there be no more mischief from you." The monkey simply chanted "re-e-er" to express his thanks to the Emperor. The Jade Emperor then ordered the two officials in charge of public works, Zhang and Lu, to build a residence for the Great Sage Equalling Heaven to the left of the Peach Orchard. In the residence there were to be two offices: a Tranquillity Office and a Calm Divinity Office. Both these offices were to have immortal clerks and senior and junior assistants. He then told the Star Lords of the Constellation Five to escort Sun Wukong to his post, and in addition gave him two bottles of imperial wine and ten golden flowers, and admonished him to settle down and keep out of mischief. The Monkey King accepted the order and went that same day with the Star Lords of the Constellation Five to his residence, where he opened the bottles of wine and drained them dry with the help of all present. He then saw the star officials off and returned to his own palace. From then on he lived in happiness and content, and enjoyed untrammelled pleasure in the Palace. Truly,

> His immortal name was for ever inscribed in the register of eternal life,
> To be transmitted for ten thousand ages, free of the wheel of rebirth.

If you don't know what happened next, listen to the explanation in the next instalment.

乱蟠桃大圣偷丹 反天宫诸神捉怪

CHAPTER FIVE

After chaos among the peaches the Great Sage
steals the pills;
In the revolt against Heaven the gods
capture the demons.

The story goes on to relate that the Great Sage Equalling
Heaven, a mere monkey devil after all, was quite satisfied that
his name was on the register of office without caring about the
grading of his job and his own rank, or the size of his salary.
The immortal clerks in the two offices in his residence were
in constant attendance on him, he had three meals a day and
a bed to sleep on at night, and he lived a free and easy life
without worries. In his spare time he would visit the other
palaces, get together with his old friends, and make new ones.
When he saw the Three Pure Ones, he would address them as
"venerable", and when he met the Four Emperors he called
them "Your Majesty". He was on fraternal terms with the
Nine Bright Shiners, the Generals of the Five Regions, the
Twenty-Eight Constellations, the Four Great Heavenly Kings,
the Gods of the Twelve Branches, the Five Ancients of the Five
Regions, the star ministers of the whole sky, and the countless
gods of the Milky Way. Today he would wander east, and tomorrow he would go west, coming and going by cloud, and
never staying anywhere for long.

When the Jade Emperor was holding his morning court one
day the Immortal Xu of Jingyang came forward from the body
of officials, kowtowed, and suggested, "The Great Sage
Equalling Heaven is spending his time in idle travel, and is
making the acquaintance of all the stars in the sky, calling them
all his friends irrespective of their rank. It would be as well

to give him some responsibility, and prevent his idleness leading to trouble later on." The Jade Emperor's response to this suggestion was to send for the Monkey King at once. He came in a cheerful mood and asked, "What promotion and reward have you summoned me here to receive, Your Majesty?" "Seeing that you are idle and have nothing to do," replied the Jade Emperor, "we are giving you a job. You are to administer the Peach Orchard, and you will give it your attention day and night." The Great Sage was overjoyed, and after expressing his thanks and chanting "re-e-er" he withdrew.

In his eagerness to be at work he went straight to the Peach Orchard to have a look round. When he got there he was stopped by a local tutelary god who asked him, "Where are you going, Great Sage?" "I've been put in charge of the Peach Orchard by the Jade Emperor, and I've come to inspect it." The local god hastened to greet him formally, and he called the men who weeded, brought water, looked after the trees, and swept the grounds to come and kowtow to the Great Sage. When Sun Wukong was taken inside this is what he saw:

> *Charming,*
> *Every tree.*
> *Charming and luxuriant the full blossom;*
> *Every tree weighed down with fruit.*
> *The fruit-laden branches are bent by balls of brocade;*
> *The blossoming trees are covered with tufts of rouge.*
> *Always blossoming, always in fruit, they are ripe for a*
>   *thousand years;*
> *They know no summer or winter, but linger for ever.*
> *The early ripeners*
> *Look red-faced and tipsy;*
> *The ones still growing*
> *Are green in stalk and skin.*
> *When the dew forms, their flesh has a touch of blue,*
> *While the sun picks out their vermilion beauty.*
> *Below the trees exotic flowers grow,*
> *Bright and unfading throughout the year.*

> *On either side stand towers and pavilions,*
> *And a rainbow always arches the sky.*
> *These are not the common breeds of the Dark Earth*
>   *Capital,*
> *But are tended by the Queen Mother of the Jade Pool.*

After taking a good look at this the Great Sage asked the local god, "How many of these trees are there?" "Three thousand six hundred all together," the local god replied. "The ones growing at the front have tiny blossoms and small fruits, and they ripen every three thousand years. Anyone who eats them becomes an immortal and understands the Way, and his body becomes both light and strong. The twelve hundred in the middle have multiple blossoms and sweet fruits, and ripen every six thousand years; whoever eats them can fly and enjoy eternal youth. The back twelve hundred are streaked with purple and have pale yellow stones. They ripen once every nine thousand years, and anyone who eats them becomes as eternal as Heaven and Earth, as long-lived as the Sun and Moon." The Great Sage was beside himself with joy on learning this, and that day he checked the number of the trees and looked over the buildings in the orchard before going back to his residence. From then on he went to admire them every three or four days. He dropped his friends, and made no more pleasure jaunts.

One day he noticed that the peaches near the end of the branches of one old tree were all but ripe, and he felt like trying one; but as the local god, the workmen, and the immortal clerks from his residence were close on his heels it was impossible. Suddenly he had an idea, and he said, "Go and wait for me outside the gates while I take a nap in this summerhouse." All the immortals thereupon withdrew, and the Monkey King took off his official hat and clothes, climbed one of the bigger trees, and chose some large, ripe peaches. When he had picked a good number he sat at his ease in the branches and ate his fill of them, then jumped down from the tree, pinned on his hat, put on his clothes, and shouted for all his attendants to go back to his residence with him. Two or three days later he thought of another trick to steal some more peaches, and he ate his fill of them.

One day the Queen Mother arranged a banquet, opening many precious pavilions for a peach banquet by the Jade Pool. She sent the Red Fairy, the Blue Fairy, the White Fairy, the Black Fairy, the Purple Fairy, the Yellow Fairy, and the Green Fairy to the Peach Orchard with their baskets to pick peaches for the feast. The seven fairies went straight to the orchard gates, the workmen of the orchard and the immortal superintendents of the two offices of the Equalling Heaven Residence were guarding the gate. The fairies went up to them and said, "We have come on the orders of the Queen Mother to pick peaches for a feast." "Wait a moment please, Immortal Beauties," said the local god. "Things are different this year. The Jade Emperor has appointed the Great Sage Equalling Heaven to be the guardian of this orchard, and we must ask him before we can open the orchard to you." "Where is the Great Sage?" the fairies asked, and the local god replied, "Inside the orchard. As he was feeling tired he is having a nap by himself in a summerhouse." "In that case, please find him without delay," requested the fairies, and the local god took them into the orchard. But all they could find of him in the summerhouse were his hat and clothes. They had no idea where he could have gone, and looked everywhere without success. The Great Sage had in fact made himself only two inches long after eating some of the peaches for fun, and he was sleeping under a large leaf at the top of one of the big trees.

"We have come by decree, and we can't go back empty-handed, even if the Great Sage is nowhere to be found," said the fairies. One of the immortal superintendents who was standing nearby replied, "As you Immortal Beauties have come by order of the Queen Mother, we must not delay you. Our Great Sage is always wandering off, so I expect that he has gone away to visit some of his friends. You had better pick the peaches; it will be all right if we inform him." The fairies did as he suggested and went into the orchard to pick peaches. First they filled two baskets from the trees in front, and then they picked three basketfuls from the trees in the middle; but when they came to the trees at the back, they saw that peaches and blossoms were few and far between. Only a few unripe fruits with furry stalks and green skins were left. All the ripe ones had been eaten up by the Monkey King. The seven fairies looked everywhere, but all they could see was a single red and white peach on a southern branch. The Blue Fairy pulled the branch down, the Red Fairy picked the peach, and then they let the branch go again. This woke up the Great Sage, who had changed himself into this peach to take a nap on this branch. He resumed his own form, took his gold-banded cudgel from his ear, shook it till it was as thick as a ricebowl, and shouted at them, "Where are you from, you thieving fiends?" The seven fairies fell on their knees in confusion. "Please don't be angry with us, Great Sage. We're not fiends but seven fairies sent by Her Majesty the Queen Mother of the West to pick peaches of immortality and open the precious halls here for a peach banquet. When we arrived here we saw the local god and other deities of the place, but we could not find you, Great Sage. We could not delay carrying out the Queen Mother's orders, so we went ahead and picked the peaches without waiting for you, Great Sage. We very much hope that you will forgive us." These words turned the Great Sage's bad mood into a good one, and he said, "Please rise, Fairy Beauties. Who is the Queen Mother inviting to this feast?" "There are old rules about who attends: The Buddha of the Western Heaven, Bodhisattvas, holy monks, Arhats, the Guanyin of the South Pole, the Merciful and Sage Emperor of the East, the Venerable Immortals of the Ten Continents and the Three Islands, the Mystic Divinity of the North Pole, and the Great Yellow-horned Immortal of the Yellow Pole at the Centre. These make up the Five Venerable Ones of the Five Regions. There will also be the Star Lords of the Five Constellation; the Three Pure Ones, the Four Emperors and the Heavenly Immortal of the Great Monad from the Eight High Caves; the Jade Emperor, the immortals of the Nine Mounds, and the gods of the Seas and Mountains from the Eight Middle Caves and the Ruler

of the Nether World and the terrestrial deities from the Eight
Lower Caves. All the major and minor gods of all the halls
and palaces will come to the Feast of Peaches." "Will I be invited?" asked the Great Sage with an ingratiating smile. "Not as
far as we've heard," the fairies replied. "I'm the Great Sage
Equalling Heaven, so why shouldn't I be an honoured guest?"
said the Great Sage. "That was what happened before: we
don't know about this time," the fairies replied. "You're right,"
he said. "Just wait here while I go and find out whether I'm
invited.

Splendid Great Sage. Making a magic with his hands as
he spoke the words of the spell, he said to the fairies, "Stay
where you are! Stay where you are!" As this was an im-
mobilizing spell, the seven fairies were left standing in a daze
under the peach tree with their eyes wide open as the Great
Sage leapt out of the orchard on a somersault cloud and headed
for the Jade Pool. As he travelled he saw that

> *The sky shimmered with auspicious light*
> *As clouds of many colours streamed across it.*
> *The white stork's cry made the heavens shake;*
> *A thousand leaves grew on the purple asphodel.*
> *Amid it all an immortal appeared,*
> *Carrying himself with heaven-sent elegance,*
> *As he danced on the rainbow, cloaked by the Milky Way,*
> *With a talisman at his waist to ward off birth and death.*
> *His name was Barefoot Immortal,*
> *And he was going to the feast of life-extending peaches.*

As the Barefoot Immortal saw him, the Great Sage
lowered his head and thought of a plan by which to trick the
Immortal and get to the banquet himself. "Where are you going, reverend sir" he asked; and the immortal replied,
"I'm going to the Peach Banquet by the invitation of the
Queen Mother." "There is something you do not know,
venerable sir," said the Great Sage. "As my somersault cloud
is so fast, the Jade Emperor has sent me everywhere to tell all
you gentlemen to go to the Hall of Universal Brightness for

a ceremony before going on to the banquet." As the immortal
was an open and upright man, he took this lie for the truth,
but wondered, "The thanksgiving ceremony is usually held by
the Jade Pool, so why are we having the ceremony in the Hall
of Universal Brightness before going to the Jade Pool for the
banquet?" Nevertheless, he turned his propitious cloud around
and went to the Hall of Universal Brightness.

As the Great Sage rode his cloud he said a spell, shook
himself, took the form of the Barefoot Immortal, and hurried
to the Jade Pool. He reached the pavilion there a moment later,
stopped his cloud, and went quietly inside. He saw

> *Fabulous perfumes coiling,*
> *A confusion of auspicious clouds;*
> *The jade tower set with colour,*
> *The precious pavilions scattering mists;*
> *The phoenix soars till almost lost to view,*
> *And jewelled flowers seem to rise and fall.*
> *Above a nine-phoenix screen*
> *A rainbow stool of the eight precious things,*
> *A coloured, golden table,*
> *Green jade bowls with a thousand flowers.*
> *On the table are dragon livers and marrow of phoenix*
> *   bone,*
> *Bears' paws and apes' lips —*
> *A hundred different dishes, and all of them good;*
> *Rare fruits and fine delicacies, every one unique.*

Everything was neatly set out, but no Immortals had yet
arrived. The Great Sage had not finished looking when he
smelt wine; and as he whirled round he saw under a portico to
the right several immortal officials in charge of brewing liquor
with some workmen who stirred the lees, a number of novices
who carried water and some boys who looked after the fires.
They were washing the vats and scrubbing the pots, having
made jade liquor and a fragrant fermentation of the less. The
Great Sage could not stop himself from drooling, and he longed
to drink some, but unfortunately all those people were there.

So he performed a spell by pulling several hairs from his body, chewing them up, spitting them up, saying the magic words, and shouting "Change"; whereupon the hairs turned into sleep insects, which flew into the faces of all the liquor-makers. Watch them as their hands go limp, their heads droop, their eyes close, and they drop their activities and all fall asleep. Whereupon the Great Sage grabbed the rare delicacies and exotic foods, then went under the portico and drank from the vats and pots until he was completely drunk. Only then did he think, "This won't do at all. When the guests come for the banquet they'll be furious with me, and I'll be for it if I'm caught. I'd better get back to the Residence as soon as I can and sleep it off."

Our dear Great Sage staggered and swayed, charging about all over the place under the influence of the liquor, and going the wrong way. He arrived not at the Equalling Heaven Residence but at the Tushita Heavenly Palace. As soon as he saw this he sobered up and said to himself, "The Tushita Palace is the highest of the thirty-three heavens, where Lord Lao Zi of the Great Monad reigns. However did I get here? Never mind, I've always wanted to see that old chap, and I've never managed to come here before. I might as well go and have a look at him now that I'm passing this way." He straightened his clothes and rushed in, but did not see Lord Lao Zi. There was no sign of anyone. This was because Lao Zi and the Ancient Buddha Dipamkara were expounding the Way from a red dais in a triple-storeyed pavilion, and all the immortal boys, generals, officials and petty functionaries were standing to right and left listening to the lecture. The Great Sage went straight to the room in which the elixir was kept, and although he could not find Lao Zi there he saw that there was a small fire in the stove beside the range over which pills were made. Around the stove were five gourds, full of golden pills of refined elixir. "This is the immortals' greatest treasure," he exclaimed in delight. "I've wanted to refine some of these golden pills to save people with ever since I understood the Way and mastered the principle of the correspondence of the Esoteric and Exoteric, but I've never had time to come here. Today I'm in luck — I've found them. As Lao Zi isn't here I'll try a few." He emptied the gourds of their contents and ate up all the pills as if he were eating fried beans.

Before long he was full of pills and quite sober. "This is terrible," he thought, "this is a frightful disaster. If the Jade Emperor is shocked by this, I'm done for. I must get out of here. I'd be much better off as a king in the lower world." He rushed out of the Tushita Palace, avoiding his usual route. Using a spell to make himself invisible, he left by the West Gate of Heaven, and went straight down to the Mountain of Flowers and Fruit by cloud. When he got there he saw flags, banners, spears and halberds gleaming in the sun: the four Stalwart Generals and the seventy-two kings of the monsters were holding military exercises. "Children, I'm back," shouted the Great Sage in a loud voice, and all the fiends dropped their weapons and fell to their knees. "You don't care, do you, Great Sage?" they said. "It's been so long since you left us, and you never came back to see us." "I haven't been long, I haven't been long," protested the Great Sage, and as they talked they walked into the innermost part of the cave. When the four Stalwart Generals had tidied the place up and made him sit down, they kowtowed to him and asked, "What office did you hold, Great Sage, during your century and more in Heaven?" The Great Sage laughed and said, "As far as I can remember it was only six months, so why do you say it was over a century?" "A day in Heaven is the same as a year on earth," the Stalwart Generals replied. "I was lucky this time," said the Great Sage. "The Jade Emperor took a liking to me and ennobled me as the Great Sage Equalling Heaven. He had an Equalling Heaven Residence built for me, complete with a Tranquillity Office and a Calm Divinity Office with immortal functionaries, attendants and guards. Later on, when he saw that I had nothing to do, he put me in charge of the Peach Orchard. Recently the Queen Mother Goddess gave a Peach Banquet, but she didn't invite me. Instead of waiting for an invitation, I went to the Jade Pool and stole all the immortal food and drink. I staggered away from the Jade Pool and blundered into Lord Lao Zi's palace, and there I ate up his five gourds of pills of immortality. Then I got out through the heavenly gates and came here because I was scared that the Jade Emperor was going to punish me."

All the fiends were delighted with what they heard, and they laid on liquor and fruit with which to welcome him back. They filled a stone bowl with coconut toddy and handed it to him, but when he tasted it the Great Sage grimaced and said, "It's awful, it's awful." Two of his Stalwart Generals, Beng and Ba, explained, "You don't find coconut toddy very tasty because you've been drinking immortal liquor and eating immortal food in the heavenly palace, Great Sage. But as the saying goes, 'Sweet or not, it's water from home'." To this the Great Sage replied, "And all of you, 'whether related to me or not, are from my home.' When I was enjoying myself beside the Jade Pool today I saw jars and jars of jade liquor under a portico there. As none of you have ever tasted it I'll go and pinch you a few jars; then you can each have a little drink, and live for ever." All the monkeys were beside themselves with glee. The Great Sage then went out of the cave, turned a somersault, made himself invisible, and went straight to the Peach Banquet. As he went through the gates of the Jade Pool he saw that the men who made the wine, stirred the lees, carried the water, and looked after the fire were still snoring away. He tucked two big jars of wine under his arms, took two more in his hands, then turned his cloud round and went back to have a feast of immortal wine with the monkey masses in the cave. They all drank several cups and were very happy, but we will not go into this.

The story returns to the seven fairies, who were only able to free themselves a whole day after Sun Wukong had immobilized them with his magic. They picked up their baskets and went back to report to the Queen Mother that they were late because the Great Sage Equalling Heaven had held them there by magic. "How many peaches did you pick?" the Queen

Mother asked. "Two baskets of little ones and three baskets of medium ones. But when we got to the back we could not find a single big one; we think that they were all eaten by the Great Sage. While we were looking for some the Great Sage suddenly appeared, and he beat and tortured us to make us tell him who had been invited to the banquet. After we had told him he immobilized us there, and we don't know where he went. We only came round and freed ourselves a moment ago."

On hearing this the Queen Mother went to see the Jade Emperor and gave him a full account of what had happened. Before she had finished, the liquor-makers arrived with their immortal officials to report that an unknown person had thrown the Grand Peach Banquet into confusion and stolen the jade liquor as well as the precious delicacies of a hundred flavours. Then came Four Heavenly Teachers to announce that the Supreme Patriarch of the Way, Lao Zi, had arrived. The Jade Emperor went out with the Queen Mother to meet him, and after doing obeisance Lao Zi said, "I had refined some Golden Pills of the Nine Transformations in my palace for a Feast of Elixir Pills with Your Majesty, but a thief has stolen them. This is what I have come to report to Your Majesty." This news made the Jade Emperor tremble with fear. Not long afterwards the immortal administrators from the Equalling Heaven Residence came to kowtow and report: "The Great Sage Sun Wukong abandoned his post and went wandering off yesterday. He has not come back yet and we do not know where he has gone." The Jade Emperor, now more suspicious than ever, then saw the Barefoot Immortal bow his head to the ground. "Your subject was going to the banquet on a summons from the Queen Mother," he reported, "when I happened to meet the Great Sage Equalling Heaven. He told me that Your Majesty had issued a decree ordering him to tell all the rest of us to go to the Hall of Universal Brightness for a ceremony before going to the banquet. Your subject went back to the Hall of Universal Brightness as he had told me to, but as I did not see the Imperial Dragon and Phoenix Chariot outside I hurried here to await orders." "This wretch has the impudence to invent fraudulent decrees and deceive eminent ministers," exclaimed the Jade Emperor with anger and astonishment. "The Miraculous Investigator is to find out at once what he has been up to."

The Miraculous Investigator left the palace in obedience to the edict, and by making thorough enquiries he found out all the details of what had happened. "The wrecker of the Heavenly Palace was Sun Wukong," he reported, and he went on to give a full account. The Jade Emperor was furiously angry, and he ordered the Four Great Heavenly Kings along with Heavenly King Li and Prince Nezha to mobilize the Twenty-eight Constellations, the Nine Bright Shiners, the Twelve Gods of the Twelve Branches, the Protectors of the Five Regions, the Four Duty Gods, the Constellations of the East and West, the Gods of the North and South, the Deities of the Five Mountains and the Four Rivers, the star ministers of all Heaven, and a total of a hundred thousand heavenly soldiers. They were to descend to the lower world with eighteen heaven-and-earth nets, surround the Mountain of Flowers and Fruit, and capture that wretch for punishment. The gods called out their troops at once, and left the heavenly palace.

> *A gusty sandstorm blotted out the heavens,*
> *Purple fog threw the earth into darkness.*
> *Just because the monkey fiend offended the Supreme*
>   *Emperor*
> *Heavenly hosts were sent down to the mortal dust.*
> *The Four Great Heavenly Kings,*
> *The Protectors of the Five Regions.*
> *The Four Great Heavenly Kings held the supreme*
>   *command,*
> *And the Protectors controlled the soldiers' movements.*
> *Li the Pagoda Carrier commanded the central corps,*
> *Nezha the deadly led the van.*
> *The star Rahu ordered the leading ranks,*
> *And the star Ketu towered behind.*
> *The Sun revealed his divinity,*

And radiance shone from the Moon.
The stars of the Five Elements were mighty in valour,
And the Nine Bright Shiners were fond of battle.
The stars of the Branches Zi, Wu, Mao and You,
Were all great heavenly warriors.
The Five Plagues and the Five Mountains were drawn up on the east and west,
While the Six Dings and Six Jias marched to right and left.
The Dragon Gods of the Four Rivers stood above and below,
And the Twenty-eight Constellations were drawn up in serried ranks:
Horn, Gullet, Base, and Chamber were the officers commanding;
Strider, Harvester, Stomach, and Mane wheeled and soared;
Dipper, Ox, Woman, Barrens, Roof, House, and Wall, Heart, Tail, and Winnower — all able stars —
Well, Ghost, Willow, Spread, Wing and Axletree
Wielded their swords and spears, showed forth their power,
Halted their clouds and descended in mists to the mortal world,
Pitching camp before the Mountain of Flowers and Fruit.

There is a poem that runs:

Many the transformations of the heaven-born Monkey King
Happy in his lair after stealing the pills and wine.
Just because he wrecked the banquet of peaches,
A hundred thousand heavenly troops now spread their nets.

Heavenly King Li gave the order for the heavenly soldiers to pitch camp and throw a watertight cordon round the Mountain of Flowers and Fruit. Above and below they spread eighteen heaven-and-earth nets, and the Nine Bright Shiners were sent out to start the battle. They took their soldiers to the outside of the cave, where they saw the monkeys, big and small, leaping and fooling around. The star officers shouted in harsh voices, "Little goblins, where's that Great Sage of yours? We are gods sent from the upper world to subdue your mutinous Great Sage. Tell him to surrender at once — and if there's so much as a hint of a 'no' from him, we will exterminate every last one of you." The little monkeys went rushing in to report, "Great Sage, a disaster, a disaster. There are nine evil gods outside who say they've been sent from the upper world to subdue you."

The Great Sage, who was just then sharing the immortal liquor with the seventy-two kings of the monsters and his four Stalwart Generals, paid no attention to the report, saying:

> "Today we have wine so today we celebrate:
> To hell with what's happening outside the gate."

But before the words were out of his mouth another group of little devils came in. "Those nine evil gods are using foul and provocative language to challenge us to fight," they announced. "Never mind them," said the Great Sage with a laugh.

> "With verse and wine we're happy today;
> Who cares when fame will come our way?"

But before these words were out of his mouth yet another group of devils came rushing in. "Sir, those nine evil gods have smashed the gates and are charging in." "The stinking gods!" exploded the Great Sage, "What bloody check! I never wanted a fight with them, so why should they come here to push us around?" He thereupon ordered the One-horned Monster King to lead the seventy-two monster kings into battle while he followed them with the four Stalwart Generals. The monster king hastily assembled the devil soldiers and sallied forth to meet the enemy. They were all stopped by a charge by the Nine Bright Shiners, who held the head of the iron bridge so that no one could enter or leave.

During the tumult the Great Sage came on the scene, and shouting "Make way" he raised his iron cudgel, shook it till it was as thick as a bowl and twelve feet long, and struck and parried as he came charging out. The Nine Bright Shiners, who were no match for him, fell back. "You reckless Protector of the Horses," they shouted when they were back in the safety of their own positions. "You have committed the most terrible crimes. You stole the peaches and the wine, wrecked the Peach Banquet, and pilfered the immortality pills of Lord Lao Zi. On top of all this you brought some of the immortal liquor you stole back here. Don't you realize that you have piled crime upon crime?" The Great Sage laughed. "It's true, it's true," he said, "but what are you going to do about it?" "In obedience to a golden edict of the Jade Emperor," the Nine Bright Shiners replied, "we have led our troops here to subdue you. Submit at once, or else all these creatures of yours will have to pay with their lives. If you refuse, we shall trample this mountain flat and turn your cave upside-down." "You hairy gods," roared the Great Sage in a fury, "what magic powers have you got to let you talk so big? Clear off, or I'll give you a taste of my cudgel." The Nine Bright Shiners did a wear-dance together, which did not frighten the Handsome Monkey King in the least. He whirled his gold-banded cudgel, parrying to right and left, and fought the Nine Bright Shiners till their muscles were weak and their strength was gone; then each of them broke ranks and fled, dragging their weapons behind them. They rushed to the command post of the central corps and reported to the Pagoda-Bearing Heavenly King Li that the Monkey King was so ferocious that they had fled from the battlefield, unable to defeat him. Heavenly King Li then sent the Four Heavenly Kings and the Twenty-eight Constellations into battle. The Great Sage, not at all frightened at this, ordered the One-horned Demon King, the seventy-two kings of the monsters, and the four Stalwart Generals to draw up their line of battle outside the gates of the cave. The ensuing melee was really terrifying:

Howling winds,
Dark, sinister clouds.
On one side flags and standards colourfully flying,
On the other side the gleam of spears and halberds.
Round helmets shine,
Layered armour gleams.
The shining round helmets reflect the sun,
Like silver bells clashing with the sky;
Gleaming layers of armour are built into cliffs
Like a mountain of ice weighing down the earth.
Long-handled swords
Flash through the clouds like lightning;
Paper-white spears
Pierce mists and fogs;
Heaven-shaped halberds,
Tiger-eye flails,
Bristling like a field of hemp;
Bronze swords,
And four-brightness spears
Drawn up like a dense forest.
Bows and crossbows, eagle-feathered arrows,
Short clubs and snaky spears to terrify the soul.
Wielding his single as-you-will cudgel,
The Great Sage fights against the heavenly gods.
Such is the slaughter that no bird flies over it;
And tigers and wolves flee in terror.
The swirling stones and clouds of sand make everything
    dark,
The dirt and the dust blot out the heavens.
The clash of arms startles the universe
As the battle strikes awe into gods and demons.

The battle started in the morning and went on till the sun
set behind the mountains in the west. By then the One-horned
Demon King and the seventy-two kings of the monsters had
all been captured by the heavenly hosts. Only the four Stalwart
Generals and the monkeys had got away, and they were now

hiding in the innermost recesses of the Water Curtain Cave. The Great Sage's solitary cudgel had fought off the Four Heavenly Kings, Li the Pagoda-bearer and Prince Nezha, who were all in the sky. After the battle had gone on for a long time the Great Sage saw that night was drawing on, so he plucked out a pinch of his hairs, munched it up, spat out the pieces and shouted, "Change!" They changed into thousands of Great Sages, all with gold-banded cudgels, who forced Prince Nezha and the five Heavenly Kings to withdraw.

After winning this victory the Great Sage put back his hair and hurried back to the cave, where the four Stalwart Generals at once led the monkeys out to kowtow at the head of the iron bridge to welcome him back. They sobbed three times and then laughed three times. "Why are you laughing and crying at the sight of me?" the Great Sage asked. "When we led all the commanders into battle against the heavenly kings this morning," replied the Stalwart Generals, "the seventy-two kings of the monsters and the One-horned Demon King were all captured by the gods, and we had to flee for our lives. That is why we cried. We laughed because you, Great Sage, have come back victorious and unharmed." To this the Great Sage replied, "Victory and defeat are all the soldier's lot. As the ancients said, 'To kill ten thousand of the enemy you must lose three thousand of your own.' Anyhow, the officers of ours who were captured were all tigers, leopards, wolves, badgers, river-deer, foxes, and racoon-dogs. Not one of our own kind was even wounded, so there's no need for us to be bothered about it. But although I forced the enemy to withdraw by dividing up my body through magic, they're still encamped at the foot of our mountain, so we'll have to remain on our guard. Meanwhile we must eat a good meal and get a good night's sleep to build up our energy. Tomorrow morning I'll use powerful magic to capture those heavenly generals and avenge our people." After the four Stalwart Generals and the other monkey commanders had drunk several cups of coconut toddy, they went to bed with their worries calmed.

When the four Heavenly Kings had withdrawn their troops

and ended the battle, those who had distinguished themselves reported what they had done. Some had captured tigers and leopards, some lions and elephants, and others wolves and racoon-dogs, but not one single monkey goblin had been taken. Then they built a mighty stockade around their camp. Commanders who had distinguished themselves were rewarded, and the soldiers who made up the heaven-and-earth nets were ordered to surround the Mountain of Flowers and Fruit, holding bells and shouting, ready for a great battle the next day. Every man heard the orders, and they were strictly obeyed. Indeed,

> *A wicked monkey made chaos, shocking heaven and earth,*
> *So they spread their nets and watched by night and day.*

Listen to the next instalment to hear how he was dealt with the following morning.

CHAPTER SIX

Guanyin comes to the feast and asks
the reason why;
The Little Sage uses his might to subdue
the Great Sage.

We shall leave for the moment the Heavenly Generals making their encirclement and the soundly sleeping Great Sage. The story goes on to tell how the Compassionate and Merciful Miraculous Saviour from Suffering, the Bodhisattva Guanyin of Mount Potaraka in the Southern Sea, having been invited by the Queen Mother to the Peach Banquet, went to the precious pavilions at the Jade Pool with her great disciple Huian the Novice. She found the place deserted and the banquet ruined. The few immortals present were not sitting at their places but talking with great agitation. When greetings were over the immortals gave the Bodhisattva an account of what had happened "If there is to be no banquet and no drinking," said the Bodhisattva, "you had better all come with me to the Jade Emperor." The Immortals were delighted to follow her, and when they arrived before the Hall of Universal Brightness the Four Heavenly Teachers, the Barefoot Immortal and many others were all there to greet the Bodhisattva. They told her that the annoyed Jade Emperor had sent heavenly armies to capture the demon, but they had not yet returned. "I wish to see the Jade Emperor," said the Bodhisattva, "so may I trouble you to inform him on my behalf?" The heavenly teacher Qiu Hongji then went to the Hall of Miraculous Mist, and the Bodhisattva was invited in. She found that Lord Lao Zi was there in the place of honour, and that the Queen Mother was behind him.

The Bodhisattva went in at the head of the others, and when

she had done obeisance to the Jade Emperor she greeted Lao
Zi and the Queen Mother. After they had all sat down she asked
what had happened at the Peach Banquet. "The banquet is held
every year, and it is normally a very happy occasion," the Jade
Emperor replied, "but this year that monkey fiend wrecked it, so
that your invitation was worth nothing." "Where does this
monkey fiend come from?" asked the Bodhisattva. "He was
born from a stone egg on the Mountain of Flowers and Fruit in
the land of Aolai in the Eastern Continent of Superior Body,"
the Jade Emperor replied. "When he was born golden beams
flashed from his eyes that reached to the star palace. At first we
paid no attention to him, but later on he became a spirit, subduing dragons and tigers, and erasing his own name from the
registers of death. The Dragon Kings and King Yama of the
underworld informed us of this in memorials, and we wanted
to capture him, but the Star of Longevity memorialized that in
the Three Worlds all beings with nine orifices can become immortals. We therefore extended education to the worthy by summoning him to the upper world and appointing him Protector
of the Horses in the Imperial Stable. But this was not good
enough for the scoundrel, who rebelled against Heaven. We sent
Heavenly King Li and Prince Nezha to accept his surrender,
extended him an amnesty, and summoned him back to the upper world. We made him a 'Great Sage Equalling Heaven',
though this carried no salary. As he had nothing to do he would
go wandering all over the place, and for fear that this might lead
to trouble we had him look after the Peach Orchard. Once again
he flouted the law by stealing and eating every single one of the
big peaches from the old trees. When the banquet was to be
held he was not invited as his position was purely an honorary
one; so he played a trick on the Barefoot Immortal, went to
the banquet looking like him, ate all the immortal delicacies, and
drank all the immortal liquor. On top of this he stole Lord Lao
Zi's pills of immortality and some imperial liquor, which he took
to his mountain for the monkeys to enjoy. This made us very
angry so we sent a hundred thousand heavenly troops to spread
heaven-and-earth nets and subdue him. But we have received

no reports today, so we do not know whether we have been victorious."

When the Bodhisattva heard this she said to Huian the Novice, "Hurry down from Heaven to the Mountain of Flowers and Fruit and find out about the military situation. If you meet with any opposition you may do your bit to help, but the important thing is to bring an accurate report back." Huian the Novice straightened his robes, took his iron staff, left the palace by cloud, and went straight to the mountain. He saw that with the layer upon layer of heaven-and-earth nets, and the men holding bells and shouting passwords at the gates of the camp, the cordon round the mountain was watertight. Huian stopped and called, "Heavenly soldiers at the gates of the camp, I would trouble you to report that I, Moksa, the second son of Heavenly King Li, also known as Huian, the senior disciple of Guanyin of the Southern Sea, have come to ask about the military situation." Then the divine soldiers of the Five Mountains inside the camp went in through the gates of the headquarters, where the Rat, the Cock, the Horse and the Hare stars reported the news to the commander of the central corps. Heavenly King Li sent a flag of command with the order that the heaven-and-earth nets were to be opened to let Huian in. The east was just beginning to grow light as Huian followed the flag in and bowed to Heavenly King Li and the four other heavenly kings. "Where have you come from, my son?" asked Heavenly King Li. "Your stupid son accompanied the Bodhisattva to the Peach Banquet, and when she found the banquet deserted and nobody at the Jade Pool, she took me and the other immortals to see the Jade Emperor. The Jade Emperor told her that you, father, and the other kings had gone down to the lower world to capture this monkey fiend. As the Jade Emperor has received no news all day on the outcome of the battle, the Bodhisattva sent me here to find out what has happened." "We arrived here and encamped yesterday," Heavenly King Li replied, "then sent the Nine Bright Shiners to challenge the enemy to battle, but that wretch used such tremendous magic powers that the Nine Bright Shiners all came back defeated. Then we led our own soldiers into action, and the wretch also drew up his line of battle. Our hundred thousand heavenly soldiers fought an indecisive engagement with him till dusk, when he used a spell to divide up his body and drive us back. When we withdrew our forces and held an investigation, we found that we had only captured wolves, tigers, leopards, and so on, and had not even taken half a monkey fiend. We have not yet given battle today."

Before he had finished speaking someone appeared outside the gates of the headquarters to report that the Great Sage was outside at the head of a crowd of monkey spirits, clamouring for battle. The four other Heavenly Kings, Heavenly King Li, and Prince Nezha were all for committing their forces, but Moksa said, "Father, when your stupid son was instructed by the Bodhisattva to come here and find out the news, I was also told that if there was a battle I could do my bit to help. May I please go and see what sort of a 'Great Sage' he is, untalented though I am?" "My boy," said Heavenly King Li, "you have been cultivating your conduct with the Bodhisattva for some years now so I suppose that you must have acquired some magic powers, but do be very careful."

The splendid Prince Moksa hitched up his embroidered robes and charged out through the gates of the headquarters waving his iron staff with both hands. "Which of you is the Great Sage Equalling Heaven?" he shouted. "I am," answered the Great Sage, brandishing his as-you-will cudgel. "But who do you think you are, asking a question like that?" "I am Prince Moksa, the second son of Heavenly King Li, and I am now a disciple and a guard before the throne of the Bodhisattva Guanyin. My Buddhist name is Huian." "Why have you come here to see me instead of staying in the Southern Sea and cultivating your conduct?" asked the Great Sage, and Moksa replied, "My teacher sent me here to find out about the military situation, but now that I've seen your savagery I've come to capture you." "You talk big, don't you," said the Great Sage. "Well then, don't go away, try a taste of my cudgel." Moksa, not in the least frightened, struck at him with his iron staff. It was a fine fight they fought, half-way up the mountainside outside the gates of the headquarters.

> The staves were matched, but made of different iron;
> The weapons clashed, but their masters were not the same.
> One was a wayward immortal known as the Great Sage,
> The other a true dragon disciple of Guanyin.
> The cast-iron staff, beaten with a thousand hammers,
> Had been forged by the art of the Dings and the Jias.
> The as-you-will cudgel once anchored the Milky Way:
> As the Treasure Stilling the Sea its magic power was great.
> When the two met they were well matched indeed,
> And they parried and lunged at each other without end.
> The sinister cudgel,
> Infinitely murderous,
> Could whirl round your waist as quick as the wind.
> The spear-catching staff,
> Never yielding an opening,
> Was irresistible, parrying to right and left.
> On the one side the flags and banners fly,
> On the other the alligator drums roll.
> Ten thousand heavenly generals in multiple encirclement;
> A cave of monkey devils densely packed together.
> Monstrous fogs and evil clouds cover the earth,
> While the smoke of deadly battle rises to the sky.
> Yesterday's fighting was bad enough;
> Today's struggle is even worse.
> The admirable skills of the Monkey King
> Put Moksa to flight, utterly defeated.

After they had fought some fifty or sixty rounds, Huian's arm and shoulders were numbed and aching, and he could resist the Great Sage no longer. Waving his staff in a feint, he turned away and ran. The Great Sage then withdrew his monkey soldiers and encamped outside the gates of the cave. The big and little heavenly soldiers at the gates of the other camp received Huian and let him go straight to the headquarters, where he gasped and panted for breath as he said to the Four Heavenly Kings, Li the Pagoda-bearer, and his brother Prince Nezha, "What a Great Sage! What a Great Sage! His magic powers are too much for me. He beat me." Startled by this news, Heavenly King Li had a request for reinforcements written and sent the Strongarm Devil King and Prince Moksa up to Heaven to submit it.

Not daring to waste a moment, the two messengers rushed out through the heaven-and-earth nets and mounted their propitious clouds. A moment later they arrived outside the Hall of Universal Brightness, where they greeted the Four Heavenly Teachers, who led them to the Hall of Miraculous Mist and handed up their memorial. Prince Moksa, or Huian, did homage to the Bodhisattva, who asked him what he had found out. "As you instructed me, I went to the Mountain of Flowers and Fruit," reported Huian, "asked them to open the gates of the heaven-and-earth nets, saw my father, and told him of the orders you had given me. His Majesty my father said that they fought against the Monkey King yesterday but did not capture a single monkey spirit — only tigers, leopards, lions, elephants and so on. While he was telling me this the Monkey King demanded battle again, so your disciple fought some fifty or sixty rounds against him with my iron staff, but I was no match for him. He beat me, and drove me back to the camp. This is why my father has sent me and the Strongarm Devil King up to Heaven to ask for reinforcements." The Bodhisattva lowered her head in deep thought.

The Jade Emperor opened the memorial and saw that it contained a request for help. "This intolerable monkey spirit has enough tricks to fight off a hundred thousand heavenly soldiers," he observed with a smile. "Heavenly King Li has asked for reinforcements. Which heavenly soldiers should we send him?" Before the words were out of his mouth, Guanyin put her hands together and said, "Do not worry, Your Majesty. I can recommend a god to capture this monkey." "Which god?" the

Jade Emperor asked, and the Bodhisattva replied, "Your Majesty's nephew, the Illustrious Sage and True Lord Erlang, who is now living at Guanjiangkou in Guanzhou, enjoying the incense that the lower beings burn to him. In the past he exterminated the Six Bogies. He has the Brothers of Plum Hill and the twelve hundred straw-headed gods, and his magical powers are enormous. He will agree to be sent though he would not obey a summons to come here, so Your Majesty might like to issue a decree ordering him to take his troops to the rescue." The Jade Emperor then issued such a decree and sent the Strongarm Devil King to deliver it.

The devil king took the decree, mounted his cloud, and went straight to Guanjiangkou. He reached the temple of the True Lord within an hour. When the demon judges guarding the gates went in to report that there was an envoy from heaven standing outside with an imperial decree, Erlang went with the brothers to receive the decree outside the gates, and incense was burned as he read

> *The Great Sage Equalling Heaven, the monkey fiend of the Mountain of Flowers and Fruit, has rebelled. Because he stole peaches, wine and pills while in Heaven and wrecked the Peach Banquet, we have despatched a hundred thousand heavenly soldiers and eighteen heaven-and-earth nets to surround the mountain and force him to submit, but we have not yet succeeded. We do now therefore especially appoint our worthy nephew and his sworn brothers to go to the Mountain of Flowers and Fruit and give their help in eliminating him. When you succeed, large rewards and high office shall be yours.*

Erlang was delighted. He told the envoy from Heaven to go back and report that he would be putting his sword to the Emperor's service. We need not describe how the devil king reported ed back to Heaven.

The True Lord Erlang called the six sworn brothers of Plum Hill — Marshals Kang, Zhang, Yao, and Li, and Generals Guo Shen and Zhi Jian — together before the hall. "The Jade Em-

peror has just ordered us to the Mountain of Flowers and Fruit
to subdue a monkey fiend," he said. "You are all coming with
me." The brothers were all eager to go, and mustering their
divine troops they unleashed a gale wind. In an instant they
had crossed the Eastern Ocean, commanding eagles and dogs,
pulling their bows and drawing their crossbows, and had reached the Mountain of Flowers and Fruit. Finding that the many
layers of heaven-and-earth nets were impenetrable, Erlang
shouted, "Listen, all you generals in charge of the heaven-and-
earth nets. I am the True Lord and the Illustrious Sage Erlang,
and I have been sent here by the Jade Emperor to capture the
monkey fiend. Open the gates of the camp and let me in at
once." Each line of gods forming the nets let them through, and
the four other Heavenly Kings and Heavenly King Li all came
to welcome him outside the headquarters. When the introductions were over he asked how the fighting had gone, and
the Heavenly Kings gave him a full account of what had happened. "Now that I, the Little Sage, have come here I shall
have to match a few transformations with him," said Erlang
with a smile. "I hope that all you gentlemen will maintain a
close cordon with your heaven-and-earth nets, but don't screen
off the top of the mountain; then I'll be able to fight him. If
he beats me I shan't need the help of you gentlemen, as I have
my brothers to support me; and if I beat him I won't have to
trouble you to tie him up as my brothers can do it. I would
just like to ask Heavenly King Li to stand in the sky and operate
this fiend-detecting mirror. I'm worried that if he's beaten he
may go and hide somewhere, so you will have to give me a clear
view of him and not let him get away." The Heavenly Kings
stayed in the four quarters, and all the heavenly soldiers were
drawn up in their battle positions.

The True Lord Erlang went out at the head of the four
marshals and the two generals — making seven sworn brothers
with himself included — to challenge the enemy to battle; and
he ordered his other officers to defend the camp firmly and keep
the eagles and dogs under control. All the straw-headed gods
acknowledged the order. Erlang then went to the outside of the

Water Curtain Cave, where he saw the monkey hordes neatly drawn up in a coiled-dragon battle line; in the middle of the central corps stood a pole with a banner on it reading "Great Sage Equalling Heaven". "What business has that loathsome fiend to call himself the equal of Heaven?" Erlang asked; and the six sworn brothers of Plum Hill replied, "Stop admiring him and challenge him to battle." When the junior monkeys at the gate of their camp saw the True Lord Erlang they rushed back to report, whereupon the Monkey King took his gold-banded cudgel, adjusted his golden armour, put on his cloud-walking shoes, felt his golden helmet, and leapt out through the gates of the camp. He saw at first sight how cool and remarkable Erlang looked, and how elegantly he was dressed. Indeed,

> *His bearing was refined, his visage noble,*
> *His ears hung down to his shoulders, and his eyes shone.*
> *The hat on his head had three peaks and phoenixes*
>   *flying,*
> *And his robe was of a pale goose-yellow.*
> *His boots were lined with cloth of gold; dragons coiled*
>   *round his socks;*
> *His jade belt was decorated with the eight jewels,*
> *At his waist was a bow, curved like the crescent moon,*
> *In his hand a double-edged trident*
> *His axe had split open Peach Mountain when he rescued*
>   *his mother,*
> *His bow had killed the twin phoenixes of Zongluo.*
> *Widespread was his fame for killing the Eight Bogies,*
> *And he had become one of Plum Hill's seven sages.*
> *His heart was too lofty to acknowledge his relatives in*
>   *Heaven;*
> *In his pride he went back to be a god at Guanjiang.*
> *He was the Merciful and Miraculous Sage of the red city,*
> *Erlang, whose transformations were numberless.*

When the Great Sage saw him he laughed with delight, raised his gold-banded cudgel, and shouted, "Where are you from, little general, that you have the audacity to challenge

me?" "You must be blind, you wretch, if you can't recognize me.
I am the nephew of the Jade Emperor, and my title is Merciful
and Miraculous King Erlang. I am here on imperial orders to
arrest you, Protector of the Horses, you rebel against Heaven,
you reckless baboon." "Now I remember who you are," replied
the Great Sage. "Some years ago the Jade Emperor's younger
sister wanted to be mortal and came down to the lower world,
where she married a Mr. Yang and gave birth to a son, who
split the Peach Mountain open with his axe. Is that who you
are? I should really fling you a few curses, but I've got no quarrel with you; and it would be a pity to kill you by hitting you
with my cudgel. So why don't you hurry back, young sir, and
tell those four Heavenly Kings of yours to come out?" When
the True Lord Erlang heard this he burst out angrily, "Damned
monkey! Where are your manners? Try this blade of mine!"
The Great Sage dodged the blow and instantly raised his gold-
banded club to hit back. There was a fine battle between the
two of them:

> *The Merciful God Erlang,*
> *The Great Sage Equalling Heaven:*
> *One was proud to be more than a match for the Hand-*
> *   some Monkey King;*
> *The other was the unknown subduer of the true cross-*
> *   beam of heaven.*
> *When the two met*
> *They were both in a fighting mood.*
> *He who had no respect before*
> *Today learnt a sense of proportion.*
> *The iron staff raced with the flying dragons,*
> *The divine cudgel seemed like a dancing phoenix.*
> *Parrying to the left, thrusting to the right,*
> *Advancing to meet a blow, flashing behind.*
> *The brothers of Plum Hill add to one side's might,*
> *While the other has the four Stalwart Generals to trans-*
> *   mit orders.*
> *As the flags wave and the drums roll each side is as one;*

Battle-cries and gongs raise everyone's morale.
The two steel blades each watch for their chance,
But neither leaves an opening as they come and go.
The gold-banded cudgel, the treasure from the sea,
Can fly and transform itself to win the victory.
A moment's delay and life is lost;
A single mistake will be the last.

After Erlang and the Great Sage had fought over three hundred rounds the outcome of the fight was still undecided. Erlang braced himself, and with a shake became ten thousand fathoms tall; in his hands his two-bladed trident looked like the peaks of Mount Hua. His face was black, his fangs were long, and his hair was bright red: he looked ferociously evil. He hacked at the Great Sage's head. The Great Sage, also resorting to magic, gave himself a body as big as Erlang's and a face as frightening; and he raised his as-you-will gold-banded cudgel, which was now like the pillar of Heaven on the summit of the Kunlun Mountain, to ward off Erlang's blow. This reduced the two ape field marshals Ma and Liu to such trembling terror that they could no longer wave their banners, while the gibbon generals Seng and Ba were too scared to use their swords. On the other side Kang, Zhang, Yao, Li, Guo Shen and Zhi Jian threw the straw-headed gods into an assault on the Water Curtain Cave, with the dogs and eagles unleashed and their bows and crossbows drawn. This attack put the four monkey generals to flight, and two or three thousand devils were captured. The monkeys threw away their spears, tore off their armour, abandoned their swords and halberds, and fled screaming. Some went up the mountain and some returned to the cave, like roosting birds frightened by an owl, or stars scattered across the sky. That is all we have to say about the sworn brothers' victory.

The story goes on to tell how the True Lord Erlang and the Great Sage, having turned themselves into figures on the scale of Heaven and Earth, were locked in battle when the Great Sage was suddenly appalled to notice that the monkey fiends in his camp had scattered in terror. Putting off his magic appearance he broke away and fled, his cudgel in his hand. Seeing him go, the True Lord Erlang hurried after him with long strides. "Where are you going?" he asked. "If you surrender at once, your life will be spared." The Great Sage, who had no heart left for the fight, was running as fast as he could. As he approached the mouth of the cave he came up against Marshals Kang, Zhang, Yao and Li, as well as Generals Guo Shen and Zhi Jian, blocking his way at the head of their armies. "Where are you going, damned monkey?" they asked, and the Great Sage hastily squeezed his gold-banded cudgel till it was the size of an embroidery needle and hid it in his ear. Then he shook himself, turned into a sparrow, flew up into a tree, and perched on one of its branches. The six sworn brothers looked for him very hard but could find him nowhere, so they all shouted in unison, "The monkey fiend has escaped, the monkey fiend has escaped."

As they were shouting the True Lord Erlang arrived and asked them, "Brothers, where had you chased him to when he disappeared?" "We had him surrounded here just now, but he vanished." Erlang opened his phoenix eyes till they were quite round and looked about him. He saw that the Great Sage had changed himself into a sparrow and was perching on a branch; so he put off his magical appearance, threw down his divine trident, and took the pellet bow from his waist. Then he shook himself, changed into a kite, spread his wings, and swooped in to attack. As soon as the Great Sage saw this he took off and turned himself into a big cormorant, soaring up into the sky. Erlang saw him, and with a quick shake of his feathers and a twist of his body he transformed himself into a crane and pierced the clouds as he tried to catch him. The Great Sage landed on a mountain stream and, changing into a fish, plunged into the water. Erlang, who had pursued him to the bank of the stream, could see no trace of him. "That macaque must have gone into the water and changed himself into some kind of fish or shrimp," he thought. "I'll transform myself again, then I'll get him." He turned into a fish-hawk and soared above the lower reaches of the stream and the first waves of the sea. He waited there for a time. Meanwhile the Great Sage, who was in the form of a fish, swam with the stream until he noticed a bird flying above him. It was quite like a blue kite, except that its feathers were not blue; it was quite like an egret, but it had no crest on its head; and it was quite like a stork, but its legs were not red. "That must be what Erlang turned himself into while waiting for me," he thought, turned round quickly, and went away. "The fish who turned round," thought Erlang when he saw this, "is like a carp but its tail isn't red; it's like a mandarin fish, but I can't see the pattern on its scales; it's like a snake-fish, but without a star on its head; and like a bream, but it has no needles on its gills. Why did it turn round the moment it saw me? It must be that monkey transformed." He swooped down and snapped at the Great Sage with his beak. The Great Sage leapt out of the water, turned into a water-snake, swam to the bank, and slid into the grass. Failing to catch the fish in his beak, Erlang saw a snake jump out of the water and realized it was the Great Sage. He changed himself at once into a red-crested grey crane, and stretched out his long beak that was like a pair of pointed pincers to eat up the water-snake. The snake gave a jump and became a bustard standing stiffly on a smartweed-covered bank. When Erlang saw that he had turned himself into so low a creature — for the bustard is the lowest and lewdest of birds, not caring whether it mates with phoenix, eagle or crow — he kept his distance, reverted to his own body, went away to fetch and load his pellet bow, and knocked him flying with a single shot.

The Great Sage seized the chance as he rolled down the precipice to crouch there and turn himself into a temple to a local god. He opened his mouth wide to look like the entrance to the temple and turned his teeth into the doors; he made his tongue into a statue of a god and his eyes into windows and lattice He could not tuck his tail away, so he stuck it up behind him as a flagpole. When Erlang came to the foot of the precipice he could not see the bustard he had shot over, and anxiously opening his phoenix eyes he looked carefully around and saw a temple with its flagpole at the back. "It

must be that monkey over there," he observed with a smile.
"He's trying to fool me again. I've seen temples before, but
never one with the flagpole at the back. I'm sure it is that beast
up to his tricks again. If he'd managed to lure me in, he'd have
been able to get me with a single bite. Of course I won't go in.
I'll smash his windows in with my fist, then I'll kick his door
down." "Vicious, really vicious," thought the Great Sage with
horror when he heard him say this. "Those doors are my teeth,
and the windows are my eyes; and if he smashes my teeth and
bashes in my eyes, what sort of a state will that leave me in?"
With a tiger leap he disappeared into the sky.

The True Lord Erlang rushed around wildly, but he could
only see his six sworn brothers, who crowded round him and
asked, "Elder brother, did you catch the Great Sage?" "That
monkey turned himself into a temple to fool me," he replied
with a laugh. "Just when I was going to smash his windows
and kick in his door he gave a jump and vanished without a
trace. Strange, very strange." They were all astonished, and
although they looked all around they could see no sign of him.
"Brothers, you patrol this area while I go to look for him above,"
said Erlang, and with a quick jump he was riding a cloud in
mid-air. When he saw Heavenly King Li holding high the
fiend-detecting mirror and standing with Nezha at the edge of
a cloud, the True Lord asked, "Your Heavenly Majesty, have
you seen that Monkey King?" "He hasn't come up here — I've
been keeping a lookout for him with this mirror," the Heavenly
King replied. The True Lord Erlang then told him how he had
used transformations and magic to capture the monkey hordes.
"He changed into a temple," Erlang went on, "but got away
just when I was going to hit him." On hearing this, Heavenly
King Li turned the fiend-detecting mirror in all four directions,
then said with a laugh, "Hurry away, True Lord, hurry away.
The monkey made himself invisible to get through the encirclement, and he's gone to your place, Guanjiangkou." Erlang took
his divine trident and returned to Guanjiangkou in pursuit.

The Great Sage had already arrived there, changed himself
into the likeness of the god Erlang with a shake of his body, put

away his cloud, and gone into the temple. The demon judges did not realize who he really was, so they all kowtowed to welcome him. He took his seat in the middle of the temple, and inspected the offerings: the beef, mutton and pork presented by one Li Hu, the ex-voto promised by a Zhang Long, the letter from a Zhao Jia asking for a son, and one Qian Bing's prayer for recovery from illness. As he was looking round it was announced that another Lord Erlang had arrived. All the demon judges hurried to look, and they were all astonished. The True Lord Erlang asked, "Has a so-called Great Sage Equalling Heaven been here?" "We haven't seen any Great Sages," they replied, "only another god who's looking around inside." The True Lord rushed in through the gates, and as soon as the Great Sage saw him he reverted to his own appearance and said, "There's no point in shouting, sir. This temple's mine now." The True Lord raised his double-bladed trident and swung at the Monkey King's head, but the Monkey King dodged the blow by magic, took his embroidery needle, shook it till it was as thick as a bowl, and rushed forward to meet the attack. Shouting and yelling, they fought their way out through the gates, and went on fighting through the mists and clouds all the way back to the Mountain of Flowers and Fruit. The Four Heavenly Kings and all their soldiers were so alarmed that they kept an even tighter guard. Marshals Kang and Zhang and the others came to meet the True Lord, and combined their efforts to surround the Handsome Monkey King. But of this no more for now.

After the Strongarm Demon King had sent the True Lord Erlang and his six sworn brothers with their troops to capture the fiend, he had gone back to Heaven to report. He found the Jade Emperor, the Bodhisattva Guanyin, the Queen Mother and all his immortal ministers in conference. "Although Erlang has joined the fight, we have had no reports on it all day," the Jade Emperor said. Guanyin put her hands together and replied, "May I suggest that Your Majesty go out through the Southern Gate of Heaven with Lord Lao Zi to see for youself what is happening." "A good idea," said the Emperor, and he went by chariot with Lao Zi, the Queen Mother, and all the immortal ministers to the Southern Gate of Heaven. Here they were met by a number of heavenly soldiers and strongmen. When the gates were opened and they looked into the distance they saw that the heavenly hosts had spread nets all around; Heavenly King Li and Nezha were standing in mid-air with the fiend-detecting mirror, and Erlang was struggling with the Great Sage within the encircling ring. The Bodhisattva addressed Lao Zi and asked, "What do you think of the god Erlang I recommended? He really does have divine powers. He's just got that Great Sage cornered, and all he has to do now is to catch him. If I give him a little help now he will certainly be able to do it." "What weapon would you use, Bodhisattva? How could you help him?" Lao Zi asked. "I'll drop that pure vase of willow twigs on the monkey's head. Even if it doesn't kill him it will knock him off balance and enable the Little Sage to catch him." "That vase of yours is made of porcelain," Lao Zi replied. "and if you hit the target that will be fine. But if it were to miss his head and smash into his iron club, it would be shattered. Just hold your hand while I give him a little help." "What sort of weapon do you have?" the Bodhisattva asked, and Lord Lao Zi replied, "I've got one all right." He pulled up his sleeve and took a bracelet off his right arm. "This weapon," he said, "is made of tempered steel to which I have added the magic elixir. It preserves my miraculous essence, can transform itself, is proof against fire and water, and can snare anything. One of its names is Diamond Jade and the other is Diamond Noose. When I went out through the Han Pass some years ago to turn into a foreigner and become a Buddha, I had a great deal to thank it for. It's the best protection at any time. Just watch while I throw it down and hit him."

As soon as he had finished speaking he threw it down from outside the heavenly gate, and it fell into the camp on the Mountain of Flowers and Fruit, hitting the Monkey King neatly on the head. The Monkey King was too preoccupied with fighting the seven sages to notice this weapon falling on him from heaven, and when it struck him on the forehead he lost his balance and stumbled, then picked himself up and started to run. The slim dog of the god Erlang caught him up and bit him in the calf, bringing him down again. As he lay on the ground he cursed at the dog "You don't bother your own master, damn you; why pick on me to bite?" He rolled over and tried unsuccessfully to get up, but the seven sages all held him down, roped him up, and put a sickle-shaped blade round his collar-bone to prevent him from making any more transformations.

Lord Lao Zi then recovered his Diamond Jade and invited the Jade Emperor, Guanyin, the Queen Mother, and all the immortal ministers to return to the Hall of Miraculous Mist. Down below, Heavenly King Li and the four other Heavenly Kings assembled their troops and pulled up the stockade. They went over to congratulate the Little Sage and said, "It was all thanks to you, Little Sage." "No, it was thanks to the great blessings of His Celestial Majesty and the might of all the gods — it was nothing I did," replied the Little Sage. "No time to talk now, elder brother," said the four marshals Kang, Zhang, Yao, and Li. "Let's take this wretch up to Heaven to see the Jade Emperor and ask what is to be done with him." "Worthy brothers," Erlang replied, "you never received any heavenly commission, so it would not be right for you to see the Jade Emperor. The heavenly soldiers can escort him while I go up there with the Heavenly Kings to report back. You should comb this mountain with your troops, and when you've finished go back to Guanjiangkou. When I've asked for our rewards I'll come back and we can celebrate together." The four marshals and the two generals accepted their orders, and the rest mounted their clouds and went to Heaven triumphantly singing victory songs. Before long they were outside the Hall of Universal Brightness. The heavenly teachers reported to the throne that the Four Great Heavenly Kings and the rest of them had captured the monkey devil, the Great Sage Equalling Heaven, and were now waiting to be summoned. The Jade Emperor then issued an edict ordering the Strongarm Demon King and the heavenly soldiers to march him to the Demon-beheading Platform, where the wretch was to have his body chopped to mincemeat. Goodness!

> *The bully and cheat now meets with a bitter punishment,*
> *The heroic spirit must now come to an end.*

If you don't know what happened to the Monkey King's life, then listen to the explanation in the next instalment.

CHAPTER SEVEN

The Great Sage escapes from the Eight
Trigrams Furnace;
The Mind Ape is fixed beneath Five
Elements Mountain.

Wealth and honour, glory and fame,
Are predetermined by fate:
No one should act against conscience to covet any of
  them.
Far-going and deep
Are the good results of true enlightenment and loyalty
Heaven punishes all wild and wicked deeds
If not at once then later on.
Ask the Lord of the East the reason why
Disasters now strike him.
It is because his ambition was high, his plans far-reach-
  ing,
He did not respect authority, and he smashed conven-
  tion.

The story goes on to tell how the Great Sage Equalling Heaven
was escorted by the hosts of heavenly soldiers to the Demon-
beheading Platform and tied to the Demon-subduing Pillar.
They hacked at him with sabres, sliced at him with axes, lunged
at him with spears and cut at him with swords, but they were
unable to inflict a single wound on him. The Southern Dipper
angrily ordered all the gods of the Department of Fire to set
him alight and burn him up, but he would not ignite. He told
the gods of the Department of Thunder to nail splinters of
thunder into him, but however hard they tried they could not
harm a hair of his body. The Strongarm Demon King and the

113

rest of them then reported this to the throne "Your Majesty," they said, "this Great Sage has learnt somewhere or other how to protect himself by magic. Although your subjects have hacked at him with sabres, sliced at him with axes, struck at him with thunder and tried to burn him with fire, we have not been able to harm a hair of his body. What are we to do?" "How can we deal with a wretch like this?" the Jade Emperor asked, and the Lord Lao Zi replied to this in a memorial: "That monkey has eaten the peaches of immortality, drunk the imperial liquor, and stolen the pills of elixir. He swallowed those five gourds of pills of mine, fresh ones and mature ones alike, which he tempered with the fire of samadhi in to one lump and made his body a diamond one that cannot be harmed. The best course would be to let me take him and put him in my Eight Trigrams Furnace, where I can refine out my elixir with slow fire and high heat and reduce him to ashes at the same time." The Jade Emperor then ordered the Six Dings and the Six Jias to untie him and hand him over to the Lord Lao Zi, who took him away in obedience to the imperial decree. At the same time the Jade Emperor summoned the Illustrious Sage Erlang to his presence and rewarded him with a hundred golden flowers, a hundred jars of imperial liquor, a hundred pills of elixir, rare jewels, lustrous pearls, brocade, embroidery, and other gifts to share with his sworn brothers. The True Lord Erlang thanked him for his bounty and returned to Guanjiangkou.

When he reached the Tushita Palace, Lord Lao Zi had the Great Sage untied, took the hook from his collar-bone, pushed him into the Eight Trigrams Furnace, and ordered the priests in charge of it and the fire-boys to fan the fire up to refine him. Now this furnace was made up of the Eight Trigrams — *Qian, Kan, Gen, Zhen, Sun, Li, Kun, and Dui* — so he squeezed himself into the "Palace of *Sun*", as *Sun* was the wind, and where there was wind there could be no fire. All that happened was that the wind stirred up the smoke, which made both his eyes red and left him somewhat blind with the illness called "fire eyes with golden pupils".

Time soon passed, and without him realizing it the seven times seven, or forty-nine, days had passed, and Lord Lao Zi's fire had reached the required temperature and burned for long enough. One day the furnace was opened for the elixir to be taken out. The Great Sage, who was shielding his eyes with both hands and wiping away his tears, heard a noise at the top of the furnace. He looked hard and saw daylight; and, unable to stand being in there a moment longer, leapt out of the furnace, kicked it over with a crash, and was off. In the ensuing chaos the fire-boys, the keepers of the furnace, the Dings and the Jias all tried to grab him, but he knocked them all down. He was like a white-browed tiger gone berserk, a single-horned dragon raving mad. Lord Lao Zi rushed up to seize him, but was thrown head over heels as the Great Sage freed himself. He took the as-you-will cudgel from his car, and shook it in the wind till it was thick as a bowl, and once more created total chaos in the Palace of Heaven, not caring in the least what he did. He laid about him to such effect that the Nine Bright Shiners shut their windows and doors, and not a sign was to be seen of the Four Heavenly Kings. Marvellous monkey spirit! As the poem has it,

> His primordial body matches the inborn nature,
> Completely natural throughout ten thousand disasters;
> Vast and passive, blended with the Great Monad;
> Always immobile, known as the Prime Mystery.
> After so much refining in the furnace he is not lead or
>   mercury;
> Having lived long outside the ordinary he is a natural
>   Immortal.
> His changes are inexhaustible, and still he has more,
> So say nothing about the Three Refuges or Five Absten-
>   tions.

Another poem says:

> A single point of magic light can fill the whole of space;
> Likewise that staff of his:

> *Longer or shorter, depending on his needs,*
> *Upright or horizontal, it can shrink or grow.*

Yet another poem runs:

> *To the ape's immortal body is matched a human mind:*
> *That the mind is an ape is deeply meaningful.*
> *It was quite true that the Great Sage equalled Heaven:*
> *The appointment as Protector of the Horse showed no*
> *   discernment.*
> *Horse and ape together make mind and thought;*
> *Bind them tightly together, and do not seek elsewhere.*
> *When all phenomena are reduced to truth they follow*
> *   a single pattern;*
> *Like the Tathagata reaching nirvana under the two*
> *   trees.*

This time the Monkey King made no distinction between high and humble as he laid about him to east and west with his iron club. Not a single god opposed him. He fought his way into the Hall of Universal Brightness outside the Hall of Miraculous Mist, where the Kingly Spirit Officer, the lieutenant of the Helpful Sage and True Lord, fortunately was on duty. When he saw the Great Sage charging around he took up his golden flail and went forward to resist him. "Where are you going, damned monkey?" he asked. "If you go wild you'll have me to deal with." The Great Sage was not in a position to argue with him, so he raised his cudgel to strike him. The Spirit Officer lifted his flail and advanced to meet him. It was a splendid fight:

> *Great is the fame of the brave and loyal officer,*
> *Evil the name of the rebel who bullied Heaven.*
> *The low one and the good one are well matched;*
> *Valiant heroes fighting each other.*
> *Vicious the iron cudgel,*
> *Quick the golden flail.*
> *Both are straight, merciless, and terrible.*

One of them is a deity formed from the Great Monad's
    thunder;
The other is the monkey spirit, the Great Sage Equalling
    Heaven.
With golden flail or iron cudgel each is a master;
Both are weapons from the palaces of the gods.
Today they show their might in the Hall of Miraculous
    Mist,
A wonderful display of courage and skill.
One in his folly wanting to capture the Palace of the
    Dipper and the Bull,
The other exerting all his strength to support the world
    of the gods.
The fight is hard and merciless: both use their magic
    powers,
As flail and cudgel struggle without result.

As they fought together without either of them emerging as victor, the True Lord sent an officer with a message to the Thunder Palace ordering the thirty-six thunder generals to surround the Great Sage. Although they all fought with the utmost ferocity, the Great Sage was not in the least frightened, and parried and blocked to left and right with his as-you-will cudgel, resisting his opponents in front and behind. Before long he found that the pressure was too great from the sabres, spears, swords, halberds, clubs, maces, claws-and-ropes, hammers, pole-axes, battle-axes, grabs, pennoned hooks, and moon-shaped bills of the thunder generals; so he shook himself and grew three heads and six arms. Then he shook his as-you-will cudgel and changed it into three cudgels, and wielding the three cudgels in his six hands he flew round and round inside the encirclement like a spinning wheel. None of the thunder generals could get anywhere near him. Indeed,

Perfectly round,
Gleaming bright,
How could mortals master these eternal weapons?
He can enter fire without being burned,

And go in the water but not be drowned.
He is as bright as a Mani pearl;
Swords and spears cannot harm him.
He is capable of good,
And capable of evil:
When faced with the choice between good and evil he
    might do either.
If he is good he becomes a Buddha or an immortal,
If bad, he grows fur and horns.
With his boundless transformations he wrecked the
    Heavenly Palace,
Nor can thunder generals and divine troops take him.

Although the gods had the Great Sage cornered, they were unable to get near him. The noise of the shouting and the fighting had already alarmed the Jade Emperor, who ordered the Miracle Official Youyi to go to the West with the Helpful Sage and True Lord and ask the Buddha to subdue him.

When these two sages received the order they went to the wonderful land of the Vulture Peak where they offered their greetings to the Four Vajrapanis and Eight Bodhisattvas before the Thunder Monastery and asked them to pass on their message. The gods went to the foot of the lotus seat to inform the Tathagata, who invited the two sages to his presence. When the sages had performed the threefold obeisance to the Buddha they stood in attendance below the throne. "Why has the Jade Emperor troubled you two sages to come here?" asked the Buddha. "A monkey," they reported, "who was born on the Mountain of Flowers and Fruit, has used his magic powers to unite all the monkeys and throw the world into confusion. The Jade Emperor sent down an edict of amnesty and appointed him Protector of the Horses, but this was not good enough for him, so he left Heaven again. When Heavenly King Li and Prince Nezha were unsuccessful in their attempt to capture him the Jade Emperor sent down another amnesty with his appointment as a 'Great Sage Equalling Heaven'. At first this appointment was purely nominal, but later he was told to look after

the Peach Orchard. But he stole the peaches and then went to
the Jade Pool where he stole the delicacies and the liquor and
wrecked the banquet. In his drunkenness he staggered into the
Tushita Palace, stole Lord Lao Zi's pills of immortality, and
left Heaven again. The Jade Emperor sent a hundred thousand
heavenly troops, but they were still unable to subdue him. Then
Guanyin recommended the True Lord Erlang and his sworn
brothers to go after the monkey, and he used many a transformation until he was finally able to capture the monkey after
the Lord Lao Zi hit him with his Diamond Jade. The monkey
was then taken to the imperial presence, and the order for his
execution was given.   But although he was hacked at with
sabres, chopped at with axes, burned with fire, and struck with
thunder, none of this did him any damage; so Lord Lao Zi requested permission to take him away and refine him with fire.
But when the cauldron was opened after forty-nine days he
jumped out of the Eight Trigrams Furnace, routed the heavenly
troops, and went straight to the Hall of Universal Brightness
in front of the Hall of Miraculous Mist.   Here he has been
stopped and engaged in fierce combat by the Kingly Spirit Officer, the lieutenant of the Helpful bage and True Lord Erlang,
thunder generals have been sent there to encircle him; but no
one has been able to get close to him. In this crisis the Jade Emperor makes a special appeal to you, the Tathagata, to save
his throne."   On hearing this the Tathagata said to the assembled Bodhisattvas, "You stay here quietly in this dharma hall
and behave yourselves in your seats of meditation while I go to
deal with the demon and save the throne."

Telling the Venerable Ananda and the Venerable Kasyapa
to accompany him, the Tathagata left the Thunder Monastery
and went straight to the gate of the Hall of Miraculous Mist,
where his ears were shaken by the sound of shouting as the
thirty-six thunder generals surrounded the Great Sage.   The
Buddha issued a decree that ran: "Tell the thunder generals
to stop fighting, open up their camp, and call on that Great
Sage to come out, so that I may ask him what divine powers
he has." The generals then withdrew, whereupon the Great

Sage put away his magic appearance and came forward in his own body. He was in a raging temper as he asked, "Where are you from? Man of religion. You've got a nerve, stopping the fighting and questioning me!" "I am the Venerable Sakyamuni from the Western Land of Perfect Bliss," replied the Buddha with a smile. "I have heard of your wild and boorish behaviour, and of your repeated rebellions against Heaven, and I would like to know where you were born, when you found the Way, and why you have been so ferocious." "I am," the Great Sage said,

> "A miracle-working Immortal born of Heaven and Earth,
> An old ape from the Mountain of Flowers and Fruit.
> My home is in the Water Curtain Cave,
> I sought friends and teachers, and became aware of the Great Mystery.

> "I have practised many a method for obtaining eternal life;
> Infinite are the transformations I have learned.
> That is why I found the mortal world too cramped,
> And decided to live in the Jade Heaven.

> "None can reign for ever in the Hall of Miraculous Mist;
> Kings throughout history have had to pass on their power.
> The strong should be honoured — he should give way to me:
> This is the only reason I wage my heroic fight."

The Buddha laughed mockingly. "You wretch! You are only a monkey spirit and you have the effrontery to want to grab the throne of the Jade Emperor. He has trained himself since childhood, and suffered hardship for one thousand, seven hundred and fifty kalpas. Each kalpa is 129,600 years, so you can work out for yourself how long it has taken him to be able to enjoy this great and infinite Way. But you are a beast who has only just become a man for the first time. How dare you

talk so big? You're not human, not even human! It'll shorten
your life-span. Accept my teaching at once and stop talking such
nonsense! Otherwise you'll be in for trouble and your life
will very shortly be over; and that will be so much the worse
for your original form too." "Although he has trained himself
for a long time, ever since he was a child, he still has no right
to occupy this place for ever," the Great Sage said. "As the
saying goes, 'Emperors are made by turn; next year it may be
me.' If he can be persuaded to move out and make Heaven
over to me, that'll be fine. But if he doesn't abdicate in my
favour I'll most certainly make things hot for him, and he'll
never know peace and quiet again." "What have you got, besides
immortality and the ability to transform yourself, that gives you
the nerve to try to seize the Heavenly Palace?" the Buddha
asked. "I can do many tricks indeed," the Great Sage replied.
"I can perform seventy-two transformations, and I can preserve
my youth for ten thousand kalpas. I can ride a somersault
cloud that takes me thirty-six thousand miles at a single jump.
So why shouldn't I sit on the throne of Heaven?" "I'll have
a wager with you then," said the Buddha. "If you're clever
enough to get out of my right hand with a single somersault,
you will be the winner, and there will be no more need for
weapons or fighting: I shall invite the Jade Emperor to come
and live in the west and abdicate the Heavenly Palace to you.
But if you can't get out of the palm of my hand you will have to
go down to the world below as a devil and train yourself for
several more kalpas before coming to argue about it again."

When he heard this offer the Great Sage smiled to himself
and thought, "This Buddha is a complete idiot. I can cover
thirty-six thousand miles with a somersault, so how could I fail
to jump out of the palm of his hand, which is less than a foot
across?" With this in his mind he asked eagerly, "Do you guarantee that yourself?" "Yes, yes," the Buddha replied, and he
stretched out his right hand, which seemed to be about the
size of a lotus leaf. Putting away his as-you-will cudgel, the
Great Sage summoned up all his divine powers, jumped into
the palm of the Buddha's hand, and said, "I'm off." Watch him

as he goes like a streak of light and disappears completely. The Buddha, who was watching him with his wise eyes, saw the Monkey King whirling forward like a windmill and not stopping until he saw five flesh-pink pillars topped by dark vapours. "This is the end of the road," he said, "so now I'll go back. The Buddha will be witness, and the Hall of Miraculous Mist will be mine." Then he thought again, "Wait a moment. I'll leave my mark here to prove my case when I talk to the Buddha." He pulled out a hair, breathed on it with his magic breath, and shouted "Change". It turned into a writing brush dipped in ink, and with it he wrote THE GREAT SAGE EQUALLING HEAVEN WAS HERE in big letters on the middle pillar. When that was done he put the hair back on, and, not standing on his dignity, made a pool of monkey piss at the foot of the pillar. Then he turned his somersault round and went back to wher he had started from. "I went, and now I'm back. Tell the Jade Emperor to hand the Heavenly Palace over to me," he said, standing in the Buddha's palm.

"I've got you, you piss-spirit of a monkey," roared the Buddha at him. "You never left the palm of my hand." "You're wrong there." the Great Sage replied. "I went to the farthest point of Heaven, where I saw five flesh-pink pillars topped by dark vapours. I left my mark there: do you dare come and see it with me?" "There's no need to go. Just look down." The Great Sage looked down with his fire eyes with golden pupils to see the words "The Great Sage Equalling Heaven Was Here" written on the middle finger of the Buddha's right hand. The stink of monkey-piss rose from the fold at the bottom of the finger. "What a thing to happen," exclaimed the Great Sage in astonishment. "I wrote this on one of the pillars supporting the sky, so how can it be on his finger now? He must have used divination to know what I was going to do. I don't believe it. I refuse to believe it! I'll go there and come back again."

The splendid Great Sage hurriedly braced himself to jump, but the Buddha turned his hand over and pushed the Monkey King out through the Western Gate of Heaven. He turned his five fingers into a mountain chain belonging to the elements Metal, Wood, Water, Fire, and Earth, renamed them the Five Elements Mountain, and gently held him down. All the thunder gods and the arhats Ananda and Kasyapa put their hands together to praise the Buddha: "Wonderful, wonderful,

> *An egg learnt to be a man,*
> *Cultivated his conduct, and achieved the Way.*
> *Heaven had been undisturbed for ten thousand kalpas,*
> *Until one day the spirits were scattered.*

> *"The rebel against Heaven, wanting high position,*
> *Insulted immortals, stole the pills, and destroyed mo-*
>   *rality.*
> *Today his terrible sins are being punished.*
> *Who knows when he will be able to rise again?"*

When he had eliminated the monkey fiend the Buddha told Ananda and Kasyapa to return with him to the western paradise. At that moment Tian Peng and Tian You hurried out of the Hall of Miraculous Mist to say, "We beg the Tathagata to wait a moment as the Jade Emperor's chariot is coming." The Buddha turned round and looked up, and an instant later he saw an eight-splendour imperial chariot and a nine-shining jewelled canopy appear to the sound of strange and exquisite music, and the chanting of countless sacred verses. Precious flowers were scattered and incense was burned. The Jade Emperor went straight up to the Buddha and said, "We are deeply indebted to the great Buddha's powers for wiping out the demon, and we hope that the Tathagata will spend a day here so that we may invite all the Immortals to a feast of thanksgiving." The Buddha did not dare refuse, so putting his hands together he replied, "This old monk only came here in obedience to Your Celestial Majesty's command. What magic powers can I pretend to? This was all due to the wonderful good fortune of Your Celestial Majesty and the other gods. How could I possibly allow you to thank me?" The Jade Emperor then ordered all the gods of the Department of Thunder to split up and invite the Three Pure Ones, the Four Emperors, the Five Ancients, the Six

Superintendents, the Seven Main Stars, the Eight Points of the Compass, the Nine Bright Shiners, the Ten Chiefs, the Thousand Immortals, and the Ten Thousand Sages to a banquet to thank the Buddha for his mercy. Then he ordered the Four Great Heavenly Teachers and the Nine Heavenly Maidens to open the golden gates of the jade capital, of the Palace of the Great Mystery, and of the Tong Yang Jade Palace, invite the Tathagata to take his seat on the Throne of the Seven Precious Things, arrange the places for all the different groups of guests, and set out the dragon liver, phoenix bone-marrow, jade liquor, and magic peaches.

Before long the Original Celestial Jade Pure One, the High Celestial Precious Pure One, the Heavenly Celestial Pure One of the Way, the True Lords of the Five Humours, the Star Lords of the Five Constellations, the Three Officers, the Four Sages, the Left Assistant, the Right Support, the Heavenly Kings, Nezha, and the whole of space responded to the invitations that had been sent out magically. Their standards and canopies came two by two as they brought shining pearls, rare jewels, fruit of longevity, and exotic flowers, and presented them to the Buddha with bows. "We thank the Tathagata for subduing the monkey fiend with his infinite powers. His Celestial Majesty has asked us all to come to his banquet to express our thanks. We beg the Tathagata to give this banquet a title." The Buddha accepted this commission and said, "Since you want a name for it, we could call it the 'Banquet to Celebrate Peace in Heaven'." "Splendid, 'Banquet to Celebrate Peace in Heaven', splendid," exclaimed all the immortals with one voice, and then they all sat down in their places, put flowers in their hair, and played the lyre. It was indeed a splendid banquet, and here are some verses to prove it:

> *The Banquet to Celebrate Peace in Heaven far surpasses*
> *The Banquet of Peaches that the monkey wrecked.*
> *Radiance shines from dragon flags and imperial chariots;*
> *Auspicious vapours float above streamers and symbols*
>   *of office.*

Melodious the fairy music and mysterious songs;
Loud sound the tones of phoenix flute and pipe of jade
The rarest of perfumes waft around the Immortals,
  assembled calm in the sky.
To congratulate the court on Pacifying the Universe.

When the immortals were all enjoying the feast the Queen Mother and a group of fairies, immortal beauties, and houris, floated through the air as they danced towards the Buddha, and after paying her respects the Queen Mother said, "My Peach Banquet was ruined by that monkey fiend, and I failed to invite the immortals and the Baddhas. This Banquet to Celebrate Peace in Heaven is being given because the Tathagata has used his great powers to chain down the evil monkey. Having nothing else with which to express my gratitude, I have picked a number of peaches of immortality with my own pure hands as an offering." They were

> *Half red, half green, sweetly fragrant,*
> *Growing every ten thousand years from immortal roots.*
> *The peaches of Wulingyuan seem laughable:*
> *How can they compare with those of Heaven?*
>
> *Purple-veined and tender, rare even in the sky,*
> *Yellow-stoned, and matchless on earth for their*
>   *sweetness.*
> *They are able to adapt the body and make it live for*
>   *ever;*
> *Those lucky enough to eat them are no ordinary beings.*

The Buddha put his hands together to thank the Queen Mother, who instructed the fairies and houris to sing and dance again, and their performance met with the praises of the whole assembly. Indeed,

> *Misty heavenly incense filled the room;*
> *A chaos of heavenly petals and flowers.*
> *Great is the splendour of the jade city and golden gates,*
> *Priceless the strange treasures and rare jewels.*

Two by two, coeval with Heaven,
Pair by pair, outliving ten thousand kalpas:
Even if land and sea changed places
They would not be astonished or alarmed.

Soon after the Queen Mother had ordered the fairies and houris to sing and dance, and when wine cups and chopsticks were weaving to and fro, suddenly

A strange scent reached their noses,
Startling the stars and constellations in the hall.
Immortals and the Buddha put down their cups,
Each of them raising their heads to look.

An old man appeared in the middle of the Milky Way
Holding a sacred mushroom.
His gourd contains ten-thousand-year elixir.
On the sacred rolls his name is written Eternal Life.

In his cave Heaven and Earth are free.
In his bottle Sun and Moon were created.
As he wanders around the Four Seas in pure idleness
Taking his ease in the Ten Continents, enjoying the
    bustle.

When he went to Peach Banquets he often got drunk
But when he came round, the moon was as bright as
    ever.
A long head, big ears and a short body,
Known as Longevity from the Southern Pole.

The Star of Longevity had arrived. When he had made his greetings to the Jade Emperor and the Buddha he made a speech of thanks. "When I heard that the monkey fiend had been taken by the Lord Lao Zi to his Tushita Palace to be refined I thought that this was bound to restore peace," he said, "and I never expected he would rebel again. Happily the demon was quelled by the Tathagata, and so when I heard that this feast was being given to thank him I came at once. As I have nothing else to offer I have brought with me purple magic

mushrooms, jasper herbs, greenish jade lotus-root, and golden
pills of immortality: these I humbly present." The poem says

> Offering the jade lotus-root and golden pills to Sakya-
> muni,
> To give him as many years as the grains of sand of the
> Ganges.
> Peace and eternal joy decorate the Three Vehicles;
> Prosperity and eternal life make the nine grades of im-
> mortals glorious.

> Within the gate of No Phenomena the true Law rules;
> Above the Heaven of Nothingness is his immortal home.
> Heaven and Earth both call him their ancestor,
> His golden body provides blessings and long life.

The Buddha happily accepted his thanks, and after the
Star of Longevity had taken his place the wine-cups started to
circulate once more. Then the Barefoot Immortal appeared,
kowtowed to the Jade Emperor, and thanked the Buddha. "I
am deeply grateful to you for subduing the monkey fiend with
your divine powers. As I have nothing else with which to express my respect, I offer you two magic pears and a number
of fire-dates."

> Sweet are the Barefoot Immortal's pears and dates,
> And long will be the life of the Buddha to whom they
> are offered.
> The lotus seat of the seven treasures is as firm as a
> mountain;
> His thousand-golden-flower throne is as gorgeous as
> brocade.

> Coeval with Heaven and Earth — this is no lie;
> It is true that his blessings are greater than a flood.
> His Western Paradise of leisure and bliss
> Truly provides all the long life and blessings one could
> hope.

The Buddha thanked him too, and telling Ananda and Kasyapa to collect together all the offerings he went over to the Jade Emperor to thank him for the banquet. When all the guests were thoroughly drunk the Miraculous Patrolling Officer reported that the Great Sage had poked his head out. "It doesn't matter," the Buddha said, producing from his sleeve a strip of paper on which were written the golden words *Om mani padme hum.* He gave this piece of paper to Ananda and told him to stick it on the summit of the mountains. The Venerable Ananda took it through the gates of Heaven and pasted it firmly to a square boulder on the top of the Five Elements Mountain. When this was done the mountain sank roots and joined up all its seams. The Monkey King was still able to breathe and he could still stick his hands out and move them. Ananda went back to Heaven and reported that he had pasted the paper in place.

The Buddha then took his leave of the Jade Emperor and all the other deities. When he and his two disciples had gone out through the gates of Heaven his merciful heart moved him to chant a spell ordering a local tutelary god and the Protectors of the Five Regions to live on the mountain and keep guard over him. When he was hungry they were to feed him iron pellets, and when he was thirsty they were to give him molten copper to drink. When the time of his punishment was over, someone would come and rescue him. Indeed,

> *The monkey fiend was bold enough to rebel against Heaven,*
> *But was subdued by the Tathagata's hand.*
> *He endures the months and years, drinking molten copper for his thirst,*
> *And blunts his hunger on iron pellets, serving his time.*
>
> *Suffering the blows of Heaven, he undergoes torment,*
> *Yet even in the bleakest time a happy fate awaits.*
> *If this hero is ready to struggle again,*
> *He will go to the West in the service of the Buddha.*

Another poem goes:

His great power grew as he humbled the mighty,
He used his wicked talents to subdue tigers and dragons.
He stole the peaches and wine as he wandered round
Heaven,
Was graciously given office in the Jade Capital.

When his wickedness went too far his body suffered,
But his roots of goodness were not severed, and his breath
still rose.
If he wants to escape from the hand of the Buddha,
He must wait till the Tang produces a saintly monk.

If you don't know in what month of what year his sufferings
ended, listen to the explanation in the next instalment.

CHAPTER EIGHT

Our Buddha creates the Scriptures and passes
on Perfect Bliss;
Guanyin obeys a decree and goes
to Chang'an.

If you try to ask about the dhyana
Or investigate the innumerable
You will waste your life and achieve nothing.
Polishing bricks to make mirrors,
Or piling up snow to turn it into grain —
How many youngsters have been misled like that?
A hair can contain an ocean,
A mustard-seed can hold a mountain,
And the golden Kasyapa only smiles.
When you are awakened you will surpass the Ten Stages
    and the Three Vehicles,
And stop the four kinds of birth and the six types of rein-
    carnation.
Who has ever heard, before the cliff of thoughts ex-
    tinguished,
Under the tree that has no shadow,
The sound of the cuckoo in a spring dawn?
The path by the Cao Stream is difficult to follow,
The Vulture Peak is high in the clouds:
Here there is no news of old friends.
On a cliff ten thousand feet high
Five-leaved lotuses bloom
As scent coils round the shutters of the old palace.
At that time

Your knowledge smashes all the currents of thought;
The Dragon King and the Three Treasures can be seen.

This lyric poem is set to the tune *Su Wu Man*. Our story
goes on to how our Buddha, the Tathagata, left the Jade Emperor and went back to the Thunder Monastery, where he saw
the three thousand Buddhas, five hundred Arhats, eight great
Vajrapanis and countless Bodhisattvas standing under the pairs
of sala trees at the foot of the Vulture Peak, all holding banners,
canopies, jewels and magical flowers. The Tathagata brought his
propitious cloud to a halt and addressed them thus:

> *"With my deep insight*
> *I surveyed the Three Worlds.*
> *The origin of nature*
> *Is ultimately emptiness,*
> *Like the great void,*
> *Containing nothing at all.*
>
> *The subjection of this evil monkey*
> *Was a mystery beyond understanding.*
> *It is called the beginning of life and death:*
> *Such is the appearance of things.*

When he had spoken a sacred light filled the sky with forty-
two rainbows that linked north and south together. All who saw
them bowed, and a moment later the Buddha gathered together
some felicitous cloud and climbed to the supreme Lotus Throne,
where he seated himself in majesty. Then the three thousand
Buddhas, the five hundred Arhats, the eight Vajrapanis and the
four Bodhisattvas came forward to bow to him with their hands
together and ask, "Who was it who wrecked the Heavenly Palace
and ruined the Peach Banquet?" they asked. "The wretch
was a monkey fiend born on the Mountain of Flowers and
Fruit," the Buddha replied, "whose towering crimes would beg-
gar description. None of the heavenly generals were able to
subdue him, and when Lord Lao Zi refined him with fire after
Erlang had captured him, he was unharmed. When I went
there he was in the middle of the thunder generals, giving a

great display of his martial prowess and his spirit. I stopped the fighting and asked him what it was all about. He said that he had divine powers, was able to do transformations, and could ride a somersault cloud for thirty-six thousand miles at a single jump. I made a wager with him that he could not jump out of my hand, then grabbed him, turned my fingers into the Five Elements Mountain, and sealed him under it. The Jade Emperor opened wide the golden gates of the Jade Palace, and invited me to be the guest of honour at a Banquet to Celebrate Peace in Heaven he gave to thank me. After that I took my leave of him and came back here." They were all delighted by the news and they congratulated him effusively, after which they withdrew group by group, each to go about his duties as all rejoiced in the divine truth. Indeed,

> Propitious vapours filled Paradise,
> Rainbows surround the Venerable One.
> The Western Paradise, known as the best,
> Is ruled by the dharma king of non-phenomenon.
> Black apes are always offering fruit,
> Deer hold flowers in their mouths;
> Blue phoenixes dance,
> Coloured birds call;
> Sacred turtles offer long life,
> Immortal cranes present magic mushrooms.
> Here they peacefully enjoy the Pure Land of the Jetava-
>   na Park,
> The infinite realms of the Dragon Palace.
> Every day flowers bloom,
> Fruit is always ripe.
> Through practising silence they return to the truth,
> Achieving reality by contemplation.
> There is no birth nor death;
> They neither wax nor wane.
> Mists follow them as they come and go;
> Untouched by heat or cold, they do not notice the years.
> There is also a poem that goes;

In his travels he comes and goes at will,
Free from fear and free from grief.
All is magnanimity in the field of bliss;
There are no springs and autumns in the eternal land.

One day, as the Buddha dwelt in the Thunder Monastery on the Vulture Peak, he called together all the other Buddhas, Arhats, guardian deities, Bodhisattvas, Vajrapanis, monks and nuns and said, "As we are beyond time, I don't know how long it has been since the crafty ape was subdued and Heaven pacified, but by earthly reckoning it must be about five hundred years. As today is a fine early autumn day and I have a precious bowl filled with a hundred kinds of rare flowers and a thousand varieties of exotic fruit, what would you say to our having an Ullambana Feast?" They all put their hands together and performed the reverence of going round him three times in acceptance. The Buddha then ordered Ananda to hold the bowl of flowers and fruit while Kasyapar laid them out. The hosts were moved to gratitude, which they expressed in verse.

The poem on happiness went:

The Star of Happiness shines bright before the Venerable
*   One;*
Gifts of happiness spread wide and deep, ever richer.
Fortune is boundless and lasts as long as the Earth;
A happy fate has the luck to be linked with Heaven.

Fields of happiness are widely sown and flourish every
*   years;*
The sea of happiness is mighty and deep, never chang-
*   ing.*
Happiness fills Heaven and Earth, leaving legacies of
*   happiness;*
Happiness grows beyond measure, eternally complete.

The poem on official rank went:

With rank as high as a mountain, coloured phoenixes
*   call;*

With rank ever increasing, we praise the evening star.
Salary raised to ten thousand bushels, and a healthy body;
Salary raised to a thousand tons, and the world at peace.

Rank and salary equalling Heaven, and eternal too;
Rank and fame as great as the sea, and even clearer.
Rank and favour continuing for ever, greatly to be admired;
Rank and nobility without bounds, like ten thousand kingdoms.

The poem on longevity went:

The Star of Longevity shines towards the Buddha;
The glories of the land of longevity start from here.
Fruits of longevity fill the bowls, glowing with good omen;
Longevity's flowers are newly plucked and placed on the lotus throne.

Poems of longevity, pure and elegant, full of rare conceits;
Songs of longevity sung with exquisite talent.
Life as long as sun and moon,
Life that will outlast both mountains and seas.

When the Bodhisattvas had presented all the poems they asked the Buddha to expound the fundamentals to them. Then the Tathagata opened his excellent mouth and expounded the great Law and retribution. He spoke about the wonderful scriptures of the Three Vehicles and the theory of the Five Aggregates as contained in the *Surangama-sutra;* the deities and nagas gathered round, and flowers came raining down in profusion. Indeed,

The meditating heart shines like the moon in a thousand rivers;
The true nature embraces ten thousand miles of sky.

When the Buddha had finished his sermon he said to the host, "I have observed that the morality of the living creatures of the four continents varies. In the Eastern Continent of Superior Body they worship Heaven and Earth, their minds are lively and they are even-tempered. In the Northern Kuru Continent they are given to killing living things, but they only do it to feed themselves; they are stupid and lazy by nature, but they do not trample much on others. Our Western Continent of Cattle-gift has people who neither covet nor kill. They nourish the vital essence and submerge the spirit; and although they produce no saints of the highest order, they all live to a ripe old age. But in the Southern Jambu Continent they are greedy and lecherous and delight in the sufferings of others; they go in for a great deal of killing and quarrelling. That continent can with truth be called a vicious field of back-biting and calumny, an evil sea of disputation. I now have Three Stores of True Scriptures with which they can be persuaded to be good." On hearing this, all the Bodhisattvas put their hands together in submission, then went forward to ask, "What Three Stores of True Scriptures does the Tathagata have?" "I have one store of the Vinaya, the law, which is about Heaven; one of Sastras, expositions which are concerned with Earth; and one of Sutras, or scriptures, which save ghosts. The Three Stores consist of fifteen thousand one hundred and forty-four scrolls in thirty-five classes. They are the scriptures for cultivating the truth, and the gate to real goodness. I want to send them to the eastern lands because it is intolerable that the beings of that quarter should all be such stupid wretches who slander and defame the true word, do not understand the gist of my Law, and have lapsed from the orthodox Yogacara Sect. How am I to find one with the magic powers to go to the east, choose a worthy believer and bid him make the arduous crossing of a thousand mountains and ten thousand rivers in search of the scriptures until he finally comes to this abode of mine to receive them? When he does come they will be sent to the East for ever to convert all living beings, which will be a blessing as big as a mountain, a cause for congratulation as deep as the sea. Is anyone willing to go and find him?" The Bodhisattva Guanyin went up to the lotus throne, and after going round the Buddha three times by way of salutation she said, "Your untalented disciple wishes to go to the East to find a man to come and fetch the scriptures." All present raised their heads to look at the Bodhisattva:

> *Her understanding filling out the four virtues,*
> *Wisdom filling her golden body.*
> *From her necklace hang pearls and jade,*
> *Her bracelet is made of jewels.*
> *Her hair is black clouds skilfully piled like coiling drag-*
>   *ons;*
> *Her embroidered girdle lightly sways, a phoenix wing.*
> *Seagreen jade buttons,*
> *A gown of white silk gauze,*
> *Bathed with sacred light;*
> *Brocade skirts,*
> *A girdle of gold,*
> *Shielded by propitious vapours.*
> *Eyebrows like crescent moon,*
> *Eyes like a pair of stars.*
> *A jade face full of heavenly happiness,*
> *Scarlet lips making a touch of red.*
> *Her pure bottle of sweet dew is ever full,*
> *The willow twigs in it are always green.*
> *She delivers from the eight disasters,*
> *Saves all living beings,*
> *Great is her compassion.*
> *She stays on Mount Tai,*
> *Lives in the Southern Sea,*
> *Rescues the suffering when she hears their cries,*
> *Never failing to answer every call,*
> *Infinitely divine and miraculous.*
> *Her orchid heart admires the purple bamboo;*
> *Her orchid nature loves the fragrant creeper.*

She is the merciful ruler of Potaraka Island,
The living Guanyin of the Tide Cave.

The Buddha was very pleased to see her. "No one but the venerable Guanyin, whose divine powers are so great, will do for this mission," he said. "What instructions have you for your disciple as she goes to the East?" Guanyin asked. "You must watch the route all the way," said the Buddha. "You may not go via the Milky Way, but if necessary you may have a little cloud or mist. As you cross mountains and rivers you must note the distances carefully to enable you to give full instructions to the man who will come to fetch the scriptures. But that true believer will, I'm afraid, have a difficult journey, so I shall give you five treasures for him." The Buddha ordered Ananda and Kasyapa to bring out a brocade cassock and a nine-ringed monk's staff. "Give this cassock and staff to him who will come to fetch the scriptures: they are for him to use. If he is determined to come here, he can avoid the Wheel of Reincarnation by wearing this cassock, and he will be free from evil if he carries this staff." The Bodhisattva bowed and took them. The Buddha then produced three bands. "These precious things are called 'tight bands'," he told the Bodhisattva as he handed them to her. "Although all three of them look the same, they have different uses. I also have three Band-tightening Spells. If you meet any devils with great magic powers on your journey you should persuade them to reform and become the disciples of the pilgrim who will come to fetch the scriptures. If they do not do as they are told these bands should be put on their heads, where they will of themselves take root in the flesh. If the appropriate spell for each one is recited the victim's eyes will bulge, his head will ache, and his forehead will split open. He will thus be certainly induced to adopt our religion."

When he finished speaking the Bodhisattva bowed eagerly and withdrew. She told Huian the Novice to accompany her, and he took his iron staff weighing a thousand pounds with him so that he could act as a demon-quelling strongman for the Bo-

dhisattva. The Bodhisattva wrapped the cassock up in a bundle
and gave it to him to carry. She then put the golden bands
away safely and went down the Vulture Peak with the staff in
her hand. This journey was to have consequences:

> *The Buddha's disciple comes back to his original vow;*
> *The Venerable Golden Cicada is dressed in sandal-*
> *wood.*

When the Bodhisattva reached the foot of the mountain
the Gold-headed Immortal of the Jade Truth Temple stopped
her at the temple gate and invited her to take some tea. But
she dared not stop for long, and so she said, "I have been given
a sacred command by the Tathagata to go to the East and
find a man who will come to fetch the scriptures." "When will
he arrive?" the Immortal asked. "It is not definite", the Bodhisattva replied, "but he will probably reach here in two or three
years' time." She took her leave of the Immortal and as she
travelled amid cloud and mist she estimated the distances.
There are some verses to prove it:

> *She cared nothing of the journey of ten thousand miles*
> *to seek him,*
> *But worried about finding the right man.*
> *Looking for the man seemed to be very chancy:*
> *But how can it be a mere coincidence?*

> *One who teaches the Way for the wrong motives will*
> *distort it;*
> *He who explains it without faith will preach in vain.*
> *Whoever tries to know it with his whole being,*
> *Is bound to have a future ahead of him.*

As the teacher and her disciple were on their journey they
suddenly noticed a thousand miles of weak water, which was the
River of Flowing Sands. "Disciple," said the Bodhisattva,
"this will be hard to cross for the man who will come to fetch
the scriptures, as he will be of impure bone and mortal flesh.
How will he do it?" "Teacher, how wide does the river look

to you?" asked Huian.   The Bodhisattva stopped her cloud
to investigate. She saw:

> Joining up with the deserts to the east,
> Reaching the foreign kingdoms in the west,
> Wuge in the south
> The Tartars in the north.
> It was about three hundred miles across,
> And three million miles long.
> As the waters flowed it was like the earth turning over,
> The waves were like rearing mountains.
> Broad and boundless,
> Vast and mighty:
> From three miles' distance the mighty flood is heard.
> Immortals' rafts do not reach here;
> Lotus leaves cannot float on it.
> The sun slants through withered plants and bathes the
>   crooked shore;
> Brown clouds block its light and darken the long bank.
> How could merchants pass this way?
> Has a fisherman ever moored here?
> No geese alight on the sandbanks,
> But apes cry on the distant shore.
> Its colour comes from bountiful red smartweed,
> While delicate white duckweed drifts together.

As the Bodhisattva was surveying the scene she heard a
splash and saw a hideous ogre leap out of the waves. He was

> Not really blue,
> Not really black,
> With an evil face;
> Neither tall,
> Nor short,
> Bare legs and a muscular body.
> His eyes flashed
> Like a pair of tortoise-shell lanterns;
> The corners of his mouth were as sinister
> As a butcher's cauldron.

Protruding fangs like swords,
Red hair, matted and unkempt.
He roared like a clap of thunder,
And ran across the waves with the speed of wind.

This ogre climbed up the bank with a pole in his hands to catch the Bodhisattva, but was stopped by Huian's staff. "Don't run away," Huian shouted as the ogre advanced towards him. The battle that ensued between them was quite terrifying:

Moksa with his iron club,
Using his divine powers to protect the Bodhisattva;
The ogre with his demon-quelling pole
Displaying his valour for all he was worth.
A pair of silver dragons dancing by the river;
Two holy monks in battle on the bank.
The one used his skill to control the River of Flowing
     Sands;
The other had distinguished himself in protecting
     Guanyin.
The one could make the waves leap and roll,
The other could breathe out fogs and gales.
When the waves leapt and rolled, Heaven and Earth
     were darkened;
In the fogs and gales, sun and moon were dimmed.
The demon-quelling pole
Was like a white tiger coming down from the mountain;
The iron club
Was like a crouching yellow dragon.
When one goes into action
It beats the undergrowth to start the snakes;
When the other lashes out,
It parts the pines to flush the sparrowhawks.
They fight till the sky goes dark
And the stars twinkle.
Then the mist rises,
And earth and sky are dim.

The one has long been unrivalled in the Weak Waters;
The other has always been the hero of Vulture Peak.

When the pair of them had fought several dozen rounds in-
conclusively the ogre blocked his opponent's iron staff and asked,
"Where are you from, monk, that you dare to take me on?" "I
am Prince Moksa, the second son of the Pagoda-bearing Heavenly King Li," the other replied. "I am also Huian the Novice.
I am now protecting my teacher on her journey to the East to
find the man who will fetch the scriptures. Which monster are
you? How dare you stand in our way?" The ogre then realized
who he was. "I remember," he said, "you used to cultivate your
conduct with Guanyin of the Southern Sea in the Purple Bamboo
Grove. Why have you come here?" "Can't you see my teacher
standing there on the bank?"

When the ogre heard this he chanted "re-e-er" several
times to show his respect, withdrew his pole and let Moksa seize
it. Then he bowed to Guanyin and said, "Forgive me, Bodhisattva, and listen to what I have to tell you. I am not a
demon, but the Curtain Raising General who used to stand in
attendance by the imperial chariot in the Hall of Miraculous
Mist. Just because I accidentally smashed a crystal dish at a
Peach Banquet the Jade Emperor had me given eight hundred
strokes of the rod, exiled me to the lower world, and made me
look like this. And on top of it all every seven days he sends
a flying sword here to stab my chest over a hundred times before
it goes back again. It's agony. I get so unbearably cold and
hungry that I have to emerge from the waves every two or three
days to devour a traveller. I never thought that in my ignorance
I would insult the merciful Bodhisattva today." "You were
exiled here for a crime against Heaven, but now you are deepening your guilt by harming living beings. I am now going to the
East on the Buddha's orders to find the man who will fetch
the scriptures. Why don't you become one of us and ensure
yourself good retribution in future by accompanying the pilgrim
as a disciple and ascending to the Western Heaven to pay
homage to the Buddha and seek the scriptures? I will see to it

that the flying sword stops coming to pierce you, and when you
are successful you will be forgiven your crimes and your old job
will be given back to you. What do you think of that?" "I am
willing to return to the truth," the ogre replied, then went closer
as he continued, "Bodhisattva, I have lost count of the number
of people I have eaten here, and I have even devoured some
pilgrims who were trying to fetch scriptures. I throw the heads
of all my victims into the river, and they all sink to the bottom
as not even goose-down will float on this water. But the
skeletons of those nine pilgrims floated and would not sink. I
was so impressed by this that I threaded them together with
rope and play with them in my spare time. But I am afraid
that the man who is to fetch the scriptures may not get this far,
which would wreck my future." "Of course he'll get here," the
Bodhisattva replied. "You should hang those skeletons from
your head and wait for him. They will come in useful." "In
that case," the ogre said, "I shall await your instructions." The
Bodhisattva then laid her hands on his head and administered
the monastic rules to him, chose for him the surname Sha
("Sand") and gave him the Buddhist name of Wujing ("Awakened to Purity"). Then he entered monkish life and took the
Bodhisattva across the river. He washed his heart, cleansed his
thoughts, and stopped killing living creatures. All he did now
was to wait for the pilgrim who would come to fetch the scriptures.

After leaving him the Bodhisattva and Huian hurried on towards the east. When they had been travelling for a long time
they saw a high mountain veiled with an evil mist, and they
were unable to climb it on foot. Just when they were intending
to cross the mountain by cloud, a gale wind blew up and a monster suddenly appeared. He too was very menacing to behold:

> *His entrails hung from his mouth, rolled up and*
>   *knotted;*
> *His ears were like rush fans, his eyes shone gold.*
> *His teeth were sharp as steel files,*
> *And when he opened his mouth it was like a brazier.*

His golden helmet was tied firmly round his cheeks;
His armour, bound with a silken sash, was a python's
    sloughed-off skin.
In his hands he held a nailed rake like a dragon's claw,
At his waist hung a curved bow the shape of a half-
    moon.
His martial might overawed the Year Planet;
His overweening spirit threatened the heavenly gods.

He rushed upon them, and without a second thought smote
at the Bodhisattva with his rake. Moksa the Novice parried his
blow, and shouted at the top of his voice, "Remember your manners, damned monster, and watch out for my staff." "Monk,"
the other replied, "you don't know how to keep yourself in one
piece. Mind my rake!" At the foot of the mountain the pair of
them rushed upon each other as they struggled for supremacy. It
was a fine battle:

The fierce and murderous ogre;
Huian, imposing and able.
The iron staff could pulverize the heart;
The rake struck at the face.
The dust thrown up darkened Heaven and Earth;
The flying sand and stones startled gods and ghouls.
The nine-toothed rake
Gleamed and flashed
As its pair of rings resounded;
The lone staff
Was ominously black
As it whirled in its owner's hands.
One was the heir of a Heavenly King;
The other was the spirit of a marshal
One defended the Law on Potaraka Island;
The other was an evil fiend in a mountain cave.
In their battle for mastery,
None knew who the winner would be.

Just when the fight was getting really good, Guanyin
threw down a lotus flower from mid-air to separate the two

weapons. The monster, shocked at the sight of it, asked, "Where are you from, monk? How dare you try to fool me with a 'flower in front of the eyes'?" "I'll get you, you stinking, flesh-eyed mortal," replied Moksa. "I am a disciple of the Bodhisattva of the Southern Sea, and this lotus was thrown down by her. Don't you know that?" "By the Bodhisattva of the Southern Sea do you mean Guanyin Who Eliminates the Three Calamities and Saves from the Eight Disasters?" the monster asked. "Who else could I mean?" retorted Moksa. The monster threw down his rake, bowed to him, and asked, "Where is the Bodhisattva, elder brother? May I trouble you to introduce me?" Moksa looked up and pointed. "There she is," he said. The monster kowtowed to her and shouted in a shrill voice, "Forgive me, Bodhisattva, forgive me." Guanyin brought her cloud down to earth, went over to him and asked, "Are you a wild boar become a devil or a pig turned monster? How dare you block my way?" "I'm neither a wild boar nor a pig," the monster replied. "I used to be Marshal Tian Peng in the Milky Way. Because I took some wine to seduce the moon maiden, the Jade Emperor sentenced me to two thousand hammer blows and exile in the mortal world. My spirit had to find a womb to occupy, but I lost my way and entered the womb of a sow. That's why I look like this. I ate up my sow mother, drove all the other pigs away, and seized this mountain, where I keep myself by eating people. I never meant to offend you, Bodhisattva. Save me, save me, I beg you." "What is this mountain called?" the Bodhisattva asked. "It's called the Mount of Blessing, and the cave in it is called the Cloud Pathway Cave. Second Sister Luan, who used to live there, saw that I knew how to fight and asked me to be the head of her household as her husband, but she died within a year and all her property became mine. As the days lengthened into years I found that I had no way of supporting myself, so I had to eat people to keep myself going as I had done before. Forgive me my sins, I beg of you, Bodhisattva." "There is an old saying," the Bodhisattva replied, "that goes, 'If you want to have a future, don't do anything with no future in it?' You broke the law in the upper world, and since then your vicious nature has not been reformed. You have further sinned by taking life, so this surely means that you will be doubly punished." "Future!" said the monster angrily. "According to you I should have lived on air! As the saying goes, 'By the government's law you're beaten to death, and by the Buddha's law you starve to death.' Clear off! Clear off! I'd do better catching myself a traveller and making a good meal of his tender flesh. I don't give a damn if it's double sinning, triple sinning, or sinning a thousand or ten thousand times over." " 'If a man wishes to be good, Heaven will certainly allow him to be'," said the Bodhisattva. "If you are prepared to submit to the truth, there are of course ways to feed yourself. There are the five kinds of food-grains, and they are sufficient to assuage hunger, so why eat people to keep alive?"

When the monster heard these words it was as if he awoke from a dream, and he said to the Bodhisattva, "I would love to reform, but isn't it true that 'a sinner against Heaven has nowhere to pray to'?" "I'm going to the East on the orders of the Buddha to find the man who will fetch the scriptures," she replied. "You can be a disciple of his and make this journey to the Western Heaven; thus you will gain merit and atone for your crimes, and I will see to it that you are freed from disaster." "I'll go with him, I'll go with him," the monster said over and over again. The Bodhisattva then laid her hands on his head and he accepted the monastic rules. She gave him the surname Zhu ("Pig") because of his appearance, and gave him the Buddhist name Zhu Wuneng ("Pig Awakened to Power"). She ordered him to adhere to the truth and eat only vegetarian food, cutting out the five pungent vegetables as well as the three forbidden things; wild goose, dog and fish. He was now to wait single-mindedly for the pilgrim who would come to fetch the scriptures.

The Bodhisattva and Moksa then took their leave of the Pig Awakened to Power and continued on their way by low-altitude cloud. As they were travelling along they heard a jade dragon call to them in mid-air. "Which dragon are you?" the

Bodhisattva asked as she went up to him. "And why are you undergoing punishment here?" "I am the son of Ao Run, the Dragon King of the Western Sea. Because I burnt up the bright pearls in the palace, my father reported me to the court of Heaven as a rebel. The Jade Emperor had me hung up in mid-air and given three hundred strokes, and I am to be executed any day now. I beg you to save me, Bodhisattva."

When she heard his plea the Bodhisattva went in through the Southern Gates of Heaven with Moksa. Here they were met by the Heavenly Teachers Qiu and Zhang, who asked them, "Where are you going?" "I would like an audience with the Jade Emperor." The two Heavenly Teachers hurried in to announce her, and the Jade Emperor came out of his palace to receive her. The Bodhisattva went forward to greet him and said, "On my way to the East on the orders of the Buddha to find the man to fetch the scriptures, I met a wicked dragon suspended in mid-air. I have come here especially to ask you to spare his life and give him to me so that I can teach him to serve the pilgrim with his legs." On hearing this the Jade Emperor issued a decree pardoning him, and he sent a heavenly general to release him and give him to the Bodhisattva. The Bodhisattva thanked him for his generosity and left. The young dragon kowtowed to show how grateful he was for having his life spared, and he obediently did what the Bodhisattva told him to. She took him to a deep ravine, where he was to wait until the pilgrim came. When that happened he was to turn into a white horse and achieve merit by going to the Western Heaven. On receiving his orders the young dragon hid himself.

The Bodhisattva led Moksa the Novice across this mountain, and they hurried on towards the east. Before they had gone much further they suddenly saw ten thousand beams of golden light and a thousand wisps of propitious vapour. "Teacher," said Moksa, "the place where all the light is coming from is the Five Elements Mountain, where the Tathagata's restriction order is posted." "This must be because that Great Sage Equalling Heaven who wrecked the Peach Banquet and threw the Heavenly Palace into chaos is imprisoned there." "That's right,"

Moksa replied, and teacher and pupil climbed the mountain together to look at the paper. On it were written the true words *Om mani padme hum*, and when the Bodhisattva saw them she sighed deeply and composed a poem that went:

"Pity the evil monkey who did not obey the lord
In his arrogance he showed off his valour in the old days,
In his folly he wrecked the Peach Banquet,
And he had the effrontery to sin in the Tushita Palace.

In the army of a hundred thousand there was none to
    match him;
His might was felt above the ninefold heavens.
But now he has been caught by our Tathagata,
Will he be able to unleash his talents and win more
    glory?"

The conversation between teacher and disciple had disturbed the Great Sage, who shouted from under the roots of the mountain, "Who's that up there getting at me with poetry?" When she heard this the Bodhisattva hurried down the mountain to visit him. At the foot of the mountainside the local gods, the mountain gods and the heavenly generals who were guarding the Great Sage all bowed to the Bodhisattva in greeting and took her to the Great Sage. She saw that he was pressed down inside a stone box, so that he could speak but could not move his body. "Monkey," the Bodhisattva said, "do you know who I am?" The Great Sage opened wide his fiery eyes with their golden pupils, nodded his head and shouted at the top of his voice, "Of course I recognize you. You, thank goodness, are the All-Compassionate, All-Merciful Deliverer from Suffering, the Bodhisattva Guanyin from Potaraka Island in the Southern Sea. You're a very welcome visitor. Every day here seems like a year, and nobody I know has ever come to see me. Where have you come from?" "I have received a mandate from the Buddha to go to the East and find the man who will fetch the scriptures," she replied, "and as I was passing this way I decided to come over and see you." "The Buddha fooled me and crushed me under this mountain — I haven't been able to stretch myself for five hundred years. I desperately hope that you will be obliging enough to rescue me, Bodhisattva." "You wretch," she replied, "you have such an appalling criminal record that I'm afraid you'd only make more trouble if I got you out." "I have already repented," he said, "and hope that you will show me the road I should follow. I want to cultivate my conduct." Indeed,

> When an idea is born in a man's mind
> It is known throughout Heaven and Earth.
> If good and evil are not rewarded and punished
> The world is bound to go to the bad.

The Bodhisattva was delighted to hear what he had to say. "The sacred scriptures say," she replied, " 'If one's words are good, they will meet with a response from even a thousand miles away; if they are bad, they will be opposed from the same distance.' If this is your state of mind, then wait while I go to the East to find the man who will fetch the scriptures; I'll tell him to rescue you. You can be his disciple, observe and uphold the faith, enter our Buddha's religion, and cultivate good retribution for yourself in the future. What do you say to that?" "I'll go, I'll go," the Great Sage repeated over and over again. "As you have reformed," she said, "I'll give you a Buddhist name." "I've already got a name. It's Sun Wukong." The Bodhisattva, very pleased, said, "I made two converts earlier, and their names both contained Wu ('Awakened'). There's no need to give you any further instructions, so I'll be off." The Great Sage, now aware of his own Buddha-nature, was converted to the Buddha's religion; and the Bodhisattva devotedly continued her search for a saintly monk.

After leaving that place she and Huian carried straight on to the east, and before long they reached Chang'an, the capital of the Great Tang. Putting away their mists and clouds, teacher and pupil turned themselves into a pair of scabby itinerant monks and went inside the city of Chang'an It was already dark, and beside the great market street they saw a shrine to a local tutelary god and went in. The local god was thrown into confusion at the sight of them, and the devil soldiers quaked

with terror; they knew that she was a Bodhisattva, and kowtowed to her in greeting. The local god then scurried off to tell
the City God, the Lord of the Altar, and the gods of all the
other shrines in Chang'an. When they knew that the Bodhisattva
had come they all went to report to her and said, "Bodhisattva,
please forgive us for our crime in being late to welcome you."
"You mustn't let a whisper of this get out," she said. "I have
come here on a decree from the Buddha to find someone to fetch
the scriptures. I shall be borrowing your temple for a few days
while I find this true monk, and then I shall go back." All the
gods returned to their own shrines, and they took the local god
to stay in the temple of the City God. Teacher and disciple disguised their true appearances. If you don't know whom they
found to fetch the scriptures, listen to the explanation in the
next instalment.

CHAPTER NINE

Chen Guangrui comes to grief on his way
to his post;
The monk of the river current avenges
his parents.

The story goes on to tell that Chang'an city in the great land of Shaanxi had been a place where emperors and kings had made their capitals for generation after generation. Ever since the Zhou, Qin and Han dynasties, the Three Prefectures had been as rich as brocade, and the eight rivers had flowed round its walls. It was indeed a famous country. At that time Emperor Taizong of the Great Tang was on the throne. He had changed the name of the reign-period to *Zhen Guan*, and had been reigning for thirteen years. It was the year *jisi* and the world was at peace; tribute was being sent in from the eight directions, and all within the four seas acknowledged themselves as subjects.

One day Taizong took his seat on the throne and assembled all his military and civilian officials. When they had finished making their greetings, the minister Wei Zheng came forward from the ranks of officials and memorialized, "As the world is now at peace and the eight directions are calm, an examination should be held in accordance with the practice of the ancients. Thus we could recruit wise scholars and select men of talent to help with our civilizing mission." "The suggestion of our wise minister is right," said the emperor, and notices inviting worthy men to compete in the examinations were posted throughout the empire. All the Confucian scholars on the civil or military rolls in every prefecture, district and county who had distinguished themselves in the three-stage examinations for their understanding of literature were to go to Chang'an for a final test.

陳光蕊赴任逢災
江流僧復讐報本

When this notice reached the district of Haizhou it was seen
by a man called Chen E, whose courtesy name was Guangrui.
He returned home and said to Madame Zhang, his mother, "The
court has issued a yellow notice saying that the Chancellery will
be opened for an examination to select men of wisdom and
talent. Your child wants to go and take part. If I am given
an official post it will bring me fame and make our family
illustrious; my wife will be given a title, my sons will be given
preferential treatment; and it will bring glory to our house. Such
is my ambition; and I have come to tell you, mother, that I am
going." "You are a scholar, my son," his mother replied, "and
it is right that 'one who studies when young should travel when
grown up'. But do take care on the journey to the examinations,
and if you are given office, come back home as soon as you can."
Chen Guangrui then ordered his servants to get his luggage
together, took his leave of his mother, and started off on his
journey. When he reached Chang'an the examination grounds
were open and he went in. Having been successful in this examination, he went to the palace for the test on policies. The
Tang Emperor personally awarded him the first place, and he
was paraded round the streets on horseback for three days.

It happened that just when the procession was passing the
gateway of the minister Yin Kaishan, the minister's unmarried
daughter Wenqiao, whose other name was Man-tang-qiao
(Beauty Throughout the Hall), was making decorations for the
house and throwing an embroidered ball to see who her future
husband would be. When Chen Guangrui passed below she saw
at once that he was exceptionally handsome, and she knew that
he had come first in the recent examinations. She was thoroughly taken with him, and when she dropped her embroidered ball
it landed squarely on his black hat. To the sound of pipes and
flutes a dozen or so maidservants and serving women hurried
downstairs to take hold of the head of Chen Guangrui's horse
and invite him into the minister's mansion to marry his daughter.
The minister and his wife came into the main hall, and when
they had called for a master of ceremonies they married their
daughter to Guangrui. When bride and groom had bowed to

Heaven, Earth and each other they both bowed to the bride's father and mother. The minister ordered a banquet, and there was a night of drinking and celebration. The bride and groom went hand in hand into the bridal chamber

At the third quarter of the fifth watch the next morning the emperor took his throne in the throne room of the palace, and the civil and military officials came to court. "What office should Chen Guangrui who came top in the examinations be given?" the emperor asked, and the minister Wei Zheng replied, "Your subject has gone through the list of the prefectures and commanderies, and found that the district of Jiangzhou needs a prefect. I beg Your Majesty to give him this office." The emperor therefore appointed him prefect of Jiangzhou and ordered him to pack his belongings and set off as he had to be there by a set date. Chen Guangrui thanked the emperor for his grace and withdrew. He went back to the minister's mansion and consulted his wife, then he took his leave of his parents-in-law and set off together with her for his post in Jiangzhou.

It was late spring as they left Chang'an at the start of their journey. Warm breezes were coaxing the willows into green, and light rain was touching the blossoms with red. Chen Guangrui was able to call at his own home on the way, so he and his bride could pay their respects to his mother, Madame Zhang, "Congratulations, my son," she said. "And you have brought a bride back with you too." "Thanks to my mother's blessings, your son was placed first in the examinations," he replied, "and given a parade through the streets on His Majesty's orders. As I was passing the gateway of minister Yin's residence, I happened to be hit by an embroidered ball, and the minister was kind enough to give me his daughter's hand. The court has appointed me prefect of Jiangzhou, so I have come to fetch you, mother, and take you with me to my post." Madame Zhang was overjoyed, and she packed her luggage and travelled with them.

One night, after they had been on the road for several days they put up at the Liu the Second's Ten Thousand Flowers Inn where Madame Zhang was suddenly taken ill. "As I'm not feeling well," she said to her son, "I'd better stay in this inn for a couple of days to get over it before going on." Chen Guangrui accepted her suggestion. The next morning he saw a man selling a golden-coloured carp in front of the inn and bought it from him for a string of copper coins, intending to have it lightly fried for his mother. Then he noticed it blinking. "It's said that if a fish or a snake blinks it is no ordinary creature," he thought. He asked the fisherman where he had caught it. "In the Hongjiang River, five miles from the prefectural capital," the fisherman replied. Chen Guangrui had the fish taken back to the Hongjiang River to be released there, then went back to the inn to tell his mother about what had happened. "It is good to release living things," his mother said, "and I am very pleased." Then Chen Guangrui said, "We have been at this inn for three days, and the time limit set for me is a tight one, so I must be on my way tomorrow morning. Are you well enough yet, mother?" "I'm still poorly," his mother replied, "and it's so hot to travel now that I'm afraid it might make me seriously ill. You had better take a couple of rooms for me and leave me some money; I'll stay here for the time being. You two can go on ahead to your post. Come back to fetch me in the autumn when it's cooler." Having discussed it with his wife he rented a wing for her and gave her some money, then they took their leave of her and set off.

It was a hard journey, setting off every day at dawn and not stopping till nightfall, and before they realized it they reached the ford over the Hongjiang Estuary. They saw two boatmen, Liu Hong and Li Biao, punt their ferry to the bank for them. This was the disaster and these were the enemies that Chen Guangrui had been fated to meet since before he was born. He told his servant to put the luggage on board, while he and his wife climbed sedately into the boat. Liu Hong stared at Miss Yin, and saw that her face was like a full moon, her eyes like autumn waves, her tiny mouth like a cherry, and her waist as supple as a willow; her charms would have made fish sink and wild geese fall from the sky, and her beauty put moon and flowers to shame. Evil thoughts surged up in him, and he conspired with Li Biao to punt the boat to a misty and deserted place and wait till the middle of the night, when they killed first the servant and then Chen Guangrui. They pushed both the corpses into the river and went away. When the young lady saw her husband killed she tried to fling herself into the water, but Liu Hong put his arms round her and said, "If you come with me, you'll be all right; but if you don't, I'll cut you in half." Unable to think of any other way out, the young lady had to agree to stay with Liu Hong for the time being at least. The murderer took the boat across to the southern bank and gave it to Li Biao. Then he dressed up in Chen Guangrui's clothes and, armed with the dead man's credentials, went with the young lady to take up his post in Jiangzhou.

The corpse of the murdered servant floated with the current, but Chen Guangrui's body sank straight to the bottom and did not move. A patrolling yaksha demon stationed at the Hongjiang Estuary saw him and rushed straight back to the dragon palace to report. He arrived just as the dragon king was entering the throne-hall. "Someone has murdered a learned gentleman at the Hongjiang Estuary, and thrown the body into the bed of the river," he reported. The dragon king had the body brought in and laid in front of him. After examining it carefully he said, "This is the benefactor who saved my life: why has he been murdered? As the saying goes, 'Always repay to kindness'. I must save his life today to repay him for the favour he did me in the past." He wrote a memorandum and sent a yaksha with it to the city god and local god of Hongzhou asking for the scholar's soul so that he could save his life. The city god and the local god told a junior devil to give Chen Guangrui's soul to the yaksha, who took it back to the palace of crystal and reported to the dragon king.

"What is your name, scholar?" asked the dragon king. "Where are you from? What brought you here, and why were you killed?" Chen Guangrui bowed to him and replied, "My name is Chen E and my courtesy name is Guangrui. I come from Hongnong County in Haizhou Prefecture. I was given first place in the recent examinations, and was on my way with my

wife to take up my post as prefect of Jiangzhou when we
boarded a ferry at the bank of this river. The boatman Liu Hong
lusted after my wife, so he killed me and threw me overboard.
I beg you to save me, Your Majesty." "So that's how things
stand," said the dragon king. "I am the golden carp you released. You saved me then, so I must help you now that you
are in trouble." He had Guangrui's body placed beside a wall
and put a "Face Preserving Pearl" in its mouth to stop it from
decomposing so that the soul could be returned to it in future
for him to obtain his revenge. "As you are now a true soul, you
shall stay in my palace for the time being as a commander," the
dragon king added. Chen Guangrui kowtowed in thanks, and
the dragon king gave a banquet to welcome him.

Miss Yin's hatred for the villainous Liu Hong was such that
she wished she could eat his flesh and spread his flayed hide on
her bed, but as she was pregnant and the child had not yet been
born she had to force herself to go with him. In the twinkling
of an eye they reached Jiangzhou. The clerks and constables all
turned out to welcome him, and the subordinate officials in the
prefecture gave a banquet for him in the main hall of his office.
"Now that I, your student, have come here, I shall be entirely
dependent on the support of all you gentlemen," said Liu Hong.
"Your honour is a great genius," the officials replied, "and you
will naturally treat the people as your own children, thus cutting
down litigation and making punishment unnecessary. We will
all be able to rely on you — your excessive modesty is uncalled
for." When the banquet was over they all went away.

Time flew by. One day, when Liu Hong was far away on
official business, the young lady was in a summerhouse in the
official residence sighing sadly as she thought of her mother-in-
law and her husband. Suddenly she felt weak and her belly
started to ache. She fell to the ground unconscious, and before
she knew it she gave birth to a son. She heard a voice in her
ear saying, "Man-tang-qiao, you must do as I tell you. I am
the Lord of the Southern Pole Star, and I have come to give
you this son on the orders of the Bodhisattva Guanyin. One day
he will be extraordinarily famous. When the villainous Liu

comes back he will certainly want to kill this boy, so you must look after him with great care. Your husband has been rescued by the dragon king; one day you will be reunited with him and your son, and your sufferings will be at an end. Remember my words. Wake up, wake up!" When the young lady came to she remembered every word he had spoken, but as she wrapped the baby tight in swaddling clothes, she could not think what to do. When Liu Hong came back he wanted to drown the child the moment he saw him, but the young lady said, "It's already dark: we can throw him in the river tomorrow."

Fortunately Liu Hong had to go a long way away on urgent business the next day. "If I wait till that villain returns my son will be killed," thought the young lady, "so the best thing would be to abandon him in the river as soon as possible and let fate determine whether he is to live or to die. If Heaven is merciful someone will rescue the boy and bring him up, and we shall be reunited one day." Then, worrying that she might not be able to recognize him, she bit open her finger and wrote a letter in blood giving a full account of his parentage and background. Then she bit off the little toe of the child's left foot to be an identifying mark, wrapped him up in one of her own shifts, and carried him out of the official residence when nobody was looking. Luckily the residence was not far from the river bank. When she reached it she wept for a while and was just going to throw him in when she noticed a board floating beside the bank. The young lady bowed to Heaven in her gratitude and tied the child to the board with her sash, placing the blood letter next to his chest. Then she pushed him out into the stream to go where he would and returned to the yamen in tears.

The boy floated downstream on the plank until he came to a stop under the Jinshan Temple. The abbot of this temple was a monk called Faming who by cultivating the Truth and being awakened to the Way had found the secret of avoiding rebirth. As he was sitting at his meditation he heard a baby crying, and he hurried anxiously down to the riverside to look. He saw a baby lying on a board beside the bank, and got him out of the water as quickly as he could. When he read the letter written in blood that was on the baby's chest he knew why he was there. He gave the child the milk-name Jiangliu, "River Current", and arranged for him to be fostered. The letter in blood he put away in a very safe place. Time passed like an arrow, and the days and months moved as fast as a shuttle. When Jiangliu reached the age of seventeen the abbot told him to have his head tonsured and enter the religious life. Giving him the Buddhist name Xuanzang he laid his hands upon his head and instructed him to observe the monastic discipline. Xuanzang was determined to cultivate the Way.

One day in late spring the whole community gathered under the shade of some pine trees to expound the scriptures, meditate and discuss the inner mysteries. A bibulous, meat-eating monk who had been confounded in a disputation by Xuanzang lost his temper and started to abuse him: "You animal, you don't know your own surname or who your parents were. Don't try any of your clever tricks here." Stung by this abuse, Xuanzang went into the temple and knelt before his teacher with tears streaming from his eyes. "All men who are born between Heaven and Earth, and who are endowed with the Positive, the Negative, and the Five Elements — all are begotten by a father and reared by a mother," he said. "How can there be any man alive who never had father and mother?" He begged over and over again to know his parents' names. "If you really wish to find out about your father and mother, come with me into my cell," said the abbot, and they went there together. The abbot lifted down a little box from on top of a massive beam, opened it, took out a letter written in blood and a shift, and gave them to Xuanzang, who unfolded the letter and read it. At last he learnt about his parents and the wrongs they had suffered.

When he had read it he collapsed, weeping and crying out, "How can I be a man if I don't avenge my father and mother? For seventeen years I haven't known my own parents, but now I know that I have a mother. I would not be alive today, teacher, had you not rescued me and brought me up. Please allow me to go and see my mother, then I will put an incense-burner on my head and rebuild the temple to repay the great kindness you have shown me." "If you want to go and look for your mother you had better take the letter written in blood and the shift with you. Go as an alms-collector to the private residence of the prefect of Jiangzhou and you will be able to see your mother."

Xuanzang did as his teacher had said and went to Jiangzhou as a mendicant monk. It happened that Liu Hong was away on business, and as Heaven had arranged for mother and son to meet, Xuanzang went straight to the gateway of the residence to beg for alms. Miss Yin had dreamt the previous night of the moon being eclipsed and then coming back to its full roundness. "I have never heard from my mother-in-law," she thought, "and my husband was murdered by that evil man. My son was abandoned on the river, and if he was rescued and brought up, he would be seventeen now. Who knows, perhaps Heaven is going to make us meet today." As she was deep in her reflections she heard someone chanting scriptures and calling for alms in front of her home, so she thought she would go out and ask him where he had come from, and he replied, "I am a disciple of Abbot Faming of the Jinshan Temple." "A disciple of Abbot Faming of the Jinshan Temple, are you?" she said. She asked him in and gave him a vegetarian meal while observing closely the way he moved and talked. He seemed very much like her husband, so she sent the servants away and asked, "Tell me, young teacher, have you been a monk since childhood or did you become one later in life? What is your name? Do you have a mother and father?" "I did not become a monk when I was a child nor when I was older," he replied. "I must tell you that I bear a hatred as deep as the sea because of a terrible wrong. My father was murdered and my mother carried off by an evil man. The Abbot Faming, my teacher, told me to come and find my mother in the residence of the prefect of Jiangzhou." "What is your mother's name?" she asked. "My mother's name is Yin Wenqiao," he replied. "My father was called Chen Guangrui. My milk-name was Jiangliu, and my Buddhist name is Xuanzang." "I am Yin Wenqiao," she said, then added, "Have you any proof?" When he learnt that she was his mother, Xuanzang fell to his knees and wept aloud. "Mother," he said, "if you don't believe me, then look at this evidence — the blood letter and the shift." As soon as she saw that they were the real ones, she and her son embraced each other and wept. Then she said, "Go away at once my child." "I can't possibly leave you, mother, on the very day I've seen you after seventeen years of not even knowing who my parents were," he said. "My child, you must go away as fast as you can," she replied. "The evil Liu will certainly kill you if he comes back. Tomorrow I'll pretend to be ill and say that I once made a vow to donate a hundred pairs of monks' shoes. I'll come to your temple to fulfil the vow, and I'll talk to you then." Xuanzang obediently bowed to her and left.

Now that she had seen her son Miss Yin was both anxious and happy. One day she said that she was ill, and she lay in her bed refusing food and tea. When Liu Hong came back and asked what was the matter she said, "When I was young I once vowed that I would donate a hundred pairs of monks' shoes. Five days ago I dreamt that a monk came with a sharp sword in his hand to demand the shoes, and since then I haven't been feeling well." "That's easily done," said Liu Hong. "Why didn't you mention it before?" He took his place in the official hall and gave instructions to yamen assistants Wang and Li that every household living in the city of Jiangzhou was to make a pair of monk's shoes and hand them in within five days.

When the common people had handed all the shoes in, Miss Yin said to Liu Hong, "Now that the shoes have been made, what temples are there here to which I can take them to fulfil my vow?" "In Jiangzhou we have the Jinshan Temple and the Jiaoshan Temple; you can go to whichever of them you prefer," replied Liu Hong. "I've long heard that the Jinshan Temple is a good one, so I'll go there," she said. Liu Hong told the yamen assistants Wang and Li to arrange a boat. Miss Yin went aboard with a trusted servant, the boatman pushed off, and they headed for the Jinshan Temple.

On his return to the temple Xuanzang gave Abbot Faming a full account of what had happened. The abbot was delighted. The next day a maid arrived at the temple to say that her mis-

tress was coming to repay a vow, and all the monks came out
to welcome her. When Miss Yin came into the temple she
prayed to the Bodhisattva, offered a rich meal to the monks
with a donation of money to each of them, and told her maid
to put the shoes and the summer socks into the offertory tray.
She then went into the Buddha-hall and worshipped with great
devotion. When she told him to, Abbot Faming went away to
distribute the gifts to the monks. Xuanzang saw that all the
other monks had gone and that there was nobody else in the
Buddha-hall, so he went up to his mother and knelt down. She
told him to take off his shoes and socks and saw that one toe
was indeed missing from his left foot. The pair of them hugged
each other and cried again, then they bowed to the abbot to
thank him for his kindness in bringing the boy up. "I'm worried
that the villain may get to know of your reunion," said the
abbot, "so you had better go back as quickly as you can to avoid
trouble." "My son," said Miss Yin, "I shall give you a sandalwood bracelet. You must go to a place called the Ten Thousand
Flowers Inn to the northwest of Hongzhou, which is about five
hundred miles from here, where we left Madame Zhang, your
paternal grandmother. I shall also write you a letter that you
must take to the house of the minister Yin Kaishan which lies
to the left of the palace inside the capital city of the Tang
Emperor. He is my father. Give him this letter and ask him
to submit a memorial to the Tang Emperor asking him to send
horse and foot to capture and kill that bandit. Then your father
will be avenged and your mother will be rescued. I must stay
no longer as I am afraid that evil man may be suspicious if I
am late back." She left the temple and went back in her boat.

Xuanzang returned to the temple in tears and told the abbot
that he was leaving at once for Hongzhou. When he reached
the Ten Thousand Flowers Inn he said to the innkeeper Liu the
Second, "How is the mother of Prefect Chen of Jiangzhou who
is staying in your inn?" "She used to stay here," replied the
innkeeper. "She went blind, and as she didn't pay any rent for
three or four years, she now lives in a ruined tile-kiln near the
southern gate and begs in the streets every day to keep herself

alive. That official went away a very long time ago and she hasn't heard from him to this day, though I don't know why." On learning this he asked the way to the ruined tile-kiln at the southern gate and found his grandmother. "You sound like my son Chen Guangrui," said his grandmother. "I'm not Chen Guangrui, I'm his son. My mother is Miss Yin Wenqiao." "Why have your father and mother not come?" she asked; and he replied, "My father was murdered by a brigand and my mother was forced to become his wife. I have a letter here and a sandalwood bracelet from my mother." His grandmother took the letter and the bracelet, and sobbed aloud. "My son came here for the sake of fame and glory. I thought that he had forgotten all feelings of decency and gratitude; it never occurred to me that he might have been murdered. What a blessing that Heaven in its mercy did not cut short my son's line, so that I now have a grandson to come and find me." "How did you go blind, granny?" asked Xuanzang. "I was always thinking of your father and longing for him to come back every day," she said, "but as he never did I wept so much that I lost the sight of both my eyes." Xuanzang fell to his knees and prayed to Heaven. "Although I am seventeen," he said, "I have been unable to avenge my parents. Today I have come on my mother's orders and found my grandmother; if Heaven is at all moved by my sincerity, may my granny's eyes see again." When he had prayed, he licked her eyes with the tip of his tongue. The licking soon opened them, and they could see once more. His grandmother looked at the little monk with a mixture of joy and sadness and said, "You really are my grandson — you're the very image of my son Guangrui." Xuanzang took her out of the kiln and reinstalled her in Liu the Second's inn, where he rented a room for her, gave her some money to live on, and told her that he would be back within a month.

Taking his leave of his grandmother, he went straight on to the capital, where he found Minister Yin's house in the Eastern Avenue of the imperial city. "I am a relation of the minister's," he said to the gatekeeper, "and I would like to see him." When the gatekeeper reported this to the minister, he said, "I am no relation of any monk." But his wife said, "I had a dream last night that our daughter Man-tang-qiao came home; perhaps he has a letter from our son-in-law." The minister had the young monk brought into the main hall, and when the monk saw the minister and his wife he wept and bowed to the floor before them, then took an envelope out of his bosom and handed it to the minister. The minister opened the letter and read it through, then wailed aloud. "What's the matter, my lord?" asked his wife, and the minister replied, "This monk is our grandson. Our son-in-law Chen Guangrui was murdered by a brigand, who forced Man-tang-qiao to become his wife." His wife too began to weep bitterly when she heard this news. "Try not to upset yourself, wife," said the minister. "I shall ask our sovereign at court tomorrow morning to be allowed to lead an army myself. I shall certainly avenge our son-in-law."

The minister went to court the next day and wrote in a memorial to the Tang Emperor: "Your subject's son-in-law, the top graduate Chen Guangrui, was murdered by the boatman Liu Hong while going with his family to take up his office in Jiang-zhou, and my daughter was forced to become his wife. This Liu Hong has usurped office for many years by masquerading as my son-in-law. This constitutes treason. I beg Your Majesty to dispatch horse and foot at once to destroy this rebellious brigand." The Tang Emperor was so angry when he read this that he ordered Minister Yin to set off at the head of sixty thousand men of the Imperial Guard. The minister left the court with the decree and went to the parade ground to muster the soldiers before setting out for Jiangzhou. By setting out at dawn every day and not stopping till night, they travelled as fast as a shooting star or a flying bird, and before they realized it they had reached Jiangzhou, where Minister Yin's army camped on the northern bank. That night he sent a messenger with a gold-inscribed tablet to summon the deputy prefect and district judge of Jiangzhou. Minister Yin explained the situation to them and told them to call out their troops to help him. They crossed the river together, and surrounded Liu Hong's yamen before dawn. Liu Hong, who was still in his dreams, heard the sound of cannon and the beating of drums and gongs; when the soldiers rushed into his residence he was helpless and soon captured. The minister ordered that Liu Hong and his gang should be tied up and taken to the execution ground, while the army was to encamp outside the city walls.

The minister went into the main hall of the yamen and asked his daughter to come out and see him. His daughter, who had been longing to go out, felt too ashamed to face her father and so was on the point of hanging herself. When Xuanzang learnt of this he went as fast as he could to save her, fell on his knees, and said, "Your son and my grandfather have come here with an army to avenge my father. That brigand has been arrested, so there is no need at all for you to kill yourself. If you die, mother, I won't be able to stay alive." The minister too came into the residence to talk her out of it. "They say that a woman should only have one husband in her life," she said to them. "I was bitterly grieved at the death of my husband at that brigand's hands, and could not bear the disgrace of marrying his murderer; but as I was carrying my husband's child I had to swallow the shame of staying alive. Now, thank goodness, my son has grown up and my father has brought an army to avenge my husband but how could I have the face to see you. The only way I can make up for it to my husband is to kill myself." "My child," said the minister, "this was not a case of abandoning morality for the sake of material gain. You acted under duress, and did nothing to be ashamed of." Father and daughter then embraced each other and wept, while Xuanzang sobbed too "There is no need for the two of you to be so distressed," said the minister, wiping away his tears. "Today I have captured our enemy, that rebel, and now I must deal with him." He got up and went to the execution ground. As it happened, the assistant prefect of Jiangzhou had sent constables to arrest the other pirate, Li Biao, and they brought him in. The minister was very pleased, and he ordered that Liu Hong and Li Biao were to be put under a close guard. They were each given a hundred strokes of the heavy pole, and statements were taken from them about how and why they had committed the wicked murder of Chen

Guangrui. Then Li Biao was nailed on a wooden donkey and pushed to the market-place, where he was sliced into a thousand pieces, after which his head was hung up on public display. Liu Hong was taken to the Hongjiang Estuary where he had murdered Chen Guangrui. The minister, his daughter and Xuanzang went to the riverside, where they made offerings and libations to the emptiness and cut out Liu Hong's heart and liver while he was still alive to sacrifice to Chen Guangrui. They also burnt a funerary address.

The bitter lamentations of the three of them startled the underwater palace. A patrolling yaksha demon handed the funerary address to the dragon king. When he had read it, the dragon king sent Marshal Turtle to ask Chen Guangrui to come and see him. "Congratulations, sir, congratulations," said the dragon king. "Your lady, your son and your father-in-law are all sacrificing to you on the bank. I shall now return your soul to you and give you an as-you-will pearl, two rolling pearls, ten pieces of mermaid silk, and a belt of jade studded with pearls. Today you will be reunited with your wife, your son and your mother." Chen Guangrui bowed to him over and over again to express his gratitude. The dragon king then told a yaksha to take Chen Guangrui's body out to the estuary, where he was to return the soul to it; and the yaksha obediently went off.

When she had wailed for her husband and sacrificed to him, Miss Yin tried to jump into the water to drown herself, but with a desperate effort Xuanzang managed to keep hold of her. Just at this tense moment they saw a corpse floating towards the bank. Miss Yin, rushing forward to see who it was, recognized it as that of her husband and started a great wailing. Everyone else had now come up to look, and they saw Chen Guangrui open his fist and stretch his foot as his body gradually began to move. Suddenly he sat up, to their great astonishment. He opened his eyes, and the first thing he saw was his wife, his father-in-law and the young monk all weeping beside him. "What are you all doing here?" he asked. "After you were killed I gave birth to this son," replied his wife, "and by a piece of good fortune he was brought up by the abbot of the Jinshan

Temple. When he came to find me I sent him to see my father; and when my father knew what had happened he submitted a memorial at court and brought an army here to arrest your murderer, whose heart and liver we have just plucked from his living body to sacrifice to you. But how is it that your soul has been returned to you, husband?" "It is all because we bought and released that golden carp when we were staying at the Ten Thousand Flowers Inn: the carp, it turned out, was the local dragon king. When that treasonous murderer pushed me into the water I was rescued by the dragon king, who has given me back my soul and presented me with all the treasures I have on me. I never had any idea that you had borne this son, or that my father-in-law had avenged me. Our sorrows are now at an end. This is a very happy moment indeed."

When the other officials heard what had happened they all came to offer their congratulations, and the minister gave a banquet to thank all his subordinates. The army set off on its return journey that same day. When they reached the Ten Thousand Flowers Inn the minister ordered them to encamp while Guangrui and Xuanzang went to the inn to find the old lady. The night before she had dreamt of a withered tree blossoming again while magpies made a clamorous din behind the building. "Perhaps my grandson has come," she thought, and while the words were still in her mind she saw Guangrui and his son at the gate of the inn. "Isn't this my grandmother?" said the little monk; and the moment Guangrui saw his aged mother he kowtowed to her. Mother and son embraced in tears; then he told her all about what had happened. The innkeeper's account was presented and settled, and then they set off for the capital. When they reached the minister's residence, Guangrui, his wife, his mother and Xuanzang all went in to see the minister's wife, who was overcome with joy and told the servants to lay on a large banquet to celebrate. "We can call today's banquet a 'reunion banquet'," said the minister, and the whole household was indeed happy.

When the Tang Emperor entered tne throne hall early the next morning, Minister Yin stepped forward and submitted a memorial giving a detailed account of what had happened, and recommending Chen Guangrui as a man whose talents could be put to great use. The Tang Emperor approved the memorial and ordered that Chen Guangrui should be appointed a Scholar in order to take part in administration at court. As Xuanzang had decided to follow the contemplative life he was sent to cultivate his conduct in the Hongfu Temple. Later on Miss Yin finally ended her own life in a quiet and honourable way, and Xuanzang went back to the Jinshan Temple to report to Abbot Faming. If you don't know what happened afterwards, listen to the explanation in the next instalment.

CHAPTER TEN

With a stupid plan the dragon king breaks
the laws of Heaven;
Minister Wei sends a letter to an officer
of Hell.

We shall not discuss how Chen Guangrui performed his duties or Xuanzang cultivated his conduct; instead we shall talk about two wise men who lived beside the banks of the River Jing outside the city of Chang'an. One was an old fisherman called Zhang Shao and the other was a woodcutter called Li Ding. They were both advanced scholars who had never taken the official examination, lettered men of the mountains. One day, when Li Ding had sold his load of firewood and Zhang Shao had sold his basketful of carp in Chang'an city, they went into a tavern, drank till they were half tipsy, and strolled slowly home along the banks of the Jing, each holding a bottle in his hand. "Brother Li," said Zhang Shao, "it seems to me that people who struggle for fame kill themselves for it; those who compete for profit die for it; those who accept honours sleep with a tiger in their arms; and those who receive imperial favours walk around with snakes in their sleeves. Taking all in all, we are much better off living free among our clear waters and blue hills: we delight in our poverty and follow our destinies." "You are right, Brother Zhang," said Li Ding, "but your clear waters have nothing on my blue hills." "Your blue hills are not a patch on my clear waters," retorted Zhang Shao, "and here is a lyric to the tune of *The Butterfly Loves the Flowers* to prove it:

> The skiff is tiny amid the misty expanse of waves;
> Calmly I lean against the single sail,

Listening to the voice of Xishi the beauty.
My thoughts and mind are cleared; I have little wealth
*　　or fame*
As I toy with the waterweed and the rushes.
"To count a few gulls is enough to make me happy.
In the reedy bend, under the willow bank,
My wife and children smile with me.
The moment I fall asleep, wind and waves are quiet;
No glory, no disgrace, and not a single worry."

"Your clear waters are no match for my blue hills," said Li Ding, "and there is another lyric to the same tune to prove it. It goes:

The cloudy woods are covered with pine blossom.
Hush! Hear the oriole sing,
As if it played a pipe with its cunning tongue.
With touches of red and ample green the spring is warm;
Suddenly the summer's here as the seasons turn.

"When autumn comes the look of things is changed;
The scented chrysanthemum
Is enough for my pleasure.
Soon the cruel winter plucks all off.
I am free through four seasons, at nobody's beck and
*　　call."*

"You don't enjoy the good things in your blue hills that I do on my clear waters," replied the fisherman, "and I can prove it with another lyric to the tune of *The Partridge Heaven*:

In this magic land we live off the cloudy waters;
With a sweep of the oar the boat takes us home.
We cut open the live fish and fry the green turtle
Then steam the purple crab and boil the red shrimps.
Green reed shoots,
Sprouts of water-lilies,
Better still, water chestnuts and the gorgon fruit,
Delicate lotus roots and seeds, tender celery,
Arrowhead, reed-hearts and birdglory blossom."

"Your clear waters cannot compare with my blue hills when it comes to the good things they provide," said the woodcutter, "and I can cite another lyric to the tune *The Partridge Heaven* as evidence:

> *Mighty crags and towering peaks reach to the sky;*
> *A grass hut or a thatched cottage is my home.*
> *Pickled chicken and duck are better than turtles or crabs,*
> *Roebuck, boar, venison, and hare beat fish and shrimps.*
> *The leaves of the tree of heaven,*
> *Yellow chinaberry sprouts,*
> *And, even better, bamboo shoots and wild tea,*
> *Purple plums and red peaches, ripe gages, and apricots,*
> *Sweet pears, sharp jujubes, and osmanthus blossom."*

"Your blue hills are really nothing on my clear waters," replied the fisherman, "and there is another lyric to the tune *Heavenly Immortal*:

> *In my little boat I can stay where I like,*
> *Having no fear of all the misty waves.*
> *Drop the hook, cast wide the net, to catch fresh fish:*
> *Even without fat or sauce,*
> *They taste delicious*
> *As the whole family eats its meal together.*
> *"When there are fish to spare I sell them in Chang'an*
>   *market*
> *To buy good liquor and get a little drunk.*
> *Under my grass cloak I sleep on the autumn river,*
> *Snoring soundly*
> *Without a care,*
> *Not giving a damn for honour and glory."*

"Your clear waters still aren't as good as my blue mountains," came back the woodcutter, "and I too have a *Heavenly Immortal* lyric to prove it:

> *Where I build a little thatched hut under the hill*
> *The bamboo, orchid, plum, and pine are wonderful.*
> *As I cross forests and mountains to look for dry firewood*

> *Nobody asks awkward questions,*
> *And I can sell*
> *As much or as little as the world wants.*
> *I spend the money on wine and I'm happy,*
> *Content with my earthenware bowl and china jug.*
> *When I've drunk myself blotto I lie in the shade of the*
> *   pine.*
> *No worries,*
> *No profits or losses;*
> *What do I care about success or failure?"*

"Brother Li," said the fisherman, "you don't make as easy a living in the hills as I do on the water, and I can prove it with a lyric to the tune *The Moon in the West River*:

> *The smartweed's flowers are picked out by the moon*
> *While the tangled leaves of rushes sway in the wind.*
> *Clear and distant the azure sky, empty the Chu river:*
> *Stir up the water, and the stars dance.*
> *Big fish swim into the net in shoals;*
> *Little ones swallow the hooks in swarms;*
> *Boiled or fried they taste wonderful —*
> *I laugh at the roaring river and lake."*

"Brother Zhang," replied the woodcutter, "the living I make in the hills is much easier than yours on the water, and I can prove it with another *Moon on the West River* lyric:

> *Withered and leafless rattan fills the paths,*
> *Old bamboo with broken tips covers the hillside.*
> *Where vines and creepers tangle and climb*
> *I pull some off to tie my bundles.*
> *Elms and willows hollow with decay,*
> *Pines and cedars cracked by the wind —*
> *I stack them up against the winter cold,*
> *And whether they're sold for wine or money is up to*
> *   me."*

"Although you don't do too badly in your hills, your life is not as elegant as mine on the water," said the fisherman, "as

I can show with some lines to the tune *The Immortal by the River*:

> *As the tide turns my solitary boat departs;*
> *I sing in the night, resting from the oars.*
> *From under a straw cape the waning moon is peaceful.*
> *The sleeping gulls are not disturbed*
> *As the clouds part at the end of the sky.*
> *Tired, I lie on the isle of rushes with nothing to do,*
> *And when the sun is high I'm lying there still.*
> *I arrange everything to suit myself:*
> *How can the court official compare with my ease*
> *As he waits in the cold for an audiences at dawn?"*

"Your life on the water may be elegant, but it's nothing compared with mine," replied the woodcutter, "and I have some lines to the same tune to demonstrate the point:

> *On an autumn day I carry my axe along the greeny path*
> *Bringing the load back in the cool of evening,*
> *Putting wild flowers in my hair, just to be different,*
> *I push aside the clouds to find my way home,*
> *And the moon is up when I tell them to open the door.*
> *Rustic wife and innocent son greet me with smiles,*
> *And I recline on my bed of grass and wooden pillow.*
> *Steamed millet and pear are spread before me,*
> *While the new wine is warm in the pot:*
> *It is all delightful to think about."*

"All this is about our livings and the ways we provide for ourselves," said the fisherman. "I can prove to you that your leisure is nowhere near as good as mine with a poem that goes:

> *Idly I watch the white cranes as they cross the sky;*
> *As I moor the boat at the river's bank, my door is half-*
> *closed.*
> *Leaning on the sail I teach my son to twist a fishing line,*
> *When rowing's done I dry the nets out with my wife.*
> *A settled nature can really know the calm of the waves;*
> *A still body feels the lightness of the breeze.*

Always to wear a green straw cape and a blue straw hat
Is better than the purple robes of the court."

"Your leisure doesn't come up to mine," replied the woodcutter, "as this poem I shall now recite demonstrates:

With a lazy eye on the white clouds in the distance,
I sit alone in a thatched hut, the bamboo door hay open.
When there's nothing to do I teach my son to read;
Sometimes a visitor comes and we play a game of chess.
When I'm happy I take my stick and walk singing along
   the paths,
Or carry my lute up the emerald hills.
Grass shoes with hempen thongs, a cloak of coarsest
   cloth,
A mind relaxed: better than wearing silk."

"Li Ding," said the other, "how truly it can be said of us
that 'by reciting some verses we become close friends: What
need for golden winecups and sandalwood clappers?' But there
is nothing remarkable in just reciting verses; what would you
say if we made couplets in which we each contributed a line
about our lives as fisherman and woodcutter?" "Brother
Zhang," said Li Ding, "that is an excellent suggestion. Please
be the one to start." Here are their couplets:

My boat is moored in the green waters amid the misty
   waves;
My home is in the wilds, deep in the mountains.

How well I like the swollen stream under the bridge in
   spring;
My delight is a mountain peak swathed in clouds at
   dawn.
Dragon-Gate fresh carp cooked at any time;
Dry, rotten, firewood always keeping one warm.

A full array of hooks and nets to support my old age;
Carrying wood and making twine will keep me till I die.

Lying back in a tiny boat watching the flying geese;
Reclining beside the grassy path and hearing the wild swans call.

I have no stall in the marketplace of tongues;
I've left no trace in the sea of disputation.

The nets hung to dry beside the brook are like brocade;
An axe well honed on rock is sharper than a spear.

Under the shining autumn moon I often fish alone;
I meet nobody on the solitary mountain in spring.

I trade my surplus fish for wine to drink with my wife;
When I've wood to spare I buy a bottle and share it with my sons.

Singing and musing to myself I'm as wild as I care to be;
Long songs, long sighs, I can let myself be crazy.

I invite my brothers and cousins and fellow boatmen;
Leading my friends by the hand I meet the old man of the wilds.

As we play guess-fingers the cups fly fast;
When we make riddles the goblets are passed round.

Sauté or boiled crab is a delight every morning;
Plenty of fried duck and chicken cooked in ashes every day.

As my simple wife brews tea, my spirits are untrammelled;
While my mountain spouse cooks supper, my mind is at ease.

At the coming of dawn I wash my stick in the ripples;
When the sun rises I carry firewood across the road.

After the rain I put on my cloak to catch live carp;
I wield my axe before the wind to fell a withered pine.

I cover my tracks and hide from the world, acting the imbecile;
I hide my name and pretend to be deaf and dumb.

"Brother Li," said Zhang Shao, "I unfairly took the first lines just now, so now it's your turn to compose the first lines while I follow you." Thus they continued:

> The man of the mountains acting mad under wind and
>   moon;
> The haughty and unwanted dotard of the river.
>
> With his share of idleness, and able to be quite free;
> No sound from his voice as he revels in his peace.
>
> On moonlit nights he sleeps secure in a cottage of thatch;
> He lightly covers himself at dusk with clothes of reed.
>
> His passion spent, he befriends the pine and the plum;
> He is happy to be the companion of cormorant and gull.
>
> Fame and profit count for nothing in his mind;
> His ears have never heard the clash of arms.
>
> One is always pouring out fresh rice-wine,
> The other has wild vegetable soup with every meal.
>
> One makes a living with two bundles of firewood;
> The other supports himself with rod and line.
>
> When at leisure he tells his boy to sharpen the axe of
>   steel;
> In his quietness the other bids his slow-witted child to
>   mend the nets.
>
> In spring one likes to see the willows turning green;
> When the seasons change the other enjoys the rushes'
>   blue.
>
> Avoiding the summer heat, one trims the new bamboo;
> The other gathers water-chestnuts on cool July evenings.
>
> When frost begins, plump chickens are killed each day;
> In mid-autumn the crabs are at their best and always in
>   the pot.
>
> When the sun is high in winter, I am still asleep;
> I keep cool in the dog days of summer.

Throughout the year I do as I please in the hills;
In all four seasons I am happy on the lake.

By gathering firewood you can become an immortal;
There is nothing worldly about fishing.

Sweet smell the wild flowers growing outside my door;
Smooth are the green waves lapping at my boat.

A contented man never speaks of high honours;
A settled nature is stronger than a city wall.

Higher than a city wall for resisting enemy armies;
More illustrious than holding high office and listening
    to imperial decrees.

Those who are happy with mountains and rivers are few
    indeed;
Thank Heaven, thank Earth, and thank the spirits.

When the two of them had recited their verses and matched couplets they came to the place where their ways parted and bowed to each other to take their leave. "Brother Li," said Zhang Shao, "look after yourself on your way home and keep a sharp look-out for tigers up in the hills. If you met with an accident then 'an old friend would be missing on the road tomorrow'." This made Li Ding angry. "You scoundrel," he said, "I'm your friend; I'd die for you. How could you put such a curse on me? If I'm killed by a tiger, you'll be capsized by a wave." "I'll never be capsized," retorted Zhang Shao. "'In nature there are unexpected storms and in life unpredictable vicissitudes'," quoted Li Ding, "so how can you be sure you'll never have an accident?" "Brother Zhang," replied the fisherman, "despite what you just said, it's your life that's insecure, whereas my life is certain: I'm sure that I shan't have an accident." "Your life on the water is very dangerous and insecure," said the woodcutter, "so how can you be so certain?" "There's something you don't know," said Zhang Shao. "Every day I give a golden carp to a fortune-teller on the West Gate Street in Chang'an, and he passes a slip into my sleeve telling me I'll catch something every time provided I go to the right place. I went to buy a forecast from him today, and he told me that if I cast my nets to the east of bend in the Jing River and lowered my lines on the western bank, I would be bound to get a full load of fish and shrimps to take home. Tomorrow I shall go into town to sell them to buy wine, and we can continue our talk then, brother." With this they parted.

How true it is that if you talk on the road there will be someone listening in the grass. A patrolling yaksha from the Jing River Palace overheard Zhang Shao's remark about always catching fish and rushed straight back to the palace of crystal to make an urgent report of disaster to the dragon king. "What disaster?" asked the dragon king, and the yaksha replied, "Your subject was patrolling in the water by the river's edge when I heard a fisherman and a woodcutter talking. Just when they were parting they sounded very dangerous. The fisherman said that there is a soothsayer on West Gate Street in Chang'an city whose predictions are very accurate. The fisherman gives him a golden carp every day, and he hands the fisherman a slip saying that he'll catch fish at every attempt. If his calculations are so accurate, won't all we water folk be wiped out? Shall we fortify the water palace, or shall we make some leaping waves to strengthen Your Majesty's prestige?" The dragon king seized his sword in a great rage, intending to go straight to Chang'an city and destroy this fortune-teller, but then his dragon sons and grandsons, shrimp officials, crab soldiers, shad generals, mandarin-fish ministers, and carp premier submitted a joint memorial that read: "We beg Your Majesty not to act in anger. As the saying goes, 'words overheard are not to be trusted.' If Your Majesty were to go now you would have to be accompanied by clouds and helped by rain; and if this frightens the common people of Chang'an, Heaven may take offence. Your Majesty is capable of making all sorts of transformations, and of appearing and vanishing unexpectedly; so you should change into a scholar for this visit to Chang'an. If you find that it is true, you will be able to punish him at your leisure; and if it turns out to be false, you will avoid killing an innocent man." Taking their advice, the dragon king put aside his sword, and without raising clouds or rain he climbed out on the bank, shook himself, and turned into a scholar dressed in white. He was

> *Handsome and noble,*
> *Towering into the clouds.*
> *His step was stately*
> *And he observed the rules of conduct.*
> *In his speech he showed his respect for Confucius and*
>   *Mencius,*
> *His manners were those of the Duke of Zhou and King*
>   *Wen.*
> *He was dressed a gown of jade-green silk,*
> *And a hat worn casually on his head.*

Once on the road he strode straight to West Gate Street in Chang'an city, where he saw a crowd of people pushing and shouting. One of them was proclaiming grandiloquently, "He who was born under the Dragon will clash with the one who belongs to the Tiger. Although the cyclical characters are supposed to be in concordance, I'm afraid that the Year Planet may be offended by the Sun." As soon as he heard this the dragon king knew that this was the place where fortunes were told, so he pushed through the crowds to look inside. He saw:

> *Four walls covered with pearls,*
> *A room full of silken embroideries,*
> *Incense ever rising from a burner,*
> *Clear water in a porcelain pot.*
> *On either side were paintings by Wang Wei;*
> *High above the seat hung a picture of the Devil Valley*
>   *Hermit.*
> *An inkstone from Duanxi County,*
> *"Golden smoke" ink,*
> *On which leant a large brush of finest hairs;*
> *A forest of fiery pearls,*
> *The predictions of Guo Pu,*

As he diligently compared them to the Tai Zheng Xin
     Jing.
He was deeply versed in the hexagrams of the Change,
A great expert on the Eight Trigrams.
He understood the principles of Heaven and Earth,
And saw into the feelings of gods and devils.
He knew all about the cyclical numbers,
And had a clear picture of the constellations.
He saw the events of the future,
The events of the past,
As if in a mirror.
Which house would rise,
Which house would fall,
He could tell with divine perception.
He knew when good and bad was coming,
Could predict death and survival.
His words hastened wind and rain;
When he wielded his writing-brush, gods and devils
     trembled.
His name was written on a signboard:
Master of Divination Yuan Shoucheng.

Who was he? He was Yuan Shoucheng, the uncle of Yuan
Tiangang the Imperial Astrologer. He was famous throughout
the country, and the leading member of his profession in
Chang'an. The dragon king went in to see him, and when they
had greeted each other he asked the dragon king to sit down,
while a servant brought tea. "What have you come to ask about,
sir?" asked the soothsayer, and the dragon king replied, "I beg
you to uncover the secrets of the sky for me." The soothsayer
passed him a slip of paper from his sleeve and said, "Clouds
obscure the mountain peak, mist covers the tree tops. If there is
to be rain, it will certainly come tomorrow." "When will it rain
tomorrow," asked the dragon king, "and how many inches of
rain will fall?" "Tomorrow the clouds will gather at midmorn-
ing; late in the morning there will be thunder; at noon it will
start to rain; and in the early afternoon the rain will finish, after

3 feet 3.48 inches have fallen," replied the soothsayer. "I trust that you are not fooling," said the dragon king. "If it rains tomorrow at the time and to the depth you have predicted I shall pay you a fee of fifty pieces of gold. If it does not rain, or if it does not rain at the time and to the depth you say it will, then I'm telling you straight that I'll smash up your shopfront, tear down your sign and run you out of Chang'an so that you won't be able to deceive the people a moment longer." "That is entirely up to you," replied the other cheerfully. "We shall meet again tomorrow after the rain."

The dragon king took his leave and went back from Chang an to his watery palace. The greater and lesser water spirits greeted him with the question, "How did Your Majesty's visit to the soothsayer go?" "It was all right," he replied, "but he was a smooth-tongued fortune-teller. When I asked him when it would rain, he said tomorrow. When I asked what time of day it would be and how much would fall, he said that at mid-morning the clouds would gather, late in the morning it would thunder, at noon it would start to rain, and early in the afternoon it would stop raining. He also said that 3 feet 3.48 inches of rain would fall. I made a wager with him that if his prediction turned out to be true, I'd give him fifty ounces of gold; but if he got it at all wrong, I'd smash up his shopfront and drive him out, so that he wouldn't be able to deceive the public any longer. The watery tribe laughed and said, "Your Majesty is the General Superintendent of the Eight Rivers and the Great Dragon God of the Rain, so only you can know whether there will be rain. How dare he talk such nonsense? That fortune-teller is bound to lose, absolutely bound to."

Just as all the dragon sons and grandsons were laughing and talking about this with the fish ministers and crab soldiers a shout was heard from the sky: "Dragon King of the Jing River, prepare to receive an Imperial Decree." They all looked up and saw a warrior in golden clothes coming towards the watery palace with a decree from the Jade Emperor in his hands. This alarmed the dragon king, who straightened his clothes, stood up solemnly, burnt incense and received the de-

cree. The gold-clad warrior returned to the sky. Giving thanks
for the imperial grace the dragon king opened the letter and
read:

> We order the Superintendent of the Eight Rivers
> to travel with thunder and lightning and succour the
> city of Chang'an with rain. . . .

The time and the amount on the decree were exactly the
same as those foretold by the soothsayer, which so startled the
dragon king that he passed out. When he came round a moment
later he said to the watery tribe, "How can there be a man of
such powers in the mortal world? He is really someone who
knows everything about Heaven and Earth — I'm bound to be
beaten by him." "Your Majesty should not worry," submitted
General Shad in a memorial. "There will be no difficulty about
beating him. Your subject has a humble plan that I can guarantee will shut that scoundrel's mouth." When the dragon king
asked what the plan was, the general replied, "Make it rain at
the wrong time and not quite enough, so that his predictions are
wrong, and then you will surely beat him. There will be nothing to stop you smashing his sign to smithereens and running
him out of town." The dragon king accepted this advice and
stopped worrying.

The next day he ordered Viscount Wind, Grandfather Thunder, the Cloud Youth and Mother Lightning to go to the sky
above the city of Chang'an. He waited till late in the morning
before spreading the clouds, unleashed the thunder at noon,
started the rain in the early afternoon, and stopped it in the late
afternoon, when only three feet and 0.4 inches had fallen. He
had thus changed the times by two hours and reduced the
amount of rain by 3.08 inches. After the rain he dismissed his
generals and his hosts and put away his clouds; then he changed
back into a white-clad scholar and charged into Yuan Shoucheng's fortune-telling stall on West Gate Street. Without even
asking for an explanation he smashed up Yuan's sign, his brush,
his inkstone, and everything else, while the fortune-teller remained calmly in his chair without moving. The dragon king bran-

dished the door in the air, ready to hit him with it, and began to pour abuse on him: "You evil man, with all your reckless talk about blessings and disasters; you stinking deceiver of the masses. Your predictions are false, and you talk nonsense. You got the time and the amount of today's rain quite wrong, but you still sit there so high and mighty. Get out at once if you want me to spare your life." Yuan Shoucheng, who was as calm and unfrightened as ever, looked up to the sky with a mocking smile. "I'm not afraid," he said, "I'm not afraid. I've committed no capital offence, but I fear that you have. You may be able to fool other people, but you can't fool me. I know who you are. You're no scholar; you're the Dragon King of the River Jing. You flouted a decree of the Jade Emperor by changing the time of the rain and cutting down the amount, which is a crime against the laws of Heaven. I'm afraid that you're for the executioner's blade on the Dragon-slicing Scaffold. Are you going to keep up that abuse of me?"

On hearing this the dragon king trembled from fear and his hair stood on end. Dropping the door at once he straightened his clothes and made gestures of submission, kneeling to the soothsayer and saying, "Please do not be angry with me, sir; I was only joking. I never thought that it would be taken seriously. Whatever am I to do if I have broken the laws of Heaven? I beg you to save me, sir. If you don't I shall haunt you after my death." "I can't save you," replied Yuan Shoucheng, "but I can suggest one way by which you may be able to save your skin." "I beg you to tell me," implored the dragon king. "Tomorrow afternoon at half past one you will have to go to the office of the official in charge of personnel, Wei Zheng, to be beheaded. If you want to stay alive you must report at once to the present Tang Emperor, Taizong, as Wei Zheng is a minister of his; and if you can get him to speak for you, you will be all right." The dragon king took his leave of the soothsayer with tears in his eyes and went away. The sun was setting in the west, and the moon and stars were coming out.

> *As clouds settle round the purple mountains the crows*
>   *fly back to roost,*
> *The travellers on long journeys find inns for the night.*
> *The returning geese sleep on a sandbank by the ford,*
> *As the Milky Way appears.*
> *While the hours push on*
> *A lamp in the lonely village burns with barely a flame.*
> *Pure is the monastery as the reed smoke curls in the*
>   *breeze;*
> *Men disappear in the butterfly dream.*
> *As the moon sinks, flower shadows climb the rails,*
> *The stars are a jumble of light.*
> *The hours are called,*
> *The night is already half way through.*

The Dragon King of the River Jing did not return to his watery palace but stayed in the sky until the small hours of the morning, when he put away his cloud and mist, and went straight to the gate of the Imperial Palace. At this very moment the Tang Emperor dreamt that he went out of the palace gate to stroll among the flowers in the moonlight. The dragon king at once took human form, went up to him and knelt and bowed before him, crying, "Save me, Your Majesty, save me." "Who are you, that we should save you?" asked Taizong. "Your Majesty is a true dragon," replied the dragon king, "and I am a wicked dragon. As I have offended against the laws of Heaven, I am due to be beheaded by Your Majesty's illustrious minister Wei Zheng, the official in charge of personnel, so I have come to beg you to save me." "If you are supposed to be beheaded by Wei Zheng, we can save you, so set your mind at rest and go along now," said the Tang Emperor. The dragon king, who was extremely happy, kowtowed in thanks and went away.

Taizong remembered his dream when he woke up. It was now half past four in the morning, so Taizong held court before the assembled civil and military officials.

> *Mist wreathed the palace gates;*
> *Incense rose to the dragon towers.*

In the shimmering light the silken screen moves;
As the clouds shake the imperial glory spreads.
Monarch and subject as faithful as Yao and Shun.
Imposing music and ritual rivalling Zhou and Han.
Pages hold lanterns,
Palace women hold fans,
In brilliant pairs.
Pheasant screens,
Unicorn halls,
Shimmering everywhere.
As the call "Long Live the Emperor" goes up,
He is wished a thousand autumns.
When the Rod of Silence descends three times,
The uniformed officials bow to the emperor.
The brightly coloured palace flowers have a heavenly
    scent;
The delicate willows on the bank sing royal songs.
Pearl curtains,
Jade curtains,
Are hung high from golden hooks;
Dragon and phoenix fans,
Landscape fans,
Rest by the royal chariot.
Elegant are the civil officials,
Vigorous the generals.
By the Imperial Way high and low are divided;
They stand by rank beneath the palace steps.
The ministers with their purple corded seals ride three
    elephants.
May the Emperor live as long as Heaven and Earth!

When the officials had all done homage they divided into
their groups. The Tang Emperor looked at them one by one
with his dragon and phoenix eyes. Among the civil officials he
observed Fang Xuanling, Du Ruhui, Xu Shiji, Xu Jingzong,
Wang Gui and others; and among the military officers he saw
Ma Sanbao, Duan Zhixian, Yin Kaishan, Cheng Yaojin, Liu
Hongji, Hu Jingde, and Qin Shubao among others. Every one

of them was standing there solemnly and with dignity, but he could not see Minister Wei Zheng among them. He summoned Xu Shiji into the palace hall and said to him, "We had a strange dream last night in which a man came and bowed to us, claiming that he was the Dragon King of the River Jing. He had broken the laws of Heaven, and was due to be beheaded by the official in the personnel department, Wei Zheng. He begged us to save him, and we agreed. Why is it that the only official missing at court today is Wei Zheng?" "If this dream is true," replied Xu Shiji, "Wei Zheng must be summoned to the palace, and Your Majesty must not let him out of doors. Once today is over the Dragon King will be saved." The Tang Emperor was overjoyed and he sent a personal aide with a decree summoning Wei Zheng to court.

That night the minister Wei Zheng had been reading the stars in his residence and was just burning some precious incense when he heard a crane calling in the sky. It was a messenger from Heaven with a decree from the Jade Emperor ordering him to behead the Dragon King of the River Jing in a dream at half past one the following afternoon. The minister thanked Heaven for its grace, fasted and bathed himself, tried out the sword of his wisdom, and exercised his soul. This was why he did not go to court. When the imperial aide came with a summons he was frightened and nonplussed; but he did not dare to delay in obeying an order from his monarch, so he hurriedly tidied his clothes, tightened his belt, and went to the palace with the summons in his hands. He kowtowed to the Emperor and admitted his fault. "We forgive you," said the Emperor. The officials had not yet withdrawn, so the Emperor now ordered the curtains to be lowered and dismissed them. The only one of them he kept behind was Wei Zheng, whom he ordered to mount the golden chariot and come to his private quarters with him, where they discussed the policies to bring peace and stability to the country. At about noon he ordered the palace ladies to bring a large *weiqi* chess set and said, "We shall now have a game of chess." The Imperial concubines brought in a chess board and set it on the Emperor's table. Thanking the Tang

Emperor for his grace, Wei Zheng started to play with him. As each moved in turn they built up their lines of battle. It was just as the *Chess Classic* says:

The Way of chess is discipline and caution.
The best place is the middle of the board,
The worst is the side,
And the corners are neither good nor bad.
This is the eternal law of chess.
The law says:
"It is better to lose a piece
Than to lose the initiative.
When you are struck on the left, look to the right,
When attacked in the rear, keep an eye on your front.
Sometimes the leader is really behind,
Sometimes the laggard is really ahead.
If you have two "live" areas do not let them be severed;
If you can survive as you are, do not link up.
Do not spread yourself out too thinly,
Do not crowd your pieces too closely.
Rather than being niggardly with your pieces,
Lose them and win the game.
Rather than moving for no reason,
It is better to strengthen your position.
When he has many and you have few,
Concentrate on survival;
When he has many and you have few,
Extend your positions.
The one who is good at winning does not have to struggle;
The one who draws up a good position does not have to fight;
The one who fights well does not lose;
The one who loses well is not thrown into confusion.
Open your game with conventional gambits,
And end by winning with surprise attacks.
When the enemy strengthens himself for no apparent

reason,
He is planning to attack and cut you off.
When he abandons small areas and does not rescue them
His ambitions are great.
The man who places his pieces at random
Has no plans;
The man who responds without thinking
Is heading for defeat.
The Book of Songs *says:*
'Be cautious and careful
As if you were walking on the edge of a precipice.'
This is what it means.

There is a poem that goes:

The board is the Earth, the chessmen Heaven,
The colours, Positive and Negative,
When you reach that subtle state when all the changes
become clear,
You can laugh and brag about the chess-playing Immortals.

As sovereign and minister played their game of chess it was half past one. Although the game was not over, Wei Zheng slumped down beside the table and started to snore, fast asleep. "Worthy minister," said Taizong with a smile, "you have exhausted your mind in strengthening the country and tired yourself out building the empire; that is why you have fallen asleep without realizing it. The emperor said no more and let him sleep. Not long afterwards Wei Zheng woke up, prostrated himself on the floor, and said, "Your subject deserves ten thousand deaths. I fell asleep without knowing what I was doing, and I beg Your Majesty to forgive your subject's criminal discourtesy to his sovereign." "What criminal discourtesy have you committed?" the emperor asked. "Rise, and take the pieces off the board so that we may start again." Wei Zheng thanked him for his grace, and was just taking the pieces in his hand when he heard shouting outside the palace gates. Qin Shubao, Xu Maogong and some others brought in a dragon's head dripping with blood, threw it to the floor in front of the emperor, and reported, "Your Majesty,

> *Seas have gone shallow and rivers have run dry,*
> *But such a sight as this was never seen by human eye."*

The emperor and Wei Zheng rose to their feet and asked where it had come from. "This dragon's head fell from a cloud at the crossroads at the end of the Thousand Yard Portico, and your humble subjects dared not fail to report it," said Qin Shubao and Xu Maogong. "What does this mean?" the Tang Emperor asked Wei Zheng in astonishment. "Your subject beheaded it in a dream just now," replied Wei Zheng, kowtowing. "But I never saw you move your hand or body when you were dozing," said the shocked Emperor, "and you had no sword, so how could you have beheaded it?" "My lord," replied Wei Zheng, "your subject

> *Was bodily in your presence,*
> *But far away in my dream.*
> *I was bodily in your presence reaching the end of a game,*
> *When I shut my eyes and felt drowsy;*
> *I went far away in my dream, riding a magic cloud,*
> *Bursting with energy.*
> *That dragon*
> *Was on the Dragon-slicing Scaffold,*
> *Where he had been tied by the officers and soldiers of Heaven.*
> *Then your minister said,*
> *'You have broken the laws of Heaven,*
> *And deserve the death penalty.*
> *I bear a heavenly mandate*
> *To behead you.'*
> *When the dragon heard he was bitterly grieved;*
> *Your subject marshalled his spirits.*
> *When the dragon heard he was bitterly grieved,*
> *Pulled in his claws, laid down his scales and gladly prepared to die.*
> *Your subject marshalled his spirits,*

*Hitched up his clothes, stepped forward and raised the
    blade.
The sword came down with a snick,
And the dragon's head fell into the void."*

Emperor Taizong's feelings on hearing this were mixed.
On the one hand he was happy, because he was proud of having
so good a minister as Wei Zheng; for with a hero like that in
his court he needed to have no worries about the safety of the
empire. On the other hand he was distressed, because although
he had promised in his dream to save the dragon, it had been
executed. He had no choice but to pull himself together and
order Qin Shubao to hang the dragon's head up in the market
place as a warning to the common people of Chang'an. He also
rewarded Wei Zheng, and then all the officials dispersed.

When he returned to the palace that evening, the Emperor
was depressed as he remembered how the dragon had wept so
bitterly in his dream, begging to be saved. Yet the dragon
had been unable to avoid its doom. After brooding over this
for a long time he felt more and more exhausted and uneasy. In
the second watch of the night he heard sobbing outside the
palace gates, which made him more frightened than ever. As
he lay in a fitful sleep, the dragon king of the River Jing reap-
peared, this time holding a head dripping with blood in his
hands. "Emperor Taizong of the Tang," he shouted, "give me
back my life, give me back my life. Last night you were full of
promises to save me, so why did you double-cross me yesterday
and order Wei Zheng, the official in charge of personnel, to behead me? Come out, come out, and we shall go to the King of
Hell's palace to have this out." He pulled at the emperor's
clothes and would not stop shouting. Taizong could find nothing to say, and struggled so hard to get away that he was pouring with sweat. Just at this most awkward moment he saw fragrant clouds and coloured mists to the south. A female immortal
came forward and waved a willow twig, at which the headless
dragon went off to the northwest, weeping pitifully. This Immortal was the Bodhisattva Guanyin, who had come to the

East in obedience to the Buddha's decree to find the man to fetch the scriptures. She was now staying in the temple of the tutelary god of Chang'an, and when she heard the devilish howling she came to chase away the wicked dragon. The dragon then went down to Hell to submit a full report.

When Taizong woke up he shouted, "A ghost, a ghost!" The empresses of the three palaces, the imperial consorts and concubines of the six compounds, the attendants and the eunuchs were all so terrified by this that they lay awake trembling for the rest of the night. Before long it was half past four, and all the military and civil officials were waiting for the morning court outside the palace gates. When dawn came and the emperor had still not come to court they were so frightened that they did not know what to do. It was not till the sun was high in the sky that a decree was brought out that read, "As our mind is not at ease all the officials are excused court." Six or seven days quickly passed, and all the officials were so anxious that they wished they could rush to the palace gates to see the emperor and ask after his health, but all that happened was that the empress issued a decree summoning the royal doctors to the palace to administer medicine. Crowds of officials gathered at the palace gates waiting for news, and when the doctors came out a little later they asked what the matter was. "His Majesty's pulse is not as it should be: it is both faint and fast. He murmurs deliriously about having seen a ghost. His pulse stops every ten beats. His five viscera lack all spirit, and I am afraid that the worst must be expected within seven days." The officials went pale from shock.

Amid all the panic it was learnt that Taizong had sent for Xu Maogong, the Duke Protector Qin Shubao, and Lord Yuchi Jingde. When the three lords received the decree they hurried to the lower storey of the side palace. When they had bowed to him, a serious-faced Taizong spoke forcefully to them. "Illustrious ministers," he said, "we started to command troops at the age of nineteen, and had many hard years of fighting from then on, conquering the north and the south, defending in the east, and wiping out our enemies in the west; but never once did we see anything sinister or evil. Yet now we are seeing ghosts." "Your Majesty has founded an empire and slaughtered men beyond number, so why should you be scared of ghosts?" asked Lord Yuchi. "You don't believe us," the emperor replied, "but outside our bedroom door at night bricks and tiles fly about and the ghosts and demons howl. It is really terrible. Daytime is passable, but the nights are unbearable.' "Don't worry, Your Majesty," said Qin Shubao. "Tonight I and Yuchi Jingde shall guard the palace doors to see whether there are any ghosts or not." Taizong agreed to his suggestion, and after thanking him for his kindness Xu Maogong and the other two generals withdrew. That evening the two of them put on their equipment and took up their positions outside the palace gates in full armour and helmet, with golden maces and battle-axes in their hands. Look how these splendid generals were dressed:

> On their heads were golden helmets bright,
> On their bodies was armour like dragon scales.
> Magic clouds glisten in front of their Heart-protecting Mirrors;
> Their lion coats are tightly buckled.
> Fresh are the colours of their embroidered belts.
> One looks up to the sky with his phoenix eyes, and the stars tremble;
> The other's eyes flash lightning and dim the moonlight.
> These true heroes and distinguished ministers
> Will be called gate-protectors for a thousand years
> And serve as door-gods for ten thousand ages.

The two generals stood beside the doors till deep into the night, and not a single demon did they see. That night Taizong slept peacefully in the palace and nothing happened. When morning came he called the two generals in and gave them rich rewards. "We had not been able to sleep for several days since we fell ill," he said, "but last night was very peaceful, thanks to the awesome might of you two generals. Please go and rest now so that you can guard us again tonight." The two generals thanked him and left. For the next two or three nights

they stood guard and all was quiet; but the Emperor ate less
and less as his illness took a turn for the worse. Not wishing
to put the two generals to any more trouble, he summoned them
to the palace with Du Ruhui and Fang Xuanling. These were
the instructions he gave them: "Although we have enjoyed peace
for the last two days, we are unhappy about the night-long or-
deals we have imposed on Generals Qin and Yuchi. We therefore wish to commission two skilled painters to make faithful
portraits of the two generals to paste on the doors so that they
may be saved trouble. What do you think?" In obedience to
the imperial decree the officials chose two men who could draw
a good likeness, and the two generals wore their armour as
before while they were painted. Then the pictures were stuck
on the doors, and there was no trouble that night.

The next two or three days were peaceful too but then the
Emperor heard bricks and tiles banging and crashing once again
at the Hou Zai Gate. He summoned his officials at dawn and
said, "There has, thank goodness, been no trouble at the front
gates for several days now, but there were noises at the back
gates last night that practically scared me to death." Xu Maogong went forward and submitted this suggestion: "When there
was trouble at the front gates Yuchi Jingde and Qin Shubao protected Your Majesty. Now there is trouble at the back gates
Wei Zheng should be ordered to stand guard." Taizong approved his suggestion, and ordered Wei Zheng to stand guard
at the back gates that night. Wei Zheng received the edict, and
that night he put on his best clothes, belted himself tightly,
and took up his vigil outside the Hou Zai Gate. He was a
true hero. He wore

> A black band of silk around his forehead,
> A brocade gown loosely belted with jade.
> His hood and billowing sleeves caught the frost and
>   dew,
> And he looked more ferocious than the ghost-quellers
>   Shenshu and Yulei.

> *On his feet he wore black boots for motionless move-*
> *ment;*
> *In his hand he wielded a keen-edged blade with great*
> *ferocity.*
> *He looked around with glaring eyes:*
> *What evil spirit would have dared approach?*

No devils were seen all night, but although nothing happen-ed at the front or back gates the emperor's condition still deterio-rated. One day the empress dowager issued an edict summon-ing the officials to discuss funeral arrangements. Taizong sent for Xu Maogong and gave him orders about affairs of state, in-structing him to look after the heir to the throne in the way that Liu Bei, the ruler of Shu, had instructed Zhuge Liang. When he had finished speaking he was bathed and put into clean clothes. All he had to do now was to wait for the end. Then in rushed Wei Zheng, who grabbed hold of his dragon robes and said, "Do not worry, Your Majesty. I can ensure Your Majesty long life." "The disease has reached my heart," re-plied the emperor, "and my life will end at any moment now, so how can you save it?" "Your subject has a letter here," said Wei Zheng, "that I am offering to Your Majesty to take with you to the underworld and give to Cui Jue, the judge of Feng-du." "Who is this Cui Jue?" asked the emperor. "He was one of the officers of Your Majesty's exalted predecessor. From being magistrate of Cizhou he was promoted to be vice-president of the Ministry of Rites. When he was alive he and I were close friends. Now that he is dead he is in charge of the Registers of Birth and Death in the underworld as judge of Fengdu, and he often comes to see me in my dreams. If you take this letter with you on your journey and give it to him, he is bound to allow Your Majesty to come back out of consideration for your humble subject. I can guarantee that Your Majesty's soul will return to the sunlight, and the dragon countenance will certainly return to the imperial capital." Taizong took the letter and put it in his sleeve, then he shut his eyes in death. The em-presses, consorts and imperial concubines of the three palaces and the six compounds, the palace servants, the heir to the throne, and the civil and military officials all grieved and dressed in mourning. The imperial coffin lay in state in the White Tiger Hall.

If you don't know how Taizong came back to life, listen to the explanation in the next chapter.

CHAPTER ELEVEN

After touring the underworld, Taizong
returns to life;
By presenting a pumpkin Liu Quan
continues his marriage.

A hundred years flow by like water;
A lifetime's career is no more than a bubble,
The face that yesterday was the colour of peach-blossom
Today is edged with snow.

When the white ants' line of battle collapses, all is illu-
sion;
"Repent, repent," is the cuckoo's urgent call.
He who does good in secret can always prolong his life;
Heaven looks after the one who asks no pity.

Taizong was in a daze as his soul went straight to the Tower
of Five Phoenixes, in front of which he saw the horsemen of
the Imperial Guard who invited him out hunting with them.
Taizong was glad to go and they went off into the distance; but
after they had been going for some time he found himself walking alone in a wasteland: the horsemen had all disappeared.
Just as he was discovering to his alarm that he could not find
his way a man appeared not far away, shouting, "Great Tang
Emperor, come here, come here." On hearing this Taizong
looked up and saw him:

A black silk turban,
A rhinoceros-horn belt.
The black silk turban has tabs blowing in the breeze;
The rhinoceros-horn belt has golden mountings.
In his hands an ivory tablet, glowing auspiciously;

His thin silk gown conceals his divine light.
He wears a pair of boots with whitened soles
As he climbs the clouds and grasps the mist,
Holding to his chest the Registers of Life and Death,
Nothing down the quick and the dead.
His tangled hair blows about his ears;
His whiskers dance and fly beside his cheeks.
Once he used to be a Tang minister,
But now he judges cases for the King of Hell.

When Taizong went up to him, he fell on his knees beside the path and said, "Your Majesty, please forgive your subject for his crime of failing to come far enough to meet you." Who are you?" asked the Emperor, "and why have you come to meet me?" "A fortnight ago your humble servant heard the Dragon King of the River Jing bringing a case against Your Majesty in the Senluo Palace because he was executed despite your promise to save him," replied the other. "The King of Qinguang of the First Palace sent devil messengers with an urgent summons to Your Majesty to be present when the case is heard between the three parties of plaintiff, defendant and witness. When I heard this I came here to meet Your Majesty. I arrived late, so I beg for forgiveness." "What is your name and position?" asked Taizon. "When your humble servant was alive I used to serve His Late Majesty. I was magistrate of Cizhou, and later made vice-president of the Ministry of Rites. My name is Cui Jue. I have now been given office in the underworld as the judge in charge of cases at Fengdu." Taizong, greatly delighted to learn this, went up to him and supported him with his imperial hands as he said, "Sir, you have made a long and exhausting journey. Wei Zheng, our minister, gave us a letter for you; how lucky that we have met." The judge thanked him and asked where the letter was. Taizong produced it from his sleeve and handed it over to Cui Jue, who received it with a bow. When he opened it he saw that it read as follows:

> Your Excellency, Metropolitan Judge, and Venerable
> Elder Brother Cui,

Remembering our former friendship; I still see and hear you as if you were alive; but many years have now flown by since I last received your lofty instruction. On feast days I set out some vegetarian dishes as a sacrifice to you, but I have been unable to divine whether they are enjoyed by you. As I have the good fortune not to have been abandoned by you and you have appeared to me in dreams, I now know that my great elder brother has risen high. But, alas, there is a great gap between the worlds of darkness and of light, and we are unable to meet each other as we are each at different ends of the universe.

As the Cultured Emperor Taizong has recently passed away of a sudden illness it seems likely that his case will be discussed in the presence of the three parties, so that he is bound to meet you, elder brother. I beseech you to remember the friendship of the days when you were alive and give His Majesty such assistance as will enable him to return to the sunlight. This would be a great favour, and I shall write again to thank you. I cannot go into all the details of the case here.

Your younger brother, who is so unworthy of your affection, kowtows to you.

Wei Zheng.

The judge was very pleased when he had read the letter "I know about how the official Wei of the personnel department beheaded the dragon in a dream the other day," he said, "and this news filled me with great admiration. He has always looked after my sons and grandsons, and now that I have a letter from him, Your Majesty need have no worries. Your humble servant can undertake to escort Your Majesty back to the light, where you will once more ascend the throne." Taizong thanked him.

As they were talking a pair of servant boys in black appeared, carrying banners and a precious canopy. "An invitation from King Yama," they shouted. Taizong and Judge Cui went along with them. A city wall appeared in front of them, and above its gates hung a large tablet on which was written DEVIL GATE OF THE WORLD OF DARKNESS in huge letters of gold.   The two lictors waved their banners and led Taizong into the city and along its streets.   Beside the road he saw his father and predecessor Li Yuan, as well as his dead brothers Jiancheng and Yuanji, who went up to him and said, "Shimin's here, Shimin's here," using his personal name.   They grabbed and hit him, demanding their lives back; and as Taizong could not avoid them they held him fast until Judge Cui ordered a blue-faced devil with terrible fangs to drive them away. Only then was Taizong able to escape from their clutches.   After another mile or so he saw a green-tiled tower rising majestically before him.

> A myriad coloured veils of haze drifting about it,
> A thousand wisps of red mist dimly appearing.
> The flying eaves had monsters at their ends;
> The matching tiles of the five roofs were gleaming bright.
> Rows of golden studs were driven into the doors;
> A length of whitest jade was placed across each threshold.
> When the windows faced the light they glowed lilke the dawn;
> Red lightning flashed from the lattice and the blinds.
> The tower soared into the azure sky,
> While porticos led to sumptuous courtyards.
> Incense from braziers shaped like animals perfumed the royal robes;
> The light from lanterns of purple gauze was thrown on palace fans.
> To the left a row of ferocious bull-headed demons;
> To the right were terrible horse-faced devils.
> Those who escorted the spirits of the dead had golden tablets;
> Those who summoned souls wore white sackcloth.
> This place was called the assembly of the underworld,
> The Palace of Yama, King of Hell.

As Taizong gazed at it from the outside, jade ornaments could be heard tinkling as they swung from the belts of officials, and rare perfumes could be smelt. In front were two pairs of attendants holding lanterns, and behind them the ten generations of kings of the underworld came down the steps. The ten kings were the King of Qinguang, the King of Chujiang, King Songdi, King Wuguan, King Yama, King Impartial, King of Mount Tai, the Metropolitan King, the King of Biancheng, and the King of the Ever-turning Wheel. They came out of the Senluo Palace and bowed to Taizong in greeting. Taizong felt too humble to go forward. "Your Majesty is a monarch in the world of light, but we are only kings in the world of darkness. It is therefore only right that we should do this, so why this excessive modesty?" "We have offended against Your Majesties," replied Taizong, "so how can we venture to talk in terms of light and darkness, or men and ghosts?" After much yielding Taizong went into the Senluo Palace, and when they had finished bowing to each other they sat down as hosts and guest.

A moment later the King of Qinguang clasped his hands together and said, "Why is it that the ghost dragon of the River Jing has brought a case against Your Majesty, saying that he was executed despite your promise to save him?" "I had a dream that an old dragon came to ask me to save him," replied Taizong, "and I did in fact promise that he would come to no harm; but as it turned out his crime was a capital one, for which he was due to be beheaded by the minister in the personnel department, Wei Zheng. We summoned Wei Zheng to come and play chess in the palace, and I never knew that he had beheaded the dragon in a dream. This happened because that officer can come and go miraculously, and also because the dragon king had committed a crime for which he deserved to die. We were in no way to blame for his death." When the Ten Kings heard his statement they bowed and replied, "Even before that dragon was born it was written in the registers of the Southern Pole Star that he was destined to die at the hands of a personnel minister, as we have long been aware. But because he argued about the matter and insisted on Your Majesty coming here to settle the case between the three parties we have already sent him on his way to reincarnation. We hope that Your Majesty will forgive us for forcing you to attend." Then they ordered the judge in charge of the Registers of Birth and Death to fetch them at once to see how long His Majesty was due to live. Judge Cui hurried to his office and took down the general register of the lengths of the reigns Heaven had allowed to the kings of all the countries of the earth. As he was looking through it he saw to his horror that Emperor Taizong of the Great Tang in the Southern Jambu Continent was due to die in year 13 of his reign. He hurriedly seized a large brush soaked in ink, changed 13 into 33, then he handed the register up. The Ten Kings started at the beginning and read it through until they saw that Taizong was due to reign for thirty-three years. "How long has Your Majesty been on the throne?" asked the shocked kings of hell. "It is now thirteen years since my accession," Taizong replied. "Then there is no need for Your Majesty to worry," said King Yama. "You have twenty years of life ahead of you. Now that you have answered these charges satisfactorily, will you please return to the World of Light." On hearing this Taizong bowed and thanked the Ten Kings, who then ordered Judge Cui and Marshal Zhu to return Taizong his soul. As he was leaving the Senluo Palace Taizong raised his hand in salutation and asked the Ten Kings about the prospects for all the members of his family in his palace. "Good," they replied, "except that Your Majesty's younger sister does not seem to be going to live much longer." Taizong bowed once more to express his thanks. "When we return to the daylight we shall have nothing with which to show our gratitude except for fruit and melons." "We have gourds, eastern melons and western melons, or water-melons, here, but no pumpkins, no southern melons," said the Ten Kings. "When we return to the world of the living we shall send some," replied Taizong, and with that they raised their clasped hands to each other, bowed, and parted.

The marshal, with a soul-guiding flag in his hand, led the way, and Judge Cui followed with Taizong as they left the office of darkness. Taizong looked up and saw that they were not going the same way as they had come. "Have we taken the wrong road?" he asked the judge, who replied, "No. In the underworld you can only go; you can never come back. We are now taking Your Majesty out through the Revolving Prayer-wheel; thus you will be able to tour the underworld on your way back to life." Taizong had no choice but to follow them as they led the way.

After a mile or two he saw a high mountain wrapped in dark clouds down to its foot, while a black mist blotted out the sky. "What's that mountain over there, Mr. Cui?" he asked; and the judge replied, "That is the Dark Mountain of the Underworld." "However shall we cross it?" Taizong asked in terror. "Have no fears, Your Majesty; your subjects will lead the way," answered the judge. Taizong followed them shivering and trembling, and when they had climbed the mountain he looked around him. He saw that it was

> *Jagged,*
> *Precipitous,*
> *High as the Sichuan ranges,*
> *Lofty as Lushan.*
> *It is not a famous peak of the world of light,*
> *But a crag of the underworld.*
> *Ogres hide in the clumps of thorn,*
> *Evil monsters lurk behind the cliffs.*
> *Your ears hear no calls of animals or birds,*
> *The eyes can only see fiends.*
> *A dark wind howls,*
> *As black fog spreads.*
> *The dark wind that howls*
> *Is the smoke breathed from the mouths of magic soldiers;*
> *The spreading black fog*
> *Is the vapour belched out by hidden trolls.*
> *Wherever you look the prospect is appalling;*
> *All you can see to left or right is unbridled evil.*
> *To be sure, there are hills,*
> *Peaks,*

Ranges,
Caves,
And gullies.
But no grass grows on the hills,
There is no sky for the peaks to touch.
No travellers cross the ranges,
The caves hold no clouds,
No water runs in the gullies.
Before the cliffs there are only goblins;
Below the ranges are trolls.
Savage ghosts shelter in the caves;
Evil spirits hide in the gullies.
All around the mountain
Ox-headed and horse-faced demons howl and roar;
Half hidden from view,
Hungry ghosts and desperate spirits sob to each other.
The judge who claims men's lives
Cannot wait to deliver the letter;
The marshal who chases souls,
Shouts and roars as he hastens along with his documents.
The swift-footed ones
Swirl like a tornado;
The catchers of souls
Stand as thick as clouds.

Thanks entirely to the protection of the judge, Taizong crossed the Dark Mountain.

As they continued on their way they went past very many courts, and from each of them piteous sounds assailed his ear, while the evil ghouls there struck terror into his heart. "What place is this?" asked Taizong. "It is the eighteen layers of hell that lie behind the Dark Mountain," the judge replied. "What are the eighteen layers?" asked Taizong. "Listen and I will tell you," the judge replied.

"The Hanging-by-the-Sinews Hell, the Hell of Injustice,
and the Hell of the Pit of Fire.
Loneliness and desolation,

Misery and suffering.
All those here committed a thousand sins,
And were sent here for punishment after death.

The Fengdu Hell, the Tongue-extraction Hell, the Flay-
    ing Hell:
Howling and wailing,
Terrible anguish.
They offended against Heaven by not being loyal or
    filial;
They have Buddha-mouths but snake hearts, so fell down
    here.

The Grinding Hell, the Pounding Hell, the Hell of
    Drawing and Quartering.
Skin and flesh ripped and torn,
Lips rubbed away till the teeth show.
In the blindness of their hearts they did evil things;
For all their fine words they harmed others in secret.

The Ice Hell, the Skin-shedding Hell, the Disembowel-
    ling Hell.
Filthy faces and matted hair,
Frowning foreheads and sad eyes.
They all used false measures to cheat the foolish,
Thus piling up disasters for themselves.

The Oil-cauldron Hell, the Hell of Blackness, the Hell
    of the Mountain of Knives.
Shivering and trembling,
In terrible agony;
Because they used violence against the good
They cower and hunch their shoulders in their suffering.

The Hell of the Pool of Blood, the Avichi Hell, the Hell
    of the Steelyard Beam,
Where skin is pulled away from the bone,
Arms are broken and tendons cut.
Because they killed for gain,
Butchering living creatures,

> They fell into these torments that will not end in a
>   thousand years;
> They will always lie here, never to escape.
>
> Every one of them is tightly bound,
> Knotted and roped.
> Red-faced demons,
> And black-faced demons,
> Are sent with their long halberds and short swords.
> Ox-headed fiends,
> And horse-faced fiends,
> With iron clubs and brazen hammers,
> Beat them till their wincing faces flow with blood.
> As they call on Heaven and Earth and get no answer
> Let no man betray his conscience:
> The devils carry out their orders and release nobody.
> Good and evil will always be rewarded:
> It is only a question of time.

Before they had gone much further a group of devil soldiers holding banners knelt down beside the road and said, "The Commissioners of the Bridges welcome you." The judge shouted to them that they were to rise and led Taizong across a golden bridge. Taizong saw that there was a silver bridge beside it over which some loyal, filial, worthy, just, and upright people were passing, led by banners. There was a third bridge on the other side with an icy wind roaring across it and waves of blood boiling below amid unbroken howls and wails. "What is that bridge called?" Taizong asked, and the judge replied, "Your Majesty, that is called the Bridge of Punishment, and you must tell people about it when you return to the world of the living. Below the bridge there are

> A narrow, precipitous path
> Over a mighty, rushing river.
> It is like a strip of cloth across the Yangtse,
> Or a fiery pit rising up to Heaven.
> The icy vapours freeze one to the bone;
> Nauseating stenches assail the nostrils.

> There is no boat to ferry you
> Across the crashing waves.
> All who appear are sinful ghosts
> With bare feet and matted hair.
> The bridge is many miles long
> And only three spans wide;
> The drop is a hundred feet,
> The water are infinitely deep.
> Above there are no railings for support,
> While trolls snatch their victims from below.
> In cangues and bonds
> They are driven along the dangerous path by the River
>   of Punishment.
> See the ferocity of the divine generals by the bridge;
> Watch how the ghosts of the wicked suffer in the river.
> On the branching trees
> Hang silken clothes in blue, red, yellow and purple;
> In front of the precipice
> Squat lewd and shameless women who swore at their
>   parents-in-law.
> Copper snakes and iron dogs feast on them at will,
> As they constantly fall in the river, never to escape.

There is a poem that goes:

> As ghosts wail and spirits howl
> The waves of blood tower high.
> Countless ghouls with heads of bulls and horses
> Guard the bridge with great ferocity.

The commissioners of the bridges had gone away while he
was speaking. Taizong's heart was once more filled with horror,
and he nodded his head and sighed silently in his distress, then
followed the judge and the marshal. Before long they crossed
the evil River of Punishment and passed the terrors of the Bowl
of Blood. Then they came to the City of the Unjustly Slain.
Amid the hubbub, shouts of "Li Shimin's here, Li Shimin's
here," could be made out, to the terror of Taizong. He saw that
his way was blocked by a crowd of maimed and headless

spectres. "Give us back our lives," they were all shouting, "give us back our lives." The panic-stricken Taizong tried to hide, yelling, "Help, Judge Cui, help, help." "Your Majesty," the judge replied, "these are the ghosts of the kings and chieftains of the sixty-four groups of rebels and the seventy-two troops of bandits. They were all killed unjustly, and nobody has given them a home or looked after them. They cannot get themselves reborn as they have no money for the journey, so they are all uncared-for cold and hungry ghosts. If Your Majesty is able to give them some money I can save you." "I came here empty-handed," Taizong replied, "so where could I possibly get any money?" "Your Majesty," the judge replied, "there is a man in the world of light who deposited a certain amount of money in the underworld. If Your Majesty is prepared to sign an I.O.U., I will endorse it, and we can borrow his store of money to distribute among these hungry ghosts; then we will be able to continue on our way." "Who is this man?" asked Taizong. "He is a man of Kaifeng in Henan," the judge replied, "and his name is Xiang Liang. He has thirteen hoards of gold and silver down here, and if Your Majesty borrows them, all you have to do is repay them when you return to the world of light." Taizong was very pleased, and only too eager to borrow one. He signed an I.O.U. at once and gave it to the judge, then borrowed a store, which he gave to the marshal to hand out. "You are to share out this gold and silver and let your Lord of the Great Tang past," said the judge. "As it is too early in his life, I am under orders from the ten kings to return his soul and tell him to hold a Great Mass when he is back in the world of light to enable all of you to be reborn, so don't be making any more trouble." When the ghosts heard what he had to say and were given the gold and silver they all withdrew, murmuring their obedient assent. The judge then told the marshal to wave his soul-leading flag, and Taizong was taken out of the City of the Unjustly Slain and floated along the highway to the daylight.

After they had been going for a long time they reached the Wheel of the Six Paths of Being. Some people were soaring in the clouds, wearing cloaks of rosy mist. Others were being given office with golden insignia to hang from their waists. Monks and nuns, clergy and lay people, beasts of the field and birds of the air, ghosts and devils — all were pouring under the wheel and each was going along his allotted path. "What's all this about?" asked the Tang Emperor. "Your Majesty is a man of deep understanding," the judge replied. "You must be sure to remember all this and tell the living about it. It is called the Wheel of the Six Paths of Being. Those who have done good deeds rise on the Path of the Immortals; those who have been loyal are reborn on the Path of Honour; those who have done their duty to their parents lead their next life on the Path of Happiness; those who have been just return to life on the Path of Man; those who have accumulated merit are reborn on the Path of Wealth; and the evildoers fall down into the Path of Devils." On hearing this the Tang Emperor nodded and said with a sigh:

> "Excellent, truly excellent,
> The virtuous come to no harm.
> The good heart is always mindful,
> The way of goodness always lies open.
>
> "Do not allow evil thoughts to arise;
> Thus you will avoid all trouble.
> Say not that there is no retribution;
> The gods and ghosts will determine it well."

The judge took Taizong straight to the Gate of Rebirth on the Path of Honour, bowed to him and said, "Your Majesty, this is the way out, where I shall have to take my leave and go back. Marshal Zhu will escort you for the next stage of your journey." "I have made you come an awfully long way, sir," said the Tang Emperor as he thanked him. "When Your Majesty returns to the world of the living you absolutely must hold a Great Mass to enable those forlorn ghosts to be reborn," replied the judge. "Don't on any account forget, as there can only be peace on earth if there are no vengeance-seeking ghosts in the underworld. Every single wrong will have to be corrected.

Teach all people to be good, and then you will be able to assure the continuity of your line and the eternal security of your empire." The Tang Emperor agreed to each of his proposals and took leave of him, then went through the gates with Marshal Zhu. Seeing a fine horse standing ready and saddled inside the gates, the marshal asked Taizong to mount it with the help of his assistants. The horse was as swift as an arrow, and it was soon at the banks of the River Wei, where a pair of golden carp could be seen sporting in the water. Taizong, captivated at the sight, pulled in his horse's reins and gazed at them. "Your Majesty," the marshal said, "please keep moving. We have to enter the city early." But all the Tang Emperor wanted to do was to look. As he would not move on the marshal grabbed him by the feet and shouted, "Get moving. What are you waiting for?" as he pushed him off his horse and into the River Wei with a splash. Taizong was now free of the underworld and back in the world of the living.

The civil and military officials of the Tang court, Xu Maogong, Qin Shubao, Yuchi Jingde, Duan Zhixian, Ma Sanbao, Cheng Yaojin, Gao Shilian, Li Shiji, Fang Xuanling, Du Ruhui, Xiao Yu, Fu Yi, Zhang Daoyuan, Zhang Shiheng, Wang Gui and the others, as well as the empresses, imperial consorts and concubines, and pages were all in the White Tiger Hall. They were discussing whether to issue an edict of mourning to inform the world so that the heir could be put on the throne. Wei Zheng was saying, "Gentlemen, stop this discussion. We must not do that. If the country is alarmed, anything might happen. If we wait for another day our master is bound to come back to life." Xu Jingzong stepped forward from the lower ranks and protested, "Minister Wei is talking nonsense. As the old saying goes, 'spilt water can't be picked up and the dead can't come back to life.' What business have you to be spreading confusion with these groundless claims?" "Mr. Xu," Wei Zheng replied, "I can say truthfully that I have been given instruction in the magic arts since childhood and my predictions are extremely accurate. I can assure you that I have saved His Majesty from death."

As they were arguing they heard loud shouts of "You're drowning me, you're drowning me," coming from the coffin. The civil officials and the generals were struck with terror; the empresses and consorts shivered. Every one of them had

> *A face as yellow as a mulberry-leaf after autumn,*
> *A waist as weak as a willow sapling before spring.*
> *The heir went weak at the knees,*
> *As he stood in full mourning, unable to hold up his staff;*
> *The attendants' souls flew away:*
> *How would it do for them to be wearing mourning hats*
>   *and clothes?*
> *The consorts and concubines collapsed,*
> *The palace beauties had to lie down.*
> *When the consorts and concubines collapsed,*
> *It was like a gale blowing down withered lotuses.*
> *When the palace beauties lay down*
> *It was like a rainstorm beating young lotuses down.*
> *All the ministers were terrified*
> *And their limbs went numb;*
> *They shivered and shook,*
> *Struck dumb and stupid.*
> *The White Tiger Hall was like a bridge collapsing,*
> *And the confusion round the coffin*
> *Was like a temple falling down.*

All the palace women fled, as not one of them dared to approach the imperial coffin. Luckily the upright Xu Maogong, the trusty Wei Zheng, the brave Qin Shubao, and the ferocious Yuchi Jingde went forward to put their hands on the coffin and shouted, "What is it that worries Your Majesty and makes you speak to us? Tell us, and do not haunt us and scare the royal family." "His Majesty is not haunting us," Wei Zheng said. "His Majesty has come back to life. Bring tools at once." They opened the coffin and found Taizong sitting up inside and still shouting, "You're drowning me. Save me, someone." Xu Maogong and the others helped him to his feet and said, "There is nothing to fear as you come round, Your Majesty. We are all here to protect you." The Tang Emperor then opened his eyes and said, "We have been having an awful time: after escaping from the evil demons of the underworld, we were drowned." "Relax, Your Majesty, there is nothing to fear. How could you have drowned?" the ministers said. "We were riding along the banks of the River Wei and watching to fishes playing when that deceitful Marshal Zhu pushed us off the horse and made us fall into the river, where we all but drowned." "Your Majesty still has something of the ghost about you," said Wei Zheng, and he ordered the Imperial Medical Academy to send medicinal potions to settle the spirit and calm the soul at once; he also sent for some thin gruel. After one or two doses of the medicine the emperor returned to normal and regained full consciousness. The Tang Emperor had been dead for three days and nights before returning to rule the world of the living once more. There is a poem to prove it:

> Since ancient times there have been changes of power;
> Dynasties have always waxed and waned.
> What deed of the kings of old could compare
> With the Emperor of Tang returning to life?

As it was evening by then the ministers asked the Emperor to go to bed, and they all dispersed.

The next day they all took off their mourning garments and put colourful clothes back on. Wearing red robes and black hats, and with their golden seals of office hanging from purple ribbons at their waists, they stood outside the gates of the court awaiting the summons. As for Taizong, after taking the medicine to settle his spirit and calm his soul and drinking some thin gruel he was helped to his bedroom by his ministers. He slept soundly all night, building up his energies, and at dawn he rose. See how he was arrayed as he summoned up his authority:

> On his head a hat that thrust into the sky;
> On his body a dark yellow robe
> Girt with a belt of Lantian jade;
> On his feet a pair of Shoes of Success.
> The dignity of his bearing

Surpasses all others at court.
His awesome majesty
Is today restored.
What a peaceful and wise Great Tang Emperor,
The king named Li who can die and rise again.

The Tang Emperor entered the throne hall, and when the two groups of civil and military officials had finished acclaiming him they divided into sections according to their ranks. When they heard the decree, "Let all those with business step forward from their sections and submit memorials, and let those with no business retire," Xu Maogong, Wei Zheng, Wang Gui, Du Ruhui, Fang Xuanling, Yuan Tiangang, Li Chunfeng, Xu Jingzong and others stepped forward on the eastern side; and on the western side Yin Kaishan, Liu Hongji, Ma Sanbao, Duan Zhixian, Cheng Yaojin, Qin Shubao, Yuchi Jingde, Xue Rengui and others stepped forward also. They advanced together, bowed low before the white jade steps, and asked in a memorial, "Why did it take Your Majesty so long to awake from your dream the other day?" To this Taizong replied, "The other day we took Wei Zheng's letter and felt our soul leaving the palace. The horsemen of the Imperial Guard asked us to go hunting with them, and as we were going along the men and their horses all vanished. His Late Majesty and our dead brothers appeared and started to shout at us in a quarrelsome way. Things were getting very awkward when we saw a man in a black hat and gown who turned out to be the judge Cui Jue. When he had shouted at my dead brothers and driven them away we gave him Wei Zheng's letter. As he was reading it some servants in black holding banners led us in and took us to the Senluo Palace, where we were invited to sit with the Ten Kings of Hell. They said that the dragon of the River Jing had falsely accused us of deliberately killing him after we had promised to save him, so we gave them a full account of what we told you about before. They said that the case had now been settled between the three parties, and ordered that the Registers of Birth and Death be brought at once so that they could see how long we were due to live. Judge Cui handed up the register, and they

saw in it that we were due to reign for thirty-three years, which
meant that we had another twenty years of life in front of us.
They told Marshal Zhu and Judge Cui to escort us back. We
took our leave of the Ten Kings and promised to send them some
pumpkins and fruit as a mark of our thanks. After leaving the
Senluo Palace we saw in the underworld how the disloyal, the
unfilial, those who do not observe the rules of propriety, wasters
of foodgrains, bullies, cheats, those who use false measures,
adulterers, robbers, hypocrites, deceivers, debauchees, swindlers
and the like undergo the agonies of being ground, burnt, pounded and sliced, and suffer the torments of being fried, boiled,
hung in mid-air, and skinned. There were tens of thousands of
them, far more than our eyes could take in.   Then we went
through the City of the Unjustly Slain where there were countless ghosts of the wrongly killed, and all of them, the chieftains
of the sixty-four groups of rebels and the spirits of the seventy-
two bands of rebels, blocking our way. Luckily Judge Cui acted
as our guarantor and lent us one of the hoards of gold and silver
of a Mr. Xiang of Henan, with which we were able to buy them
off and continue on our way. Judge Cui told us that when we
returned to the world of the living we had an inescapable obliga-
tion to hold a Great Mass to enable all those forlorn ghosts to
be reborn, and with these instructions he took his leave. When
we came out under the Wheel of the Six Paths of Being Marshal
Zhu invited us to mount a horse. This horse seemed to fly
to the banks of the River Wei, where we saw a pair of fish
sporting in the water. Just as we were enjoying this sight the
marshal grabbed our legs and tipped us into the water, and with
that we returned to life." When the ministers had heard this they
all congratulated him and they compiled a record of it; and all
the prefectures and counties of the empire sent in memorials of
felicitation.

Taizong issued a decree of amnesty for all the convicted
criminals in the empire and ordered inquiries into the cases of
all those held in jail on serious charges. The inspectors submitted to the throne the names of more than four hundred
criminals who had been sentenced by the Ministry of Punish-

ments to beheading or strangulation, and Taizong gave them a stay of execution, allowing them to go home to see their families and give their property to their relations; on the same day the following year they were to report to the authorities for their sentences to be carried out. The criminals thanked him for his mercy and withdrew. He also issued a notice about charity for orphans and released three thousand women of all ages from the palace to be married to members of the army. From then on all was well within and without the palace. There is a poem to prove it:

> Vast is the mercy of the great Tang Emperor;
> He surpasses Yao and Shun in making the people prosper.
> Four hundred condemned men all left their prisons,
> Three thousand mistreated women were released from the palace.
>
> All the officials of the empire proclaim the monarch's long life;
> The ministers at court congratulate the Great Dragon.
> Heaven responds to the thoughts of the good heart,
> Its blessing will protect his seventeen successors.

When he had released the women from the palace and let the condemned men out of prison he issued a notice that was posted throughout the empire. It read:

> "Great are Heaven and Earth;
> Sun and Moon shine clearly.
> Although the universe is vast,
> Earth and sky have no room for evil plots.
>
> If you use your wits and skill to cheat people,
> You will get retribution in this life;
> If you are good at giving and ask for little,
> You are sure to find a reward before your future life.
>
> A thousand cunning plans
> Cannot compare with living according to one's lot;

Ten thousand contrivances to gain wealth by force
Are no match for those who live frugally and accept their
*   fate.*

If you are good and merciful in thought and deed,
What need is there to bother to read the scriptures?
If your mind is full of malice towards others,
To read the whole of the Buddha's canon would be a
*   waste of time."*

From then on everyone in the country did good deeds. Another notice was issued calling for a worthy man to take pumpkins to the underworld, and at the same time Yuchi Jingde, the Duke of E, was sent to Kaifeng in Henan to visit Xiang Liang and pay him back a hoard of gold and silver from the treasury. Some days after the notice had been issued a worthy man called Liu Quan from Junzhou came forward to deliver the pumpkins. He came from a family worth ten thousand strings of cash. When his wife Li Cuilian had taken a gold pin from her hair to give as an offering to a monk at the gate, Liu Quan had cursed her for being a loose wife who would not stay in the women's quarters. Li Cuilian, bitterly resenting this, had hanged herself, leaving a little boy and girl who had been crying night and day ever since. Liu Quan, unable to bear it any longer, wanted only to end his own life and abandon his family and his children. For this reason he had volunteered to deliver the pumpkins in death and came to the Tang Emperor with the imperial notice in his hand. The emperor ordered him to go to the Golden Pavilion, where he was to put a pair of pumpkins on his head and some gold in his sleeve and drink poison.

Liu Quan drank the poison and died. In an instant his soul appeared at the Devil Gate with the pumpkins on his head. The demon officer at the gate asked, "Who are you, and how did you come here?" "I have come on the orders of Emperor Taizong of the Great Tang to present some pumpkins to the Ten Kings of Hell." The officer was only too pleased to let him in, and he went straight to the Senluo Palace, and when he was given audience with the Kings of Hell he presented the pumpkins to them and said, "I have brought these pumpkins a great distance in obedience to the decree of the Tang Emperor, who wishes to thank Your Majesties for their great mercy to him." "How splendid of the Tang Emperor to be as good as his word," exclaimed the ten delighted kings as they accepted the pumpkins. Then they asked him what he was called and where he was from. "I am a commoner of the city of Junzhou," hse replied, "and my name is Liu Quan. As my wife Miss Li hanged herself and left a boy and a girl with nobody to look after them I wanted to abandon my family and children by giving my life for my country, so I brought this offering of pumpkins on behalf of my sovereign, who wanted to thank Your Majesties for your great mercy." On hearing this the Ten Kings ordered a search for Liu Quan's wife, Miss Li. The devil messengers soon brought her to the Senluo Palace, outside which Liu Quan was reunited with her. They thanked the Ten Kings for their kindness and told each other about what had happened. On consulting the Registers of Birth and Death, the kings found that they were fated to become immortals, so they ordered demon officers to take them back at once. The demon officers, however, asked in a report, "As Li Cuilian has been dead for some time her body has perished, so what is her soul to be attached to?" "Li Yuying, the sister of the Tang Emperor, is due to die a sudden death today," said the Kings of Hell, "so we can borrow her body to put Li Cuilian's soul back into." On receiving this order the demon officers took Liu Quan and his wife out of the underworld to be brought back to life. If you don't know how they returned to life, listen to the explanation in the next instalment.

CHAPTER TWELVE

The Tang Emperor keeps faith and holds
a Great Mass;
Guanyin appears to the reincarnated
Golden Cicada.

When the devil officers left the underworld with Liu Quan and
his wife, a dark and whirling wind blew them straight to the
great capital Chang'an, where Liu Quan's soul was sent to the
Golden Pavilion and Li Cuilian's to an inner courtyard of the
palace, where Princess Yuying could be seen walking slowly
beside some moss under the shade of some blossoming trees.
Suddenly the devil officers struck her full in the chest and
knocked her over; they snatched the soul from her living body
and put Li Cuilian's soul into the body in its place. With that
they returned to the underworld.

When the palace serving-women saw her drop dead they
rushed to the throne hall to report to the three empresses that
Her Royal Highness the Princess had dropped dead. The
shocked empresses passed the news on to Taizong who sighed
and said, "We can well believe it. When we asked the Ten
Lords of Hell if young and old in our palace would all be well,
they replied that they would all be well except that our younger
sister was going to die suddenly. How true that was." He and
everyone else in the palace went with great sorrow to look at
her lying under the trees, only to see that she was breathing
very lightly. "Don't wail," the Tang Emperor said, "don't
wail; it might alarm her." Then he raised her head with his
own hand and said, "Wake up, sister, wake up." All of a
sudden the princess sat up and called out, "Don't go so fast,
husband. Wait for me." "Sister, we're waiting for you here,"

said the Emperor. The princess lifted her head, opened her eyes, and looked at him. "Who are you?" she asked. "How dare you put your hands on us?" "It's your august brother, royal sister," replied Taizong. "I've got nothing to do with august brothers and royal sisters," said the princess. "My maiden name is Li, and my full name is Li Cuilian. My husband is Liu Quan, and we both come from Junzhou. When I gave a gold hairpin to a monk at the gate three months ago my husband said harsh words to me about leaving the women's quarters and not behaving as a good wife should. It made me so angry and upset that I hanged myself from a beam with a white silk sash, leaving a boy and a girl who cried all night and all day. As my husband was commissioned by the Tang Emperor to go to the underworld to deliver some pumpkins, the Kings of Hell took pity on us and let the two of us come back to life. He went ahead, but I lagged behind. When I tried to catch him up I tripped over. You are all quite shameless to be mauling me like this. I don't even know your names." "We think that Her Royal Highness is delirious after passing out when she fell," said Taizong to the palace women. He sent an order to the Medical Academy for some medicinal potions, and helped Yuying into the palace.

When the Tang Emperor was back in his throne-hall, one of his aides came rushing in to report, "Your Majesty, Liu Quan, the man who delivered the pumpkins, is awaiting your summons outside the palace gates." The startled Taizong immediately sent for Liu Quan, who prostrated himself before the vermilion steps of the throne. "What happened when you presented the pumpkins?" asked the Tang Emperor. "Your subject went straight to the Devil Gate with the pumpkins on my head. I was taken to the Senluo Palace where I saw the Ten Kings of Hell, to whom I presented the pumpkins, explaining how very grateful my emperor was. The Kings of Hell were very pleased. They requested me to send their respects to Your Majesty and said, 'How splendid of the Tang Emperor to be as good as his word.' " "What did you see in the underworld?" asked the Emperor. "I did not go very far there so I did not see much.

But when the kings asked me where I was from and what I was called, I told them all about how I had volunteered to leave my family and my children to deliver the pumpkins because my wife had hanged herself. They immediately ordered demon officers to bring my wife, and we were reunited outside the Senluo Palace. Meanwhile they inspected the Registers of Births and Deaths and saw that my wife and I were both due to become immortals, so they sent devil officers to bring us back. I went ahead with my wife following behind, and although I was fortunate enough to come back to life, I don't know where her soul has been put." "What did the Kings of Hell say to you about your wife?" asked the astonished Emperor. "They didn't say anything," replied Liu Quan, "but I heard a demon officer say, 'As Li Cuilian has been dead for some time her body has decomposed.' To this the Kings of Hell said, 'Li Yuying of the Tang house is due to die today, so we can borrow her body to put Li Cuilian's soul back into.' As I don't know where this Tang house is or where she lives, I haven't been able to go and look for her yet."

The Tang Emperor, who was now very pleased, said to his officials, "When we were leaving the Kings of Hell, we asked them about our family. They said all its members would be well except for my sister. She collapsed and died under the shade of some blossoming trees, and when we hurried over to support her she came to, shouting 'Don't go so fast, husband. Wait for me.' We thought at the time that she was just talking deliriously after passing out, but when we asked her to tell us more her story tallied precisely with Liu Quan's." "If Her Royal Highness died suddenly and came to shortly afterwards talking like this, then it means that Liu Quan's wife must have borrowed her body to come back to life," said Wei Zheng. "Things like this do happen. The princess should be asked to come out so that we can hear what she says." "We have just ordered the Imperial Medical Academy to send some medicine, so we don't know whether it will be possible," said the Tang Emperor, who then sent a consort into the palace to ask her to come out. The princess, meanwhile, was shouting wildly inside the palace, "I'm taking none of your medicine. This isn't my home. My home is a simple tiled house, not like this jaundiced, yellow place with its flashy doors. Let me out, let me out."

Four or five women officials and two or three eunuchs appeared while she was shouting and helped her go straight to the throne hall. where the Tang Emperor asked, "Would you recognize your husband if you saw him?" "What a thing to ask! We were engaged since we were children, and I've given him a son and a daughter, so of course I'd recognize him." The emperor told his attendants to help her down and she went down from the throne hall. As soon as she saw Liu Quan in front of the white jade steps she seized hold of him. "Husband," she explained, "where did you go? Why didn't you wait for me? I tripped over, and all these shameless people surrounded me and shouted at me. Wasn't that shocking?" Although Liu Quan could hear that it was his wife talking, she looked like somebody else, so he did not dare to recognize her as his wife. "Indeed," said the Emperor,

> "Sometimes mountains collapse and the earth yawns
>   open,
> But few men will shorten their lives to die for another."

As he was a good and wise monarch he gave all of the princess' dressing-cases, clothes and jewellery to Liu Quan as if they were a dowry, presented him with an edict freeing him from labour service for life, and told him to take the princess home with him. Husband and wife thanked him before the steps and returned home very happily. There is a poem to prove it:

> Life and death are pre-ordained;
> Some have many years, others few.
> When Liu Quan came back to the light after taking the
>   pumpkins,
> Li Cuilian returned to life in a borrowed body.

After leaving the Emperor the pair went straight back to the city of Junzhou, where they found that their household and their

children were all well. There is no need to go into how the two
of them publicized their virtue rewarded.

The story turns to Lord Yuchi, who went to Kaifeng in
Henan with a hoard of gold and silver for Xiang Liang, who
made a living by selling water and dealing in black pots and
earthenware vessels with his wife, whose maiden name was
Zhang, at the gate of their house. When they made some money
they were content to keep enough for their daily expenses, giving
the rest as alms to monks or using it to buy paper ingots of gold
and silver, which they assigned to various hoards in the underworld and burnt. That was why they were now to be so well
rewarded. Although he was only a pious pauper in this world,
he owned mountains of jade and gold in the other one. When
Lord Yuchi brought them the gold and silver, Mr. and Mrs.
Xiang were terrified out of their wits. Apart from his lordship
there were also officials from the local government office, and
horses and carriages were packed tight outside their humble
cottage. The two of them fell to their knees dumbfounded and
began to kowtow. "Please rise," said Lord Yuchi. "Although I
am merely an imperial commissioner, I bring gold and silver
from His Majesty to return to you." Shivering and shaking,
Xiang Liang replied, "I've lent out no silver or gold, so how
could I dare to accept this mysterious wealth?" "I know that
you are a poor man," said Lord Yuchi, "but you have given
monks everything they need and bought paper ingots of gold
and silver which you have assigned to the underworld and
burnt, thus accumulating large sums of money down there.
When His Majesty the Emperor Taizong was dead for three
days before returning to life he borrowed one of your hoards of
gold and silver down there, which he is now repaying to you in
full. Please check it through so that I can go back and report
that I have carried out my instructions." Xiang Liang and his
wife just went on bowing to Heaven and refused to take the
gold and silver. "If humble folk like ourselves took all this gold
and silver it'd soon be the death of us. Although we have
burned some paper and assigned it to various stores, it was a
secret. Anyhow, what proof is there that His Majesty — may he

live for ten thousand years — borrowed gold and silver down
there? We refuse to accept it." "The emperor said that Judge
Cui was his guarantor when he borrowed your money, and this
can be verified, so please accept it," replied Lord Yuchi. "I
would sooner die than do so," said Xiang Liang.

Seeing how earnestly he refused Lord Yuchi had to send a
man back with a detailed report to the throne. On reading this
report that Xiang Liang had refused to accept the gold and
silver, Taizong said, "He really is a pious old fellow." He sent
orders to Yuchi Jingde that he was to build a temple in his
name, erect a shrine to him, and invite monks to do good deeds
on his behalf: this would be as good as paying him back the
gold and silver. On the day this decree reached him Yuchi
Jingde turned towards the palace to thank the Emperor, and
read it aloud for all to hear. Then he bought of land at a place
inside the city that would not be in the way from either the civil
or the military point of view, and here work was begun on a
monastery to be called The Imperially Founded Xiang Guo
Monastery. To its left was erected a shrine to Mr. and Mrs.
Xiang with an inscribed tablet that read "Built under the super-
vision of Lord Yuchi". This is the present Great Xiang Guo
Monastery.

When he was informed that work had been completed Taizong was very pleased, and assembling the multitude of officials
he issued a notice summoning monks to come and hold a Great
Land and Water Mass for the rebirth of those lonely souls in the
underworld. As the notice travelled throughout the empire the
local officials everywhere recommended holy and venerable
monks to go to Chang'an for the service. By the end of the
month many monks had arrived in Chang'an from all over the
empire. The Emperor issued a decree ordering Fu Yi, the Deputy Annalist, to select some venerable monks to perform Buddhist ceremonies. On hearing this command Fu Yi sent up a
memorial requesting a ban on the building of pagodas and saying that there was no Buddha. It read:

> By the Law of the West there are no distinctions
> between ruler and subject or between father and son;

the Three Paths and the Six Roads are used to deceive the foolish; past sins are chased away to filch future blessings; and Sanskrit prayers are recited in attempts to avoid retribution. Now birth, death and the length of life are in fact decided by nature; and punishments, virtue, power and blessings come from the lord of men. But these days vulgar believers distort the truth and say that they all come from Buddha. In the time of the Five Emperors and Three Kings of antiquity this Buddha did not exist, yet rulers were enlightened, subjects were loyal, and prosperity lasted for many a long year. When foreign gods were first established in the time of Emperor Ming of the Han Dynasty, sramanas from the West began to propagate their religion. This is in reality a foreign encroachment on China, and it does not merit belief.

When he had heard this read to him Taizong tossed it to his other officials for debate. The minister Xiao Yu stepped forward from the ranks, kowtowed and said, "The Buddha's law has flourished for several dynasties, and by spreading good and preventing evil it gives unseen help to the state; there is no reason why it would be abolished. Buddha was a sage. Those who deny sages are lawless. I request that he be severely punished." Fu Yi argued with Xiao Yu, pointing out that correct behaviour was derived from serving one's parents and one's sovereign, whereas the Buddha turned his back on his parents, resisting the Son of Heaven although he was but a commoner, and rebelling against his mother and father with the body that they gave him. Xiao Yu had not lost his father soon after birth, but he honoured a religion that denied fathers; this indeed proved that he who had no sense of filial piety denied his father. All Xiao Yu did was to put his hands together and say, "Hell must have been made for men such as him." Taizong sent for the High Chamberlain Zhang Daoyuan and the Head of the Secretariat Zhang Shiheng to ask them how effectively Buddhist ritual obtained blessings. "The Buddha dwells in purity, benevolence and mercy," the two officers replied, "and the True Result is Buddha-emptiness. Emperor Wu of the Northern Zhou Dynasty placed the Three Teachings in an order. The Chan Master Dahui wrote a poem in praise of the distant and mysterious which the masses always remembered without sinking into oblivion. The Five Patriarchs came down to their mothers' wombs, and Bodhidharma appeared. From remotest antiquity everyone has said that the Three Teachings are highly venerable and cannot be destroyed or abolished. We humbly beg Your Majesty to give us his perceptive ruling." "Your submission makes sense," said the delighted Taizong. "If anyone else makes further comments, he will be punished." He then ordered Wei Zheng, Xiao Yu and Zhang Daoyuan to invite all the monks and select one of great virtue to be Master of Ceremonies. They all bowed to thank him and withdrew. From then on there was a new law: anyone who injured a monk or slandered the Buddha would lose his arm.

The next day the three court officials assembled all the monks at the altar among rivers and hills, and they went through them all one by one. From among them they chose a venerable and virtuous monk. Do you know who he was?

> Fully versed in the basic mystery, his title was Golden
>   Cicada;
> But because he did not want to hear the Buddha preach
> He transferred to the mortal world to suffer torment,
> Was born among the common mortals to fall into the
>   net.
> From the moment he entered the womb he met with evil;
> Before he left it he encountered a gang of villains.
> His father was Top Graduate Chen from Haizhou,
> His grandfather a senior imperial commander.
> His birth offended the meteor that dropped into the
>   water;
> He drifted with the current and followed the waves.
> Jinshan Island had a great destiny:
> The abbot Qian'an brought him up.

Only at seventeen did he meet his mother,
And go to the capital to find his grandfather.
Commander Yin Kaishan, raising a great army,
Wiped out and punished the bandits at Hongzhou. .
Graduate Chen Guangrui escaped from the heavenly net,
And father and son were happily reunited.
Accepting the invitation he receives once more the
    monarch's grace,
And his fame is spread as he climbs the lofty tower.
Refusing to take office he wants to be a monk,
So as sramana of the Hongfu Temple he learns about
    the Way,
The child of an ancient Buddha who used to be called
    Jiangliu,
And took the dharma-name of Chen Xuanzang.

That day the Reverend Xuanzang was chosen from among
all the monks. He had been a monk from infancy, and ever
since birth he had eaten vegetarian food and observed the prohibitions. His maternal grandfather was an imperial commander,
Yin Kaishan. His father Chen Guangrui had come top in the
Palace Examination and had been appointed a grand secretary
in the Imperial Library. Xuanzang, however, had no interest
in honour and glory, and his only joy was to cultivate Nirvana.
Investigation revealed that his origins were good and his virtue
great; of the thousand sutras and ten thousand holy books there
was not a single one that he did not know; he could sing every
Buddhist chant and knew all the religious music. The three officials took him to the imperial presence, where they danced
and stirred up the dust. When they had bowed they reported,
"Your subject Xiao Yu and the rest of us have chosen a venerable monk called Chen Xuanzang in obedience to the imperial
decree." On hearing his name Taizong thought deeply for a
long time and then asked, "Is that the Xuanzang who is the son
of Grand Secretary Chen Guangrui?" "Your subject is he" replied Xuanzang with a kowtow. "Then you were indeed well
chosen," said the Emperor with satisfaction. "You are indeed

a monk of virtuous conduct of a mind devoted to meditation. I give you the offices of Left Controller of the Clergy, Right Controller of the Clergy, and Hierarch of the Empire." Xuanzang kowtowed to express his thanks and accepted the appointments. The Emperor then gave him a multicoloured golden cassock and a Vairocana mitre, telling him to be sure he conscientiously continued to visit enlightened monks, and giving him the position at the top of the hierarchy. He gave him a decree in writing ordering him to go to the Huasheng Temple to pick a propitious day and hour on which to begin the recitations of the scriptures.

Xuanzang bowed, took the decree, and went to the Huasheng Temple where he assembled many monks, had meditation benches made, prepared for the mass, and chose the music. He selected a total of twelve hundred high and humble monks of enlightenment, who he divided into an upper, a middle and a lower hall. All the holy objects were neatly arranged before all the Buddhas. The third day of the ninth month of that year was chosen an auspicious day on which to start the seven times seven days of the Great Land and Water Mass. This was all reported to the throne, and at the appointed time Taizong, the high civil and military officials, and the royal family went to the service to burn incense and listen to the preaching. There is a poem to prove it that goes:

> At the dragon assembly in the thirteenth year of Zhen Guan
> The Emperor called a great meeting to talk about the scriptures.
> At the assembly they began to expound the unfathomable law,
> While clouds glowed above the great shrine.
> The Emperor in his grace orders the building of a temple;
> The Golden Cicada sheds his skin to edify the West.
> He spreads the news that rewards for goodness save from ill,

*Preaching the doctrine of the three Buddhas of past and
future.*

In the year *jisi*, the thirteenth of *Zhen Cuan*, on the day
jiaxu, the third of the ninth month, the Hierarch Chen Xuanzang
assembled twelve hundred venerable monks at the Huasheng
Temple in the city of Chang'an for a chanting of all the holy
scriptures. After morning court was over the Emperor left the
throne hall in his dragon and phoenix chariot at the head of
a host of civil and military officials and went to the temple to
burn incense. What did the imperial chariot look like? Indeed

Propitious vapours filled the sky
That shone with ten thousand beams of sacred light.
A mellow breeze blew softly;
The sunlight was strangely beautiful.
*A thousand officials with jade at their belts walked in
    due order.*
*The banners of the five guards are drawn up on either
    side.*
Holding golden gourds,
Wielding battle-axes,
They stand in pairs;
Lamps of purple gauze,
Imperial censers,
Make majestic clouds.
Dragons fly and phoenixes dance,
Ospreys and eagles soar.
True is the enlightened Son of Heaven;
Good are his just and loyal ministers.
*This age of prosperity surpasses the time of Shun and
    Yu;*
*The eternal peace he has given outdoes that of Yao and
    Tang.*
Under a parasol with curved handle
The dragon robe sweeps in,
Dazzling bright.
Interlocking jade rings,

> *Coloured phoenix fans,*
> *Shimmer with a magic glow.*
> *Pearl crowns and belts of jade,*
> *Gold seals on purple cords.*
> *A thousand regiments of soldiers protect the imperial chariot,*
> *Two lines of generals support the royal chair.*
> *Bathed and reverent, the Emperor comes to worship the Buddha,*
> *Submitting to the True Achievement as he joyfully burns incense.*

When the carriage of the Tang Emperor reached the temple, orders were given to stop the music as he descended from the vehicle and went at the head of his officials to bow to the Buddha and burn incense. When he had walked round the Buddha's image three times he looked up and saw what a magnificent assembly it was:

> *Dancing banners,*
> *Flying canopies.*
> *When the banners dance*
> *The sky shake with the clouds of silk;*
> *When the canopies fly*
> *The sun gleams as the red lightning flashes.*
> *Perfect the image of the statue of the Honoured One,*
> *Mighty the grandeur of the Arhats' countenances.*
> *Magic flowers in a vase,*
> *Censers burning sandalwood and laka.*
> *As the fairy flowers stand in vases*
> *Trees like brocade fill the temple with their brightness.*
> *As the censers burn sandalwood and laka*
> *Clouds of incense rise to the azure heaven.*
> *Fresh fruit of the season is piled in vermilion dishes,*
> *Exotic sweets are heaped on the silk-covered tables.*
> *Serried ranks of holy monks intone the sutras*
> *To save abandoned souls from suffering.*

Taizong and his civil and military officials all burned incense, bowed to the golden image of the Lord Buddha, and paid their respects to the Arhats. The Hierarch Chen Xuanzan then led all the monks to bow to the Emperor, and when this was over they divided into their groups and went to their meditation places while the hierarch showed the Emperor the notice about the delivery of the lonely ghosts. It read:

> "Mysterious is the ultimate virtue, and the Sect of Meditation leads to Nirvana. The purity of the truth is all-knowing; it pervades the Three Regions of the universe. Through its countless changes it controls the Negative and Positive; unbounded are the embodiments of the eternal reality. In considering those forlorn ghosts one should be deeply distressed. At the sacred command of Taizong we have assembled some chosen monks for meditation and preaching. He has opened wide the gates of enlightenment and rowed far the boat of mercy, saving all the beings in the sea of suffering, and delivering those who had long been afflicted by the six ways of existence. They will be led back to the right road and revel in the great chaos; in action and in passivity they will be at one with primal simplicity. For this wonderful cause they are invited to see the purple gates of the pure capital, and through our assembly they will escape from the confines of Hell to climb to the World of Bliss and be free, wandering as they please in the Paradise of the West. As the poem goes:
>
> *A burner of incense of longevity,*
> *A few spells to achieve rebirth.*
> *The infinite Law is proclaimed,*
> *The boundless mercy of Heaven is shown.*
>
> *When sins are all washed away.*
> *The neglected souls leave Hell.*
> *We pray to protect our country;*
> *May it stay at peace and be blessed."*

When he had read this the Tang Emperor's heart was filled
with happiness and he said to the monks, "Hold firm to your
sincerity and never allow yourselves a moment's slackness in the
service of the Buddha. Later on, when the Assembly is over,
you will be blessed and we shall richly reward you. You shall
certainly not have laboured in vain."   The twelve hundred
monks all kowtowed to thank him. When the three vegetarian
meals for the day were over the Tang Emperor went back to
the palace. He was invited to come back to the Grand Assembly
to burn incense once more on the seventh day. As evening was
now drawing in all the officials went away. It was a fine evening:

> *A light glow suffused the boundless sky;*
> *A few crows were late in finding their roosts.*
> *Lamps were lit throughout the city as all fell still;*
> *It was just the hour for the monks to enter the trance.*

We will omit a description of the night or of how the monks
intoned the scriptures when their master took his seat again the
next morning.

The Bodhisattva Guanyin from Potaraka Island in the
Southern Sea had long been in Chang'an, looking on the Buddha's orders for the man to fetch the scriptures, but she had
not yet found anyone really virtuous. Then she heard that Taizong was propagating the True Achievement and selecting
venerable monks for a Grand Assembly, and when she saw that
the master of ceremonies was the monk Jiangliu who was really a Buddha's son come down from the realms of supreme bliss,
an elder whom she herself had led into his earthly mother's
womb, she was very pleased. She took her disciple Moksa and
the treasures that the Buddha had given her out on the street
to offer them for sale. Do you know what these treasures were?
There was a precious brocade cassock and a monastic staff with
nine rings. She also had those three golden bands, but she put
them away safely for future use; she was only selling the cassock
and the staff.

There was a monk in Chang'an city too stupid to be chosen for the service but who nonetheless had some ill-gotten banknotes. When he saw the bald, scabby, barefoot figure wearing a tattered robe — the form the Bodhisattva had taken — offering the cassock of dazzling beauty for sale he went up and asked, "How much d'you want for that cassock, Scabby?" "The price of the cassock is five thousand ounces of silver and the staff two thousand," replied the Bodhisattva. The stupid monk roared with laughter. "You must be a nutcase, Scabby, or else a dope. Those two lousy things wouldn't be worth that much unless they gave you immortality and turned you into a Buddha. No deal. Take 'em away."

Not bothering to argue, the Bodhisattva walked on with Moksa. After they had been going for quite a long time they found themselves in front of the Donghua Gate of the palace, where the minister Xiao Yu happened to be returning home from morning court. Ignoring the crowd of lictors who were shouting to everyone to get out of the way, the Bodhisattva calmly went into the middle of the road with the cassock in her hands and headed straight for the minister. When the minister reined in his horse to look he saw the cassock gleaming richly and sent an attendant to ask its price. "I want five thousand ounces of silver for the cassock and two thousand for the staff," said the Bodhisattva. "What's so good about the cassock to make it worth that much?" asked Xiao Yu. "On the one hand it is good and on the other it isn't," replied the Bodhisattva. "On the one hand it has a price and on the other it hasn't." "What's good about it and what isn't?" asked the minister. "Whoever wears this cassock of mine will not sink into the mire, will not fall into Hell, will not be ensnared by evil and will not meet disaster from tiger or wolf: these are its good points. But as for a stupid monk who is greedy and debauched, who takes delight in the sufferings of others, does not eat vegetarian food, and breaks the monastic bans; or a common layman who harms the scriptures and slanders the Buddha — such people have great difficulty even in seeing this cassock of mine: that is its disadvantage." "What did you mean by saying that it both has a price and hasn't got one?" asked the minister, continuing his questions. "Anyone who doesn't obey the Buddha's Law or honour the Three Treasures but still insists on buying the cassock and the staff will have to pay seven thousand ounces for them: in that case they have a price. But if anyone who honours the Three Treasures, takes pleasure in goodness, and believes in our Buddha, wants to have them, then I'll give him the cassock and staff as a gift. In that case they have no price." Xiao Yu's cheeks coloured, showing that he was a good man, and he dismounted to greet the Bodhisattva. "Elder of the Great Law," he said, "forgive me. Our Great Tang Emperor is a true lover of goodness, and every one of the civil and military officials in his court acts piously. This cassock would be just right for the Hierarch, Master Chen Xuanzang, to wear in the Great Land and Water Mass that is now being conducted. You and I shall go into the palace to see His Majesty."

The Bodhisattva gladly followed him as he turned around and went straight in through the Donghua Gate. The eunuchs reported their arrival, and they were summoned to the throne hall. Xiao Yu led the two scabby monks in, and they stood beneath the steps of the throne. "What have you come to report, Xiao Yu?" the Emperor asked. Xiao Yu prostrated himself in front of the steps and replied, "When your subject went out through the Donghua Gate I met two monks who were selling a cassock and a staff. It occurred to me that this cassock would be suitable for Master Xuanzang to wear, so I have brought the monks for an audience with Your Majesty." The delighted Taizong asked how much the cassock cost. Still standing beneath the steps, and not making any gestures of courtesy, the Bodhisattva and Moksa replied, "The cassock costs five thousand ounces of silver, and the staff two thousand." "What advantages does the cassock have to make it worth so much?" the Emperor asked. To this the Bodhisattva replied:

> "This cassock
> Has a strand of dragon cape,
> To save from being eaten by the Roc,

And a thread of a stork jacket,
To deliver from mortality and lead to sainthood.
When one sits
Ten thousand spirits come to pay homage;
In all your actions
The Seven Buddhas will be with you.

"This cassock is made of silk reeled from giant ice-
    worms,
Twisted into yarn by skilful craftsmen,
Woven by fairy beauties,
Finished by goddesses.
The strips of cloth are joined with embroidered seams,
Each piece thick with brocade.
The openwork decoration has a flower pattern
Shimmering with colour, shining with jewelled beauty.
The wearer of the cassock is wreathed in red mist,
And when it is taken off, coloured clouds fly.
Its primal light slipped out through the Three Gates of
    Heaven,
The magic vapour arose before the Five Sacred Peaks.
It is embroidered with layer upon layer of passion-
    flowers,
And gleams with pearls that shine like stars.
At the four corners are night-shining pearls;
Set at the top is an emerald.
Although it does not completely illuminate the Original
    Body
It shines with the light of the Eight Treasures.

"This cassock
Is normally kept folded,
And will only be worn by a sage.
When kept folded,
A rainbow shines through its thousand layers of wrap-
    ping;
When it is worn by a sage,
It will astonish the heavenly spirits and scare all demons.

> On top is an as-you-wish pearl,
> A Mani pearl,
> A dust-repelling pearl,
> And a wind-calming pearl;
> There is also red agate,
> Purple coral,
> Night-shining pearls,
> And relics of the Buddha.
> They steal the white of the moon,
> Rival the sun in redness.
> Their magic essence fills the sky;
> Their auspicious light honours the sage.
> Their magic essence fills the sky,
> Shining through the gates of Heaven;
> Their auspicious light honours the sage,
> Illuminating the whole world.
> Shining on mountains and rivers,
> The essence frightens tigers and leopards;
> Illuminating oceans and islands,
> The light startles fishes and dragons.
> At the side are two rows of gold-plated hooks,
> At the neck are loops of whitest jade."

There is a poem that goes:

> "Great are the Three Jewels, and honoured be the Way;
> The Four Kinds of Life and Six Paths are all explained.
> Whoever knows and teaches the law of Man and
>   Heaven,
> Can pass on the lamp of wisdom when he sees his
>   original nature.
> It protects the body and makes it a world of gold,
> Leaves body and mind pure as an ice-filled jar of jade.
> Ever since Buddha made his cassock
> No one will ever dare to end the priesthood."

When the Tang Emperor heard these words spoken in his throne hall he was filled with joy, and he asked another question: "Monk, what is so wonderful about your nine-ringed staff?" "This staff of mine," the Bodhisattva replied, "is:

> A nine-ringed iron staff inlaid with copper,
> A nine-sectioned immortal's cane to preserve eternal youth.
> Held in your hand it stops bones aging;
> As you go down the mountain it brings white clouds.
>
> The Fifth Patriarch took it through the gates of Heaven;
> When Lo Bu searched for his mother he used it to smash the gates of Earth.
> Untouched by the filth of mortal dust,
> It gladly accompanies the godly monk as he climbs the jade mountain."

The Tang Emperor then ordered that the cassock be unfolded. On examining it from top to bottom he saw that it was indeed a fine article. "Elder of the Great Law," he said, "I tell you truthfully that I am now propagating the good word and widely sowing seeds of blessing. At this moment many monks are assembled at the Huasheng Monastery for recitation of the sutras. Among them is one monk of outstanding virtue whose Buddha-name is Xuanzang, and we wish to buy those two treasures of yours to give him. So what is your price?" The Bodhisattva and Hoksa put their hands together, intoned the name of the Buddha, and bowed. "If he really is a virtuous monk," she said, "I shall give them to him, and I refuse to accept any money for them." With that she turned and left. The Emperor immediately told Xiao Yu to stop her as he rose to his feet and called out, "You told us that you wanted five thousand ounces for the cassock and two thousand for the staff, but now that we have said we shall buy them, you refuse to take any money. Are you going to say that I abused my power to seize your things? We would never dream of it. We shall pay the price you asked, and will take no refusal." Raising her hand, the Bodhisattva said, "I made a vow that I would give them free to anyone who honoured the Three

Treasures, delighted in goodness, and believed in our Buddha.
Now I have seen that Your Majesty is a good and virtuous
respecter of our Buddhist faith, and have heard that there is
a monk of virtuous conduct who preaches the Great Law, it is
only right that I should offer them to him; I don't want any
money for them. I am leaving the things here. Goodbye." The
Tang Emperor was very pleased with the monk's sincerity, and
ordered that a large vegetarian banquet be given to thank him
in the Imperial Kitchen. This the Bodhisattva refused to accept
and went airily off. There is no need to describe how she returned to her hide-out in the local god's temple.

Taizong arranged for a court to be held at midday and sent
Wei Zheng with a decree summoning Xuanzang to attend. He
found the monastic official assembling the monks as he climbed
the rostrum for the chanting of sutras and gathas. The moment
he heard the decree he came down from the rostrum, tidied his
clothes, and went with Wei Zheng to the imperial presence.
"Up till now we have had nothing suitable with which to
thank you, Your Grace, for your efforts in acquiring merit. This
morning Xiao Yu met two monks who have vowed to give you
a precious brocade cassock and a nine-ringed monk's staff. We
have therefore sent for you, Master, to come and receive them,"
said the Emperor. Xuanzhang kowtowed in thanks. "If you do
not reject it, Your Grace, let us see what it looks like on you."
Xuanzang shook it open, draped it across his shoulders, took
the staff in his hand, and stood respectfully before the steps of
the throne. The monarch and all his ministers were overjoyed.
He truly was a son of the Tathagata. Look at him:

> How elegant his imposing features;
> His Buddha-vestments fit as if made for him.
> The glow radiating from them fills Heaven and Earth,
> While the colours crystallize in the sky.
>
> Rows of gleaming pearls above and below,
> Layers of golden threads joining front and back.
> A hood edged with brocade,
> Embroidered with ten thousand strange designs.

*Patterns of the Eight Treasures hold the threads of the
    buttons,*
*While the golden collar is fastened with catches of
    velvet.*
The Buddha Heavens are set out in order of eminence,
While to left and right are the high and humble stars.

Great is the destiny of Xuanzang, Master of the Law,
Who is worthy to accept this gift at present.
He is just like a living Arhat,
Excelling the Enlightened One of the West.

On the monkish staff the nine rings clink,
And richly glows the Vairocana mitre.
How true that he is a Buddha's son;
It is no lie that he has surpassed enlightenment.

All the civil and military officials cried out with admiration,
and the Emperor was delighted. Telling the Master of the Law
to put the cassock on properly and take the staff, he granted
him two bands of ceremonial attendants and had a host of officials see him out of the palace and walk with him to his monastery. It was just like the procession for a top graduate in
the palace examination. Xuanzang bowed once more to thank
the Emperor and then set out, striding majestically along the
highway. All the travelling merchants, the shop-keepers, the
fashionable young men, the professional scribes, the men and
women, young and old, in the city of Chang'an fought to get a
look at him and praise him. "What a splendid Master of the
Law," they said. "He's an Arhat come down to earth, a living
Bodhisattva come to see us mortals." Xuanzang went straight
to his monastery, where all the monks left their places of meditation to welcome him. When they saw the cassock he was wearing and the staff in his hand they all said that King Ksitigarbha
had come, did homage to him, and stood in attendance to right
and left. Ascending the main hall, Xuanzang burned incense
and worshipped Buddha, and when he had given an account
of the Emperor's grade they all returned to their seats for med-

itation. Nobody noticed that the red wheel of the sun was now sinking in the west.

> As the sun sinks, plants and trees are veiled in mist
> While the capital echoes to the bell and drum.
> After three chimes of the bell nobody moves;
> The streets throughout the city are still.

> The monastery gleams with the light of its lamps;
> The village is lonely and silent.
> The Chan monks enter their trance and repair damaged
> sutras.
> A good way to purify oneself of evil and nourish the
> true nature.

Time passed in the snap of a finger, and it was time for the special assembly on the seventh day, so Xuanzang wrote a memorial inviting the Tang Emperor to come and burn incense. His reputation for piety had now spread throughout the empire. Taizong therefore led a large number of civil and military officials and his empresses, consorts and their families to the monastery in a procession of carriages to the temple early that morning. Everyone in the city, whether young or old, humble or mighty, went to the temple to hear the preaching. The Bodhisattva said to Moksa, "Today is a special day of the Great Land and Water, Mass, which will go on from this first seventh day to the seventh seventh day, as is proper. You and I are going to mingle with the crowds for three reasons: to see the service, to see the Golden Cicada enjoying the blessing of wearing our treasure, and to hear what branch of the scriptures he preaches on." The pair of them went to the temple. They were fated to meet their old acquaintance, just as the Wisdom returned to its own preaching place. When they went inside the monastery they saw that this great and heavenly dynasty surpassed and other in the world; while the Jetavana Monastery and Sravasti were no match for this temple. Sacred music sounded clear above the shouting of Buddha names. When the Bodhisattva approached the preaching dais she saw in Xuanzang the likeness of the wise Golden Cicada. As the poem goes:

Pure in every image, free of every speck of dirt,
The great Xuanzang sat on his lofty dais.
The lonely souls who have been delivered come
*   secret,*
While the well-born arrive to hear the Law.

Great is his wisdom in choosing suitable methods;
All his life he has opened the doors of the scriptures.
As they watch him preach the infinite Law,
The ears of young and old alike are filled with joy.

As Guanyin went to the temple preaching hall
She met an old acquaintance who was no common mor-
*   tal.*
He spoke about every current matter,
And mentioned the achievements of many a mortal era.

The clouds of the Dharmas settle over every mountain;
The net of the teaching spreads right across the sky.
If one counts the number of pious thoughts among
*   humans*
They are as plentiful as raindrops on red blossom.

On his dais the Master of the Law read through the *Sutra to Give Life and Deliver the Dead*, discussed the *Heavenly Charm to Protect the Country* and preached on the *Exhortation to Cultivate Merit*. The Bodhisattva went up to the dais, hit it, and shouted out at the top of her voice, "Why are you only talking about the doctrine of the Little Vehicle, monk? Can't you preach about the Great Vehicle?" On hearing these questions a delighted Xuanzang leapt down from the preaching dais, bowed to the Bodhisattva, and said, "Venerable teacher, your disciple has sinned grievously in failing to recognize you. We monks who stand before you only preach the Law of the Little Vehicle, and we know nothing of the doctrine of the Great Vehicle." "That doctrine of the Little Vehicle of yours will never bring the dead to rebirth; it's only good enough for a vulgar sort of enlightenment. Now I have the Three Stores of the Buddha's Law of the Great Vehicle that will raise the dead up to Heaven,

deliver sufferers from their torments, and free souls from the
eternal coming and going."

As the Bodhisattva was talking, the Master of Incense, an
official who patrolled the temple, made an urgent report to the
Tang Emperor that just when the Master of the Law was in
the middle of preaching the wonderful Law a pair of scabby
itinerant monks had dragged him down and were engaging him
in wild argument. The emperor ordered them to be arrested
and brought before him, and a crowd of men hustled the two
of them into the rear hall of the monastery. When they saw
Taizong they neither raised their hands in greeting nor bowed,
but looked him in the eye and said, "What does Your Majesty
want to ask us about." Recognizing them, the Emperor asked,
"Are you not the monk who gave us the cassock?" "That's
right," replied the Bodhisattva. "If you came here to listen to
the preaching you should be satisfied with getting something to
eat," said Taizong. "Why did you start ranting at the Master
of the Law, disturbing the scripture hall and interfering with
our service to the Buddha?" "That master of yours was only
teaching the doctrine of the Little Vehicle, which will never
send the dead up to Heaven," replied the Bodhisattva. "I have
the Three Stores of the Buddha's Law of the Great Vehicle,
which can save the dead, deliver from suffering, and ensure that
the body will live for ever without coming to harm." Showing
no signs of anger, Taizong earnestly asked where the Buddha's
Law of the Great Vehicle was. "It is in the Thunder Monastery
in the land of India in the West, where our Buddha lives," the
Bodhisattva replied, "and it can untie the knots of all injustice
and save the innocent from disaster." "Can you remember it?"
the Emperor asked, and the Bodhisattva answered "Yes". Taizong then gave orders that this Master of the Law was to lead
the way to the dais and the Bodhisattva invited to preach.

The Bodhisattva and Moksa flew up to the dais, then soared
into the sky on magic clouds. She appeared in her own form
as the Deliverer from Suffering, holding a twig of willow in a
vase, and Moksa stood beside her as Huian, holding a stick
and bristling with energy. The Tang Emperor was so happy

that he bowed to Heaven, while his civil and military officials all fell to their knees and burned incense. Everyone in the temple — monks, nuns, clerics, lay people, scholars, workmen and merchants — all bowed down and prayed, "Good Bodhisattva, good Bodhisattva." There is a description of her appearance:

> The sacred radiance shines around her,
> The holy light protects her Dharma body.
> In the glory of the highest Heaven
> Appears a female immortal.
> The Bodhisattva
> Wore on her head
> Marvellous pearl tassels
> With golden clasps,
> Set with turquoise,
> And gleaming golden.
> She wore on her body
> A plain blue robe with flying phoenixes,
> Pale-coloured,
> Patterned with running water,
> On which curled golden dragons.
> Before her breast hung
> A moon-bright,
> Wind-dancing,
> Pearl-encrusted,
> Jade-set circlet full of fragrance.
> Around her waist was
> A skirt of embroidery and brocade from the Jade Pool
> Made from the silk of ice-silkworms,
> With golden seams,
> Supported by coloured clouds.
> Before her went
> A white and yellow red-beaked parrot,
> To fly across the Eastern Ocean,
> And all over the world
> In gratitude and duty.
> The vase she held gave grace and salvation;

And in the vase was a sprig of
Weeping willow to sweep away the fog,
Scattering water on the heavens.
Cleansing all evil.
Rings of jade looped over brocade buttons
And her golden-lotus feet were concealed.
She was able to visit the three heavens,
For she was Guanyin, the rescuer from suffering.

Taizong was so entranced that he forgot all about his empire; the ministers and generals were so captivated that they forgot all about court etiquette; and the masses all intoned, "Glory be to the Bodhisattva Guanyin." Taizong ordered that a skilled painter was to make a true likeness of the Bodhisattva, and no sooner had the words left his mouth than the brilliant and enlightened portrayer of gods and immortals, Wu Daozi, was chosen. He was the man who later did the pictures of distinguished ministers in the Cloud-piercing Pavilion. Wielding his miraculous brush, he painted a true likeness on the spot. The Bodhisattva's magic cloud slowly faded into the distance, and a moment later the golden light could be seen no more. All that was visible was a note drifting down from the sky on which could be read the following brief address in verse:

"Greetings to the lord of the Great Tang.
In the West are miraculous scriptures.
Although the road is sixty thousand miles long,
The Great Vehicle will offer its help.
When these scriptures are brought back to your country
They will save ghosts and deliver the masses.
If anyone is willing to go for them,
A golden body will be his reward."

When he had read these lines Taizong issued an order to the assembly of monks: "Suspend this service until we have sent someone to fetch the scriptures of the Great Vehicle, and then you shall once more strive sincerely to achieve good retribution." The monks all obeyed his instructions. The Emperor then asked those present in the monastery, "Who is willing to accept our

commission to go to the Western Heaven to visit the Buddha
and fetch the scriptures?" Before he had finished his question,
the Master of the Law came forward, bowed low in greeting,
and said, "Although I am lacking in ability, I would like to
offer my humble efforts to fetch the true scriptures for Your
Majesty and thus ensure the eternal security of your empire."
The Tang Emperor, who was overjoyed to hear this, went forward to raise him to his feet. "Master," he said, "if you are
prepared to exert your loyalty and wisdom to the full, not fearing the length of the journey or the rivers and mountains you will
have to cross, I shall make you my own sworn brother." Xuanzang kowtowed to thank him. As the Tang Emperor was indeed a man of wisdom and virtue he went to a place before the
Buddha in the monastery where he bowed to Xuanzang four
times, calling him "younger brother" and "holy monk". Xuanzang thanked him effusively. "Your Majesty," he said, "I have
no virtue or talent that fits me for the sacred honour of being
treated as your kinsman. On this journey I shall give my all
and go straight to the Western Heaven. If I fail to reach there
or to obtain the true scriptures, then I shall not return to this
country even in death, and shall fall for eternity into Hell."
He burned incense in front of the Buddha to mark this vow.
The happy Emperor ordered his chariot to take him back to the
palace; later on an auspicious day would be chosen on which
Xuanzang would be given a passport and set out. With that
he returned and everyone dispersed.

Xuanzang went back to the Hongfu Monastery, where the
many monks and his few personal disciples had already heard
that he was going to fetch the scriptures. They came to ask
if it was true that he had vowed to go to the Western Heaven.
On being told by Xuanzang that it was indeed true, his pupils
said, "Teacher, we have heard that the journey to the Western
Heaven is a long one, and that there are many tigers, leopards,
fiends, and demons on the way. We are afraid that you may
lose your life and never come back." "I have sworn a great
vow that I shall fall into Hell for eternity if I do not get the
true scriptures," replied Xuanzang. "Besides, as I have been

so favoured by His Majesty, I shall have to show my loyalty to the utmost if I am to repay the country for his honour. But it will be a journey into the unknown, and there is no saying what my fate will be. My pupils," he went on to say, "two or three years after I set out, or it may be as much as six or seven, that pine tree inside the monastery gate will turn to the east, which will mean that I am coming back. If it does not, you can be sure that I will not return." All his disciples committed his words most carefully to memory.

At court the next morning Taizong assembled his civil and military officials and wrote out the document Xuanzang would need to fetch the scriptures, stamping it with the imperial seal that gave the right to travel freely. When an imperial astrologer reported that this day was under an auspicious star for setting out on a long journey, the Tang Emperor was delighted. A eunuch official came in to report, "The Imperial Younger Brother, the Master of the Law, awaits a summons outside the palace doors." Calling him into the throne hall, Taizong said, "Brother, today is a lucky one for starting on a journey, and here is the pass that will let you through the checkpoints. I am also giving you a golden bowl with which you may beg for food on your journey, in addition to choosing two experienced travellers to accompany you and presenting you with a horse to carry you on your long journey. You may now set out." Xuanzang, who was very happy to hear this, thanked the Emperor and took the presents. He was now more eager than ever to be off. Taizong and a host of officials went by carriage to accompany him to the checkpoint. When they got there they found that the monks of the Hongfu Monastery and Xuanzang's own disciples were waiting outside with his summer and winter clothing. As soon as he saw this the Tang Emperor ordered that it be packed and horses be provided, then told an official to pour out some wine. Raising his cup he asked, "Brother, what is your courtesy name?" "As I am not of the world, I do not have one," replied Xuanzang. "The Bodhisattva said yesterday that there are Three Stores (*san zang*) of scriptures in the Western Heaven. You, brother, should take a courtesy name from this   What about Sanzang?" Thanking the Emperor for his kindness, he accepted the cup of wine with the words, "Your Majesty, liquor is the first of the things from which a monk must abstain, and so I have never drunk it." "Today's journey is exceptional," Taizong replied, "and besides, this is a non-alcoholic wine, so you should drink this cup and let us feel that we have seen you off properly." Unable to refuse any longer, Sanzang took the wine, and was on the point of drinking it when he saw Taizong bend down, take a pinch of dust in his fingers, and flick it into his cup. Seeing Sanzang's incomprehension, Taizong laughed and said, "Dear brother, when will you return from this journey to the Western Heaven?" "I shall be back in this country within three years," Sanzang replied. "The days and years will be long, the mountains will be high, and the road will lead you far away," said Taizong, "so you should drink this wine to show that you have more love for a pinch of dust from home than for thousands of ounces of foreign gold." Only then did Sanzang understand the significance of the pinch of dust, and thanking the Emperor once more he drained the cup, took his leave of him, and went out through the checkpoint. The Emperor went back to the palace. If you don't know what happened on the journey, listen to the explanation in the next instalment.

CHAPTER THIRTEEN

He falls into the tiger's den and is saved
by the Great White Planet;
On Double-Forked Peak Boqin entertains
the Priest.

The Great Tang Emperor issued an edict
Sending Sanzang to learn the Dhyana teachings.
With firmness and patience he seeks the dragon's lair,
Determined to carry on till he climbs the Vulture Peak.

On his long journey he will visit many a country;
Thousands of cloud-capped mountains lie before him.
Now he leaves the Emperor and sets out for the West
Cleaving to the faith. and aware of the Great Void.

It has been told already how Sanzang was seen off at the checkpoint outside Chang'an by the Tang Emperor and a host of
officials on the twelfth day of the ninth month in the thirteenth
year of *Zhen Guan*. For two days his horse's hoofs were never
still, and he soon reached the Fa Men Monastery, where the
abbot came out to meet him at the head of five hundred and
more monks drawn up in two lines. Taking Sanzang inside,
he greeted him, offered him tea, and then gave him a monastic
meal. By the time the meal was over night had fallen.

As it approached the Milky Way,
The moon was free from any dust.
The wild goose called to the distant traveller,
While washing-boards could be heard by neighbours.

Roosting birds perch in the withered trees;
The Dhyana monks chant Sanskrit music.

On their seats with hassocks of rushes
They sit until the middle of the night.

In the lamplight the monks were discussing the true teach-ings of the Buddhist faith and the reasons for going to the Western Heaven to fetch the scriptures. Some said that there would be wide rivers and high mountains to cross, some that there would be many a tiger and leopard along the way, some that the lofty ranges and cliffs would be hard to cross, and some that there would be evil demons and foul fiends difficult to subdue. Sanzang kept his lips sealed; he said nothing, only pointing to his heart and nodding occasionally. The monks, unable to understand what he meant, put their hands together and asked, "Why do you point to your heart and nod your head, Master?" "When the heart and mind live," Sanzang replied, "every kind of evil lives; but when they are extinguished, evil is extinguished too. I made a great vow to the Buddha in the Huasheng Monastery, and I must do everything in my power to fulfil it. I am determined to reach the Western Heaven, where I may see the Buddha and ask for the scriptures, so that the Wheel of the Law may revolve, and our sage emperor enjoy eternal security." On hearing his words the monks all expressed their admiration, saying as if with one voice, "What a loyal and brave Hierarch." With praises still on their lips they invited the Master to go to bed and wished him a peaceful night's sleep.

Before long the bamboo clappers were sounding for the setting moon, while the cocks greeted the dawn with their crow-ing. The monks all got up and prepared tea and breakfast. Sanzang put on his cassock and went to worship the Buddha in the main hall. "Your disciple Chen Sanzang," he said, "is going to the Western Heaven to fetch the scriptures, but my fleshly eye is too dim to see the true image of the living Buddha. I now vow that whenever I come across a temple on my journey I shall burn incense; whenever I see a Buddha's image I shall worship it; and whenever I pass a stupa I shall sweep it. My only wish is that Buddha in his mercy will soon appear to me in his golden body and give me the true scriptures to take back

and propagate in the land of the East." When he had prayed
he went back to the abbot's room for breakfast. After breakfast his two attendants saddled the horse and set off at a good
pace. At the gate of the monastery Sanzang took his leave of
the monks, who were so unwilling to be parted from him that
they accompanied him for some three miles before turning back
with tears in their eyes, while Sanzang carried on westwards.
It was autumn weather:

> Leafless the village trees, and fallen the reed flowers;
> The red leaves had dropped from maple.
> The way was foggy and damp, and few were the friends
>   that he met.
> Beautiful the yellow chrysanthemums,
> Delicate the mountain spurs;
> Sad to see the lotus withered now the water was cold.
> White duckweed and red smartweed were turned to
>   snow by the frost.
> Solitary ducks came down from the clouds, dropping
>   from the sky,
> Where pale and wispy clouds were scudding.
> The swallows had departed,
> The migrant geese were here,
> And their honking shattered the night.

When the master and his attendants had been travelling
for several days they reached the city of Gongzhou, where all
the local officials were waiting to greet them and take them
into the city. After a night's rest they set out again the next
morning. They ate when they were hungry and drank when
they were thirsty, travelling by day and stopping at night. Two
or three days later they reached the garrison city of Hezhou,
which was on the frontier of the Great Tang Empire. The
garrison commander and the local Buddhist monks and priests
had all heard that the Master of the Law, the Imperial Younger
Brother, was going to the West on His Majesty's orders to see
the Buddha, so they were all very respectful. The Director
of Monks took him into the city, provided him with all he need-

ed, and invited him spend the night in the Fuyuan Monastery. All the monks of the monastery came to pay their respects to him, and when he had finished the meal they prepared for him he told his attendants to give the horse a good feed as they would be setting out before dawn. As soon as the cocks started to crow he called for his attendants, thus disturbing the monks, who brought him tea and food. When he had eaten he crossed the frontier.

In his impatience Sanzang had got up too soon. As it was late autumn the cocks had crowed very early, and it was still only about two in the morning. The three of them — four, including the horse — covered about a dozen miles through the frost, finding their way by the light of the moon, until they saw a large mountain in front of them. They had to push the undergrowth aside as they looked for their way, and the going was indescribably rough and difficult. Just when they were wondering whether they were lost, all three of them and the horse stumbled and fell into a pit. Sanzang was thrown into a panic, and his attendants were trembling with fear, when to add their terror they heard roars coming from further inside and loud shouts of , "Get 'em! Get 'em!" With a ferocious blast of wind a crowd of fifty or sixty fiends fell upon them and dragged them out. When the shivering and shaking Master of the Law took a stealthy look he saw a thoroughly evil demon king sitting above them. Truly he was

> *Mighty of stature,*
> *Ferocious of face.*
> *His eyes flashed like lightning;*
> *His thunderous voice shook the four quarters.*
>
> *Protruding, saw-edged teeth;*
> *Bared fangs like chisels.*
> *His body was clad in brocade,*
> *And his back was covered with its patterns.*
>
> *A beard of steel concealing his face;*
> *Hooked claws sharp as frost:*

> *The white-browed king of the southern mountain,*
> *Feared by the Yellow Lord of the Eastern Sea.*

The sight of him frightened Sanzang out of his wits and made his two attendants feel their bones turn to jelly and their muscles go numb. When the demon king roared out an order to tie them up the fiends bound them with rope. He was just on the point of devouring them when a great noise was heard outside and the arrival of Mountain Lord Bear and Hermit Ox was announced. Sanzang looked up and saw that one of them was a dark fellow. Can you imagine what he looked like?

> *A hero of great courage,*
> *Light and strong in body,*
> *Powerful in crossing rivers,*
> *Showing his awesome might as he runs through the woods.*
> *Always blessed with lucky dreams,*
> *He now revealed his unique valour.*
> *He could uproot and snap a green tree,*
> *And when he felt cold he could forecast the weather.*
> *Clearly he shows his miraculous powers,*
> *For which he is known as the Mountain Lord.*

Behind him Sanzang saw a fat man. Do you know what he looked like?

> *A hat with two towering horns,*
> *His shoulders squarely set.*
> *He liked to wear dull-coloured clothes,*
> *And his pace was always sluggish.*

> *His male ancestors were called Bull;*
> *His mother was known as Cow.*
> *As he could work for farmers,*
> *His name was Hermit Ox.*

When these two came swaggering in, the demon king rushed out to greet them. "General Yin," said Mountain Lord Bear, "I must congratulate you: you're always so successful." "General Yin," said Hermit Ox, "my felicitations on being ever-victorious." "How have things been with you two gentlemen recently?" asked the demon king. "Much as usual," replied Mountain Lord. "I get by," answered the Hermit. These preliminaries over, the three of them sat down to laugh and joke together.

Sanzang's two attendants meanwhile were howling pitifully in their bonds. "How did those three get here?" asked the dark fellow. "They delivered themselves to the front door," the demon king replied. "Will you be serving them to your friends?" asked the Hermit with a smile. "I should be honoured to," answered the demon king. "We won't need them all," remarked the Mountain Lord. "We could eat two and keep the third." With a "re-e-er" of obedience the demon king told his servants to cut open the two attendants, scoop their hearts out, and chop their bodies into mince. He presented the heads, hearts, and livers to his two guests, eating the limbs himself and dividing the rest of the flesh and bones among the fiends. All that could be heard was a crunching and a munching that sounded just like tigers devouring lambs, and in a few moments it had all been eaten up. Sanzang was almost dead with fright, yet this was only his first tribulation, coming so soon after leaving Chang'an.

In his despair he noticed that the east was beginning to grow light, and when dawn broke the two monsters left, saying, "We have been handsomely entertained today, and we shall repay your hospitality in full another day." With that they both rushed out. A moment later the red sun rose high in the sky, but Sanzang was too befuddled to know where he was. Just when all seemed lost, an old man appeared, walking towards him with the help of a stick. He came up to Sanzang, broke all his bonds with a wave of his hand, and revived him by blowing into his face. Sanzang fell to his knees and bowed low to him, saying, "Thank you, venerable ancient, for saving my humble life." The old man returned his bow and said, "Get up. Have you lost anything?" "My attendants have been eaten by monsters, and I don't know where my baggage or my horse is," replied Sanzang. The old man pointed with his stick and asked, "Isn't that a horse with two baggage-rolls over there?" When Sanzang turned round he saw that his things had not been lost after all, which somewhat relieved his anxiety. "Venerable sir," he asked, "what is this place, and how did you get here?" "This is the Double Forked Mountain, where tigers and leopards make their dens. How did you fall in here?" "I crossed the frontier at the garrison city of Hezhou at cock-crow, not realizing that I had got up too early," replied Sanzang. "Just as we were making our way through frost and dew we suddenly fell into this pit. A dreadfully ferocious demon king appeared and had me and my attendants tied up. Then a dark fellow called Mountain Lord Bear and a fat one called Hermit Ox came in, and they addressed the demon king as General Yin. The three of them ate up my two attendants, and their party only ended at dawn. I cannot imagine why I should have been fated with the good fortune of you coming to rescue me, venerable sir." "The Hermit is a wild bull spirit, the Mountain Lord is a bear spirit, and General Yin is a tiger spirit," the old man replied. "The fiends who serve him are mountain spirits, tree devils, monsters, and wolves. The reason they did not eat you was because your fundamental nature is enlightened. Come with me and I'll show you the way." Overcome with gratitude, Sanzang put the packs on his horse and led it by the bridle as he followed the old man out of the pit and on to the main road. Tying the horse to a bush beside the road, he turned round to bow low to the old man and thank him, but the old man changed into a puff of wind and rose into the sky on the back of a red-crested white crane. All that could be seen was a piece of paper drifting down in the wind with four lines of verse written on it:

> "I am the Great White Planet of the Western Heaven,
> Who came to save your life.
> In the journey ahead divine disciples will come to your
>   aid:
> Do not in your troubles blame the scriptures."

When he had read this Sanzang worshipped Heaven and said, "Many thanks, Planet, for delivering me from this danger." This done, he continued on his difficult journey, feeling very lonely as he led his horse along. On this mountain there were

Cold rains and winds howling in the trees,
Streams splashing noisily down gullies,
Fragrant wild flowers,
Screens of rocks and boulders.
Deer and ape made raucous howls,
Roebuck and muntjac ran in herds.
Many were the songs of birds.
But there was no trace of man.
The abbot
Was trembling and uneasy;
His horse
Could barely lift its hoofs.

Sanzang did not spare himself as he pressed ahead amid the mountain peaks. He had been going for many hours without seeing any sign of a human house; he was hungry and finding the going heavy. Just at this critical moment he saw in front of him a pair of ferocious tigers roaring, while two long snakes were coiled up behind him. To his left were venomous reptiles, and to his right were terrible monsters. Being by himself and unable to think of a way out, Sanzang prepared to abandon his mind and body and let Heaven do as it would. Besides, the horse's back was now so tired and its legs so bent that it fell to its knees on the ground and collapsed. Sanzang could not move it, either by blows or by dragging at its bridle. The poor Master of the Law, who had nowhere to shelter, was feeling thoroughly wretched, convinced that nothing could save him from death. But when his troubles were at their worst someone came to his rescue. Just when all seemed lost he saw the venomous reptiles and the evil monsters flee, while the tigers and the snakes hid themselves. Sanzang looked up and saw a man coming across the hillside with a steel trident in his hand and bow and arrows at his waist. Just look and see what a fine chap he was:

> *On his head*
> *A leopardskin hat with artemisia patterns;*
> *On his body*
> *A coat of woollen cloth.*
> *Round his waist was tied a lion belt,*
> *On his feet a pair of deerskin boots.*
> *His eyes bulged like a hanged man's;*
> *His curly beard was like the evil god.*
> *From his waist hung a bow with poisoned arrows;*
> *And in his hand was a steel-tipped trident.*
> *The thunder of his voice would make a wild beast trem-*
> *ble,*
> *And his ferocity terrified the pheasants.*

Seeing him approach, Sanzang knelt down beside the path, put his hands together, and shouted at the top of his voice, "Spare me, bandit king, spare me." The man went over to him, put down his trident, and raised him to his feet. "Don't be frightened, venerable monk," he said, "I'm not a bad man; I'm a hunter who lives in these mountains. My name is Liu Boqin and I am known as the warden of the mountain. I came along here because I wanted a couple of animals for the pot. I never expected to meet you here — I must have offended you." "I am a monk sent by the Emperor of the Great Tang to visit the Buddha in the Western Heaven and ask for the scriptures," Sanzang replied. "I had just got here when I found myself completely surrounded by wolves, tigers, snakes and other creatures, which meant that I could go no further. Then suddenly you appeared, High Warden, and saved my life. Thank you very much indeed." "Those of us who live here," replied Liu Boqin, "can only support ourselves by killing tigers and wolves, and catching snakes and other reptiles, which is why all those animals fled in terror from me. As you are from the Tang Empire, we are compatriots. This is still the territory of the Great Tang, and I am a Tang citizen. Both of us depend

on the emperor's lands and rivers for our food and drink, and
we are fellow-countrymen, so there is nothing to fear. You must
come with me to my hut, and your horse can rest. I'll take
you on your way tomorrow." Sanzang, who was delighted to
hear this, thanked him and went along behind him, leading the
horse.

When they had crossed the mountainside they heard a sound
like the howling of a wind. "Sit down here and don't move,
venerable monk," said Boqin. "That noise like a wind means
that a mountain cat is coming. Just wait a moment while I
catch it, then I can take it home to feed you with." This news
so terrified Sanzang that he dared not move. The high warden
was striding forward, brandishing his trident, to meet the
animal, when a striped tiger appeared in front of him. At the
sight of Liu Boqin the animal turned to flee, but the high
warden let out a thunderclap of a shout: "Where d'you think
you're going, wretch?" When the tiger realized that Liu Boqin
was in hot pursuit, it turned and charged him, baring its claws.
The high warden raised his trident to meet his opponent. At the
sight of all this Sanzang collapsed on the grass, paralyzed with
fear; never had he seen anything so terrifying in all his born
days. The tiger and the high warden fought a magnificent battle
under the mountain:

> *Bursting with anger,*
> *Mad with rage.*
> *Bursting with anger,*
> *The warden bristled, immensely strong.*
> *Mad with rage,*
> *The striped tiger snorted out red dust as it showed its*
>   *might.*
> *One bared its teeth and brandished its claws,*
> *The other twisted and turned.*
> *The trident thrust against the heavens and blotted out*
>   *the sun;*
> *The patterned tail stirred up mist and clouds.*
> *One made wild stabs at the chest,*

The other struck at the head.
To avoid the blows was to win a new life;
A hit was an appointment with the King of Hell.
All that could be heard was the tiger bellowing
And the high warden shouting.
When the tiger bellowed,
Mountains and rivers split open, to the terror of birds
    and beasts.
At the high warden's shouts,
The sky was parted and the stars revealed.
The tiger's golden eyes were bulging with fury,
The hunter's valiant heart was full of wrath.
How admirable was high warden Liu of the mountain,
How splendid the lord of the beasts of the land.
As man and tiger fought for victory
Whoever weakened would lose his life.

After the pair of them had been fighting for about two hours the tiger's claws began to slacken as it grew tired, and just then the high warden smote him full in the chest with his trident. Its points pierced the animal's liver and heart, a pitiful sight. Within an instant the ground was covered with its blood as the hunter dragged it along the path by its ears. What a man! Without panting, and with his expression unchanged, he said to Sanzang, "What a piece of luck. This mountain cat will be enough to feed you for a whole day." Sanzang was full of praise for him. "High Warden, you really are a mountain god." "It was nothing," said Liu Boqin, "so please don't exaggerate. This is all the result of your blessings. Come on, let's skin it and boil up some of its meat as soon as we can so as to get you fed." Holding his trident in one hand and dragging the tiger with the other he led the way, while Sanzang followed, leading his horse. As they wound their way across the mountain, a cottage suddenly came into view. In front of its gate there were:

Ancient trees reaching to the sky,
Wild creepers covering the path.
Cool were the wind and dust in the valleys,

Strange vapours coiled around the cliffs.
The scent of wild flowers was all along the path,
Deep, deep the green of the bamboos.
A thatched gatehouse,
A fenced yard,
Both pretty as a picture.
A stone bridge,
Whitewashed mud walls:
A rare and charming sight.
The loneliness of autumn,
Airy isolation.
Yellow leaves lay fallen beside the path,
White clouds drifted above the peaks.
Mountain birds sang in the woods
While a puppy barked outside the gate.

When he reached the gate, the high warden Liu Boqin threw down the tiger and shouted, "Where are you, lads?" Three or four servants of strange and repulsive appearance came out, and with much pulling and tugging they carried the tiger in. Boqin told them to skin it at once and prepare it to offer to their guest, then turned round to welcome Sanzang in. When they had formally greeted each other Sanzang bowed to Boqin to thank him for taking pity on him and saving his life. "Why bother to thank me? We're fellow countrymen." When Sanzang had been offered a seat and served with tea, an old woman came out to greet him followed by a young one. Liu Boqin explained that they were his mother and his wife. "Madam, please take the highest seat while I bow to you," said Sanzang. "You are a guest from afar, venerable monk, so let us each preserve our dignity and neither bow to the other," the old woman replied. "Mother," said Liu Boqin, "he has been sent by His Majesty the Tang Emperor to go to the Westen Heaven to see the Buddha and fetch the scriptures. I met him on the mountain, and I thought that as we were fellow-countrymen I should invite him home to rest before I take him on his way tomorrow." The old woman was delighted. "Good, good," she said. "But it would be even better to ask him to stay longer. Tomorrow is the an-

niversary of your father s passing away, and I would like to
trouble the venerable monk to say some prayers and read a
sutra for him; you could take him on his way the day after."
Although this Boqin was a tiger-killer and the high warden of
the mountain, he was a dutiful son, and when he heard this suggestion he made ready paper money and incense and asked Sanzang to stay.

While they talked they had not noticed the evening drawing
in. The servants set out a table and stools, then brought in
several dishes of tender tiger-meat, which they placed steaming
hot on the table. Liu Boqin asked Sanzang to help himself while
he served the rice. Putting his hands together in front of his
chest, Sanzang replied, "This is wonderful, but I must tell you
frankly that I have been a monk ever since I left my mother's
womb, so I am quite unable to eat meat." Boqin thought for
a while before replying, "Venerable monk, our family has not
eaten vegetarian food for generations. When we cut bamboo
shoots, pick fungus, gather wild vegetables for drying, or make
bean-curd we always cook them in the fat of roebuck, deer, tiger
or leopard, so even they aren't really vegetarian; and our two
cooking pots are steeped in fat, so what are we to do? I'm
afraid it was wrong of me to ask you here." "There's no need
to worry," Sanzang answered. "Please go ahead and eat. I'd
go without food for four or five days, or even starve, rather than
break the monastic rule about vegetarian food." "But we can't
have you starving to death," protested Liu Boqin. "Thanks to
your great kindness, High Warden, I was saved from the packs
of tigers and wolves. Even if I were to starve to death, it
would be better than providing a meal for tigers." Liu Boqin's
mother, who had been listening to their conversation, said,
"Don't talk nonsense, son. I've got some vegetarian things that
we can offer to him." "Where did you get them from?" Liu Boqin asked, to which mother replied, "Never you mind how, but
I've got them." She told her daughter-in-law to take down the
little cooking-pot, burn the fat out of it, scrub it and wash it
several times over, then put it back on the stove. Then they
half filled it with boiling water that they threw away Next

she poured boiling water on mountain-elm leaves to make tea,
boiled up some millet, and cooked some dried vegetables. This
was then all put into two bowls and set on the table. Then
the old woman said to Sanzang, "Please eat, venerable monk.
This is completely pure tea and food that I and my daughter-
in-law have prepared." Sanzang thanked them and sat down
in the seat of honour. Another place was laid for Liu Boqin,
where were set out bowls and dishes full of the meat of tiger,
roebuck, snake, fox, and hare, as well as dried venison, all cooked without salt or sauce, which he was going to eat while San
zang had his vegetarian meal. He had just sat down and was on
the point of picking up his chopsticks when he noticed Sanzang
put his hands together to recite some scripture, which so alarmed him that instead of picking up his chopsticks he stood beside
him. When Sanzang had recited a few lines he urged Boqin to
eat. "Are you a short-sutra monk then?" Boqin asked. "That
wasn't a sutra, it was a grace before eating." "You monks are
very particular. Fancy reciting sutras at mealtimes," was Boqin's
comment.

When the meal was over and the dishes had been cleared
away, Liu Boqin invited Sanzang out into the gathering darkness
for a stroll at the back. They went along an alley and came
to a thatched hut. On pushing the door open and going in
Sanzang saw bows and crossbows hanging on the walls and
quivers filled with arrows. From the beams were slung two
gory and stinking tiger-skins, and at the foot of the wall were
stood many spears, swords, tridents and clubs. In the middle
were two seats. Liu Boqin urged Sanzang to sit down, but
Sanzang could not bear to stay there long among the horrifying
filth, and so he went outside. Going further to the back they
came to a large garden full of clumps of yellow chrysanthemums
and red maple-trees. Then with a whinnying noise about a doz-
en plump deer and a large herd of roebuck ran out; they were
docile and unfrightened on seeing humans. "Were those roebuck
and deer raised by you?" asked Sanzang. "Yes," replied Boqin.
"When you Chang'an people have some money you buy valua-
bles, and when you have land you accumulate grain; but we

hunters can only keep a few wild animals for a rainy day." Dusk had fallen unnoticed as the two of them talked, and now they went back to the house to sleep.

Early the next morning the whole family, young and old, got up and prepared vegetarian food for the monk, and then they asked him to start reciting sutras. Sanzang washed his hands, went to the family shrine of the high warden, burned incense there, and worshipped, then beat his "wooden fish" as he recited first a prayer to purify his mouth, then a holy spell to purify his body and mind, and finally the *Sutra to Deliver the Dead*. When he had finished, Boqin asked him to write out a letter of introduction for the dead man and also recite the *Diamond Sutra* and the *Guanyin Sutra*. Sanzang recited them in a loud, clear voice and then ate lunch, after which he read out the several chapters of the *Lotus Sutra*, the *Amitabha Sutra*, as well as one chapter of the *Peacock Sutra* and told the story of the cleansing of the bhikshu. By now it was dark, and when they had burned all kinds of incense, paper money, and paper horses for all the gods, and the letter of introduction for the dead man, the service was over and everyone went to bed and slept soundly.

The soul of Boqin's father, now delivered from being a ghost of perdition, drowned in the sea of suffering, came to the house that night and appeared in a dream to everyone in the family. "I suffered long in the underworld, unable to find deliverance," he said, "but now that the saintly monk has wiped out my sins by reading some scriptures. King Yama has had me sent back to the rich land of China to be reborn in an important family. You must reward him generously, and no half measures. Now I'm going." Indeed,

> Great is the significance of the majestic Law,
> That saves the dead from suffering and perdition.

When they all awoke from their dreams, the sun had already risen in the east. Boqin's wife said, "Warden, your father came to me in a dream last night. He said that he had suffered long in the underworld, and couldn't find deliverance. Now that the saintly monk has wiped out his sins by reading some scriptures, King Yama has had him sent back to the rich land of China to be reborn in an important family. He told us to thank him generously, and no half measures. When he'd said this he went out through the door and drifted away. He didn't answer when I called, and I couldn't make him stay. Then I woke up and realized that it was a dream." "I had a dream just like yours," replied Liu Boqin. "Let's go and tell mother about it." As they were on the point of doing this they heard his mother shout, "Come here, Boqin my son. There's something I want to tell you." The two of them went in to her to find the old woman sitting on the bed. "My child, I had a happy dream last night. Your father came home and said that thanks to his salvation by the venerable monk, his sins have been wiped out and he has gone to be reborn in an important family in the rich land of China." Husband and wife laughed for joy and her son said, "I and my wife both had this dream, and we were just coming to tell you when you called to us. So now it turns out that you had it too." They told everyone in the house to get up to thank Sanzang and get his horse loaded and ready. They all bowed to him and he said, "Many thanks, venerable monk, for recommending my father for delivery from his sufferings and for rebirth. We can never repay this debt of gratitude." "What powers have I that you should thank me?" replied Sanzang.

Boqin told him about what the three of them had been told in their dreams, and Sanzang was happy too. Then they gave him his breakfast and an ounce of silver as an expression of their thanks, but he would not take a single penny of it, although the whole family begged and beseeched him to do so. "If in your mercy you could escort me for the next stage of my journey I would be deeply touched," he said. All that Boqin, his mother, and his wife could do then was to prepare some scones of coarse wheaten flour as his provisions, and make sure that Boqin escorted him a long way. Sanzang gladly accepted the food. On his mother's orders the high warden told two or three servants to bring hunting gear as they set off together along the road. They saw no end of wild mountain scenery.

When they had been travelling for some time they saw a mountain in front of them, a high and precipitous one that towered right up to the azure sky. Before long they had reached its base. The high warden climbed it as if he were walking on level ground, and when they were half-way over it he turned round, stood beside the path and said, "Venerable monk, I must ask you to take yourself on from here. I have to go back." On hearing this Sanzang tumbled out of his saddle to say, "Please, please, take me another stage, High Warden." "You don't seem to know that this is called Double Boundary Mountain," said the high warden. The eastern part belongs to our Great Tang, but the western part is Tatar territory. The tigers and wolves on that side are not subject to my control, which is why I can't cross the boundary. You must go on by yourself." The monk was so alarmed to hear this that he waved his arms around and grabbed hold of the hunter's clothes and sleeves, weeping and refusing to let him go. When at last Sanzang was bowing repeatedly to the hunter to take his leave, a shout like thunder came from under the mountain: "My master's come, my master's come." Sanzang stood frozen with fear at the sound of it, and Boqin had to hold him up. If you don't know who it was who shouted, listen to the explanatoin in the next instalment.

CHAPTER FOURTEEN

The mind-ape returns to truth;
The six bandits disappear without trace.

Buddha is the mind, the mind is Buddha:
Mind and Buddha have always needed things.
When you know that there are no things and no mind
Then you are a Buddha with a true mind and a Dharma
    body.

A Dharma-bodied Buddha has no form;
A single divine light contains the ten thousand images.
The bodiless body is the true body,
The imageless image is the real image.

It is not material, not empty, and not non-empty;
It does not come or go, nor does it return.
It is not different nor the same, it neither is nor isn't.
It can't be thrown away or caught, nor seen or heard.

The inner and outer divine light are everywhere the
    same;
A Buddha-kingdom can be found in a grain of sand.
A grain of sand can hold a thousand worlds;
In a single body and mind, all dharmas are the same.

For wisdom, the secret of no-mind is essential,
To be unsullied and unobstructed is to be pure of karma.
When you do no good and do no evil,
You become a Kasyapa Buddha.

The terror-stricken Liu Boqin and Sanzang then heard another shout of "My master's come." "That must be the old monkey who lives in a stone cell under this mountain shouting," said the servants. "Yes, yes," said the high warden. "What old

261

monkey?" asked Sanzang, and the high warden replied, "This mountain used to be called Five Elements Mountain, and its name was only changed to Double Boundary Mountain when our Great Tang Emperor fought his western campaign to pacify the country. I once heard an old man say that in the days when Wang Mang usurped the Han throne, Heaven sent down this mountain and crushed a monkey under it. This monkey doesn't mind heat or cold and neither eats nor drinks. He's guarded by a local tutelary god who gives him iron pellets when he's hungry and molten copper when he's thirsty. Although he's been there since ancient times, he hasn't died of cold or hunger. It must have been him shouting; there's nothing for you to be afraid of, venerable sir. Let's go down and have a look." Sanzang had to follow him, leading his horse down the mountain. A mile or two later they saw that there really was a monkey poking out his head out of a stone cell, and making desperate gestures with his outstretched hands as he shouted, "Master, why didn't you come before? Thank goodness you're here, thank goodness. If you get me out of here I guarantee that you'll reach the Western Heaven." Do you know what the venerable monk saw when he went forward for a closer look?

> *A pointed mouth and sunken cheeks,*
> *Fiery eyes with golden pupils.*
> *His head was thick with moss,*
> *And climbing figs grew from his ears.*
> *By his temples grew little hair but plentiful grass,*
> *Under his chin there was sedge instead of a beard.*
> *Dirt between his eyebrows,*
> *And mud on his nose*
> *Made him an utter mess;*
> *On his coarse fingers*
> *And thick palms*
> *Was filth in plenty.*
> *He was so happy that he rolled his eyes*
> *And made pleasant noises.*
> *Although his tongue was nimble,*

He could not move his body.
He was the Great Sage of five hundred years ago,
Who today ended his suffering and escaped the net of Heaven.

High Warden Liu showed great courage in going up to him, pulling away the grass that was growing beside his temples and the sedge under his chin, and asking, "What have you got to say?" "I've got nothing to say," the monkey replied. "You just tell that monk to come over here while I ask him a question." "What question do you want to ask me?" said Sanzang. "Are you the fellow sent to the Western Heaven by the emperor of the East to fetch the scriptures?" asked the monkey. "Yes, I am," Sanzang replied. "Why do you ask?" "I am the Great Sage Equalling Heaven who wrecked the Heavenly Palace five hundred years ago. The Lord Buddha put me under this mountain for my criminal insubordination. Some time ago the Bodhisattva Guanyin went to the East on the Buddha's orders to find someone who could fetch the scriptures. When I asked her to save me she told me that I was to give up evil-doing, return to the Buddha's Law, and do all I could to protect the traveller when he went to the Western Paradise to worship Buddha and fetch the scriptures; she said that there'll be something in it for me when that's done. Ever since then I've been waiting day and night with eager anticipation for you to come and save me, Master. I swear to protect you on your way to fetch the scriptures and to be your disciple." Sanzang, delighted to hear this, said, "Although you now have these splendid intentions and wish to become a monk thanks to the teaching of the Bodhisattva, I've no axe or chisel, so how am I to get you out?" "There's no need for axes or chisels. As long as you're willing to save me, I can get myself out," the monkey replied. "I'm willing to save you," Sanzang said, "but how are you going to get out?" "On the top of this mountain there is a detention order by the Tathagata Buddha written in letters of gold. If you climb the mountain and tear it off, I'll be straight out." Accepting his suggestion. Sanzang turned round to ask Liu Boqin if

he would go up the mountain with him. "I don't know whether he's telling the truth or not," said Boqin, at which the
monkey shouted at the top of his voice, "It's true.   I wouldn't
dare lie about that." So Liu Boqin told his servants to lead
the horse while he helped Sanzang up the mountain. By hanging
on to creepers they managed to reach the summit, where they
saw a myriad beams of golden light and a thousand wisps of
propitious vapour coming from a large, square rock on which
was pasted a paper seal bearing the golden words *Om mani
padme hum*. Sanzang went up and knelt down before the rock,
then read the golden words and bowed his head to the ground
a number of times. He looked to the west and prayed, "I am the
believer Chen Xuanzang sent on imperial orders to fetch the
scriptures. If I am fated to have a disciple, may I be able to tear
off the golden words and release the divine monkey to come with
me to the Vulture Peak. If I am not fated to have a disciple,
and this monkey is an evil monster who has deceived me and will
do me no good, then may I be unable to remove it." When he
had prayed he bowed again, after which he went up and gently
tore the paper seal off. A scented wind blew in his face and
carried the paper up into the sky as a voice called, "I am the
Great Sage's guard. Now that his sufferings are over I am going
back to see the Tathagata and hand in this seal." The startled
Sanzang, Liu Boqin, and the rest of them all bowed to Heaven,
then went down the mountain to the stone cell, where they said
to the monkey, "The restriction order has been torn off, so you
can come out." The delighted monkey said, "Master, please
stand well clear so that I don't give you a fright when I come
out."

On hearing this Liu Boqin took Sanzang and the rest of
them to the east, and when they had covered some two or three
miles they heard the monkey shout, "Further, further!" So Sanzang went much further until he was off the mountain.   Then
there was a great noise as the mountain split open. As they
were all shaking with terror, the monkey appeared kneeling
stark naked in front of Sanzang's horse and saying, "Master,
I'm out." He bowed four times to Sanzang, then jumped up,

addressed Liu Boqin with a respectful noise, and said, "Thank you, elder brother, for escorting my master, and thank you too for weeding the grass off my face." He then picked up the luggage and put it on the horse's back. At the sight of him the horse felt so weak and trembling that it could not stay on its feet. Because the monkey had once been the Protector of the Horses and looked after the dragon steeds of Heaven, and mortal horses were terrified at the very sight of him.

Seeing that his intentions were indeed good and that he really was now a Buddhist, Sanzang asked him what was his surname. "My surname's Sun," replied the Monkey King. "I'll give you a Buddhist name that I can call you by," said Sanzang. "There's no need to trouble yourself," said the Monkey King, "I've already got one: Sun Wukong — Monkey Awakened to Emptiness." "That's just right for our sect," exclaimed the monk. "As you look so much like a young novice, I'll give you another name and call you Brother Monkey. Is that all right?" "Yes, yes, yes," said Sun Wukong, and from then on he was also called Brother Monkey, or Sun the Novice.

When he saw that Brother Monkey was determined to go, the high warden turned to Sanzang, chanted a noise of respect and said, "It's splendid that you have got so good a disciple, venerable sir. He'll certainly make the journey. I must now take my leave." Sanzang bowed to him in thanks, saying, "I have brought you a long way, and am deeply indebted to you. When you return home please convey my respects to your venerable mother and your wife; I caused them a lot of trouble, and hope that I shall be able to come and thank them on my return." Boqin returned his bow, and with that they parted.

Brother Monkey asked Sanzang to mount the horse while he ambled ahead, stark naked, carrying the luggage on his back. Before long they were over the Double Boundary Mountain.

Suddenly a ferocious tiger rushed at them, roaring and lashing about with its tail. Sanzang on his horse was terrified. Brother Monkey, who was standing beside the path, put down the luggage and said happily, "Don't be scared, Master, it's just bringing me my clothes." He pulled a needle out of his ear and shook it in the wind, turning it into an iron cudgel as thick as a bowl. "I haven't used this little treasure in over five hundred years," he said, holding it in his hand. "Today I'm bringing it out to get myself some clothes to wear." Just watch as he rushes at the tiger, shouting, "Where d'you think you're going, wretch?" The tiger crouched in the dust, not daring to move, as the cudgel smashed into its head. Thousands of drops of red brain and many a pearly piece of tooth flew everywhere, so terrifying Sanzang that he fell out of the saddle, biting on his finger and crying, "Heavens, the high warden had to fight for ages before killing the striped tiger the other day, but this Sun Wukong has smashed a tiger to pulp with a single blow. He really is a tough's tough."

"Sit down for a moment, Master, while I strip the clothes off him to wear on the journey," said Brother Monkey as he dragged the tiger over. "But he hasn't got any clothes," Sanzang protested. "Don't bother yourself about it, I know how to cope." The splendid Monkey King pulled a hair from his body, breathed some magic breath on it, and said "Change!", on which it turned into a pointed knife shaped like a cow's ear. Cutting into the skin on the tiger's belly, he took it all off in a single stroke, chopped off the head and claws, then held up the square hide to get an idea of its size. "It's on the big side," he said, "so I could make two kilts out of it," and with these words he took his knife and cut it in two. One piece he put away, and the other he wrapped round his waist to cover the lower half of his body and tied firmly with a creeper he pulled down from beside the path. "Let's go on, Master, let's go on," he said. "The sewing can wait till we reach a house where we can borrow a needle and thread." He pinched his iron cudgel to make it as small as a needle again, put it back in his ear, took the luggage on his back, and asked Sanzang to mount the horse.

As the two of them went along the venerable monk asked from the horse's back, "Wukong, why has the iron cudgel you used to kill the tiger disappeared?" "What you don't know, Master," replied Brother Monkey with a laugh, "is that I got it from the dragon palace of the Eastern Sea, and that it's called

the 'Magic Iron to Hold the Bed of the Milky Way in Place'
or 'As-You-Will Gold-Banded Cudgel'. When I raised my
great rebellion against the Heavenly Palace in the old days it
served me well. It can change into anything and be whatever
size I want it to be. Just now I turned it into an embroidery
needle and put it away in my ear. I only take it out when I
need it." Concealing his delight at hearing this, Sanzang went
on to ask, "Why didn't that tiger move when it saw you? Why
on earth did it let you hit it?" "I can tell you in all truthfulness,
Master, that not just tigers but even dragons have to be on
their best behaviour when they meet me. I know a few tricks
for putting them in their place and have the power to make
rivers run backwards and stir up the seas. I can tell what things
are really like from appearances alone, and sort out the truth
behind what is said. When I want to make myself big I measure
myself against the universe, and when I shrink I can be held
on a downy hair. There's no limit to the transformations I can
perform, and nobody can tell when I'm going to vanish or when
I'm going to reappear. There was nothing wonderful about
skinning that tiger. Wait till I show you a thing or two." This
took a great load off Sanzang's mind, and he whipped his horse
on. As master and disciple went along their way talking together, the sun was sinking in the west, and they saw:

> In the fiery glow of the setting sun
> The clouds return to ends of the sky and the sea.
> The birds on a thousand mountains chirrup and call,
> Flying in flocks to the woods for the night.
>
> The wild beasts go two by two;
> All species return to their dens.
> A crescent moon breaks through the dusk,
> As countless points of starlight shimmer.

"You must hurry up, Master, as it's late," said Monkey.
"There must be a house in that clump of trees over there, so
let's get there as soon as possible to settle down for the night."
Sanzang whipped on his horse and galloped to the house, where
he dismounted. Brother Monkey put down the luggage, went

up to the gate, and shouted, "Open up, open up." An old man came out, leaning on a bamboo stick, and the gate creaked as he opened it. At the sight of Monkey's ugly face and the tiger-skin wrapped around him, which made him look like the god of thunder, the old man was so terrified that his legs turned to jelly and his body went numb. "A devil.... A devil," he muttered deliriously. Sanzang went up to support him, saying, "Don't be afraid, aged benefactor. He's no devil, he's my disciple." When the old man looked up and saw Sanzang's pure face he felt steady on his feet at once, and he asked what monastery Sanzang was from, and why had he brought that evil- looking creature to his house. "I come from the Tang Court," said Sanzang, "and I am going to the Western Heaven to visit the Buddha and ask for the scriptures. As we were passing this way at nightfall we came to your mansion, good benefactor, to ask for a night's lodging. We shall be off before dawn tomorrow. I very much hope that you will be able to help us." "You may be a Tang man," the old fellow replied, "but that ugly brute certainly isn't." "You've got no eyes in your head, you silly old man," shrieked Brother Monkey. "He's my master and I'm his disciple. I'm no Tang man or Spike man, I'm the Great Sage Equalling Heaven. Some of the people who live in this house must know me, and I've seen you before." "Where've you seen me?" the old man asked. "Didn't you gather firewood in front of my face and pick wild vegetables from my cheeks when you were a child?" said Sun Wukong. "Rubbish," retorted the old man. "Where did you live and where did I live when I was supposed to gather firewood and wild vegetables in front of your face?"

"It's you who's talking rubbish, my child," replied Sun Wukong. "You don't know who I am, but I'm the Great Sage from the stone cell under the Double Boundary Mountain. Take another look and see if you can recognize me now." The old man at last realized who he was and said, "I suppose you do look a bit like him, but however did you get out?" Sun Wukong told him the whole story of how the Bodhisattva had converted him and told him to wait till the Tang Priest came to take off the seal and release him. Then the old man went down on his knees and bowed his head, inviting the Tang Priest inside and calling his wife and children to come and meet him; they were all very happy when they heard what had happened. When they had drunk tea he asked Sun Wukong, "How old are you, Great Sage?" "How old are you, then?" said Sun Wukong. "In my senile way I have reached a hundred and thirty." "Then you could be my remote descendant," said Brother Monkey. "I can't remember when I was born, but I spent over five hundred years under that mountain." "True, true," remarked the old man, "I remember my grandfather saying that this mountain fell from heaven to crush a magical monkey, and you weren't able to get out before now. When I saw you in my childhood, grass grew on your head and there was mud on your face, so I wasn't afraid of you. But now that the mud and grass have gone you look thinner, and the tiger-skin round your waist makes you as near a devil as makes no difference."

This conversation made everyone roar with laughter, and as he was a kind old man he had a vegetarian meal set out. When the meal was over Sanzang asked him his surname. "Chen," the old man replied. On hearing this, Sanzang raised his hands in greeting and said, "Venerable benefactor, you are of the same clan as myself." "Master," protested Brother Monkey, "you're called Tang, aren't you, so how can you belong to the same clan as him?" "My secular surname is Chen, and I am from Juxian Village, Hongnong Prefecture, Haizhou, in the Tang Empire. My Buddhist name is Chen Xuanzang. But as our Great Tang Emperor Taizong called me his younger brother and gave me the surname Tang, I am known as the Tang Priest." The old fellow was delighted to hear that they shared a surname. "Chen, old fellow," said Monkey, "I'm afraid this will be putting your family out, but I haven't washed for over five hundred years, so could you go and boil up some water for me and my master to have a bath before we set out again? Thank you." The old man gave instructions for water to be boiled and a tub brought, and he lit the lamp. When master and disciple had bathed they sat down by the lamp, and Brother Monkey asked once more, "Old Chen, there's another thing I'd like to ask you: could you lend me a needle and thread?" "Yes, of course," the old man replied, sending his wife to fetch them and then handing them to Monkey. Monkey's sharp eyes had observed his master take off a short white cotton tunic, which he did not put on again, so Monkey grabbed it and put it on himself. Then he took off his tiger skin, joined it up with a pleat, wrapped it round his waist again, tied it with a creeper, went up to his master, and asked, "How would you say these clothes compared with what I was wearing before?" "Splendid, splendid," replied Sanzang, "it makes you look quite like a real monk. If you don't mind cast-offs," he added, "you can go on wearing that tunic." Sun Wukong chanted a "re-e-er" of obedience and thanked him, then went off to find some hay for the horse. When all the jobs were finished, master and disciple went to bed.

Early the next morning Sun Wukong woke up and asked his master to set out. Sanzang dressed and told Monkey to pack the bedding and the rest of the luggage. They were just on the point of leaving when the old man appeared. He had prepared hot water for washing as well as breakfast. After breakfast they set out, Sanzang riding the horse and Brother Monkey leading. They ate when they were hungry and drank when they were thirsty, travelling by day and resting by night. Thus they went on until they realized it was early winter.

> When the frost destroys the red leaves the woods are
>   sparse;
> On the ridge only pine and cypress flourish.
> The unopened plum buds exhale a dark perfume,
> Warming the short days,
> A touch of spring.
> When the chrysanthemum and lotus is finished, the wild
>   camellia blossoms.
>
> By the cold bridge and the ancient trees the birds quar-
>   rel for branches.
> In the twisting gully the waters of the spring run low,

Pale snow clouds drift across the sky.
The north wind blows strong,
Tugging at your sleeves:
Who can bear the cold towards evening?

When master and disciple had been travelling for a long time they heard a whistle from beside the path, and six men rushed out with spears, swords, cutlasses, and strongbows. "Where do you think you're going, monk?" they roared. "If you give us your horse and luggage we'll spare your life." Sanzang fell from his horse, scared out of his wits and unable to utter a word. Brother Monkey helped him to his feet and said, "Dont worry, Master, it's nothing serious. They've come to bring us some clothes and our travelling expenses." "Are you deaf, Wukong?" the other asked. "They told us to give them our horse and luggage, so how can you ask them for clothes and money?" "You look after the clothes, the luggage and the horse while I go and have a bash at them. We'll see what happens." "A good hand is no match for two fists," said Sanzang, "and a pair of fists is no match for four hands. They are six big men against little you, all by yourself. You can't possibly have the nerve to fight them."

The brave Brother Monkey did not stop to argue. Instead he stepped forward, folded his arms across his chest, bowed to the six bandits and said, "Why are you gentlemen obstructing our way?" "We are mighty robber kings, benevolent lords of the mountain. We have been very famous for a long time, although you don't seem to have heard of us. If you abandon your things at once, we'll let you go on your way; but if there's even a hint of a 'no' from you, we'll turn your flesh into mincemeat and your bones into powder." "I too am a hereditary robber king, and have ruled a mountain for many years, but I've never heard of you gentlemen." "Since you don't know our names, I'll tell them to you: Eye-seeing Happiness, Ear-hearing Anger, Nose-smelling Love, Tongue-tasting Thought, Mindborn Desire, and Body-based Sorrow." Sun Wukong laughed at them. "You're just a bunch of small-time crooks. You can't see that I'm your lord and master although I'm a monk, and you have the effrontery to get in our way. Bring out all the jewels you've stolen, and the seven of us can share them out equally. I'll let you off with that." This made the bandits happy, angry, loving, thoughtful, desirous, and sorrowful respectively, and they all charged him, yelling, "You've got a nerve, monk. You've got nothing to put in the kitty, but you want to share our stuff." Waving their spears and swords they rushed him, hacking wildly at his face. Seventy or eighty blows crashed down on him, but he simply stood in the middle of them, ignoring everything. "What a monk!" the bandits said. "He's a real tough nut." "I can get by reasonably well," said Brother Monkey with a smile. "Your hands must be tired after all that bashing. Now it's my turn to bring out my needle for a bit of fun." "This monk must have been an acupuncturist" said the bandits. "There's nothing wrong with us. Why is he talking about needles?"

Taking the embroidery needle from his ear, Brother Monkey shook it in the wind, at which it became an iron cudgel as thick as a ricebowl. With this in his hand he said, "Stick around while I try my cudgel out." The terrified bandits tried to flee in all directions, but Monkey raced after them, caught them all up, and killed every one of them. Then he stripped the clothes off them, took their money, and went back with his face wreathed in smiles. "Let's go, Master; I've wiped those bandits out," he said. "Even though they were highwaymen, you're really asking for trouble," Sanzang replied. "Even if they had been arrested and handed over to the authorities, they wouldn't have been sentenced to death. You may know a few tricks, but it would be better if you'd simply driven them away. Why did you have to kill them all? Even taking a man's life by accident is enough to stop someone from becoming a monk. A person who enters the religious life

> *Spares the ants when he sweeps the floor,*
> *Covers the lamps to save the moth.*

What business did you have to slaughter the lot of them, without caring which of them were the guilty and which were innocent?

You haven't a shred of compassion or goodness in you. This time it happened in the wilds, where nobody will be able to trace the crime. Say someone offended you in a city and you turned murderous there. Say you killed and wounded people when you went berserk with that club of yours. I myself would be involved even though I'm quite innocent." "But if I hadn't killed them, they'd have killed you, Master," protested Sun Wukong. "I am a man of religion, and I would rather die than commit murder," said Sanzang. "Had I died, there'd only have been me dead, but you killed six of them, which was an absolute outrage. If the case were taken to court, you couldn't talk your way out of this even if the judge were your own father." "To tell you the truth, Master, I don't know how many people I killed when I was the monster who ruled the Mountain of Flowers and Fruit," said Sun Wukong, "but if I'd acted your way I'd never have become the Great Sage Equalling Heaven." "It was precisely because you acted with such tyrannical cruelty among mortals and committed the most desperate crimes against Heaven that you got into trouble five hundred years ago," retorted Sanzang. "But now you have entered the faith, you'll never reach the Western Heaven and never become a monk if you don't give up your taste for murder. You're too evil, too evil."

Monkey, who had never let himself be put upon, flared up at Sanzang's endless nagging. "If you say that I'll never become a monk and won't ever reach the Western Heaven, then stop going on at me like that. I'm going back." Before Sanzang could reply, Monkey leapt up in a fury, shouting, "I'm off." Sanzang looked up quickly, but he was already out of sight. All that could be heard was a whistling sound coming from the east. Left on his own, the priest nodded and sighed to himself with great sadness and indignation. "The incorrigible wretch," he reflected. "Fancy disappearing and going back home like that just because I gave him a bit of a telling-off. So that's that. I must be fated to have no disciples or followers. I couldn't find him now even if I wanted to, and he wouldn't answer if I called him. I must be on my way." So he had to strive with all his might to reach the West, looking after himself with nobody to help.

Sanzang had no choice but to gather up the luggage and tie it on the horse. He did not ride now. Instead, holding his monastic staff in one hand and leading the horse by the reins with the other, he made his lonely way to the West. Before he had been travelling for long he saw an old woman on the mountain path in front of him. She was holding an embroidered robe, and a patterned hat was resting upon it. As she came towards him he hurriedly pulled the horse to the side of the path to make room for her to pass. "Where are you from, venerable monk," the old woman asked, "travelling all alone and by yourself?" "I have been sent by the great king of the East to go to the West to visit the Buddha and ask him for the True Scriptures," he replied. "The Buddha of the West lives in the Great Thunder Monastery in the land of India, thirty-six thousand miles away from here. You'll never get there, just you and your horse, without a companion or disciple." "I did have a disciple, but his nature was so evil that he would not accept a little reproof I administered to him and disappeared into the blue," said Sanzang. "I have here an embroidered tunic and a hat inset with golden patterns that used to be my son's," the woman said, "but he died after being a monk for only three days. I've just been to his monastery to mourn him and say farewell to his master, and I was taking this tunic and this hat home to remember the boy by. But as you have a disciple, venerable monk, I'll give them to you." "Thank you very much for your great generosity, but as my disciple has already gone, I couldn't accept them." "Where has he gone?" "All I heard was a whistling sound as he went back to the east." "My home isn't far to the east from here," she said, "so I expect he's gone there. I've also got a spell called *True Words to Fix the Mind*, or the Band-tightening Spell. You must learn it in secret, and be sure to keep it to yourself. Never leak it to anyone. I'll go and catch up with him and send him back to you, and you can give him that tunic and hat to wear. If he's disobedient again, all you have to do is recite the spell quietly. That will stop him committing any more murders or running away again."

Sanzang bowed low to thank her, at which she changed into a beam of golden light and returned to the east. He realized in his heart that it must have been the Bodhisattva Guanyin who had given him the spell, so he took a pinch of earth as if he were burning incense and bowed in worship to the east most reverently. Then he put the tunic and hat in his pack, sat down beside the path, and recited the *True Words to Calm the Mind* over and over again until he knew them thoroughly, and had committed them to his memory.

Let us turn to Sun Wukong, who after leaving his master went straight back to the Eastern Ocean on his somersault cloud. Putting his cloud away, he parted the waters and went straight to the undersea palace of crystal. His approach had alarmed the dragon king, who came out to welcome him and took him into the palace, where they sat down. When they had exchanged courtesies the dragon king said, "I'm sorry that I failed to come and congratulate you on the end of your sufferings, Great Sage. I take it that you are returning to your old cave to put your immortal mountain back in order." "That's what I wanted to do," Monkey replied. "But I've become a monk instead." "A monk? How?" the dragon king asked. "The Bodhisattva of the Southern Sea converted me. She taught me to work for a good reward later by going to the West with the Tang Priest from the East, visiting the Buddha, and becoming a monk. And my name has been changed to Brother Monkey." "Congratulations, congratulations," said the dragon king. "You've turned over a new leaf and decided to be good. But in that case why have you come back to the East instead of going West?" Monkey laughed. "Because that Tang Priest doesn't understand human nature. He started nagging away at me about a few small-time highwaymen I killed, and said that everything about me was wrong. You know how I can't stand people going on at me, so I left him to come home to my mountain. I looked in on you first to ask for a cup of tea." "Delighted to oblige," said the dragon king, and his dragon sons and grandsons came in with some fragrant tea which they presented to Monkey.

When he had drunk his tea, Monkey looked round and saw a picture called, "Presenting the Shoe at the Yi Bridge" hanging on the wall behind him. "What's that a view of?" asked Monkey. "You wouldn't know about it because it happened after your time," the dragon king replied. "It's called 'Presenting the Shoe Three Times at the Yi Bridge'." "What's all that about?" Monkey asked. "The Immortal is Lord Yellow Stone, and the boy is Zhang Liang, who lived in Han times," the dragon king replied. "Lord Yellow Stone was sitting on the bridge when suddenly he dropped one of his shoes under it and told Zhang Liang to fetch it for him. The boy Zhang Liang did so at once, and knelt down to present it to him. Lord Yellow Stone did this three times, and because Zhang Liang never showed a trace of arrogance or disrespect, Lord Yellow Stone was touched by his diligence. One night he gave Zhang Liang some heavenly books and told him to support the Han cause. Later he won victories hundreds of miles away through his calculations within the walls of his tent. When peace came he resigned his office and went back to roam on his mountain with Master Red Pine and achieve the Way of Immortality through enlightenment. Great Sage, if you don't protect the Tang Priest with all your might, and if you reject his instruction, then you might as well stop trying to win yourself a good later reward, because it will mean you're only an evil Immortal after all." Monkey hummed and hawed, but said nothing. "Great Sage," said the dragon king, "you must make your mind up. Don't ruin your future for the sake of any easy life now." "Enough said. I'll go back and look after him," replied Sun Wukong. The dragon king was delighted. "In that case I shan't keep you. I ask you in your mercy not to leave your master waiting for long." Being thus pressed to go, Monkey left the sea palace, mounted his cloud, and took leave of the dragon king.

On his way he met the Bodhisattva Guanyin. "What are you doing here, Sun Wukong?" she asked. "Why did you

reject the Tang Priest's teaching and stop protecting him?"
Brother Monkey frantically bowed to her from his cloud and
replied, "As you had predicted, Bodhisattva, a monk came from
the Tang Empire who took off the seal, rescued me, and made
me his disciple. I ran away from him because he thought I was
wicked and incorrigible, but now I'm going back to protect
him." "Hurry up then, and don't have any more wicked
thoughts." With that they each went their separate ways.

A moment later Monkey saw the Tang Priest sitting gloomily
beside the path. He went up to him and said, "Why aren't you
travelling, Master? What are you still here for?" Sanzang
looked up. "Where have you been?" he asked. "I couldn't move
without you, so I had to sit here and wait till you came back."
"I went to visit the Old Dragon King of the Eastern Sea to
ask him for some tea," Monkey replied. "Disciple, a religious
man shouldn't tell lies. How can you say that you went to
drink tea at the dragon king's place when you haven't been
gone two hours?" "I can tell you quite truthfully," replied
Monkey with a smile, "that with my somersault cloud I can
cover thirty-six thousand miles in a single bound. That's
how I got there and back." "When I spoke to you a little severely you resented it and went off in a huff," said Sanzang. "It was
all right for a clever person like you — you begged yourself some
tea. But I couldn't go, and had to stay here hungry. You ought
to be sorry for me." "If you're hungry, Master, I'll go and beg
you some food," suggested Monkey. "No need," his master replied, "there are still some dry provisions in my bundle that the
high warden's mother gave me. Take that bowl and fetch some
water. When we have eaten some of it we can be on our way."

Opening the bundle, Brother Monkey found some scones
made of coarse flour, which he took out and gave to his master.
He also noticed the dazzling brocade tunic and the hat with
inlaid golden patterns. "Did you bring this tunic and hat with
you from the east?" he asked. Sanzang had to make something
up on the spot. "I used to wear them when I was young. With
that hat on you can recite scriptures without ever having been
taught them, and if you wear that tunic you can perform the

rituals without any practice." "Dear Master, please let me
wear them," Monkey pleaded. "I don't know whether they'll
fit you, but if you can get them on, you can wear them." Monkey
took off the old white tunic, put the brocade one on instead,
and found that it was a perfect fit. Then he put the hat on
his head. As soon as he had the hat on, Sanzang stopped eating
and silently recited the Band-tightening Spell. "My head
aches, my head aches," cried Brother Monkey, but his master
went on and recited the spell several times more. Monkey,
now rolling in agony, tore the hat to shreds, and Sanzang stopped reciting the spell for fear he would break the golden band.
The moment the spell stopped the pain finished. Reaching up to
feel his head, Monkey found something like a golden wire
clamped so tightly around it that he could not wrench or snap
it off. It had already taken root there. He took the needle
out of his ear, forced it inside the band, and pulled wildly at it.
Sanzang, again frightened that he would snap it, started to
recite the spell once more. The pain was so bad this time that
Monkey stood on his head, turned somersaults, and went red
in the face and ears. His eyes were popping and his body went
numb. Seeing the state he was in, Sanzang had to stop, and
the pain stopped again too. "Master," said Monkey, "What
a curse you put on me to give me a headache like that." "I
didn't put a curse on you, I recited the Band-tightening Spell,"
Sanzang replied. "Say it again and see what happens," said
Monkey, and when Sanzang did as he asked, Monkey's head
ached again. "Stop, stop," he shouted, "the moment you started
reciting it my head ached. Why did you do it?" "Will you accept my instruction now?" Sanzang asked. "Yes," Monkey replied. "Will you misbehave again in future?" "I certainly
won't," said Monkey.

 Although he had made this verbal promise, he was still
nurturing evil thoughts, and he shook his needle in the wind
till it was as thick as a ricebowl. He turned on the Tang Priest,
and was on the point of finishing him off when the terrified
Sanzang recited the spell two or three more times. The Monkey
dropped his cudgel and fell to the ground, unable to raise his

arm, "Master," he shouted, "I've seen the light. Stop saying the spell, please stop." "How could you have the perfidy to try to kill me?" asked Sanzang. "I'd never have dared," said Brother Monkey, adding, "who taught you that spell, Master?" "An old lady I met just now," replied Sanzang. Monkey exploded with rage. "Tell me no more," he said, "I'm sure and certain the old woman was that Guanyin. How could she do this to me? Just you wait. I'm going to the Southern Sea to kill her." "As she taught me this spell," Sanzang replied, "she's bound to know it herself. If you go after her and she recites it, that will be the end of you." Seeing the force of his argument, Monkey changed his mind and gave up the idea of going. He knelt down and pleaded pitifully, "Master, she's used this to force me to go with you to the West. I shan't go to make trouble for her, and you must recite scriptures instead of saying that spell all the time. I promise to protect you, and I shall always be true to this vow." "In that case you had better help me back on he horse," Sanzang replied. Monkey, who had been plunged into despair, summoned up his spirits, tightened the belt round his brocade tunic, got the horse ready, gathered up the luggage, and hurried off towards the West. If you want to know what other stories there are about the journey, then listen to the explanation in the next instalment.

CHAPTER FIFTEEN

On the Coiled Snake Mountain the gods
give secret help;
In the Eagle's Sorrow Gorge the thought-horse
is reined in.

Monkey looked after the Tang Priest as they headed west. They had been travelling for several days in the twelfth month of the year, with its freezing north winds and biting cold. Their path wound along overhanging precipices and steep cliffs, and they crossed range after range of dangerous mountains. One day Sanzang heard the sound of water as he rode along, and he turned around to shout, "Monkey, where's that sound of water coming from?" "As I remember, this place is called Eagle's Sorrow Gorge in the Coiled Snake Mountain. It must be the water in the gorge." Before he had finished speaking, the horse reached the edge of the gorge. Sanzang reined in and looked. He saw:

> A thin cold stream piercing the clouds,
> Deep, clear waves shining red in the sun.
> The sound shakes the night rain and is heard in the quiet valley,
> Its colour throws up a morning haze that obscures the sky.
> A thousand fathoms of flying waves spit jade;
> The torrent's roar howls in the fresh wind.
> The current leads to the misty waves of the sea;
> The egret and the cormorant never meet by a fisherman.

As master and disciple watched they heard a noise in the gorge as a dragon emerged from the waves, leapt up the cliff, and grabbed at Sanzang. In his alarm Monkey dropped the luggage, lifted Sanzang off his horse, turned, and fled. The dragon, unable to catch him up, swallowed the white horse, saddle and all, at a single gulp, then disappeared once more beneath the surface of the water. Monkey made his master sit down on a high peak and went back to fetch the horse and the luggage. When he found that the horse had gone and only the luggage was left, he carried the luggage up to his master and put it down before him. "Master," he said, "that damned dragon has disappeared without a trace. It gave our horse such a fright that it ran away." "However are we going to find the horse, disciple?" "Don't worry, don't worry, wait here while I go and look for it."

He leapt into the sky, whistling. Putting up his hand to shade his fiery eyes with their golden pupils, he looked all around below him, but saw no sign of the horse. He put his cloud away and reported, "Master, that horse of ours must have been eaten by the dragon — I can't see it anywhere." "Disciple," Sanzang protested, "how could that wretched creature have a mouth big enough to swallow a horse that size, saddle and all? I think the horse must have slipped its bridle in a panic and run into that valley. Go and have a more careful look." "You don't know about my powers," Monkey replied. "These eyes of mine can see what's happening three hundred miles away, and within that range I can even spot a dragonfly spreading its wings. There's no way I could miss a big horse like that." "But we will never get across those thousands of mountains and rivers without it." As he spoke, his tears fell like rain. The sight of him crying was too much for Brother Monkey, who flared up and shouted, "Stop being such an imbecile, Master. Sit there and wait while I find that wretch and make him give us back our horse." "You mustn't go," said Sanzang, grabbing hold of him. "I'm frightened that he'll come creeping out again and kill me this time. Then I'll be dead as well as the horse, and that would be terrible." This made Monkey angrier than ever, and he roared with a shout like thunder, "You're hopeless, absolutely hopeless. You want a horse to ride but you won't let me go. This way you'll be sitting there looking at the luggage for the rest of your life."

As he was yelling ferociously in a flaming temper, a voice was heard in the sky that said, "Don't be angry, Great Sage; stop crying, younger brother of the Tang Emperor. We are gods sent by the Bodhisattva Guanyin to give hidden protection to the pilgrim who is fetching the scriptures." At these words Sanzang immediately bowed, but Monkey said, "Tell me your names, you lot." "We are the Six Dings, the Six Jias, the Protectors of the Five Regions, the Four Duty Gods, and the Eighteen Guanlian of the Faith; we shall take it in turns to be in attendance every day." "Who starts today?" "The Dings and Jias, the Four Duty Gods, and the Guanlian of the Faith will take turns. Of the Protectors of the Five Regions, the Gold-headed Protector will always be with you by day and by night." "Very well then," said Monkey, "all those of you who are not on duty may withdraw. The Six Ding Heavenly Generals, the Duty God of the Day, and the Protectors will stay here to protect my master, while I shall go to find that evil dragon in the gorge and make him give our horse back." The gods all did as they were told, and Sanzang, now greatly relieved, sat on the cliff and asked Monkey to be careful. "There's no need for you to worry," said the splendid Monkey King as he tightened the belt round his brocade tunic, folded up his tiger-skin kilt, grasped his cudgel, went to the edge of the gorge, and stood amid clouds and mist above the water. "Give us back our horse, mud loach, give us back our horse," he shouted.

Now when the dragon had eaten Sanzang's white horse it lay low in the stream, hiding its miraculous powers and nourishing its vital nature. When it heard someone shouting and cursing it and demanding the horse back, it was unable to hold back its temper. Leaping up through the waves it asked, "How dare you make so free with your insults?" The moment he saw it, Monkey roared, "Don't go! Give us back our horse!" and swung his cudgel at the dragon's head. Baring its fangs and waving its claws, the dragon went for him. It was a noble battle that the pair of them fought beside the ravine.

The dragon stretched its sharp claws;
The monkey raised his gold-banded cudgel.
The beard of one hung in threads of white jade;
The other's eyes flashed like golden lamps.
The pearls in the dragon's beard gave off a coloured
   mist;
The iron club in the other's hands danced like a whirl-
   wind.
One was a wicked son who had wronged his parents;
The other, the evil spirit who had worsted heavenly
   generals.
Both had been through trouble and suffering,
And now they were to use their abilities to win merit.

Coming and going, fighting and resting, wheeling and turn-ing, they battled on for a very long time until the dragon's strength was exhausted and his muscles numb. Unable to re-sist any longer, it turned around, dived into the water, and lay low at the bottom of the stream. It pretended to be deaf as the Monkey King cursed and railed at it, and did not emerge again.

Monkey could do nothing, so he had to report to Sanzang, "Master, I swore at that ogre till it came out, and after fighting me for ages it fled in terror. It's now in the water and won't come out again." "Are you sure that it really ate our horse?" Sanzang asked. "What a thing to say," said Monkey, "If it hadn't eaten the horse, it wouldn't have dared to say a word or fight against me." "When you killed that tiger the other day you said you had ways of making dragons and tigers submit to you, so how comes it that you couldn't beat this one today?" Monkey had never been able to stand provocation, so when Sanzang mocked him this he showed something of his divine might. "Say no more, say no more. I'll have another go at it and then we'll see who comes out on top."

The Monkey King leapt to the edge of the ravine, and used a magical way of throwing rivers and seas into turmoil to make the clear waters at the bottom of the Eagle's Sorrow Gorge as turbulent as the waves of the Yellow River in spate. The evil dragon's peace was disturbed as he lurked in the depths of the waters, and he thought, "How true it is that blessings never come in pairs and troubles never come singly. Although I've been accepting my fate here for less than a year since I escaped the death penalty for breaking the laws of Heaven, I would have to run into this murderous devil." The more he thought about it, the angrier he felt, and unable to bear the humiliation a moment longer he jumped out of the stream cursing, "Where are you from, you bloody devil, coming here to push me around?" "Never you mind where I'm from," Monkey replied. "I'll only spare your life if you give back that horse." "That horse of yours is in my stomach, and I can't sick it up again, can I? I'm not giving it back, so what about it?" "If you won't give it back, then take this! I'm only killing you to make you pay for the horse's life." The two of them began another bitter struggle under the mountain, and before many rounds were up the little dragon could hold out no longer. With a shake of his body he turned himself into a water-snake and slithered into the undergrowth.

The Monkey King chased it with his cudgel in his hands, but when he pushed the grass aside to find the snake the three gods inside his body exploded, and smoke poured from his seven orifices. He uttered the magic word *om*, thus calling out the local tutelary god and the god of the mountain, who both knelt before him and reported their arrival. "Put out your ankles," Monkey said, "while I give you five strokes each of my cudgel to work off my temper." The two gods kowtowed and pleaded pitifully, "We beg the Great Sage to allow us petty gods to report." "What have you got to say?" Monkey asked. "We didn't know when you emerged after your long sufferings, Great Sage," they said, "which is why we didn't come to meet you. We beg to be forgiven." "In that case," Monkey said, "I won't beat you, but I'll ask you this instead: where does that devil dragon in the Eagle's Sorrow Gorge come from, and why did he grab my master's white horse and eat it?" "Great Sage, you never had a master," said the two gods, "and you were a supreme immortal with an undisturbed essence who would not submit to Heaven or Earth, so how does this master's horse come in?" "You two don't know that either," Monkey replied. "Because of that business of offending against Heaven, I had to suffer for five hundred years. Now I've been converted by the Bodhisattva Guanyin, and she's sent a priest who's come from the Tang Empire to rescue me. She told me to become his disciple and go to the Western Heaven to visit the Buddha and ask for the scriptures. As we were passing this way we lost my master's white horse." "Ah, so that's what's happening," the gods said. "There never used to be any evil creatures in the stream, which ran wide and deep with water so pure that crows and magpies never dared to fly across it. This was because they would mistake their own reflections in it for other birds of their own kind and often go plummeting into the water. That's why it's called Eagle's Sorrow Gorge. Last year, when the Bodhisattva Guanyin was on her way to find a man to fetch the scriptures, she rescued a jade dragon and sent it to wait here for the pilgrim without getting up to any trouble. But when it's hungry it comes up on the bank to catch a few birds or a roedeer to eat. We can't imagine how it could be so ignorant as to clash with the Great Sage." "The first time he and I crossed swords we whirled around for a few rounds," Brother Monkey replied. "The second time I swore at him but he wouldn't come out, so I stirred up his stream with a spell to throw rivers and seas into turmoil, after which he came out and wanted to have another go at me. He didn't realize how heavy my cudgel was, and he couldn't parry it, so he changed himself into a water snake and slithered into the undergrowth. I chased him and searched for him, but he's vanished without a trace." "Great Sage, you may not be aware that there are thousands of interconnected tunnels in this ravine, which is why the waters here run so deep. There is also a tunnel entrance round here that he could have slipped into. There's no need for you to be angry, Great Sage, or to search for it. If you want to catch the creature, all you have to do is to ask Guanyin to come here, and it will naturally submit."

On receiving this suggestion Monkey told the local deity and the mountain god to come with him to see Sanzang and tell him all about what had happened previously. "If you go to ask the Bodhisattva to come here, when will you ever be back?" he asked, adding, "I'm terribly cold and hungry." Before the words were out of his mouth they heard the voice of the Gold headed Protector shouting from the sky, "Great Sage, there's no need for you to move. I'll go and ask the Bodhisattva to come here." Monkey, who was delighted, replied, "This putting you to great trouble, but please be as quick as you can." The Protector then shot off on his cloud to the Southern Sea. Monkey told the mountain god and the local deity to protect his master, and sent the Duty God of the Day to find some vegetarian food, while he himself patrolled the edge of the ravine.

The moment the Gold-headed Protector mounted his cloud he reached the Southern Sea. Putting away his propitious glow, he went straight to the Purple Bamboo Grove on the island of Potaraka, where he asked the Golden Armour Devas and Moksa (or Huian) to get him an audience with the Bodhisattva. "What have you come for?" the Bodhisattva asked. "The Tang Priest," the Protector replied, "has lost his horse in the Eagle's Sorrow Gorge, and the Great Sage Sun Wukong is desperate, because they can neither go forward nor back. When the Great Sage asked the local deity he was told that the evil dragon you sent to the ravine, Bodhisattva, had swallowed it, so he has sent me to ask you to subdue this dragon and make it give back the horse." "That wretched creature was the son of Ao Run, the Dragon King of the Western Sea, whom his father reported for disobedience when he burned the palace jewels. The heavenly court condemned him to death for it, but I went myself to see the Jade Emperor and asked him to send the dragon down to serve the Tang Priest as a beast of burden. Whatever made it actually eat the Tang Priest's horse? I'd better go and look into it." The Bodhisattva descended from her lotus throne, left her magic cave, and crossed the Southern Sea, travelling on propitious light with the Protector. There is a poem about it that goes:

Paramita is in the Buddha's words that fill Three Stores
of scripture;
The Bodhisattva's goodness is longer than the Great
Wall.
The wonderful words of the Mahayana fill Heaven and
Earth;
The truth of the prajna rescues ghosts and souls.

It even made the Golden Cicada shed his cocoon once
more,
And ordered Xuanzang to continue cultivating his con-
duct.
Because the road was difficult at the Eagle's Sorrow
Gorge,
The dragon's son returned to the truth and changed into
a horse.

The Bodhisattva and the Protector reached the Coiled Snake Mountain before long, and stopping their cloud in mid-air they looked down and saw Brother Monkey cursing and shouting at the edge of the ravine. When the Bodhisattva told him to call Monkey over, the Protector brought his cloud to land at the edge of the ravine. Instead of going to see Sanzang first, he said to Monkey, "The Bodhisattva's here." Monkey leapt straight into the air on his cloud and shouted at her at the top of his voice, "Teacher of the Seven Buddhas, merciful head of our religion, why did you think up this way of hurting me?" "I'll get you, you outrageous baboon, you red-bottomed ape," she replied. "I was at my wit's end two or three times over to fetch that pilgrim, and I told him to save your life. But so far from coming to thank me for saving you, you now have the effrontery to bawl at me." "You've been very good to me, I must say," retorted Monkey. "If you'd let me out to roam around enjoying myself as I pleased, that would have been fine. It was all right when you met me above the sea the other day, spoke a few unkind words, and told me to do all I could to help the Tang Priest. But why did you give him that hat he tricked me into wearing to torture me with? Why did you make this band grow into my head? Why did you teach him that Band-tightening Spell? Why did you make that old monk recite it over and over again so that my head ached and ached? You must be wanting to do me in." "You monkey," the Bodhisattva smiled. "You don't obey the commands of the faith, and you won't accept the true reward, so if you weren't under control like this you might rebel against Heaven again or get up to any kind of evil. If you got yourself into trouble as you did before, who would look after you? Without this monstrous head, you'd never be willing to enter our Yogacarin faith." "Very well then," Monkey replied, "let's call this object my monstrous head. But why did you send that criminal and evil dragon to become a monster here and eat my master's horse? Letting evil creatures out to run amuck like that is a bad deed." "I personally asked the Jade Emperor to put the dragon here as a mount for the pilgrim," said the Bodhisattva. "Do you think an ordinary horse would be able to cross the thousands of mountains and rivers to reach the Buddha-land on the Vulture Peak? Only a dragon horse will be able to do it." "But he's so afraid of me that he's skulking down there and won't come out, so what's to be done?" Monkey asked. The Bodhisattva told the Protector to go to the edge of the ravine and shout, "Come out, Prince Jade Dragon, son of the Dragon King Ao Run, to see the Bodhisattva of the Southern Sea," on which he would emerge. The Protector went to the edge of the gorge and shouted this twice, on which the young dragon leapt up through the waves, took human form, stepped on a cloud, and greeted the Bodhisattva in mid-air. "In my gratitude to you, Bodhisattva, for saving my life, I have been waiting here for a long time, but I have had no news yet of the pilgrim who is going to fetch the scriptures." The Bodhisattva pointed to Brother Monkey and said, "Isn't he the pilgrim's great disciple?" "He's my enemy," the young dragon replied when he looked at him. "I ate his horse yesterday because I was starving, so he used some powers of his to fight me till I returned exhausted and terrified, then swore at me so that I had to shut myself in, too frightened to come out. He never said a word about anyone fetching scriptures." "You never asked me my name, so how could I have told you?" Monkey retorted. "I asked you 'Where are you from, you bloody devil?' and you yelled, 'Never mind where I'm from, and give me back that horse,'" said the dragon. "You never so much as breathed the word 'Tang'." You monkey, you are so proud of your own strength that you never have a good word for anyone else," said the Bodhisattva. "There will be others who join you later on your journey, and when they ask you any questions, the first thing you must mention is fetching the scriptures. If you do that, you'll have their help without any trouble at all."

Monkey was happy to accept instruction from her. The Bodhisattva then went forward, broke off some of the pearls from the dragon's head, soaked the end of her willow twig in the sweet dew in her bottle, sprinkled it on the dragon's body, and breathed on it with magic breath, shouted, and the dragon turned into the exact likeness of the original horse. "You must concentrate on wiping out your past sins," she told him, "and when you have succeeded, you will rise above ordinary dragons and be given back your golden body as a reward." The young dragon took the bit between his teeth, and her words to heart. The Bodhisattva told Sun Wukong to take him to see Sanzang as she was returning to the Southern Sea. Monkey clung to her, refusing to let her go. "I'm not going," he said, "I'm not going. If the journey to the West is as tough as this, I can't possibly keep this mortal priest safe, and if there are many such more trials and tribulations, I'll have enough trouble keeping alive myself. How can I ever achieve any reward? I'm not going, I'm not going." "In the old days, before you had learnt to be a human being," the Bodhisattva replied, "you were prepared to work for your awakening with all your power. But now that you have been delivered from a Heaven-sent calamity, you have grown lazy. What's the matter with you? In our faith, to achieve nirvana you must believe in good rewards. If you meet with injury or suffering in future, you have only to call on Heaven and Earth for them to respond; and if you get into a really hopeless situation I shall come to rescue you myself. Come

over here as I have another power to give you." The Bodhisattva plucked three leaves from her willow twig, put them on
the back of Brother Monkey's head, and shouted "Change", on
which they turned into three life-saving hairs. "When the time
comes when nobody else will help you," she said, "they will
turn into whatever is needed to save you from disaster."

After hearing all these fine words, Monkey finally took his
leave of the All-merciful Bodhisattva, who went back to
Potaraka amidst scented breezes and coloured mists.

Monkey brought his cloud down to land, and led the dragon
horse by the mane to see Sanzang. "Master," he said, "we've
got our horse." Sanzang cheered up the moment he saw it.
"Why is it sturdier than it was before?" he asked. "Where did
you find it?" "Master, you must have been dreaming. The
Golden-headed Protector asked the Bodhisattva to come here,
and she turned the dragon in the gorge into our white horse.
The colouring is the same, but it hasn't got a saddle or a bridle,
which is why I had to drag it here." Sanzang was astounded.
"Where's the Bodhisattva? I must go and worship her," he
said. "She's back in the Southern Sea by now, so don't bother,"
Monkey replied. Sanzang took a pinch of earth as if he were
burning incense, knelt down, and bowed to the south. When
he had finished he got up and helped Monkey put their things
together for the journey. Monkey dismissed the mountain god
and the local deity, gave orders to the Protector and the Duty
Gods, and invited his master to mount the horse. "I couldn't
possibly ride it — it's got no saddle or bridle," his master replied, "but we can sort this out when we've found a boat to
ferry us across the stream." "Master, you seem to have no common sense at all. Where will a boat be found in these wild
mountains? This horse has lived here for a long time and is
bound to know about the currents, so you can ride him and use
him as your boat." Sanzang had no choice but to do as Monkey
suggested and ride the horse bareback to the edge of the stream
while Monkey carried the luggage.

An aged fisherman appeared upstream, punting a raft along
with the current. As soon as he saw him, Monkey waved his

hand and shouted, "Come here, fisherman, come here. We're
from the East, and we're going to fetch the scriptures. My
master is having some trouble crossing the river, so come and
ferry him over." The fisherman punted towards them with all
speed, while Monkey asked Sanzang to dismount and helped
him on board the raft. Then he led the horse on and loaded
the luggage, after which the fisherman pushed off and started
punting with the speed of an arrow. Before they realized it they
had crossed the Eagle's Sorrow Gorge and were on the western
bank. When Sanzang told Brother Monkey to open the bundle
and find a few Great Tang coins and notes to give the fisherman, the old man pushed his raft off from the shore with the
words, "I don't want your money, I don't want your money,"
and drifted off into mid-stream. Sanzang was most upset, but
could do nothing except put his hands together and thank him.
"There's no need to thank him, Master," Monkey said. "Can't
you see who he is? He's the water god of this stream, and I
should be giving him a beating for not coming to welcome me.
He should consider himself lucky to get off the beating — how
could he possibly expect money too?" His master, who was only
half-convinced, mounted the saddleless horse once more and
followed Monkey to join the main path, and then they hurried
on towards the West. Indeed,

> *The great truth landed on the opposite bank,*
> *The sincere heart and complete nature climbed Vulture*
>   *Peak.*

As disciple and master went forward together, the sun slipped down in the west and evening drew in.

> *Pale and ragged clouds,*
> *The moon dim over the mountains,*
> *As the cold frost fills the heavens,*
> *And the wind's howl cuts through the body.*
> *With the lone bird gone, the grey island seems vast;*
> *Where the sunset glows, the distant mountains are low.*
> *In the sparse forests a thousand trees moan,*
> *On the deserted peak a lonely ape screams.*

The path is long, and bears no footprints,
As the boat returns for thousands of miles at the night.

As Sanzang was gazing into the distance from the back of his horse, he noticed a farm-house beside the path. "Monkey," he said, "let's spend the night in the house ahead of us and go on in the morning." Monkey looked up and replied, "Master, it's not a farm-house." "Why not?" "A farm-house wouldn't have all those decorative fishes and animals on the roof. It must be a temple or a nunnery."

As they were talking they reached the gate, and when Sanzang dismounted he saw the words TEMPLE OF THE WARD ALTAR written large above the gate and went inside. Here an old man with a rosary of pearls hanging round his neck came out to meet them with his hands held together and the words, "Please sit down, master." Sanzang quickly returned his courtesies and entered the main building to pay his respects to the divine image. The old man told a servant to bring tea, and when that had been drunk Sanzang asked the old man why the temple was dedicated to the ward altar. "This place is in the territory of the western land of Hami," the old man replied, "and behind the temple lives the devout farm family which built it. 'Ward' means the ward of a village, and the altar is the altar of the local tutelary deity. At the time of the spring ploughing, the summer weeding, the autumn harvest, and the storing away in winter they all bring meat, flowers, and fruit to sacrifice to the altar. They do this to ensure good fortune throughout the four seasons, a rich crop of the five grains, and good health for the six kinds of livestock." On hearing this Sanzang nodded and said in approval, "How true it is that 'Go three miles from home, and you're in another land.' We have nothing as good as this in our country." The old man then asked him where his home was. "I come from the land of the Great Tang in the East," Sanzang replied, "and I have imperial orders to go to the Western Heaven to worship the Buddha and ask for the scriptures. As our journey brought us this way and it is almost night, we have come to this holy temple to ask for a night's loding. We shall set off at dawn." The old man, who was very pleased to hear this, apologized profusely for having failed in his hospitality and told the servant to prepare a meal. When Sanzang had eaten he thanked the old man.

Monkey's sharp eyes had noticed a clothes-line under the eaves of the building. He went over, tore it down, and hobbled the horse with it. "Where did you steal that horse from?" the old man asked with a smile. "You don't know what you're talking about, "Monkey replied. "We're holy monks going to visit the Buddha, so how could we possibly steal a horse." "If you didn't steal it," the old man continued the smile still on his lips, "then why do you have to break my clothes-line because it's got no saddle, bridle or reins?" Sanzang apologized for Monkey and said to him, "You're too impatient, you naughty monkey. You could have asked the old gentleman for a piece of rope to tether the horse with. There was no need to snap his clothes-line. Please don't be angry, sir," Sanzang went on, addressing the old man. "This horse isn't stolen, I can assure you. When we reached the Eagle's Sorrow Gorge yesterday I was riding a white horse complete with saddle and bridle. We did not know that there was an evil dragon in the stream who had become a spirit, and this dragon swallowed my horse saddle, bridle and all, in a single gulp. Luckily this disciple of mine has certain powers, and he brought the Bodhisattva Guanyin to the side of the gorge, where she caught the dragon and changed it into a white horse, exactly like the original one, to carry me to the Western Heaven to visit the Buddha. It's been less than a day from when we crossed that stream to when we reached your holy shrine, sir, and we haven't yet saddle or bridle for it." "Please don't be angry, Father. I was only joking," the old man replied. "I never thought your respected disciple would take it seriously. When I was young I had a bit of money, and I was fond of riding a good horse, but after many years of troubles and bereavement and a fire that burned my house down, I've come to this miserable end as a sacristan looking after the incense. Luckily the benefactor who owns the farm behind here provides me with the necessities of life. As it happens, I still have a saddle and bridle — I was so fond of them in the old days that I have never been able to bring myself to sell them, poor as I am. Now that I have heard, venerable master, how the Bodhisattva saved the divine dragon and changed it into a horse to carry you, I feel that I must help too, so I shall bring that saddle and bridle out tomorrow for you to ride on. I beg you to be gracious enough to accept them." Sanzang thanked him effusively. The servant boy had by now produced the evening meal, and when it was over they spread out their bedding, lamp in hand, and all went to sleep.

When Monkey got up the next morning he said, "Master, that old sacristan promised us the saddle and bridle last night. You must insist and not let him off." Before the words were out of his mouth, the old man appeared with the saddle and bridle in his hands, as well as saddle-cloth, saddle-pad, reins, muzzle and all the other trappings for a horse. Nothing was missing. As he put it all down in front of the verandah he said, "Master, I humbly offer this saddle and bridle." When Sanzang saw them he accepted them with delight. Then he told Monkey to put them on the horse to see if they fitted him. Monkey went over and picked them up to look at them one by one: they were all fine pieces. There are some verses to prove it that go

> *The well-carved saddle shines with silver stars;*
> *The jewelled stirrups gleam with golden light.*
> *Several layers of saddle-pads are made from wool;*
> *The lead-rope is plaited from purple silk.*

> *The reins are inlaid with flashing flowers;*
> *The blinkers have dancing animals outlined in gold.*
> *The bit is made of tempered steel,*
> *And woollen tassels hang from either end.*

Monkey, who was secretly very pleased, put the saddle and bridle on the horse and found that they fitted as if they had been made to measure. Sanzang knelt and bowed to the old man in thanks, at which the old man rushed forward and said, "No, no, how could I allow you to thank me?" The old man did not try to keep them a moment longer, and bade Sanzang mount the horse. When he was out of the gate Sanzang climbed into the saddle, while Monkey carried the luggage. The old man then produced a whip from his sleeve and offered it to Sanzang as he stood beside the road. Its handle was of rattan bound with leather, and its thong of tiger sinew bound at the end with silk. "Holy monk," he said, "I would also like to give you this as well." As Sanzang took it sitting on horseback, he thanked the old man for his generosity.

As Sanzang was on the point of clasping his hands together to take his leave of him, the old man disappeared, and on turning round to look at the temple, the monk could see nothing but a stretch of empty land. He heard a voice saying in the sky, "Holy monk, I have not shown you much courtesy. I am the mountain god and the local deity of Potaraka Island, and I was sent by the Bodhisattva Guanyin to give you the saddle and bridle. You two are now to make for the west as fast as you can, and not to slacken your pace for a moment." Sanzang tumbled out of the saddle in a panic, and worshipped the heavens, saying, "My eyes of flesh and my mortal body prevented me from recognizing you, noble gods; forgive me, I beg you. Please convey my gratitude to the Bodhisattva for her mercy." Look at him, kowtowing to the sky more often than you could count. The Great Sage Sun Wukong, the Handsome Monkey King, was standing by the path overcome with laughter and beside himself with amusement. He went over and tugged at the Tang Priest. "Master," he said, "get up. He is already much too far away to hear your prayers or see your kowtows, so why ever are you doing that?" "Disciple," Sanzang replied, "what do you mean by standing beside the path sneering at me and not even making a single bow while all those kowtows?" "You don't know anything," Monkey retorted. "A deceitful one like him deserve a thrashing. I let him off out of respect for the Bodhisattva. That's quite enough: he couldn't expect me to bow to him too, could he? I've been a tough guy since I was a kid, and I don't bow to anyone. Even when I meet the Jade Emperor or the Supreme Lord Lao Zi I just chant a 're-e-er' and that's all." "You inhuman beast," said Sanzang, "stop talking such nonsense. Get moving, and don't hold us up a moment longer." With that Sanzang rose to his feet and they set off to the west.

The next two months' journey was peaceful, and they only met Luoluos, Huihuis, wolves, monsters, tigers, and leopards. The time passed quickly and it was now early spring. They saw mountains and forests clad in emerald brocade as plants and trees put out shoots of green; and when all the plum blossom had fallen, the willows started coming into leaf. Master and disciple travelled along enjoying the beauties of spring, and they saw that the sun was setting in the west. Sanzang reined in his horse to look into the distance, and in the fold of a mountain he dimly discerned towers and halls. "Wukong," he said, "can you see if there's anywhere there we can go?" Monkey looked and said, "It must be a temple or a monastery. Let's get there quickly and spend the night there." Sanzang willingly agreed, and giving his dragon horse a free rein he galloped towards it. If you don't know what sort of place it was that they were going to, listen to the explanation in the next instalment.

CHAPTER SIXTEEN

The monks of the Guanyin Monastery plot
to take the treasure;
The monster of the Black Wind Mountain
steals the cassock.

The master whipped on his horse and hurried straight to the
temple gate with his disciple to have a look. They saw that it
was indeed a monastery:

> Hall upon hall,
> Cloister after cloister.
> Beyond the triple gates
> Countless coloured clouds are massed;
> Before the Hall of Five Blessings
> Coil a thousand wisps of red mist.
> Two rows of pine and bamboo,
> A forest of locust and cypress trees.
> The two rows of pine and bamboo
> Are ageless in their elegant purity;
> The forest of locust and cypress trees
> Has colour and beauty.
> See how high the drum and bell towers are,
> How tall the pagoda.
> In peaceful mediation the monks make firm their na-
>   tures,
> As birds sing in the trees outside.
> Peace beyond mortal dust is the only true peace;
> Emptiness with the Way is the real emptiness.

As the poem goes,

A supreme Jetavana hidden in a green valley,
A monastery set in scenery unbeaten in the world.
Such pure lands are·rare on earth;
On most of the famous mountains dwell monks.

Sanzang dismounted, Monkey laid down his burden, and they were just on the point of going in when a crowd of monks came out. This is how they were dressed:

On their heads they wore hats pinned on the left;
On their bodies were clothes of purity.
Copper rings hung from their ears,
And silken belts were tied around their waists.

Slowly they walked on sandals o, straw,
As they held wooden clappers in their hands.
With their mouths they were always chanting
Their devotion to the Wisdom.

When Sanzang saw them he stood respectfully beside the gate and greeted them. A monk hastily returned his greeting and apologized for not noticing them before. "Where are you from?" he asked. "Please come to the abbot's rooms and have some tea." "I have been sent from the East on an imperial mission to worship the Buddha in the Thunder Monastery and ask for the scriptures," Sanzang replied, "and as it is almost night we would like to ask for a night's lodging now that we are here." "Come inside and sit down, come inside and sit down," the monk said. When Sanzang told Monkey to lead the horse over, the monk was frightened at the sudden sight of him and asked, "What's that thing leading the horse?" "Keep your voice down," Sanzang urged, "keep your voice down. He has a quick temper, and if he hears you referring to him as 'that thing', he will be furious. He is my disciple." The monk shuddered and bit his finger as he remarked, "Fancy taking a monstrously ugly creature like that for a disciple." "He may not look it," Sanzang replied, "but ugly as he is, he has his uses."

The monk had no choice but to go through the monastery gate with Sanzang and Monkey, and inside they saw the words CHAN MONASTERY OF GUANYIN written in large letters on the main hall. Sanzang was delighted. "I have often been the grateful beneficiary of the Bodhisattva's divine mercy," he exclaimed, "but I have not yet been able to kowtow to her in thanks. To worship her in this monastery will be just as good as seeing her in person." On hearing this, the monk told a lay brother to open the doors and invited Sanzang to go in and worship. Monkey tethered the horse, put the luggage down, and went up into the hall with Sanzang, who prostrated himself and put his head on the floor before the golden statue. When the monk went to beat the drum, Monkey started striking the bell. Sanzang lay before the image, praying with all his heart, and when he had finished the monk stopped beating the drum. Monkey, however, was so engrossed in striking the bell, sometimes fast and sometimes slow, that he went on for a very long time. "He's finished his devotions," a lay brother said, "so what are you still beating the bell for?" Monkey threw down the bell hammer and said with a grin, "You're ignorant, aren't you? 'Whoever is a monk for a day strikes the bell for a day': that's me." By then all the monks in the monastery, senior and junior, as well as the abbot and his assistant, had been so startled by the wild noises from the bell that they all came crowding out to ask what savage was making such a din with the bell and drum. Monkey jumped out and cursed them: "Your grandfather Sun Wukong was having some fun." All the monks collapsed with shock at the sight of him and said as they knelt on the ground, "Lord Thunder God, Lord Thunder God." "The Thunder God is my great grandson," Monkey replied. "Get up, get up, you've nothing to fear. I'm a lord from the land of the Great Tang Empire in the East." The monks all bowed to him, and could not feel easy until Sanzang appeared. "Please come and drink tea in my rooms," said the abbot of the monastery. The horse was unloaded and led off, while they went round the main hall to a room at the back where they sat down according to their seniority.

The abbot gave them tea and arranged for food to be brought, and after the meal it was still early. As Sanzang was expressing his thanks, two servant boys appeared behind them supporting an aged monk. This is what he looked like:

> A Vairocana mitre on his head,
> Topped with a gleaming cat's-eye jewel.
> On his body a gown of brocade,
> Edged with gold-mounted kingfisher feathers.
> A pair of monkish shoes studded with the Eight Treas-
>   ures,
> A walking stick inlaid with clouds and stars.
> A face covered with wrinkles,
> Like the Old Goddess of Mount Li;
> A pair of purblind eyes,
> Like the Dragon King of the Eastern Sea.
> His mouth can't keep out the wind as his teeth have gone;
> His back is bent because his muscles are stiff.

"The Patriarch has come," the monks all said. Sanzang bowed low to him in greeting and said, "Your disciple pays his respects, venerable abbot." The aged monk returned his greeting and they both sat down. "The youngsters have just told me that gentlemen have come from the Tang Empire in the East," he said, "so I have come out to see you." "Please forgive us for blundering into your monastery so rudely," Sanzang replied. "Dont put it like that," the aged monk said, going on to ask, "How long a journey is it from the eastern lands to here?" "It was over sixteen hundred miles from Chang'an to the Double Boundary Mountain, where I took on this disciple," Sanzang replied. "We travelled on together through the land of Hami, and as that took two months we must have covered getting on for another two thousand miles before reaching here." "Over three thousand miles," said the aged monk. "I have spent a life of piety and have never been outside the monastery gates, so you could really say that I have been 'looking at heaven from the bottom of a well,' and call mine a wasted life." "How great is your age, venerable abbot?" Sanzang asked. "In my stupid way I have lived to be two hundred and seventy," the old monk replied. "Then you're my ten-thousandth-great grandson," put in Monkey. "Talk properly," said Sanzang, glaring at him, "Don't be so disrespectful and rude." "How old are you, sir?" the aged monk asked. "I don't venture to mention it," Monkey replied. The aged monk then thought that he must have been raving, so he put the matter out of his mind, said no more about it, and ordered tea to be brought for them. A young page brought in three *cloisonné* teacups on a jade tray the colour of mutton fat, and another carried in a white alloy teapot from which he poured out three cups of fragrant tea. It had a better colour than pomegranate blossom, and its aroma was finer than cassia. When Sanzang saw all this he was full of praise. "What splendid things, he said, "what splendid things. Wonderful tea in wonderful vessels." "They're not worth looking at," the old monk replied. "After all, sir, you come from a superior and heavenly court, and have seen many rare things in your wide travels; so how can you give such exaggerated praise to things like that? What treasures did you bring with you from your superior country that I could have a look at?" "I'm afraid our eastern land has no great treasures, and even if it did, I would have been unable to bring them on so long a journey."

"Master," put in Monkey, who was sitting beside him, "isn't that cassock I saw in our bundle the other day a treasure? Why don't I take it out for him to see?" When the monks heard him mention the cassock, they smiled sinister smiles. "What are you smiling at?" Monkey asked. "We thought it was very funny when you said that a cassock was a treasure," the abbot of the monastery replied. "A priest of my rank has two or three dozen, and our Patriarch, who has been a monk here for two hundred and fifty or sixty years, has seven or eight hundred." He ordered them to be brought out and displayed. The old monk, who was also in on the game, told the lay brothers to open the storerooms, while friars carried twelve chests out into the courtyard, and unlocked them. Then they set up clothes frames, put rope all around, shook the cassocks open one by one, and hung them up for Sanzang to see. Indeed, the whole building was full of brocade, and the four walls covered with silk.

Monkey examined them one by one and saw that some were made of brocade and some were embroidered with gold. "Enough, enough, enough," he said. "Put them away, put them away. I'll bring ours out for you to take a look at." Sanzang drew Monkey aside and whispered to him, "Disciple, never try to compete with other people's wealth. You and I are alone in this foreign land, and I'm afraid that there may be trouble." "What trouble can come from letting them look at the cassock?" Monkey asked. "You don't understand," Sanzang replied. "The ancients used to say, 'Don't let greedy and treacherous men see rare or amusing things.' If he lays his eyes on it, his mind will be disturbed, and if his mind is disturbed, he's bound to start scheming. If you were cautious, you would only have to give it to him when he asks for it; but as it is, this is no trifling matter, and may well be the end of us." "Don't worry, don't worry," said Brother Monkey, "I'll look after everything." Watch as without another word of argument he rushes off and opens the bundle, which is already giving off a radiant glow. It still had two layers of oiled paper round it, and when he removed it to take out the cassock and shake it open the hall was bathed in red light and clouds of coloured vapours filled the courtyard. When the monks saw it their hearts were filled with delight and their mouths with praise. It really was a fine cassock.

> Hung with pearls of unrivalled quality,
> Studded with Buddhist treasures infinitely rare.
> Above and below a dragon beard sparkles,
> On kapok-cloth edged with brocade.
>
> If it is worn, all demons are extinguished;
> When donned it sends all monsters down to hell.
> It was made by the hands of heavenly immortals,
> And none but a true monk should dare put it on.

When the aged monk saw how rare a treasure it was, his heart was indeed disturbed. He went up to Sanzang and knelt before him.   "My fate is indeed a wretched one," he lamented, tears pouring down his cheeks.   Sanzang helped him to his feet again and asked, "Why do you say that, venerable Patriarch?" "You have unfolded this treasure of yours, sir," the aged monk replied   "when it is already evening, so that my eyes are too dim to see it clearly. That is why I say my fate is wretched." "Send for a candle and take another look," Sanzang suggested. "My lord, your precious cassock is already shining brightly, so I don't think I would see more distinctly even if a candle were lit," replied the aged monk.   "How would you like to look at it then?" asked Sanzang. "If, sir, you were in your mercy to set aside your fears and let me take it to my room to examine it closely during the night, I will return it to you in the morning to take to the West.   What do you say to that?" This request startled Sanzang, who grumbled at Brother Monkey, "It's all your fault, all your fault." "He's nothing to be frightened of." Monkey replied with a grin.   "I'll pack it up and tell him to take it away to look at.   If anything goes wrong, I'll be responsible."   As there was nothing he could do to stop him, Sanzang handed the cassock to the old monk with the words, "I'll let you take it, but you must give it back to me tomorrow morning in its present condition.   I won't have you getting it at all dirty."   The old monk gleefully told a page to take the cassock to his room, and instructed the other monks to sweep out the front meditation hall, move two rattan beds in, spread out the bedding on them, and invite the two gentlemen to spend the night there; he also arranged for them to be given breakfast and seen off the next morning.   Then everyone went off to bed. Sanzang and his disciple shut the doors of the meditation hall and went to sleep.

Now that the old monk had tricked them into giving him the cassock, he held it under the lamp in the back room as he wept and wailed over it. This so alarmed the monks that none of them dared go to sleep before he did.   The young page, not knowing what to do, went to tell the other monks, "Grandad's still crying although it's getting on for eleven."   Two junior monks, who were among the old man's favourites, went over to ask him why he was crying. "I'm crying because my accursed fate won't allow me to see the Tang Priest's treasure," he said; to which they replied, "Grandad, in your old age you have succeeded. His cassock is laid before you, and all you have to do is open your eyes and look. There's no need for tears." "But I can't look at it for long," the aged monk answered. "I'm two hundred and seventy this year, and I've collected all those hundreds of cassocks for nothing. However am I to get hold of that one of his? However am I to become like the Tang Priest?" "Master, you've got it all wrong," the junior monks said. "The Tang Priest is a pilgrim far from home. You should be satisfied with your great seniority and wealth; why ever would you want to be a pilgrim like him?" "Although I live at home and enjoy my declining years, I've got no cassock like his to wear," the aged monk replied. "If I could wear it for a day, I would close my eyes in peace. I wouldn't have been a monk in this world in vain." "What nonsense," the junior monks said. "If you want to wear his cassock, there'll be no problem about that. We'll keep him for another day tomorrow, and you can wear it for another day. Or we can keep him for ten days and you can wear it for ten days. So why get so upset about it?" "Even if we kept him for a year," the old monk replied, "I'd only be able to wear it for a year, which wouldn't bring me any glory. I'll still have to give it to him when he went: I can't keep him here for ever."

As they were talking a young monk called Broad Wisdom spoke out. "Grandad," he said, "if you want it for a long time, that's easy to arrange too." "What brilliant idea have you got, child?" the aged monk asked, cheering up. "That Tang Priest and his disciple were so exhausted after their journey that they are both asleep by now," Broad Wisdom replied. "If we arm some strong monks with swords and spears to break into the meditation hall and kill them, they can be buried in the back garden, and nobody but us will be any the wiser. This way we get their white horse and their luggage as well as the cassock, which will become an heirloom of the monastery. We would be doing this for posterity." The old monk was very pleased with this suggestion, and he wiped the tears from his eyes as he said, "Very good, very good, a marvellous plan."

Another young monk called Broad Plans, a fellow-student of Broad Wisdom's, came forward and said, "This plan's no good. If we are to kill them, we'll have to keep a sharp eye on them. That old pale-faced one looks easy enough, but the hairy-faced one could be tricky; and if by any chance we fail to kill him, we'll·be in deep trouble. I have a way that doesn't involve using weapons, but I don't know what you'll think of it." "What do you suggest, my child?" the aged monk asked "In my humble opinion," he replied, "we should assemble the head monks of all the cells, senior and junior, and get everyone to put a bundle of firewood outside the meditation hall. When it's set alight, those two will have no escape, and will be burnt to death together with their horse. Even if the people who live around this mountain see the blaze, they'll think that those two burnt down the meditation hall by carelessly starting a fire. This way they'll both be burnt to death and nobody will know how it happened. Then the cassock will become our monastery's treasure for ever." All the monks present were pleased with this suggestion, exclaiming, "Great, great, great; an even better plan." The head of every cell was told to bring firewood, a scheme that was to bring death to the venerable and aged monk, and reduce the Guanyin Monastery to ashes. Now there were seventy or eighty cells in the monastery, and over two hundred junior and senior monks. They shifted firewood all night, piled it up all round the meditation hall so that there was no way out, and prepared to set it alight.

Although Sanzang and he had gone to bed, the magical Monkey's spirit remained alert and his eyes half open even when he was asleep. His suspicions were aroused by the sound of people moving around outside and the rustling of firewood in the breeze. "Why can I hear footsteps in the still of the night?" he wondered. "Perhaps bandits are planning to murder us." He bounded out of bed, and was on the point of opening the door· to take a look when he remembered that this might disturb his

master, so instead he used his miraculous powers to turn himself
into a bee with a shake of his body.

> *Sweet his mouth and venomous his tail,*
> *Slender his waist and light his body.*
> *He flew like an arrow, threading through willows and*
>   *flowers,*
> *Seeking their nectar like a shooting star.*
> *A tiny body that could bear great weights,*
> *Carried on the breeze by his frail and buzzing wings.*
> *Thus did he emerge from under the rafters,*
> *Going out to take a look.*

He saw that the monks had piled firewood and straw all
around the meditation hall were setting it alight. Smiling
to himself he thought, "So my master was right. This is
their idea. They want to kill us and keep our cassock. I wish
I could lay into them with my cudgel. If only I wasn't forbidden to use it, I could kill the lot of them; but the master would
only be angry with me for murdering them. Too bad. I'll just
have to take my chances as they come, and finish them off."
The splendid Monkey leapt in through the Southern Gate of
Heaven with a single somersault, startling the heavenly warriors Pang, Liu, Gou and Bi into bowing, and Ma, Zhao, Wen
and Guan into bending low as they all said, "Oh no, oh no!
The fellow who turned Heaven upside down is here again."
"There's no need to stand on courtesy or be alarmed, gentlemen," said Monkey with a wave of his hand, "I've come to find
the Broad-Visioned Heavenly King."

Before the words were out of his mouth the Heavenly King
was there and greeting Monkey with, "Haven't seen you for
ages. I heard the other day that the Bodhisattva Guanyin
came to see the Jade Emperor to borrow the four Duty Gods,
the Six Dings and Jias and the Protectors to look after the Tang
Priest on his pilgrimage to the Western Heaven to fetch the
scriptures. They were also saying that you were his disciple, so
how is it that you have the spare time to come here?" "Let's
cut the cackle," said Monkey. "The Tang Priest has run into

some villains who have started a fire to burn him to death. It's very urgent, which is why I've come to ask you for the loan of your Anti-fire Cover to save him with. Fetch it at once; I'll bring it straight back." "You've got it all wrong," the Heavenly King replied. "If villains are trying to burn him, you should rescue him with water. What do you need my Anti-fire Cover for?" "You don't understand," Monkey continued. "If I try to save him with water, he may still be hurt even if he isn't burnt up. I can only keep him free from injury if you lend me that cover; and with that it doesn't matter how much burning they do Buck up, buck up! It may be too late already. Don't mess up what I've got to do down there." "You monkey," said the Heavenly King with a laugh, "You're as wicked as ever, thinking only of yourself and never of others." "Hurry up, hurry up," Monkey pleaded. "You'll ruin everything if you go on nattering." The Heavenly King, no longer able to refuse, handed the cover to Monkey.

Taking the cover, Monkey pressed down on his cloud and went straight to the roof of the meditation hall, where he spread the cover over the Tang Priest, the dragon horse, and the luggage. Then he went to sit on top of the aged monk's room to protect the cassock. As he watched them starting the fire he kept on reciting a spell and blew some magic breath towards the southwest, at which a wind arose and fanned the flames up into a wild and roaring blaze. What a fire!

> *Spreading black smoke,*
> *Leaping red flames;*
> *The spreading black smoke blotted out all the stars in*
>   *the sky.*
> *The leaping red flames made the earth glow red for*
>   *hundreds of miles.*
> *When it started*
> *It was a gleaming golden snake;*
> *Later on*
> *It was a spirited horse.*
> *The Three Spirits of the South showed their might,*

The Fire God Huilu wielded his magic power.
The bone-dry kindling burned ferociously,
As when the Emperor Suiren drilled wood to start a fire.
Flames leapt up from the boiling oil before the doors,
Brighter than when Lord Lao Zi opens his furnace.
As the cruel fire spreads,
What can stop this wilful murder?
Instead of dealing with the disaster
They abetted it.
As the wind fanned the fire,
The flames flew many miles high;
As the fire grew in the might of the wind,
Sparks burst through the Nine Heavens.
Cracking and banging,
Like firecrackers at the end of the year;
Popping and bursting,
Like cannon-fire in battle.
None of the Buddha statues could escape the blaze,
And the guardian gods in the eastern court had nowhere to hide.
It was fiercer than the fire-attack at Red Cliff,
Or the burning of the Epang Palace.

A single spark can start a prairie fire. In a few moments the raging wind had blown the fire up into an inferno, and the whole Guanyin Monastery was red. Look at the monks as they move away boxes and baskets, grabbing tables and carrying cooking-pots on their heads. The whole monastery was full of the sound of shouting and weeping. Brother Monkey protected the abbot's rooms at the back, and the Anti-fire Cover covered the meditation hall in front; everywhere else the fire raged, its red flames reflected in the sky and its dazzling brightness shining through the wall.

When the fire broke out, all the animals and devils of the mountain were disturbed. Seven miles due south of the Guanyin Monastery was the Black Wind Mountain, on which there

was a Black Wind Cave. In this cave a monster awoke and
sat up. Seeing light streaming in through his window, he
thought it must be dawn, but when he got up to take a better
look he saw a fire blazing to the north. "Blimey," the monster
exclaimed with astonishment, "those careless monks must have
set the Guanyin Monastery on fire. I'd better go and help
them." The good monster leapt off on a cloud and went down
below the smoke and flames that reached up to the sky. The
front halls were all empty, and the fire was burning bright in
the cloisters on either side. He rushed forward with long
strides and was just calling for water when he noticed that the
rooms at the back were not burning as there was someone on
the roof keeping the wind away. The moment he realized this
and rushed in to look, he saw a magic glow and propitious
vapours coming from a black felt bundle on the table. On opening it he found it contained a brocade cassock that was a rare
treasure of the Buddhist religion. His mind disturbed by the
sight of this valuable object, he forgot about putting out the
fire or calling for water and grabbed the cassock, which he made
off with in the general confusion. Then he went straight back
to his cave by cloud.

The fire blazed on till dawn before burning itself out. The
naked monks howled and wailed as they searched through the
ashes for bronze and iron, and picked over the cinders to find
gold and silver. Some of them fixed up thatched shelters in
what remained of the frames of the buildings, and others were
rigging up pots to cook food at the bases of the exposed walls.
We will not describe the weeping, the shouting and the confused hubbub.

Brother Monkey grabbed the Anti-fire Cover, took it back
to the Southern Gate of Heaven with a single somersault, and
returned it to the Heavenly King Virupaksa with thanks.
"Great Sage," said the Heavenly King as he accepted it. "You
are as good as your word. I was so worried that if you didn't
give me back my treasure, I'd never be able to find you and get
it off you. Thank goodness you've returned it." "Am I the
sort of bloke who'd cheat someone to his face?" asked Monkey.

"After all, 'If you return a thing properly when you borrow it, it'll be easier to borrow it next time.'" "As we haven't met for so long, why don't you come into the palace for a while?" said the Heavenly King. "I'm no longer the man to 'sit on the bench till it rots, talking about the universe'," Monkey replied. "I'm too busy now that I have to look after the Tang Monk. Please excuse me." Leaving with all speed, he went down on his cloud, and saw that the sun was rising as he went straight to the meditation hall, where he shook himself, turned into a bee, and flew in. On reverting to his true form he saw that his master was still sound asleep.

"Master, get up, it's dawn," he called. Sanzang woke up, rolled over, and said, "Yes, so it is." When he had dressed he opened the doors, went outside, and saw the walls reddened and in ruins, and the halls and towers gone. "Goodness," he exclaimed in great astonishment, "why have the buildings all disappeared? Why is there nothing but reddened walls?" "You're still asleep," Monkey replied. "There was a fire last night." "Why didn't I know about it?" Sanzang asked. "I was protecting the meditation hall, and as I could see you were asleep, Master. I didn't disturb you," Monkey replied. "If you were able to protect the meditation hall, why didn't you put out the fire in the other buildings?" Sanzang asked. Monkey laughed. "I'll tell you, Master. What you predicted actually happened. They fancied that cassock of ours and planned to burn us to death. If I hadn't noticed, we'd be bones and ashes by now." "Did they start the fire?" asked Sanzang who was horrified to learn this. "Who else?" replied Monkey. "Are you sure that you didn't cook this up because they were rude to you?" Sanzang asked. "I'm not such a rascal as to do a thing like that," said Monkey. "Honestly and truly, they started it. Of course, when I saw how vicious they were I didn't help put the blaze out. I helped them with a slight breeze instead." "Heavens! Heavens! When a fire starts you should bring water, not wind." "You must know the old saying — 'If people didn't harm tigers, tigers wouldn't hurt people.' If they hadn't started a fire, I wouldn't have caused a wind." "Where's the cassock?

Don't say that it's been burnt too." "It's all right; it hasn't been burnt. The abbots' cell where it was kept didn't catch fire." "I don't care what you say. If it has come to harm, I'll recite that spell till it kills you." "Don't do that," pleaded Monkey desperately, "I promise to bring that cassock back to you. Wait while I fetch it for you, and then we'll be on our way." With Sanzang leading the horse, and Monkey carrying the luggage, they went out of the meditation hall and straight to the abbot's lodgings at the back.

When the grief-stricken monks of the monastery suddenly saw master and disciple emerge with horse and luggage from the meditation hall they were terrified out of their wits, and screamed, "Their avenging ghosts have come to demand our lives." "What do you mean, avenging ghosts coming to demand your lives?" Monkey shouted. "Give us back our cassock at once." The monks all fell to their knees and kowtowed, saying, "Masters, wrongs are always avenged, and debts always have to be paid. If you want lives, it's nothing to do with us; It was the old monk and Broad Plans who cooked up the plot to kill you. Please don't punish us." Monkey snorted with anger and roared, "I'll get you, you damned animals. Who asked for anyone's life? Just bring out that cassock and we'll be on our way." Two brave men from among the monks said, "Masters, you were burnt to death in the meditation hall, and now you come back to ask for the cassock. Are you men or ghosts?" "You cattle," sneered Monkey, "there wasn't any fire. Go and look at the meditation hall and then we'll see what you have to say." The monks rose to their feet, and when they went forward to look, they saw that there was not even the slightest trace of scorching on the door and the window-frames. The monks, now struck with fear, realized that Sanzang was a divine priest, and Monkey a guardian god. They all kowtowed to the pair of them and said, "Our eyes are blind. We failed to recognize saints sent down from Heaven. Your cassock is in the abbot's rooms at the back." Sanzang went past a number of ruined walls and buildings, sighing endlessly, and saw that the abbot's rooms at the back had indeed not been burnt. The monks all rushed in shouting, "Grandad, the Tang Priest is a saint, and instead of being burnt to death he's wrecked our home. Bring the cassock out at once and give it back to him."

Now the old monk had been unable to find the cassock, which coming on top of the destruction of the monastery had him distraught with worry. When the monks asked him for it, he was unable to reply. Seeing no way out of his quandary, he bent his head down and dashed it against the wall. He smashed his skull open and expired as his blood poured all over the floor. There are some verses about it:

> Alas that the aged monk in his folly
> Lived so long a life for nothing.
> He wanted the cassock as an heirloom for the monastery,
> Forgetting that what is Buddha's is not as mortal things.
>
> As he took the changeable for the eternal,
> His sorry end was quite inevitable.
> What use were Broad Wisdom and Broad Plans?
> Harming others for gain will always fail.

The other monks began to howl in desperation, "Our Patriarch has dashed his brains out, and we can't find the cassock, so whatever shall we do?" "I think you've hidden it somewhere," Monkey said. "Come out, all of you, and bring me all the registers. I'm going to check that you're all here." The senior and junior abbots brought the two registers in which all the monks, novices, pages, and servants were registered. There were a total of two hundred and thirty names in them. Asking his master to sit in the place of honour, Monkey called out and marked off each of the names, making the monks open up their clothes for his inspection. When he had checked each one carefully there was no sign of the cassock. Then he searched carefully through all the boxes and baskets that had been saved from the flames, but again he could find no trace of it. Sanzang, now absolutely furious with Brother Monkey, started to recite the spell as he sat up high. Monkey fell to the ground in great agony, clutching his head and pleading, "Stop, stop,

I swear to return the cassock to you." The monks, trembling at the sight, begged him to stop, and only then did he shut his mouth and desist. Monkey leapt to his feet, took his iron cudgel from behind his ear, and was going to hit the monks when Sanzang shouted, "You ape, aren't you afraid of another headache? Are you going to misbehave again? Don't move your hand or hurt anyone. I want you to question them again instead." The monks all kowtowed to him and entreated him most pitifully to spare their lives. "We've honestly not seen it. It's all that dead old bastard's fault. After he saw your cassock yesterday evening he cried till late into the night, not even wanting to look at it as he worked out a plan by which it could belong to the monastery for ever. He wanted to burn you to death, masters, but when the fire started, a gale wind blew up, and we were all busy trying to put the blaze out and move away what stuff we could. We don't know where the cassock went."

Monkey went into the abbot's quarters at the back in a great rage and carried out the corpse of the old monk who had killed himself. When he stripped the body he found no treasures on it, so he dug up the floor of his room to a depth of three feet, again without finding a sign of the cassock. Monkey thought for a moment and then asked, "Are there any monsters turned spirits around here?" "If you hadn't asked, sir, I'd never have imagined you wanted to know," the abbot replied. "There is a mountain due south of here called the Black Wind Mountain, and in the Black Wind Cave on it there lives a Great Black King. That old dead bastard of ours was always discussing the Way with him. There aren't any other evil spirits apart from him." "How far is the mountain from here?" Monkey asked. "Only about seven miles," the abbot replied. "It's the mountain you can see over there." Monkey smiled and said to Sanzang, "Don't worry, Master, there's no need to ask any more questions. No doubt about it: it must have been stolen by that black monster." "But his place is seven miles from here, so how can you be sure it was him?" Sanzang asked. "You didn't see the fire last night,"

Brother Monkey retorted. "The flames were leaping up hundreds of miles high, and the glow penetrated the triple heavens. You could have seen it seventy miles away, let alone seven. I'm convinced that he saw the glare and took the chance to slip over here quietly. When he saw that our cassock was a treasure, he must have stolen it in the confusion. Just wait while I go and find him." "If you go, who's going to protect me?" asked Sanzang. "Don't worry, gods are watching over you in secret, and in the visible sphere I'll make these monks serve you." With that he called the community together and said, "I want some of you to go and bury that old ghost, and some of you to serve my master and look after our white horse." The monks all assented obediently, and Monkey continued, "I won't have you agreeing glibly now but not waiting on them when I've gone. Those of you who look after my master must do so with pleasant expressions on your faces, and those who feed the horse must make sure he gets the right amount of hay and water. If there's the slightest mistake, I'll hit you like this." He pulled out his cudgel, and smashed a fire-baked brick wall to smithereens; the shock from this shook down seven or eight more walls. At the sight of this the monks' bones turned to jelly, and they knelt down and kowtowed to him with tears pouring down their cheeks. "Don't worry, Master, you can go — we'll look after him. We promise not to show any disrespect." The splendid Monkey then went straight to the Black Wind Mountain with a leap of his somersault cloud to look for the cassock.

> The Golden Cicada left the capital in search of the truth,
> Leaning on his staff as he went to the distant west.
> Along his route were tigers, leopards and wolves;
> Few were the artisans, merchants, or scholars he met.
> In a foreign land he encountered a stupid and covetous monk,
> And depended entirely on the mighty Great Sage Equalling Heaven.

When fire and wind destroyed the monastery,
A black bear came at night to steal the silken cassock.

If you don't know whether the cassock was found on this journey or how things turned out, listen to the explanation in the next instalment.

CHAPTER SEVENTEEN

Brother Monkey makes trouble on
the Black Wind Mountain;
Guanyin subdues the Bear Spirit.

As Monkey leapt up with a somersault, the senior and junior monks, the novices, the page-boys, and the servants of the monastery all bowed low to the sky and said, "Master, you must be a cloud-riding immortal come down from Heaven. No wonder that fire can't burn you. Damn that stupid old skinflint of ours: he destroyed himself with his own scheming." "Please rise, gentlemen," replied Sanzang. "There's no need to hate him. If my disciple finds the cassock our troubles will all come to an end; but if he doesn't find it, he has rather a nasty temper, and I'm afraid that none of you will escape with your lives." When they heard this warning, the monks' hearts were in their mouths, and they implored Heaven to let him find the cassock and spare their lives.

Once in mid-air, the Great Sage Sun Wukong reached the Black Wind Mountain with one twist of his waist. Stopping his cloud while he took a careful look around, he saw that it was indeed a fine mountain. It was a spring day:

> *The myriad valley's streams compete,*
> *A thousand precipices vie in beauty.*
> *Where the birds call, no man is;*
> *When the blossoms fall, the trees are still fragrant.*
> *After the rain, the sky and the lowering cliff are moist;*
> *As the pines bend in the wind, they spread an emerald*
>   *screen.*
> *The mountain herbs grow,*
> *The wild flowers blossom,*

Hanging over beetling crags;
The wild fig thrives
And fine trees flourish
On craggy range and flat-topped hill.
You meet no hermits,
And can find no wood-cutters.
Beside the stream a pair of cranes drink,
And wild apes gambol on the rocks.
Peaks like mussel-shells, gleaming black,
Lofty and green as they shine through the mist.

As Monkey was looking at the mountain scenery he heard voices from in front of the grassy slope. He slipped off to conceal himself under the rock-face and take a discreet look. He saw three fiends sitting on the ground. At the head was a dark fellow, to his left was a Taoist, and to his right a white-robed scholar, and they were all talking about lofty and broad matters: about refining cinnabar and mercury with tripods and cauldrons; and about the white snow, mercury, the yellow sprout, lead, and other esoteric teachings. In the middle of this the dark fellow said, "As it's my birthday tomorrow, I hope you two gentlemen will do me the honour of coming along." "We celebrate your birthday every year, Your Majesty," the white-robed scholar replied, "so of course we shall come this year." "I came by a treasure last night," the dark fellow went on, "a brocade cassock for a Buddha, and it's a wonderful thing. I'm going to give a big banquet for it the day after tomorrow and I'm inviting all you mountain officials to come and congratulate me, which is why I'm calling it a 'Buddha's Robe Banquet'." "Wonderful, wonderful," the Taoist exclaimed with a smile. "Tomorrow I'll come to congratulate you on your birthday, and the day after I'll come again for the banquet." As soon as Monkey heard him mention the Buddha's robe he was sure it was their treasure, and unable to hold back his anger he leapt out from the cliff brandishing his gold-banded cudgel with both hands and shouting, "I'll get you, you gang of devils. You stole our cassock, and now you think you're going to have a 'Buddha's Robe Banquet'. Give it back to me at once." "Don't move," he barked, swinging the cudgel and bringing it down towards the monster's head. The dark fellow turned into a wind to flee in terror, and the Taoist rode off on a cloud, so Monkey was only able to slay the white-robed scholar with a blow from the club. When he dragged the body over to look at it, he saw that it was a white-patterned snake spirit. In his anger he picked the corpse up and tore it to pieces, then went into the recesses of the mountain in search of the dark fellow. Rounding a sharp pinnacle and traversing a dizzy precipice, he saw a cave palace in the cliff:

> Thick, misty clouds,
> Dense with cypress and pine.
> The thick and misty clouds fill the gates with colour;
> The dense stands of cypress and pine surround the door
>   with green.
> For a bridge there is a dried-out log,
> And wild fig coils around the mountain peaks.
> Birds carry red petals to the cloud-filled valley;
> Deer tread on scented bushes as they climb the stone
>   tower.
> Before the gates the season brings out flowers,
> As the wind wafts their fragrance.
> Around the willows on the dike the golden orioles sing;
> Butterflies flit among the peach-trees on the bank.
> This ordinary scene can yet compete
> With lesser views in Fairyland.

When he reached the gates Monkey saw that they were very strongly fastened, and above them was a stone tablet inscribed with the words Black Wind Cave of the Black Wind Mountain in large letters. He brandished his cudgel and shouted, "Open up!" at which the junior devil who was on the gates opened them and asked, "Who are you, and how dare you come and attack our immortals' cave?" "You damned cur," Monkey railed at him. "How dare you call a place like this an 'immortals' cave'? What right have you to use the word 'immortal'? Go

in and tell that dark fellow of yours that if he gives back my
cassock at once, I'll spare your lives." The junior devil rushed
in and reported, "The 'Buddha's Robe Banquet' is off, Your
Majesty. There's a hairy-faced thunder god outside the gates
who's demanding the cassock." The dark fellow, who had barely had time to shut the gates and had not even sat down properly since Brother Monkey chased him away from the grassy
slope, thought on hearing this news, "This wretch has come from
I don't know where, and now he has the effrontery to come yelling at my gates." He called for his armour, tightened his belt,
and strode out of the gates with a black-tasselled spear in his
hands. Monkey appeared outside the gates holding his iron
cudgel and glaring wide-eyed at that ferocious-looking monster.

> His bowl-shaped iron helmet shone like fire;
> His black bronze armour gleamed.
> A black silk gown with billowing sleeves,
> A dark green silken sash with fringes.
>
> In his hands a spear with black tassels,
> On his feet a pair of dark leather boots.
> Lightning flashed from his golden pupils;
> He was indeed the Black Wind King of the mountains.

"This wretch looks as though he's been a brick-burner or a
coal-digger," Monkey thought as he smiled to himself. "He's
so black he must be the local soot-painter." "What gives you
the nerve to act so big round here, monk, and what the hell
are you?" shouted the monster at the top of his voice. Monkey
rushed him with his cudgel and roared, "Cut the cackle, and give
me back the cassock at once, kid." "What monastery d'you come
from? Where did you lose the cassock? Why come and ask
for it here?" "My cassock was in the back abbot's lodgings at
the Guanyin Monastery due north of here. When the monastery caught fire you made the most of the confusion to do a bit
of looting and brought it back here, you wretch, and now you're
planning to hold a 'Buddha's Robe Banquet'. Don't try to brazen it out. Give it back at once, and I'll spare your life, but if

even a hint of a 'no' gets past your teeth I'll push the Black Wind Mountain over, trample your cave flat, and pound every one of you fiends into powder."

The monster laughed evilly and replied, "You've got a nerve. You were the one who started the fire last night. You were sitting on the roof of the abbot's lodgings and calling up a wind to make it worse. What's it to you if I did take a cassock? Where are you from? Who are you? You must have a lot of tricks up your sleeve if you have the nerve to talk so big." "You can't recognize your own grandfather," Brother Monkey replied. "I, your grandfather, am the disciple of His Highness the Patriarch Sanzang, the younger brother of the Emperor of the Great Tang. My name is Brother Sun Wukong. If you want to know about my tricks, just give me the word. I'll slaughter you here and now, and send your souls flying." "I've never heard of these tricks of yours, so you'd better tell me about them." "Stand still and listen to me, my child," Monkey replied, and went on to say:

> "Great have been my magic powers since childhood;
> Changing with the wind, I show my might.
> Nourishing my nature and cultivating the truth, I have
>   lived out the days and months,
> Saving my life by jumping beyond the cycle of rebirth.
> With sincerity I searched for the Way,
> Climbing the Spirit Terrace Mountain to pick medicinal
>   herbs.
> On that mountain lives an ancient immortal
> One hundred and eight thousand years old.
> I took him as my master,
> Hoping that he would show me a road to immortality.
> He said that the elixir is in one's own body —
> It is a waste of effort to seek it outside.
> I learnt a great spell of immortality
> Without which I could scarcely have survived.
> Turning my gaze inwards, I sat and calmed my mind,
> While the sun and moon in my body intermingled.

Ignoring the affairs of the world, I made my desires few.
When senses, body, and mind were purified, my body
*   was firm.*
Reversing the years and returning to youth is then easily
*   done;*
The road to immortality and sagehood was not long.
Not letting anything leak for three whole years I acquired
*   a magic body*
That did not suffer like a common one.
I wandered around the Ten Continents and Three
*   Islands,*
The corners of the sea and the edge of the sky.
I was due to live over three hundred years
But could not yet fly up to the Nine Heavens.
I got a real treasure for subduing sea dragons:
An iron cudgel banded with gold.
On the Mountain of Flowers and Fruit I was supreme
*   commander;*
In the Water Curtain Cave I assembled the fiendish
*   hosts.*
The Great Jade Emperor sent me a decree
Conferring high rank and the title 'Equalling Heaven'.
More than once I wrecked the Hall of Miraculous Mist,
And stole the Queen Mother's peaches several times.
A hundred thousand heavenly soldiers came in serried
*   ranks*
With spears and swords to put me down.
I sent the heavenly kings back up there in defeat,
Made Nezha flee in pain at the head of his men.
I fought hard and equalled in power
The True Lord Erlang, skilled at transformations.
Lao Zi, Guanyin and the Jade Emperor
Watched me being subdued from the Southern Gate of
*   Heaven.*
As he was given some help by Lord Lao Zi,
Erlang captured me and took me to Heaven.
I was tied to the Demon-subduing Pillar,

And divine soldiers were ordered to cut off my head.
Though hacked with swords and hammered I remained
*   unharmed,*
So then I was struck with thunder and burned with fire.
As I really do have magic powers,
I was not in the slightest bit afraid.
They took me to Lord Lao Zi's furnace to be refined:
The Six Dings roasted me slowly with divine fire.
When time was up and the furnace opened, out I jumped,
And rushed round Heaven, my cudgel in my hand.
No one could stop me making trouble everywhere,
And I caused chaos in the thirty-three Heavens.
Then our Tathagata Buddha used his Dharma power
And dropped Five Elements Mountain on my back.
There I lay crushed for full five hundred years,
Until Sanzang came from the land of Tang.
Now I have reformed and am going to the West
To climb the Thunder Peak and see the Buddha.
Enquire throughout the Four Seas, Heaven and Earth:
You'll find that I'm the greatest monster ever.

On hearing this the fiend laughed and said, "So you're the Protector of the Horses who wrecked Heaven, are you?" Monkey, who got angrier at being addressed by this title than at anything else, was furious. "You vicious monster. You steal the cassock and refuse to give it back, and on top of that you insult your lord and master. Just hold it, and see how you like my club." The dark fellow dodged the blow and then riposted with his spear. The pair of them fought a fine battle.

An as-you-will cudgel,
A black-tasselled spear,
And two men showing their toughness at the mouth of
*   a cave.*
One stabs at heart and face,
The other tries for arm and head.
This one strikes cunning sideswipes with a club,
That one brandishes his spear in three swift movements.

The white tiger climbs the mountain to extend his claws;
The yellow dragon lying on the road turns round fast.
Snorting out coloured mists,
Disgorging rays of light,
The two immortal fiends are hard to choose between:
One is the Sage Equalling Heaven who has cultivated the
*   truth;*
The other is the Great Black King become a spirit.
On this battlefield in the mountains
The pair of them fight for the cassock.

The fiend fought some ten inconclusive rounds with Monkey, and as the sun was now rising steadily towards the zenith, the dark fellow raised his halberd to block the iron cudgel and said, "Brother Monkey, let's lay down our arms. I'll come back and fight you again after I've eaten." "You accursed beast," Monkey replied, "how can you call yourself a real man? If you were, you wouldn't be needing to eat after only half a day. I never even tasted water once in those five hundred years I spent under the mountain, but I wasn't hungry. Stop making excuses, and don't go. I'll let you have your meal if you give me back my cassock." The fiend waved his halberd in a feint, withdrew into the cave, and shut the doors fast behind him. Summoning his junior goblins, he ordered that a banquet be spread and wrote invitations asking all the devil kings of the mountain to come to the celebratory feast.

Monkey charged the gates but was unable to force them open, so he had to go back to the Guanyin Monastery, where the monks had buried the old patriarch and were now all in attendance on the Tang Priest in the abbot's quarters. Breakfast was over, and lunch was being brought in. Just as they were bringing soup and more hot water, Monkey descended from the sky. The monks all bowed low and took him into the abbot's room to see Sanzang. "Ah, you're back, Wukong," he said. "What about the cassock?" "I've found the answer. We misjudged these monks. It was in fact stolen by a fiend from the Black Wind Mountain. I went to have a quiet look for him and found him sitting in front of a grassy slope talking to a white-gowned scholar and an old Taoist. He's a self-confessed monster, and he said with his own mouth that he was inviting all the evil spirits to come and celebrate his birthday tomorrow, and that as he had come by a brocade Buddha's robe last night he wanted to celebrate that too, so he was going to give a great feast that he called an 'Assembly for the Celebration and Admiration of the Buddha's Robe'. I rushed him and took a swipe at him with my club, but the dark fellow turned into a puff of wind and fled. The Taoist disappeared too, and I was only able to kill the white-clad scholar, who was a white snake turned spirit. I went to the mouth of his cave as fast as I could and told him to come out and fight me. He admitted that he had carried it off. We fought for half a day without either of us winning, and then the monster went back to his cave for lunch and shut the stone gates behind him. He was too scared to come out again, so I came back to give you this news, Master. Now we know where the cassock is, there's no need to worry that he won't give it back."

On hearing this, the monks put their hands together or kowtowed as they invoked Amitabha Buddha and exclaimed, "He's found where it is — we're saved." "Don't be so happy about it," Monkey warned, "I haven't got it yet, and my master hasn't left your monastery yet. You'll have to wait till I've recovered the cassock and my master has been seen off properly from here before you can consider yourselves safe. And if there is the slightest mistake, remember that I'm a very quick-tempered boss. Have you given my master the best food and tea? Have you given my horse the best fodder?" "Yes, yes, yes," the monks hastened to assure him. "We haven't been remiss in any way while looking after his Reverence." "While you were away all morning I've drunk tea three times and eaten twice, and they have not been at all offhand with me," Sanzang explained. "You'd better go back and do everything possible to recover that cassock." "Don't be in such a hurry," Monkey replied. "I know where it is, and I guarantee that I'll capture this wretch and return the cassock to you. There's no need to worry."

As he was talking the senior abbot came in, set out the vegetarian meal, and invited Lord Monkey to eat. After swallowing a few mouthfuls, Monkey mounted his magic cloud once more and went off on his hunt. On his way he saw a junior goblin going along the main path with a rosewood box under his left arm. Guessing that there must be some kind of letter in the box Monkey raised his cudgel and brought it down on his head. The blow did not just kill the goblin: it left him looking like a hamburger. Throwing his remains aside, Brother Monkey wrenched open the box and saw that it contained an invitation:

> Your pupil Bear presents his humble greetings to Your Excellency, the Supreme and Venerabe One of the Golden Pool:
>
> I am deeply grateful for the magnificent kindness that I have so frequently received from you. When I saw the fire last night I failed to put it out, but I am sure that your divine intelligence will have suffered no harm from it. As your pupil has been lucky enough to obtain a Buddha's robe, I am giving a banquet, to which I hope you will come to appreciate the robe. I would be profoundly grateful if you would honour me with your presence at the appointed time. Written two days beforehand.

On reading this, Monkey roared with laughter and said, "That crooked old monk. He thoroughly deserved to be killed. He'd been ganging up with evil spirits, had he? It's odd that he should have lived to be two hundred and seventy. I suppose that evil spirit must have taught him a few tricks about controlling his vital essence, which was why he lived so long. I can remember what he looked like, so I think I'll make myself look like him and go into that cave. This way I can see where he's put that cassock, and if I'm lucky I'll be able to get back and save a lot of trouble.

The splendid Great Sage recited a spell, faced the wind,

and made himself look just like the old monk. He hid his cudgel, walked straight to the entrance of the cave, and shouted, "Open up." The junior goblin opened up, and as soon as he saw him he rushed back to report, "Your Majesty, the Elder of the Golden Pool is here." The monster was astounded. "I've only just sent a youngster with an invitation for him, and the message can't have reached him yet. How could he possibly have got here so fast? The youngster can't even have met him. Obviously Brother Monkey has sent him here to ask for the cassock. Steward, hide that cassock somewhere where he won't see it."

As he came to the front gates Monkey saw that the court-yard was green with bamboo and cypress, while peach and plum trees vied in beauty amid blossoming shrubs and fragrant or-chids. It was a cave paradise. He also saw a couplet inscribed on the gates that read:

> *In peaceful retirement deep in the hills, one is free of vulgar worries;*
> *Dwelling quietly in a magic cave, happy in divine sim-plicity.*

"This wretch has escaped from the dirt and dust of the world," thought Monkey, "and is a fiend who understands life." Going through the gates he went further inside and pass-ed through a triple gate. Here were carved and painted beams, light windows and coloured doors. He saw that the dark fellow was wearing a dark green silken tunic over which was slung a black patterned silk cloak; on his head was a soft black hat, and on his feet a pair of dusky deerskin boots. When he saw Monkey approaching he straightened his clothes and came down the steps to greet him with the words, "I've been looking forward to seeing you for days, Golden Pool. Please take a seat." Monkey returned his courtesies, and when they had finished greeting each other they sat down and drank tea. Then the evil spirit bowed and said, "I sent you a note just now asking you to come over the day after tomorrow. Why is it that you've come to see me today, old friend?" "I was on my way here to visit you when I happened to see your message that you were giving a 'Buddha's Robe Banquet', so I hurried over to ask you to let me have a look." "You've misunderstood, old friend," replied the evil monster with a smile. "It's the Tang Priest's cassock, and as he's been staying at your place you must have seen it there. Why come here to see it?" "When I borrowed it," Monkey said, "it was too late at night for me to be able to look at it. Since then, to my great surprise, it has been taken by Your Majesty. On top of that, the monastery has been burnt down and I have lost everything I own. That disciple of the Tang Priest's is quite a bold fellow, but he could not find it anywhere. I have come here to look at it as Your Majesty has had the great good fortune to recover it." As they were talking, a junior goblin came in from patrolling the mountain to announce, "Your Majesty, a terrible thing's happened. Brother Monkey has killed the lieutenant who was taking the invitation by the main path, and taken the chance of making himself look like the Elder of the Golden Pool to come here and trick the Buddha's robe out of you." "I wondered why the elder came today," the monster thought, "and why he came so soon, and now I see that it's really *him*." He leapt to his feet, grabbed his halberd, and thrust at Monkey. Monkey pulled the cudgel from his ear in a flash, reverted to his true form, parried the halberd's blade, jumped out from the main room into the courtyard, and fought his way back out through the front gates. This terrified all the fiends in the cave, scaring the wits out of young and old alike. The fine combat on the mountain that ensued was even better than the previous one.

> The courageous Monkey King was now a monk;
> The cunning dark fellow had hidden the Buddha's robe.
> At matching words they were both masters;
> In making the most of chances there was nothing be-
>   tween them.
> The cassock could not be seen, whatever one wished:
> A hidden treasure is a true wonder.

*When the junior demon on mountain patrol announced
    a disaster,*
The old fiend in his fury showed his might.
*Monkey transformed himself and fought his way out of
    the cave,*
As halberd and cudgel strove to decide the issue.
*The club blocked the lengthy halberd with resounding
    clangs;*
The halberd gleamed as it parried the iron club.
Sun Wukong's transformations were rare on earth;
Few could rival the foul fiend's magic.
One wanted to take the robe to celebrate his birthday;
One had to have the cassock to return with honour.
This bitter struggle was not to be broken up:
Even a Living Buddha could not have resolved it.

From the mouth of the cave the pair of them fought to the top of the mountain, and from the top of the mountain they battled their way beyond the clouds. They breathed out wind and mist, set sand and stones flying, and struggled till the red sun set in the west, but the contest was still undecided. Then the monster said, "Stop for the moment, Monkey. It's too late to go on fighting tonight. Go away, go away. Come back tomorrow, and we'll see which of us is to live and which to die." "Don't go, my child," Monkey shouted back. "If you want to fight, fight properly. Don't use the time of day as an excuse to get out of it." With that he struck wildly at the dark fellow, who changed himself into a puff of wind, went back to his cave, and fastened the stone gates tightly shut.

Monkey could think of no alternative to going back to the Guanyin Monastery. Bringing his cloud down, he called to his master, who had been waiting for him anxiously until he appeared suddenly before his eyes. Sanzang was very glad, until seeing that there was no cassock in Monkey's hands his happiness turned to fear. "Why haven't you got the cassock this time either?" he asked. Brother Monkey produced the invitation from his sleeve, and as he handed it to Sanzang he said,

"Master, that fiend was friends with that dead crook. He sent a junior goblin with this invitation asking him to go to a 'Buddha's Robe Banquet'. I killed the goblin, made myself look like the old monk, went into the cave, and tricked a cup of tea out of them. I asked him to let me see the cassock, but he wouldn't bring it out. Then as we were sitting there a mountain patrolman of some sort gave the game away, so he started to fight me. We fought till just now, and neither of us was on top, when he saw that it was late, shot back to his cave and shut the stone doors behind him. This meant that I had to come back for the moment." "How do your tricks compare with his?" Sanzang asked. "I'm not much better than him," Monkey replied, "and I can only keep my end up." Sanzang read the invitation and handed it to the prelate. "Can it be that your Patriarch was an evil spirit?" he said. The prelate fell to knees as fast as he could and said, "My lord, he was human. But because that Great Black King was cultivating the ways of humanity he often came to our temple to discuss the scriptures with our Patriarch, and taught him some of the arts of nourishing the divine and controlling the vital essence. That was why they were on friendly terms." "None of these monks have anything satanic about them," Monkey said. "They all have their heads in the air and their feet on the ground, and are taller and fatter than I am. They're not evil spirits. Do you see where it says 'Your pupil Bear' on the invitation? He must be a black bear who has become a spirit." To this Sanzang said, "There's an old saying that 'Bears and baboons are alike'. If they are all animals, how can they become spirits?" Monkey laughed and replied, "I'm an animal too, but I became the Great Sage Equalling Heaven. I'm just the same as him. All the creatures on heaven and earth that have nine openings to their bodies can cultivate their conduct and become immortals." "Just now you said his abilities were the same as yours, so how are you going to beat him and get the cassock back?" Sanzang went on to ask. "Don't worry, don't worry," Monkey replied, "I can manage."

As they were talking, the monks brought their evening meal and invited them to eat. Then Sanzang asked for a lamp

and went to bed in the front meditation hall as before. The
monks all slept under thatched shelters rigged up against the
walls, leaving the abbot's quarters at the back for the senior and
junior prelate. It was a peaceful night.

> The Milky Way was clear,
> The jade firmament free of dust.
> The sky was full of coruscating stars,
> A single wave wiped out the traces.
> Stilled were all sounds,
> And the birds were silent on a thousand hills.
> The fisherman's light beside the bank was out,
> The Buddha-lamp in the pagoda dimmed.
> Last night the abbot's bell and drum had sounded;
> This evening the air was filled with weeping.

This night he spent asleep in the monastery. Sanzang, however, could not sleep for thinking about the cassock. He turned
over, and seeing that the sky was growing light outside the
window, got straight out of bed and said, "Monkey, it's light,
go and get the cassock." Brother Monkey bounded out of bed,
and in an instant a host of monks was in attendance, offering
hot water. "Look after my master properly," he said. "I'm
off." Sanzang got out of bed and seized hold of him. "Where
are you going?" he asked. "I've been thinking," said Monkey,
"that this whole business is the Bodhisattva Guanyin's fault.
Although this is her monastery and she receives the worship of
all these monks, she allows that evil spirit to live in the neighbourhood. I'm going to the Southern Sea to find her and ask
her to come here herself to make that evil spirit give us back
the cassock." "When will you come back?" Sanzang asked.
"After you've finished breakfast at the earliest, and by midday
at latest, I'll have done the job. Those monks had better look
after you well. I'm off now."

No sooner were the words out of his mouth than he had
disappeared without a trace and reached the Southern Sea.
Stopping his cloud to take a look, he saw:

A vast expanse of ocean,
Waters stretching till they joined the sky.
Propitious light filled the firmament;
Auspicious vapours shone over mountains and rivers.
A thousand snow-capped breakers roared at the azure
*   vault;*
A myriad misty waves reared at the sky.
Water flew in all directions;
Torrents poured everywhere.
As the water flew in all directions it echoed like
*   thunder;*
As the torrents poured everywhere they crashed and
*   thunder;*
Let us leave the sea,
And consider what lay in it:
A precious mountain in many a misty colour —
Red, yellow, purple, black, green, and blue.
Then did he see the beautiful land of Guanyin,
Potaraka Island in the Southern Sea.
What a wonderful place to go —
Towering peaks
Cutting through the sky,
With a thousand kinds of exotic flowers below them,
And every type of magical herb.
The wind shook priceless trees,
The sun shone on lotuses of gold.
Guanyin's palace was roofed with glazed tiles;
The gates of the Tide Cave were set with tortoise shell.
In the shade of green willows parrots talked,
While peacocks called amid purple bamboo.
On the marbled stone
The protecting gods were majestically severe;
Before the agate strand
Stood the mighty Moksa.

Not pausing to take in the whole of this exotic scene, Monkey brought his cloud straight down to land under the bamboo grove. A number of devas were already there to meet him, and they said, "The Bodhisattva told us some time ago that you had been converted, Great Sage, and praised you very warmly. But if you are now protecting the Tang Priest, how have you found the time to come here?" "Because something has happened while I've been escorting him on his journey. Please go and tell the Bodhisattva that I'd like an audience with her." When the devas went into the cave to report this, Guanyin summoned him inside. Monkey did as he was told and bowed to her beneath the lotus throne. "What have you come for?" the Bodhisattva asked. "My master's journey has brought him to a monastery of yours," Monkey replied, "and I find that although you accept incense from its monks, you allow a black bear spirit to live in the neighbourhood, and have let him steal my master's cassock. I've tried to take it off him a number of times but got nowhere, so now I've come to ask you to demand it from him." "What nonsense, you ape," the Bodhisattva retorted. "Even if a bear spirit has stolen your cassock, what business have you to ask me go and demand it for you? It all happened because you wanted to show it off, you big-headed and evil baboon, in front of petty-minded people. On top of that, in your wickedness you called up the wind to spread the fire that burnt down my monastery. And now you have the nerve to try your tricks here." These words from the Bodhisattva made Monkey realize that she knew all about the past and the future, so he hastily bowed down in reverente and pleaded, "Bodhisattva, forgive your disciple his sins. Everything you say is true. All the same, my master will recite that spell again because that monster won't give back the cassock, and I couldn't bear the agonizing headache. That's why I came to bother you, Bodhisattva. I beg you in your mercy to help me catch that evil spirit, get the cassock back, and carry on towards the west." "That monster's magical powers are certainly no weaker than yours," the Bodhisattva said. "Very well then, out of consideration for the Tang Priest I'll go there with you." Monkey thanked her and bowed again, asked her to come out, and rode on the same magic cloud as her. In next to no time they reached the Black Wind Mountain, where they landed the cloud and headed for the cave on foot.

As they were on their way, a Taoist-priest appeared on the mountain slope. He was carrying a glass salver on which were two pills of the elixir of immortality. Monkey was immediately suspicious of him, so he struck straight at his head with the iron cudgel, sending blood splattering out from brain and chest. "Are you still as wild as this, you ape?" the shocked Bodhisattva asked. "He didn't steal your cassock, you didn't even know him, and he was no enemy of yours. Why kill him?" "You may not know him, Bodhisattva," Monkey replied, "but he was a friend of the Black Bear Spirit. Yesterday they and a white-clad scholar were sitting talking in front of the grassy mountain-side. Today is the Black Spirit's birthday, and tomorrow he was coming to the 'Buddha's Robe Banquet'. That's why I recogniz ed him. I'm sure that he was coming to greet that monster on his birthday." "If that is how it is, very well then," said the Bodhisattva. Monkey then went to lift up the Taoist to take a look at him, and he saw that he had been a grey wolf. There was an inscription under the glass salver that lay beside him. It read, "Made by Master Emptiness-reached".

Brother Monkey laughed and said, "What luck, what luck. This helps me and will save you trouble too, Bodhisattva. This monster has confessed of his own free will, and the other monster there can be finished off today." "What do you mean?" the Bodhisattva asked. "I have a saying," he replied, "that goes 'beat him at his own game'. Are you willing to let me do things my way?" "Tell me about it," the Bodhisattva said. "The two pills of immortality you see on that salver will be the pres-ent we take to visit him with," said Monkey, "and the words inscribed underneath — 'Made by Master Emptiness-reached' — are the bait we'll set for him. If you do as I say, I have a plan for you that does not call for force or fighting. The fiend will collapse before our eyes, and the cassock will appear. If you won't let me have my way, then you go west, I'll go east, we can say goodbye to the Buddha's robe, and Sanzang will be up the creek." "You've got a cheek, you ape," replied the Bodhisattva with a smile. "No, no, I really have got a plan,"

Monkey protested. "Tell me about it then," said Guanyin. "You know it says on the salver, 'Made by Master Emptiness-reached.' Well, Master Emptiness-reached must be his name. Bodhisattva, if you're prepared to let me have my way, then change yourself into that Taoist. I shall eat one of those pills and then change myself into a pill, though I'll be a bit on the big side. You are to take the tray with the two pills on it and go to wish the fiend many happy returns. Give him the bigger of the pills, and when he's swallowed me, I'll take over inside him. If he doesn't hand the cassock over then, I'll weave a substitute out of his guts."

The Bodhisattva could only nod her agreement. "What about It then?" said the laughing Monkey, and at this the Bodhisattva in her great mercy used her unbounded divine power and her infinite capacity for transformation to control her will with her heart and her body with her will — in an instant she turned into Master Emptiness-reached.

> The wind of immortality blew around his gown,
> As he hovered, about to rise to emptiness.
> His dark features were as ancient as a cypress,
> His elegant expression unmatched in time.
> Going and yet staying nowhere,
> Similar but unique.
> In the last resort all comes down to a single law,
> From which he is only separated by an evil body.

"Great, great," exclaimed Brother Monkey at the sight. "Are you a Bodhisattva disguised an evil spirit, or a Bodhisattva who really is an evil spirit?" "Monkey," she replied with a laugh, "evil spirit and Bodhisattva are all the same in the last analysis — they both belong to non-being." Suddenly enlightened by this, Monkey curled up and turned himself into a pill of immortality:

> Rolling across the plate but not unstable,
> Round and bright without any corners.
> The double three was compounded by Ge Hong,
> The double six was worked out by Shao Weng.

> *Pebbles of golden flame,*
> *Pearls that shone in the daylight.*
> *On the outside were lead and mercury,*
> *But I cannot reveal the formula.*

The pill he changed himself into was indeed a little larger than the other one. The Bodhisattva noted this and went with the glass salver to the entrance of the fiend's cave. Here she saw

> *Towering crags and lofty precipices,*
> *Where clouds grow on the peaks;*
> *Blue cypresses and green pines*
> *Where the wind soughs in the forest.*
> *On towering crags and lofty precipices*
> *The devils come and go, and few men live.*
> *The blue cypresses and green pines*
> *Inspire immortals to cultivate the hidden Way.*
> *The mountains have gullies,*
> *The gullies have springs,*
> *Whose gurgling waters sing like a guitar,*
> *Refreshing the ear.*
> *Deer on its banks,*
> *Cranes in the woods,*
> *Where the reticent immortal's pipe is casually played*
> *To delight the heart.*
> *Here an evil spirit can attain enlightenment,*
> *And the boundless vow of the Buddha extends its mercy.*

When the Bodhisattva saw this she thought, "If the beast has chosen this cave, there must be some hope for him." And from then on she felt compassion for him. When she reached the entrance of the cave, the junior goblins at the gates greeted her with the words, "Welcome, Immortal Elder Emptiness-reached." As some of them ran in to announce her, the monster came out of the gates to meet her and say, "Master Emptiness-reached, how good of you to put yourself to this trouble. This is an honour for me." "Allow me to present you with this magic pill that, I venture to say, will confer immortality on you," the Bodhisattva replied. When the two of them had finished exchanging greetings they sat down, and the monster started to talk about the events of the previous day. The Bodhisattva quickly changed the subject by passing the salver to him and saying, "Please accept this token of my regard for you." She observed which was the bigger one and handed it to him with the words, "I wish Your Majesty eternal life." The monster handed the other pill to her and said, "I hope, Master Emptiness-reached, that you will share it with me." When they had finished declining politely, the fiend picked up the pill and was on the point of swallowing it when it went rolling into his mouth. Then Monkey resumed his true form and struck up some acrobatic postures, at which the fiend fell to the ground. The Bodhisattva too resumed her true form and asked the monster for the Buddha's cassock. As Monkey had now emerged through the monster's nostrils, she was worried that the evil spirit might misbehave again, so she threw a band over his head. He rose to his feet, ready to run them through with his spear, but Monkey and the Bodhisattva were already up in mid-air, where she began to recite the spell. As the monster's head began to ache, he dropped the spear and writhed in agony on the ground. The Handsome Monkey King collapsed with laughter in the sky, while the Black Bear Spirit rolled in torment on the earth.

"Beast, will you return to the truth now?" asked the Bodhisattva. "I swear to, I swear to, if only you spare my life," the monster repeated over and over again. Monkey wanted to finish him off with no more ado, but the Bodhisattva stopped him at once: "Don't kill him — I've got a use for him." "What's the point in keeping that beast alive instead of killing him?" Monkey asked. "I've got nobody to look after the back of my Potaraka Island," she replied, "so I shall take him back with me to be an island-guarding deity." "You certainly are the all-merciful deliverer who doesn't allow a single soul to perish," said Monkey with a laugh. "If I knew a spell like that one of yours, I'd say it a thousand times over and finish off all the black bears I could find." Although the bear spirit had come round and the spell had stopped, he was still in great pain as he knelt on the ground and begged pitifully, "Spare my life and I promise I'll return to the truth." The Bodhisattva descended in a ray of light, placed her hands on his head, and administered the monastic discipline to him; then she told him to take up his spear and accompany her. The black bear's evil intentions ceased from that day on, and his unbounded perversity came to an end. "Sun Wukong," ordered the Bodhisattva, "go back now. Serve the Tang Priest well, don't be lazy, and don't start trouble." "I'm very grateful to you for coming so far, Bodhisattva, and I must see you home," Monkey said.   "That will not be necessary," she replied. Monkey took the cassock, kowtowed to her, and departed. The Bodhisattva took Bear back to the sea, and there is a poem to prove it:

> *A magic glow shines round the golden image,*
> *Ten thousand rays of glorious light.*
> *She saves all men, giving of her pity,*
> *Surveying the whole universe and revealing the golden*
>   *lotus.*
>
> *She comes today to preach the scriptures' meaning,*
> *And when she goes she leaves no flaw behind.*
> *The demon subdued and converted, she returns to the*
>   *sea:*
> *The religion of Emptiness has recovered the brocade*
>   *cassock.*

If you don't know how things developed, listen to the explanation in the next chapter.

CHAPTER EIGHTEEN

The Tang Priest is rescued in
the Guanyin Temple;
The Great Sage removes a monster from
Gao Village.

Taking his leave of the Bodhisattva, Monkey brought his cloud
in to land, hung the cassock on a *nanmu* tree, pulled out his
cudgel, charged into the Black Wind Cave, and found not a
single goblin inside. This was because the appearance of the
Bodhisattva in her true form had set the old monsters rolling
on the ground and fleeing in all directions. Evil thoughts welled
up in Brother Monkey, and after piling dry firewood all around
the multi-storeyed gate he set it alight, turning the Black Wind
Cave into a Red Wind Cave. Then he went back to the north
on a beam of magic light.

Sanzang, who had been anxiously waiting for him, was
beginning to wonder why he had not come back. Had the
Bodhisattva not come when asked to, or had Monkey just made
up a story to escape? As he was being racked by these desperate thoughts, a shimmering cloud appeared in mid-air and
Monkey came down and knelt before him. "Master, here's the
cassock," he announced, to Sanzang's great joy. All the monks
of the temple were delighted too, and they exclaimed, "Wonderful, wonderful, our lives are safe at last." "Monkey," said
Sanzang as he took the cassock from him, "when you set out
this morning you reckoned that it would only take the length of
a meal, or until midday at longest. Why have you only come
back now, at sunset?" When Monkey gave him a full account of
how he had asked the Bodhisattva to transform herself to subdue the monster, Sanzang set up an incense table and bowed

虹庵
虹庵弄
傳院弄末
名末雅
雅弄
大
傳
熊

low to the south. That done, he said, "Disciple, now that we have the Buddha's robe, pack our luggage as quickly as you can." "Not so fast, not so fast," Monkey replied. "It's already evening, too late to hit the road. Let's set out tomorrow morning." The monks all knelt and said, "Lord Monkey is right. For one thing it's too late, and for another we made a vow. Now that all is well and the treasure has been recovered, we would like to carry out that vow and invite Your Lordships to share in the thanksgiving meal. Tomorrow morning we'll see you off on your way west." "Yes, yes," urged Monkey. The monks then emptied their bags and produced everything that was left of what they had saved from the fire to make an offering of food. Then they burnt some paper to bring blessings and recited some sutras to ward off disaster. The ceremonies were finished that evening.

The next morning the horse was curried and the luggage packed, and then they set out. The monks escorted them a long distance before turning back, after which Monkey led the way. It was now early spring.

> The grass cushions the horse's hooves,
> New leaves emerge from the willow's golden threads.
> Apricot vies for beauty with the peach;
> The wild fig round the path is full of life.
> On sun-warmed sandbanks sleep mandarin ducks;
> In the flower-scented gully the butterflies are quiet.
> After autumn, winter, and half of spring,
> Who knows when the journey will end as they find the
>   true word?

One evening, after they had been travelling along a desolate path for six or seven days, master and disciple saw a distant village. "Monkey," said Sanzang, "do you see the village not far over there? Let's go and ask them to put us up for the night; we can set off again tomorrow morning." "Wait till I've made sure it's all right before deciding," Monkey replied, gazing at the village as his master pulled on the silken rein. He saw

Close-planted bamboo fences,
Many a thatched roof.
Outside the gates soar lofty trees;
Houses are mirrored in the waters under a bridge.
Green grow the willows beside the road;
Fragrant bloom the flowers in the gardens.
As sun sets in the west
Birds sing in the wooded hills.
The smoke of evening rises from the stoves
Along the paths roam sheep and cattle.
Well-fed chickens and pigs sleep under the eaves,
While the drunk old man sings his song next door.

When he had surveyed the scene, Brother Monkey said, "Go ahead, Master. It's definitely a good village. We can spend the night there." Sanzang urged his horse forward, and in a few moments they were at the beginning of the main street. A young man appeared wearing a silken turban, a blue jacket, a pair of trousers tied at the ankles, and a pair of straw sandals. He was carrying an umbrella in his hand and a pack on his back. He was a fine sight as he walked briskly down the street. Monkey grabbed him and asked, "Where are you going? I want to ask you something — where is this?" The fellow, who was trying to break loose, shouted, "Why ask me? I'm not the only person in the village." "Don't be angry, kind sir," replied Monkey, all smiles. "To help others is to help yourself. What harm can it do to tell me what the place is called? We might be able to bring your troubles to an end, you know." Struggle as he might, the fellow could not break loose, which made him leap around with fury. "Damn it, damn it," he shouted, "I get more bullying from the old man than I can stand, and now I've got to run into you, baldy. You've got it in for me too." "If you're good for anything, get out of my grip," Monkey said. "Do that and I'll let you go." The young man twisted and turned, but he could not break free — it was as if he were held in a pair of pliers. In his temper he threw down his umbrella and his bundle, and tore at Monkey with both hands, trying to get hold of him.

Monkey was holding the luggage in one hand, and with the other he was keeping the young man under control, and no matter how hard the fellow tried he could not get a grip on him. Monkey, however, was now holding him more firmly than ever, which made him furious. "Monkey," Sanzang said, "here comes someone else you can ask. Why keep such a tight grip on him? Let him go." "You don't understand, Master," replied Monkey with a smile. "It would be no fun to ask anyone else. I have to ask him if there's to be anything to be got out of this." Seeing that Monkey would not let him go, the fellow started to talk. "This is Old Gao Village in the country of Stubet, and it's called that because practically everyone here has the surname Gao. Now let me go." "From your get-up, you're going on a long journey," Monkey went on. "Tell me where you're going and what you're up to, then I'll let you go."

The poor fellow had no option but to tell Monkey the truth. "I'm Gao Cai from the family of Squire Gao. His youngest daughter is twenty and not yet married, but three years ago an evil spirit came and took her. He's been staying with us for three years, and the old man isn't at all pleased. There's no future in having a girl marry an evil spirit, he says. It's ruining our family, and we don't get a family of in-laws to visit. He's always wanted to get rid of the evil spirit, but he refuses to go. Now he's shut the girl up in the back building for the best part of a year, and he won't let any of the family see her. My old man gave me two ounces of silver and sent me to find a priest to capture the monster. I've been on the go for ages now, and asked three or four of them, but they were all hopeless monks or pimples of Taoists — none of them could control him. The old man's just been swearing at me as an utter idiot, given me another half an ounce of silver as travelling expenses, and told me to find a good priest who'll deal with the monster. Then I was grabbed by you, you evil star, and that's made me later than ever. No wonder I shouted at you: I'm pushed around at home and pushed around when I go out. I never thought you'd be such a good wrestler that I wouldn't be able to break out of your clinch. Let me go now — I've told you everything."

"You're in luck — we're in the business," Monkey replied. "This is quite convenient; you needn't go any further or spend any of your money. We're not hopeless monks or pimples of Taoists. We've got some real magic powers, and we know how to deal with evil spirits. This'll do both of us a bit of good. Go back and tell the head of your houschold that my master is a saintly monk, and the younger brother of the Emperor of the East, who has sent him to visit the Buddha in the Western Heaven and seek the scriptures. We are very good at controlling devils and capturing monsters." "Don't lie to me," the young man replied. "I've had enough of being pushed around. If you're tricking me, you haven't really got any special powers, and you can't capture that fiend, you'll only be getting me into more trouble than ever." "I swear I'm not fooling you," answered Monkey. "Show us the way to your front door." The young man saw that there was nothing for it but to pick up his bundle and umbrella, turn round, and take the two of them to his gate, where he said to them, "Reverend gentlemen, would you mind sitting here on the verandah for a moment while I go in and tell the master?" Only then did Monkey let go of him, put down the carrying-pole, take the horse's reins, and stand beside his master, who sat down by the gate.

The young man went in through the gate and straight to the main hall, where he happened to meet Squire Gao. "Well, you savage, why have you come back instead of going to find someone?" Squire Gao demanded. Putting down his bundle and umbrella, the young man replied, "I must report to you, sir, that I had just got to the end of the street when I met a couple of monks. One was on horseback, and the other had a carrying-pole on his shoulder. He grabbed me and wouldn't let me go, and asked me where I was going. I refused to tell him several times, but he had me locked in a grip I couldn't get out of, so I had to tell him all about the mission you gave me, sir. He was absolutely delighted when he heard about it, and wanted to catch that monster for us." "Where are they from?" Squire Gao asked. "He says that his master is a saintly monk, the younger brother of the Emperor of the East, who has sent him to visit the Buddha in the Western Heaven and seek the scriptures," the young man replied. "But if they're monks from far away, they may really be capable of something. Where are they now?" "Waiting outside the gate."

The old man quickly put on his best clothes and went out with the youngster to greet them, addressing them as "Venerable Elders". Sanzang turned hurriedly round when he heard this, and found them standing before him. The older man was wearing a black silk turban, an onion-white robe of Sichuan brocade, a pair of calf-skin boots the colour of unpolished rice, and a belt of black silk. He came forward and said with a smile, "Greetings, Venerable Elders," as he bowed, holding his hands together. Sanzang returned his bow, but Monkey stood there immobile. At the sight of Brother Monkey's ugly face the old man decided not to bow to him. "Why won't you pay your respects to me?" Monkey asked, at which the old man, somewhat frightened, said to the young man, "You'll be the death of me, you little wretch. We've already got one hideous monster at home as a son-in-law we can't get rid of, so why ever did you have to bring this thunder god here to ruin us?" "Gao, old chap, you've been living all these years for nothing — you've still got no sense. It's completely wrong to judge people by their faces. I may be no beauty, but I'm quite clever. I'll grab that evil spirit for you, catch that demon, seize your son-in-law, and give you back your daughter. I'll be doing you a good turn, so there's no need to fuss about my looks." The old man, now shaking with fear, pulled himself together and asked them in. Monkey took the horse's bridle, told the young man to carry the luggage, and went in with Sanzang. In his usual devil-may-care way he tethered the horse to one of the pillars of an open-air pavilion, pulled up a gleaming lacquered armchair, and told his master to sit down. Then he brought over a chair for himself and sat beside him. "The younger venerable elder has already made himself at home," Squire Gao remarked. "I'd feel at home here if you entertained us for six months," Brother Monkey replied.

When they were all seated the old man said, "The boy told

me a moment ago that you were from the East." "That's right,"
Sanzang replied. "The court has sent me to worship the Buddha
in the Western Heaven and ask for the scriptures. As we are
passing this way on our journey, we would like to spend the
night here before continuing on our way tomorrow morning."
"If you two gentlemen just want to spend the night here, why
all the talk about catching monsters?" "As we'll be spending the
night here," Monkey put in, "we thought it would be fun to
catch a few monsters while we're about it. May I ask how many
there are in your residence?" "Good heavens," the old man
exclaimed, "however many do you want? We've only got this
monster of a son-in-law, and he's ruined our lives." "Tell me
all about this monster from the beginning," Monkey said. "I
must know about his magic powers if I'm to capture him for
you." "This village has never had any trouble from ghosts, demons or evil spirits before. It was my misfortune to have no
son, and three daughters, of whom the eldest is called Fragrant
Orchid, the second Jade Orchid, and the third Blue Orchid.
The other two were betrothed to men from the village when
they were children and have been married off. I wanted the
third to marry a man who would live here to support me in my
old age, look after the household, and do jobs about the place.
About three years ago a good-looking young fellow turned up
who said that his name was Zhu and he came from the Mountain of Blessing. He told me that he had no parents or brothers,
and wanted to marry and live with his in-laws. As he had no
family commitments I offered him my daughter's hand, old fool
that I am, and from the moment he became a member of our
family he worked very hard. He ploughed and hoed without
using oxen or tools; and he didn't need a scythe or a stick to
harvest the crops. As day followed day, there was nothing
wrong with him, except that he started to look different."
"How?" Monkey asked. "At first he was a plump, dark chap,
but later on he became a long-nosed, big-eared idiot with thick
black hairs running down from the back of his head and a great,
thick body. His face is just like a pig's. His appetite is enormous, too. He needs several bushels of grain at every main

meal, and over a hundred griddle-cakes for breakfast. Luckily
he is a vegetarian. If he ate meat and wine he would have
ruined us in six months." "He has to eat so much because he
works so hard," Sanzang commented. "But that's not the main
thing," Squire Gao continued. "He can also summon up a
wind, make clouds and mist come and go, and send pebbles and
sand flying. He's terrified our neighbours, who don't feel safe
living here any longer. He's shut my daughter away in the
building at the back, and nobody's seen her for six months. We
don't even know if she's still alive. That is how we know he's
an evil monster, and why we want a priest to come and get rid
of him." "No difficulty there," Monkey replied. "Don't worry,
old chap, I guarantee that I'll get him tonight, make him write
out a document divorcing your daughter, and bring her back to
you. What do you say to that?" "Because I thought there'd be
no harm in offering him my daughter, I've ruined my reputation
and estranged all my relations," Squire Gao replied. "If you
can catch him, why bother with a divorce document? Wipe him
out for me, if you please." "Easy, easy," said Monkey. "I'll
get him tonight."

The old man was delighted. He had a table and chairs set
out and wiped clean, and a vegetarian meal brought in. When
the meal was over and he was about to go to bed, the old man
asked, "What weapons and how many men will you need? I'll
get everything ready in good time." "I have a weapon," Monkey
replied. "You two gentlemen only have your monastic staves —
how will you be able to kill the fiend with them?" the old man
asked. Monkey produced the embroidery needle from his ear,
held it between his fingers, and shook it in the wind. It turned
into the gold-banded cudgel as thick as a rice-bowl. Monkey
turned to Squire Gao and asked, "How does this cudgel compare
with the weapons you have in here? Will it do to kill the
monster?" "So you have the weapon," the old man went on,
"but what about the men?" "I can do it single-handed,"
Monkey replied, "though I would like a few respectable old
gentlemen to come in and keep my master company while I'm
away from him. When I've captured the monster they can

witness his confession before I wipe him out for you." The old man thereupon sent his servants to ask a few old friends over, and before long they had all arrived. When the introductions were over Monkey said, "Master, you sit here and don't worry. I'm off."

Just watch Monkey as with his cudgel in his hand he takes hold of the old man and says, "Take me to the building at the back. I want to see where this evil spirit lives." Squire Gao led him to the door of the back building, and Monkey told him to bring the key at once. "Look here," the old man answered, "if a key would have done the trick, I wouldn't have had to ask for your services." "Can't you tell at your age when someone's joking?" Monkey asked. "I was only teasing. You shouldn't have taken me seriously." He felt the lock and found that molten copper had been poured into it, so he struck it a vicious blow with his cudgel and shattered it. Pushing the doors open, he saw that it was pitch-black inside. "Call your daughter's name, Old Gao, to see whether she's in here," he said. The old man summoned up his courage and called her name, and the daughter, recognizing her father's voice, answered feebly, "Dad, I'm in here." With a roll of his golden pupils Monkey peered into the darkness to take a closer look at her. Do you know what she was like?

> Her cloudy hair was tangled and unkempt,
> Her face was filthy and unwashed.
> Her orchid heart was as pure as ever,
> But her beauty lay in ruins.
> There was no blood or life in her cherry lips,
> And her limbs were crooked and bent.
> A sad frown on her forehead,
> Her eyebrows pale;
> Weak and frightened,
> Only daring to whisper.

When she came out and saw her father, she grabbed hold of him, put her hand round his head, and wept. "Don't cry," Monkey said, "don't cry. Where has the monster gone?" "I don't know. These days he's been setting out at dawn and only coming back in the middle of the night. There's always so much cloud and mist that I can't tell where he goes. He knows that my father wants to exorcise him, so he's always on the alert. That's why he comes back late and leaves at dawn." "Of course he would," Monkey remarked, adding, "old fellow, take the girl to the front building. You two can have a good long talk; I'm going to wait for the monster here. Don't be surprised if he doesn't turn up; but if he does, I'll wipe him out for you." The old man happily took his daughter to the front building.

Monkey then used some of his magic powers to turn himself into the likeness of the girl with a shake of his body. Then he sat down in the room to wait for the evil spirit. Before long there was a marvellous wind that sent stones and dust flying:

> At first it was a gentle breeze,
> That gradually became a mighty gale.
> When it was a gentle breeze, it filled Heaven and Earth,
> When it grew, nothing could withstand it.
>
> It stripped off flowers and snapped willows like stalks of hemp,
> Uprooting forests as if picking vegetables.
> It threw rivers and seas into turmoil, to the fury of gods and devils,
> Splitting rocks and mountains as Heaven and Earth watched in horror.
>
> The flower-eating deer lost their way;
> The fruit-plucking monkeys did not know where they were.
> Seven-storeyed iron pagodas fell on the Buddha's head;
> The streamers in the temple fell on the jewelled canopy.
>
> Golden beams and pillars of jade were shaken from their roots;
> Tiles flew from the roof like swallows.
> As the boatman raised his oar he made a vow,

Quickly sacrificing a pig and a goat as he pushed off.
The guardian god of the city ward abandoned his shrine;
The Dragon Kings of the Four Seas bowed to Heaven.
The yaksha demons' boats were wrecked on the coast,
And half the length of the Great Wall was blown down.

As this gale wind passed, an evil spirit appeared in mid-air. He was certainly ugly with his dark face, stubbly hair, long nose, and big ears. He wore a cotton tunic that was somewhere between black and blue, and round his waist was a patterned cotton cloth. "So that's what he's like," thought Monkey with a secret smile, and without greeting him or asking him anything he lay down on the bed, breathing heavily and pretending to be ill. Not knowing who this really was, the monster came straight in, put his arms around him and was going to kiss him. Monkey laughed to himself again as he thought, "So he really wants to do me." Then he thrust his hand up under the monster's long nose to throw him off balance. The monster fell off the bed. As the monster pulled himself up he leaned on the edge of the bed and said, "Darling, why are you so angry with me today? Is it because I'm late?" "I'm not angry," Monkey replied, "not angry at all." "If you're not angry with me, why did you make me fall over?" "You should have been more thoughtful and not tried hugging me and kissing me although I'm not feeling very well today. If I'd been my usual self I'd have been waiting for you at the door. Take your clothes off and come to bed." Not realizing what he was up to, the monster undressed. Monkey jumped out of bed and sat on the pot as the monster went back to bed and groped around without finding the girl. "Where've you gone, darling?" he asked. "Take your clothes off and come to bed." "Go to sleep," Monkey replied, "I'm doing a shit." The monster did as he was told. Monkey sighed and said, "What terrible luck." "What are you so fed up about?" the monster asked. "What do you mean by 'terrible luck'? I may have eaten some food and drunk some tea since marrying you, but I haven't been idle either. I've swept for your family and dug ditches, I've shifted bricks and tiles, I've built walls for you, I've ploughed and weeded your fields, I've sown your wheat, and I've transplanted your rice. I've made your family's fortune. These days you dress in brocade and have golden pins in your hair. You have fruit and flowers in all four seasons, and vegetables for the pot throughout the year. But despite this you're still not satisfied, groaning and moaning like that and complaining about your 'terrible luck'." "I didn't mean that," Monkey replied. "Today I could hear my parents through the wall. They were smashing up bricks and tiles and pretending to curse and beat me." "Why should they want to do that?" the monster asked. "They said that since we married and you became their resident son-in-law, all respectability has gone by the board. They were complaining about having such an ugly fellow as you around, and about never meeting any brother-in-law or other relations of yours. Besides, with all that wind and cloud whenever you come in or go out, they wonder who on earth you can be and what you are called. You're ruining their reputation, and disgracing the family. That's why they were so angry that they went through the motions of beating and cursing me." "I may be a bit of an eyesore," the monster said, "but if you want me to be a good-looker I can fix that without any difficulty. When I first came I had a word with your father, and he agreed to the marriage of his own free will. Why is he talking like this now? My home is the Cloud Pathway Cave on the Mount of Blessing. My surname, Zhu, is like my face — piggy — and my correct name is Zhu Ganglie, Iron-Haired Pig. You tell them all that if they ask you again."

"He's an honest monster," thought Monkey with delight. "If he came out with all this without being tortured. Now I know who he is and where he's from, I'm sure I can catch him." "He's sent for a priest to come and catch you," Monkey said aloud. "Come to bed, come to bed, and forget about him," the monster said with a laugh. "I can do as many transformations as the Plough, and I have my nine-pronged rake too, so what have I to fear from priests, monks or Taoists? Even if your old man were holy enough to summon the Demon-destroying Patriarch down from the Ninth Heaven, he's an old friend of mine and

wouldn't do anything to harm me." "My father said that he'd
asked that fellow by the name of Sun, the Great Sage Equalling
Heaven who made such trouble up in the Heavenly Palace some
five hundred years ago, to come and capture you." The monster
was somewhat taken aback on hearing this name, and said, "In
that case I'm off. We're through." "You can't just go like that,"
said Monkey. "You wouldn't know," the monster replied, "but
that Protector of the Horses who made such trouble in the Heavenly Palace is quite a fighter. I might not be able to beat him,
and my name would be mud." With these words he pulled on
his clothes, opened the door, and was just going out when Monkey grabbed him, gave his own face a rub, and changed back
into his real form. "Where d'you think you're going, my fine
monster?" he roared, adding, "take a look and see who I am."
The monster turned round and saw Monkey's protruding teeth,
pinched face, fiery eyes with golden pupils, bald head and hairy
face. At the sight of this thunder god incarnate his hands were
numbed and his legs paralyzed; then with a great tearing sound
he broke free, ripping his clothes, and escaped in the form of
a hurricane. Monkey rushed after him, grabbed his iron cudgel,
and took a swipe at the wind. The monster then changed into
ten thousand sparks and went straight back to his mountain.
Monkey mounted his cloud and went after him shouting, "Where
d'you think you're going? If you go up to Heaven, I'll chase you
as far as the Dipper and Bull Palace, and if you go into the
Earth, I'll pursue you as far as the Hell of the Unjustly Slain."

Goodness! If you don't know how far he chased the monster,
or who won in the end, listen to the explanation in the next
chapter.

CHAPTER NINETEEN

In the Cloud Pathway Cave Sun Wukong
wins over Zhu Bajie;
On Pagoda Mountain Xuanzang receives
the *Heart Sutra*.

The monster shot forward as a stream of sparks, with the Great
Sage behind him on his coloured cloud. As he was racing along,
Monkey saw a tall mountain appear in front of them. Here the
monster put himself together again by reassembling the sparks,
rushed into a cave, and came out with a nine-pronged rake in his
hand to do battle. "Wretch," shouted Monkey, "where are you
from? How do you know my name, you evil demon? What
powers have you got? Tell me honestly, and I'll spare your
life." "You don't know what I can do," the monster replied.
"Come a little nearer and stand still while I tell you:

> *I was born stupid,*
> *An idler and a slacker.*
> *I never nourished my nature or cultivated the truth,*
> *But spent my time in primal ignorance.*
> *Then I happened to meet a true immortal,*
> *Who sat down with me and chatted about the weather,*
> *Advised me to reform and not to sink among mortals,*
> *For taking life was a heinous sin.*
> *One day, when my life came to an end,*
> *It would be too late to regret the punishments in store,*
> *His words moved me to seek reform,*
> *And my heart longed for miraculous spells.*
> *I was lucky enough to have him as my teacher;*
> *He showed me the gates of Heaven and Earth.*

He taught me the Nine Changes and the Great Return
　　of Cinnabar,
As we worked by night and day with never a break.
It reached up to the Mud Ball Palace in my head,
And down to the Bubbling Spring in my feet.
The circulating magic liquid reached the Flowery Pool
　　under my tongue,
And the Cinnabar Field in my abdomen was given extra
　　warmth.
The Babe, lead, and the Girl, mercury, were married,
And combining together, they divided into sun and
　　moon.
The Dragon and the Tiger were harmonized;
The Sacred Tortoise drank the Golden Crow's blood.
The Three Flowers gathered at the top and returned to
　　the root;
The Five Essences faced the Origin and flowed in all
　　directions.
When their work was done, I could fly,
And the immortals of Heaven came in pairs to greet me.
Coloured clouds grew beneath my feet,
As I faced the Heavenly Palace gates with a body light
　　and strong.
The Jade Emperor gave a banquet for all the immortals,
And all lined up according to their grades.
I was made Field Marshal in charge of the Milky Way,
Commanding all the sailors on that river in the sky.
When the Queen Mother gave a Peach Banquet,
She invited many guests to the Jade Pool.
As drunkenness clouded my mind that day,
I lurched and staggered around.
As I charged in drunken pride into the Cool Broad
　　Palace
I was greeted by an exquisite immortal maiden.
At the sight of her beauty my soul was captivated,
And I could not repress my mortal passions of old.
Losing all sense of rank and dignity,

I seized the beauty and asked her to sleep with me.
Three times, four times she refused,
Dodging and trying to hide in her distress.
Great was the courage of my lust, and I roared like
*   thunder,*
All but toppling the gates of heaven.
The Miraculous Inspecting Officer reported to the Jade
*   Emperor,*
And from that day I was doomed.
The Cool Broad Palace was closely surrounded.
I could neither advance nor retreat: escape was impos-
*   sible.*
Then I was arrested by the gods,
But as I was still drunk I was not scared.
I was marched to the Hall of Miraculous Mist to see the
*   Jade Emperor,*
And, after questioning, sentenced to death.
Luckily the Great White Planet
Stepped forward, bowed low, and interceded.
My sentence was commuted to two thousand strokes of
*   the heavy rod,*
Which tore my flesh and all but smashed my bones.
I was released alive and driven out of Heaven,
So I tried to make a living on the Mount of Blessing.
For my sins I was reborn from the wrong womb,
And now I am known as Iron-haired Pig."

"So you are an earthly reincarnation of Marshal Tian Peng,"
said Brother Monkey when he heard this. "No wonder you knew
my name." "Ha," the monster snorted angrily. "Your insane rebellion caused trouble for very many of us, Protector of the
Horses. Have you come here to throw your weight around
again? I'll teach you some manners. Take this!" Monkey was
in no mood to spare him after this, and he struck at the monster's
head with his cudgel. The pair of them fought a magnificent
midnight battle on that mountainside:

Monkey's golden pupils flashed with lightning;
The monster's glaring eyes sparked silver.
One disgorged coloured mist,
The other breathed out red clouds.
The red clouds lit up the night;
The coloured mists illuminated the darkness
A gold-banded cudgel,
A nine-toothed rake,
And two splendid heroes.
One a Great Sage down among the mortals,
The other a marshal banished from Heaven.
One had been misbehaving and become a monster,
The other had been saved taking service with a priest.
When the rake attacked, it was like a dragon stretching
*   its claws;*
The cudgel blocked it as nimbly as a phoenix flying
*   through flowers.*
Pig said,
"In wrecking my marriage your crime is as great as pat-
*   ricide."*
Monkey replied,
"You deserve to be arrested for raping that young girl."
Amid these exchanges
And wild shouts,
The cudgel and the rake crossed and clashed.
They fought each other till the day began to dawn,
And the monster's arms were tired right out.

They fought from the second watch of the night until the sky began to grow light in the east. The monster, no longer able to resist his enemy, broke away and fled, turning himself into a hurricane again. He went straight back to his cave, shut the gates behind him, and did not come out. Monkey saw a stone tablet outside the cave on which was inscribed CLOUD PATH-WAY CAVE. The monster did not come out again and it was now broad daylight, so Monkey thought that as his master might be waiting for him he had better go back to see him. He could come back later to catch the monster. He gave his cloud a kick and was back in Old Gao Village in an instant.

Sanzang, meanwhile, had been talking all night with the elders about things ancient and modern, and had not slept a wink. Just as he was beginning to think that Brother Monkey would not come back, Monkey appeared in the courtyard, put away his iron club, straightened his clothes, and entered the main room. "Master, I'm here," he announced, giving the old men such a surprise that they all fell to their knees and thanked him for his efforts. "You've been out all night, Monkey," Sanzang said. "Where did you catch that evil spirit?" "He's no common or garden ghost, Master," Monkey replied, "and he isn't an ordinary wild animal turned monster. He is Marshal Tian Peng, who was exiled to the mortal world. As he was placed in the wrong womb he has a face like a wild boar, but he's still kept his original divine nature. He says that he takes his name from his looks and is called Zhu Ganglie, Iron-haired Pig. I was going to kill him in the building at the back, but he turned into a hurricane and fled. When I struck at this wind, he changed into sparks, went straight back to his cave, came out with a nine-pronged rake, and fought me all night. He broke off the engagement in terror as the dawn broke and shut himself in his cave. I was going to smash down the gates and have it out with him, but then it occurred to me that you might be worried after waiting for me so long, so I came back to put you in the picture first."

After Monkey had made his report, Squire Gao came up and knelt before him saying, "Venerable sir, I'm afraid that although you've chased him away, he'll come back after you've gone; so this is no real solution. Please, I beg of you, catch him for me and exterminate him to prevent trouble later. I promise you that I shall not be remiss if you do this for me, and there will, of course, be rich rewards. I shall write a deed, witnessed by my relations and friends, giving you half of my property and my land. Please, please eradicate this evil weed and save the honour of the family." "You've got no sense of what's proper, old man," replied Monkey with a grin. "He told me that although he may have put away a lot of your rice and tea, he's also done you a deal of good. You've made a pile in the past few years, and it's all thanks to his efforts. He says he hasn't been eating your food in idleness, and wants to know why you're trying to have him exorcised. He maintains that he is a heavenly immortal come down to earth who has been working for your family and has never harmed your daughter. I would say that he is a very fitting son-in-law for you, who does your family's name no harm. You really ought to keep him." "Venerable sir", the old man replied, "he may never have done anything wicked, but it does our reputation no good to have a son-in-law like him. Whether he does anything or not, people say that the Gaos have asked a monster to marry into the family, and I simply can't bear to hear a thing like that." "Go and have it out with him, and then we'll see what to do," said Sanzang. "I'll try a trick on him this time," Monkey replied. "I guarantee to bring him back this time for you to look at. So don't worry about it." "Old Gao," he continued, addressing the old man, "look after my master well. I'm off."

By the time the words were out of his mouth, he had disappeared. He leapt up the mountain and smashed the gates of the cave to splinters with a single blow of his cudgel, shouting, "Come out and fight Monkey, you chaff-guzzling moron." The monster, who had been snoring inside, heard the gates being smashed and the insulting "chaff-guzzling moron", and went wild with fury. Seizing his rake and summoning up·his spirit, he rushed out and shrieked, "You shameless Protector of the Horses. What have I ever done to you to make you smash down my gates? You'd better take a look at the statute book: there's the death penalty for breaking and entering." "You fool," laughed Monkey, "I've got a very good justification for smashing your gates — you abducted a girl by force, without matchmakers or witnesses, and without giving proper presents or observing the right ceremonies. You're a fine one to talk about who deserves to have his head cut off." "Stop talking such nonsense and see how this rake of mine strikes you," the monster replied. Blocking the blow with his cudgel, Monkey retorted, "Is that

the rake you used when you were tilling the fields and growing
vegetables for the Gaos as their hired hand? What's so wonderful about it that I should be afraid of you?" "You don't
realize that it's no ordinary weapon," the monster replied.
"You'd better listen while I tell you about it:

> This was refined from divine ice-iron,
> Polished till it gleamed dazzling white,
> Hammered by Lord Lao Zi himself,
> While Ying Huo fed the fire with coal-dust.
> The Five Emperors of the Five Regions applied their
>   minds to it;
> The Six Dings and Six Jias went to great efforts.
> They made nine teeth of jade,
> Cast a pair of golden rings to hang beneath them,
> Decorated the body with the Six Bright Shiners and the
>   Five Planets,
> Designed it in accordance with the Four Seasons and
>   the Eight Divisions.
> The length of top and bottom match Heaven and Earth.
> Positive and Negative were to left and right, dividing
>   the sun and moon.
> The Six Divine Generals of the Oracular Lines are there,
>   following the Heavenly Code;
> The constellations of the Eight Trigrams are set out in
>   order.
> It was named the Supremely Precious Gold-imbued
>   Rake,
> And served to guard the gates of the Jade Emperor's
>   palace.
> As I had become a great immortal,
> I now enjoyed eternal life,
> And was commissioned as Marshal Tian Peng,
> With this rake to mark my imperial office.
> When I raise it, fire and light stream forth;
> When I lower it, a snowy blizzard blows.
> It terrifies the Heavenly Generals,

And makes the King of Hell too quake with fear.
There is no other weapon matching it on Earth;
Nothing of iron can rival it throughout the world.
It changes into anything I like,
And leaps about whenever I say the spell.
For many a year I've carried it around,
Keeping it with me every single day.
I will not put it down even to eat,
Nor do I when I sleep at night.
I took it with me to the Peach Banquet,
And carried it into the celestial court.
When I sinned my sin in drunken pride,
I used it to force compliance with my evil will.
When Heaven sent me down to the mortal dust,
I committed all kinds of wickedness down here.
I used to devour people in this cave,
Until I fell in love and married in Gao Village.
This rake has plunged beneath the sea to stir up dragons,
And climbed high mountains to smash up tigers' dens.
No other blade is worth a mention
Besides my rake, the sharpest weapon ever.
To win a fight with it requires no effort;
Of course it always brings me glory.
Had you an iron brain in a brazen head and a body of
    steel,
This rake would scatter your souls and send your spirit
    flying."

Monkey put his cudgel away and replied, "Stop shooting your mouth off, you idiot. I'm now sticking my head out for you to hit. Let's see you scatter my souls and send my spirits flying." The monster raised his rake and brought it down with all his might, but although flames leapt forth, it did not even scratch Monkey's scalp. The monster's arms and legs turned to jelly with fright as he exclaimed, "What a head, what a head." "You wouldn't know," Monkey replied. "When I was captured by the Little Sage for wrecking the Heavenly Palace, stealing the pills of immortality and the heavenly peaches, and filching the imperial wine, I was marched to a place outside the Dipper and Bull Palace, where all the gods of Heaven hacked at me with axes, hit me with maces, cut at me with swords, stabbed at me with daggers, tried to burn me with lightning, and pounded me with thunder; but none of it hurt me in the slightest. Then I was taken off by the Great High Lord Lao and put in the Eight Trigrams Furnace, where I was refined with divine fire, so that my eyes are now fiery, my pupils golden, my head brazen, and my shoulders of iron. If you don't believe me, try a few more blows to see whether you can hurt me or not." "I remember you, you baboon," the monster replied. "When you made trouble in Heaven, you lived in the Water Curtain Cave on the Mountain of Flowers and Fruit in the land of Aolai in the Continent of Divine Victory. I haven't heard of you for a very long time. What brings you here, and why are you bullying me in front of my own gates? Surely my father-in-law didn't go all that way to ask you to come here?" "No," said Monkey, "he didn't. I have turned away from evil and been converted to good. I have given up Taoism and become a Buddhist. I am protecting the Patriarch Sanzang, the younger brother of the Great Tang Emperor, on his journey to the Western Heaven to visit the Buddha and ask for the scriptures. We happened to ask for a night's lodging when we came to Gao Village, and in the course of our conversation Old Gao asked me to rescue his daughter and capture you, you chaff-guzzling moron."

The monster dropped his rake to the ground, chanted a respectful "re-e-er", and said, "Where's this pilgrim? Please take me to meet him." "What do you want to see him for?" Monkey asked. "Guanyin converted me and told me to obey the monastic rules and eat vegetarian food here till I could go with that pilgrim, the one who's going to the Western Heaven to worship the Buddha and ask for the scriptures. I'll be able to make up for my sins through this good deed, and win a good reward. I've been waiting for him for years, but there's been no news of him till now. If you're a disciple of his, why didn't you say something about fetching the scriptures before, instead of making this vicious attack on me in my own home?" "This had better not be a trick to soften me up and make me let you get away," said Monkey. "If you really want to protect the Tang Priest and you aren't trying to kid me, then you'd better make a vow to Heaven, and I'll take you to meet my master." The monster fell to his knees with a thud, and kowtowed to the sky so often that he looked like a rice pestle. "Amitabha Buddha," he cried out, "if I'm not completely sincere, cut me up into ten thousand bits for breaking the laws of Heaven." After hearing him swear this oath, Monkey said, "Very well then, now light a brand and burn this place of yours out. If you do that, I'll take you." The monster piled up some reeds and brambles, lit a brand, and set the Cloud Pathway Cave on fire; it burned as well as a brick kiln that has got out of control. "I've no second thoughts," he said, "so please take me to see him." "Give me that rake of yours," Monkey ordered, and the monster obediently handed it over. Monkey then plucked out a hair, blew on it with magic breath, and shouted, "Change!" It turned into three lengths of hempen rope, with which he bound the monster's hands behind his back; the monster docilely put his hands there and let Monkey tie him up. Then Monkey seized him by the ear and led him off with the words, "Quick march." "Take it easy," the monster pleaded. "You're pulling so hard you're hurting my ear." "Can't be done," Monkey replied. "Can't show you any favours. As the old saying has it, 'even a good pig must be handled roughly.' Wait until you've seen my master. If you really are sincere, you'll be released then." The two of them went back through cloud and mist to Gao Village, and there is a poem to prove it:

> The nature of metal is stronger than Wood,
> The Mind-ape could bring the Wooden Dragon to submission.
> When Metal obeyed and Wood was tamed they were at one;
> When Wood was loving and Metal kind they worked together.

One host and one guest with nothing to keep them apart:
With the three in harmony they had a mysterious power.
Nature and feelings both rejoiced as they joined in the
*   Supreme Principle;*
They both promised without reservation to go to the
*   West.*

In a moment they were back at the village. Holding the monster's rake in one hand and twisting his ear with the other, he said, "Do you know who that is sitting up straight in the main hall? It's my master." When Old Gao and all his friends and relations saw Monkey coming, tugging the bound monster by his ear, they all came into the courtyard and said happily, "Venerable sir, this is the son-in-law all right." The monster went forward, fell to his knees, and kowtowed to Sanzang with his hands behind his back. "Master," he shouted, "Your disciple failed to welcome you. Had I known, Master, that you were staying in my father-in-law's house, I'd have come to greet you and do homage, and I'd have been saved all this agony." "How did you make him submit and come to pay homage?" Sanzang asked Monkey. Monkey then let the monster go, hit him with the handle of the rake, and yelled, "Tell him, fool." The monster then told Sanzang all about how he had been converted by the Bodhisattva.

Sanzang was so pleased that he asked Squire Gao for an incense table to be brought, which was done at once. Sanzang then washed his hands, burnt incense, bowed low to the south, and said, "Thanks be to the Bodhisattva for her divine grace." The elders also burnt incense and bowed low in worship. When this was done, Sanzang took the seat of honour in the hall and told Monkey to untie the monster. Monkey shook himself to take his hairs back, and the ropes untied themselves. The monster bowed to Sanzang once more and vowed to go to the West with him. Then he bowed to Monkey as his elder brother because he had joined first, addressing him as "elder brother" from then on. "If you wish to earn a good reward by going with me as my disciple, I'll give you a Buddhist name to call you by."

"Master," he replied, "when the Bodhisattva laid her hands upon my head and told me to obey the prohibitions, she gave me a Buddhist name — Zhu Wuneng, Pig Awakened to Power." "Wonderful, wonderful," said Sanzang with a smile. "Your elder brother is called Wukong, Awakened to Emptiness, and you're called Awakened to Power. That makes us members of the same sect in the Buddhist faith." "Master," said Pig, "I have been instructed by the Bodhisattva and I never eat the five stinking foods and the three forbidden meats — wild goose, dog, and snake-fish. I've eaten vegetarian food in my father-in-law's house and never touched the stinking foods; but now that I have met you, Master, I'm freed from these restrictions." "You are not," Sanzang replied. "You are not to eat the five stinking foods and the three forbidden meats, and I'm giving you another name: Eight Prohibitions, or Bajie." "I shall obey my master's command," the idiot happily replied, and from then on he was known as Zhu Bajie, or Eight Prohibitions Pig.

Squire Gao was happier than ever to see that he had turned from evil to good, and he ordered his servants to set out banquet with which to thank the Tang Priest. Pig went over to Squire Gao, tugged at his coat, and said, "Sir, may my wife come out and pay her respects to these two gentlemen?" "Brother," said Monkey with a laugh. "You've entered the church now and become a monk. Don't ever talk about a wife again. Only Taoist priests can have families — we Buddhist monks never marry. Let's all sit down and eat a vegetarian meal, then we can set off early tomorrow morning on our journey to the West." Squire Gao had the table and chairs set out and asked Sanzang take the seat of honour. Monkey and Pig sat on his left and right, and all the relations sat below them. Squire Gao opened a jar of wine, from which he filled a cup and poured a libation to Heaven and Earth before handing it to Sanzang. "Frankly, sir," Sanzang said, "I have been a vegetarian from the womb, and have not consumed strong-flavoured food since my earliest childhood." "Venerable Master, I know that you are a vegetarian," Squire Gao replied, "which is why I haven't pressed any meat or strong-flavoured food upon you. But this wine

is made from vegetable matter, so a cup of it will do no harm."
"I don't drink either," Sanzang explained, "as alcohol is the
first of the prohibitions of the priesthood." "Master," Pig hastily
interjected, "I may be a vegetarian, but I haven't given up liquor." "And although I haven't a strong head for the stuff and
can't finish a whole jar of it, I haven't given it up either,"
Monkey added. "In that case you two had better drink some;
but don't get drunk and ruin everything," said Sanzang. The
pair of them then took the first cup, after which everyone sat
down again as the vegetarian dishes were brought in. Words
could not describe the flowing cups, the well-filled dishes, and
the splendid food.

When master and disciples had eaten, Squire Gao brought
pieces of gold and silver to the weight of two hundred ounces
on a red lacquer tray and offered them to the three pilgrims to
help with the expenses of their journey. Then he produced three
brocade-collared gowns that could serve as overcoats. "We are
mendicant monks," said Sanzang, "who beg for our food in the
villages and other places through which we pass, so we could
not possibly accept gold, silver, or cloth." Monkey then marched up and grabbed a handful of the money. Then he addressed
the young man, Gao Cai. "Yesterday," he said, "I troubled you
to lead my master here, and today he's recruited another disciple, but we haven't been able to show our gratitude. So take
these pieces of gold and silver as your fee for guiding us, and
buy yourself a pair of straw sandals. If you have any more evil
spirits in future, and you help us again, we'll be able to show
even more appreciation." The young man Gao Cai took the gold
and silver, then kowtowed to express his thanks. "If you won't
take gold or silver," Squire Gao said, "please be good enough
to accept these rough clothes as a mark of our gratitude." "If we
monks accepted a single thread, we would have to atone for it
for a thousand ages," replied Sanzang. "It will suffice if we
take the pancakes and fruit that we haven't eaten with us as
provisions for the journey." "Master, elder brother," said Pig,
who was standing beside them, "it's all right for you two to refuse them, but I was a son-in-law in this family for several years,

and I deserves three bushels of grain to take with me. Oh yes, father-in-law, my tunic was torn by elder brother yesterday and my shoes have split, so please give me a black brocade cassock and a good pair of new shoes." Old Squire Gao, who could scarcely refuse this request, gave him the new shoes and a tunic in exchange for his old ones.

Pig swaggered over to Old Gao, chanted a "re-e-er" of respect, and said, "Please inform my mother-in-law, my sisters-in-law, my brothers-in-law and my uncles that as from today I'm a monk, and ask them to excuse me for not saying goodbye to them in person. Father-in-law, look after my wife well. If we don't get the scriptures, I'll go back to lay life and work for you as a son-in-law again." "Idiot," shouted Monkey, "stop talking nonsense." "I'm doing nothing of the sort," Pig replied, "I am thinking that if things go wrong I'd be wasting my time as a monk, and my wife's marriage would have been ruined, both for nothing." "Enough of your idle chatter," said Sanzang, "let's be on our way at once." Their luggage was hung from a carrying-pole on Pig's shoulders. When the white horse was saddled, Sanzang mounted it, and Monkey led the way with his iron cudgel over his shoulder. Thus the three of them left Squire Gao, his relations, and his friends, and headed west. There is a poem to prove it that goes:

> The trees tower above the misty earth
> As the Tang disciples of Buddha toil and suffer.
> When hungry, they beg their food from a thousand
> homes;
> When cold they wear cloaks with a thousand patches.
>
> Do not allow the Thought-horse to run wild,
> And don't let the stubborn Mind-ape howl at will.
> With passions stilled and one's nature firm, all destinies
> are in harmony;
> When the full moon of contemplation is reached, you
> will be pure.

After travelling peacefully westwards for a month, the three of them left the territory of Stubet and saw a mountain soaring up above their heads. Sanzang stopped whipping his horse on, reined him in, and said, "Monkey, Monkey, that's a high mountain in front of us, so please go and reconnoitre it." "No need," said Pig. "It's called Pagoda Mountain, and there's a Rook's Nest Hermit who cultivates his conduct on it. I've met him." "What does he do?" Sanzang asked. "He has some powers," Pig replied. "He once invited me to cultivate my conduct with him, but I didn't go." As master and disciples talked they were soon on the mountain. It was a splendid mountain at that:

> South of it were blue pines and verdant locust trees;
> To the north were green willows and red peach-blossom.
> Cawing noisily,
> The wild birds talked to each other;
> Soaring gracefully,
> The cranes flew together.
> Rich in fragrance
> Were the thousands of different flowers;
> Softly dark
> Were the endless kinds of herbs.
> In the gullies were bubbling green streams;
> The crags were wreathed in auspicious cloud.
> It was indeed a scene of rare and elegant beauty,
> Lonely, where no man came or went.

As the master surveyed the scene from his horse he noticed a grass hut in front of a fragrant locust tree. To the left of it were David's-deer with flowers in their mouths, and to the right were monkeys holding offerings of fruit, while phoenixes of many colours wheeled around the top of the tree, in which cranes and golden pheasants had gathered. Pig pointed and said, "That's the Rook's Nest Hermit." Sanzang gave his horse the rein, whipped it on, and went straight to the foot of the tree.

When the hermit saw the three of them coming he jumped down from his bird's nest. Sanzang dismounted and bowed to him, and only then the hermit reply, helping him up, "Please arise, holy priest. I'm sorry I did not welcome you properly." "Greetings, venerable hermit," said Pig. "Aren't you the Iron-

haired Pig from the Mount of Blessing? How have you had the
great good fortune of travelling with a holy monk?" "Last
year," replied Pig, "I was converted by the Bodhisattva Guanyin, and I swore that I'd go with him as his disciple." "Wonderful, wonderful," exclaimed the delighted hermit, who then
pointed at Monkey and asked, "Who is this gentleman?" "Old
hermit," said Monkey, "how is it that you know him but didn't
recognize me?" "Please excuse my ignorance," the hermit replied. "He is Sun Wukong, the senior of my disciples," explained Sanzang. "I apologize for my discourtesy," said the
hermit.

Sanzang bowed again and asked him the way to the Great
Thunder Monastery in the Western Heaven. "Far away," the
other replied, "far away. The journey is a long one and there
are many tigers and leopards along the way. It will be difficult."
"How far is it?" asked Sanzang with great interest. "Although
the journey is a long one," the hermit replied, "you are bound
to get there in the end. But there will be evil influences that
you'll find hard to dispel. I have a *Heart Sutra*, a total of 270
words in 54 sentences, and if you recite it when you encounter
evil influences you will come to no harm." Sanzang prostrated
himself on the ground and begged the hermit to tell him it, and
the hermit recited it to him. It went:

> When the Bodhisattva Avalokitesvara* was meditat-
> ing on the profound prajna-paramita, he perceived that
> all the five aggregates are void and empty, and he was
> thereupon freed from all sufferings and calamities.
> Sariputra, matter is not different from voidness and
> voidness is not different from matter: matter is voidness
> and voidness is matter. Such is also the case with sen-
> sation, perception, discrimination and consciousness.

---

* Avalokitesvara (Guanyin) has many different forms of incarnation. In
China *he* is usually worshipped in the form of a woman, but in India *she* is
a man. In order to avoid this confusion the first sentence of the *Heart Sutra*
may also be translated as:

While meditating on the profound prajna-paramita, the Bodhisattva Avalokitesvara perceived that all the five aggregates are void and empty, and
was thereupon freed from all sufferings and calamities.

Sariputra, all these things are void in nature, having neither beginning nor end, being neither pure nor impure, and having neither increase nor decrease. Therefore, in voidness there is no matter, no sensation, no perception, no discrimination and no consciousness; there is no eye, no ear, no nose, no tongue, no body and no mind; there is no sight, no sound, no smell, no taste, no touch and no mental process; there is no category of eye nor is there a category of consciousness; no ignorance nor the cessation of ignorance; no old age and death, nor the cessation of old age and death; there is no suffering, no causes of suffering, no cessation of suffering, and no way leading to the cessation of suffering; and there is no wisdom, nor anything to be gained. As nothing is to be gained, a Bodhisattva depending on prajna-paramita becomes free in his mind, and as he is free in his mind he has no fear and is rid of dreamlike thoughts of unreality and enjoys ultimate Nirvana. By means of prajna-paramita, all Buddhas of the past, the present and the future realize anuttara-samyak-sambodhi. Therefore, we know prajna-paramita is a great, divine spell, a great enlightening spell, a supreme spell, and a spell without a parallel, that can do away with all sufferings without fail. Thus we recite the Prajna-paramita Spell and say: Gate, gate, paragate, parasamgate, bodhi, svaha!

As the Patriarch from the Tang had already the origins of enlightenment inside himself, he was able to remember the *Heart Sutra* after only one hearing, and it has been passed on down to this very day. This sutra is the kernel of the cultivation of the truth, and it is the gateway to becoming a Buddha. When the hermit had recited it, he started to rise up to his crow's nest by cloud, but Sanzang tugged at him and said that he wanted to know about the way to the Western Heaven. To this the hermit replied with a smile:

"*The journey will not be difficult,*
If you try to follow my instructions.

There will be a thousand mountains, a thousand deep
  rivers.
Many evil miasmas, and many a devil.
If you reach the crags touching the edge of the sky
Do not worry or be afraid.
If you come to Precipitous Cliff
Walk with your feet placed sideways.
Be careful in the Black Pine Forest,
Where many an evil fox may block your path.
The capital cities will be full of spirits,
And demon kings will live in the mountains.
Tigers will sit in the music rooms;
Wolves will be in charge of documents.
Lions and elephants will all be kings,
With tigers and leopards for ministers.
A wild boar will carry your luggage;
A water monster will lead the way.
A very old stone monkey
Has no cause to be angry.
Ask those friends of yours —
They know the way to the West."

Monkey smiled bitterly and said, "Let's go. No need to
ask him; you can ask me." Sanzang did not understand what
he meant. The hermit changed himself into a beam of golden
light and went up to his nest, while the venerable Sanzang bowed to him in gratitude. Monkey, now furiously angry, raised his
iron cudgel and was just going up to wreck the place when ten
thousand lotus flowers appeared, protected by a thousand miraculous mists. Brother Monkey, you are strong enough to stir up
the ocean or turn a river upside-down; but don't even dream
of touching a twig of that nest! When Sanzang saw what he
was going to do, he grabbed hold of him and said, "Wukong,
what do you mean by trying to wreck this Bodhisattva's nest?"
"He insulted us two disciples," Monkey replied. "He did not
insult you," said Sanzang. "He was talking about the way to
the Western Heaven." "You wouldn't be able to understand,"
Monkey said. "When he said, 'A wild boar will carry your

luggage', he was insulting Pig; and 'A very old stone monkey'
was an insult to me. You didn't get his meaning, of course."
"Don't be angry," said Pig. "That hermit knows about the past
and the future as well. We don't yet know whether his talk
about a water monster leading the way will come true or not.
Let him off." Monkey saw the lotus blossoms and the miraculous mists draw in round the nest, and could but ask his
master to mount the horse and go down the mountain to the
west. On this journey,

> *Although they knew blessings rare on earth,*
> *There was many a demon and disaster in the hills.*

If you don't know what lay in store for them, listen to the explanation in the next instalment.

CHAPTER TWENTY

The Tang Priest meets trouble on
the Yellow Wind Ridge;
Pig wins mastery halfway up the mountain.

The Dharma is born in the mind,
And in turn is destroyed by the mind.
Who do life and death come from?
Decide for yourself.
If it is all from your own mind,
Why do you need others to tell you?
All you need to do is work hard,
Squeezing blood out of iron.
Thread a silken rope through your nose,
And fasten yourself to emptiness.
Tie it to the tree of non-action,
To prevent it from collapsing.
Don't acknowledge bandits as your sons,
Or you will forget the Dharma and the mind.
Do not allow yourself to be deceived by others —
Smash them first with a punch.
When the mind appears it is non-existent,
When the Dharma appears, it ceases.
When the boy and the ox both disappear,
The blue sky is absolutely clear.
All is as round as an autumn moon,
And this and that can no longer be distinguished.

This *gatha* refers to how the Patriarch Xuanzang came to awareness and understanding of the *Heart Sutra* and thus opened the gate. As that venerable elder recited it constantly, a ray of miraculous light penetrated through to him.

Eating and sleeping in the open, the three of them travelled on, and before long the heat of summer was upon them.

The blossoms were over, the butterflies' passion spent;
High in the trees the cicadas screeched.
Wild silkworms spun cocoons amid pomegranate blossom,
As lotus flowers opened in the pool.

As they were travelling along one evening they saw a cottage beside the road. "Look," said Sanzang, "the sun is setting behind the western hills, hiding its mirror of fire, and the moon is rising from the eastern sea to show its wheel of ice. How lucky that there is a family living by our path. Let's spend the night here and set off again tomorrow morning." "Well said," put in Pig. "I'm a bit hungry, and if we begged some food from that house I'd have more strength for carrying the luggage." "Homesick ghost," remarked Brother Monkey, "you've only been away from home for a few days, but you're already regretting that you came." "Elder brother," Pig replied, "I can't live on wind and mist like you. You couldn't realize how the hunger's been gnawing at my stomach all these days I've been following our master." "Pig," said Sanzang, "if your heart is still at home, you are not intended for a religious life, and you'd better go back." The oafish Pig fell to his knees and pleaded, "Master, please don't pay any attention to what my elder brother says: it's an insult. He says I wish I hadn't come, but in fact I've had no regrets at all. I may be stupid, but I'm straight. I just said that I was hungry and want to beg for some food, and he starts calling me a homesick ghost. But the Bodhisattva told me about the prohibitions, and you have been so kind to me; so I really do want to serve you on your journey to the West. I'll never have any regrets, I swear I won't. This is what they call 'cultivating conduct the hard way'. What right have you to say I shouldn't be a monk?" "Very well then," said Sanzang, "up you get."

The idiot leapt up, and picked up the carrying-pole, chattering incessantly. Then he pressed grimly on. Before long they

reached the roadside house, where Sanzang dismounted as
Monkey took the bridle and Pig put down his burden. They
all stood in a green shade. Sanzang took his nine-ringed monastic staff, straightened his rattan hat, and hurried to the gates,
where he saw an old man lying back on a bamboo bed mumbling
Buddhist scriptures to himself. Not wanting to shout loudly,
Sanzang said in a quiet voice, "Greetings, benefactor." The old
man sprang to his feet, straightened his clothes, and came out
through the gate to return his greeting. "Excuse my discourtesy,
venerable sir," he said, going on to ask, "Where are you from,
and why have you come to my humble abode?" "I am a monk
from the Great Tang in the East," Sanzang replied, "and I bear
an imperial command to worship the Buddha in the Thunder
Monastery and ask for the scriptures. As we find ourselves in
this district at nightfall, I would be enormously obliged if you
could allow us to spend the night in your mansion." "You'll
never get there," said the old man with a wave of his hand and
a shake of his head. "It's impossible to get scriptures from the
Western Heaven. If you want scriptures you'd better go to the
Eastern Heaven." Sanzang said nothing as he asked himself why
the old man was telling them to go east when the Bodhisattva
had instructed them to go west. How could the scriptures be
obtained in the east, he asked himself. In his embarrassment he
was at loss for words, so he made no reply.

Monkey, who was rough by his very nature, could not stand
for this, so he went up to the old man and shouted, "Old fellow,
you may be very ancient but you're a complete fool. We holy
men from far away come to ask for lodging, but all you can do
is to try to put us off. If your house is too poky and there isn't
room for us to sleep in it, we'll sit under the trees all night and
won't trouble you any further." The old man grabbed hold of
Sanzang and said, "Master, you didn't warn me that you had
a disciple with such a twisted face and no chin to speak of, looking like a thunder god with his red eyes. You shouldn't let a
demon of sickness like him alarm and offend a person of my
age." "You're completely lacking in judgement, old man,"
Monkey said with a laugh. "Those pretty boys may look good

but, as they say, they don't taste good. I may be little but I'm tough, and under my skin it's all muscle."

"I suppose you must have some powers," the old man remarked. "Without wishing to boast," Monkey replied, "I can get by." "Where is your home," the old man asked, "and why did you shave your head and become a monk?" "My ancestral home is the Water Curtain Cave on the Mountain of Flowers and Fruit in the land of Aolai which lies across the sea to the east of the Eastern Continent of Superior Body. I learnt how to be an evil monster from childhood, and my name was Wukong, or Awakened to Emptiness. I used my abilities to make myself the Great Sage Equalling Heaven, but as I declined heavenly office and raised a great rebellion against the Heavenly Palace, I brought a disaster down on my own head. My sufferings are now over. I've turned to the Buddhist faith and am seeking a good reward for the future by escorting His Tang Excellency, my master, on his journey to the Western Heaven to visit the Buddha. I'm not afraid of high mountains with precipitous paths, or of broad rivers with huge waves. I can catch monsters and subdue demons, capture tigers or dragons, walk in the sky, or burrow into the earth. If your house has any poltergeists throwing brisks around, breaking tiles, making the pans call out or opening doors, I'll settle them."

After hearing this speech, the old man said with a chuckle, "So you're a monk with the gift of the gab who suddenly switched destinies." "You're the gabber, my child," retorted Monkey. "I'm too tired after the strain of the journey with my master to be able to talk." "It's as well you are," the old man replied, "or you'd be talking me to death. If you have all these powers you'll be able to reach the West. How many of you are there? Please come into my cottage for the night." "Thank you very much for not losing your temper with him," Sanzang said. "There are three of us." "Where is the third?" the old man asked. "Your eyes are very dim, old man," said Monkey, pointing as he continued, "Can't you see him standing in the shade there?" When the old man, whose eyes were indeed dim, looked carefully and saw Pig's face he was so terrified that he ran into the house shouting, "Shut the gates, shut the gates, there's a monster here." Monkey ran after him and grabbed him. "Don't be afraid, old fellow," he said, "he's not an evil monster, he's a fellow-disciple of mine." "Very well then," replied the old man, who was trembling all over, "but what a hideous creature to be a monk."

As the old man was talking to the three monks in front of the gates, two young men appeared at the southern end of the farm bringing an old woman and three or four children back from transplanting rice-seedlings, for which reason their clothes were tucked up and their feet were bare. When they saw the white horse and the carrying pole with luggage and heard the shouting at the gates of their home, they did not know what was up, so they rushed forward and asked, "What are you doing?" Pig turned round, flapped his ears, and thrust his snout at them, at which they all collapsed in terror or fled. In the confusion Sanzang kept calling out, "Don't be afraid, don't be afraid, we are good men, we are monks going to fetch the scriptures." The old man then came out again, and helped the old woman to her feet. "Up you get, wife," he said, "there's no call for panic. This holy father is from the Tang court, and although his disciples are a bit ugly, their hearts are in the right place. Please take the youngsters inside." The old woman clung to the old man while the two young men took the children inside.

As he sat on a bamboo chair in the gatehouse, Sanzang said indignantly, "Disciples, the pair of you are ugly to look at, and your language is too coarse. You gave that whole family a terrible fright, and got me into trouble." "I tell you truthfully, Master," Pig replied, "that I've grown better-looking since I've been following you. When I lived in Gao Village I looked so awful that I often used to scare twenty or thirty people to death by making a face and waggling my ears." "Don't exaggerate, stupid," said Monkey with a smile, "and tidy that ugly mug of yours up a bit." "What nonsense you're talking, Monkey," said Sanzang. "He was born that way, so how can you expect him to tidy his face up?" "He could stick his rake of a snout into his chest, and not bring it out; and he could lay those fan-shaped ears down behind his head and not waggle them. That would tidy his appearance up." Pig then tucked his snout away and laid his ears back, and stood beside Sanzang with his head bowed. Brother Monkey took the luggage inside and tethered the white horse to a post.

The old man came out again with a young man who was carrying a tray with three cups of tea on it, and when it had been drunk he gave instructions for a vegetarian meal to be prepared. The young man then brought out an old, dented, and unlacquered table, as well as a pair of benches with chipped tops and broken legs, which he put in a cool spot before asking the three of them to sit down. Sanzang then asked the old man his surname, and was told, "Your humble servant's surname is Wang." "How many descendants have you?" "Two sons and three grandchildren." "Congratulations, congratulations," said Sanzang; then he asked the old man how old he was. "I have lived in my stupidity to sixty-one." "Splendid, splendid, you have begun a new cycle," said Sanzang. "Benefactor," he continued, "why did you say at first that it would be impossible to fetch the scriptures from the Western Heaven?" "There is no problem about actually getting the scriptures," the old man replied, "it's just that the journey will be very difficult. Only some twelve miles to the west of here is a mountain called the three-hundred mile Yellow Wind Ridge, and it's full of evil monsters. That's why I said it would be impossible to get the scriptures. But as this younger gentleman says he has so many magic powers, you will be able to get there." "Certainly, certainly," said Monkey. "With me and my fellow-disciple, no devils, however fierce, will dare to provoke us."

As he spoke the youth came in with food, which he put on the table with the words, "Please eat." Sanzang put his hands together and started to recite the grace. By then Pig had already swallowed a bowlful, and the moron finished three more before the short prayer was over. "What a chaff-guzzler," said Monkey. "We do seem to have run into a hungry ghost." Old Wang, however, found the speed at which Pig ate very amusing, and said, "This reverend gentleman must be very hungry. Give him more rice at once." The stupid creature indeed had a large stomach. Look at him, keeping his head down as he devours at least a dozen bowls. Sanzang and Monkey had not been able to finish two bowls, but the idiot would not stop and was still eating. "As this is far from being haute cuisine, I cannot press you too hard, but please take another mouthful." "We have eaten enough," said Sanzang and Monkey; but Pig said, "What are you going on about, old fellow? Who's been telling your fortune? Is that why you're going on about quizzing? Anyhow, if there's rice left, give me some more." In a single meal the idiot ate all the rice in the house, and still said that he was only half full. Then the table was cleared away, bamboo beds were set out for them in the gatehouse, and they went to sleep.

At dawn the next morning Monkey went to saddle the horse while Pig packed the luggage. Old Wang told his wife to prepare some pastries and hot water for them, after which the three of them thanked him and said goodbye. "If anything goes wrong on your journey," the old man said, "you must come to our place." "Don't be so discouraging, old fellow," said Monkey. "We're dedicated, and there's no turning back for us." With that they whipped the horse, picked up the carrying-pole, and headed west.

Alas! On their journey there was no good path to the West, and there were undoubtedly demons and great disasters in store for them. Before they had been going for half a day, they reached the mountain. It was most precipitous. Sanzang rode as far as the edge of a cliff, then dismounted to have a look.

> *High was the mountain,*
> *Craggy the ridge;*
> *Steep the cliffs,*
> *Deep the valleys.*
> *Springs could be heard,*
> *And sweet smelt the flowers.*
> *Was that mountain high?*
> *Its summit touched the azure heavens.*
> *Were the gorges deep?*

At their bottom you could see the Underworld.
In front of the mountain
Were rolling white clouds,
And towering crags.
There were no end of myriad-fathom, soul-snatching
  cliffs,
In which were twisting caves for dragons,
Caves full of stalactites dripping with water.
He saw deer with branching antlers,
And river-deer gazing with fixed stare,
Coiled, red-scaled pythons,
And mischievous, white-faced apes.
At evening tigers climbed the hills to find their dens;
Dragons emerged from the waves at dawn,
To enter their caves with thunderous roars.
Birds flying in the grass
Rose in a flurry;
Beasts walking in the woods
Hurried helter-skelter.
Suddenly a pack of wolves ran past,
Making the heart pound hard with fear.
This was a place where caves were linked with caves,
And mountains stood with mountains.
The green of the peak made it like ten thousand feet of
  jade,
As a myriad clouds were piled above it like a cover of
  bluish gauze.

While Sanzang urged his silvery steed slowly forward, Monkey strolled ahead on his cloud and Pig ambled along with the carrying-pole. As they looked at the mountain they heard a whirlwind blowing up, and Sanzang was alarmed. "Wukong," he said, "there's a whirlwind coming." "What's there to be afraid of about a wind?" said Monkey. "It's only weather, after all, and nothing to be scared of." "But this is a very evil wind, not like a natural wind at all," Sanzang replied. "How can you tell?" Monkey asked. "Just look at it," said Sanzang:

"Mighty and majestic it howls and roars,
Coming out of the distant heavens.
As it crosses the ridge the trees all moan;
The trunks bend when it enters the wood.

"The willow on the bank is shaken to its roots,
And flowers and leaves go swirling round the garden.
Gathering in nets on fishing boats they pull hard on the
*   cables;*
Ships lower their sails, and all cast anchor.

"The traveller loses his way in mid-journey,
The woodcutter in the hills cannot carry his load.
The monkeys scatter in the orchards of fairy fruit,
The deer flee from the clumps of rare flowers.

"Locust trees and cedars collapse before the cliff,
While pine and bamboo in the valley are stripped of
*   leaves.*
There are stinging blasts of dirt and sand,
And waves boil on rivers and seas."

Pig went up to Monkey and grabbed hold of him. "Brother," he said, "this is a terrific storm. Let's take shelter." "You're useless, brother," replied Monkey with a mocking laugh. "If a big wind makes you want to hide, what are you going to do when you meet an evil spirit?" "Elder brother, have you never heard the saying, 'Avoid a pretty girl as you would an enemy, avoid a wind as you would an arrow'?" Pig replied. "There's no reason why we shouldn't take shelter." "Stop talking, will you, while I get a hold on that wind and take a sniff at it," said Monkey. "You're talking through your hat again," said Pig with a grin. "As if you could get a hold on a wind. Besides, even if you did, your hand would go through it." "What you don't know, brother, is that I have a magic way of catching winds," Monkey replied. Letting the head of the wind pass, the splendid Monkey grabbed the tail and sniffed at it. It had rather a foul stench. "It certainly isn't a good wind," he remarked. "It smells like either a tiger wind or a monster wind. There's definitely something suspicious about it."

Before the words were out of his mouth, a ferocious striped tiger leapt out at the foot of the slope, slashing with its tail and rushing towards them. Sanzang was so scared that he could no longer keep his seat in his carved saddle, but fell head first off his white horse and lay sprawled in a witless heap beside the path. Pig threw down the luggage, grabbed his rake and, not letting Monkey move forward, roared, "Animal, where d'you think you're going?" He went straight after it and smote it on the head. The tiger stood up on its hind legs, and with a swing of its front left claws ripped at its own chest. There was a tearing noise as its skin all came off, and then the creature stood beside the path. Just see how hideous it was:

> A gory, skinned body,
> Round, red legs and feet.
> Fiery, matted hair,
> And straight, bristling eyebrows.
>
> Four sinister steely white fangs,
> A pair of glittering golden eyes.
> With soaring spirits it gave a mighty roar,
> A mighty and majestic shout.

"Not so fast," it yelled, "not so fast. I am none other than the Commander of the Vanguard for the Great Yellow Wind King. I bear His Majesty's strictest command to patrol the mountain and catch a few common mortals as titbits for him to nibble with his wine. Where are you from, monk, and how dare you wound me with that weapon of yours?" "I'll get you, you beast," replied Pig abusively. "You don't seem to realize that I'm not just any old passing traveller: I'm a disciple of Sanzang, the younger brother of the Tang Emperor of the East, who has been sent by the Emperor to visit the Buddha in the Western Heaven and ask for the scriptures. If you clear off, stop blocking our path, and don't frighten my master any more, I'll spare your life. But if you go on raging about like that, there'll be no mercy for you."

Not bothering to argue, the evil spirit rushed at Pig, feinted, and clawed at his face. Pig dodged nimbly and swung his rake

at the monster, who turned and fled as he was unarmed. With
Pig at his heels he made for the bottom of the slope and produced
two bronze swords from the tangled undergrowth there; then,
brandishing them, he turned to face Pig. The two of them
battled away at the foot of the hill, lunging and hitting at each
other. Monkey, who was helping the Tang Priest to sit up, said,
"Don't be afraid, Master. You sit here while I help Pig to
defeat that monster, then we can be on our way." Sanzang, who
had managed to sit up, was shaking all over and intoning the
Heart Sutra.

Monkey grabbed his cudgel and shouted, "Get it." Pig made
a tremendous effort, and the monster fled from the scene of
battle. "Don't let him get away," yelled Monkey. "You've got
to catch it." The pair of them chased the monster down the
mountain, waving the rake and the cudgel. The monster was so
hard-pressed that it did a "golden cicada shedding its skin" trick.
It reverted to its real form — a ferocious tiger — with a somersault, but Monkey and Pig would still not let it get away, and
were hot on its heels, determined to destroy it. When the monster
saw how close they were, it ripped at its chest and tore off its
skin again, then laid it over a rock that was shaped like a crouching tiger. Then it abandoned its real body, turned into a hurricane, and went straight back to the path, where it noticed Sanzang reciting the *Heart Sutra*. Sanzang was grabbed by the
monster and carried away on the wind. Poor Sanzang:

> *The Monk of the River was fated to suffer much;*
> *In the faith of Nirvana it is hard to win merit.*

Carrying the Tang Priest to the mouth of the cave, the monster stilled the hurricane and said to the gatekeepers, "Report
to His Majesty at once that the Tiger of the Vanguard has caught
a monk and is awaiting further instructions outside the gates."
He was then admitted on the orders of the chieftain. With his
two bronze swords stuck in his belt and holding the Tang Priest
in both hands, he went forward and genuflected before the
chieftain. "Your Majesty," he said, "your humble underling was
patrolling the mountain as ordered when suddenly I met a monk.

He is the Patriarch Sanzang, the younger brother of His Majesty the Great Tang Emperor, and he was going to the West to visit the Buddha and ask for the scriptures. I have captured him and now offer him as a dish for your table."

The chieftain was astonished at the news. "I've heard tell of the Patriarch Sanzang, the holy priest sent by the Great Tang Emperor to fetch the scriptures. He has a disciple called Brother Monkey whose magical powers are tremendous and whose cunning is considerable. However did you manage to catch him?" "He has two disciples. The first one to come at me was a fellow with a long nose and big ears who wields a nine-pronged rake, and the second one has a gold-banded iron cudgel and fiery eyes with golden pupils. When the pair of them were after me and about to attack, I used a 'golden cicada shedding its skin' trick to make my getaway, then I caught this monk to offer to Your Majesty as a snack." "He's not to be eaten yet," the chieftain said. "You must be off your food, Your Majesty, if you won't eat what's put before you," said the Tiger of the Vanguard. "You don't get my point," the chieftain replied. "It's not eating him that worries me, but the thought that those two disciples of his may come here to make trouble, which would be dangerous. Tie him to the wind-settling stake in the garden at the back, and leave him there for a few days till we're sure his disciples won't be coming to make trouble for us. This way he'll be nice and clean, and we can do what we like with him without any arguments. Whether we have him boiled, steamed, fried or scrambled, we can eat him at our leisure." "Your Majesty's plans are most far-sighted, and you are quite right," said the Tiger of the Vanguard, who then ordered his underlings to take Sanzang away.

Seven or eight of them crowded forward to tie up Sanzang and take him away; they were like hawks seizing bramblings as they bound him tightly. Then did the unfortunate Monk of the River long for Brother Monkey; the holy priest in his troubles wished Pig would come. "Disciples," he called out, "I don't know on what mountain you are catching monsters, or where you're subduing evil spirits, but I've met with disaster and been

captured by a demon. Alas, when will I ever see you again?
If you come soon, you can save my life, but if you are too long
about it I will be finished." His tears poured down like rain as
he moaned and sighed.

As Monkey and Pig chased the tiger down the mountain side
they saw that it had reached the bottom and was crouching at
the foot of the cliff. Monkey raised his cudgel and brought it
down as hard as he could, thus hurting his own hands. Pig took
another swipe at the beast with his rake, which made its prongs
splay apart. The Tiger turned out to be only a tiger skin spread
over a rock shaped like crouching tiger. "This is terrible," said
Monkey, "he's tricked us." "How?" Pig asked. "The trick is
called 'the golden cicada shedding its skin'. He put his tiger-
skin over this rock and got away. We'd better go back and see
that our master comes to no harm." The two of them rushed
back to find that Sanzang had disappeared. "Whatever shall
we do?" cried Monkey in a voice as loud as thunder. "It's caught
our master." Pig led the horse over and said through his tears,
"Heaven help us. Wherever shall we look for him?" "Don't
cry," said Monkey, raising his head, "don't cry. If you cry you'll
dampen our spirits. I'm convinced he must be somewhere on
this mountain. We must start searching for him."

The two of them hurried deep into the mountain, going
through passes and crossing ridges, and after they had been going
for a long time they saw a cave palace at the foot of a rock-face.
They stopped to gaze at it, and saw an awe-inspiring sight:

> *Screened by many a jagged peak,*
> *With ancient paths winding around.*
> *Green pines merged with bluish bamboo;*
> *The softness of willows and* wutong *trees.*
> *Odd boulders stood in pairs before the cliff,*
> *While birds made couples hidden in the woods.*
> *The water in the gully splashed against the rock-wall,*
> *As the spring waters trickled over the sandbank.*
> *Under the billowing clouds,*
> *Rare herbs grew lush.*

Fox spirits and crafty hares darted around;
Horned deer and river-deer fought for mastery.
Ancient creepers hung across the rocks,
And a thousand-year cypress was suspended in a chasm.
In pinnacled majesty it vied with Mount Hua;
The flowers and birdsong rivalled Tiantai Peak.

"Worthy brother," said Monkey, "put our baggage in the wind-storing valley, let the horse out to pasture, and lie low while I go to the gates of that place and fight it out with them. I must catch that evil spirit before I can rescue our master." "There's no need to give me instructions," Pig replied. "Go at once." Monkey straightened his tunic, tightened his tiger-skin kilt, and went straight to the gate with his cudgel in his hands. Above the gate he saw YELLOW WIND CAVE OF THE YELLOW WIND RIDGE written in large letters. Taking a firm stance and brandishing the club he shouted, "Evil monsters, send my master out if you don't want this den of yours turned upside down and your home trampled flat."

When the junior fiends heard this they were terrified, and they ran trembling inside to announce, "Your Majesty, a disaster." "What is it?" asked the Yellow Wind Monster who was sitting inside. "There's a hairy-faced monk with a mouth like the thunder god outside with a great thick iron cudgel in his hands, and he wants his master back," they said. The alarmed chieftain sent for the Tiger of the Vanguard and said to him, "When I sent you to patrol the mountain you were only supposed to catch mountain oxen, wild boar, deer, and goats. Why on earth did you bring that Tang Priest here? It's provok-ed his disciple into coming to make trouble. What are we to do?" "There is no need for Your Majesty to worry," the Tiger replied. "Your incompetent underling will take fifty junior of-ficers out with me and bring back that Brother Monkey as a second course for the meal." "Apart from the higher and lower ranking commanders, we have about six hundred junior officers here," said the chieftain. "Take as many of them as you like with you. If you catch that Monkey, we can dine off the priest at our leisure, and I promise to make you my sworn brother. But I'm afraid that you won't be able to get him, and that he'll kill you. If that happens, don't blame me."

"Rest assured," the tiger monster said, "rest assured. I'll soon be back with him." Mustering fifty strong and spirited young fiends, he charged out of the gates with drums rolling and banners waving; his two bronze swords were tied to his body. "Where are you from, ape monk?" he shrieked at the top of his voice. "What do you mean by all this yelling and shouting?" "You skinned beast," Monkey retorted, "you played that trick of skinning yourself to capture my master, and you have the nerve to ask me what I'm doing! Bring my master out at once and I'll spare your life." "Yes, I captured your master," the monster replied, "and he's going to be served up at His Majesty's dinner table. If you have any sense, go away. Otherwise I'll catch you too, and you'll be served up with him. I've got one of you, and I'll take the other thrown in. Monkey was now furious, and he gnashed his steely teeth as his fiery eyes opened wide in a terrible glare. "What powers have you," he roared, brandishing his iron cudgel, "to give you the nerve to talk so big? Hold it a moment, and take this." The tiger put his hands on his swords, and a terrible fight ensued as each of them showed off his powers.

> The monster was like a goose egg,
> Monkey was an egg-shaped stone.
> Trying to ward off Monkey with bronze swords
> Was like throwing eggs at a stone.
> How can a crow or jackdaw fight a phoenix?
> What chance has a pigeon against a hawk?
> The monster snorted out winds that covered the mountain with dust,
> But Monkey breathed a fog that blotted out the sun.
> After fighting it out for many a round,
> The Vanguard was exhausted, his strength all gone.
> He turned away, defeated, to flee for his life,
> Only to have Monkey harry him to death.

When he could defend himself no longer, the monster turned to flee. As he had talked so boastfully in front of his chieftain he dared not return to the cave, so he tried to escape up
the mountainside. Monkey, who had no intention of letting him
go, chased him as fast as he could, waving his cudgel, roaring,
and howling. He chased him as far as the hollow where the
wind was stored, where Pig could be seen pasturing the horse.
As soon as Pig heard the shouting he turned to look, and when
he saw Monkey pursuing the defeated tiger monster he let go
of the horse, raised his rake, and struck the tiger diagonally
across the head. The poor monster, who thought he had made
his way out of the silken net, never realized that he had been
caught by a fish-trapper. Pig's rake made nine holes from which
the blood gushed, and the brains all spurted out. There is a
poem to prove it that goes:

> Converted to the true faith several years before,
> He avoided meat and was awakened to emptiness.
> Determined with all his heart to defend Sanzang
> He won this merit early in his religious life.

Planting his foot in the middle of the monster's back, Pig
swung the rake with both hands and smote him again. When
Monkey saw this he was delighted, and he said, "That's the
way, brother. He led a few dozen petty fiends out to do battle
with me, but I beat him. Instead of running back to the cave he
came this way, as if he wanted to die. If you hadn't been here
to meet him, he'd have got away again." "Was he the one who
made a gale and carried off our master?" Pig asked. "The very
one," Monkey replied. "Did you ask him where our master is?"
Pig asked. "He took our master into the cave and wanted to
give him to his chieftain to eat with his rice. This made me
so angry that I fought him all the way to here, where you
finished him off. The credit for this must go to you, brother.
You'd better go on looking after the horse and our things while
I drag that monster's body over to the cave and challenge them
to another fight. We must capture the chief monster if we're
to rescue our master." "You're right," said Pig, "so off you go.

If you beat that chief monster, mind you chase him this way for me to corner and kill." Splendid Monkey went straight to the mouth of the cave with his cudgel in one hand and the dead tiger in the other. Indeed,

> *When the patriarch was in danger from evil monsters,*
> *Emotion and Nature combined to subdue the demons.*

If you don't know whether he defeated the evil monsters and saved Sanzang, listen to the explanation in the next instalment.

CHAPTER TWENTY-ONE

The Guardians of the Faith build a farm
for the Great Sage;
Lingji from Sumeru pacifies the wind devil.

The fifty petty devils fled routed into the cave, their banners
and drums smashed, to report, "Your Majesty, the Tiger of the
Vanguard is no match for the hairy-faced monk, who has chased
him down the mountain." The old fiend was very angry at the
news, and he sat silent with his head bowed as he thought over
what to do. Then the petty demons from the gate came
in to announce, "Your Majesty, the hairy-faced monk has killed
the Tiger of the Vanguard and dragged his body to the gates,
where he's insulting us to provoke us to fight." The old fiend
was angrier than ever when he heard this, and he said, "This
wretch doesn't know what he's doing, killing my Commander
of the Vanguard although I haven't eaten his master. Hateful
beast. Bring my armour. I've heard of this Brother Monkey,
and now I think I'll go out to have a look at this nine-headed,
eight-tailed monk. I'll capture him to avenge my Tiger of the
Vanguard." The junior devils brought the armour as fast as
they could, and when the old fiend had put it all on properly,
he took his steel trident and led his devilish host out of the
cave. He was full of martial dignity as he came out, and you
can see how he was equipped:

> His golden helmet shone in the sun,
> And light was reflected from his golden armour.
> A pheasant's tail floated above his helmet,
> And the thin silk robe over his armour was pale goose-
> yellow.
> The belt that girded his armour was dragon-brilliant;
> His shining breastplate dazzled the eye.

His deerskin boots
Were the colour of locust-tree blossom;
His brocade kilt
Was patterned with willow leaves.
With a sharp steel trident in his hand,
He was no less awesome than the Little Sage Erlang.

As he came out of his cave the old fiend shouted at the top of his voice, "Are you Brother Monkey?" Monkey, who was jumping up and down on the tiger monster's corpse and brandishing his cudgel, replied, "Your grandfather, Monkey, is here. Send my master out." The evil spirit looked carefully at Monkey and saw that he had a miserable little body and a pinched face, and did not even stand four feet tall. "Poor little thing," he said with a laugh. "I'd imagined that you were some sort of invincible hero, but now I see what a little sick devil you really are, all skin and bone." Monkey smiled back and said, "You've no eyes in your head, my child. I may be tiny, but if you hit me on the head with the handle of your trident, I'll grow another six feet." "Make your head hard then," the monster replied, "here it comes." The Great Sage did not flinch as the monster hit him, then with a bend of his waist he grew six feet taller, making himself ten feet tall altogether, to the astonishment of the monster, who put his trident down and shouted, "Brother Monkey, why do you come and do these defensive transformations at my gate? Stop fooling around, and come over here so we can compare tricks." "My child," Monkey replied, "as the saying goes, 'If you have any warm feelings, don't raise your hand in anger; and if you raise your hand in anger, put all feelings aside.' I have a very heavy hand, and I'm afraid that you may not be able to stand my cudgel." No longer wishing to talk, the monster whirled his trident round and lunged at Monkey's chest. With unrushed expertise Monkey did a "Black Dragon Pawing the Ground" movement to parry the trident with his cudgel before striking at the monster's head. There followed a fine duel between the pair of them at the mouth of the Yellow Wind Cave:

The demon king was furious;
The Great Sage showed his might.
The furious demon king
Wanted to catch Monkey to avenge his Vanguard Commander;
The mighty Great Sage
Intended to capture the evil spirit and rescue his master.
When the trident came the cudgel parried;
When the cudgel struck the trident blocked.
One was supreme commander of the mountain;
The other was the Handsome Monkey King, Protector of the Law.
At first they fought in the dust,
But then they rose into mid-air.
The steel-tipped trident
Was bright-pointed and deadly sharp;
The as-you-will cudgel
Was black and banded with gold.
Whoever was run through would go to the Underworld;
Anyone who was hit he would surely meet King Yama.
All depended on a fast hand and a quick eye;
Strength and vigour were essential.
Each was mindless of life or death:
Who would survive, and who would be killed?

After some thirty rounds of combat between the old fiend and the Great Sage the issue was still not settled. As Monkey wanted to win glory he used an "extra body" trick: plucking a hair out, he chewed it into little bits, blew them all out, and shouted, "Change!" They turned into well over a hundred Monkeys, all dressed like him and wielding iron cudgels. They surrounded the monster in mid-air, and in his fright he countered with a trick of his own. He turned his head sharply to the southeast opened his mouth three times, and blew. A yellow hurricane suddenly arose. It was really terrible.

As it howled and moaned all was changed;
Without sign or shadow the yellow dust whirled,

Whistling through forests, toppling mountains, and uprooting trees,
Picking up dust to blot out the tumbling ridge.
The Yellow River's waters were all in turmoil,
While the Xiang River's waves were blown backwards.
The Polar Palace was rocked in the sky;
The Senluo Palace in the Underworld was all but blown down.
Heaven was filled with the shouting of Arhats;
The Eight Great Vajrapanis were all yelling wildly.
Manjusri's black-coated lion fled;
Samantabhadra's white elephant was nowhere to be found.
The True Martial Emperor's tortoise and snake were missing;
Zi Tong's mule was blown away by its saddle-cloth.
Travelling merchants called on Heaven;
Boatmen made vows to the gods as they sought safety.
Lives were washed away in the torrent;
Fortune or death was decided by the waters.
The cave palace on the magic mountain was murky dark,
And Penglai, island of joy, was wrapped in gloom.
Lao Zi could hardly manage to look after his furnace;
The Star of Longevity put away his fan of dragon's beard grass.
The Queen Mother, on her way to a Peach Banquet,
Had the pendants at her waist blown in a tangle.
Erlang could not find his city of Guanzhou;
Nezha could scarcely draw his sword from its scabbard.
Heavenly King Li lost sight of the pagoda in his hand;
Lu Ban the carpenter dropped his gold-tipped awl.
Three storeys of the pagoda at Thunder Monastery fell,
And the stone bridge at Zhaozhou collapsed.
The red wheel of the sun sent out no light,
And all the stars in the sky were dimmed.
The birds of the southern hills were carried to the north;
The waters of the east lake flowed to the west.

Husband was parted from wife,
Mother snatched from child.
The dragon king searched the seas for his yakshas;
The thunder god hunted everywhere for his lightning.
The Ten Kings of Hell looked for the judge,
While the bull-headed demons searched for the horse-
*   faced.*
This hurricane overturned Potaraka Island,
Rolling up one of Guanyin's scriptures.
The white lotus went flying beyond the seas,
And the twelve courts of the Bodhisattva were all blown
*   down.*
Pan Gu, who had seen all winds since creation,
Had never seen one as fierce as this.
Howl, howl —
As mountains and seas trembled,
Heaven and Earth were all trembling.

The hurricane that the monster had summoned up made all the little Monkeys that the Great Sage had produced from his hair whirl round in mid-air like so many spinning-wheels, and so far from being able to use their cudgels, they could not even control their own bodies. At this critical moment Monkey shook his hair and put it back on his body, then advanced to give battle with his iron cudgel held high. The monster blew another yellow hurricane at him, and it was so strong that Monkey had to shut his fiery eyes with their golden pupils tight. Opening them was out of the question. Unable to use his iron cudgel, he had to flee from the scene of battle, at which the monster put his wind away and went back to his cave.

When Pig saw the great yellow hurricane blow up and cast Heaven and Earth into darkness, he held on to the horse and kept a grip on the carrying pole while he crouched in the hollow on the mountain side, not daring to open his eyes or raise his head as he invoked the Buddha and made all sorts of vows to him. He did not know whether Monkey had won or lost, or whether their master was still alive. As he worried about all this the wind died down and the sky became clear again. He raised his head to look towards the entrance of the cave, but he could neither see any weapons nor hear any gongs or drums. The idiot did not want to get any nearer to those gates, and there was nobody else to look after the horse and the baggage, so he was stuck there, not knowing what to do, and feeling miserable. His gloomy thoughts were interrupted by the sound of Monkey shouting to the west of him. Pig half rose to his feet to welcome him and said, "That was quite a wind, elder brother. Where've you been?" "That was terrible," said Monkey, "Never in my life have I known such a hurricane. That old fiend came out to fight me with a steel trident, and after we'd been at it for thirty rounds I used my extra body trick to surround him. This made him so worried that he deliberately summoned up the wind. It was really vicious — it blew so hard I couldn't stand my ground, so I had to put my tricks away and clear out. What a wind, what a wind! I can call up wind or rain, but I've never produced anything as vicious as his." "Can that evil monster fight well?" Pig asked. "He's not bad at all," Monkey replied, "and he has a very neat way with his trident. We were evenly matched, apart from that foul wind, which makes him unbeatable." "Then how are we going to rescue our master?" Pig asked. "His rescue will have to wait," Monkey replied. "I wonder if there's an oculist near here to treat my eyes." "What's happened to them?" Pig asked. "When that monster blew his wind at me," said Monkey, "it made my eyes very sore, and they keep on watering." "We're halfway up a mountain, and night's falling," said Pig. "Never mind about an oculist, there's nowhere for us to shelter for the night." "There's no problem about shelter," Monkey replied. "I don't think that evil spirit will dare to do our master any harm, so let's find the main path and look for a house to stay in tonight. We can come back here at first light to subdue that fiend." "Very well, very well," Pig replied.

Leading the horse and carrying the baggage, they came out of the hollow and went along the path. The dusk was gradually deepening when they heard dogs barking under a hill to the south of the path. They stopped to look and saw a farmhouse with a lamp shining brightly in its window. The pair of them stopped bothering to look for the path and cut straight through the grass to the gate. They saw

> Dark magic fungus,
> Greeny white rocks.
> The magic fungus was dark among the many herbs,
> The white rocks were green with moss.
> Some tiny fireflies made dots of light
> Against the dense ranks of the forest trees.
> Heavy was the fragrance of the orchid,
> And the tender bamboo had been newly planted.
> A pure spring flowed along a winding bed,
> An ancient cypress hung over a cliff.
> No travellers came to this remote spot,
> And only wild flowers bloomed before the gate.

As they did not want to march straight in, the two of them shouted, "Open up, open up." An old man came out at the head of several farm hands carrying forks, rakes and brooms. "Who are you," he asked, "who are you?" "We are the disciples of the holy priest of the Great Tang in the East," replied Monkey with a bow. "We were crossing these mountains on our way to the West to visit the Buddha and ask for the scriptures when the Great King of the Yellow Wind snatched our master away. We haven't been able to rescue him yet, but as it is getting dark we have come to beg for a night's lodging in your mansion, and we hope very much that you will help us." The old man returned his bow and said, "I'm sorry I didn't welcome you properly. This is a place where we see a lot of clouds but very few people, and when I heard you shouting at the gate I feared it might be fox-spirits, tigers, bandits from the mountains, or something of the sort. I am afraid that I have stupidly offended you: I did not realize it would be two reverend gentlemen. Please come in." Taking the horse and the luggage with them they went inside, tethered the animal, put down the carrying pole, bowed to the old man, and sat down. A

servant came in with tea, and when they had drunk it some
bowls of sesame meal were produced. After they had eaten,
the old man had beds prepared for them and suggested that they
went to bed. "We don't need to sleep yet," Monkey replied,
adding, "may I ask you, kind sir, if eye ointment is sold anywhere around here?" "Do you have a chronic eye complaint,
reverend sir?" the old man asked. "I can tell you truthfully,
sir," Monkey replied, "that we religious men have never been
ill before, and I've never had trouble with my eyes before."
"Then why are you asking for ointment?" the old man asked.
"We were trying to rescue our master on the Yellow Wind
Ridge today," Monkey explained, "when that monster started
blowing his wind at me, which made my eyes ache. They're
streaming with tears now, which is why I want to find some
eye ointment." "A fine story," the old man commented. "How
could you tell such lies, a reverend gentleman, and so young a
one at that? The Great King of the Yellow Wind's hurricane
is really terrible. It can't be compared with spring winds, autumn winds, pine and bamboo winds, or north, south, east and
west winds." "It must be a brain-snatching wind," interrupted
Pig, "or a goat's ear wind, or a hemp wind, or a head-twisting
wind." "No, no," the old man said, "it's called a Divine Samadhi Wind." "What's it like?" Monkey asked.

> *"It can darken Heaven and Earth,*
> *Make gods and devils gloomy,*
> *Split rocks open and bring cliffs down,*
> *And it doesn't stop till you're dead,"*

the old man replied. "If you'd encountered that wind, you
couldn't possibly have survived. Only a god or an immortal
would be able to survive such a wind." "Quite right," Monkey
replied, "quite right. Although we're not gods or immortals
ourselves, I regard them as my juniors, and this life of mine
is extremely hard to snuff out — all the wind could do was
to make my eyes very sore." "If what you say is true," the
old man said, "you must really be somebody. Although there
is nowhere that sells eye ointment here, I sometimes suffer from

watering eyes myself when I'm in the wind, and I once met an unusual person who gave me a prescription for 'Three Flower Nine Seed Ointment'. This cures all inflammations of the eye." Monkey bowed his head, chanted a respectful "re-e-er", and said, "Please put a little on my eyes for me to try." The old man consented, went inside, and brought out a tiny agate bottle. Removing the stopper, he dipped a jade hairpin inside and put a tiny amount in Monkey's eyes, then told him not to open them. He could go to sleep without worrying, and in the morning he would be cured. When he had finished applying it he put the stopper back the bottle and gave it to a servant to put away inside. Pig opened their bundles, spread out their bedding, and told Monkey to go to bed. Monkey groped about so wildly with his eyes shut that Pig laughed at him and said, "Would you like a blind man's stick, sir?" "Chaff-guzzling moron," Monkey retorted, "do you want to make a blind man of me?" The idiot chuckled himself quietly to sleep, but Monkey sat thinking on the bed until midnight before he dozed off.

At about five the next morning, just before the break of day, Brother Monkey rubbed his face, opened his eyes and said, "It certainly is good ointment — I can see far, far more clearly than ever." He turned round to look behind him, and to his astonishment there was no house, windows, or doors; all that could be seen were some ancient locust trees and tall willows. The pair of them were sleeping on cushions of green sedge. "What are you shouting for?" asked Pig as he woke up. "Open your eyes and look," replied Monkey. The idiot raised his head, and when he saw that there was nobody there, he leapt up in a panic with the words, "Where's our horse?" "Over there, tied to a tree," said Monkey. "What about the luggage?" "There, beside your head." "The wretches," said Pig, "why didn't they tell us they were going to move? If they'd let me know I'd have given them some tea and fruit. They must have been illegal residents clearing off in the middle of the night so the village head wouldn't know about it. Damn it, we must have been almost dead asleep. However did they dismantle the house without us hearing a thing?" "Idiot," said Monkey with a snigger, "don't go shouting all over the place. Can you see what that piece of paper on the tree over there is?" Pig went over, tore it down, and saw that there were four lines of verse on it:

> *"This farm was not inhabited by mortals;*
> *The Guardians of the Dharma produced the house by*
> *magic.*
> *We gave you good medicine to cure your eyes:*
> *Subdue demons with all your heart, and never hesitate."*

"So those tough gods came to play their tricks although I haven't called the roll since they changed the dragon into a horse," said Monkey. "Don't show off, brother," said Pig. "How could they possibly answer to your roll-call?" "You don't realize," Monkey replied, "that the Guardians of the Faith, the Six Dings, the Six Jias, the Protectors of the Five Regions and the Four Duty Gods have all been ordered by the Bodhisattva to give secret protection to our master. They reported their names to me then, but as I've had you with me recently I haven't needed them again, which is why I haven't called the roll." "Brother," Pig replied, "if they have been ordered to protect our master in secret, then of course they can't appear in their true forms. That was why they produced the magic farm. You mustn't be angry with them. Yesterday they gave you eye ointment and fed us — they did all they could. Don't be angry with them. Let's go and rescue the master instead." "How right you are," said Monkey. "It's not far from here to the Yellow Wind Cave, so there's no need for you to move. You'd better stay in the wood and look after the horse and the luggage while I go to the cave to see what I can find out about where our master is before fighting the monster again." "Yes," said Pig, "find out for sure whether he's alive or dead. If the master's dead, we'd better each go our own way, and if he's alive we'll do everything we can to save him." "Stop talking such nonsense," replied Monkey. "I'm off."

With a single jump he arrived at the entrance to the cave, where the gates were still locked as everyone was asleep. Mon-

key did not call on them to open the gates as he did not want
to alarm the monsters. Instead he said a spell, made a magic
movement with his hand, shook himself, and turned into a
neat little mosquito. There are some lines about it that go:

> Its troublesome little body has a sharp bite,
> Its faint buzz echoes like thunder.
> Clever at getting through the curtains round the bed,
> It particularly loves the summer's warm weather.
> It fears only smoke and fly-swatters,
> And loves the brilliance of the lamp.
> Light and tiny, it flies straight in,
> Entering the evil spirit's cave.

Seeing that the lowly demon on the gate was fast asleep
and snoring, Monkey bit him on the face, at which he woke up
and said, "My lord! What an enormous mosquito! It's raised a
huge lump with a single bite." Then he opened his eyes and
announced, "It's light." The two gates creaked open, and
Monkey flew inside with a buzz to see the old demon giving
orders that a very close watch was to be kept at all the gates,
and all the weapons were to be assembled at such-and-such a
spot. "I'm afraid that yesterday's wind may not have killed
Brother Monkey," he was saying, "and I think he's bound to
come back today. When he does, I'll finish him off."

When he heard this, Monkey flew across to the back of the
hall where he saw a door that was tightly closed. He slipped
through the crack between the two leaves of the door and found
himself in a large empty garden, on one side of which was the
wind-settling stake with the Tang Priest tied to it. The tears
were pouring down Sanzang's face as he wondered where
Monkey and Pig were. Monkey stopped flying as he stung his
shaven pate and called, "Master." "Monkey," said Sanzang,
recognizing his voice, "I'm missing you so much it's almost killing me. Where are you calling me from?" "I'm on your head,
Master. Don't be anxious or worried. We are sure to catch that
evil spirit and save your life." "How long will it be till you
catch that evil spirit, disciple?" "Pig has already killed the

tiger monster who captured you," Monkey replied, "but that old fiend has a terrible way with a hurricane. All the same, I'm certain that I can catch him today, so don't worry and stop crying. I'm off now."

With those words he buzzed away to the front hall, where he saw the old monster sitting on his throne and reviewing his captains. A junior evil spirit suddenly rushed in with a command flag in his hands and announced, "I had just gone out to patrol the mountain, Your Majesty, when I saw a monk with a long snout and big ears sitting in the woods. If I hadn't run as fast as I could, he'd have caught me. But I didn't see that hairy-faced monk." "If Brother Monkey wasn't there," the old fiend said, "he must have been killed by the wind, and he won't be going off to get soldiers to rescue his master." "If the wind killed him, Your Majesty," the other devils said, "we are in luck. But if he wasn't killed and went to fetch divine soldiers instead, what's to be done?" "What's so frightening about divine soldiers?" the old fiend said. "None of them can put down my wind except the Bodhisattva Lingji, so there's no need to fear the rest of them."

When Monkey heard this as he sat on a roof-beam, he was beside himself with delight. Flying straight out, he reverted to his real form and went back to the wood, calling, "Brother." "Where have you been?" Pig asked. "I chased an evil spirit with a command flag away just now." "Good for you," said Monkey with a smile, "good for you. I changed myself into a mosquito and went into the cave to see our master. He was tied to a wind-settling stake in there and crying. I told him not to cry, flew up to a roof-beam, and had a good listen. I saw the one with the command flag come puffing and panting in to report that you'd chased him away and that he hadn't seen me. The old fiend was making some wild guesses. First he said that I had been killed by his wind, then he said I'd gone to ask for the help of divine soldiers. It's wonderful — he gave the fellow's name away." "Whose name?" Pig asked. "He said that no divine soldier could suppress his wind except the

Bodhisattva Lingji," Monkey continued, adding, "but I don't know where the Bodhisattva Lingji lives."

As they were wondering what to do, and old man came along the road. Look at him:

> He was strong enough not to need a stick,
> But his beard was like ice and his flowing hair snowy.
> Although his gold-flecked sparkling eyes seemed some-
> what dim,
> His aged bones and muscles had not lost their strength.
> Slowly he walked, back bent, and head bowed down,
> But his broad brow and rosy cheeks were those of a
> boy.
> If you gave him a name from his looks,
> The Star of Longevity had come out of his cave.

When Pig saw him he said with delight, "Brother, you know the saying, 'If you want to know the way down the mountain, ask a regular traveller.' Why don't you ask him?" The Great Sage put his iron cudgel away, unhitched his clothes, and went up to the old man. "Greetings, grandfather," he said. Half replying to him and half not, the old man returned his bow and asked, "Where are you from, monk, and what are you doing in this desolate spot?" "We are holy monks going to fetch the scriptures," Monkey replied. "Yesterday we lost our master here, and we would like to ask you, sir, where the Bodhisattva Lingji lives." "Lingji lives a thousand miles due south of here," the old man said, "on a mountain called Little Mount Sumeru. There is a holy place there which is the monastery where he preaches the scriptures. Are you going to fetch scriptures from him." 'No," Monkey replied, "we're going not to fetch scriptures from him, but to trouble him over something else. How does one got there?" The old man pointed south and said, "That twisting path will take you." Thus tricking the Great Sage into turning round to look, the old man turned into a puff of wind and disappeared from sight. All that could be seen of him was a piece of paper he had left beside the road. On it there were four lines of verse that read:

> *"I report to the Great Sage Equalling Heaven,*
> *That I am Morning Star Li.*
> *On Sumeru Mountain there is a Flying Dragon Staff,*
> *The weapon the Buddha once gave to Lingji."*

Brother Monkey took the note turned, and set off. "What lousy luck we've been having for the last few days, brother," said Pig. "For the last couple 'of days we've been seeing ghosts even in broad daylight. Who was that old man who turned into a wind?" Monkey handed the piece of paper to him, and when he had read it he said, "Who is this Morning Star Li?" "He's the Great White Planet of the west," Monkey replied. Pig immediately bowed low and said, "My benefactor, my benefactor. If he hadn't put in a memorial to the Jade Emperor, I don't know what would have become of me." "So you re capable of feeling gratitude," said Monkey. "Meanwhile, you're to hide deep in these woods without showing yourself, and keep a close watch on the baggage and the horse while I go to Mount Sumeru to ask the Bodhisattva to come." "Understood," said Pig, "understood. You go as fast as you can. I've learnt the tortoise's trick, and can pull my head in when I have to."

The Great Sage Monkey leapt into the air and headed south on his somersault cloud at tremendous speed. He could cover a thousand miles with a nod of his head, and do eight hundred stages with a twist of his waist. It was only an instant before he saw a high mountain surrounded by auspicious clouds and a propitious aura. In a valley on the mountain there was a monastery from which the distant sounds of bells and stone chimes could be heard, and a haze of incense smoke hung above it. Monkey went straight to the gate, where he saw a lay brother with prayer beads round his neck who was invoking the Buddha. "Greetings, lay brother," said Monkey, clasping his hands in salutation. The lay brother bowed to him in reply and said, "Where are you from, sir?" "Is this where the Bodhisattva Lingji preaches the scriptures?" Monkey asked. "Yes, this is the place," the lay brother replied. "Have you a message

for him?" "I would like you to tell him that I am Brother Sun
Wukong, the Great Sage Equalling Heaven, a disciple of the
Patriarch Sanzang, the younger brother of His Majesty the
emperor of the Great Tang in the East, and there is a matter
about which I should like to see the Bodhisattva." "That's far
too many words for me to remember, sir," said the lay brother
with a smile. "Then tell him that the Tang Priest's disciple Sun
Wukong is here," Monkey replied. The lay brother did as he
asked and went into the preaching hall to pass on the message.
The Bodhisattva put on his cassock, burnt some incense, and
prepared to receive him. As the Great Sage went through the
gate and looked inside he saw:

> A hall full of brocade,
> A room of awe-inspiring majesty.
> All the monks were chanting the Lotus Sutra
> While the aged head priest lightly struck the golden
>   chime.
> The offerings made to the Buddha
> Were magic fruit and magic flowers;
> Set out on tables
> Were meatless delicacies.
> Dazzling candles
> Sent golden flames up to the rainbow;
> From fragrant incense
> Jade smoke rose to the translucent mist.
> With the sermon over and the mind at peace, a trance
>   was entered;
> White clouds coiled around the tops of the pine trees.
> When the sword of wisdom is sheathed, the demon has
>   been beheaded;
> Great are the powers of the prajnaparamita.

The Bodhisattva straightened his clothes and came out to
meet Monkey, who climbed the steps into the hall and sat in
the guest's seat. When the orders were given for tea to be
brought, Monkey said, "I won't trouble you to give me tea.

My master is in troube on the Yellow Wind Mountain, and I have come to ask you, Bodhisattva, to use your great powers to subdue the demon and rescue my master." "I have been ordered by the Tathagata Buddha to guard over the Yellow Wind Monster," the Bodhisattva replied. "The Tathagata gave me a Wind-settling Pill and a Flying Dragon Staff. When I captured that monster before, I spared his life and exiled him to live in seclusion on this mountain, where he is not allowed to kill or do any other evil. I never imagined that he would want to murder your master today. I must hold myself responsible for this as I have failed to carry out my orders." The Bodhisattva wanted to keep Monkey for a meal and a talk, but in response to Monkey's urgent pleading he took his Flying Dragon Staff and rode off with the Great Sage by cloud.

A moment later they reached the Yellow Wind Mountain, and the Bodhisattva said, "Great Sage, as this evil monster is a bit scared of me, I'd better stay here inside the cloud while you go down and challenge him to come out and fight. Once you've lured him out, I can use my divine power." Doing as he suggested, Monkey brought his cloud down to land; and without more ado he smashed down the gates of the cave with his iron cudgel. "Fiendish monster," he shouted, "give my master back." The junior fiends on the gate all rushed back to report this, and the old monster said, "That damned ape really has a cheek — instead of behaving himself properly, he comes to smash my gates down. This time I'll use a magic wind that will certainly blow him to death." Putting on his armour and taking his trident as before, he went out through the gate, and the moment he saw Monkey, he thrust straight at his chest with his trident, not uttering a single word. Monkey sidestepped to dodge it and hit back at the monster's face with his cudgel. When only a few rounds had been fought, the monster turned to the southeast and was just going to open his mouth and blow out a wind when the Bodhisattva Lingji appeared in mid-air and dropped the Flying Dragon Staff on him. While the monster recited all sorts of spells, an eight-clawed golden dragon grabbed him with two of its claws and smashed him several times against a rock-face. At this the monster reverted to his real form — a brown marten.

Monkey rushed at it and had raised his cudgel to kill it when the Bodhisattva stopped him and said, "Don't kill it, Great Sage. I must take it back to see the Tathagata. He used to be a marten who had obtained the Way underneath the Vulture Peak, and once he stole some of the pure oil from a crystal lamp. When the lamp went out he was so afraid of being caught by a Vajrapani that he ran away and became a spirit monster here. The Tathagata decided that as this was not a capital offence I should be sent to keep guard over him; but if he took life or committed any other evil deeds he was to be taken to the Vulture Peak. As he has now offended you, Great Sage, and captured the Tang Priest with the intention of murdering him, I must take him to see the Tathagata to be sentenced for his crime before this business can be regarded as cleared up." After hearing this, Monkey thanked the Bodhisattva, who then returned to the west.

Pig, meanwhile, who had been wondering about Monkey as he waited in the wood, heard a shout from the mountain side, "Pig, bring the luggage and the horse out." Recognizing the voice as Monkey's, the idiot rushed out of the wood with the things and asked Monkey, "How did it go?" "I asked the Bodhisattva Lingji to come, and he used his Flying Dragon Staff to capture the evil spirit, who turned out to have been the spirit of a brown-coated marten and was taken off to the Vulture Peak by the Bodhisattva to see the Buddha. We two had better go into the cave to rescue out master." The idiot was very pleased to hear the news.

The pair of them charged into the cave and killed all the evil hares, fox-fiends, roebuck, and deer inside with the iron club and the rake. Then they went into the garden at the back to rescue their master. When he was outside he asked, "How did you two capture that evil spirit? How did you manage to rescue me?" Monkey told him all about how Lingji had subdued the fiend, and Sanzang expressed his gratitude at great

length while the two prepared a meal from the meatless food
that there was in the cave. Then they left the cave and looked
for the main path west once more. If you don't know what happened later, listen to the explanation in the next instalment.

CHAPTER TWENTY-TWO

Pig fights a great battle in the Flowing
Sands River;
Moksa obeys the Dharma and wins
Friar Sand over.

The story tells how the Tang Priest and his two disciples escaped from their troubles and pressed forward. Before long they had crossed the Yellow Wind Ridge and were heading west across a plain. The time passed rapidly, and summer gave way to autumn. Cold cicadas sang in moulting willow trees, and the Great Fire Star sank below the western horizon. As they were travelling one day they saw the mighty waves of a great river, boiling and raging. "Disciple," called out Sanzang from his horse, "do you see that broad river in front of us? Why are there no boats on it, and how are we going to get across?" "Those are really terrible waves," said Pig when he saw the river, "and there aren't any boats to ferry us over." Monkey sprang into the sky, shaded his eyes with his hand, and looked. "Master," he said with horror, "we're in big trouble here. I can cross a river like this with a twist of my waist, but I'm afraid you'll never be able to cross it in ten thousand years." "How wide is it, then?" Sanzang asked. "I can't see the other bank from here." "About three hundred miles," Monkey replied. "How can you be so sure of the distance, brother?" Pig asked. "These eyes of mine can see what's happening three hundred and fifty miles away in daytime," Monkey replied. "When I took a look from up in the air just now I couldn't make out the length of the river, but I could see that it was a good three hundred and fifty miles wide." Depressed and worried, Sanzang reined in his horse and noticed a stone tablet beside the river. The three of them went to look at it, and they saw the words FLOWING SANDS RIVER inscribed on it in the ancient curly style. On the base of the tablet were four lines in the standard script:

"Three hundred miles of flowing sands,
Three thousand fathoms of weak water,
On which a goose feather will not float,
And the flower of a reed will sink."

As the three of them were looking at this tablet they heard the waves make a roar like a collapsing mountain as a most hideous evil spirit emerged from the water:

A head of matted hair, as red as fire,
A pair of staring eyes, gleaming like lamps.
An indigo face, neither black nor green,
A dragon's voice like drums or thunder.

On his body a cloak of yellow goose-down,
Tied at the waist with white creeper.
Nine skulls hung around his neck,
And in his hands was an enormous staff.

The monster came to the bank in a whirlwind and rushed straight at the Tang Priest. Monkey picked Sanzang up at once, turned, and made off up the high bank. Pig dropped his carrying-pole, grabbed his rake, and struck at the evil spirit, who parried the blow with his staff. Each of them showed his prowess on the banks of the Flowing Sands River, and it was a fine battle:

The nine-pronged rake,
And the ogre-quelling staff:
Two men fighting on the banks of the river.
One was the great commander Tian Peng,
The other the banished Curtain-lifting General.
They used to meet in the Hall of Miraculous Mist,
But now they were locked in ferocious combat.
The rake had dug deep into clawed dragons;

The staff had defeated tusked elephants.
When either was held defensively, it was rock-solid;
In attack they cut into the wind.
While one clawed at head and face,
The other never panicked or left an opening.
One was the man-eating monster of the Flowing Sands
River,
The other was a believer, a general cultivating his
conduct.

The pair of them battled on for twenty rounds, but neither emerged as the victor. The Great Sage, who was holding on to the horse and looking after the luggage after carrying the Tang Priest to safety, became worked up into such a fury at the sight of Pig and the monster fighting that he ground his teeth and clenched his fists. When he could hold himself back no longer, he pulled out his cudgel and said, "Master, you sit here and don't be afraid. I'm going to play with him." Ignoring San-zang's pleas for him to stay, he whistled, jumped down to the side of the river, and found that the fight between Pig and the ogre was at its height. Brother Monkey swung his cudgel and aimed it at the ogre's head, but the ogre made a lightning turn and plunged straight into the river. Pig was hopping mad. "Nobody asked you to come, elder brother," he said. "That ogre was tiring and he could hardly fend my rake off. With few more rounds I would have captured him, but you gave him such a fright that he ran away, damn it." "Brother," said Monkey with a smile, "I must tell you frankly that the sight of you fighting so beautifully gave me an uncontrollable itch. I haven't used my cudgel for a whole month since we came down the mountain after dealing with the Yellow Wind Monster — I just had to join in the fun. How was I to know that the monster wouldn't want to play and was going to run away?"

The two of them then clasped hands and went back talking and laughing to see Sanzang, who asked, "Did you catch the ogre?" "No," Monkey said, "he couldn't take any more and dived back into the water." "He has lived here for a long time, disciple," Sanzang said, "and must know the shallows and deeps here. We must have a water expert to lead us across this vast expanse of weak water that has no boats." "Yes," said Monkey, "as the saying goes, 'What's near cinnabar goes red. and what's next to ink turns black.' As that ogre lives here he must be a water expert, so if we catch him we shouldn't kill him — we should make him take you across, Master, before finishing him off." "There's no time to lose, brother," said Pig. "You go and catch him while I look after the master." "This is something I can't talk big about," said Monkey with a smile. "I'm not all that good at underwater stuff. Even to walk underwater I have to make a magic hand movement and recite a water-repelling spell before I can move. The only other way I can get about there is by turning myself into a fish, a shrimp, a crab or a turtle. I can manage any strange and wonderful magic on a mountain or in the clouds that you can do, but when it comes to underwater business, I'm useless." "When I was the commander of the Milky Way, the heavenly river, in the old days," said Pig, "I had a force of eighty thousand sailors, so I know a bit about water. But I'm afraid that he might have generations of clansmen down there, and that would be too much for me. And if they got me, we'd be in a real mess." "You go into the water and start a fight with him there," said Monkey. "Don't fight hard, and don't win. You must lose and lure him out, then I can finish him off for you." "Very well then, I'll be off," said Pig. After stripping off his brocade tunic and removing his shoes he swung his rake in both hands and made his way into the water, where the tricks he had learnt years back enabled him to go through the waves to the river-bed, across which he advanced.

The ogre had now recovered his breath after his earlier defeat, and when he heard someone pushing the waters aside he leapt to his feet to look. Seeing that it was Pig brandishing his rake, the monster raised his staff and shouted at him, "Where do you think you're going, monk? Watch out, and take this." Pig warded off the blow with his rake and replied. "Who are you, evil spirit, and why are you blocking the way?" "You

may not realize who I am," the monster replied, "but I'm no
fiend, demon, ghost or monster, and I don't lack a name either."
"If you're not a fiend, a demon, or a monster, then why do you
live here taking life? Tell me your name truthfully and I'll
spare your life." "I," the monster replied,

> "Have had a divine essence since childhood,
> And have wandered all over heaven and earth.
> I have won glory among the he.oes of the world,
> And brave knights have taken me as their model.
>
> I travelled at will over countries and continents,
> Going where I liked in lakes and seas,
> To study the Way I went to the sky's edge,
> And I roamed the wastes in search of teachers.
>
> In those days I had a cassock and an alms-bowl,
> And I kept my mind and spirit well controlled.
> I travelled the earth by cloud some dozen times,
> Visiting everywhere on a hundred journeys.
>
> The Immortal I finally managed to find
> Led me along the great and shining Way.
> First I gathered mercury and lead,
> Then I let go of the Mother of Wood and Metal's Father.
>
> The kidney-water behind my brow entered my mouth,
> And the liver-fire in my windpipes entered my heart.
> With three thousand accomplishments won, I bowed to
>   the heavenly countenance;
> Piously I worshipped him in his glory.
>
> The Great Jade Emperor then promoted me
> To be the General Who Lifts the Curtain.
> I was honoured within the Southern Gate of Heaven,
> Supreme before the Hall of Miraculous Mist.
>
> At my waist was hung the tiger tally;
> In my hand I held my demon-quelling staff.
> My golden helmet shone like sunlight,
> And on my body gleamed a suit of armour.

I led the escort for the emperor's carriage,
Always took precedence when he entered or left court.
But then the queen mother gathered the peaches
And invited all the generals to feast at the Jade Pool.

I carelessly smashed some jade and crystal,
To the horror of all of the heavenly gods.
The Jade Emperor in his terrible fury
Put his hands together and turned to the vice-premier.

My hat and armour were removed, and I was stripped
*   of office,*
Then marched to the place of execution.
Then, to my good fortune, the great Barefoot Immortal
Stepped forward to ask for my reprieve.

Death was commuted; I was exiled
To the east bank of the Flowing Sands River.
When well fed I sleep in the river waters;
When hungry I burst through the waves in search of
*   food.*

If a woodcutter meets me his life is finished —
No fisherman sees me and survives.
In one way and another I've eaten many a man,
Cloaked as I am in an atmosphere of death.

As you have come to make trouble at my gates,
My belly will have something to look forward to today.
No matter if you're coarse and don't taste good,
When I've caught you I can cut you up for salted mince."

Pig was extremely angry to hear this, and he replied,
"You're completely blind, wretch. I can catch bubbles in my
fingers, so how dare you say that I'm so coarse you'll cut me
up for salted mince? So you take me to be a very well-cured
side of ham! Damned cheek — take a dose of this rake."
When the monster saw the rake coming at him he did a "phoenix
nod" to avoid it. The two of them fought their way up to the
surface of the water, where each of them trod on the waves as

they struggled in a combat that was even fiercer than their previous one.

> The Curtain-lifting General,
> And Marshal Tian Peng;
> Each gave a splendid show of magic powers.
> The ogre-quelling staff wheeled around the head;
> The nine-pronged rake was swift in the hand.
> As they leapt on the waves, they shook hills and rivers,
> Darkening the world as they pushed the waters aside.
> As terrible as the Disaster Star striking banners and
>   pendants,
> As frightening as lifting the canopy off the Death Star.
> One was the loyal defender of the Tang Priest,
> The other, a criminal, was an ogre of the waters.
> Where the rake struck it left nine scars;
> When the staff smote, all souls were scattered.
> Cheerfully fighting for all they were worth,
> They put all their hearts into the combat.
> Only for the sake of the pilgrim fetching scriptures
> His unrestrained anger burst against the sky.
> Such was the chaos that the fishes lost their scales,
> While the soft shells of terrapins were crushed;
> Red prawns and purple crabs all lost their lives,
> And the gods of the water palace all prayed to heaven.
> The only sound was the thunder of crashing waves;
> Sun and moon were dark, to the horror of earth and sky.

They battled on for four hours, but the issue was still undecided. It was as if a brass pan was fighting an iron brush, or a jade chime competing with a golden bell.

The Great Sage, who was standing beside the Tang Priest to guard him, watched the fight on the water with longing, unable to do anything. Then Pig feinted with his rake, pretended to be beaten, and made for the eastern bank with the ogre rushing after him. When he had almost reached the bank, Monkey could hold himself back no longer. Abandoning his master, he sprang down to the river's edge with his cudgel in his hand and took a swing at the ogre's head. Not daring to face him, the monster went straight back into the river. "Protector of the Horses," Pig shouted, "you impatient ape. You should have taken it a bit more slowly and waited till I'd drawn him up to high ground, and then cut him off from the river-bank. Then he wouldn't have been able to go back and we'd have caught him. But now he's gone back in, he'll never come out again." "Don't shout, idiot," Monkey said with a smile, "don't shout. Let's go back and see our master."

When Pig reached the top of the bank with Monkey, Sanzang bowed to him and said, "You've had a hard time, disciple." "I wouldn't say that," Pig replied. "But if we'd captured that evil spirit and made him take you across the river, that would have been the perfect solution." "How did your battle with the evil spirit go?" Sanzang asked. "He's as good as me," Pig replied. "When I pretended to be beaten in the fight he chased me to the river's edge; but then he saw elder brother waving his cudgel, so he ran away." "So what are we going to do?" Sanzang asked. "Relax, Master," said Monkey, "there's no need to worry. It's getting late, so you'd better sit on the bank while I go and beg some food. When you've eaten that you can go to sleep, and we can decide what to do tomorrow morning." "Good idea," said Pig. "Be as quick as you can."

Monkey leapt up on his cloud, went due north to a house where he begged some food, and came back to give it to his master. Seeing him come back so soon, Sanzang said to him, "Monkey, let's go to the house where you begged this food and ask them how to cross this river. That would be better than having to fight this ogre." "But that house is a long way away," laughed Monkey. "It's about two thousand miles from here. What would be the point in asking them about this river? They wouldn't know anything about it." "You're telling tall stories again," Pig said. "If it's two thousand miles away, how did you get there and back so fast?" "You wouldn't know, of course," Brother Monkey replied, "that my somersault cloud can cover thirty-six thousand miles with a single bound. To do a mere two-thousand-mile return journey takes only a couple of nods and a bow — there's nothing to it." "If it's so easy, brother," said Pig, "you should carry the master on your back, take him across with just a couple of nods and a bow, and save us all the trouble of fighting the monster." "You can ride clouds, can't you?" said Monkey. "Why don't you carry the master across?" "The master's mortal flesh and bones are heavier than Mount Tai," said Pig, "so although I can ride clouds I could never lift him. Nothing but your somersault will do the trick." "My somersault is the same as cloud-riding," Monkey said, "except that it takes you further. I'm no more able to carry him than you are. As the old saying goes; 'Mount Tai is as easy to move as a mustard seed, but a mortal cannot be dragged away from the earthly dust.' When that other poisonous monster of a fiend made a magic wind I could only move the master by dragging and tugging him along the ground. Of course, I can do tricks like that, and all those other ones like making myself invisible or shrinking land. But although our master cannot escape from the sea of suffering he wants to go to a foreign land, so he finds every inch of the way heavy going. All we can do is escort him and see that he comes to no harm. We can't undergo all that suffering on his behalf, nor can we fetch the scriptures for him. Even if we went ahead to see the Buddha, he wouldn't give the scriptures to you or me. After all, if we could get them that easily, we'd have nothing to do." The idiot accepted everything Monkey said, then they ate some plain rice without any vegetables, after which the three of them went to sleep on the eastern bank of the Flowing Sands River.

"Monkey," said Sanzang the next morning, "what are we going to do about it today?" "There's nothing for it but to send Pig back under the water," Monkey replied. "You're making me go underwater because you want to stay dry, brother," Pig protested. "I won't be impatient this time," Monkey said. "I'll let you lure him out onto the bank and then I'll cut him off from the river. That way we'll be bound to catch him."

Dear Pig rubbed his face, summoned up his energy, took his rake in both hands, went down to the river, and parted the waters as he went back to the monster's lair once more. The ogre, who had only just woken up, turned to see what was happening the moment he heard the waters being pushed apart. Observing that a rake-wielding Pig was upon him, he sprang to his feet to stop him, shouting, "Not so fast, not so fast. Take this." Pig blocked the blow from the staff with his rake and said, "What do you mean by telling your ancestor to 'take this' from that mourner's staff of yours?" "You know nothing, you wretch," the monster replied, continuing:

> "Great is the fame of this staff of mine,
> Made from a Sala tree on the moon.
> Wu Gang cut down a branch of it,
> For Lu Ban to work with his unrivalled skill.
>
> A strip of gold goes right through its heart,
> And it is set with countless pearls.
> It is a precious staff, fine for subduing fiends;
> It could quell all demons when it guarded the Heavenly
>   Palace.
>
> When I was commissioned as High General
> The Jade Emperor gave it me to use.
> It can be any length I wish,
> Thick or thin, responding to my will.
>
> It protected the Emperor at Peach Banquets,
> Attended at court in the upper world.
> When I was at the palace, it met all the sages,
> When I lifted the curtain, it greeted the Immortals.
>
> I nurtured it and made it a divine weapon —
> This is no ordinary earthly arm.
> When I was sent down from Heaven in exile
> I roamed at will throughout the world.
>
> I do not need to boast about this staff,
> Unmatched by any spear or sabre in the world.
> Look at that rusty rake of yours,
> Only good for farming or vegetable-growing."

"I'll give you the beating you deserve, damn you," said Pig. "Never mind about vegetable-growing — one swipe from it and you'll have nowhere left to put ointment, because your blood will be pouring out from nine holes. Even if it doesn't kill you, you'll have tetanus for the rest of your days." The ogre dropped his defensive posture and fought with Pig from the river-bed to the surface of the water. This battle was fiercer than the earlier ones:

> The precious staff whirled,
> The deadly rake struck,
> And no word passed between the two foes.
> Because the Mother of Wood conquered the Medicine Measure
> The pair of them had to fight each other twice.
> With no victory,
> And no defeat,
> The waves were overturned and knew no peace.
> How could the one hold back his anger?
> How could the other bear his humiliation?
> As the staff parried the rake's blows, they showed their prowess;
> Each was most vicious as the Flowing Sands River rolled.
> Towering rage,
> Strenuous efforts,
> All because Sanzang wanted to go West.
> The rake was thoroughly murderous,
> The staff was wielded with expertise.
> Pig grabbed his enemy, trying to drag him ashore,
> While the other in turn tried to pull Pig under water.
> The thunderous noise disturbed fish and dragons;
> Gods and ghosts lay low as the sky was darkened.

The battle went on for thirty rounds, but neither emerged victorious. Pig feigned defeat once again, and fled trailing his rake behind him. The ogre charged through the waves after him as far as the bank, when Pig shouted at him, "I'll get you, you damned ogre. Come up on this higher ground where we can fight with dry land under our feet." "You're trying to lure me up there, damn you," the monster replied, "for your mate to come and get me. Come back and fight in the water." The fiend, who had more sense than to go up the bank again, stood at the river's edge, shouting it out with Pig.

When Monkey saw that the monster was not coming up on the bank he seethed with frustration at not being able to catch him. "Master," he said, "you sit here while I do a 'Hungry Eagle Falling on Its Prey' on him." He somersaulted into mid-air, then plummeted down to catch the ogre, who heard the noise of a wind as he was yelling at Pig, turned immediately, and saw Monkey descending from the clouds. He put his staff away, plunged into the water with a splash, and was seen no more. "Brother," said Monkey to Pig as he landed on the bank, "the monster's got a lot more clever. Whatever are we to do if he won't come on to the bank again?" "It's impossible," said Pig, "we'll never be able to beat him Even if I put everything I've got into it, I can only hold my own against him." "Let's go and see the master," Monkey said.

The two of them climbed the bank and told the Tang Priest about the difficulty of capturing the ogre. "It's so hard," said Sanzang, tears streaming down his cheeks. "However are we going to cross?" "No need to worry, Master," said Monkey. "The monster is lurking deep down on the river-bed, where it's very hard to move around. You stay here and look after the master, Pig, and don't fight with the ogre again. I'm going to the Southern Sea." "What for?" Pig asked. "This whole business of fetching the scriptures was started by the Bodhisattva Guanyin, and it was she who converted us. Now we are stuck here at the Flowing Sands River nobody but she can sort this one out. It's better to ask for her help than to fight that monster." "Yes, yes," said Pig, "and when you're there, please thank her for converting me." "If you're going to ask the Bodhisattva to come," Sanzang said, "don't waste a moment, and be back as quickly as possible."

Monkey then somersaulted off on his cloud towards the Southern Sea, and before an hour was up he saw Potaraka

Island. An instant later he landed outside the Purple Bamboo Grove, where the twenty-four devas came forward to greet him with the words, "Why have you come, Great Sage?" "Because my master is in trouble," Monkey replied, "I have come for an audience with the Bodhisattva." The deva on duty that day asked Monkey to sit down while he went in to report, whereupon he went into the Tide Cave to announce that Sun Wukong was seeking an audience on business. The Bodhisattva was leaning on a balcony looking at the blossoms in the Precious Lotus Pool with the Dragon Princess Peng Zhu when she heard the news. She went back into her cloudy cave, opening the door and summoning Monkey to her presence. The Great Sage greeted her with grave reverence.

"Why aren't you looking after the Tang Priest," she asked. "and why have you come to see me?" "My master won a new disciple at Gao Village, Bodhisattva," Brother Monkey reported. "He's called Zhu Bajie and also has the Buddhist name Wuneng thanks to you. We have now reached the Flowing Sands River after crossing the Yellow Wind Ridge, but it's a thousand miles of Weak Water and my master cannot cross it. On top of this there's an evil monster in the river who's a great fighter, and although our Pig had three great battles with him on the surface of the water, he couldn't beat the ogre, who is still blocking our way and preventing my master from crossing. This is why I've come to see you and ask you in your mercy to help him across." "You have revealed your conceit once again, you ape," said the Bodhisattva. "Why didn't you tell the monster that you were protecting the Tang Priest?" "We wanted to catch him," Monkey replied, "and make him take our master across the river. As I'm not up to much in the water and Pig was the only one who could find the ogre's den and did all the talking. I expect he never mentioned fetching the scriptures." "The ogre of the Flowing Sands River is the mortal incarnation of the Great Curtain-lifting General," said Guanyin, "and is a believer whom I converted myself and instructed to protect those who would be coming to fetch the scriptures. If you had told him that you had come from the East to fetch the scriptures, so far from

JOURNEY TO THE WEST

fighting you, he would certainly have joined you." "But the craven monster is now skulking in the river, too frightened to come out," Monkey said, "so how are we to make him join us, and how is my master to cross the weak water?"

The Bodhisattva sent for her disciple Huian and produced a red bottle-gourd from her sleeve. "Take this gourd," she said, "and go with Sun Wukong to the Flowing Sands River. Shout 'Wujing' — 'Awakened to Purity' — and he'll come out. First take him to submit to the Tang Priest, and then make him thread his nine skulls on a string like the nine palaces of the Pole Star. If he puts this gourd in the middle of them, it will make a dharma boat to ferry the Tang Priest across the river." In obedience to the Bodhisattva's command, Huian and the Great Sage took the gourd with them from the Tide Cave and the Purple Bamboo Grove. There are some lines to describe it:

> *The Five Elements were combined to form a heavenly truth,*
> *Recognizing their mistress of the old days.*
> *They have been sufficiently refined to achieve great things,*
> *When true and false are distinguished, origins are seen.*
> *When Metal joins Nature, like joins like;*
> *When Wood seeks the Passions, both are lost.*
> *When the two Earths achieve nirvana,*
> *Fire and Water will combine, and worldly dust be no more.*

A little later the pair of them brought their clouds down to land on the bank of the Flowing Sands River. Recognizing Huian as Moksa the Novice, Pig led his master forward to meet him. When Moksa had exchanged courtesies with Sanzang, he greeted Pig. Then Pig said, "Thanks to Your Holiness's instruction, I was able to meet the Bodhisattva, and since then I have obeyed the Buddhist law and had the pleasure of becoming a monk. As I have been travelling since then, I've been too busy to go and thank you. Please forgive me." "Don't be so long-winded," said Monkey. "Let's go and call to that wretch."

"Call to whom?" asked Sanzang. "I saw the Bodhisattva," said Monkey, "and told her what had happened. She said that the ogre of the Flowing Sands River is the mortal incarnation of the Great Curtain-lifting General, who was thrown down to this river as a monster because of a crime he had committed in Heaven. He has been converted by the Bodhisattva and has vowed to go to the Western Heaven with you. If we'd told him we were going to fetch the scriptures, there would have been none of this bitter fighting. The Bodhisattva has now sent Moksa to give this gourd to that fellow to make a dharma boat that will ferry you across." Sanzang bowed in reverence to the Bodhisattva many times when he heard it, and also bowed to Moksa with the words, "Please do this as quickly as you can, Your Holiness." Moksa then went by cloud and stood over the river with the gourd in his hands. "Wujing, Wujing," he shouted at the top of his voice, "the pilgrims who are going to fetch the scriptures have been here for a long time. Why haven't you submitted to them?"

The ogre, who had gone back to the river-bed for fear of the Monkey King, was resting in his den when he heard his Buddhist name being called and realized that this was a message from the Bodhisattva Guanyin. On hearing that the pilgrims were there, his fears of being attacked melted away, and he pushed his head up through the waves to see that it was Moksa the Novice. Look at him as he bows to Moksa, his face wreathed in smiles. "I'm sorry I did not welcome you properly, Your Holiness," he said. "Where is the Bodhisattva?" "She didn't come," Moksa replied. "She sent me to tell you to be the Tang Priest's disciple. You are to take the nine skulls you wear round your neck, arrange them with this gourd in the pattern of the nine palaces of the Pole Star, and make a dharma boat to ferry him across this weak water." "Where is the pilgrim?" Wujing asked. "There he is, sitting on the bank," said Moksa, pointing at Sanzang. Wujing then noticed Pig and said, "I don't know where that bloody creature is from, but he fought with me for two whole days and never said a word about fetching scriptures. And as for this one," he added, noticing Monkey, "he's that one's accomplice and a real terror. I'm not going with them." "That one is Zhu Bajie, and this one is Brother Monkey. They are both disciples of the Tang Priest who have been converted by the Bodhisattva, so you have nothing to fear from them. Let me present you to the Tang Priest." Wujing put away his staff, straightened his yellow brocade tunic, jumped ashore, knelt before the Tang Priest, and said, "Master, your disciple's eyes have no pupils in them — I beg you to forgive me for attacking your followers instead of recognizing who they were." "You pustule," said Pig, "why did you fight me instead of submitting? What did you mean by it?" "You can't blame him, brother," said Monkey. "We didn't tell him our names or even mention fetching the scriptures." "Do you believe in our teachings with all your heart?" Sanzang asked. "I was converted by the Bodhisattva," Wujing replied, "and she gave me this river's name as a surname and called me by the Buddhist name of Sha Wujing, or Sand Awakened to Purity, so of course I must follow you, Master." "In that case," said Sanzang, "bring the razor over, Monkey, and cut his hair off." The Great Sage obediently shaved the monster's head, who then bowed to Sanzang, Monkey, and Pig with appropriate degrees of reverence. When Sanzang saw him do this just like a real monk he gave him another name — Friar Sand. "Now that you have entered the faith," said Moksa, "there's no need to waste time talking. Make that dharma boat at once."

Friar Sand took the skulls from round his neck without delay and tied them into the pattern of the nine palaces of the Pole Star with the Bodhisattva's gourd in the middle. Then he asked Sanzang to board it, and Sanzang found when he sat on it that it was as stable as a small dinghy. Pig and Friar Sand supported him to left and right, while Monkey led the dragon horse through the clouds behind him, and Moksa stood above him on guard. Sanzang thus made a calm and windless crossing of the weak water of the Flowing Sands River. He moved with the speed of an arrow, and it was not long before he climbed ashore on the other side. He was neither wet nor muddy, and his hands and feet were completely dry. Thus it was that master and disciples trod on dry land again without any trouble. Moksa then landed his cloud, and took back the gourd. The nine skulls changed into nine gusts of wind and disappeared. Sanzang bowed to Moksa to thank him and worshipped the Bodhisattva, after which

> *Moksa returned to the Eastern Ocean,*
> *While Sanzang remounted and headed west.*

If you don't know when they won their reward and fetched the scriptures, listen to the explanation in the next chapter.

CHAPTER TWENTY-THREE

Sanzang does not forget the basic;
The four holy ones have their piety tested.

> Long is the road as they travel west;
> In the rustling autumn breeze the frost-killed flowers
>   fall.
> The cunning ape is firmly chained — do not unite him;
> The wicked horse is tightly reined — don't whip him on.
>
> The Mother of Wood and Father of Metal were originally
>   combined;
> Between the Yellow Mother and the Red Babe there
>   was no difference.
> When the iron pill is bitten open, truth is revealed;
> The Prajnaparamita has reached that person.

Although this book is about the journey to fetch the scriptures, it never leaves the subject of how the individual strives for the basic. The four of them, having understood the truth, shaken off the chains of the mortal world, and leapt away from the flowing sands of the sea of nature, headed along the main road west free of all impediment. They crossed blue mountains and green rivers, and saw no end of wild flowers. The time flew by, and before long it was autumn. They saw:

> Hills covered with red maple leaves,
> Yellow chrysanthemums braving the evening breeze,
> Aging cicadas singing with less vigour,
> Miserable crickets endlessly worried.
>
> The lotus was losing its green silken leaves,
> The fragrant orange tree was covered with golden globes.
> Lines of wild geese, alas,
> Spread out like dots across the distant sky.

As they were travelling along one day, evening drew in, and Sanzang said, "Where are we going to sleep, disciples, now that it's getting late?" "That's not the right thing to say, Master," said Monkey. "We monks are supposed to eat the wind and drink the rain, and sleep under the moon and in the frost. Our home is wherever we are. So why ask where we're going to sleep?" "You may think that you've had an easy journey," said Pig, "but you don't give a damn about other people being tired. Ever since we crossed the Flowing Sands River we've been going over mountain ranges, and this heavy load has fairly worn me out. We've got to find a house where we can beg some tea and food and have a good rest — it's only fair." "It sounds to me, idiot, as though you're having regrets," said Monkey. "I'm afraid you can't have such an easy life now as you did back in Gao Village. If you want to be a monk, you have to suffer — it's the only way of being a true disciple." "How heavy do you think this load is?" Pig asked. "I haven't carried it since you and Friar Sand joined us, so how should I know?" Monkey replied. "Just add it up," said Pig. "'There are

> Four bundles wrapped in yellow bamboo mats,
> Eight ropes of assorted lengths.
> Then, to keep out rain and damp,
> Three or four layers of felt around it all.
> The carrying-pole is terribly slippery
> With nails at either end.
> Then there's a bronze and iron nine-ringed staff
> And a cape made of bamboo and creeper.

With all this luggage to carry day after day of course I find the going heavy. While you're allowed to be the master's disciple, I'm treated as a hired hand." "Who do you think you're talking to, idiot?" Monkey asked. "I'm talking to you, elder brother," said Pig. "You shouldn't be complaining about this to me," Monkey replied. "My job is to look after the master's safety, while you and Friar Sand look after the horse and the luggage. And if there's any slacking from you, you'll feel a heavy stick about your ankles." "Don't threaten me with a beating, brother," said Pig. "That'd be bullying. I know that you're too high and mighty to carry the luggage, but the master's horse is a big, sturdy animal to be carrying only one old monk. I'd be very happy if it could carry a few pieces of luggage."

"Do you think he's a horse?" Monkey asked. "He's no ordinary horse. He was the son of Ao Run, the Dragon King of the Western Sea, and his name is Prince Dragon-horse. Because he burnt the palace pearls his father reported on him as an offender against the Heavenly Code. Luckily for him, his life saved by the Bodhisattva Guanyin, and he waited a long time for the master in the Eagle's Sorrow Gorge. He was honoured by another visit from the Bodhisattva, who took off his scales and horns, removed the pearls from under his neck, and turned him into this horse, which has sworn to carry the master to the Western Heaven to visit the Buddha. This is a matter of him winning merit for himself, so you'd better leave him alone." "Is he really a dragon?" asked Friar Sand when he heard this. "Yes," Monkey replied. "I've heard an old saying," Pig remarked, "that dragons can breathe out clouds, make the dust and sand fly, pull mountain ranges up by their roots, and turn oceans upside down. How is it that he's moving so slowly now?" "If you want to see him go fast," Monkey replied, "I'll make him go fast for you." The splendid Great Sage gripped his iron cudgel, and countless luminous clouds sprang from it. When the horse saw him grab the cudgel he thought he was going to be hit with it, and in his terror he shot off at the speed of lightning. Sanzang was too weak to rein him in as he galloped right up the mountain side for all his evil nature was worth before he slackened his pace. As Sanzang began to get his breath back, he looked up and saw some fine houses in the shade of a bamboo grove:

> *Cypresses were bending over the gates*
> *Of the houses near the blue mountain,*
> *There were several spreading pines*
> *And a stand of mottled bamboo.*

Wild chrysanthemum outside the fence, beautiful in the
    frost;
The orchid by the bridge reflected red in the water.
A whitewashed, plastered wall
Surrounded it all.
Handsome was the lofty hall,
Peaceful the main building.
There was no sign of oxen, sheep, chickens or dogs;
It seemed to be the slack season after harvest.

Sanzang stopped the horse to take a longer look, and then
he saw Monkey and the others arrive. "You didn't fall off
the horse, Master?" asked Monkey. "You gave this horse a
terrible fright, you filthy ape," Sanzang said, "but I kept my
seat." "Don't tell me off, Master," said Monkey, putting on a
smile. "It was only because Pig said the horse was going too
slowly that I made him speed up a bit." The blockhead Pig,
who had been running quite fast after the horse, was puffing
and panting as he mumbled, "Enough of this. When you're
bent double you can't relax. Although I'm carrying a load so
heavy I can't pick it up, you make me go running after the
horse." "Disciple," said Sanzang, "do you see the farm over
there? Let's ask if we can spend the night there." Monkey
immediately looked up, saw that the sky above it was full of
clouds of blessing, and knew that the farm had been miraculously
produced by the Buddha or some immortals. Not daring to
give away the secrets of Heaven, however, he only said, "Splendid, splendid, let's ask if we can lodge there."

Dismounting from his horse, Sanzang saw a gate-house with
pillars like elephants' trunks and beams that had been painted
and carved. Friar Sand put down the carrying-pole and Pig
said as he held the horse, "This is a very wealthy house." Monkey was on the point of going in when Sanzang said, "No, we
men of religion should avoid incurring suspicion. You mustn't
go charging in. We should wait till somebody comes out and
then ask politely for lodging." Pig tethered the horse at the
sloping base of the wall while Sanzang sat on a stone stool, and

Friar Sand and Monkey sat beside the steps. When nobody appeared for a long time Monkey jumped up impatiently and went through the gate to have a look. He saw a large hall facing south whose tall windows were shaded with bamboo curtains. Over the doorway dividing the inner and outer parts of the house was a horizontal landscape painting symbolizing long life and blessings, and on the gold-painted columns flanking the door was pasted a pair of scrolls reading:

> *"The tender willow leaves sway in the evening by the*
> *bridge;*
> *When the plum-blossom looks like snowflakes it is spring*
> *in the courtyard."*

In the middle of the room was an incense table whose black lacquer had been polished, an ancient animal-shaped bronze incense-burner standing on it, and six chairs. Pictures of the four seasons were hung on the walls at either end of the hall.

As Monkey was peeping inside he heard footsteps from behind the door at the back. A woman, neither old nor young, came out and asked in a charming voice, "Who has forced his way into this widow's house of mine?" The Great Sage hastened to greet her respectfully and say, "I am a humble monk from the Great Tang in the East, under imperial orders to go to the West to worship the Buddha and ask for the scriptures. There are four of us altogether, and since our journey has brought us this way as evening is drawing in, we have come to your mansion, divine patroness, to beg for a night's lodging." She returned his greeting with a smile and said, "Where are the other three gentlemen, venerable sir?" at which Monkey shouted, "Master, come in." Sanzang, Pig and Friar Sand then came in, bringing the horse and the luggage with them. As the woman came out of the hall to welcome them, Pig stole a glance at her with greedy eyes.

> *She wore a green silk gown,*
> *And over it a pale red jacket;*
> *A skirt of yellow brocade,*
> *Below which showed thick-soled shoes.*

Her fashionable coiffure was veiled in black,
Which suited her greying locks, coiled like a dragon;
Palace-style ivory combs shone with red and green,
And two golden pins adorned her hair.
Her half-grey tresses soared like a phoenix in flight;
Two rows of pearls hung from her ear-rings.
Free of powder and paint, her beauty was natural;
She was as attractive as a younger girl.

When she saw the three others she was more pleased than ever, and she invited them into the main room. When all the introductions had been made, she asked them to sit down and have some tea. A servant girl with her hair in plaits came in through the door leading to the back of the house; she was carrying a golden tray on which were set white jade cups of steaming hot tea as well as exotic fruits that smelt delicious. Her sleeves were wide, and with her fingers as slender as bamboo shoots in spring she handed each of them a jade bowl and bowed. When the tea had been drunk, the mistress ordered a meatless meal to be prepared "What is your name, venerable Bodhisattva?" asked Sanzang, spreading out his hands. "And what is this place called?" "This is the Western Continent of Cattle-gift, or Godaniya," she replied. "My maiden name is Jia,* and my husband's name was Mo.** In my childhood I had the misfortune of losing both my parents, and I married to continue the ancestral enterprise. Our family is worth ten thousand strings of cash, and we own fifteen thousand acres of good arable land. We were not fated to be given sons, and we only had three daughters. The year before last I suffered the great misfortune of losing my husband. I have remained a widow, and this year I have come out of mourning. There are no other relations to inherit the family estate besides myself and my daughters. I would like to remarry, but not at the price of abandoning the estate. Now that you have come here, venerable sir, with your three disciples, I think it should be you. I

---

* A pun on "false".
** A pun on "nobody".

and my three daughters want to marry while staying at home, and you four gentlemen would suit us nicely. I wonder if you would be prepared to consent." Sanzang sat there pretending to be deaf and dumb, with his eyes shut and his mind kept calm. He made no reply.

"We have over fifty acres of paddy fields, and over five thousand each of dry land and of orchards on hillsides," she continued, "as well as over a thousand head of oxen and water buffalo, herds of mules and horses, and more pigs and sheep than you could count. There are sixty or seventy farm buildings and barns. We have more grain in the house than we could eat in eight or nine years, and more than enough silk to clothe us for a decade — to say nothing of more gold and silver than you could spend in a life-time. You'll be even better off than those ancients who 'kept beauties behind brocade curtains' and girls in two rows whose 'hair was heavy with golden pins'. If you and your disciples are prepared to change your minds and live in this house as our husbands, you can enjoy wealth and ease. Wouldn't that be better than a difficult journey to the West?" Sanzang sat there silent, as if he were an imbecile.

"I was born at the hour *chou* of the third day of the third month of the year *dinghai*," she continued. "My late husband was three years older than me, and I am now forty-four. My eldest daughter, Zhenzhen, is nineteen; my second, Aiai is seventeen; and Lianlian, the youngest, is fifteen.* None of them have been betrothed. Although I am rather ugly myself, the girls are all quite good-looking, and they have all the feminine accomplishments. As my late husband had no sons, he gave them a boy's education, teaching them to read the Confucian classics from an early age and training them to recite poems and make couplets. Although they live in this mountain farmhouse you couldn't consider them boorish, and I think that they would be good partners for all you reverend gentlemen. If you are willing to broaden your outlook and let your hair grow, you could be head of the family and wear silks and brocades. Wouldn't that

---

* The three names together mean "true love".

be far better than your earthenware begging-bowl, rough clothes, straw sandals, and rain-hats?"

Sanzang sat in the place of honour as still as a child terrified by thunder or a toad soaked in a rainstorm. He seemed to be in a trance as he leant back with his eyes turned up towards the sky. Pig, however, felt an itch in his mind that was hard to scratch when he heard about all this wealth and beauty. He fidgeted on his chair as if needles were being stuck into his back-side, and finally could bear it no longer. He went up to his master, tugged at his clothes, and said, "Master, why are you paying no attention to what the lady is saying? You really ought to take some notice." Sanzang glared at him angrily, made a furious noise, and shouted at him to go away. "Evil beast," he said, "We are men of religion. It's disgraceful to allow yourself to be moved by the thought of wealth, honour or sex."

"Poor, poor things," said the woman with a smile. "What good can there be in being men of religion?" "What good can there be in being of the world, Bodhisattva?" Sanzang replied. "Please sit down, reverend sir, while I tell you about the advantages of being in the world," she said. "There is a poem to describe them that goes:

> For our spring fashions we wear new silk;
> In summer we change to light gauze and admire the
> lotus;
> In autumn comes delicious rice-wine newly brewed;
> In winter the house is warm, and our faces are red with
> drink.
>
> We have all that's needed in the four seasons,
> The treasures and delicacies of the whole year.
> Brocade clothes, silken sheets and a wedding night
> Are better than plodding along and worshipping
> Buddha."

"Bodhisattva," said Sanzang, "it is, of course, very good to enjoy wealth and honour with plenty of food and clothes and a family. But what you don't realize is that the religious life has advantages, which are described in this poem:

It is no light matter to decide to enter religion:
You have to demolish the love and gratitude you felt
*   before.*
Externals are created no longer, and your mouth is tight-
*   ly shut;*
Negative and positive exist within your body.

When all has been achieved, you face the golden gates;
See your nature, clarify your mind, and return home.
This is better than staying in the world to be greedy for
*   blood and food*
While your stinking flesh grows aged and decrepit."

"You insolent monk," the woman said in great anger. "If it weren't for the fact that you've come a long, long way from the East, I'd drive you out of my house. I invite you four with all sincerity to marry us and enjoy our wealth, and you repay my kindness with insults. If you have accepted the prohibitions and made your vows, you could at least let me have one of your underlings as a son-in-law. Why are you being such a stickler for the rules?" As she had lost her temper, Sanzang had to soothe her, so he said, "Monkey, you stay here." "I've never been able to do that sort of thing," Monkey replied. "Why not let Pig stay?" "Stop teasing, elder brother," Pig said. "We should all decide what's the best thing to do." "If neither of you will stay, I must ask Friar Sand to stay," said Sanzang; but Friar Sand replied, "What a thing to say, Master. I was converted by the Bodhisattva, agreed to obey the prohibitions, and waited till you came, and since taking me as your disciple you've taught me more. I haven't been with you for two months yet, and I've had no time win any merit at all. How could I possibly want wealth and position? I want to go to the Western Heaven even if it costs me my life, and I'm certainly not going to frustrate my hopes by doing that." In the face of their refusals the woman turned round, went out through the door leading to the back of the house, and slammed it behind her, leaving master and disciples outside with neither food nor tea. Nobody else came out to see them. "That's not the way to handle things, Master," grumbled an angry Pig. "You should have been more flexible and given her some noncommittal answer, then you'd have got some food out of her. That way we'd have eaten well tonight, but would still have been able to refuse to marry them in the morning. We're going to have a lousy night with nothing to eat if that inside door is shut and nobody comes out to us."

"Brother Pig, you should stay here and marry one of the girls," said Friar Sand. "Stop getting at me," Pig replied. "We must decide what's the best thing to do." "Why bother?" said Monkey. "If you want to marry one of them, you'll make our master and the woman in-laws, and you can be a husband living with his in-laws. A family as rich as this is bound to give a good dowry, as well as a feast for relations which will do us all a bit of good. So it's in all our interests for you to return to worldly life here." "It sounds all right," said Pig, "but it would mean going back to the world after leaving it, and marrying again after ending another marriage."

"Did you have a wife before, then?" asked Friar Sand. "So you still don't know," said Monkey, "that he used to be the son-in-law of Squire Gao in Gao Village in the land of Stubet. After I defeated him and the Bodhisattva converted him and made him promise to observe the prohibitions, we managed to force him to become a monk. So he left his wife and joined our master for the journey to the Buddha in the West. I think that now he's been away from her for so long he's remembering all that business again. When he heard this woman's offer, it revived his old ideas. Blockhead," he continued, addressing Pig, "marry into this family as a son-in-law. I won't report on you provided you bow to me a few times." "Nonsense, nonsense," said Pig. "You've all been thinking the same thoughts, but you pick on me to make an exhibition of. It's always said that 'a monk among pretty women is a hungry ghost', and that goes for all of us. But by acting so high and mighty you've ruined our chances of doing well here. We haven't cast our eyes on so much as a cup of tea, and there isn't even anyone to light the lamps for us. We may be able to stick it out for a night, but

that horse will have to carry our master again tomorrow, and
if he gets nothing to eat all night he'll collapse. You lot sit here
while I take him out for a feed." He untied the animal and
dragged it out in a great hurry, at which Monkey said, "Friar
Sand, you sit here with the master while I follow him and see
where he pastures that horse." "If you want to keep an eye on
him, you may do so," Sanzang said, "but don't play any tricks
on him." "I understand," said Monkey, and as he went out of
the room he shook himself, turned into a red dragonfly, flew out
of the main gate, and caught up with Pig.

Instead of letting the horse eat what grass there was, the
blockhead chivied and dragged it round to the back door of the
house, where he saw the woman and her three daughters admiring some chrysanthemums. When they saw Pig coming, the
three girls rushed inside, while their mother remained standing
in front of him. "Where are you going, reverend sir?" she
asked. The idiot dropped the horse's bridle, greeted her respectfully, and said, "I'm pasturing the horse, mother." "That master
of yours is too prim and proper," she said. "Wouldn't you
rather marry here than go on plodding west as a travelling
monk?" "They're under orders from the Tang Emperor," Pig
replied with a grin, "and are too scared of disobeying him to
do a thing like this. When they put the pressure on me in the
hall just now I was in a very awkward spot. I hope you don't
mind about my long snout and big ears." "I don't mind," she
said, "as long as we can have a man about the house, though
my girls might not find you very attractive." "Tell your girls
not to be so particular about a husband," said Pig. "That Tang
Priest may be very handsome, but he's completely useless.
Although I'm as ugly as they come, I have something to say for
myself." "What would that be?" she asked. His reply was:

> "I may be not much to look at,
> But I certainly get things done.
> Six thousand acres
> I can plough without an ox.
> Just by using my rake

I plant crops that come up well.
I can summon rain in a drought,
Call up a wind when there's none.
If you find your house too small,
I can add two more storeys, or three.
If the ground needs sweeping, I'll sweep it;
If the ditches are blocked, I'll make them run.
I can carry out all sorts of household duties,
And do odd jobs around the home."

"Very well then," she said, "if you can manage the work about the place you'd better go and talk it over with your master. If there are no problems, then you can marry one of the girls." "There's no need to talk it over with him," Pig said. "He's not my father or mother, and it's entirely up to me whether I do it or not." "Very well then," she said, "Wait while I tell the girls." With that she went in and shut the door behind her. Pig still did not let the horse graze but dragged it round towards the front of the house. Unbeknown to him, Monkey, who knew all about what had happened, flew back, changed back into his own form, and said to the Tang Priest, "Master, Pig is leading the horse back." "If he hadn't led it, it might have got excited and run away," Sanzang said, at which Monkey burst out laughing and told him all about what had taken place between Pig and the woman. Sanzang did not know whether to believe him or not.

A moment later the blockhead led the horse in and tethered it. "Have you grazed the horse?" Sanzang asked. "I couldn't find any grass that was good enough," said Pig, "so I couldn't graze it." "You may not have been able to graze the horse," said Monkey, "but you managed do some horse-trading." This jibe made the idiot realize that the cat was out of the bag, so he hung his head and did not say a word. There was a creak as a side door opened and the woman and her three daughters — Zhenzhen, Aiai and Lianlian — came in with a pair of lamps glowing red and two portable incense burners from which sweet-smelling smoke curled up as the jade ornaments at their waists tinkled. The three girls greeted the pilgrims, standing in a row in the middle of the room and bowing. They were undoubtedly beauties:

> *All had moth-eyebrows glistening blue,*
> *Pale and springlike faces.*
> *Seductive beauties who could tumble kingdoms,*
> *Disturbing men's hearts with their quiet charm.*
> *Elegant were their ornaments of golden flowers;*
> *Their embroidered sashes floated above the worldly*
> *   dust.*
> *Their hint of a smile was a bursting cherry;*
> *Their breath was perfumed as they walked with slow*
> *   steps.*
> *Their hair was covered with pearls and jade.*
> *Trembling under countless jewelled ornament;*
> *Their whole bodies were fragrant,*
> *Covered with delicate flowers of gold.*
> *Why mention the beauty of the woman of Chu,*
> *Or the charms of Xi Zi?*
> *They really were like fairies from the Ninth Heaven,*
> *Or the Lady of the Moon coming out of her palace.*

While Sanzang put his hands together and bowed his head the Great Sage pretended not to notice and Friar Sand turned away. But Pig gazed at them with a fixed stare, his mind seething with lewd thoughts as his lust overwhelmed him. "Thank you, divine angels, for coming to see us," he said, fidgeting, "but could you ask the girls to go, please, mother?" The three girls went out through the door, leaving a pair of gauze-shielded lanterns behind them. "Will you four reverend gentlemen please decide which of you is to marry one of the girls?" the woman said. "We've already made up our minds that Mr. Pig is to be your son-in-law," Friar Sand replied. "Don't pick on me, brother," said Pig, "we should discuss this together." "No need to," said Monkey. "You've already fixed everything up at the back door and called her 'mother', so there's nothing to discuss. Our master can represent the groom's family, this lady is the bride's family, I can be best man, and Friar Sand can be the matchmaker. There's no need to consult the almanac to select a lucky day. Today is a most auspicious one full of heavenly grace. So bow to the master and go in to be her son-in-law." "Impossible," said Pig, "impossible. I couldn't do a thing like that."

"Stop trying to cover up, blockhead," said Monkey. "You've already called her 'mother' umpteen times: there's nothing impossible about it at all. Hurry up and fulfil your promise so that we can have some wedding wine, which will be one good thing about it." Seizing Pig with one hand and grabbing the woman with the other he said, "As the bride's mother, you should take your son-in-law inside." The idiot Pig hesitated, wanting to go in, and the woman said to the servants, "Bring table and chairs and give these three relatives of ours a meatless supper. I'm taking our son-in-law inside." Then she told the cooks to prepare a banquet for their friends and relations the following morning. The servants did as they were told, and the other three pilgrims ate their supper, spread their bedding, and went to sleep in their places.

Pig followed his mother-in-law inside, and as he lost count of the number of rooms he went through, constantly tripping over the thresholds. "Don't go so fast, mother," he said, "and please guide me as I don't know the way." "These are all granaries, storehouses, and milling rooms," she said. "We haven't reached the kitchens yet." "What an enormous house," said Pig, as he went round many a corner, tripping and bumping into things, until he reached the inner apartments of the house. "Your brother said that today was a very auspicious day," the woman said, "which is why I've brought you inside. But as we're doing things in such a rush, I haven't had time to call in a fortune-teller or arrange a proper ceremony with the scattering of fruit. You must just bow eight times, and that will have to do." "A good idea, mother," said Pig. "You sit in the seat of honour and I'll bow to you a few times — that can be the wedding ceremony and thanking the bride's family rolled into one, which will save trouble." "Very well then," said the woman with a laugh. "You are a most capable and practical son-in-law. I'll sit here while you bow to me."

In the room glittering with silver candlesticks the idiot bowed to her, then asked which of the girls would be married to him. "That's the problem," his mother-in-law said. "If I give you the eldest, the second one will be upset; and if I give you the second one, I'm afraid the third one will be; and if I give you the third, the eldest will be — so I haven't decided yet." "If there's any danger of them quarrelling," said Pig, "then give me all of them, to save the family from being troubled with arguments and squabbles." "What a suggestion," his mother-in-law exclaimed. "You're certainly not having all my daughters to yourself." "Don't be silly, mother. What's unusual about three or four wives? Even if there were several more of them, I'd take them on with a smile. When I was young I learnt the art of 'protracted warfare', and I can guarantee to keep every one of them happy." "No, no," the woman said. "I have a handkerchief here. Tie it round your head to cover your face, and we can let Heaven decide which one you'll marry. I'll tell the girls to walk in front of you while you stretch your arms out. The one you catch will be yours." The blockhead obediently tied the handkerchief round his head, and there is a verse to prove it:

> *The fool, not knowing his own fate,*
> *Was wounded by the sword of sex as he harmed himself*
> *   in secret*
> *There have always been proper wedding rites,*
> *But today the groom blindfolded himself.*

When he had tied the handkerchief on firmly, the idiot said, "Mother, please ask the girls to come out." "Zhenzhen, Aiai, Lianlian," she called, "come out to see which of you Heaven will marry to my new son-in-law." He heard the tinkling of jade ornaments and smelt rare perfumes as if fairies were there, so he reached out to grab one. He groped about to his left and his right, but without success. There were so many girls running about, and he had no chance of catching one. When he stretched

east he only put his arms round a pillar, and when he stretched
west he felt only the wall. As he rushed from one end of the
room to the other he felt so dizzy that he lost his balance and
kept tripping over. He stumbled into the door when he went
forward, and collided with the brick wall when he went back,
bumping, crashing and falling over till his snout was swollen
and his head blue with bruises. Finally he sat on the floor and
said as he gasped for breath, "Mother, your daughters are so
slippery I can't catch a single one of them. Whatever shall I
do?"

"They're not slippery," she said, taking off the handkerchief,
"they're all too shy to marry you." "If they won't marry me,"
Pig said, "then you marry me." "What a son-in-law!" she said.
"He doesn't care whether they're young or old — he even wants
his own mother-in-law. Now each of these clever girls of mine
has made a brocade shirt sewn with pearls. I'll tell whichever
girl it is whose shirt you put on to marry you." "Great, great,
great," said Pig. "'Bring out all three shirts for me to try on,
and if I can get them all on, I'll marry them all." The woman
went back inside, and brought out only one shirt, which she
handed to Pig. The idiot took off his own black cloth tunic and
pulled on the shirt, but before he could tie the belt at the waist
he fell to the ground with a thump and found himself tightly
bound with many ropes. He was in great pain, and the women
had all disappeared.

When Sanzang, Monkey, and Friar Sand woke up, the east
was already lightening, and as they opened their eyes and looked
around them they saw none of the lofty buildings that had been
there. There were no carved and painted beams or rafters
either: they had all been sleeping in a grove of pine and cypress.
Sanzang called for Monkey in terror, and Friar Sand said,
"Elder brother, we're done for, done for — they were demons."
"What do you mean?" asked Monkey, who understood what
had happened, with a trace of a smile. "Look where we've
been sleeping," said Sanzang. "We're very comfortable here
under the pine trees," said Monkey, "but I wonder where that
idiot is being punished." "Who's being punished?" asked San-

zang. "The woman and the girls last night were some Bodhisattvas or other appearing to us in disguise," replied Monkey
with a grin, "and I suppose they went away in the middle of
the night. I'm afraid Pig is being punished." On hearing this,
Sanzang put his hands together and worshipped, and then they
saw a piece of paper hanging from a cypress tree and fluttering
in the breeze. Friar Sand hurried over to fetch it and show it to
their master, who saw that there were eight lines of verse on it:

> "The Old Woman of Mount Li had no yearning for the
>   world,
> But the Bodhisattva Guanyin persuaded her to come.
> Samantabhadra and Manjusri were both present
> Disguised as pretty girls among the trees.
> The holy monk were too virtuous to return to lay life,
> But the unreligious Pig was worse than worldly.
> From now on he must calm his mind and reform —
> If he misbehaves again, the journey will be hard."

As Sanzang, Monkey, and Friar Sand read out these lines
they heard loud shouts from the depths of the wood: "Master,
they've tied me up and left me to die. I'll never do it again if
you save me." "Is that Pig shouting, Friar Sand?" asked Sanzang, and Friar Sand said, "Yes." "Although that idiot is
obstinately stupid in mind and nature," said Sanzang, "he is
an honest fellow. Besides, he is very strong and can carry the
luggage — and we should also remember that the Bodhisattva
saved him and told him to come with us. I don't think he'll
have the nerve to do it again." Friar Sand then rolled up the
bedding and arranged the luggage, while Monkey untied the
horse and led it along as he guided the Tang Priest into the
wood to investigate. Indeed,

> In the pursuit of righteousness you must be careful,
> And sweep away desires in your return to the truth.

If you don't know whether the blockhead survived or not,
listen to the explanation in the next instalment.

CHAPTER TWENTY-FOUR

On the Mountain of Infinite Longevity
a great immortal entertains an old friend;
In the Wuzhuang Temple Monkey steals
manfruit

The three of them went into the wood and saw the idiot tied
up under a tree, yelling and howling in unbearable pain.
Monkey went over to him and said with a laugh, "What a son-
in-law! So late, and you still haven't got up to thank your
mother-in-law or come to tell the good news to the master. Why
are you still playing around here? Where's your mother-in-law?
Where's your wife? You make a fine, strapped-up, well-beaten
son-in-law!" The blockhead, burning with humiliation at being
thus mocked, gritted his teeth to stop himself howling in his
agony. Friar Sand was overcome with pity when he saw him,
and putting down the luggage he went over and untied him.
The idiot kowtowed to him in gratitude. He was suffering
terrible remorse. There is a poem to the tune *The Moon in the
West River* to prove it:

> *Sex is a sword that wounds the body:*
> *Whoever lusts for it will suffer.*
> *A pretty girl of sixteen*
> *Is far more dangerous than a yaksha demon.*
>
> *There is only one Origin,*
> *And there are no extra profits to stuff in the sack.*
> *Better store all your capital away,*
> *Guard it well, and don't squander it.*

Pig used a pinch of earth to represent burning incense and bowed
in worship to Heaven. "Did you recognize the Bodhisattva?"

439

Monkey asked. "I was lying here in a faint and my eyes were seeing stars, so I couldn't tell who it was." Monkey handed him the piece of paper, and when he saw the divine message, Pig was more ashamed than ever. "You're very lucky," said Friar Sand with a laugh, "you've got four Bodhisattvas as your relations now." "Please don't talk about it," said Pig. "It was very wicked of me. I'll never misbehave again in future, and even if the effort breaks my bones, carrying our master's luggage to the West only means getting my shoulder a bit rubbed." "That's more like it," said Sanzang.

Monkey then led his master along the main road. After they had been going for a long time, walking and resting, they saw a high mountain blocking their way. "Disciples," said Sanzang as he reined in the horse and stopped giving it the whip, "we must be very careful on that mountain. I'm afraid there may be fiends and demons on it who will attack us." "With us three followers," said Monkey, "you needn't fear demons." Sanzang, his worries ended, pressed forward. The mountain was certainly a fine one:

> The mountain was very high,
> And craggy was its majesty.
> Its roots joined the Kunlun range;
> Its summit touched the Milky Way.
> White crane came to perch in its locust and cypress trees;
> Dark apes hung upside-down from its creepers.
> When the sun shone bright on its forests,
> It was enveloped in red haze;
> When winds sprang from dark valleys,
> Coloured clouds scudded across the sky.
> Hidden birds called in the green bamboo;
> Pheasants fought among the wild flowers.
> Thousand-year peaks,
> Five-blessing peaks,
> Lotus peaks,
> Majestically reflecting a delicate light;
> Ten thousand year rocks,

Tiger-tooth rocks,
Three Heavens rocks,
Wreathed in subtle and auspicious vapours.
Luxuriant grass in front of the cliff,
The scent of plum blossom on the ridge.
Dense grew the jungle of thorns;
Pure and pale were the orchids.
Deep in the woods the birds gathered round the phoenix;
In an ancient cave a unicorn was chief of the animals.
A delightful stream in a gully
Twisted and turned as it wandered around;
Endless peaks
Coiled about in layer upon layer.
Then there were the green locust trees,
Mottled bamboo,
And bluish pines,
That had been competing in splendour for a thousand
      years.
White plum blossom,
Red peach,
And emerald willows
Were brilliant as they vied in beauty during spring.
Dragons called and tigers roared;
Cranes danced and apes howled.
Deer emerged from the flowers,
Pheasants sang to the sun.
This was a land of blessing, an immortals' mountain,
Just like Penglai or Langyuan.
Flowers opened and withered on the mountain top,
Clouds came and went above the peaks along the ridge.

"Disciples," said Sanzang with delight as he sat on his horse, "I've crossed many mountains on my journey west, and they were all steep and rocky, but none of them could be compared to the extraordinarily beautiful scenery here. If this isn't far from the Thunder Monastery, we had better put ourselves in a solemn and reverent mood to meet the Buddha." "It's early days yet," said Monkey with a laugh. "That's not an easy place to get to." "How far are we from Thunder Monastery, elder brother?" asked Friar Sand. "Thirty-six thousand miles," Monkey replied, "and we haven't covered a tenth of it." "How many years will it take us to get there?" Pig asked. "You two younger brothers of mine could manage it in ten days or so, and I could go there fifty times over in a single day and still be back before sunset. But for our master it doesn't bear thinking about." "Tell me, Monkey, how long will it take?" asked Sanzang. "If you went from childhood to old age," said Monkey, "and from old age back to childhood again, and you did it a thousand times over, you'd still find it hard to get there. But if you see your true nature, are determined to be sincere, and always remember to turn your head back to enlightenment, then you will have reached Vulture Peak." "Even if this isn't the Thunder Monastery," said Friar Sand, "good people must live amid such fine scenery as this." "Quite right," said Monkey, "there couldn't be any evil creatures here. This must be the home of holy monks or immortals. Let's look around here and take our time over it."

This mountain was called the Mountain of Infinite Longevity, and there was a Taoist temple on it called the Wuzhuang Temple. In this temple lived an immortal whose Taoist name was Zhen Yuan Zi. He was also known as Conjoint Lord of the Age. The temple had a rare treasure, a miraculous tree that had been formed when primeval chaos was first being divided, before the separation of Heaven and Earth. In the four great continents of the world, only the Western Continent of Cattlegift's Wuzhuang Temple had this treasure that was known as "Grass-returning Cinnabar" or "manfruit". It took three thousand years to blossom, three thousand years to form the fruit, and another three thousand years for the fruit to ripen, so that very nearly ten thousand years had to pass before the fruit could be eaten. Only thirty fruit were formed each ten thousand years, and they were shaped just like a newborn baby, complete with limbs and sense organs. Anyone whose destiny permitted him to smell one would live for three hundred and sixty years, and if you ate one you would live for forty-seven thousand years.

That day the Great Immortal Zhen Yuan had received an invitation from the Original Celestial Jade Pure One inviting him to the Miluo Palace in the Heaven of Supreme Purity to hear a lecture on the Product of Undifferentiated Unity. The immortals who had studied under this great immortal were too numerous to count, and he now had forty-eight disciples who had all attained to the full truth of the Way. That day, the Great Immortal took forty-six of them with him to hear the lecture in the upper world, leaving the two youngest, Pure Wind and Bright Moon, to look after the temple. Pure Wind was 1,320 years old, and Bright Moon had just turned 1,200. The Great Immortal gave his instructions to the two boys: "As I must obey the summons of the Original Celestial Jade Pure One and go to the Miluo Palace to hear a lecture, you two will have to look after the temple carefully. An old friend of mine will be coming this way before long, and you must entertain him very well indeed. You can pick two manfruits for him as a token of our old friendship." "Who is this old friend of yours, master?" the boys asked. "Please tell us who he is so that we can entertain him properly." "He is a priest sent by the Tang Emperor in the East," the Great Immortal replied, "and he is known as Sanzang. He is the monk going to worship the Buddha and ask for the scriptures in the Western Heaven." "Confucius said, 'Don't have anything to do with people of a different Way'," replied the boys with smiles. "Ours is the esoteric sect of the Great Monad, so why ever are you friends with that Buddhist monk?" "You are not aware," the Great Immortal replied, "that he is a reincarnation of the Golden Cicada, the second disciple of the Tathagata Buddha, that ancient sage of the West. I made his acquaintance at an Ullambana assembly where he gave me tea with his own hands. As this disciple of the Buddha paid me such an honour, I regard him as an old friend."

When the two immortal boys heard this, they accepted their master's orders. Just as he was on the point of setting out, the Great Immortal gave them some more instructions: "There are a limited number of those manfruits. You must only give two, and not one more." "When the garden was opened we all shared two," said the boys, "and there are twenty-eight now left on the tree. We won't use more than two." "Although the Tang Priest is an old friend of mine," said the Great Immortal, "you must be on your guard against his gangster underlings, and you mustn't let them know about the manfruit." The Great Immortal then flew up to Heaven with the rest of his disciples.

The Tang Priest and his three followers, meanwhile, were enjoying themselves strolling on the mountain when they noticed some tall buildings rising above a bamboo grove. "What do you think that is?" Sanzang asked Monkey, who replied, "It's either a Taoist temple or a Buddhist one. Let's go over and find out." It did not take them long to reach the gate, and they saw

> A cool pine-covered slope,
> A tranquil path through the bamboo.
> White cranes brought floating clouds;
> Monkeys and apes offered fruit.
> Before the gate was a wide pool, and the shadows of the trees were long;
> In the cracks of the rocks grew moss.
> Many a purple hall was massed together;
> A red aura enveloped the lofty towers.
> It certainly was a blessed place,
> A cloud cave on Penglai.
> In its pure emptiness little happened;
> Its stillness gave birth to thoughts of the Way.
> Green birds often brought letters from the Queen Mother;
> Purple pheasants carried the classics of Lord Lao Zi.
> There was a majestic air of the Way and its Power —
> It was indeed a divine immortal's home.

Sanzang dismounted and saw that there was a stone tablet outside the gate on which was inscribed in large letters:

BLESSED LAND OF THE MOUNTAIN
OF INFINITE LONGEVITY
CAVE HEAVEN OF THE WUZHUANG TEMPLE

"You were right," said Sanzang, "it is a Taoist temple." "Good people must live in this temple," said Friar Sand, "set as it is in such fresh, light scenery. Let's go in and have a look round. When we go back to the East at the end of our journey, this will be one of the finest sights we'll have seen." "Well spoken," said Monkey, and they all went in. On the next gate was pasted the couplet:

"Residence of Divine Immortals Who Never Grow Old;
Home of Taoists as Ancient as Heaven."

"This Taoist tries to intimidate people by talking big," said Monkey with a laugh. "When I wrecked the Heavenly Palace five hundred years ago I never saw anything like that over the gate of the Supreme Lord Lao Zi." "Never mind him," said Pig. "Let's go in. This Taoist may well be quite a decent bloke."

As they went through the second gate they saw two boys come scurrying out. This is what they looked like:

Pure bones, lively spirits, pretty faces,
And hair tied in childish tufts.
Their Taoist robes naturally wreathed in mist,
The sleeves of their feather clothes were floating in the
wind.
Their jade belts were tied with dragon-head knots,
Their grass sandals lightly fastened with silk.
In their elegance they were unlike common mortals —
The Taoist boys Pure Wind and Bright Moon.

The two boys bowed and came out to greet them. "We are sorry we did not welcome you properly, venerable master," they said. "Please sit down." Sanzang was delighted, and he accompanied the two boys up to the main hall of the temple, which faced south. There was a patterned lattice window that let through the light on top of the door that the boys pushed open.

They asked the Tang Priest to come in, and he saw two huge
words executed in many colours hanging on the wall — Heaven
and Earth. There was an incense table of red carved lacquer
on which stood a pair of golden censers and a supply of incense.

Sanzang went over to the table and put a pinch of incense
in the censers with his left hand while performing triple rev-
erences. Then he turned round to the boys and said, "This
temple is a home of immortals in the Western Continent, so
why don't you worship the Three Pure Ones, the Four Emperors,
and all the ministers of Heaven? Why do you burn incense to
the two words 'Heaven' and 'Earth'?" "To be frank with you,
venerable teacher," the boys replied with smiles, "it's quite right
to worship the top word, 'Heaven', but the bottom one, 'Earth',
gets no incense from us. Our teacher only put them up to ingratiate himself." "How does he ingratiate himself?" Sanzang
asked. "The Three Pure Ones and the Four Emperors are our
teacher's friends," the boys replied, "the Nine Bright Shiners
are his juniors, and the Constellations are his underlings."

When Monkey heard this he collapsed with laughter, and
Pig asked him, "What are you laughing at?" "They say that
I get up to no good, but these Taoist boys really tell whoppers."
"Where is your teacher?" Sanzang asked them. "He had an
invitation from the Original Celestial Jade Pure One and has
gone to the Palace in the Heaven of Supreme Purity to hear a
lecture on the Product of Undifferentiated Unity, so he's not
at home."

At this Monkey could not help roaring, "Stinking Taoist
boys, you don't know who you're talking to. You play your dirty
tricks in front of our faces and pretend to be oh-so-innocent.
What Heavenly Immortal of the Great Monad lives in the Miluo
Palace? Who invited your cow's hoof of a master to a lecture?"
Sanzang was worried that now he had lost his temper the boys
would answer back and spark off a disastrous fight, so he said,
"Don't quarrel with them, Wukong. We'll be going in a
minute, so we obviously need have nothing to do with them.
Besides, as the saying goes, 'egrets don't eat egret flesh'. Their
master isn't here anyway, so there would be no point in wrecking

the place. Go and graze the horse outside the gate. Friar Sand, you look after the luggage, and tell Pig to take some rice from our bundles and use their kitchen to make our meal. When we go we shall give them a few coppers for the firewood. All do as I've told you and leave me here to rest. When we have eaten we shall be on our way again." The three of them went off to do their jobs.

Bright Moon and Pure Wind were meanwhile quietly praising Sanzang to each other: "What a splendid monk. He is indeed the beloved sage of the West in mortal form, and his true nature is not at all befuddled. The master told us to entertain him and give him some manfruit as a token of their old friendship, and he also warned us to be on our guard against those gangsters of his. They have murderous-looking faces and coarse natures. Thank goodness he sent them away, because if they were still with him, we wouldn't be able to give him the manfruit." "We don't yet know whether this monk is our master's old friend or not," said Pure Wind. "We'd better ask him to make sure." The two of them then went over to Sanzang and said, "May we ask you, venerable master, whether you are the Sanzang of the Great Tang who is going to the Western Heaven to fetch the scriptures?" "Yes, I am," said Sanzang, returning their bows. "How did you know who I was?" "Our master told us before he went," they replied, "to go out to meet you long before you got here, but as you came faster than we expected we failed to do so. Please sit down, teacher, while we fetch you some tea." "I am honoured," said Sanzang. Bright Moon hurried out and came back with a cup of fragrant tea for him. When Sanzang had drunk the tea, Pure Wind said to Bright Moon, "We must do as our teacher told us and fetch the fruit."

The two boys left Sanzang and went to their room, where one of them picked up a golden rod and the other a red dish, on which he put many a silk handkerchief as cushioning. They went into the manfruit orchard, where Pure Wind climbed the tree and tapped the fruit with the golden rod while Bright Moon waited below to catch them in the dish. They only took a few moments to knock down and catch a couple, which they took to the front hall to offer to Sanzang with the words, "This temple of ours is on a remote and desolate mountain, master Sanzang, and there is no local delicacy we can offer you except these two pieces of fruit. We hope they will quench your thirst." At the sight of the manfruit the monk recoiled some three feet, shaking with horror. "Goodness me!" he exclaimed. "How could you be so reduced to starvation in this year of plenty as to eat human flesh? And how could I possibly quench my thirst with a newborn baby?" "This monk has developed eyes of flesh and a mortal body in the battlefield of mouths and tongues and the sea of disputation," thought Pure Wind, "and he can't recognize the treasures of this home of immortals." "Venerable master," said Bright Moon, "this is what is called 'manfruit', and there is no reason why you should not eat one." "Nonsense, nonsense," said Sanzang. "They were conceived by their fathers and mothers and had to go through no end of suffering before they were born. How can you treat them as fruit when they haven't been alive for three days yet?" "They really and truly grew on a tree," said Pure Wind. "Stuff and rubbish," Sanzang replied. "Babies don't grow on trees. Take them away. It's very wicked."

As he refused absolutely to eat them, the two boys had to take the dish away and go back to their room. This fruit was rather difficult to handle, and did not keep for long without becoming hard and inedible, so the boys sat on their beds and ate one each.

Oh dear! What a thing to happen! There was only a wall separating their room from the kitchen, where their whispering could be clearly heard. Pig was in there cooking the rice when he heard them talk as they fetched the golden rod and the red dish. Later he heard them saying that the Tang Priest had not recognized the manfruit, which was why they took them back to their room to eat. "I'd love to try one, but I don't know how," thought Pig, unable to prevent his mouth from watering. Too stupid to do anything about it himself, he had to wait until he could talk it over with Brother Monkey. He had now lost all interest in stoking the stove as he stood in front of it, con-

stantly poking his head outside the kitchen to look for Monkey.
Before long Monkey appeared leading the horse, which he
tethered to a locust tree. As he came round to the back, the
blockhead waved frantically to him and said, "Come here, come
here." Monkey turned round, came to the kitchen door, and
said, "What are you yelling for, idiot? Not enough food for
you? Let the old monk eat his fill, then we two can go to the
next big house that lies ahead and beg for some more." "Come
in," said Pig, "it's not that. Do you know that there's a treasure in this temple?" "What treasure?" Monkey asked. "I
can't describe it because you've never seen it," said Pig, "and if
I gave it to you, you wouldn't know what it was." "Don't try
to make a fool of me, idiot," said Monkey. "When I studied
the Way of Immortality five hundred years ago I travelled on
my cloud to the corners of the ocean and the edge of the sky.
I've seen everything." "Have you seen manfruit then?" Pig
asked. "No, I haven't," said Monkey with astonishment. "But
I've heard that manfruit is Grass-returning Cinnabar, and that
anyone who eats it lives to a great old age. Where can we get
some?" "Here," said Pig. "Those boys gave two to our master,
but that old monk didn't know what they were and thought they
were newborn babies. He wouldn't eat them. Those boys are
disgraceful — instead of giving them to us as they should have
done they sneaked off into their room and had one each, gobble,
gobble, gobble — I was drooling. I wish I knew how I could
try one. Surely you've got some dodge for getting into the
orchard and pinching a few for us to taste. You have, haven't
you?" "Easy," said Monkey. "I'll go in and pick some." As
he rushed out Pig grabbed him and said, "I heard them saying
in their room that they needed a golden rod to knock them down
with. You must do this very carefully — nobody must know
about it." "I know, I know," replied Monkey.

The Great Sage made himself invisible and slipped into the
boys' room, only to find that after eating the fruit they had
gone to the front hall, where they were talking to Sanzang.
Monkey looked all around the room for the golden rod until he
saw a two-foot length of gold hanging from the window lattice.

It was about as thick as a finger. At the bottom was a lump like a bulb of garlic, and at the top was a hole through which was fastened a green silk tassel. "So this must be what they call the golden rod," he thought as he took it down. He left the room and pushed open a pair of gates at the back. Goodness! He saw a garden

With red, jewelled balconies
And a twisting artificial hill.
Rare flowers tried to outshine the sun;
The bamboo attempted to be bluer than the sky.
Outside the Floating Cup Pavilion
A curve of willows hung like mist;
Before the Platform to Admire the Moon
Clumps of lofty pines made splashes of indigo.
Bright, bright red,
The pomegranate orchard;
Deep, deep green,
The cushions of grass.
Richly blue
Were the jade-coloured orchids;
Rushing and powerful
The water in the stream.
Crimson cassia blazed beside golden wells and wutong
  trees;
Brocade-rich locust trees flanked red balconies and steps.
There was peach blossom in pink and white,
Yellow and fragrant chrysanthemums that have seen
  nine autumns.
Trellises of raspberries
Flourish by the peony pavilion;
Banks of hibiscus
Led to beds of tree-peonies.
There was no end of noble bamboos that had held out
  against frost,
Or of lordly pines that defied the snows.
Then there were nests of cranes and houses for deer,

Square ponds and round pools,
Spring water like fragments of jade,
Golden heaps of flowers.
The north wind burst the white plum blossom open.
When spring came, it touched the crab-apple with red.
It could be rightly called the most splendid view on
    Earth,
The finest garden in the west.

Before Monkey had time to take all of this in he saw another
gate.   When he pushed it open he saw

Vegetables for each of the four seasons —
Spinach, celery, beetroot, ginger, and kelp,
Bamboo shoots, sweet potato, melons, oblong gourd and
    wild rice stem,
Onions, garlic, coriander, scallion and shallots,
Lettuce, artemisia, and bitter alisma,
Gourds and aubergines that must be planted,
Turnips, radishes, docks,
Red amaranth, green cabbage, and purple mustard-plant.

"So they're Taoists who grow their own food," thought
Monkey, smiling to himself. When he had crossed the vegetable
garden he saw yet another gate, and when he opened it there
was a huge tree in front of him with fragrant branches and
shade-giving green leaves shaped rather like those of plantains.
The tree was about a thousand feet high, and its trunk was some
seventy or eighty feet round.   Monkey leant against it and
looked up, and on a branch that was pointing south he saw a
manfruit, which really did look just like a newborn child. The
stem came from its bottom, and as it hung from the branch its
hands and feet waved wildly around and it shook its head.
Monkey was thoroughly delighted, and he thought in admiration, "What a splendid thing — a real rarity, a real rarity." And
with that thought he went shooting up the tree.
Now there is nothing that monkeys are better at than climbing trees to steal fruit, and one blow from the golden rod sent
the manfruit tumbling down. He jumped down to fetch it, but

it was nowhere to be seen. He searched the grass all around, but could find not a trace of it. "That's odd," he thought, "very odd indeed. It must be able to use its feet — but even then it won't be able to get past the wall. No, I've got it. The local deity of this garden has hidden it away to stop me stealing it." He made some finger magic and uttered the sacred sound "*Om*," which forced the garden deity to come forward, bow and say, "You summoned me, Great Sage. What are your orders?" "Surely you know," Monkey said, "that I am the most famous criminal on earth. When I stole the sacred peaches, the imperial wine, and the elixir of immortality some years ago, nobody dared to try and take a cut. How comes it that when I take some fruit today you pinch my very first one? This fruit grows on a tree, and the birds of the air must have their share of it, so what harm will be done if I eat one? Why did you snatch it the moment it fell down?" "Great Sage," the deity replied, "don't be angry with me. These treasures belong to the immortals of the Earth, and I am a ghost immortal, so I would never dare take one. I've never even had the good fortune even to smell one." "If you didn't take it, why did it disappear the moment I knocked it down from the tree?" Monkey asked. "You may know that these treasures give eternal life, Great Sage," the deity replied, "but you don't know about their origin."

"Where do they come from, then?" Monkey asked. "These treasures," the deity replied, "take three thousand years to blossom, another three thousand to form, and three thousand more to ripen. In almost ten thousand years only thirty grow. Anyone lucky enough to smell one will live for three hundred and sixty years, and if you eat one you will live to be forty-seven thousand. These fruit fear only the Five Elements." "What do you mean, 'fear only the Five Elements'?" Monkey asked. "If they meet metal," the deity said, "they fall; if they meet wood they rot; if they meet water they dissolve; if they meet fire they are burnt; and if they meet earth they go into it. If you tap them you have to use a golden rod, otherwise they won't drop; and when you knock them down you must catch them in a bowl padded with silk handkerchiefs. If they come in contact with wooden utensils they rot, and even if you eat one it won't make you live any longer. When you eat them you must do so off porcelain, and they should be cooked in clear water. If they come in contact with fire they become charred and useless, and they go into any earth they touch. When you knocked one to the ground just now it went straight in, and as the earth here will now live for forty-seven thousand years you wouldn't be able to make any impression on it even with a steel drill: it's much harder than wrought iron. But if a man eats one he wins long life. Try hitting the ground if you don't believe me." Monkey raised his gold-ringed cudgel and brought it down on the ground. There was a loud noise as the cudgel sprank back. The ground was unmarked. "So you're right," said Monkey, "you're right. This cudgel of mine can smash rocks to powder and even leave its mark on wrought iron, but this time it did no damage at all. This means that I was wrong to blame you. You may go back now." At this the local deity went back to his shrine.

The Great Sage now had a plan. He climbed the tree and then held the rod in one hand while he undid the lapel of his cloth tunic and made it into a kind of pouch. He pushed the leaves and branches aside and knocked down three manfruits, which he caught in his tunic. He jumped out of the tree and went straight to the kitchen, where a smiling Pig asked him if he had got any. "This is the stuff, isn't it?" said Monkey. "I was able to get some. We mustn't leave Friar Sand in the dark, so give him a shout." "Come here, Friar Sand," Pig called, waving his hand. Friar Sand put the luggage down, hurried into the kitchen, and asked, "Why did you call me?" "Do you know what these are?" Monkey asked, opening his tunic. "Manfruits," said Friar Sand as soon as he saw them. "Good," said Monkey, "you know what they are. Where have you eaten them?" "I've never eaten them," Friar Sand replied, "but when I was the Curtain-lifting General in the old days I used to escort the imperial carriage to the Peach Banquets, and I saw some that immortals from over the seas brought as birthday presents for the Queen Mother. I've certainly seen them, but I've never tasted one. Please give me a bit to try." "No need to ask," said Monkey. "We're having one each."

So each of them had one manfruit to eat. Pig had both an enormous appetite and an enormous mouth, and had, moreover, been suffering pangs of hunger ever since hearing the Taoist boys eating. So the moment he saw the fruit he grabbed one, opened his mouth, and gulped it down whole; then he put on an innocent expression and shamelessly asked the other two what they were eating. "Manfruit," Friar Sand replied. "What does it taste like?" Pig asked. "Ignore him, Friar Sand," said Monkey. "He's already eaten his, and he's no business to ask you." "Brother," said Pig, "I ate mine too fast. I didn't nibble it delicately and taste the flavour like you two. I don't even know if it had a stone or not as I gulped it straight down. You should finish what you've started: you've whetted my appetite, so you ought to get me another to eat slowly." "You're never satisfied," Monkey replied. "These things aren't like rice or flour — you can't go stuffing yourself full of them. Only thirty grow in every ten thousand years, so we can think ourselves very lucky indeed to have a whole one each. Come off it, Pig, you've had enough." He got up and tossed the golden rod back into the Taoist boys' room through the window, paying no more attention to Pig, who went on grumbling.

Before long the Taoist boys were back in their room, and they heard Pig moaning, "I didn't enjoy my manfruit; I wish I could have another." Pure Wind's suspicion were aroused, and he said to Bright Moon, "Did you hear that long-snouted monk saying he wished he could have another manfruit? Our master told us when he went that we were to be careful of those gangsters and not let them steal our treasures." "This is terrible, terrible," said Bright Moon. "What's the golden rod doing on the floor? We'd better go into the garden and take a look around." The two of them hurried out and found the garden gates open. "We shut this gate," said Pure Wind, "so why is it open?" They rushed round the flower garden, found the vegetable garden gate open too, and tore into the manfruit garden. They leant on the tree and looked up into it to count the fruit, but however often they added the number up, it always came to twenty-two. "Can you do arithmetic?" Bright Moon asked, and Pure Wind replied, "Yes. Tell me the figures." "There were originally thirty manfruits," said Bright Moon. "When our master opened the garden two were divided up and eaten, which left twenty-eight. Just now we knocked two down to give the Tang Priest, which left twenty-six. But there are only twenty-two now, which means that we're four short. It goes without saying that those evil men must have stolen them. Let's go and tell that Tang Priest what we think of him."

The two of them went from the garden to the front hall, where they pointed at Sanzang and poured the most filthy and stinking abuse on him, calling him "baldy" this and "baldy" that. It was more than Sanzang could stand, so he said, "What are you making all this fuss about, immortal boys? Please stop. I wouldn't mind you being a bit offhand with me, but you can't talk in this outrageous way." "Are you deaf?" Pure Wind asked. "We're not talking a foreign language, and you can understand us perfectly well. You've stolen our manfruit, and you've no right to forbid us to mention it." "What does manfruit look like?" Sanzang asked. "It's what we offered you just now and you said looked like babies." "Amitabha Buddha!" Sanzang exclaimed. "I shook with terror at the very sight of them — I couldn't possibly steal one. Even if I were being racked by the most terrible greed, I could never commit the crime of eating one of those. What do you mean by making so unjust an accusation?" "Although you didn't eat any," said Pure Wind, "those underlings of yours stole and ate some." "Even if they did, you shouldn't shout like that. Wait till I've questioned them. If they stole some, I'll see that they make it up to you." "Make it up?" said Bright Moon. "They are things that money can't buy." "Well then," said Sanzang, "if money won't buy them, 'decent behaviour is worth a thousand pieces of gold,' as the saying goes. I'll make them apologize to you, and that will be that. Besides, we still don't know whether they did it." "Of course they did," retorted Bright

Moon. "They're still quarrelling in there because they were divided unfairly." "Come here, disciples," called Sanzang.

"We've had it," said Friar Sand when he heard Sanzang calling. "The game's up. Our master is calling us and the young Taoists are swearing and cursing. The cat must be out of the bag." "How disgraceful," said Monkey, "all that fuss about some food. But if we confess it, they'll say it was stealing food; the best thing is not to admit it at all." "Quite right, quite right, we'll cover it up," said Pig, and three of them went from the kitchen to the hall. If you don't know how they denied it, listen to the explanation in the next instalment.

CHAPTER TWENTY-FIVE

The Immortal Zhen Yuan captures
the pilgrim priest;
Monkey makes havoc in the
Wuzhuang Temple.

"The meal is cooked," the three disciples said as they entered the hall. "What did you call us for?" "I'm not asking about the meal, disciples," said Sanzang. "'This temple has things called manfruit or whatever that look like babies. Which of you stole and ate some?" "I don't know anything about it, honest I don't — I never saw any," said Pig. "That grinning one did it," said Pure Wind, "that grinning one." "I've had a smile on my face all my life," shouted Monkey. "Are you going to stop me smiling just because you can't find some fruit or other?" "Don't lose your temper, disciple," said Sanzang. "As men of religion we should control our tongues and not eat anything against our conscience. If you ate their fruit you should apologize to them, instead of trying to brazen it out like this."

Seeing that his master was talking sense, Brother Monkey began to tell the truth. "I didn't start it, master," he said. "Pig heard the Taoist boys eating something called manfruit next door to him and wanted to try one himself. He made me go and get three so that we three disciples could have one each. But now they've been eaten, that's that. What about it?" "How can these priests deny that they are criminals when they've stolen four of our manfruits?" said Bright Moon. "Amitabha Buddha," exclaimed Pig, "if he pinched four of them why did he only share out three? He must have done the dirty on us." He continued to shout wildly in this vein.

Now that they knew that the fruit really had been stolen,

457

the two boys started to abuse them even more foully. The Great Sage ground his teeth of steel in his fury, glaring with his fiery eyes and tightening his grip on his iron cudgel. "Damn those Taoist boys," he thought when he could restrain himself no longer. "If they'd hit us we could have taken it, but now they're insulting us to our faces like this, I'll finish their tree off, then none of them can have any more fruit." Splendid Monkey. He pulled a hair out from the back of his head, breathed a magic breath on it, said "Change", and turned it into an imitation Monkey who stayed with the Tang Priest, Pig and Friar Sand to endure the cursing and swearing of the Taoist boys, while the real Monkey used his divine powers to leap out of the hall by cloud. He went straight to the garden and struck the manfruit tree with his gold-banded cudgel. Then he used his supernatural strength that could move mountains to push the tree over with a single shove. The leaves fell, the branches splayed out, and the roots came out of the ground. The Taoists would have no more of their "Grass-returning Cinnabar". After pushing the tree over Monkey searched through the branches for manfruit, but he could not find a single one. These treasures dropped at the touch of metal, and as Monkey's cudgel was ringed with gold, while being made of iron, another of the five metals, one tap from it brought them all tumbling down, and when they hit the ground they went straight in, leaving none on the tree. "Great, great, great," he said, "that'll make them all cool down." He put the iron cudgel away, went back to the front of the temple, shook the magic hair, and put it back on his head. The others did not see what was happening as they had eyes of mortal flesh.

A long time later, when the two Taoist boys felt that they had railed at them for long enough, Pure Wind said to Bright Moon, "These monks will take anything we say. We've sworn at them as if we were swearing at chickens, but they haven't retorted anything. I don't think they can have stolen any, after all. The tree is so tall and the foliage is so dense that we may well have miscounted, and if we have, we shouldn't be cursing them so wildly. Let's go and check the number again." Bright

Moon agreed, and the pair of them went back to the garden. When they saw that the tree was down with its branches splayed out, the leaves fallen, and the fruit gone, they were horror-struck. Pure Wind's knees turned soft and he collapsed, while Bright Moon trembled and shook. Both of them passed out, and there is a verse to describe them:

> When Sanzang came to the Mountain of Infinite Longevity,
> Monkey finished the Grass-returning Cinnabar.
> The branches were splayed out, the leaves fallen, and the tree down.
> Bright Moon and Pure Wind's hearts both turned to ice.

The two of them lay in the dirt mumbling deliriously and saying, "What are we to do, what are we to do? The elixir of our Wuzhuang Temple has been destroyed and our community of immortals is finished. Whatever are we going to say to the master when he comes back?" "Stop moaning, brother," said Bright Moon. "We must tidy ourselves up and not let those monks know anything's wrong. That hairy-faced sod who looks like a thunder god must have done it. He must have used magic to destroy our treasure. But it's useless to argue with him as he'll deny everything, and if we start a quarrel with him and fighting breaks out, we two haven't a chance against the four of them. We'll have to fool them and say that no fruit is missing. We'll pretend we counted wrong before, and apologize to them. Their rice is cooked, and we can give them a few side dishes to eat with it. The moment they've each got a bowl of food you and I will stand on either side of the door, slam it shut, and lock it. After that we can lock all the gates, then they won't be able to get away. When our master comes back he can decide what to do with them. That old monk is a friend of his, so our master may want to forgive him as a favour. And if he doesn't feel forgiving, we've got the criminals under arrest and may possibly not get into trouble ourselves." "Absolutely right," said Pure Wind.

The two of them pulled themselves together, forced themselves to look happy, and went back to the front hall. "Master," they said, bowing low to Sanzang, "we were extremely rude to you just now. Please forgive us." "What do you mean?" asked Sanzang. "The fruit is all there," they replied. "We couldn't see it all before as the tree is so tall and the foliage so thick but when we checked just now the number was right." "You're too young to know what you're doing," said Pig, taking the chance to put the boot in. "Why did you swear and curse at us, and try to frame us up? It's wicked." Monkey, who understood what the boys were up to, said nothing and thought, "Lies, lies. The fruit is all finished. Why ever are they saying this? Can it be that they know how to bring the tree back to life?" "Very well then," Sanzang was saying meanwhile, "bring our rice in and we'll be off after eating it."

Pig went off to fill their bowls and Friar Sand arranged a table and chairs. The two boys hurried out and fetched some side dishes — salted squash, salted eggplant, turnips in winelees, pickled bean, salted lettuce, and mustard plant, some seven or eight plates in all. These they gave to the pilgrims to eat with their rice, and then they waited on them with a pot of good tea and two cups. As soon as the four pilgrims had their ricebowls in their hands, the boys, who were on either side of the doorway, slammed the doors to and locked them with a doublesprung bronze lock. "You shouldn't do that, boys," said Pig with a smile. "Even if the people round here are a bit rough there's no need to shut the doors while we eat." "Yes, yes," said Bright Moon, "we'll open them after lunch." Pure Wind, however, was abusive. "I'll get you, you greedy, bald-headed food-thief," he said. "You ate our immortal fruit and deserve to be punished for the crime of stealing food from fields and gardens. On top of that you've pushed our tree over and ruined our temple's source of immortality. How dare you argue with us? Your only chance of reaching the Western Heaven and seeing the Buddha is to be reborn and be rocked in the cradle again." When Sanzang heard this he dropped his ricebowl, feeling as if a boulder was weighing down his heart. The two boys went and locked the main and the inner gates of the temple,

then came back to the main hall to abuse them with filthy language and call them criminals and bandits till evening, when
they went off to eat. The two of them returned to their rooms
after supper.

"You're always causing trouble, you ape," grumbled Sanzang at Monkey. "You stole their fruit, so you should have let
them lose their temper and swear at you, then that would have
been the end of it. Why on earth did you push their tree over?
If they took this to court you wouldn't be able to get off even if
your own father were on the bench." "Don't make such a row,
Master," said Monkey. "Those boys have gone to bed, and
when they're asleep we can do a midnight flit." "But all the
gates have been locked," said Friar Sand, "and they've been
shut very firmly, so how can we possibly get away?" "Don't let
it bother you," said Monkey, "I have a way." "We weren't
worried that you wouldn't have a way," said Pig. "You can
turn yourself into an insect and fly out through the holes in the
window lattice. But you'll be leaving poor old us, who can't
turn ourselves into an insect and fly out through the holes in the
can for you." "If he does a trick like that and doesn't take us
with him I'll recite that old sutra — he won't get away scot-
free then." Pig was both pleased and worried to hear this.
"What do you mean, Master?" he said. "I know that the
Buddha's teachings include a *Surangama Sutra*, a *Lotus Sutra*, a
Peacock Sutra, an *Avalokitesvara Sutra*, and a *Diamond Sutra*,
but I never heard of any *Old Sutra*." "What you don't know,
brother," said Monkey, "is that the Bodhisattva Guanyin gave
this band I have round my head to our master. He tricked me
into wearing it, and now it's virtually rooted there and I can't
take it off. The spell or sutra for tightening this band is what
he meant by the 'old sutra'. If he says it, my head aches. It's a
way he has of making me suffer. Please don't recite it, Master.
I won't abandon you. I guarantee that we'll all get out.

It was now dark, and the moon had risen in the east. "It's
quiet now," said Monkey, "and the moon is bright. This is the
time to go." "Stop fooling about, brother," said Pig. "The
gates are all locked, so where can we possibly go?" "Watch

this trick," said Monkey, and gripping his cudgel in his hand he pointed at the doors and applied unlocking magic to them. There was a clanking sound, and the locks fell from all the doors and gates, which he pushed them open. "Not half clever," said Pig. "A locksmith with his skeleton keys couldn't have done it anything like as fast." "Nothing difficult about opening these doors," said Monkey. "I can open the Southern Gates of Heaven just by pointing at them." Then he asked his master to go out and mount the horse. Pig shouldered the luggage, Friar Sand led the horse, and they headed west. "You carry on," Monkey said, "while I go back to make sure that those two boys will stay asleep for a month." "'Mind you don't kill them, disciple," said Sanzang, "or you'll be on a charge of murder in the pursuit of theft as well." "I'm aware of that," replied Monkey and went back into the temple. Standing outside the door of the room where the boys were sleeping, he took a couple of sleep insects from his belt which he had won from the Heavenly King Virudhaka at the Eastern Gate of Heaven in a drinking game. Now he threw them in through a gap in the window lattice. They landed straight on the boys' faces, and made them fall into a deeper sleep from which they would not wake up for a long time. Then he streaked back by cloud and caught up with Sanzang. They headed west along the main road.

That night the horse never stopped, and they kept on till dawn. "You'll be the death of me, you ape," said Sanzang. "Because of your greed I've had to stay awake all night." "Stop grumbling," said Monkey. "Now that it's light you can rest in the forest beside the road and build your strength up before we move on." Sanzang obediently dismounted and sat down on the roots of a pine tree, using it as a makeshift meditation platform. Friar Sand put down the luggage and took a nap, while Pig pillowed his head on a rock and went to sleep. Monkey, the Great Sage, had his own ideas and amused himself leaping from tree to tree.

After the lecture in the palace of the Original Celestial Jade Pure One the Great Immortal Zhen Yuan led his junior Immortals down from the Tushita Heaven through the jade sky on auspicious clouds, and in a moment they were back at the gates of the Wuzhuang Temple. The gates, he saw, were wide open, and the ground was clean. "So Pure Wind and Bright Moon aren't so useless after all," he said. "Usually they're still in bed when the sun is high in the sky. But now, with us away, they got up early, opened the gates, and swept the grounds." All the junior immortals were delighted. Yet when they went into the hall of worship there was no incense burning and nobody to be seen. Where were Bright Moon and Pure Wind, they wondered. "They probably thought that with us not here they could steal some stuff and clear out." "What an outrageous idea," said the Great Immortal. "As if men cultivating immortality could do anything so evil! I think they must have forgotten to shut the gates before they went to sleep last night and not have woken up yet." When the immortals went to look in their room they found the doors closed and heard the boys snoring. They hammered on the doors and shouted for all they were worth, but the boys did not wake up. They forced the doors open and pulled the boys from their beds: the boys still did not wake up. "Fine immortal boys you are," said the Great Immortal with a smile. "When you become an immortal your divine spirit should be so full that you do not want to sleep. Why are they so tired? They must have been bewitched. Fetch some water at once." A boy hastily handed him half a bowl of water. He intoned a spell, took a mouthful of the water, and spurted it on their faces. This broke the enchantment. The two of them woke up, opened their eyes, rubbed their faces, looked around them, and saw the Great Immortal as well as all their immortal brothers. Pure Wind bowed and Bright Moon kowtowed in their confusion, saying, "Master, that old friend of yours, the priest from the East ... a gang of bandits ... murderous, murderous. ..."

"Don't be afraid," said the Great Immortal with a smile. "Calm down and tell us all about it." "Master," said Pure Wind, "the Tang Priest from the East did come. It was quite soon after you had left. There were four monks and a horse — five of them altogether. We did as you had ordered us and picked two manfruits to offer him, but the venerable gentleman was too vulgar and stupid to know what our treasures were. He said that they were newborn babies and refused to eat any, so we ate one each. Little did we imagine that one of his three disciples called Brother Sun Wukong, or Monkey, would steal four manfruits for them to eat. We spoke to him very reasonably, but he denied it and secretly used his magic. It's terrible...." At this point the two boys could no longer hold back the tears that now streamed down their cheeks. "Did the monk strike you?" asked the immortals. "No," said Bright Moon, "he only felled our manfruit tree."

The Great Immortal did not lose his temper when he heard their story, "Don't cry," he said, "don't cry. What you don't realize is that Monkey is an immortal of the Supreme Monad, and that he played tremendous havoc in the Heavenly Palace. He has vast magic powers. But he has knocked our tree over. Could you recognize those monks?" "I could recognize all of them." replied Pure Wind. "In that case come with me," said the Great Immortal. "The rest of you are to prepare the instruments of torture and be ready to flog them when we come back."

The other immortals did as they were told while the Great Immortal, Bright Moon and Pure Wind pursued Sanzang on a beam of auspicious light. It took them but an instant to cover three hundred miles. The Great Immortal stood on the edge of the clouds and gazed to the west, but he did not see Sanzang; then he turned round to look east and saw that he had left Sanzang over two hundred and fifty miles behind. Even riding all night that venerable gentleman had covered only forty miles, which was why the Great Immortal's cloud had overshot him by a great distance. "Master," said one of the immortal boys, "there's the Tang Priest, sitting under a tree by the side of the road." "Yes, I'd seen him myself," the Great Immortal replied. "You two go back and get some ropes ready, and I'll catch him myself." Pure Wind and Bright Moon went back.

The Great Immortal landed his cloud, shook himself, and

turned into an itinerant Taoist. Do you know what he looked like?

> He wore a patchwork gown,
> Tied with Lü Dongbin sash.
> Waving a fly-whisk in his hand
> He tapped a musical drum.
> The grass sandals on his feet had three ears;
> His head was wrapped in a sun turban.
> As the wind filled his sleeves
> He sang The Moon Is High.

"Greetings, venerable sir," he called, raising his hands. "Oh, I'm sorry I didn't notice you before," replied Sanzang hastily. "Where are you from?" the Great Immortal asked. "And why are you in meditation during your journey?" "I have been sent by the Great Tang in the East to fetch the scriptures from the Western Heaven," Sanzang said, "and I'm taking a rest along the way." "You must have crossed my desolate mountain if you have come from the East." "May I ask, immortal sir, which mountain is yours?" "My humble abode is the Wuzhuang Temple on the Mountain of Infinite Longevity."

"We didn't come that way," said Monkey, who realized what was happening. "We've only just started out." The Great Immortal pointed at him and laughed. "I'll show you, you damned ape. Who do you think you're fooling? I know that you knocked our manfruit tree down and came here during the night. You had better confess: you won't get away with concealing anything. Stay where you are, and give me back that tree at once." Monkey flared up at this, and with no further discussion he struck at the Great Immortal's head with his cudgel. The Great Immortal twisted away from the blow and went straight up into the sky on a beam of light, closely pursued by Monkey on a cloud. In mid-air the Great Immortal reverted to his true appearance, and this is what he looked like:

> A golden crown on his head,
> A No-worries cloak of crane's down on his body.

> *A pair of turned-up sandals on his feet,*
> *And round his waist a belt of silk.*
> *His body was like a child's;*
> *His face was that of a beautiful woman.*
> *A wispy beard floated down from his chin,*
> *And the hair on his temples was crow-black.*
> *He met Monkey unarmed*
> *With only a jade-handled whisk in his hands.*

Monkey struck wildly at him with his club, only to be parried to left and right by the Great Immortal's whisk. After two or three rounds the Great Immortal did a "Wrapping Heaven and Earth in His Sleeve" trick, waving his sleeve gently in the breeze as he stood amid the clouds, then sweeping it across the ground and gathering up the four pilgrims and their horse in it. "Hell," said Pig, "We're all caught in a bag." "It isn't a bag, you idiot," said Monkey, "he's caught us all in his sleeve." "It doesn't matter, anyhow," said Pig. "I can make a hole in it with a single blow of my rake that we can all get through. Then we'll be able to drop out when he relaxes his grip on us." But however desperately he struck at the fabric he could make no impression on it: although it was soft when held in the hand it was harder than iron when hit.

The Great Immortal turned his cloud round, went straight back to the Wuzhuang Temple, landed, sat down, and told his disciples to fetch rope. Then, with all the junior immortals in attendance, he took the Tang Priest out of his sleeve as if he were a puppet and had him tied to one of the pillars of the main hall. After that he took the other three out and tied each of them to a pillar. The horse was taken out, tethered, and fed in the courtyard, and their luggage he threw under the covered walk. "Disciples," he said, "these priests are men of religion, so we cannot use swords, spears or axes on them. You'd better fetch a leather whip and give them a flogging for me — that will make me feel better about the manfruit." The disciples immediately produced a whip — not an oxhide, sheepskin, deerskin or calfskin whip, but a seven-starred dragon-skin one — and were told to soak it in water. A brawny young immortal was told to take a firm grip on it. "Master," he said, "which of them shall I flog first?" "Sanzang is guilty of gross disrespect," the Great Immortal replied, "flog him first."

"That old priest of ours couldn't stand a flogging," thought Monkey when he heard this, "and if he died under the lash the fault would be mine." Finding the thought of this unbearable, he spoke up and said, "You're wrong, sir. I stole the fruit, I ate the fruit, and I pushed the tree over. Why flog him first when you ought to be flogging me?" "That damn monkey has a point," said the Great Immortal with a smile, "so you'd better flog him first." "How many strokes?" the junior Immortal asked. "Give him thirty," the Great Immortal replied, "to match the number of fruits." The junior immortal whirled the lash and started to bring it down. Monkey, frightened that the immortal might have great magical powers, opened his eyes wide and looked carefully to see where he was going to be hit. It turned out to be on his legs. He twisted at the waist, shouted "Change!", turned them into a pair of wrought-iron legs, and watched the blows fall. The junior immortal gave him thirty lashes, one after the other, until it was almost noon. "Sanzang must be flogged too," the Great Immortal commanded, "for training his wicked disciple so slackly and letting him run wild." The junior immortal whirled the lash again and was going to strike Sanzang when Monkey said, "Sir, you're making another mistake. When I stole the fruit, my master knew nothing about it — he was talking to those two boys of yours in the main hall of the temple. This plot was hatched by us three disciples. Anyhow, even if he were guilty of slackness in training me, I'm his disciple and should take the flogging for him. Flog me again." "That damn monkey may be cunning and vicious, but he does have some sense of his obligations to his master. Very well then, flog him again." The junior immortal gave him another thirty strokes. Monkey looked down and watched his legs being flogged till they shone like mirrors but still he felt no pain. It was now drawing towards evening, and the Great Immortal said, "Put the lash to soak. We can continue the flogging tomorrow." The junior immortal took the lash away to be soaked while everyone retired to their quarters, and after supper they all went to bed.

"It was because you three got me into this trouble that I was brought here to be punished," moaned the venerable Sanzang to his three disciples as tears streamed down from his eyes. "What are you going to do about it?" "Don't grumble," Monkey replied. "I was the one to be flogged first, and you haven't felt the lash, so what have you got to groan about?" "I may not have been flogged," Sanzang replied, "but it's agony being tied up like this." "We're tied up too to keep you company," said Friar Sand. "Will you all stop shouting?" said Monkey. "Then we can be on our way again when we've taken a rest." "You're showing off again, elder brother," said Pig. "They've tied us up with hempen ropes and spurted water on them, so we're tightly bound. This isn't like the time we were shut in the hall of the temple and you unlocked the doors to let us out." "I'm not boasting," said Monkey. "I don't give a damn about their three hempen ropes sprayed with water. Even if they were coir cables as thick as a ricebowl they would only be an autumn breeze." Apart from him speaking, all was now silence. Splendid Monkey made himself smaller, slipped out of his bonds, and said, "Let's go, Master." "Save us too, elder brother," pleaded a worried Friar Sand. "Shut up, shut up," Monkey replied, then freed Sanzang, Pig and Friar Sand, straightened his tunic, tightened his belt, saddled the horse, collected their luggage from under the eaves, and went out through the temple gates with the others. "Go and cut down four of the willow-trees by that cliff," he told Pig, who asked, "Whatever do you want them for?" "I've got a use for them," Monkey replied. "Bring them here immediately."

The idiot Pig, who certainly had brute strength, went and felled each of them with a single bite, and came back holding them all in his arms. Monkey stripped off their tops and branches and told his two fellow-disciples to take the trunks back in and tie them up with the ropes as they themselves had been tied up. Then Monkey recited a spell, bit the tip of his tongue open, and spat blood over the trees. At his shout of "Change!" one of the trees turned into Sanzang, one turned into Monkey, and the other two became Friar Sand and Pig. They were all perfect likenesses; when questioned they would reply, and when called by their names they responded. The three disciples then hurried back to their master, and once more they travelled all night without stopping as they fled from the Wuzhuang Temple.

By the time it was dawn the venerable Sanzang was swaying to and fro as he dozed in the saddle. "Master," called Monkey when he noticed, "you're hopeless. You're a man of religion — how can you be finding it so exhausting? I can do without sleep for a thousand nights and not feel a bit tired. You'd better dismount and spare yourself the humiliation of being laughed at by a passer-by. Take a rest in the hollow place under this hill where you can shelter from the wind before we go any further."

We shall leave them resting beside the path to tell how the Great Immortal got up at dawn, ate his meatless breakfast, and went to the hall. "Today Tang Sanzang is to be lashed," he announced as he sent for the lash. The junior whirled it around and said to the Tang Priest, "I'm going to flog you." "Flog away," the willow tree replied. When he had given it thirty resounding lashes he whirled the whip around once more and said to Pig, "Now I'm going to flog you." "Flog away," the willow tree replied. When he came to flog Friar Sand, he too told him to go ahead. But when he came to flog Monkey, the real Monkey on the road shuddered and said, "Oh, no!" "What do you mean?" Sanzang asked. "When I turned the four willow trees into the four of us I thought that as he had me flogged twice yesterday he wouldn't flog me again today, but now he's lashing the magic body, my real body is feeling the pain. I'm putting an end to this magic." With that he hastily recited an incantation to break the spell.

Look at the terror of the Taoist boys as they throw down their leather whips and report, "Master, we started by flogging the Priest from the Great Tang, but all we are flogging now are willow trunks." The Great Immortal laughed bitterly on hearing this and was full of admiration. "Brother Monkey really is a splendid Monkey King. I had heard that when he turned the Heavenly Palace upside-down, he could not even be caught with a Heaven and Earth Net, and now I see it must be true. I wouldn't mind your escaping, but why did you leave four willows tied up here to impersonate you? He shall be shown no mercy. After him!" As the words "After him" left his mouth, the Great Immortal sprang up on a cloud and looked west to see the monks carrying their bundles and spurring their horse as they went on their way. Bringing his cloud down he shouted, "Where are you going, Monkey? Give me back my manfruit tree." "We're done for," exclaimed Pig, "our enemy's come back." "Put all your piety away for now, Master," said Monkey, "while we finish him off once and for all with a bit of evil; then we'll be able to escape." The Tang Priest shivered and shook on hearing this, and before he could answer, the three disciples rushed forward, Friar Sand wielding his staff, Pig with his rake held high, and the Great Sage Monkey brandishing his iron cudgel. They surrounded the Great Immortal in mid-air and struck wildly at him. There are some verses about this terrible fight:

> Monkey did not know that the immortal Zhen Yuan,
> The Conjoint Lord of the Age, had even deeper powers.
> While the three magic weapons fiercely whirled,
> His deer-tail fly-whisk gently waved.
> Parrying to left and right, he moved to and fro,
> Blocking blows from front and back he let them rush
>   around.
> When night gave way to dawn they still were locked in
>   combat.
> If they tarried here they would never reach the Western
>   Heaven:

The three of them went for him with their magic weapons, but the Great Immortal kept them at bay with his fly-whisk. After about an hour he opened wide his sleeve and caught up master, disciples, horse, and baggage in it once more. Then he turned his cloud around and went back to his temple, where all the Immortals greeted him. After taking his seat in the hall he took them out of his sleeve one by one. He had the Tang Priest tied to a stunted locust tree at the foot of the steps, with Pig and Friar Sand tied to trees next to him. Monkey was tied up upside down, which made him think that he was going to be tortured and interrogated. When Monkey was tightly bound, the Great Immortal sent for ten long turban-cloths. "What a kind gentleman, Pig," said Monkey, "he's sent for some cloth to make sleeves for us — with a bit less he could have made us cassocks." The junior immortals fetched home-woven cloth, and on being told by the Great Immortal to wrap up Pig and Friar Sand with it, they came forward to do so. "Excellent," said Monkey, "excellent — you're being encoffined alive." Within a few moments the three of them were wrapped up, and lacquer was then sent for. The immortals quickly fetched some lacquer that they had tapped and dried themselves, with which they painted the three bandaged bodies all over except for the heads. "Never mind about our heads, sir," said Pig, "but please leave us a hole at the bottom to shit through." The Great Immortal then sent for a huge cauldron, at which Monkey said with a laugh, "You're in luck, Pig. I think they must have brought the cauldron out to cook us some rice in." "Fine," said Pig, "I hope they give us some rice first — we'll make much better-looking ghosts if we die with our bellies full." The immortals carried out the large cauldron and put it under the steps, and the Great Immortal called for dry wood to be stacked up round it and set ablaze. "Ladle it full of pure oil," he commanded, "and when it is bubbling hot, deep-fry Monkey in it to pay me back for my manfruit."

Monkey was secretly delighted to hear this. "This is just what I want," he thought. "I haven't had a bath for ages, and my skin's getting rather itchy. I'd thoroughly appreciate a hot bath." Very soon the oil was bubbling and Monkey was having reservations: he was afraid that the immortal's magic might be hard for him to fathom, and that at first he might be unable to use his limbs in the cauldron. Hastily looking around him, he saw that there was a sundial to the east of the dais and a stone lion to the west. Monkey rolled towards it with a spring, bit off the end of his tongue, spurted blood all over the stone lion, and shouted "Change", at which it turned into his own image, tied up in a bundle like himself. Then he extracted his spirit and went up into the clouds, from where he looked down at the Taoists.

It was just at this moment that the junior immortals reported, "The oil's boiling hard." "Carry Monkey down to it," the Great Immortal ordered, but when four of them tried to pick him up they could not. Eight then tried and failed, and four more made no difference. "This earth-infatuated ape is immovable," they said. "He may be small, but he's very solid." Twelve junior immortals were then told to pick him up with the aid of carrying-poles, and when they threw him in there was a loud crash as drops of oil splashed about, raising blisters all over the junior immortals' faces. "There's a hole in the cauldron — it's started leaking," the scalded immortals cried, but before the words were out of their mouths the oil had all run out through the broken bottom of the cauldron. They realized that they had thrown a stone lion into it.

"Damn that ape for his insolence," said the Great Immortal in a terrible rage. "How dare he play his tricks in my presence! I don't mind so much about your getting away, but how dare you wreck my cauldron? It's useless trying to catch him, and even if you could it would be like grinding mercury out of sand, or trying to hold a shadow or the wind. Forget about him, let him go. Untie Tang Sanzang instead and fetch another pot. We can fry him to avenge the destruction of the tree." The junior immortals set to and began to tear off Sanzang's lacquered bandages.

Monkey could hear all this clearly from mid-air. "The master will be done for," he thought. "If he goes into that cauldron the first time it bubbles it'll kill him, the second time it'll fry him to a frazzle, and by the fourth or fifth time he'll be a real mess of a monk. I must go back down and save him." The splendid Great Sage brought his cloud down to land, clasped his hands in front of him, and said, "Don't spoil the lacquered bands, and don't fry my master. Put me in the cauldron of oil instead." "I'll get you, you baboon," raged the Great Immortal in astonishment. "Why did you use one of your tricks to smash my cooking-pot?" "You must expect to be smashed up if you meet me — and what business is it of mine anyhow? I was going to accept your kind offer of some hot oil, but I was desperate for a shit and a piss, and if I'd done them in your cauldron, I'd have spoilt your oil and your food wouldn't have tasted right. Now I've done my stuff I'm ready for the cauldron. Please fry me instead of my master." The Great Immortal laughed coldly, came out of the hall, and seized him. If you don't know how the story goes or how he escaped, listen to the explanation in the next instalment.

CHAPTER TWENTY-SIX

Sun Wukong looks for the formula in
the Three Islands;
Guanyin revives the tree with a spring
of sweet water.

As the poem goes,

When living in the world you must be forbearing;
Patience is essential when training oneself.
Although it's often said that violence is good business,
Think before you act, and never bully or be angry.

True gentlemen who never strive are famed for ever;
The virtue-loving sages are renowned to this day.
Strong men always meet stronger than themselves,
And end up as failures who are in the wrong.

The Great Immortal Zhen Yuan held Monkey in his hand
and said, "I've heard about your powers and your fame, but
this time you have gone too far. Even if you manage to remove
yourself, you won't escape my clutches. You and I shall argue
it out as far as the Western Heaven, and even if you see that
Buddha of yours, you'll still have to give me back my manfruit-
tree first. Don't try any of your magic now." "What a small-
minded bloke you are, sir," Monkey replied with a laugh. "If
you want your tree brought back to life, there's no problem.
If you'd told me earlier we could have been spared all this
quarrelling." "If you hadn't made trouble I'd have forgiven
you," said the Great Immortal. "Would you agree to release
my master if I gave you back the tree alive?" Monkey asked.
"If your magic is strong enough to revive the tree," the Great

Immortal replied, "I shall bow to you eight times and take you as my brother." "That's easy then," said Monkey. "Release them and I guarantee to give you back your tree alive."

Trusting him not to escape, the Great Immortal ordered that Sanzang, Pig and Friar Sand be set free. "Master," said Friar Sand, "I wonder what sort of trick Monkey is up to." "I'll tell you what sort of trick," retorted Pig. "A pleading for favour trick. The tree's dead and can't possibly be revived. Finding a cure for the tree is an excuse for going off by himself without giving a damn for you or me." "He wouldn't dare abandon us," said Sanzang. "Let's ask him where he's going to find a doctor for it. Monkey," he continued, "why did you fool the immortal elder into untying us?" "Every word I said was true," Monkey replied. "I wasn't having him on." "Where will you go to find a cure?" "There's an old saying that 'cures come from over the sea'. I'll go to the Eastern Sea and travel round the Three Islands and Ten Continents visiting the venerable immortals and sages to find a formula for bringing the dead back to life. I promise that I'll cure that tree." "When will you come back?" "I'll only need three days." "In that case I'll give you three days. If you are back within that time, that will be all right, but if you are late I shall recite that spell." "I'll do as you say," said Monkey.

He immediately straightened up his tiger-skin kilt, went out through the door, and said to the Great Immortal, "Don't worry, sir, I'll soon be back. Mind you look after my master well. Give him tea three times a day and six meals, and don't leave any out. If you do, I'll settle that score when I come back, and I'll start by holing the bottoms of all your pans. If his clothes get dirty, wash them for him. I won't stand for it if he looks sallow, and if he loses weight you'll never see the back of me." "Go away, go away," the Great Immortal replied. "I certainly won't let him go hungry."

The splendid Monkey King left the Wuzhuang Temple with a bound of his somersault cloud and headed for the Eastern Sea. He went through the air as fast as a flash of lightning or a shooting star, and he was soon in the blessed land of Penglai. As he landed his cloud he looked around him and saw that it was indeed a wonderful place. A poem about it goes:

> *A great and sacred land where the immortal sages*
> *Still the waves as they come and go.*
> *The shade of the jasper throne cools the heart of the sky;*
> *The radiance of the great gate-pillars shimmers high*
>   *above the sea.*
> *Hidden in the coloured mists are flutes of jade;*
> *The moon and the stars shine on the golden leviathan.*
> *The Queen Mother of the Western Pool often comes*
>   *here*
> *To give her peaches to the Three Immortals.*

Gazing at the enchanted land that spread out before him, Brother Monkey entered Penglai. As he was walking along, he noticed three old men sitting round a chess table under the shade of a pine tree outside a cloud-wreathed cave. The one watching the game was the Star of Longevity, and the players were the Star of Blessings and the Star of Office. "Greetings, respected younger brothers," Monkey called to them, and when they saw him they swept the pieces away, returned his salutation, and said, "Why have you come here, Great Sage?" "To see you," he replied. "I've heard," said the Star of Longevity, "that you have given up the Way for the sake of the Buddha, and have thrown aside your life to protect the Tang Priest on his journey to fetch the scriptures from the Western Heaven. How can you spare the time from your endless crossings of waters and mountains just to see us?" "To tell you the truth," said Monkey, "I was on my way to the West until a spot of bother held us up. I wonder if you could do me a small favour." "Where did this happen?" asked the Star of Blessings, "what has been holding you up? Please tell us and we'll deal with it." "We've been held up because we went via the Wuzhuang Temple on the Mountain of Infinite Longevity," said Monkey. "But the Wuzhuang Temple is the palace of the Great Immortal Zhen Yuan," exclaimed the three Immortals with alarm. "Don't say that you've stolen some of his manfruit!" "What if I had stolen and eaten some?" asked Monkey with a grin. "You ignorant ape," the three immortals replied. "A mere whiff of that fruit makes a man live to be three hundred and sixty, and anyone who eats one will live forty-seven thousand years. They are called 'Grass-returning Cinnabar of Ten Thousand Longevities', and our Way hasn't a patch on them. Manfruit makes you as immortal as Heaven with the greatest of ease, while it takes us goodness knows how long to nourish our essence, refine the spirit, preserve our soul, harmonize water and fire, capture the *kan* to fill out the *li*. How can you possibly ask whether it would matter? There is no other miraculous tree like it on earth." "Miraculous tree," scoffed Monkey, "miraculous tree! I've put an end to that miraculous tree." "What? Put an end to it?" the three immortals asked, struck with horror. "When I was in his temple the other day," Monkey said, "the Great Immortal wasn't at home. There were only a couple of boys who received my master and gave him two manfruits. My master didn't know what they were and said that they were newborn babies; he refused to eat them. The boys took them away and ate them themselves instead of offering them to the rest of us, so I went and pinched three, one for each of us disciples. Those disrespectful boys swore and cursed at us no end, which made me so angry that I knocked their tree over with a single blow. All the fruit disappeared, the leaves fell, the roots came out, and the branches were smashed up. The tree was dead. To our surprise the two boys locked us in, but I opened the lock and we escaped. When the Great Immortal came home the next day, he came after us and found us. Our conversation didn't go too smoothly and we started to fight him, but he dodged us, spread his sleeve out, and caught us all up in it. After being tied up then flogged and interrogated for a day, we escaped again, but he caught up with us and captured us again. Although he had not an inch of steel on him, he fought us off with his whisk, and even with our three weapons we couldn't touch him. He caught us the same way as before. He had my master and two brothers wrapped up in bandages and lacquered, and was going to throw me into a cauldron of oil, but I used a trick to take my body away and escape, smashing that pan of his. Now that he has realized he can't catch me and keep me he's getting a bit scared of me, and I had a good talk with him. I told him that if he released my master and my brothers I'd guarantee to cure the tree and bring it back to life, which would satisfy both parties. As it occurred to me that 'cures come from over the sea' I came here specially to visit you three brothers of mine. If you have any cures that will bring a tree back to life, please tell me one so that I can get the Tang Priest out of trouble as quickly as possible."

"You ape," the Three Stars said gloomily when they heard this. "You don't know who you're up against. That Master Zhen Yuan is the Patriarch of the immortals of the earth, and we are the chiefs of the divine immortals. Although you have become a heavenly immortal, you are still only one of the irregulars of the Great Monad, not one of the elite. You'll never be able to escape his clutches. If you'd killed some animal, bird, insect or reptile, Great Sage, we could have given you some pills made from sticky millet to bring it back to life, but that manfruit tree is a magic one and can't possibly be revived. There's no cure, none at all." When he heard that there was no cure, Monkey's brows locked in a frown, and his forehead was creased in a thousand wrinkles. "Great Sage," said the Star of Blessing, "even though we have no cure here, there may be one somewhere else. Why be so worried?" "If there were anywhere else for me to go," Monkey replied, "it would be easy. It wouldn't even matter if I had to go to the furthest corner of the ocean, or to the cliff at the end of the sky, or if I had to penetrate the Thirty-sixth Heaven. But the trouble is that the Tang Patriarch is very strict and has given me a time-limit of three days. If I'm not back in three days he'll recite the Band-tightening Spell." "Splendid, splendid," laughed the three stars. "If you weren't restricted by that spell you'd go up to Heaven again." "Calm down, Great Sage," said the Star of Longevity, "there's no need to worry. Although that Great Immortal is senior to us he is a friend of ours, and as we haven't visited him for a long time and would like to do you a favour we'll go and see him. We'll explain things for you and tell that Tang monk not to recite the Band-tightening Spell. We won't go away until you come back, however long you take, even if it's a lot longer than three to five days." "Thank you very much," said Monkey. "May I ask you to set out now as I'm off?" With that he took his leave.

The Three Stars went off on beams of auspicious light to the Wuzhuang Temple, where all present heard cranes calling in the sky as the three of them arrived.

> *The void was bathed in blessed glow,*
> *The Milky Way heavy with fragrance.*
> *A thousand wisps of coloured mist enveloped the feath-*
> *er-clad ones;*
> *A single cloud supported the immortal feet.*
>
> *Green and red phoenixes circled and soared,*
> *As the aroma in their sleeves wafted over the earth.*
> *These dragons leant on their staffs and smiled,*
> *And jade-white beards waved before their chests.*
>
> *Their youthful faces were untroubled by sorrow;*
> *Their majestic bodies were rich with blessing.*
> *They carried star-chips to count their age.*
> *And at their waists hung gourds and talismans.*
>
> *Their life is infinitely long,*
> *And they live on the Ten Continents and Three Islands.*
> *They often come to bring blessings to mortals,*
> *Spreading good things a hundredfold among humans.*
>
> *The glory and blessings of the universe*
> *Came now as happiness unlimited.*
> *As these three elders visited the Great Immortal on aus-*
> *picious light,*
> *There was no end to good fortune and peace.*

"Master," the immortal youths rushed to report when they saw them, "the Three Stars from the sea are here." The Great Immortal Zhen Yuan, who was talking with the Tang Priest,

came down the steps to welcome them when he heard this.
When Pig saw the Star of Longevity he went up and tugged at
his clothes. "I haven't seen you for ages, old meat-head," he
said with a grin. "You're getting very free and easy, turning
up without a hat." With these words he thrust his own clerical
hat on the star's head, clapped his hands, and roared with
laughter. "Great, great. You've been 'capped and promoted'
all right." Flinging the hat down, the Star of Longevity cursed
him for a disrespectful moron. "I'm no moron," said Pig, but
you're all slaves." "You're most certainly a moron," the Star
of Blessing replied, "so how dare you call us slaves?" "If you
aren't slaves then," Pig retorted, "why do people always ask
you to 'bring us long life', 'bring us blessings', and 'bring us a
good job'?"

Sanzang shouted at Pig to go away, then quickly tidied
himself up and bowed to the Three Stars. The Three Stars
greeted the Great Immortal as befitted members of a younger
generation, after which they all sat down. "We have not seen
your illustrious countenance for a long time," the Star of Office
said, "which shows our great lack of respect. The reason we
come to see you now is because the Great Sage Monkey has
made trouble in your immortal temple." "Has Monkey been
to Penglai?" the Great Immortal asked. "Yes," replied the Star
of Longevity. "He came to our place to ask for a formula to
restore the elixir tree that he killed. As we have no cure for
it, he has had to go elsewhere in search of it. We are afraid
that if he exceeds the three-day time-limit the holy priest has
imposed, the Band-tightening Spell may be said. We have
come in the first place to pay our respects and in the second to
ask for an extension of the limit." "I won't recite it, I promise,"
answered Sanzang as soon as he heard this.

As they were talking Pig came rushing in again to grab hold
of the Star of Blessing and demand some fruit from him. He
started to feel in the star's sleeves and rummage round his waist,
pulling his clothes apart as he searched everywhere. "What sort
of behaviour is that?" asked Sanzang with a smile. "I'm not
misbehaving," said Pig. "This is what's meant by the saying,

'blessings wherever you look'." Sanzang shouted at him to go away again. The idiot withdrew slowly, glaring at the Star of Blessing with unwavering hatred in his eyes. "I've never offended you, you moron," said the star, "so why do you hate me so?" "I don't hate you," said Pig. "This is what they call 'turning the head and seeing blessing'." As the idiot was going out he saw a young boy came in with four tea ladles, looking for bowls in the abbot's cell in which to put fruit and serve tea. Pig seized one of the ladles, ran to the main hall of the temple, snatched up a hand-bell, and started striking it wildly. He was enjoying himself enormously when the Great Immortal said, "This monk gets more and more disrespectful." "I'm not being disrespectful," Pig replied. "I'm 'ringing in happiness for the four seasons'."

While Pig was having his jokes and making trouble, Monkey had bounded away from Penglai by auspicious cloud and come to the magic mountain Fangzhang. This was a really wonderful place. As the poem goes,

> *The towering Fangzhang is another heaven,*
> *Where gods and immortals meet in the Palace of the*
>   *Great Unity.*
> *The purple throne illuminates the road to the Three Pure*
>   *Ones,*
> *The scent of flowers and trees drifts among the clouds.*
>
> *Many a golden phoenix comes to rejoice around its*
>   *flowery portals;*
> *What makes the fields of magical mushrooms glisten*
>   *like jade?*
> *Pale peaches and purple plums are newly ripened,*
> *Ready to give even longer life to the Immortals.*

But as Monkey brought his cloud down he was in no mood to enjoy the view. As he was walking along he smelt a fragrance in the wind, heard the cry of the black stork, and saw an immortal:

The sky was filled with radiant light,
As multicoloured clouds shone and glowed.
Red phoenixes looked brighter than the flowers in their
    beaks;
Sweetly sang green ones as they danced in flight.
His blessings were as great as the Eastern Sea, his age
    that of a mountain;
Yet his face was a child's and his body was strong.
In a bottle he kept his pills of eternal youth,
And a charm for everlasting life hung from his waist.
He had often sent blessings down to mankind,
Several times saving mortals from difficulties.
He once gave longer life to Emperor Wu,
And always went to the Peach Banquets at the Jade
    Pool.
He taught all monks to cast off worldly fates;
His explanations of the great Way were clear as lightn-
    ing.
He had crossed the seas to pay his respects,
And had seen the Buddha on the Vulture Peak.
His title was Lord Emperor of Eastern Glory,
The highest-ranked immortal of the mists and clouds.

When Brother Monkey saw him he hailed him with the words, "I salute you, Lord Emperor." The Lord Emperor hastened to return his greeting and say, "I should have welcomed you properly, Great Sage. May I ask you home for some tea?" He led Monkey by the hand to his palace of cowrie-shells, where there was no end of jasper pools and jade towers. They were sitting waiting for their tea when a boy appeared from behind an emerald screen. This is how he looked:

A Taoist robe that sparkled with colour hung from his
    body,
And light gleamed from the silken sash round his waist.
On his head he wore a turban with the sign of the stars
    of the Dipper,

*And the grass sandals on his feet had climbed all the
    magical mountains.*
He was refining his True Being, shuffling off his shell,
*And when he had finished he would reach unbounded
    bliss.*
His understanding had broken through to the origins,
And he had come to know himself without mistakes.
*Avoiding fame and enjoying the present he had won long
    life*
And did not care about the passing of time.
*He had been along the crooked portico, climbed to the
    precious hall,*
And three times received the peaches of Heaven.
*Clouds of incense appeared to rise from behind the
    emerald screen;*
This young immortal was Dongfang Shuo himself.

"So you're here, you young thief," said Monkey with a smile
when he saw him. "There are no peaches for you to steal here
in the Lord Emperor's palace." Dongfang Shuo greeted him
respectfully and replied, "What have you come for, you old
thief? My master doesn't keep any pills of immortality here for
you to pinch."

"Stop talking nonsense, Manqian," the Lord Emperor shouted, "and bring some tea." Manqian, for such was Dongfang
Shuo's Taoist name, hurried inside and brought out two cups of
tea. When the two of them had drunk it, Monkey said, "I came
here to ask you to do something for me. I wonder if you'd be
prepared to." "What is it?" the Lord Emperor asked. "Do
tell me." "I have been escorting the Tang Priest on his journey
to the West," Monkey replied, "and our route took us via the
Wuzhuang Temple on the Mountain of Infinite Longevity. The
youths there were so ill-mannered that I lost my temper and
knocked their manfruit tree over. We've been held up for a
while as a result, and the Tang Priest cannot get away, which
is why I have come to ask you, sir, to give me a formula that
will cure it. I do hope that you will be good enough to agree,"

"You thoughtless ape," the Lord Emperor replied, "you make trouble wherever you go. Master Zhen Yuan of the Wuzhuang Temple has the sacred title Conjoint Lord of the Age, and he is the Patriarch of the immortals of the Earth. Why ever did you clash with him? That manfruit tree of his is Grass-returning Cinnabar. It was criminal enough of you to steal some of the fruit, and knocking the tree over makes it impossible for him ever to make it up with you." "True," said Monkey. "When we escaped he caught up with us and swept us into his sleeve as if we were so many sweat-rags, which made me furious. However, he had to let me go and look for a formula that would cure it, which is why I've come to ask your help." "I have a nine-phased returning pill of the Great Monad, but it can only bring animate objects back to life, not trees. Trees are lives compounded of the Wood and Earth elements and nurtured by Heaven and Earth. If it were an ordinary mortal tree I could bring it back to life, but the Mountain of Infinite Longevity is a blessed land before Heaven, the Wuzhuang Temple is the Cave Paradise of the Western Continent of Cattle-gift, and the manfruit tree is the life-root from the time when Heaven and Earth were separated. How could it possibly be revived? I have no formula, none at all."

"In that case I must take my leave," replied Monkey, and when the Lord Emperor tried to detain him with a cup of jade nectar he said, "This is too urgent to allow me to stay." He rode his cloud back to the island of Yingzhou, another wonderful place, as this poem shows:

> Trees of pearls glowed with a purple haze;
> The Yingzhou palaces led straight to the heavens.
> Blue hills, green rivers, and the beauty of exquisite
>   flowers;
> Jade mountains as hard as iron.
> Pheasants called at the sunrise over the sea,
> Long-lived phoenixes breathe in the red clouds.
> People, do not look so hard at the scenery in your jar:
> Beyond the world of phenomena is an eternal spring.

On reaching Yingzhou he saw a number of white-haired immortals with the faces of children playing chess and drinking under a pearl tree at the foot of a cinnabar cliff. They were laughing and singing. As the poem says, there were

> Light-filled auspicious clouds,
> Perfume floating in a blessed haze.
> Brilliant phoenixes singing at the mouth of a cave,
> Black cranes dancing on a mountain top.
> Pale green lotus-root and peaches helped their wine
>   down;
> Pears and fiery red dates gave them a thousand years of
>   life.
> Neither of them had ever heard an imperial edict,
> But each was entered on the list of immortals.
> They drifted and floated with the waves,
> Free and easy in unsullied elegance.
> The passage of the days could not affect them;
> Their freedom was guaranteed by Heaven and Earth.
> Black apes came in pairs,
> Looking most charming as they present fruit;
> White deer, bowing two by two,
> Thoughtfully offered flowers.

These old men were certainly living a free and happy life. "How about letting me play with you?" Monkey shouted at the top of his voice, and when the immortals saw him they hurried over to welcome him. There is a poem to prove it that goes:

> When the magic root of the manfruit tree was broken,
> The Great Sage visited the immortals in search of a cure.
> Winding their way through the vermillion mist, the Nine
>   Ancients
> Came out of the precious forest to greet him.

Monkey, who knew the Nine Ancients, said with a smile, "You nine brothers seem to be doing very nicely." "If you had stayed on straight and narrow in the old days, Great Sage," they replied, "and not wrecked the Heavenly Palace you would

be doing even better than we are. Now we hear that you have
reformed and are going West to visit the Buddha. How did
you manage the time off to come here?" Monkey told them how
he was searching for a formula to cure the tree. "What a terrible thing to do," they exclaimed in horror, "what a terrible
thing. We honestly have no cure at all." "In that case I must
take my leave of you."

The Nine Ancients tried to detain him with jasper wine and
jade lotus-root, but Monkey refused to sit down, and stayed on
his feet while he drank only one cup of wine and ate only one
piece of lotus-root. Then he hurried away from Yingzhou and
back to the Great Eastern Ocean. When he saw that Potaraka
was not far away, he brought his cloud down to land on the
Potara Crag, where he saw the Bodhisattva Guanyin expounding the scriptures and preaching the Buddha's Law to all the
great gods of heaven, Moksa, and the dragon maiden in the
Purple Bamboo Grove. A poem about it goes:

> *Thick the mists round the lofty city of the sea's mistress,*
> *And no end to the greater marvels to be seen.*
> *Her mysterious teachings went beyond everything,*
> *Revealing subtle meanings of the first importance.*
> *Through them the four kinds of holy ones made their*
>   *achievements,*
> *And the six types of mortals won emancipation.*
> *This Shaolin Temple really had the true flavour,*
> *With the scent of flowers and fruit and the trees all red.*

The Bodhisattva saw Monkey arrive and ordered the Great
Guardian God of the Mountain to go and welcome him. The
god emerged from the bamboo grove and shouted, "Where are
you going, Monkey?" "You bear monster," Monkey shouted
back, "how dare you address me as 'Monkey'? If I hadn't
spared your life that time you'd have been just a demon's corpse
on the Black Wind Mountain. Now you've joined the Bodhisattva, accepted enlightenment, and come to live on this
blessed island where you hear the Law being taught all the
time. Shouldn't you address me as 'sir'?" It was indeed thanks

to Monkey that the black bear had been enlightened and was now guarding the Bodhisattva's Potaraka as one of the great gods of heaven, so all he could do was to force a smile and say, "The ancients said, Great Sage, that a gentleman does not bear grudges. Why should you care about what you're called? Anyhow, the Bodhisattva has sent me to welcome you." Monkey then became grave and serious as he went into the Purple Bamboo Grove with the Great God and did obeisance to the Bodhisattva.

"How far has the Tang Priest got, Monkey?" she asked. "He has reached the Mountain of Infinite Longevity in the Western Continent of Cattle-gift," Monkey replied. "Have you met the Great Immortal Zhen Yuan who lives in the Wu-zhuang Temple on that mountain?" she asked. "As your disciple didn't meet the Great Immortal Zhen Yuan when I was in the Wuzhuang Temple," replied Monkey, bowing down to the ground, "I destroyed his manfruit tree and offended him. As a result my master is in a very difficult position and can make no progress." "You wretched ape," said the Bodhisattva angrily now that she knew about it, "you have no conscience at all. That manfruit tree of his is the life-root from the time when Heaven and Earth were separated, and Master Zhen Yuan is the Patriarch of the Earth's immortals, which means even I have to show him a certain respect. Why ever did you harm his tree?" Monkey bowed once more and said, "I really didn't know. He was away that day and there were only two immortal youths to look after us. When Pig heard that they had this fruit he wanted to try one, so I stole three for him and we had one each. They swore at us no end when they found out, so I lost my temper and knocked the tree over. When he came back the next day he chased us and caught us all up in his sleeve. We were tied up and flogged for a whole day. We got away that night but he caught up with us and put us in his sleeve again. All our escape attempts failed, so I promised him I'd put the tree right. I've been searching for a formula all over the seas and been to all three islands of immortals, but the gods and immortals are all useless, which is why I decided to come and worship you, Bodhisattva, and tell you all about it. I beg you in your mercy to grant me a formula so that I can save the Tang Priest and have him on his way west again as soon as possible." "Why didn't you come and see me earlier instead of searching the islands for it?" the Bodhisattva asked.

"I'm in luck," thought Monkey with delight when he heard this, "I'm in luck. The Bodhisattva must have a formula." He went up to her and pleaded for it again. "The sweet dew in this pure vase of mine," she said, "is an excellent cure for magic trees and plants." "Has it ever been tried out?" Monkey asked. "Yes," she said. "How?" he asked. "Some years ago Lord Lao Zi beat me at gambling," she replied, "and took my willow sprig away with him. He put it in his elixir-refining furnace and burnt it to a cinder before sending it back to me. I put it back in the vase, and a day and a night later it was as green and leafy as ever." "I'm really in luck," said Monkey, "really in luck. If it can bring a cinder back to life, something that has only been pushed over should be easy." The Bodhisattva instructed her subjects to look after the grove as she was going away for a while. Then she took up her vase, and her white parrot went in front singing while Monkey followed behind. As the poem goes,

> The jade-haired golden one is hard to describe to
> mortals;
> She truly is a compassionate deliverer.
> Although in aeons past she had known the spotless
> Buddha,
> Now she had acquired a human form.
> After several lives in the sea of suffering she had purified
> the waves,
> And in her heart there was no speck of dust.
> The sweet dew that had long undergone the miraculous
> Law
> Was bound to give the magic tree eternal life.

The Great Immortal and the Three Stars were still in lofty conversation when they saw Monkey bring his cloud down and

heard him shout, "The Bodhisattva's here. Come and welcome
her at once." The Three Stars and Master Zhen Yuan hurried
out with Sanzang and his disciples to greet her. On bringing
her cloud to a stop, she first talked with Master Zhen Yuan
and then greeted the Three Stars, after which she climbed to
her seat. Monkey then led the Tang Priest, Pig, and Friar Sand
out to do obeisance before the steps, and all the immortals in
the temple came to bow to her as well. "There's no need to
dither about, Great Immortal," said Monkey. "Get an incense
table ready at once and ask the Bodhisattva to cure that
whatever-it-is tree of yours." The Great Immortal Zhen Yuan
bowed to the Bodhisattva and thanked her: "How could I be
so bold as to trouble the Bodhisattva with my affairs?" "The
Tang Priest is my disciple, and Monkey has offended you, so it
is only right that I should make up for the loss of your priceless
tree." "In that case there is no need for you to refuse," said
the Three Stars. "May we invite you, Bodhisattva, to come
into our orchard and take a look?"

The Great Sage had an incense table set up and the orchard
swept, then he asked the Bodhisattva to lead the way. The
Three Stars followed behind. Sanzang, his disciples, and all the
immortals of the temple went into the orchard to look, and they
saw the tree lying on the ground with the earth torn open, its
roots laid bare, its leaves fallen and its branches withered.
"Put your hand out, Monkey," said the Bodhisattva, and
Brother Monkey stretched out his left hand. The Bodhisattva
dipped her willow spray into the sweet dew in her vase, then
used it to write a spell to revive the dead on the palm of
Monkey's hand. She told him to place it on the roots of the
tree until he saw water coming out. Monkey clenched his fist
and tucked it under the roots; before long a spring of clear
water began to form a pool. "That water must not be sullied
by vessels made of any of the Five Elements, so you will have
to scoop it out with a jade ladle. If you prop the tree up and
pour the water on it from the very top, its bark and trunk will
knit together, its leaves will sprout again, the branches will be
green once more, and the fruit will reappear." "Fetch a jade

ladle this moment, young Taoists," said Monkey. "We poor monks have no jade ladle in our destitute temple. We only have jade tea-bowls and wine-cups. Would they do?" "As long as they are jade and can scoop out water they will do," the Bodhisattva replied. "Bring them out and try." The Great Immortal then told some boys to fetch the twenty or thirty tea-bowls and the forty or fifty wine-cups and ladle the clear water out from under the roots. Monkey, Pig and Friar Sand put their shoulders under the tree, raised it upright, and banked it up with earth. Then they presented the sweet spring water cup by cup to the Bodhisattva, who sprinkled it lightly on the tree with her spray of willow and recited an incantation. When a little later the water had all been sprinkled on the tree the leaves really did become as dense and green as ever, and there were twenty-three manfruits growing there. Pure Wind and Bright Moon, the two immortal boys, said, "When the fruit disappeared the other day there were only twenty-two of them; so why is there an extra one now that it has come back to life?" "'Time shows the truth about a man'," Monkey replied. "I only stole three that day. The other one fell on the ground, and the local deity told me that this treasure always entered earth when it touched it. Pig accused me of taking it as a bit of extra for myself and blackened my reputation, but at long last the truth has come out."

"The reason why I did not use vessels made from the Five Elements was because I knew that this kind of fruit is allergic to them," said the Bodhisattva. The Great Immortal, now extremely happy, had the golden rod fetched at once and knocked down ten of the fruits. He invited the Bodhisattva and the Three Stars to come to the main hall of the temple to take part a Manfruit Feast to thank them for their labours. All the junior immortals arranged tables, chairs, and cinnabar bowls. The Bodhisattva was asked to take the seat of honour with the Three Stars on her left, the Tang Priest on her right, and Master Zhen Yuan facing her as the host. They ate one fruit each, and there are some lines about it:

> *In the ancient earthly paradise on the Mountain of In-*
> *   finite Longevity*
> *The manfruit ripens once in nine thousand years.*
> *When the magic roots were bared and the branches dead,*
> *The sweet dew brought leaves and fruit back to life.*
> *The Three Stars were happy to meet old friend;*
> *It was fated that the four monks would encounter one*
> *   another.*
> *Now that they had eaten the manfruit at this feast,*
> *They would all enjoy everlasting youth.*

The Bodhisattva and the Three Stars ate one each, as did the Tang Priest, who realized at last that this was an immortal's treasure, and Monkey, Pig and Friar Sand. Master Zhen Yuan had one to keep them company and the immortals of the temple divided the last one between them. Monkey thanked the Bodhisattva, who went back to Potaraka, and saw the Three Stars off on their journey home to the island of Penglai. Master Zhen Yuan set out some non-alcoholic wine and made Monkey his sworn brother. This was a case of "if you don't fight you can't make friends", and their two households were now united. That night Sanzang and his disciples went to bed feeling very happy. That venerable priest had now

> *Been lucky enough to eat the Grass-returning Cinnabar,*
> *Gaining long life and resistance to fiends and monsters.*

Listen to the next instalment to hear how they took their leave the next day.

CHAPTER TWENTY-SEVEN

The corpse fiend thrice tricks
Tang Sanzang;
The holy monk angrily dismisses the
Handsome Monkey King.

At dawn the next day Sanzang and his three disciples packed
their things before setting off. Now that Master Zhen Yuan had
made Monkey his sworn brother and was finding him so con-
genial, he did not want to let him go, so he entertained him for
another five or six days. Sanzang had really become a new man,
and was livelier and healthier now that he had eaten the Grass-
returning Cinnabar. His determination to fetch the scriptures
was too strong to let him waste any more time, so there was
nothing for it but to be on their way.

Soon after they had set out again, master and disciples saw
a high mountain in front of them. "I'm afraid that the mountain
ahead may be too steep for the horse," Sanzang said, "so we
must think this over carefully." "Don't worry, master," said
Monkey, "we know how to cope." He went ahead of the horse
with his cudgel over his shoulder and cleared a path up to the
top of the cliff. He saw no end of

> Row upon row of craggy peaks,
> Twisting beds of torrents.
> Tigers and wolves were running in packs,
> Deer and muntjac moving in herds.
> Countless river-deer darted around,
> And the mountain was covered with fox and hare.
> Thousand-foot pythons,
> Ten-thousand-fathom snakes;

The great pythons puffed out murky clouds,
The enormous snakes breathed monstrous winds.
Brambles and thorns spread beside the paths;
Pines and cedars stood elegant on the ridge.
There were wild fig-trees wherever the eye could see,
And sweet-scented flowers as far as the horizon.
The mountain's shadow fell north of the ocean,
The clouds parted south of the handle of the Dipper.
The towering cliffs were as ancient as the Primal Es-
    sence,
The majestic crags cold in the sunlight.

Sanzang was immediately terrified, so Monkey resorted to some of his tricks. He whirled his iron cudgel and roared, at which all the wolves, snakes, tigers and leopards fled. They then started up the mountain, and as they were crossing a high ridge Sanzang said to Monkey, "Monkey, I've been hungry all day, so would you please go and beg some food for us somewhere." "You aren't very bright, Master," Monkey replied with a grin. "We're on a mountain with no village or inn for many miles around. Even if we had money there would be nowhere to buy food, so where am I to go and beg for it?" Sanzang felt cross, so he laid into Monkey. "You ape," he said, "don't you remember how you were crushed by the Buddha in a stone cell under the Double Boundary Mountain, where you could talk but not walk? It was I who saved your life, administered the monastic vows to you, and made you my disciple. How dare you be such a slacker? Why aren't you prepared to make an effort?" "I always make an effort," said Monkey. "I'm never lazy." "If you're such a hard worker, go and beg some food for us. I can't manage on an empty stomach. Besides, with the noxious vapours on this mountain we'll never reach the Thunder Monastery." "Please don't be angry, master, and stop talking I know your obstinate character — if I'm too disobedient you'll say that spell. You'd better dismount and sit here while I find somebody and beg for some food."

Monkey leapt up into the clouds with a single jump, and

shading his eyes with his hand he looked around. Unfortunately he could see nothing in any direction except emptiness. There was no village or house or any other sign of human habitation among the countless trees. After looking for a long time he made out a high mountain away to the south. On its southern slopes was a bright red patch. Monkey brought his cloud down and said, "Master, there's something to eat." Sanzang asked him what it was. "There's no house around here where we could ask for food," Monkey replied, "but there's a patch of red on a mountain to the south that I'm sure must be ripe wild peaches. I'll go and pick some — they'll fill you up." "A monk who has peaches to eat is a lucky man," said Sanzang. Monkey picked up his bowl and leapt off on a beam of light. Just watch as he flashes off in a somersault, a whistling gust of cold air. Within a moment he was picking peaches on the southern mountain.

There is a saying that goes, "If the mountain is high it's bound to have fiends; if the ridge is steep spirits will live there." This mountain did indeed have an evil spirit who was startled by Monkey's appearance. It strode through the clouds on a negative wind, and on seeing the venerable Sanzang on the ground below thought happily, "What luck, what luck. At home they've been talking for years about a Tang Monk from the East who's going to fetch the Great Vehicle; he's a reincarnation of Golden Cicada, and has an Original Body that has been purified through ten lives. Anyone who eats a piece of his flesh will live for ever. And today, at last, he's here." The evil spirit went forward to seize him, but the sight of the two great generals to Sanzang's left and right made it frightened to close in on him. Who, it wondered, were they? They were in fact Pig and Friar Sand, and for all that their powers were nothing extraordinary, Pig was really Marshal Tian Peng while Friar Sand was the Great Curtain-lifting General. It was because their former awe-inspiring qualities had not yet been dissipated that the fiend did not close in. "I'll try a trick on them and see what happens," the spirit said to itself.

The splendid evil spirit stopped its negative wind in a hollow and changed itself into a girl with a face as round as the

moon and as pretty as a flower. Her brow was clear and her
eyes beautiful; her teeth were white and her lips red. In her
left hand she held a blue earthenware pot and in her right a
green porcelain jar. She headed east towards the Tang Priest.

> *The holy monk rested his horse on the mountain,*
> *And suddenly noticed a pretty girl approaching.*
> *The green sleeves over her jade fingers lightly billowed;*
> *Golden lotus feet peeped under her trailing skirt.*
> *The beads of sweat on her powdered face were dew on*
>   *a flower;*
> *Her dusty brow was a willow in a mist.*
> *Carefully and closely he watched her*
> *As she came right up to him.*

"Pig, Friar Sand," said Sanzang when he saw her, "don't
you see somebody coming although Monkey said that this was
a desolate and uninhabited place?" "You and Friar Sand stay
sitting here while I go and take a look." The blockhead laid
down his rake, straightened his tunic, put on the airs of a gentleman, and stared at the girl as he greeted her. Although he
had not been sure from a distance, he could now see clearly that
the girl had

> *Bones of jade under skin as pure as ice,*
> *A creamy bosom revealed by her neckline.*
> *Her willow eyebrows were black and glossy,*
> *And silver stars shone from her almond eyes.*
> *She was as graceful as the moon,*
> *As pure as the heavens.*
> *Her body was like a swallow in a willow-tree,*
> *Her voice like an oriole singing in the wood.*
> *An opening peony displaying her Charm,*
> *She was wild apple-blossom enmeshing the sun.*

When the idiot Pig saw how beautiful she was his earthly
desires were aroused, and he could not hold back the reckless
words that came to his lips. "Where are you going, Bodhisattva," he said, "and what's that you're holding?" Although she

was obviously an evil fiend he could not realize it. "Venerable sir," the girl replied at once, "this blue pot is full of tasty rice, and the green jar contains fried gluten-balls. I've come here specially to fulfil a vow to feed monks." Pig was thoroughly delighted to hear this. He came tumbling back at breakneck speed and said to Sanzang, "Master, 'Heaven rewards the good'. When you sent my elder brother off begging because you felt hungry, that ape went fooling around somewhere picking peaches. Besides, too many peaches turn your stomach and give you the runs. Don't you see that this girl is coming to feed us monks?" "You stupid idiot," replied Sanzang, who was not convinced, "we haven't met a single decent person in this direction, so where could anyone come from to feed monks?" "What's she then, master?" said Pig.

When Sanzang saw her he sprang to his feet, put his hands together in front of his chest, and said, "Bodhisattva, where is your home? Who are you? What vow brings you here to feed monks?" Although she was obviously an evil spirit, the venerable Sanzang could not see it either. On being asked about her background by Sanzang, the evil spirit immediately produced a fine-sounding story with which to fool him. "This mountain, which snakes and wild animals won't go near, is called White Tiger Ridge," she said. "Our home lies due west from here at the foot of it. My mother and father live there, and they are devout people who read the scriptures and feed monks from far and near. As they had no son, they asked Heaven to bless them. When I was born they wanted to marry me off to a good family, but then they decided to find me a husband who would live in our home to look after them in their old age and see them properly buried." "Bodhisattva, what you say can't be right," replied Sanzang. "The *Analects* say, 'When father and mother are alive, do not go on long journeys; if you have to go out, have a definite aim.' As your parents are at home and have found you a husband, you should let him fulfil your vow for you. Why ever are you walking in the mountains all by yourself, without even a servant? This is no way for a lady to behave." The girl smiled and produced a smooth reply at once: "My husband is hoeing with some of our retainers in a hollow in the north of the mountain, reverend sir, and I am taking them this food I've cooked. As it's July and all the crops are ripening nobody can be spared to run errands, and my parents are old, so I'm taking it there myself. Now that I have met you three monks from so far away, I would like to give you this food as my parents are so pious. I hope you won't refuse our paltry offering." "It's very good of you," said Sanzang, "but one of my disciples has gone to pick some fruit and will be back soon, so we couldn't eat any of your food. Besides, if we ate your food your husband might be angry with you when he found out, and we would get into trouble too." As the Tang Priest was refusing to eat the food, the girl put on her most charming expression and said, "My parents' charity to monks is nothing compared to my husband's, master. He is a religious man whose lifelong pleasure has been repairing bridges, mending roads, looking after the aged, and helping the poor. When he hears that I have given you this food, he'll love me more passionately than ever." Sanzang still declined to eat it. Pig was beside himself. Twisting his lips into a pout, he muttered indignantly, "Of all the monks on earth there can't be another as soft in the head as our master. He won't eat ready-cooked food when there are only three of us to share it between. He's waiting for that ape to come back, and then we'll have to split it four ways." Without allowing any more discussion he tipped the pot towards his mouth and was just about to eat.

At just this moment Brother Monkey was somersaulting back with his bowl full of the peaches he had picked on the southern mountain. When he saw with the golden pupils in his fiery eyes that the girl was an evil spirit, he put the bowl down, lifted his cudgel, and was going to hit her on the head when the horrified Sanzang held him back and said, "Who do you think you're going to hit?" "That girl in front of you is no good," he replied. "She's an evil spirit trying to make a fool of you." "In the old days you had a very sharp eye, you ape," Sanzang said, "but this is nonsense. This veritable Bodhisattva is feeding us with the best of motives, so how can you call her an evil spirit?" "You wouldn't be able to tell, Master," said Monkey with a grin. "When I was an evil monster in the Water Curtain Cave I used to do that if I wanted a meal of human flesh. I would turn myself into gold and silver, or a country mansion, or liquor, or a pretty girl. Whoever was fool enough to be besotted with one of these would fall in love with me, and I would lure them into the cave, where I did what I wanted with them. Sometimes I ate them steamed and sometimes boiled, and what I couldn't finish I used to dry in the sun against a rainy day. If I'd been slower getting here, Master, you'd have fallen into her snare and she'd have finished you off." The Tang Priest refused to believe him and maintained that she was a good person. "I know you, Master," said Monkey. "Her pretty face must have made you feel randy. If that's the way you feel, tell Pig to fell a few trees and send Friar Sand look off to for some grass. I'll be the carpenter, and well build you a hut here that you and the girl can use as your bridal chamber. We can all go our own ways. Woudn't marriage be a worthwhile way of living? Why bother plodding on to fetch some scriptures or other?" Sanzang, who had always been such a soft and virtuous man, was unable to take this. He was so embarrassed that he blushed from his shaven pate to his ears.

While Sanzang was feeling so embarrassed, Monkey flared up again and struck at the evil spirit's face. The fiend, who knew a trick or two, used a magic way of abandoning its body: when it saw Monkey's cudgel coming it braced itself and fled, leaving a false corpse lying dead on the ground. Sanzang shook with terror and said to himself, "That monkey is utterly outrageous. Despite all my good advice he will kill people for no reason at all." "Don't be angry, Master," said Monkey. "Come and see what's in her pot." Friar Sand helped Sanzang over to look, and he saw that so far from containing tasty rice it was full of maggots with long tails. The jar had held not gluten-balls but frogs and toads, which were now jumping around on the ground. Sanzang was now beginning to believe Monkey. This was not enough, however, to prevent a furious Pig from deliberately making trouble by saying, "Master, that girl was a local countrywoman who happened to meet us while she was taking some food to the fields. There's no reason to think that she was an evil spirit. My elder brother was trying his club out on her, and he killed her by mistake. He's deliberately trying to trick us by magicking the food into those things because he's afraid you'll recite the Band-tightening Spell. He's fooled you into not saying it."

This brought the blindness back on Sanzang, who believed these trouble-making remarks and made the magic with his hand as he recited the spell. "My head's aching, my head's aching," Monkey said. "Stop, please stop. Tell me off if you like." "I've nothing to say to you," replied Sanzang. "A man of religion should always help others, and his thoughts should always be virtuous. When sweeping the floor you must be careful not to kill any ants, and to spare the moth you should put gauze round your lamp. Why do you keep murdering people? If you are going to kill innocent people like that there is no point in your going to fetch the scriptures. Go back!" "Where am I to go back to?" Monkey asked. "I won't have you as my disciple any longer," said Sanzang. "If you won't have me as your disciple," Monkey said, "I'm afraid you may never reach the Western Heaven." "My destiny is in Heaven's hands," replied Sanzang. "If some evil spirit is fated to cook me, he will; and there's no way of getting out of it. But if I'm not to be eaten, will you be able to extend my life? Be off with you at once." "I'll go if I must," said Monkey, "but I'll never have repaid your kindness to me." "What kindness have I ever done you?" Sanzang asked. Monkey knelt down and kowtowed. "When I wrecked the Heavenly Palace," he said, "I put myself in a very dangerous position, and the Buddha crushed me under the Double Boundary Mountain. Luckily the Bodhisattva Guanyin administered the vows to me, and you, Master, released me, so if I don't go with you to the Western Heaven I'll look like a 'scoundrel who doesn't return a kindness, with a name that will be cursed for ever'." As Sanzang was a compassionate and holy monk this desperate plea from Monkey persuaded him to relent. "In view of what you say I'll let you off this time, but don't behave so disgracefully again. If you are ever as wicked as that again I shall recite that spell twenty times over." "Make it thirty if you like," replied Monkey. "I shan't hit anyone else." With that he helped Sanzang mount the horse and offered him some of the peaches he had picked. After eating a few the Tang Priest felt less hungry for the time being.

The evil spirit rose up into the air when it had saved itself from being killed by Monkey's cudgel. Gnashing its teeth in the clouds, it thought of Monkey with silent hatred: "Now I know that those magical powers of his that I've been hearing about for years are real. The Tang Priest didn't realize who I was and would have eaten the food. If he'd so much as leant forward to smell it I could have seized him, and he would have been mine. But that Monkey turned up, wrecked my plan, and almost killed me with his club. If I spare that monk now I'll have gone to all that trouble for nothing, so I'll have another go at tricking him."

The splendid evil spirit landed its negative cloud, shook itself, and changed into an old woman in her eighties who was weeping as she hobbled along leaning on a bamboo stick with a crooked handle. "This is terrible, Master," exclaimed Pig with horror at the sight of her. "Her mother's come to look for her." "For whom?" asked the Tang Priest. "It must be her daughter that my elder brother killed," said Pig. "This must be the girl's mother looking for her." "Don't talk nonsense," said Monkey. "That girl was eighteen and this old woman is eighty. How could she possibly have had a child when she was over sixty? She must be a fake. Let me go and take a look." The splendid Monkey hurried over to examine her and saw that the monster had

> Turned into an old woman
> With temples as white as frozen snow.
> Slowly she stumbled along the road,
> Making her way in fear and trembling.
> Her body was weak and emaciated,
> Her face like a withered leaf of cabbage.
> Her cheekbone was twisted upwards,
> While the ends of her lips went down.

How can old age compare with youth?
Her face was as creased as a pleated bag.

Realizing that she was an evil spirit, Monkey did not wait to argue about it, but raised his cudgel and struck at her head. Seeing the blow coming, the spirit braced itself again and extracted its true essence once more. The false corpse sprawled dead beside the path. Sanzang was so horrified that he fell off the horse and lay beside the path, reciting the Band-tightening Spell twenty times over. Poor Monkey's head was squeezed so hard that it looked like a narrow-waisted gourd. The pain was unbearable, and he rolled over towards his master to plead, "Stop, Master. Say whatever you like." "I have nothing to say," Sanzang replied. "If a monk does good he will not fall into hell. Despite all my preaching you still commit murder. How can you? No sooner have you killed one person than you kill another. It's an outrage." "She was an evil spirit," Monkey replied. "Nonsense, you ape," said the Tang Priest, "as if there could be so many monsters! You haven't the least intention of reforming, and you are a deliberate murderer. Be off with you." "Are you sending me away again, Master?" Monkey asked. "I'll go if I must, but there's one thing I won't agree to." "What," Sanzang asked, "would that be?" "Master," Pig put in, "he wants the baggage divided between you and him. He's been a monk with you for several years, and hasn't suceeded in winning a good reward. You can't let him go away empty-handed. Better give him a worn-out tunic and a tattered hat from the bundle."

This made Monkey jump with fury. "I'll get you, you long-snouted moron," he said. "I've been a true Buddhist with no trace of covetousness or greed. I certainly don't want a share of the baggage." "If you're neither covetous nor greedy," said Sanzang, "why won't you go away?" "To be quite honest with you, Master," he replied, "when I lived in the Water Curtain Cave on the Mountain of Flowers and Fruit and knew all the great heroes, I won the submission of seventy-two other demon kings and had forty-seven thousand minor demons under me. I used to wear a crown of purple gold and a yellow robe with a belt of the finest jade. I had cloud-treading shoes on my feet and held an as-you-will gold-banded cudgel in my hands. I really was somebody then. But when I attained enlightenment and repented, I shaved my head and took to the Buddhist faith as your disciple. I couldn't face my old friends if I went back with this golden band round my head. So if you don't want me any longer, Master, please say the band-loosening spell and I'll take it off and give it back to you. I'll gladly agree to you putting it round someone else's head. As I've been your disciple for so long, surely you can show me this kindness." Sanzang was deeply shocked. "Monkey," he said, "the Bodhisattva secretly taught me the Band-tightening Spell, but not a band-loosening one." "In that case you'll have to let me come with you," Monkey replied. "Get up then," said Sanzang, feeling that he had no option, "I'll let you off again just this once. But you must never commit another murder." "I never will," said Monkey, "never again." He helped his master mount the horse and led the way forward.

The evil spirit, who had not been killed when hit the second time by Monkey either, was full of admiration as it floated in mid-air. "What a splendid Monkey King," it thought, "and what sharp eyes. He saw who I was through both my transformations. Those monks are travelling fast, and once they're over the mountain and fifteen miles to the west they'll be out of my territory. Any other fiends and monsters who catch them will be laughing till their mouths split, and I'll be heartbroken with sorrow. I'll have to have another go at tricking them." The excellent evil spirit brought its negative wind down to the mountainside and with one shake turned itself into an old man.

> His hair was as white as Ancient Peng's,
> His temples as hoary as the Star of Longevity.
> Jade rang in his ears,
> And his eyes swam with golden stars.
>
> He leant on a dragon-headed stick,
> And wore a cloak of crane feathers.

In his hands he fingered prayer-beads
While reciting Buddhist sutras.

When Sanzang saw him from the back of his horse he said with great delight, "Amitabha Buddha! The West is indeed a blessed land. That old man is forcing himself to recite scriptures although he can hardly walk." "Master," said Pig, "don't be so nice about him. He's going to give us trouble." "What do you mean?" Sanzang asked. "My elder brother has killed the daughter and the old woman, and this is the old man coming to look for them. If we fall into his hands you'll have to pay with your life. It'll be the death penalty for you, and I'll get a long sentence for being your accomplice. Friar Sand will be exiled for giving the orders. That elder brother will disappear by magic, and we three will have to carry the can." "Don't talk such nonsense, you moron," said Monkey. "You're terrifying the master. Wait while I go and have another look." Hiding the cudgel about his person he went up to the monster and said, "Where are you going, venerable sir? And why are you reciting scriptures as you walk along?" The monster, failing to recognize the key man, thought that the Great Sage Monkey was merely a passer-by and said, "Holy sir, my family has lived here for generations, and all my life I have done good deeds, fed monks, read the scriptures, and repeated the Buddha's name. As fate has it I have no son, only a daughter, and she lives at home with her husband. She went off to the fields with food early this morning, and I'm afraid she may have been eaten by a tiger. My wife went out to look for her, and she hasn't come back either. I've no idea what's happened to them, so I've come to search for them. If they have died, I shall just have to gather their bones and take them back for a decent burial." "I'm a master of disguise," replied Monkey with a grin, "so don't try to pull the wool over my eyes. You can't fool me. I know that you're an evil spirit." The monster was speechless with fright. Monkey brandished his cudgel and thought, "If I don't kill him he'll make a getaway; but if I do, my master will say that spell. Yet if I don't kill him," he went on to reflect, "I'll take a lot of

thought and effort to rescue the master when this monster seizes
some other chance to carry him off. The best thing is to kill him.
If I kill him with the cudgel the master will say the spell, but
then 'even a vicious tiger doesn't eat her own cubs'. I'll be able
to get round my master with my smooth tongue and some well-
chosen words." The splendid Great Sage uttered a spell and
called out to the local deities and the gods of the mountain,
"This evil spirit has tried to trick my master three times, and I'm
now going to kill it. I want you to be witnesses in the air around
me. Don't leave!" Hearing this command, the gods all had to
obey and watch from the clouds. The Great Sage raised his
cudgel and struck down the monster. Now, at last, it was dead.

The Tang Priest was shaking with terror on the back of his
horse, unable to speak. Pig stood beside him and said with a
laugh, "That Monkey's marvellous, isn't he! He's gone mad.
He's killed three people in a few hours' journey." The Tang
Priest was just going to say the spell when Monkey threw himself
in front of his horse and called out, "Don't say it, Master, don't
say it. Come and have a look at it." It was now just a pile of
dusty bones. "He's only just been killed, Wukong," Sanzang said
in astonishment, "so why has he turned into a skeleton?" "It was
a demon corpse with magic powers that used to deceive people
and destroy them. Now that I've killed it, it's reverted to its
original form. The writing on her backbone says that she's called
'Lady White Bone'." Sanzang was convinced, but Pig had to
make trouble again. "Master," he said, "he's afraid that you'll
say those words because he killed him with a vicious blow from
his cudgel, and so he's made him look like this to fool you."
The Tang Priest, who really was gullible, now believed Pig, and
he started to recite the spell. Monkey, unable to stop the pain,
knelt beside the path and cried, "Stop, stop. Say whatever it is
you have to say," "Baboon," said Sanzang, "I have nothing more
to say to you. If a monk acts rightly he will grow daily but in-
visibly, like grass in a garden during the spring, whereas an
evildoer will be imperceptibly worn away day by day like a
whetstone. You have killed three people, one after the other, in
this wild and desolate place, and there is nobody here to find

you out or bring a case against you. But if you go to a city or some other crowded place and start laying about you with that murderous cudgel, we'll be in big trouble and there will be no escape for us. Go back!" "You're wrong to hold it against me, Master," Monkey replied, "as that wretch was obviously an evil monster set on murdering you. But so far from being grateful that I've saved you by killing it, you would have to believe that idiot's tittle-tattle and keep sending me away. As the saying goes, you should never have to do anything more than three times. I'd be a low and shameless creature if I didn't go now. I'll go, I'll go all right, but who will you have left to look after you?" "Damned ape," Sanzang replied, "you get ruder and ruder. You seem to think that you're the only one. What about Pig and Friar Sand? Aren't they people?"

On hearing him say that Pig and Friar Sand were suitable people too, Monkey was very hurt. "That's a terrible thing to hear, Master," he said. "When you left Chang'an Liu Boqin helped you on your way, and when you reached the Double Boundary Mountain you saved me and I took you as my master. I've gone into ancient caves and deep forests capturing monsters and demons. I won Pig and Friar Sand over, and I've had a very hard time of it. But today you've turned stupid and you're sending me back. When these birds have all been shot this bow is put away, and when the hares have all been killed the hounds are stewed.' Oh well! If only you hadn't got that Band-tightening Spell." "I won't recite it again," said Sanzang. "Don't be so sure," replied Monkey. "If you're ever beset by evil monsters from whom you can't escape, and if Pig and Friar Sand can't save you, then you'll think of me and you won't be able to stop yourself from saying the spell again, my head will ache even if I'm many tens of thousands of miles away. But if I do come back to you, never say it again."

The Tang Priest grew angrier and angrier as Monkey talked on, and tumbling off his horse he told Friar Sand to take paper and brush from the pack. Then he fetched some water from a stream, rubbed the inkstick on a stone, wrote out a letter of dismissal, and handed it to Monkey. "Here it is in writing," he

said. "I don't want you as my disciple a moment longer. If I
ever see you again may I fall into the Avichi Hell." Monkey
quickly took the document and said, "There's no need to swear
an oath, Master. I'm off." He folded the paper up and put it
in his sleeve, then tried once more to mollify Sanzang. "Master,"
he said, "I've spent some time with you, and I've also been
taught by the Bodhisattva. Now I'm being fired in the middle of
the journey, when I've achieved nothing. Please sit down and
accept my homage, then I won't feel so bad about going." The
Tang Priest turned away and would not look at him, muttering,
"I am a good monk, and I won't accept the respects of bad people like you." Seeing that Sanzang was refusing to face him, the
Great Sage used magic to give himself extra bodies. He blew a
magic breath on three hairs plucked from the back of his head
and shouted, "Change!" They turned into three more Monkeys,
making a total of four with the real one, and surrounding the
master on all four sides they kowtowed to him. Unable to avoid
them by dodging to left or right, Sanzang had to accept their
respects.

The Great Sage jumped up, shook himself, put the hairs
back, and gave Friar Sand these instructions: "You are a good
man, my brother, so mind you stop Pig from talking nonsense
and be very careful on the journey. If at any time evil spirits
capture our master, you tell them that I'm his senior disciple.
The hairy devils of the West have heard of my powers and
won't dare to harm him." "I am a good monk," said the Tang
Priest, "and I'd never mention the name of a person as bad as
you. Go back." As his master refused over and over again to
change his mind Monkey had nothing for it but to go. Look at
him:

> Holding back his tears he bowed goodbye to his master,
> Then sadly but with care he gave instructions to Friar
>   Sand.
> His head pushed the hillside grass apart,
> His feet kicked over the creepers on the ground.
> He spun between Heaven and earth like a wheel;

At flying over mountains and seas none could beat him.
Within an instant no sign of him could be seen;
He retraced his whole journey in a flash.

Holding back his anger, Monkey left his master and went straight back to the Water Curtain Cave on the Mountain of Flowers and Fruit on his somersault cloud. He was feeling lonely and miserable when he heard the sound of water. When he looked around from where he was in mid-air, he realized that it was the waves of the Eastern Sea. The sight of it reminded him of the Tang Priest, and he could not stop the tears from rolling down his cheeks. He stopped his cloud and stayed there a long time before going. If you don't know what happened when he went, listen to the explanation in the next instalment.

CHAPTER TWENTY-EIGHT

On the Mountain of Flowers and Fruit
the devils rise;
Sanzang meets a monster in the
Black Pine Forest.

The Great Sage was gazing at the Eastern Ocean, sighing sadly at being driven away by the Tang Priest. "I haven't been this way for five hundred years," he said. As he looked at he sea,

> *Vast were the misty waters,*
> *Boundless the mighty waves.*
> *The vast and misty waters stretched to the Milky Way;*
> *The boundless and mighty waves were linked to the*
>   *earth's arteries.*
> *The tides came surging,*
> *The waters swirled around.*
> *The surging tides*
> *Roared like the thunder in spring;*
> *The whirling tides*
> *Howled like a summer hurricane.*
> *The blessed ancients riding on dragons*
> *Surely must have frowned as they came and went;*
> *Immortal youths flying on cranes*
> *Certainly felt anxious as they passed above.*
> *There were no villages near the coast,*
> *And scarcely a fishing boat beside the sea.*
> *The waves' crests were like immemorial snows;*
> *The wind made autumn in July.*
> *Wild beasts roamed at will,*
> *Shore birds bobbed in the waves.*
> *There was no fisherman in sight,*

And the only sound was the screaming of the gulls.
Though the fish were happy at the bottom of the sea,
Anxiety gripped the wild geese overhead.

With a spring Monkey leapt over the Eastern Ocean and was soon back at the Mountain of Flowers and Fruit. As he brought his cloud down and gazed around him, he saw that all the vegetation on the mountain had gone and the mists had disappeared completely. The peaks had collapsed and the woods were shrivelled and dead. Do you know why? It was because when Monkey was taken to the upper world after wrecking the Heavenly Palace, the god Erlang and the Seven Brothers of Meishan had burnt it all down. This made the Great Sage even more miserable than ever. There is a poem in the ancient style about the ruined landscape of the mountain:

I came back to the immortal mountain in tears;
On seeing it, my sorrow is doubled.
I used to think that it was safe from harm,
But now I know that it has been destroyed.

If only Erlang had not defeated me;
Curse you for bullying me like that.
I shall dig up the graves of your ancestors,
And not stop at destroying their tombs.

Gone, gone, the mists that filled the sky;
Scattered the winds and clouds that covered the earth.
On the eastern ridge the tiger's roar is silent.
The apes howl no more on the western mountain.

No sign of hare or fox in the northern valley;
No shadow of a deer in the southern ravine.
The blue rock was burnt to a thousad cinders,
The jade-green sands are now just mud.

The lofty pines outside the cave all lean askew;
Few are the cypresses before the cliff.
Cedar, fir, locust, chestnut, juniper, and sandalwood —
*   all are burnt.*
Peach, apricot, plum, pear, and jujube — gone every
*   one,*

How are the silkworms to be fed without cudrania and
   mulberry?
The birds cannot nest with no willow or bamboo.
The crags and boulders have been turned to dust,
The springs have dried up, and weeds grow in the
   stream-beds.

The earth is black in front of the cliff, and no orchids
   grow.
Creepers crawl in the brown mud by the path.
Where did the birds of yesterday fly?
To what other mountain did the animals go?

Leopards and pythons dislike this ruined spot;
Cranes and snakes avoid the desolation.
My criminal thoughts of those days past
Brought on the disaster of today.

The Great Sage, deep in gloom, heard a sound from a thorny
hollow in front of a grassy slope as seven or eight little monkeys
leapt out, rushed up to him, and surrounded him kowtowing.
"Great Sage," they shouted, "have you come home today?"
"Why aren't you playing?" the Handsome Monkey King asked
them. "Why were you all hiding? I was here for ages without
seeing a sign of you. Why?" Tears poured from the eyes of the
other monkeys as they told him, "Ever since you were taken up
to Heaven as a prisoner, Great Sage, the hunters have given us
a terrible time. What with their powerful bows and crossbows,
their brown falcons and evil hounds, their nets, loops, hooks,
and spears, we are all too afraid for our lives to come out and
play. We have to hide deep in our caves and keep away from
our usual dens. When we're hungry we filch some grass from
the hillside, and we drink the fresh spring water from the
stream. We've only just heard you, Great Sage, Your Majesty,
and come out to greet you. Please, please help us." The Great
Sage felt more depressed than ever on hearing this, and he went
on to ask, "How many of you are there left on this mountain?"
"Only about a thousand of all ages." "In the old days," said the

Great Sage, "I had forty-seven thousand demons. Where have they all gone now?" "After you went away the god Erlang set fire to the mountain and most of us were killed in the blaze. Some of us squatted at the bottom of wells, or hid in gullies, or took cover under the iron bridge, and escaped with our lives. When the fire burnt itself out and the smoke cleared we came out to find that there were no more plants or fruit to feed us. Life was almost impossible, so half of the survivors went away. The rest of us have been having a very lean time on this mountain, and half of those left have been caught by hunters in the past two years." "What do they do that for?" Monkey asked. "We hate the very name 'hunters'," the other monkeys replied. "They shoot us with arrows, spear us, poison us, and beat us death. They take us away to skin us and cut the flesh from our bones before boiling us in soy sauce, steaming us with vinegar, frying us in oil, or stir-cooking us with salt. Then they eat us to help their rice down. Those of us who are caught in nets or loops are taken away alive and made to dance in a ring, act, do somersaults and handstand, play drums and gongs in the street, and make fools of themselves in every posisble way."

"Who's in charge in the cave?" asked Monkey, now thoroughly angry. "Marshals Ma and Liu and Generals Ben and Ba," they replied, "are still in command." "Then tell them that I'm here," said Monkey. The junior fiends rushed in to report, "His Majesty the Great Sage has come home." As soon as they heard this Ma, Liu, Ben and Ba rushed out to kowtow and welcome him into the cave. The Great Sage sat in the middle of it, with his fiendish hosts prostrating themselves before him and asking, "Why have you come back to your mountain instead of going to the West, Your Majesty? We heard recently that you had come back to life and were escorting the Tang Priest to fetch scriptures from the Western Heaven." "What you don't know, my little ones," said Monkey, "is that Sanzang can't tell a good man when he sees one. I captured monsters and demons for him all along the way, and I used every one of my magical powers to kill evil spirits for him. But he called me a murderer and wouldn't have me as his disciple any longer. He sent me

back here and gave me a letter of dismissal to certify that he'll
never employ me again."

All the monkeys clapped their hands for joy. "What luck,"
they said, "what luck. Now you're home again after being some
kind of monk or other, you can be our leader for the next few
years." "Lay on some coconut toddy at once to welcome His
Majesty back," someone ordered. "No," said the Great Sage,
"don't let's drink. How often do the hunters come to our mountain?" "Great Sage," replied Marshals Ma and Liu, "they come
here in all seasons and harass us for days on end." "Then why
haven't they come today?" Monkey asked. "They'll be here soon
enough," replied the marshals. "Little ones," Monkey ordered,
"you are all to go out, gather those broken cinders that were
burnt brittle in the fire, and pile them up. I want twenty to
thirty or fifty to sixty in a pile. I have a use for them." Like a
swarm of bees the little monkeys rushed around making piles
all over the place. When Monkey saw them he said, "Go and
hide in the cave, little ones, while I do some magic."

When the Great Sage went up to the mountain peak to look
around he saw over a thousand men with horses approaching
from the south. They were beating drums and gongs, and they
all had falcons, hounds, swords or spears. Examining them closely the Monkey King saw that they were most menacing — fine
lads and brave ones.

> With fox skins over their shoulders,
> And brocade covering their chests.
> Their quivers were full of wolf-fanged arrows,
> And carved bows hung by their legs.
>
> The men were like tigers that comb the hills,
> The horses like ravine-leaping dragons.
> They came in hordes, leading their hounds,
> And their arms were packed with falcons.
>
> In thornwood baskets they carried muskets,
> And powerful eagles were fastened to their belts,
> They had sticky poles by the hundred
> And bare forks by the thousand.

Bull-headed nets blocked the paths;
Their knotted ropes were like demon kings.
As they all roared their ferocious cries
They swarmed over the hill like the stars in the sky.

The Great Sage was furious at the sight of them spreading all over his mountain. He made a spell with his fist, muttered the words that went with it, breathed in a mouthful of air from the quarter that the winds came from, and puffed it out again. It was now a hurricane, a splendid hurricane,

Picking up the dust and earth,
Blowing down trees and whole forests.
Waves reared up as high as mountains,
As they beat in thousands upon the shore.
Heaven and Earth were thrown into gloom,
Sun and moon cast into darkness.
One gust shook the pines with a tiger's roar,
Howling like a dragon through the bamboo.
Heaven belched angrily through all its orifices,
As flying dirt and stones brought injury and death.

The hurricane that the Great Sage had called up made the piles of broken stone whirl wildly around, and the thousand men with their horses were reduced to a pathetic state.

The aconite was smashed to pieces by the stones,
While the flying dirt injured all the sea horses.
Ginseng and cassia were in panic by the ridge,
And blood stained the cinnabar ground.
The aconite was stranded away from home,
The betel-nut could not return to its own town.
Corpses lay scattered like powder on the mountainside
Leaving the red lady* waiting anxiously at home.

As another poem says,

* The insect *Lycorma delicatula*. The whole verse refers to traditional Chinese medicines.

With men and horses all dead, they could not go back —
Ghosts and lonely spirits in terrible confusion.
Alas that the martial and heroic generals
Should bleed in the sand for trusting fools.

Bringing his cloud down, the Great Sage clapped his hands and laughed aloud. "What luck," he said, "what luck. Ever since I submitted to the Tang Priest and became a monk, he was always telling me 'if you do good for a thousand days you still won't have done enough, but if you do ill for one day that will be too much.' How true it was. I killed a few evil spirits when I was with him and he regarded me as a murderer; and now I've come home I've wiped out all these hunters." "Come out, little ones," he shouted, and now that the hurricane was over and the Great Sage had called them, the monkeys came bounding out one after the other. "Go and strip the clothes off the dead hunters at the foot of the southern mountain," he said, "bring them back here, and wash the bloodstains out. Then you can wear them to keep warm. Push all the corpses into the pool that's ten thousand fathoms deep, and when you've dragged all the dead horses here, strip off their hides to make into boots, and pickle their flesh — it'll feed us for a long time. I'll give you all those bows, arrows, spears and swords for you to practise your military skills with. And bring me back all those many coloured flags and banners for us to use." The monkeys all accepted his orders.

The Great Sage had the banners unstitched and washed, then put them all together as one multicoloured banner which bore the legend, Great Sage Equalling Heaven, Restorer of the Mountain of Flowers and Fruit, Recreator of the Water Curtain Cave. They hung the banner from a pole outside the cave, and for days on end he invited demons and held gatherings of the wild beasts. He accumulated provisions, and the word "monk" was never mentioned. As he was so generous and his powers so great he was able to go and borrow some sweet magic waters from the dragon kings of the four seas with which to bathe the mountain and make it green again. In front of it he planted elms and willows, and behind it pines and cedars; he also put in peaches, greengages, jujubes, and plums. Thus he led a happy and carefree life.

Let us return to the Tang Priest, who had trusted the word of crafty Nature and dismissed the Mind-ape. He climbed into his saddle, and with Pig leading the way and Friar Sand carrying the luggage they carried on westwards. After crossing the White Tiger Ridge they saw a range of forested hills of which it could truthfully be said that creepers climbed and twisted among the bluish cypresses and green pines. "Disciples," said Sanzang, "this rough mountain path is very hard going, and we must be careful in the dense pine forests ahead as I'm afraid there may be evil spirits and monsters." At this the idiot Pig summoned up his spirits and, telling Friar Sand to guide the horse, cleared a path with his rake along which he led the Tang Priest into the forest. As they were going along, the venerable Sanzang reined in his horse and said to Pig, "I'm really starving today. Is there anywhere you could find some food for me?" "Please dismount, Master," Pig replied, "and wait here while I go and find some." Sanzang dismounted, while Friar Sand put down his load, took out his begging bowl, and handed it to Pig. "I'm off," said Pig, and when asked by Sanzang where he was going he replied, "Don't let that bother you. I'll beg you some food even if it's like cutting through ice to get fire, or even if it means squeezing oil out of snow."

He travelled west about four miles from the pine forest without meeting anybody. It was indeed a lonely place inhabited only by wolves and tigers. The idiot found the going heavy, and he muttered to himself, "When Monkey was with us the old priest could have anything he wanted, but now I have to do it all. How true it is that 'you have to keep house to realize how expensive rice and firewood are, and raise sons to understand parental love'. There's nowhere at all to beg on this road." By now he felt sleepy after all this walking and he thought, "If I go back now and tell the old monk that there's nowhere I can beg food, he may not believe I've come this far. I'd better hang around here for another hour or two before reporting back. Oh well, I may as well take a snooze in that grass." With that the idiot pillowed his head in the grass and went to sleep. He had only meant to take forty winks and then get up again, not realizing that he was so exhausted by the journey that he would be sound asleep as soon as his head was down.

Let us leave Pig asleep there and return to Sanzang in the forest. As he was feeling anxious and unsettled he said to Friar Sand, "It's late now. Why isn't Pig back from begging for food?" "Master," said Friar Sand, "you still don't understand him. He's found out that many of these westerners give food to monks, and with his big belly he won't be bothering about you. He won't be back till he's eaten his fill." "True," said Sanzang. "If he's greedily stuffing himself somewhere far away we need not concern ourselves with him. It's getting late and this is no place to spend the night. We must find somewhere to stay." "There's no rush, Master," said Friar Sand. "You sit and wait here while I go and find him." "Very well," said Sanzang, "very well. Never mind about the food. It's somewhere for the night that matters." Clasping his precious staff, Friar Sand went off through the pine forest in search of Pig.

Sanzang felt thoroughly tired and miserable as he sat alone in the forest, so he summoned up his spirits, leapt to his feet, hid all the luggage in a cache, tethered the horse to a tree, took off his reed hat, and drove his staff into the ground. Then he straightened out his black robes and took a leisurely stroll among the trees to cheer himself up. As he looked at all the wild flowers he did not hear the calls of the birds returning to their nests. The grass was deep and the forest paths were narrow, and in his distraction he lost his way. He had started out to cheer himself up and also to find Pig and Friar Sand; what he did not realize was that they had headed due west while he, after wandering in all directions, was going south. He came out of the forest and looked up to see a dazzling golden light. On closer examination he saw that it was the golden roof of a pagoda gleaming in the setting sun. "What a sad destiny my disciples have," he thought. "When I left the land of the East, I vowed that I would burn incense in every temple I passed, would worship every Buddha statue I saw, and sweep out every pagoda I encountered. Isn't that a golden pagoda gleaming over there? Why didn't we go that way? There's bound to be a monastery at the foot of the pagoda, and the monastery must surely contain monks. Iet me have a look. The luggage and the white horse can come to no harm in that uninhabited spot. If there is some suitable place we can all spend the night here when my disciples come back."

Alas! The venerable Sanzang was once more the victim of delusion. He strode over to the pagoda, and what he saw was

A cliff ten thousand fathoms high,
A lofty mountain reaching to the firmament.
Its roots sunk deep into the earth,
Its peak thrust up into the sky.
On either side were trees by the thousand,
While creepers stretched many miles around.
The wind made shadows as it bent the tips of the
*   flowers;*
The moon had no root where waters flowed under the
*   clouds.*
A fallen tree spanned a deep ravine;
Withered creepers were knotted round the gleaming
*   peak.*
Under the stone bridge
Ran the water from a spring;
On the sacred altar
The ever-burning lamp was as bright as chalk.
From a distance it looked like the Three Islands of
*   Paradise;*
Close to, it resembled the blessed land of Penglai.
Fragrant pine and purple bamboo grew round the moun-
*   tain brooks,*
Magpies, monkeys, crows, and apes roamed the lofty
*   ridge.*
Outside the door of a cave
Animals came and went in orderly groups.
Among the trees
Flocks of birds were briefly seen.

Luxuriant grew the green and scented herbs,
As the wild flowers bloomed in all their glory.
This was clearly an evil place
That the deluded priest approached.

Sanzang stepped out and was soon at the gate of the pagoda. Seeing a curtain of speckled bamboo hanging inside, he lifted it up and went in. He raised his head and saw an evil monster sleeping on a stone bed. Do you know what he looked like?

A dark blue face,
White fangs,
A huge gaping mouth.
On either side of it were matted hairs
All stained with fat and grease.
The purple tufts of his beard and moustache
Made one think of splayed-out lichee shoots.
His nose was as hooked as a parrot's beak
His eyes as dim as stars in the dawn.
His two fists
Were the size of a monk's begging bowl;
His indigo-blue feet
Were like a pair of logs.
The pale yellow robe that was flung across him
Was grander than a brocade cassock.
The sword in his hand
Gleamed and flashed;
The rock on which he slept
Was exquisite, smooth and flawless.
As a little fiend he had marshalled ant formations;
When a senior demon he had sat in the wasps' head-
    quarters.
As the sight of his awe-inspiring might
All would shout out,
Calling him master.
He had created three men drinking in the moonlight,
And had magicked out of the wind cups of refreshing
    tea.

Consider his tremendous supernatural powers —
In the wink of an eyelid
He could be at the ends of the earth.
In wild forests he could sing like a bird;
Deep in the bush he would stay with snakes and tigers.
When an immortal farms the land it bears white jade;
When a Taoist master tends the fire he produces elixir.
Although this little cave-mouth
Did not lead to the Avichi Hell,
Yet this ferocious monster
Was a bull-headed demon.

Sanzang was so terrified at the sight of him that he shrank back, his whole body numb with terror. No sooner had he turned to go than the monster, whose powers really were tremendous, opened a fiendish eye with a golden pupil and shouted, "Who is that outside the door, little ones?" A junior devil poked his head out to look, saw a shaven-headed priest, and ran in to report, "A monk, Your Majesty. He has a large face and a round head, and his ears hang down to his shoulders. His flesh looks most tender and his skin extremely delicate. He's a very promising monk." The monster cackled and said, "This is what they call 'a fly landing on a snake's head, or food and clothing presenting themselves to you'. Go and catch him for me, lads, and bring him back here. I'll reward you well." The junior demons rushed out after Sanzang like a swarm of bees; and Sanzang, in his alarm, started to run so fast he seemed to fly. But he was so terrified that his legs were soon like numb jelly, and on top of this the path was very uneven and it was twilight in the deep forest. He could not move fast enough, and the junior demons picked him up and carried him back.

A dragon in shallows falls victim to shrimps;
A tiger on the plain can be put upon by dogs.
Although good deeds always run into trouble,
The Tang Priest on his westward journey has been most
*   unlucky.*

The junior devils carried the Tang Priest as far as the bamboo curtain and put him down outside it as they announced with great delight, "We've brought the monk back, Your Majesty." The old demon stole a look and saw that Sanzang, who was holding his head high with dignity, must be a fine monk. "So fine a monk," he thought, "must be a superior person, so I mustn't treat him as a nobody. If I don't overawe him he won't submit to me." Like a fox pretending to be as awe-inspiring as a tiger, he made his red whiskers bristle, his bloody hair stand on end, and his eyeballs bulge in a glare. "Bring that monk in," he roared. "Yes sir," the other fiends shouted in chorus, pushing Sanzang inside. As the saying goes, "You have to bow your head under low eaves," and Sanzang was obliged to put his hands together and greet him. "Where do you live, monk?" the monster asked. "Where have you come from, and where are you going? Tell me at once." "I am a priest from the Tang country, and I am going to the West on the command of His Majesty the Tang Emperor to ask for holy scriptures. As I was passing your distinguished mountain, I came over to visit the holy men of this pagoda. I did not realize that I would disturb Your Excellency, and I beg you to forgive me. When I return East with the scriptures from the West I shall see to it that your fame will be eternally celebrated." "I thought you must be someone from a superior country,'" said the fiend, bellowing with laughter, "and as that's who you are, I'm going to eat you up. It was splendid of you to come, splendid — otherwise we might have let you slip. You were fated to be the food in my mouth, so of course you came rushing here. We'll never let you go, and you'll never escape." Then he ordered the junior demons to tie him up. They rushed upon him and bound him tight to a soul-fixing stake.

Holding his sword in his hands, the old fiend asked, "How many of you are there altogether? You wouldn't have the guts to go to the Western Heaven all by yourself." Eyeing the sword in his hand, Sanzang had to answer truthfully. "I have two disciples, Your Majesty," he said, "called Pig and Friar Sand. They have both gone begging for food outside the pine forest.

Apart from them there is a load of baggage and a white horse that I left in the wood." "More luck," said the fiend. "Two disciples as well makes three of you, four counting the horse, which is enough for a meal." "We'll go and get 'em," the junior fiends said. "No," the old monster said, "don't go. Lock the front gate. As they've gone begging for food they'll have to find their master for him to eat it, and when they can't find him they're bound to come searching for him here. As the saying goes, 'it's easiest to do business at home.' Just wait and we'll catch them all in good time." The junior demons shut the front gate.

We will leave the unlucky Sanzang and return to Friar Sand, who was now three or four miles outside the forest in his search for Pig but had not yet seen any village. As he stood on a hillock looking around him, he heard a voice in the undergrowth; and sweeping the tall grass aside with his staff, he discovered the idiot talking in his sleep. Pig woke up when Friar Sand twisted his ear. "You idiot," said Friar Sand, "who said you could sleep here instead of begging for food as our master told you?" Pig, waking up with a start, asked, "What's the time, brother?" "Get up at once," replied Friar Sand. "The master told us two to find somewhere to stay whether we can beg any food or not."

Holding his begging bowl and his rake, the drowsy Pig headed straight back with Friar Sand, and when they looked for their master in the wood they could not see him. "It's all because you didn't come back from begging for food, you idiot," said Friar Sand indignantly. "Master must have been carried off by an evil spirit." "Don't talk nonsense, brother," replied a grinning Pig. "This forest is a very proper sort of place and couldn't possibly have any evil spirits in it. I expect the old monk got bored sitting here and went off somewhere to look around. Let's go and find him." They took the horse's bridle, picked up the shoulder-pole with the luggage, collected Sanzang's hat and staff, and left the pine wood in search of their master.

But Sanzang was not fated to die this time. When the two

had been looking for him without success for a while, they say
a shimmering golden light due south of them. "Blessed indeed
are the blessed, brother," said Pig. "Look where the master
must be staying. That light is coming from a pagoda, and they
would be bound to look after him well. I expect they've laid
on a meal and are making him stay to eat it. Let's get a move
on and have some of it ourselves." "It certainly can't be anything sinister," replied Friar Sand. "We must go and have a
look."

As the pair of them arrived at the gates they found them
closed. Above the gates they saw a horizontal tablet of white
jade on which were carved the words MOON WATERS
CAVE, BOWL MOUNTAIN. "Brother," said Friar Sand,
"this is no temple. It's an evil spirit's cave. If our master is in
there we'll never see him." "Never fear," replied Pig. "Tether
the horse and mind the luggage while I ask for news of him."
With that the idiot raised his rake and shouted at the top of
his voice, "Open up, open up." The junior devil who was on
gate duty opened the gates, and at the sight of the pair of them
he rushed inside to report, "Your Majesty, we're in business."
"What sort of business?" the old monster asked. "There are two
monks outside the gates," the junior demon replied. "One has
a long snout and big ears and the other looks down on his luck,
and they are shouting at us to open up." "That means Pig and
Friar Sand have come looking for him," said the old monster.
"Ha! They were bound to. What brought them here? They
look sinister, but I'd better treat them with respect." He called
for his armour to be put on him, and when the junior demons
had brought it and fastened it on, he took his sword in his hand
and marched straight out of the cave.

When Pig and Friar Sand, who were waiting outside, saw
the ferocious demon come out this is what he looked like:

> *A blue face, a red beard, and scarlet hair blowing free;*
> *Golden armour dazzling bright.*
> *Around his waist was a belt of cowries,*
> *And his armour was strapped to his chest with cloud-*
> *walking cords.*

As he stood before the mountain the winds all roared;
Mighty were the waves when he roamed across the seas.
A pair of indigo, muscled hands
Held a soul-chasing, life-snatching sword.
If you would know this creature's name,
The title that he bore was Yellow Robe.

As the old monster Yellow Robe came out through the gates he asked, "Where are you monks from, and why are you yelling at my gates?" "Don't you recognize me, son?" said Pig. "I'm your father. I've been sent by the Great Tang on a mission to the Western Heaven. My master is Sanzang, the emperor's younger brother. If he's here, send him out at once and save me the trouble of having to smash my way in with this rake." "Yes indeed," laughed the monster, "there is a Tang Priest in my place. I haven't showed him any discourtesy, and I've laid on a meal of human-flesh dumplings for him. Why don't you two come in and have some?"

The idiot would have gone in quite trustingly if Friar Sand had not held him back and said, "He's luring you in, brother. Besides, when did you start eating human flesh again?" The idiot saw the light at last, and he struck at the evil monster's face with his rake. The monster sidestepped and parried with his steel sword. They both showed their magic powers as they leapt up on clouds to continue the fight in mid-air. Friar Sand abandoned the baggage and the white horse and rushed to Pig's aid. It was a fine battle up in the clouds between the two wolfish monks and the evil monster:

When the staff was raised it was met by the sword;
The same sword parried the rake's blow.
One devil general displaying his prowess,
A pair of divine monks revealing their transformations.
The nine-pronged rake was quite magnificent;
The demon-submitting staff was truly terrifying.
They came from before and behind, from left and right,
But Yellow Robe was calm and unafraid.
See how his blade of tempered steel shines like silver;

Great indeed were his magical powers.
Their fighting filled the sky
With mists and clouds;
Amid the mountains
Cliffs crashed and fell.
One was fighting for fame
So how could he stop?
The others, fighting for their master,
Were completely unafraid.

The three of them fought dozens of rounds in mid-air without issue. They were all fighting for their very lives, and nothing could have kept them apart. If you don't know how they saved the Tang Priest, listen to the explanation in the next instalment.

CHAPTER TWENTY-NINE

Sanzang, delivered, crosses a border;
A grateful Pig tours mountains and forests.

A poem says

If wild thoughts are not firmly suppressed
There is no point in seeking for the Truth;
If you wish to cultivate your nature before the Buddha,
Why stay halfway between awakening and confusion?

Once awakened you can achieve the Right in an instant;
The confused will drift for ten thousand aeons.
If you can cultivate the Truth with a single thought,
Sins countless as the Ganges sands can be wiped out.

Pig and Friar Sand had fought thirty inconclusive rounds with the monster. Do you know why they were inconclusive? As far as skill went not even twenty monks, let alone two, would have been a match for that evil spirit. Yet because the Tang Priest was not fated to die he was being secretly protected by Dharma-guarding deities. There were also the Six Dings, the Six Jias, the Protectors of the Five Regions, the Four Duty Gods, and the Eighteen Guardians of the Faith helping Pig and Friar Sand in mid-air.

We must leave the three of them locked in struggle and return to Sanzang sobbing his heart out in the cave and speculating about his disciples. "I wonder if you have met a benefactor in a village somewhere, Pig," he thought, tears streaming down his face, "and have been overcome by your greed for the offerings. Wherever are you looking for him, Friar Sand? Will you find him? Little do you know of my sufferings at the hands of this fiend I have run into. When will I see you again and be delivered from my troubles so that we can hurry to the Vulture Peak?" As he fretted and wailed he saw a woman come out from the innermost part of the cave. "Venerable father," she said, leaning on the soul-fixing stake, "where have you come from? Why has he tied you here?" When Sanzang heard this he sneaked a quick look at her through his tears and observed that she was about thirty. "Don't ask me that, Bodhisattva," he said, "I was fated to die: I walked into your home. Eat me if you must, but don't ask me why." "I don't eat people," she replied. "My home is over a hundred miles west of here in the city called Elephantia. I'm the third daughter of the king, and my childhood name was Prettier-than-a-flower. Thirteen years ago, on the fifteenth night of the eighth month, the Moon Festival, that evil monster came and snatched me away in a whirlwind while we were out enjoying the full moon. I have been his wife all these thirteen years and borne him sons and daughters, but I've never been able to send any message home. I miss my parents, and I can never see them. Where did you come from to be caught by him?" "I was sent to the Western Heaven to fetch the scriptures," replied Sanzang. "I never realized when I set out for a stroll that I would stumble into this. Now he's going to capture my two disciples and steam us all together, then eat us." "Don't worry, venerable sir," said the princess with a smile. "As you are going to fetch scriptures I can save you. Elephantia lies on the main route to the west, and if you will take a letter to my parents for me, I'll make him spare your life." "If you save my wretched life, Bodhisattva," said Sanzang with a bow, "I promise to be your messenger."

The princess hurried back inside, wrote a letter to her family, sealed it, released Sanzang from the stake, and handed him the letter. "Bodhisattva," he said, taking the letter now that he was free, "I am very grateful to you for saving my life. When I reach your country I shall give this to the king. My only worry is that after all these years your parents may not believe that the letter is from you, and what would I do then? I could not have them thinking that I was trying to deceive them." "That's no problem. My father has only us three daughters and no sons. If they see this letter they'll feel that they're seeing me." Tucking the letter securely into his sleeve, he took his leave of the princess, and was on the point of going out when she pulled him back and said, "You won't be able to get out through the front gate. All those big and little monsters are outside the gates waving banners, shouting war-cries, and beating drums and gongs to help the monster king in his battle with your two disciples. You'd better go out the back way. If the monster king catches you he'll interrogate you under torture, and if the junior fiends grab you they'll kill you without a qualm. I'll go to see him and talk him over. If he's prepared to let you go, your disciples can ask his permission for all three of you to go together." Sanzang kowtowed and, as she had told him, left her, slipped out through the back door, and hid among the thorns rather than travel alone.

The princess, who had thought out a clever plan, hurried out through the front gates and made her way through the hosts of demons great and small to hear the furious clash of arms. Pig and Friar Sand were still fighting with the monster in mid-air. "Lord Yellow Robe," she shouted at the top of her voice, and as soon as he heard her the demon king left Pig and Friar Sand, landed his cloud, and, grasping his steel sword, took his wife by the arm. "What is it, wife?" he asked. "I was lying in bed asleep just now, husband," she replied, "and I dreamt that I saw a god in golden armour." "What sort of god in golden armour?" he asked. "Why did he come here?" "When I was a child in the palace," she said, "I made a secret vow that if I married a good husband I would climb holy mountains, visit immortals, and give alms to monks. I have now been happily married to you for thirteen years without ever mentioning the vow before, and the god in golden armour came to make me fulfil it. His shouting made me wake up, and then I realized it was a dream. I tidied myself up and came straight to tell you about it. To my surprise I found a monk tied to the stake. I beg you, lord and master, so respect my vow and spare that monk in your mercy. This will count as feeding monks and will fulfil my vow. Will you do this?" "What a fusser you are, wife," he replied. "Nothing to it. If I want to eat people

I can easily catch a few more. If that's how things stand, let
the monk go." "Please may he be released through the back
door, husband?" "What a thing to bother me with. Let him
go, and I don't care whether it's by the front way or the back
way." The monster then grasped his sword once more and
shouted, "Come here, Pig. I'm not afraid of you, but I'm not
fighting you any longer. For my wife's sake I've spared your
master, so hurry round and find him at the back door and carry
on west. If you set foot in my territory again I won't let you
off a second time."

This news made Pig and Friar Sand feel as if they had been
let out through the gates of Hell. They scurried away with the
horse and the baggage, and going round to the other end of the
Moon Waters Cave they called "Master" outside the back entrance. Sanzang recognized their voices and called back from
among the thorn bushes. Friar Sand made his way through the
undergrowth, helped his master out, and hurriedly helped him
mount the horse.

> When he was threatened by the terrible blue-faced
>   monster
> He was lucky to meet the devout princess.
> Escaping from the golden hook, the turtle
> Swam off through the waves with a flick of his tail.

With Pig leading and Friar Sand bringing up the rear, they
left the pine forest and travelled along the main track. The two
disciples grumbled and complained, while Sanzang tried to con-
ciliate them. Every evening they would find lodgings, and they
would be up again at cock-crow. They covered stage after stage
of their journey, sometimes longer and sometimes shorter, and
before they realized it they had done ninety-nine miles. Suddenly they looked up and there was a fine city in front of them.
This was Elephantia, and it was a splendid place:

> Distant clouds,
> A long road;
> Although this was a distant land,
> The scenery was as fine as home.

Auspicious mists enshrouded the city;
Fresh breezes were blowing under the clear moon.
Towering mountains, seen from afar,
Were spread out like a picture.
Rivers flowed rippling,
Like streams of crushed jasper.
There were fields upon fields of farmland
Where new crops sprouted close together.
A handful of fishermen worked three stretches of water;
A wood-gatherer carried twigs from a couple of hills.
The outer wall
And the inner wall of the city,
Were rock-solid.
The houses
And homes
Vied in elegance.
Nine-storied pavilions were like palaces,
High towers like imperial columns.
There was a Hall of the Great Ultimate,
A Flowery Canopied Hall,
A Hall of Incense,
A Hall of Literary Perusal,
A Hall of Policy Proclaimed,
A Hall of Talent Invitied,
All with steps of jade and gold
Where civil and military officers stood in their ranks.
There was also a Great Brightness Palace,
A Palace of Shining Radiance,
A Palace of Eternal Joy,
A Palace of Illustrious Purity,
A Palace of Established Enlightenment,
A Palace of Inexhaustible Glory.
In every palace were gongs, drums, pipes and flutes,
Lamenting the sorrows of spring and the harem's woes
Then there were imperial parks
Where dew bathed the flowers' tender petals;
And royal canals

Where willows bent their slender waists in the wind.
On the highways
Were belted gentlemen in official hats,
Attired in all their splendour
As they rode in five-horsed chariots;
In remote corners
Were archers with bows and arrows
Whose shots split the clouds apart
And skewered pairs of hawks.
What with the willow-lined streets,
And the houses full of music,
This spring scene rivalled the Luoyang Bridge.
The pilgrim seeking the sutras
Was torn with nostalgia for the Great Tang;
The disciples accompanying their master
In a rest-house found happiness in dreams.

Gazing at the view of Elephantia the master and his two disciples dealt with the luggage and the horse and settled down in a rest-house.

The Tang Priest went on foot to the palace gates, where he said to the High Custodian of the gate, "I beg you to report that there is a monk from the Tang Court who has come for a personal audience with His Majesty and has a letter of credentials." A eunuch messenger hurried to the white jade steps and announced, "Your Majesty, a distinguished priest from the Tang Court has come for an audience as he has a letter of credentials to deliver." The king was delighted to hear that he was from the mighty land of Tang and was himself a venerable and holy monk, so he gave his approval at once with the words, "Call him in." Sanzang was summoned to the golden steps, where he performed the court ritual of obeisance and called out the correct greeting. On either side the many civil and military officers all sighed with admiration and said, "What an impressive grasp of music and ritual this gentleman from that distinguished country has." "Venerable sir, why have you come to my country?" the king asked. "I am a Buddhist from the land of Tang,"

Sanzang replied, "and I am going to the Western Heaven on the Emperor's orders to fetch the scriptures. I am carrying a letter of credentials, and now that I have arrived in Your Majesty's country it seems proper to hand it to you. Not knowing whether to advance or retreat, I must apologize for disturbing the Dragon Countenance." "If you have Tang credentials," the king replied, "bring them here for me to see." Sanzang handed the letter up respectfully with both hands and unfolded it on the king's table. It read:

From the Tang Emperor of the Great Tang Kingdom, who reigns by order of Heaven, in the Southern Continent of Jambudvipa.

Despite our feeble virtues we have succeeded to the throne, and in worshipping the gods and ruling the people we are as careful morning and night as if we were on the edge of a precipice or treading on thin ice. Because we failed to save the Dragon King of the Jing River, punishment was visited on our august self; our souls were rushed to the underworld and we became a guest in the land of death. As our lifespan was not yet over, the Lord of Darkness sent us back to the world of the living. We held a Great Assembly of monks and built a holy altar where the souls of the dead could be brought over to the other side. To our great gratitude the Bodhisattva Guanyin, the deliverer from suffering, appeared in person and told us that there is a Buddha in the West who has scriptures that will save the lost and bring lonely souls who have nobody to help them over to the other side. We have therefore especially commissioned the Patriarch Xuanzang to make the long journey across countless mountains to seek for the scriptures and psalms. Should he come to any countries in the West we hope that on seeing this letter they will allow him to go on his way and not impede this predestined good deed. This is addressed to whom it may concern. Given by His Imperial Majesty on an auspicious day in the autumn of the thirteenth year of *Zhen Guan* of the Great Tang.

When he had read this letter, which bore nine imperial seals, the king sealed it with his great seal and handed it back to Sanzang, who thanked him as he took it. "Not only did I have a letter of credentials to present," he reported, "I have also brought a family letter to deliver to Your Majesty." The king was delighted and asked what it was. "I happened to meet Your Majesty's third princess, who was carried off by the Yellow-Robed Monster of the Moon Waters Cave in the Bowl Mountain, and she gave me this letter to deliver to you." Tears poured from the king's eyes at the news, and he said, "It is thirteen years since I saw her last, and I don't know how many military and civil officers I have had dismissed or degraded, and how many of the ladies-in-waiting, serving maids, and eunuchs I have had beaten to death since then because of her. I imagined that she had wandered out of the palace and lost her way, and I looked for her everywhere. Even when all the ordinary citizens were interrogated I could find no news of her whereabouts. I never thought that an evil monster could have carried her off. Hearing this all of a sudden makes me weep for sorrow." Sanzang produced the letter from his sleeve and handed it to the king, who on seeing the words, "All is well" on the outside felt so weak in his hands that he could not open it. He ordered a Grand Scholar from the Academy of Letters to climb the steps of the throne and read it aloud. As the Grand Scholar climbed the steps of the throne, the civil and military officials in front of the throne room and the empresses, royal consorts, and palace ladies behind it all listened intently. The Grand Scholar opened it and read aloud:

> Your unworthy daughter Prettier-than-a-flower kowtows one hundred times to His Most Excellent Majesty the King her father in the Dragon and Phoenix Palace, to her Majesty the Queen her mother outside the Palace of Shining Radiance, and to all the noble ministers and generals of the court; it is my pleasure to send news to

you and thank you for the infinite trouble you have taken on my behalf. But I am unable to devote myself to cheering Your Majesty and carry out my filial duties to the full.

Thirteen years ago, on the festive fifteenth night of the eighth month, when banquets were being given in all the palaces in accordance with Your Majesty's benevolent command, we were enjoying the moonlight and the clear stars. In the middle of our rejoicing a sudden gust of fragrant wind blew up, and from it emerged a demon king with golden pupils, a blue face, and green hair, who seized your daughter and carried her away on a magic cloud to a desolate mountain far from human habitation. There was no way I could stop him forcing me to be his wife, and I have had to endure this for thirteen years. I have borne him two fiendish sons, and they are both complete monsters. I would not have written to you and sullied you with the news of my uncivilized and disgraceful experiences, but I was afraid that after my death nobody would know what had happened to me. Just as I was missing my parents and angry about my fate, a Tang monk also happened to be captured by the monster, so with tears in my eyes I am boldly writing this letter and sending it to you as a token of my feelings. I beg you, Majesty, to take pity on me and send a general to the Moon Waters Cave in Bowl Mountain to capture the Yellow-robed Monster, rescue me, and take me back to the palace, this would make me profoundly grateful. Please excuse the hasty and disrespectful tone of this letter.

With more kowtows,

> Your disobedient daughter,
> Prettier-than-a-flower.

When the Grand Scholar had read it through, the king wept aloud, the ladies of the palace were all in tears, and the officials were all saddened. Everyone was miserable.

After weeping for a long time the king asked the civil and military officials which of them would lead troops to capture the monster and rescue Princess Prettier-than-a-flower for him. He asked them all serveral times, but nobody would accept. The generals looked as though they were carved out of wood, and the officials might have been moulded from clay. The king was highly agitated, and floods of tears were pouring down his face when the civil and military officials all prostrated themselves before him and said, "Please don't be so disturbed, Your Majesty. The princess has been lost for thirteen years now without anything being heard of her, so we cannot yet know whether she really met this Tang priest and sent a letter by him. Besides, we are all mere mortals, and the military manuals and books of strategy we have studied only cover the deployment of soldiers in battle, making encampments, and what else is necessary to protect the country from the disaster of invasion. That evil spirit travels by cloud and mist, and we would never even be able to catch sight of him, let alone capture him and rescue the Princess. Now that Easterner who is going to fetch scriptures is a holy priest from a great country. This monk must have demon-subduing powers as his 'high qualities overawe the dragons and tigers, and his great virtues give him power over devils and gods.'

"As the old saying goes, 'The man who comes to argue about rights and wrongs is usually the wrongdoer himself.' Far and away the best plan would be to ask this venerable gentleman to subdue the fiend and rescue the princess."

"If you have any supernatural skills, venerable sir," the king said, turning at once to Sanzang, "then use your dharma powers to capture this evil monster and bring my daughter back to the palace. If you do that there will be no need to travel to the West and visit the Buddha. You can let your hair grow and I will make you my brother. We shall sit together on the dragon throne and share my wealth and honour. What about it?" "My only humble skill," Sanzang hastened to reply, "lies in invoking the Buddha's name, and I really cannot subdue fiends." "If you can't subdue fiends," the king retorted, "how can you have the courage to go to visit the Buddha in the Western Heaven?" Sanzang now told him about the two disciples as he could not keep them a secret any longer. "Your Majesty," he said, "I could scarcely have come this far by myself. I have two disciples, both skilled at finding ways across mountains and at bridging rivers, who have escorted me here." "You have behaved disgracefully, monk," said the king angrily. "As you have disciples, you should have brought them with you to see me. Even if we could have offered them no presents they would have liked, they would at least have been given a meal." "My disciples are so hideous," Sanzang replied, "that I dared not bring them to court for fear of offending Your Majesty's dignity." "What a monkish thing to say," observed the king with a smile. "You don't really think I would be afraid of them, do you?" "Oh, no," said Sanzang. "The surname of the older one is Pig; his personal names are Wuneng, Awakened to Power, and Bajie, Eight Prohibitions. He has a long snout, vicious fangs, bristles of steel and ears as big as fans. He is so heftily built that he makes a breeze as he walks. The surname of the second disciple is Sand, and his Buddhist name is Monk Awakened to Purity. He is twelve feet tall, and his arms are four feet thick. His face is the colour of indigo, and his mouth is like a bowl of blood. His eyes burn and flash, and his teeth are like rows of nails. It was because they both look so terrible that I did not dare bring them with me." "Even after you have told me about them," said the king, "I know that I have nothing to fear. Have them summoned here." With that a messenger with a golden tablet was sent to the rest-house to invite them to the palace.

On receiving the invitation the idiot said to Friar Sand, "Brother, do you still think he shouldn't have delivered the letter? Now you can see the advantages of delivering it. I reckon that when the master delivered it, the king must have thought that the person who brought such a message could not be treated rudely and so laid on a banquet for him. As our master has such a weak appetite he must have remembered us and mentioned our names. This is why the messenger was sent here.

After a meal we'll be able to make a good start tomorrow." "This must have been in our destiny," said Friar Sand. "Let's go." Entrusting their baggage and the horse to the manager of the hostel they accompanied the messenger to court; they kept their weapons with them. When they reached the white jade steps they stood below them and chanted a "re-e-er" of respect then stood there without moving. Every one of the civil and military officials was horrified. "Apart from being hideous," they said to each other, "they are far too coarse and vulgar. Why are they standing bolt upright after a mere "re-e-er" instead of prostrating themselves before His Majesty? Shocking, quite shocking." Overhearing this, Pig said, "Please don't make rude comments on us, gentlemen, This is the way we look, and although we seem ugly at first sight, after a while we become quite bearable."

The king, who had been quite frightened at the sight of their brutishness, trembled so violently on hearing the idiot Pig talking that he lost his balance and fell off his dragon throne. Fortunately the gentlemen-in-waiting were on hand to help him up again. This threw Sanzang into such a panic that he fell to his knees and kowtowed without stopping, saying, "Your Majesty, I deserve to die ten thousand deaths, ten thousand deaths. I said that my disciples were too hideous for me to dare to bring them to court for fear of harming your dragon dignity, and now I have given Your Majesty this fright." The king walked shakily over to him, raised him to his feet, and said, "Thank goodness you warned me about them beforehand, venerable sir. Otherwise I would undoubtedly have died of shock at the sight of them." When the king had taken some time to calm himself down he asked Pig and Friar Sand which of the two of them was better at subduing fiends. "I am," said the shameless idiot. "How do you do it, pray?" the king asked. "I am Marshal Tian Peng," Pig replied, "and I was exiled to this mortal world for offending against part of the Heavenly Code. Happily I have now returned to the truth and become a monk. I am the best fiend-subduer of all of us who have come here from the East." "If you are a heavenly general turned

mortal," said the king, "you must be good at transformations."
"I wouldn't say that much," Pig replied, "but I can do one or
two." "Show me one," said the king. "Tell me what you want
me to turn into," said Pig. 'Turn into a giant, then," said the
king.

Pig, who could do thirty-six transformations, now showed
off his powers before the steps of the throne. Clenching his
fist and reciting the words of the spell he shouted "Grow!"
bowed forward, and grew eighty or ninety feet tall. He looked
like one of the paper gods carried at the head of funeral pro-
cessions. The civil and military officials trembled with fright;
monarch and subjects alike gazed at him in stupefaction. Then
the General Guarding the Palace said, "You have certainly
grown very tall, venerable sir. How much taller could you grow
before you had to stop?" "It depends on the wind," replied
the idiot, talking in his idiotic way. "I can manage quite well
in an east or a west wind, and if a south wind blows up I can
make a big dent in the sky." "Then give your magic powers
a rest," said the king, more frightened than ever. "We are sure
you can do that." Pig contracted himself to his real size and
stood in attendance at the foot of the steps once more.

"What weapon will you use to fight the monster on this
mission?" the king asked. Pig pulled his rake from his belt and
said, "This rake." "But that would disgrace us," said the king
with a smile. "Here we have steel whips, maces, claws on
chains, war-hammers, cutlasses, halberds, pole-axes, battle-axes,
swords, bills, spears, and battle-scythes. Choose one that suits
you — that rake doesn't count as a real weapon." "What Your
Majesty doesn't realize," Pig replied, "is that although it's
crude I've carried it around with me since I was a child. I depended on it completely when I commanded eighty thousand
sailors and marines as marshal of the Milky Way, the Heavenly
River. Down in this world as my master's escort I've used it to
smash the dens of tigers and wolves in the mountains and to
turn the nests of dragons and leviathans upside-down in rivers."
The king was thoroughly delighted and convinced on hearing
this, so he ordered nine of his Royal Consorts to fetch a bottle

of his own royal wine with which to send the venerable Pig off; then he filled a goblet and presented it to Pig with the words, "May this cup of wine, venerable father, express my gratitude for the service you are going to render. When you capture the evil monster and bring back my daughter you will be rewarded with a state banquet and a thousand pieces of gold." For all his coarseness the idiot accepted it with style. "Master," he said to Sanzang after chanting a "re-e-er" of respect, "you should drink this wine first, but His Majesty gave it to me and I dare not disobey him. Please allow me to drink first as it will brace my spirits for the capture of the monster." He drained the cup in one gulp, refilled it, and handed it to Sanzang, who said, "As I cannot touch alcohol you two must drink it for me." Friar Sand came over and took it. Clouds now sprouted under Pig's feet and he shot up into mid-air. "Venerable Pig," exclaimed the king, "you can walk on clouds too!"

When Pig had gone Friar Sand drained his cup of wine at one draught too and said, "When the Yellow-robed Monster· captured you, master, the pair of us were only just a match for him in combat. I'm afraid that my elder brother won't be able to beat him by himself." "Yes," Sanzang replied. "You'd better go and help him." When Friar Sand too sprang up into the air on a cloud and went off, the anxious king grabbed hold of Sanzang and said, "Stay here with me, venerable sir. Don't you go flying off on a cloud too." "I, alas, cannot take a single step by cloud," We leave the two of them talking to each other in the palace.

"I'm here, brother," said Friar Sand as he caught Pig up. "Why?" Pig asked. "The master told me to come and lend you a hand," replied Friar Sand. "Good, it's as well you've come. We two'll do our damnedest and capture this fiend. Even though it won't be anything very big, it'll at least make us famous in this country."

> *On shimmering clouds they left the country,*
> *Departing from the capital in a blaze of magic light.*

On the king's command they came to the mountain cave
To fight hard side by side to capture the evil spirit.

Before long they reached the mouth of the cave and landed their cloud. Pig brought his rake down with all his might on the door of the cave and made a hole the size of a bucket in it. The junior demons guarding it were so frightened that they opened up the gates; at the sight of the pair of them they rushed inside to report, "Bad news, Your Majesty. The long-snouted monk with big ears and the other one with a horrible face have come back and smashed down our doors." "Pig and Friar Sand again?" exclaimed the monster in astonishment. "How dare they come and break down my door after I've spared their master's life?" "Perhaps they've come to fetch something they left behind," suggested a junior demon. "Nonsense," snorted the monster. "Would they break the gate down if they'd just left something behind?" He hastily tied on his armour, took his steel sword, went outside and asked, "Monks, what do you mean by smashing down my door? I spared your master, didn't I?" "Will you do a decent thing, wretched ogre?" said Pig. "What?" asked the old monster. "You forced the Third Princess of the land of Elephantia to come to your cave," said Pig, "and you've made her stay here for thirteen years. You should send her back now. We've come here to capture you on the king's orders, so you'd better hurry in and tie yourself up if you don't want me to hit you." The old fiend was now furious. Just watch him as he gnashes his fangs of steel, glares so hard that his eyes become round with fury, raises his sword, and hacks at Pig's head. Pig avoided the blow and struck back at the monster's face with his rake, after which Friar Sand rushed forward to join in the fight with his staff. This battle on the mountain was not the same as the earlier one:

Saying the wrong things can make men angry;
Wicked intentions and hurt feelings give birth to wrath.
The great steel sword of the demon king
Sliced down at the head;
Pig's nine-toothed rake

Went for the face.
As Friar Sand let fly with his staff
The demon king parried with his magic weapon.
One wild ogre,
Two holy monks,
Moving to and fro with the greatest of calm.
One said,
"You deserve to die for your crime against the country."
The other replied,
"Interfering fellow, trying to put the world to rights."
"By seizing the princess you have insulted the ,state,"
    said the one.
"Just mind your own business," said the other.
It was all because of the letter,
That the monks and the monster were now in combat.

When they had fought eight or nine bouts on the mountain side Pig was beginning to tire; his strength was flagging and he could only raise his rake with difficulty. Do you know why they could not hold out against the monster this time? In the first battle all the guardian gods had been helping Pig and Friar Sand as Sanzang was in the cave, so that they had then been a match for the ogre. This time the guardian gods were all looking after Sanzang in Elephantia, which was why Pig and Friar Sand could not hold out against the fiend.

"You come forward and fight him, Friar Sand," said the idiot, "while I go off for a shit." Then with no further thought for Friar Sand he streaked off into the undergrowth of grass, wild figs, thorns and creepers, diving straight in and not bothering about the scratches on his face. Then he fell into a doze, too frightened to come out again. He kept an ear cocked for the sound of clashing weapons.

Seeing Pig flee, the monster charged at Friar Sand, who could do nothing to stop the ogre from seizing him and carrying him into the cave. The junior fiends tied him up hand and foot. If you don't know what became of him, listen to the explanation in the next chapter.

CHAPTER THIRTY

An Evil Monster harms the true law;
The Thought-Horse remembers the Mind-Ape.

Now that he had tied up Friar Sand, the monster did not kill
him, hit him, or even swear at him. Instead he raised his sword
and thought, "Coming from so great a country the Tang Priest
must have a sense of propriety — he can't have sent his disciples
to capture me after I spared his life. Hmm. That wife of mine
must have sent some kind of letter to her country and let the
secret out. Just wait till I question her." The monster became
so furious that he was ready to kill her.

The unwitting princess, who had just finished making herself
up, came out to see the ogre knitting his brows and gnashing his
teeth in anger. "What is bothering you, my lord?" she asked
with a smile. The monster snorted and started to insult her.
"You low bitch," he said, "you haven't a shred of human decency. You never made the slightest complaint when I first
brought you here. You wear clothes of brocade and a crown
of gold, and I go out to find anything you need. You live in
luxury all four seasons of the year, and we've always been very
close to each other. So why do you think only of your mother
and father? Why do you have no wifely feelings?" This so
frightened the princess that she fell to her knees and said,
"What makes you start talking as if you are going to get rid of
me?" "I'm not sure whether I'm getting rid of you or you're getting rid of me," the monster replied. "I captured that Tang
Priest and brought him here to eat, but you released him without asking me first. You must have secretly written a letter and
asked him to deliver it for you. There's no other explanation
for why these two monks should have made an attack on this
place and be demanding your return. It's all your fault, isn't

it?" "Don't blame me for this, my lord," she replied. "I never wrote such a letter." "Liar," he said. "I've captured one of my enemies to prove it." "Who?' she asked. "Friar Sand, the Tang Priest's second disciple." Nobody likes to accept their death, even at their last gasp, so she could only try to keep up the pretence. "Please don't lose your temper, my lord," she said. "Let's go and ask him about it. If there really was a letter I'll gladly let you kill me; but if there wasn't, you'd be killing your slave unjustly." With no further argument the monster grabbed her by her bejewelled hair with his fist the size of a basket and threw her to the floor in front of him. Then he seized his sword to question Friar Sand. "Friar Sand," he roared, "when you two had the impertinence to make your attack was it because the king of her country sent you here after getting a letter from her?"

When the bound Friar Sand saw the evil spirit throw the princess to the ground in his fury then take hold of his sword to kill her, he thought, "It's obvious she must have sent a letter. But she did us a very great favour by sparing our master. If I tell him about it, he'll kill her. No, that would be a terrible thing to do after what she did for us. Besides, I haven't done any good deeds all the time I have been with our master, so as a prisoner here I can pay back my master's goodness to me with my life." His mind made up, he shouted, "Behave yourself, evil monster. She sent no letter, so don't you mistreat her or murder her. "I'll tell you why we came to demand the princess. When my master was your prisoner in this cave he saw what the princess looked like. Later on, when he presented his credentials to the king of Elephantia, the king showed him her picture and asked him if he'd seen her on his journey. The king had this picture of her painted long ago, and made enquiries about her all over the place. My master told the king about her, and when he heard this news of his daughter the king gave us some of his imperial wine and sent us to bring her back to the palace. This is the truth. There was no letter. If you want to kill anybody, kill me, and don't be so wicked as to slaughter an innocent woman."

Impressed by Friar Sand's noble words, the monster put aside his sword and took the princess in his arms, saying, "Please forgive me for being so boorishly rude." Then he put her hair up again for her, and turning tender again urged her to go inside with him. He asked her to take the seat of honour and apologized to her. In her female fickleness the princess was prompted by his excess of courtesy to think of an idea. "My lord," she said, "could you have Friar Sand's bonds loosened a little for the sake of our love?" The old fiend ordered his underlings to untie Friar Sand and lock him up there instead. On being untied and locked up, Friar Sand got up and thought, "The ancients said that a good turn to someone else is a good turn to yourself. If I hadn't helped her out, she wouldn't have had me untied."

The old fiend then had a banquet laid on to calm his wife and make it up to her. When he had drunk himself fairly tipsy he put on a new robe and girded a sword to his waist. Then he fondled the princess and said, "You stay at home and drink, wife. Look after our two sons and don't let Friar Sand get away. While the Tang Priest is in Elephantia I'm going to get to know my relations." "What relations?" she asked. "Your father," he replied. "I'm his son-in-law and he's my father-in-law, so why shouldn't we get acquainted?" "You mustn't go," was her reply. "Why not?" he asked. "My father," she answered, "didn't win his country by force of arms; it was handed down to him by his ancestors. He came to the throne as a child and has never been far from the palace gates, so he's never seen a tough guy like you. You are a bit on the hideous side with that face of yours, and it would be very bad if a visit from you terrified him. You'd do better not to go and meet him." "Then I'll make myself handsome," he said. "Try it and show me," said the princess.

The splendid fiend shook himself, and in the middle of the banquet he changed himself into a handsome man.

> *Elegant he was, and tall.*
> *He spoke like a high official;*

His movements were those of a youth.
He was as brilliant as the poet Cao Zhi,
Handsome as Pan An to whom women threw fruit.
On his head was a hat with magpie feathers,
To which the black clouds submitted;
He wore a robe of jade-coloured silk
With wide and billowing sleeves.
On his feet were black boots with patterned tops,
And at his waist hung a gleaming sword.
He was a most imposing man,
Tall, elegant and handsome.

The princess was thoroughly delighted at the sight of him. "Isn't this a good transformation?" he asked her with a smile. "Wonderful," she replied, "wonderful. When you go to court like that the king will be bound to accept you as his son-in-law and make his civil and military officials give you a banquet, so if you have anything to drink you must be very careful not to show your real face — it wouldn't do to let the secret out." "You don't need to tell me that," he said, "I understand perfectly well myself."

He sprang away on his cloud and was soon in Elephantia, where he landed and walked to the palace gates. "Please report," he said to the High Custodian of the gate, "that His Majesty's third son-in-law has come for an audience." A eunuch messenger went to the steps of the throne and reported, "Your Majesty's third son-in-law has come for an audience and is waiting for your summons outside the palace gates." When the king, who was talking with Sanzang, heard the words "third son-in-law" he said to the assembled officials, "I only have two sons-in-law — there can't be a third." "It must be that the monster has come," the officials replied. "Then should I send for him?" the king asked. "Your Majesty," said Sanzang in alarm, "he is an evil spirit, so we mortals can do nothing about him. He knows about the past and the future and rides on the clouds. He will come whether you send for him or not, so it would be better to send for him and avoid arguments."

The king accepted the proposal and sent for him. The fiend came to the bottom of the steps and performed the usual ritual movements and chanting. His handsome looks prevented any of the officials from realizing that he was a demon; instead they took him in their mortal blindness for a good man. At the sight of his imposing figure the king thought that he would be a pillar and the saviour of the state. "Son-in-law," he asked him, "where do you live? Where are you from? When did you marry the princess? Why haven't you come to see me before?" "I come," the monster replied, knocking his head on the ground, "from the Moon Waters Cave in Bowl Mountain." "How far is that from here?" asked the king. "Not far," he replied, "only a hundred miles." "If it's a hundred miles away," said the king, "how did the princess get there to marry you?" The monster gave a cunning and deceptive answer. "My lord," he said, "I have been riding and shooting since childhood, and I support myself by hunting. Thirteen years ago as I was out hunting one day with falcons, hounds, and a few score retainers when I saw a ferocious striped tiger carrying a girl on its back down the mountains side. I fitted an arrow to my bow and shot the tiger, then took the girl home and revived her with hot water, which saved her life. When I asked her where she was from she never mentioned the word 'princess' — had she said that she was Your Majesty's daughter, I would never have had the effrontery to marry her without your permission. I would have come to your golden palace and asked for some appointment in which I might have distinguished myself. As she said she was the daughter of ordinary folk I kept her in my home. With her beauty and my ability we fell in love, and we have been married all these years. When we were married I wanted to kill the tiger and serve him up at a banquet for all my relations, but she asked me not to. There was a verse that explained why I should not:

> "'Thanks to Heaven and Earth we are becoming man
>   and wife;
> We will marry without matchmaker or witnesses.

> *A red thread must have united us in a former life,*
> *So let us make the tiger our matchmaker.'*

"When she said that I untied the tiger and spared its life. The wounded beast swished its tail and was off. Little did I realize that after escaping with its life it would have spent the past years making itself into a spirit whose sole intention is to deceive and kill people. I believe that there was once a group of pilgrims going to fetch scriptures who said that they were priests from the Great Tang. The tiger must have killed their leader, taken his credentials, and made himself look like the pilgrim. He is now in this palace trying to deceive Your Majesty. That man sitting on an embroidered cushion is in fact the very tiger who carried the princess off thirteen years ago. He is no pilgrim."

The feeble-minded king, who in his mortal blindness could not recognize the evil spirit, believed that his tissue of lies were the truth and said, "Noble son-in-law, how can you tell that this monk is the tiger who carried the princess off?" "Living in the mountains," he replied, "I eat tiger, dress in tiger, sleep amid tigers, and move among tigers. Of course I can tell." "Even if you can tell," said the king, "turn him back into his real form to show me." "If I may borrow half a saucer of water," answered the fiend, "I will turn him back into his real form." The king sent an officer to fetch some water for his son-in-law. The monster put the water in his hand, leapt forward, and did an Eye-deceiving Body-fixing Spell. He recited the words of the spell, spurted a mouthful of water over the Tang Priest, and shouted "Change!" Sanzang's real body was hidden away on top of the hall, and he was turned into a striped tiger. To the king's mortal eyes the tiger had

> *A white brow and a rounded head,*
> *A patterned body and eyes of lightning.*
> *Four legs,*
> *Straight and tall;*
> *Twenty claws,*
> *Hooked and sharp.*

Jagged fangs filled his mouth;
Pointed ears grew from his brow.
Fierce and powerful, formed like a giant cat,
Wild and virile as a brown bull-calf.
His bristling whiskers shone like silver,
Acrid breath came from his spiky tongue.
He was indeed a savage tiger
Whose majesty dominated the palace hall.

One look at him sent the king's souls flying from his body, and all the officials fled in terror except for a handful of gallant generals. They charged the tiger at the head of a group of officers, hacking wildly with every kind of weapon. If the Tang Priest had not been fated to survive, even twenty of him would have been chopped to mince. Luckily for him the Six Dings, the Six Jias, the Protectors, the Duty Gods, and the Guardians of the Faith were all protecting him in mid-air and preventing him from being wounded by any of the weapons. After a turmoil that continued until evening they finally caught the tiger, chained it, and put it in an iron cage in one of the palace chambers.

The king then ordered his household department to lay on a large banquet to thank his son-in-law for saving his daughter from being killed by the monk. That evening, when the court had been dismissed, the monster went to the Hall of Silvery Peace. Eighteen Palace Beauties and Junior Concubines had been selected, and they made music, sang and danced, urging the fiend to drink and be merry. The ogre sat alone in the seat of honour, and to left and right of him were all these voluptuous women. When he had been drinking until the second watch of the night he became too intoxicated to restrain his savagery any longer. He jumped up, bellowed with laughter, and turned back into his real self. A murderous impulse came upon him, and stretching out his hand as big as a basket he seized a girl who was playing a lute, dragged her towards him, and took a bite from her head. The seventeen other palace women fled in panic and hid themselves.

The Palace Beauties were terrified,
The Junior Concubines were panic-stricken.
The terrified Palace Beauties
Were like lotuses beaten by the rain at night;
The panic-stricken Concubines
Were like peonies swaying in the spring breezes.
Smashing their lutes, they fled for their lives,
Trampling on zithers as they ran away.
As they went out through the doors they knew not where
  they went;
In their flight from the hall they rushed everywhere,
Damaging their faces of jade
And bumping their pretty heads.
Every one of them fled for her life;
All of them ran away to safety.

The women who had fled did not dare to shout as they did not want to disturb the king in the middle of the night, so they all hid trembling under the eaves of walls, where we shall leave them.

The monster, still in his seat of honour, thought for a moment then drank another bowl of wine, dragged the woman towards him, and took two more gory mouthfuls of her. While he was enjoying himself inside the palace the news was being spread outside that the Tang Priest was really a tiger spirit. The rumour spread like wildfire, and it soon reached the government hostel. Nobody else was there but the white horse, who was eating fodder from a trough. This horse had once been a young dragon prince from the Western Sea who as a punishment for offending against the Heavenly Code had lost his horns and scales and been turned into a white horse to carry Sanzang to the West to fetch the scriptures. When he heard it being said that the Tang Priest was a tiger spirit he thought, "'My master is clearly a good man. That evil spirit must have changed him into a tiger to harm him. Whatever shall I do? Monkey's been gone for ages, and there's no news of the other two." By the middle of the night he could wait no longer. He jumped up and said,

"If I don't rescue the Tang Priest I'll win no merit at all." He
could restrain himself no longer, so he snapped his halter, shook
his bridle and girths loose, and changed himself back into a
dragon. Then he went straight up on a black cloud to the Ninth
Heaven. There is a poem to prove it that goes:

> On his journey west to worship the Buddha
> Sanzang met an evil demon.
> Now that he had been changed into a tiger
> The white horse came to his rescue, trailing its halter.

From up in the air the dragon saw the bright lights in the
Hall of Silvery Peace, where eight wax candles were burning
on eight great candlesticks. Bringing his cloud down for a closer
look he saw the monster sitting by himself in the seat of honour
and drinking as he ate human flesh. "Hopeless beast," thought
the dragon with a grin, "giving his game away like that he's
ruined everything for himself! Eating people's a fine thing to
do! Now I know what has happened to our master: he's met
this foul ogre. I'll try to fool him. If it comes off there's still time
to rescue our master."

With a shake the splendid dragon king turned himself into
a slim and seductive Palace Beauty. Hurrying inside he greeted
the ogre and said, "If you spare my life, Your Highness, I'll hold
your cup for you." "Pour me out more wine," he said. The
young dragon took the pot and used a Water-controlling Spell
to fill his cup so full that the wine stood half an inch higher
than the rim without spilling. The monster, who did not know
this piece of magic, was delighted with the trick; and when the
dragon asked, "Shall I fill it higher still?" he replied, "Yes,
yes." The dragon lifted the pot and poured and poured.
The wine rose till it towered as tall as a thirteen-storeyed
pagoda, and still hardly any spilled over. The ogre opened his
mouth wide and swallowed the lot, then pulled the dead girl
towards him and took another bite. "Can you sing?" he asked,
and the dragon replied, "Yes, in a way." He sang a short song
and handed the ogre another cup of wine. "Can you dance?"
the ogre asked. "Yes, in a way," he replied, "but I can't dance

well empty-handed." The ogre pushed his robe aside, brought out the sword he wore at his waist, unsheathed it, and handed it to the dragon, who took it and did a sword dance in front of the banqueting table.

As the monster gazed pop-eyed the dragon stopped dancing and hacked at his face. The ogre side-stepped and immediately seized a cast-iron candlestick that must have weighed a good hundred weight with its stand with which to parry the sword. As the pair of them came out of the Hall of Silvery Peace, the dragon reverted to his true form and went up into mid-air on a cloud to continue the fight. It was a really vicious combat:

> One was a monster born and bred on Bowl Mountain;
> The other was a dragon exiled from the Western Sea.
> One shone as if he were breathing out lightning;
> The other's vigour seemed to burst through the clouds.
> One was like a white-tusked elephant in a crowd;
> The other was a golden-clawed wildcat leaping down
>   to earth.
> One was a pillar of jade, towering to heaven,
> The other was one of the ocean's golden beams.
> The silver dragon danced,
> The yellow monster soared,
> As the blade cut tirelessly to left and right,
> And the lantern flashed to and fro without a pause.

The old monster was as strong as ever, after eight or nine rounds of their battle in the clouds the young dragon was tiring and unable to keep up the fight, so he hurled his sword at the monster. The ogre used a magic trick to catch it, went for the helpless dragon, throwing the candlestick at him and hitting him on the hind leg. The dragon brought his cloud straight down to earth, where the canal in the palace saved his life: once he had dived in, the ogre could not find him. Instead he went back to the Hall of Silvery Peace, clutching the sword and the candlestick. There he drank himself to sleep.

The dragon hid at the bottom of the canal for an hour, by which time all was quiet. Gritting his teeth against the pain

from his leg, he leapt out of the water and went back to the
hostel on a black cloud, where he turned himself back into a
horse and bent over the trough once more. The poor animal
was covered with sweat, and his leg was scarred.

> The Thought-horse and the Mind-ape had scattered,
> The Lord of Metal and the Mother of Wood were dis-
>   persed.
> The Yellow Wife was damaged, her powers divided,
> The Way was finished, and how could it be saved?

We will leave Sanzang in danger and the dragon in defeat
to return to Pig who had been hiding in the undergrowth ever
since he abandoned Friar Sand. He had made himself a pigsty
there, and slept through to the middle of the night. When he
woke up he could not remember where he was. He rubbed his
eyes, pulled himself together, and cocked up his ear. In these
wild mountains no dogs barked and no cocks crowed. From
the position of the stars he worked out that it was around
midnight, and thought, "I must go back and rescue Friar Sand.
It's all too true that 'You cannot make thread with a single
strand, or clap with a single hand.' No, no. I'd better go back
to the city, see the master, and report on this to the king. He
can give me some more brave soldiers to help me rescue Friar
Sand."

The idiot went back to the city on his cloud as fast as he
could, and in an instant he was back at the hostel. It was a still,
moonlit night, and he could not find his master in either wing
of the building. There was only the white horse asleep there,
his body covered in sweat, and with a greenish wound the size
of a dish on his hind leg. "This is double trouble," thought Pig
in horror. "Why is this wretch covered with sweat and injured
on his leg? He hasn't been anywhere. Some crooks must have
carried off the master and wounded the horse." Seeing Pig,
the horse suddenly called out, "Elder brother." Pig collapsed
from shock, got up again, and was about to flee when the horse
took his clothes between his teeth and said, "Brother, don't be
afraid of me." "Why ever have you started to talk today?"

asked Pig, who was shaking all over. "Something terrible must have happened to make you do it." "Do you know that our master is in danger?" the horse asked. "No," Pig replied. "You wouldn't," said the horse. "When you and Friar Sand were showing off in front of the king you thought you'd be able to catch the monster and be rewarded for it. Little did you imagine that his powers would be too much for you. You should be ashamed of the way you've come back by yourself without even having any news to report. That monster turned himself into a handsome scholar, came to the palace, and made the king accept him as his son-in-law. He changed our master into a tiger, who was captured by the officials and put in a cage in the court waiting room. The news made me feel as if my heart were being sliced to pieces. It was already two days since you two went, and for all I knew you might have been killed, so I had to turn back into a dragon and try to rescue our master. When I reached the court I couldn't find him, though I saw the monster outside the Hall of Silvery Peace. I changed into a Palace Beauty to trick him. He made me do a sword dance for him, and when I had him fascinated I took a cut at him. He dodged the blow, picked up a giant candlestick in both hands, and soon had me on the run. I flung my sword at him, but he caught it, and wounded me on the hind leg by throwing the candlestick at me. I escaped with my life by hiding in the palace canal. The scar is where he hit me with the candlestick."

"Is this all true?" asked Pig. "Don't think I'm trying to fool you," said the dragon. "What are we to do?" said Pig. "Can you move?" "What if I can?" said the dragon. "If you can move," said Pig, "then make your way back to the sea. I'll take the luggage back to Gao Village and be a married man again." The dragon's reaction to this was to bite hard on Pig's tunic and not let him go. Tears rolled down his face as he said, "Please don't give up, elder brother." "What else can I do but give up?" said Pig. "Friar Sand's been captured by him, and I can't beat him, so what can we do but break up now?"

The dragon thought for a moment before replying, still in tears, "Don't even talk about breaking up, brother. All you

need do to rescue the master is to ask someone to come here."
"Who?" asked Pig. "Take a cloud back to the Mountain of
Flowers and Fruit as fast as you can, and ask our eldest brother
Monkey to come here. With his tremendous ability to beat demons he ought to be able to rescue the master and avenge our
defeat." "Can't we ask someone else?" said Pig. "He hasn't
been on the best of terms with me since he killed the White
Bone Spirit on White Tiger Ridge. He's angry with me for
encouraging the master to say the Band-tightening Spell. I only
meant it as a joke — how was I to know the old monk would
really say it and drive him away? Goodness knows how furious
he is with me. He definitely won't come. I'm no match for
him with my tongue, and if he's disrespectful enough to hit me
a few times with that murderous great cudgel of his, it'll be
the death of me." "Of course he won't hit you," said the
dragon. "He's a kind and decent Monkey King. When you
see him don't tell him that the master's in trouble. Just say, 'The
master's missing you.' Once you've lured him here and he sees
the situation he won't possibly be angry. He's bound to want
to fight the monster. I guarantee that he'll capture the monster
and save our master." "Oh well," said Pig, "oh well. As you're
so determined I'll have to go, or else I'll look half-hearted. If
Monkey's prepared to come, I'll come back with him; but if he
isn't, then don't expect me — I won't be back." "Go," said
the dragon. "I promise he'll come."

The idiot picked up his rake, straightened his tunic, leapt
up on a cloud, and headed east. Sanzang was fated to live. Pig
had a following wind, so he stuck up his ears for sails and was
at the Eastern Ocean in no time. He landed his cloud. Without
his noticing it the sun rose as he made his way into the mountains.

As he was going along he suddenly heard voices. He looked
carefully and saw Monkey in a mountain hollow with hordes
of demons. He was perched on a rock, and in front of him over
twelve hundred monkeys were drawn up in ranks and chanting,
"Long live His Majesty the Great Sage." "He's doing very
nicely," thought Pig, "very nicely indeed. No wonder he want-

ed to come home instead of staying a monk. He has it really nice here, with a big place like this and all those little monkeys at his beck and call. If I'd had a mountain like this I'd never have become a monk. But what am I to do now I'm here? I must go and see him." As he was rather overawed, Pig did not dare walk boldly over to see him. Instead he made his way round a grassy cliff, slipped in among the twelve hundred monkeys, and started to kowtow with them.

Little did he expect that the sharp-eyed Monkey would see him from his high throne and say, "There's a foreigner bowing all wrong among the ranks. Where's he from? Bring him here." The words were hardly out of his mouth before some junior monkeys swarmed round him, shoved him forward, and threw him to the ground. "Where are you from, foreigner?" asked Monkey. "If I may be permitted to argue," replied Pig, his head bowed, "I'm no foreigner. I'm an old friend of yours." "All my monkey hordes look exactly the same," replied the Great Sage, "but from the look of your stupid face you must be an evil demon from somewhere else. Never mind though. If, as an outsider, you want to join my ranks you must first hand in a curriculum vitae and tell us your name before we can put you on the books. If I don't take you on, you've no business to be bowing to me like a madman." Pig put his arms round his head, which he still kept low, and replied, "I'm sorry. It's an ugly mug. But you and I were brothers for several years; you can't pretend not to recognize me and say that I'm a foreigner." "Raise your head," said Monkey. The idiot did so and said, "Look even if you won't recognize the rest of me, you'll remember my face." "Pig!" said Monkey with a smile. When Pig heard this he leapt to his feet and said, "Yes, yes. I'm Pig," thinking that Monkey would be easier to deal with now he had recognized him.

"Why have you come here instead of going to fetch the scriptures with the Tang Priest?" Monkey asked. "Have you offended the master and been sent back too? Show me your letter of dismissal." "I haven't offended him," Pig replied. "He hasn't given me a letter of dismissal, or driven me away."

"Then why have you come here?" asked Monkey. "The master sent me here to ask you back as he's missing you," answered Pig. "He hasn't asked me back," said Monkey, "and he doesn't miss me. He swore an oath by Heaven and wrote a letter of dismissal, so he couldn't possibly miss me or have sent you all this way to ask me back. It certainly wouldn't be right for me to go." "He's really missing you," said Pig, lying desperately, "he really is." "Why?" asked Monkey. "He called out 'disciple' when he was riding along. I didn't hear, and Friar Sand is deaf, so he started missing you and saying that we two were hopeless. He said that you were intelligent and clever, and that you always answered whenever he called. This made him miss you so badly that he sent me over here specially to ask you to come back. Please, please come back with me. You'll save him from disappointment and me from a long, wasted journey." Monkey jumped down from his rock, lifted Pig to his feet, and said, "Dear brother, it's been good of you to come so far. Won't you come and take a look round with me?" "It's been a long journey," replied Pig, "and I'm afraid that the master would miss me, so I'd better not." "'Now that you're here," said Monkey, "you really should have a look at my mountain." Not wanting to insist too hard, the idiot went off with him.

The two of them walked hand in hand with the monkey horde following behind as they climbed to the summit of the Mountain of Flowers and Fruit. It was a beautiful mountain. In the few days since he had been back, Monkey had made it as neat as it ever had been.

> It was as green as flakes of malachite,
> So high it touched the clouds.
> All around it tigers crouched and dragons coiled,
> Amid the calls of apes and cranes.
> In the morning the peak was covered with cloud;
> The evening sun would set between the trees.
> The streams splashed like a tinkle of jade;
> Waterfalls tumbled with the sound of lutes.

In the front of the mountain were cliffs and rock-faces;
At the back were luxuriant plants and trees.
Above it reached to the Jade Girl's washing bowl;
Below it jointed the watershed of the River of Heaven.
In its combination of Earth and Heaven it rivalled the
*   Penglai paradise;*
Its blend of pure and solid made it a true cave palace.
It defied a painter's brush and colours;
Not even a master could have drawn it.
Intricate were the strange-shaped boulders,
Adorning the mountain peak.
In the sun's shadow shimmered a purple light;
A magical glow shone red throughout the sea of clouds.
Cave-heavens and paradises do exist on Earth,
Where the whole mountainside is covered with fresh
*   trees and new blossoms.*

As Pig gazed at it he said with delight, "What a wonderful place, brother. It's the finest mountain in the world." "Could you get by here?" asked Monkey. "What a question," said Pig with a grin. "This mountain of yours is an earthly paradise, so how could you talk about getting by?" The two talked and joked for a while then went back down. They saw some young monkeys kneeling beside the path and holding huge, purple grapes, fragrant dates and pears, deep golden loquats, and rich, red tree-strawberries. "Please take some breakfast, Your Majesty," they said. "Brother Pig," replied Monkey with a smile, "your big appetite won't be satisfied with fruit. Never mind though — if you don't think it too poor you can eat a littele as a snack." "Although I do have a big appetite," said Pig, "I always eat the local food. Bring me a few to taste."

As the pair of them ate the fruit the sun was rising, which made the idiot worry that he might be too late to save the Tang Priest. "Brother," he said, trying to hurry Monkey up, "the master is waiting for us. He wants us back as soon as possible." "Come and look round the Water Curtain Cave," was Monkey's reply. "It's very good of you to offer," said Pig, "but I mustn't

keep the master waiting, so I'm afraid I can't visit the cave."
"Then I won't waste your time," said Monkey. "Goodbye."
"Aren't you coming?" Pig asked. "Where to?" Monkey replied. "There's nobody to interfere with me here and I'm free to do just as I like. Why should I stop having fun and be a monk? I'm not going. You can go and tell the Tang Priest that as he's driven me away he can just forget about me." The idiot did not dare press Monkey harder in case he lost his temper and hit him a couple of blows with his cudgel. All he could do was mumble a farewell and be on his way.

As Monkey watched him go he detailed two stealthy young monkeys to follow him and listen to anything he said. The idiot had gone hardly a mile down the mountainside when he turned round, pointed towards Monkey, and started to abuse him. "That ape," he said, "he'd rather be a monster than a monk. The baboon. I asked him in all good faith and he turned me down. Well, if you won't come, that's that." Every few paces he cursed him some more. The two young monkeys rushed back to report, "Your Majesty, that Pig is a disgrace. He's walking along cursing you." "Arrest him," shouted Monkey in a fury. The monkey hordes went after Pig, caught him, turned him up-side-down, grabbed his bristles, pulled his ears, tugged his tail, twisted his hair, and thus brought him back. If you don't know how he was dealt with or whether he survived, listen to the explanation in the next instalment.

Pig moves the Monkey King through
his goodness;
Sun the Novice subdues the ogre through
cunning.

They swore to become brothers,
And the Dharma brought them back to their true nature.
When Metal and Wood were tamed, the True Result
*   could be achieved;*
The Mind-ape and the Mother of Wood combined to
*   make the elixir.*
Together they would climb to the World of Bliss,
And share the unique faith.
The scriptures are the way of self-cultivation,
To which the Buddha has given his own divinity.
The brothers made up a triple alliance
With devilish powers to cope with the Five Elements.
Sweeping aside the six forms of existence,
They head for the Thunder Monastery.

As he was being dragged and carried back by the crowd of
monkeys, Pig's tunic was shreds. "I'm done for," he grumbled
to himself, "done for. He'll kill me now." Before long he was
back at the mouth of the cave, where Monkey, sitting on top of
a rockface, said to him angrily, "You chaff-guzzling idiot. I let
you go, so why swear at me?" "I never did, elder brother,"
said Pig on his knees, "May I bite off my tongue if ever I did.
All I said was that as you weren't coming I'd have to go and
tell the master. I'd never have dared to swear at you." "You
can't fool me," Monkey replied. "If I prick my left ear up I can
hear what they're saying in the Thirty-third Heaven, and if I

point my right ear down I can know what the Ten Kings of Hell and their judges are discussing. Of course I could hear you swearing at me as you walked along." "Now I see," said Pig. "With that devilish head of yours you must have changed yourself into something or other to listen to what I said." "Little ones," shouted Monkey, "bring some heavy rods. Give him twelve on the face, then twelve on the back. After that I'll finish him off with my iron cudgel." "Elder brother," pleaded Pig, kowtowing desperately, "I beg you to spare me for our master's sake." "That good and kind master? Never." said Monkey. "If he won't do," begged Pig, "then spare me for the Bodhisattva's sake." The mention of the Bodhisattva made Monkey relent slightly. "Now you've said that I won't have you flogged," he replied. "But you must tell me straight and without lying where the Tang Priest is in trouble — which is presumably why he sent you to try and trick me." "He isn't in trouble," Pig protested, "he's honestly missing you." "You really deserve a beating," said Monkey, "for still trying to hoodwink me, you moron. Although I've been back in the Water Curtain Cave, I've stayed with the pilgrim in my mind. The master must have been in trouble at every step he has taken. Tell me about it at once if you don't want that flogging." Pig kowtowed again and said, "Yes, I did try to trick you into coming back. I didn't realize that you would see through it so easily. Please spare me a flogging and let me go, then I'll tell you." "Very well then," replied Monkey, "get up and tell me." The junior monkeys untied his hands. He leapt to his feet and began looking around wildly. "What are you looking at?" asked Monkey. "I'm looking at that wide empty path for me to run away along," said Pig. "That wouldn't get you anywhere," Monkey said. "Even if I gave you three days' start I'd still be able to catch you up. Start talking. If you make me lose my temper, that'll be the end of you."

I'll tell you the truth," said Pig. "After you came back here Friar Sand and I escorted the master. When we saw a dark pine forest the master dismounted and told me to beg for some food. When I'd gone a very long way without finding anyone I was so tired that I took a snooze in the grass; I didn't realize that the master would send Friar Sand after me. You know how impatient the master is: he went off for a stroll by himself, and when he came out of the wood he saw a gleaming golden pagoda. He took it for a monastery, but an evil spirit called the Yellow-robed Monster who lived there captured him. When I and Friar Sand came back to find him, all we saw was the white horse and the baggage. The master had gone. We searched for him as far as the entrance to the cave and fought the monster. Luckily the master found someone to save him in the cave. She was the third daughter of the king of Elephantia and she'd been carried off by the monster. She gave the master a letter to deliver to her family and persuaded the ogre to let him go. When we reached the capital and delivered the letter the king asked our master to subdue the monster and bring the princess home. I ask you, brother, could the master catch a monster? We two went off to fight him, but his powers were too much for us: he captured Friar Sand and made me run away. I hid in the undergrowth. The monster turned himself into a handsome scholar and went to court, where he introduced himself to the king and turned the master into a tiger. The white horse changed himself back into a dragon in the middle of the night and went to look for the master. He didn't find him, but he did see the monster drinking in the Hall of Silvery Peace, so he turned himself into a Palace Beauty. He poured wine and did a sword dance for the ogre in the hope of finding a chance to cut him down, but the ogre wounded his hind leg with a candlestick. It was the white horse who sent me here to fetch you. 'Our eldest brother is a good and honourable gentleman,' he said, 'and gentlemen don't bear grudges. He's sure to come and rescue the master.' Please, please remember that 'if a man has been your teacher for a day, you should treat him as your father for the rest of his life'. I beg you to save him."

"Idiot," said Monkey, "I told you over and over again before leaving that if any evil monsters captured the master you were to tell them I am his senior disciple. Why didn't you mention me?" Pig reflected that to a warrior a challenge was more

effective than an invitation and said, "It would have been fine
if we hadn't used your name. It was only when I mentioned
you that he went wild." "What did you say?" asked Monkey.
"I said, 'Behave yourself, kind monster, and don't harm our
master. I have an elder brother called Brother Monkey who
is an expert demon-subduer with tremendous magic powers. If
he comes he'll kill you, and you won't even get a funeral.' This
made the ogre angrier than ever, and he said, 'I'm not scared
of Monkey. If he comes here I'll skin him, tear his sinews out,
gnaw his bones, and eat his heart. Although monkeys are on the
skinny side, I can mince his flesh up and deep-fry it.' " This so
enraged Monkey that he leapt around in a fury, tugging at his
ear and scratching his cheek. "Did he have the bloody cheek
to say *that* about me?" he asked. "Calm down, brother," said
Pig. "I specially remembered all his insults so as to tell you."
"Up you get," said Monkey, "I didn't have to go before, but
now he's insulted me I've got to capture him. Let's be off.
When I wrecked the Heavenly Palace five hundred years ago
all the generals of Heaven bowed low at the sight of me and
called me 'Great Sage'. How dare that fiend have the nerve to
insult me behind my back! I'm going to catch him and tear his
corpse to shreds to make him pay for it. When I've done that
I'll come back here." "Quite right," said Pig. "When you've
captured the monster and got your own back on him, it'll be
up to you whether you come on with us."

The Great Sage jumped down from the cliff, rushed into the
cave, and took off all his devil clothes. He put on an embroidered tunic, tied on his tigerskin kilt, seized his iron cudgel,
and came out again. His panic-stricken monkey subjects tried
to stop him, saying, "Where are you going, Your Majesty, Great
Sage? Wouldn't it be fun to rule us for a few more years?"
"What are you saying, little ones?" replied Monkey. "I have to
protect the Tang Priest. Everyone in Heaven and Earth knows
that I'm the Tang Priest's disciple. He didn't really drive me
away. He just wanted me to take a trip home and have a little
relaxation. Now I've got to attend to this. You must all take
good care of our household. Plant willow and pine cuttings at

the right season, and don't let things go to pieces. I must escort the Tang Priest while he fetches the scriptures and returns to the East. When my mission is over I'll come back to this happy life with you here." The monkeys all accepted his orders.

Taking Pig's hand, Monkey mounted a cloud and left the cave. When they had crossed the Eastern Sea he stooped at the western shore and said, "You carry on at your own speed while I take a bath in the sea." "We're in a terrible hurry," said Pig. "You can't take a bath now?" "You wouldn't understand," Monkey replied. "While I was at home I developed rather a devil-stink, and I'm afraid that with his passion for cleanliness the master would object." Only then did Pig realize that Monkey really was being sincere and single-minded.

After Monkey's dip they were back on their clouds and heading west again. When they saw the gleam of the golden pagoda Pig pointed at it and said, "That's where the Yellow-robed Monster lives. Friar Sand is still there." "You wait for me up here," said Monkey, "while I take a look around the entrance before fighting the evil spirit." "No need," said Pig, "as he's not at home." "I know," said Monkey. The splendid Monkey King landed his gleaming cloud and looked around outside the entrance. All he could see was two children, one of about ten and the other of eight or nine, hitting a feather-stuffed ball with curved sticks. Without bothering to find out whose children they were, Monkey rushed up at them as they played, grabbed them by the tufts of hair that grew on the top of their heads, and flew off with them. The sobs and curses of the terrified boys alarmed the junior devils of the Moon Waters Cave, who rushed in to tell the princess that someone, they did not know who, had carried her sons off. These boys, you see, were the children of the princess and the ogre.

The princess ran out of the cave to see Monkey holding her sons on the top of a cliff and about to hurl them over.

"Hey, you, I've never done you any harm," she screamed desperately, "so why are you kidnapping my sons? Their father won't let you get away with it if anything happens to them, and he's a killer." "Don't you know who I am?" said Monkey.

"I'm Monkey, the senior disciple of the Tang Priest. If you release my brother Friar Sand from your cave, I'll give you your sons back. You'll be getting a good bargain — two for one." The princess hurried back into the cave, told the junior demons who were on the door to get out of her way, and untied Friar Sand with her own hands. "Don't let me go, lady," said Friar Sand, "or I'll be letting you in for trouble with that monster when he comes back and askes about me." "Venerable sir," the princess replied, "what you said about the letter saved my life, so I was going to let you go anyhow, and now your elder brother Monkey has come here and told me to release you."

At the word "Monkey" Friar Sand felt as though the oil of enlightenment had been poured on his head and the sweet dew had enriched his heart. His face was all happiness and his chest filled with spring. He looked like someone who has heard that a friend has arrived, or like someone who has found a piece of gold or jade. He brushed his clothes down with his hands, went out, bowed to Monkey and said, "Brother, you've dropped right out of the blue. I beg you to save my life." "Did you say one word to help me, Brother Sand, when the master said the Band-tightening Spell?" asked Monkey with a grin. "Talk, talk, talk. If you want to rescue your master you should be heading west instead of squatting here." "Please don't bring that up," said Friar Sand. "A gentleman doesn't bear a grudge. We've been beaten, and we've lost the right to talk about courage. Please rescue me." "Come up here," Monkey replied, and Friar Sand sprang up on the cliff with a bound.

When Pig saw from up in the air that Friar Sand had come out of the cave, he brought his cloud down and said, "Forgive me, forgive me, Brother Sand." "Where have you come from?" asked Friar Sand on seeing him. "After I was beaten yesterday," said Pig, "I went back to the capital last night and met the white horse, who told me that the master was in trouble. The monster has magicked him into a tiger. The horse and I talked it over and we decided to ask our eldest brother back." "Stop chattering, idiot," said Monkey. "Each of you take one of these children to the city. Use them to provoke the monster into coming back here to fight me." "How are we to do that?" asked Friar Sand. "You two ride your clouds, till you're above the palace," said Monkey, "harden your hearts, and drop the children on the palace steps. When you're asked, say they're the sons of the Yellow-robed Monster, and that you two brought them there. The ogre is bound to come back when he hears that, which will save me the trouble of going into town to fight him. If we fought in the city, the fogs and dust storms we stirred up would alarm the court, the officials and the common people." "Whatever you do, brother," said Pig with a laugh, "you try to trick us." "How am I tricking you?" asked Monkey. "These two kids have already been scared out of their wits," Pig replied. "They've cried themselves hoarse, and they're going to be killed at any moment. Do you think the monster will let us get away after we've smashed them to mince? He'll want our necks. While you get away scot free, with not even a witness against you. It's obvious you're tricking us." "If he goes for you," said Monkey, "fight your way back here, where there's plenty of room for me to have it out with him." "That's right," said Friar Sand, "what our eldest brother says is quite right. Let's go." The pair of them were an awe-inspiring sight as they went off, carrying the two boys.

Monkey then jumped down from the cliff to the ground in front of the pagoda's gates, where the princess said to him, "You faithless monk. You said you'd give me back my children if I released your brother. Now I've let him go, but you still have the boys. What have you come back for?" "Don't be angry, princess," said Monkey, forcing a smile. "As you've been here so long, we've taken your sons to meet their grandfather." "Don't try any nonsense, monk," said the princess. "My husband Yellow Robe is no ordinary man. If you've frightened those children, you'd better calm them down."

"Princess," said Monkey with a smile, "do you know what's the worst crime you can commit on earth?" "Yes," she replied. "You're a mere woman, so you don't understand anything," said Monkey. "I was educated by my parents in the palace ever since I was a child," she said, "and I remember what the ancient book said: "There are three thousand crimes, and the greatest is unfilial behaviour.' " "But you're unfilial," replied Monkey. " 'My father begot me, my mother raised me. Alas for my parents. What an effort it was to bring me up.' Filial piety is the basis of all conduct and the root of all goodness, so why did you marry an evil spirit and forget your parents? Surely this is the crime of unfilial behaviour." At this the princess' face went red as she was overcome with shame. "What you say, sir, is so right," she said. "Of course I haven't forgotten my parents. But the monster forced me to come here, and he is so strict that I can hardly move a step. Besides, it's a long journey and nobody could deliver a message. I was going to kill myself until I thought that my parents would never discover that I hadn't run away deliberately. So I had nothing for it but to drag out my wretched life. I must be the wickedest person on earth." As she spoke the tears gushed out like the waters of a spring. "Don't take on so, princess," said Monkey. "Pig has told me how you saved my master's life and wrote a letter, which showed you hadn't forgotten your parents. I promise that I'll catch the monster, take you back to see your father, and find you a good husband. Then you can look after your parents for the rest of their lives. What do you say to that?" "Please don't get yourself killed, monk," she said. "Your two fine brothers couldn't beat Yellow Robe, so how can you talk about such a thing, you skinny little wretch, all gristle and no bone? You're like a crab, the way your bones all stick out. You don't have any magic powers, so don't talk about capturing ogres." "What a poor judge of people you are," laughed Monkey. "As the saying goes, 'A bubble of piss is big but light, and a steelyard weight can counterbalance a ton.' Those two are big but useless. Their bulk slows them down in the wind as they walk, they cost the earth to clothe, they're hollow inside, like fire in a stove, they are weak and they give no return for all the food they eat. I may be small, but I'm very good value." "Have you really got magic powers?" the princess asked. "You've never seen such magic as I have," he replied. "I have no rival when it comes to subduing monsters and demons."

"Are you sure you won't let me down?" said the princess. "Yes," said Monkey. "As you're so good at putting down demons, how are you going to catch this one?" "Hide yourself away and keep out of my sight," said Monkey. "Otherwise I may not be able to deal with him properly when he comes back. I'm afraid you may feel more friendly towards him and want to keep him." "Of course I won't want to keep him," she protested. "I've only stayed here under duress." "You've been his wife for thirteen years," said Monkey, "so you must have some affection for him. When I meet him it won't be for a child's game. I shall have to kill him with my cudgel and my fists before you can be taken back to court."

The princess did as she had been told and went off to hide in a quiet place. As her marriage was fated to end she had met the Great Sage. Now that the princess was out of the way the Monkey King turned himself with a shake of his body into the very image of the princess and went back into the cave to wait for the ogre.

Pig and Friar Sand took the children to the city of Elephantia and hurled them down on the palace steps, where the wretched boys were smashed to mincemeat; their blood splashed out and their bones were pulverized. The panic-stricken courtiers announced that a terrible thing had happened — two people had been thrown down from the sky. "The children are the sons of the Yellow-robed Monster," shouted Pig at the top of his voice, "and they were brought here by Pig and Friar Sand."

The monster, who was still asleep in the Hall of Silvery Peace, heard someone calling his name as he was dreaming, turned over, and looked up to see Pig and Friar Sand shouting from the clouds. "I'm not bothered about Pig," he thought, "but Friar Sand was tied up at home. However did he escape? Could my wife have let him go? How did he get to catch my sons? Perhaps this is a trick Pig is using to catch me because I won't come out and fight with him. If I'm taken in by this I'll have to fight him, and I'm still the worse for wear after all that wine. One blow from his rake would finish off my prestige and my plan would be given away. I'll go home and see whether they are my sons before arguing with them."

Without taking leave of the king, the monster went back across the forested mountains to his cave to find out what had happened. By now the palace knew he was an evil spirit. The seventeen other women who had fled for their lives when he ate the Palace Beauty had told the king all about it early the next morning, and his unannounced departure made it even clearer that he was an ogre. The king told the officials to look after the false tiger.

When Monkey saw the monster coming back to the cave he thought of a way to trick him. He blinked till the tears came down like rain, started to wail for the children, and jumped and beat his breasts as if in grief, filling the cave with the sound of his sobbing. The monster failed to recognize who Monkey really was and put his arms round him. "What makes you so miserable, wife?" he asked. "Husband," said Monkey, weeping as he concocted his devilish lies, "How true it is that 'A man without a wife has no one to look after his property; a woman who loses her husband is bound to fail'. Why didn't you come back yesterday after going to the city to meet your father-in-law? Pig came and seized Friar Sand this morning, and then they grabbed our sons and refused to spare them despite all my pleas. They said they were taking them to the palace to meet their grandfather, but I haven't seen them all day. I don't know what's become of them, and you were away. I've been so miserable at losing them that I can't stop crying." The monster was furious. "My sons?" he asked. "Yes," Monkey replied, "Pig carried them off."

The monster, now jumping with rage, said, "Right that's it. He's killed my sons. He'll die for this. I'll make that monk pay for it with his life. Don't cry, wife. How are you feeling now? Let me make you better." "There's nothing wrong with me," said Monkey, "except that I've cried so much my heart aches." "Never mind," the monster replied. "Come over here. I've got a treasure here that you just have to rub on your pain to stop it hurting. But be very careful with it and don't flick it with your thumb, because if you do you'll be able to see my real body." Monkey was secretly delighted. "What a well-behaved fiend," he thought, "giving that away without even being tortured. When he gives me the treasure I'll flick it to see what kind of monster he really is." The ogre then led him to a remote and secluded part of the cave and spat out a treasure about the size of a hen's egg. It was a magic pill skilfully fashioned from a piece of a conglomeration of internal secretion. "What a splendid thing," Monkey thought. "Goodness knows how many times it had to be worked, refined and mated before becoming such a magic relic. Today it was fated to meet me." The ape took it, rubbed it over his pretended pain, and was just going to flick it with his thumb when the monster took fright and tried to grab it from him. The crafty Monkey popped it into his mouth and swallowed it. The monster clenched his fist, and hit at him, but Monkey parried the blow, rubbed his face, and reverted to his real form with a shout of, "Behave yourself, ogre. Take a look and see who I am."

"Wife," said the shocked monster, "however did you get that terrible face?" "I'll get you, you damned fiend," said Monkey. "I'm not your wife. Can't you even recognize your own grandfather?" The monster, now beginning to see the light, said, "You do look a bit familiar." "Take another look," said Monkey, "I won't hit you." "I know you by sight," the monster said, "but I can't remember your name. Who are you? Where are you from? Where have you hidden my wife? Why did you swindle me out of my treasure? This is a disgusting way to behave." "As you don't know who I am," said Monkey, "let me tell you that I am Sun Wukong, Brother Monkey, the Tang Priest's senior disciple. I'm your ancestor by a clear five hundred years." "Nonsense," the ogre replied, "nonsense. I know that the Tang Priest only had two disciples when I captured him. They were called Pig and Friar Sand. Nobody mentioned anyone by the name of Monkey. You must be a fiend from somewhere or other who has come to trick me." "I didn't come here with the other two," said Monkey, "because my master is a kind and merciful man who sent me back home

for killing too many evil spirits.   You ought to know your ancestors' name." "What sort of man are you?" asked the monster.
"How can you have the face to come back after your master
has sent you away?" ""You wouldn't understand, you damned
monster," said Monkey, "that when a man has been your teacher
for a single day, you should treat him as your father for the rest
of his life, and that father and son should never let the sun set
on a quarrel. You've harmed my master, so of course I've come
to rescue him. Even if I could ignore that, it's quite outrageous
that you insulted me behind my back." "I never insulted you,"
said the monster. "Pig told me you did," replied Monkey. "You
shouldn't believe that sharp-tongued old gossip," said the
monster. "Let's stop beating about the bush," said Monkey.
"You've treated me very shabbily for a guest from far away.
You may not have any wine or fine delicacies to feed me but
you do have a head, so stretch it out and let me hit it with my
cudgel — that'll do instead of tea."   The mention of hitting
made the monster bellow with laughter. "You've got it all
wrong this time, Monkey," he said, "You shouldn't have come
in if you wanted to fight me. I have over a hundred devils of
all sizes in here. Even if you were covered with arms you'd
never be able to fight your way out." "Nonsense," replied
Monkey. "Never mind a hundred or so — if you had thousands
or tens of thousands of them I'd only need to see them clearly
for my every blow to strike home. I'll wipe the lot of you out."

The monster at once ordered all the fiends and ogres in and
around the cave to muster with their weapons and put a close
blockade on all the doors. Monkey was delighted to see them,
and wielding his cudgel with both hands he shouted "Change!"
and suddenly had six arms and three heads. Then he shook
his gold-banded cudgel and turned it into three gold-banded
cudgels.   He went into action with his six arms and three
cudgels. He was a tiger in a sheepfold, a hawk in a chicken run.
The poor little demons had their heads smashed to pulp, while
their blood flowed like water. He rushed to and fro as if there
was nobody else there until only the old ogre was left. He followed Monkey outside and said, "Insolent ape. How dare you

come here and bully us?" Monkey turned, beckoned to him and
said, "Come here, come here. Let me win the credit for killing
you."

The monster struck at the head with his sword, and Monkey
riposted to the face with his cudgel. They fought it out amid
the mists on the mountain top.

> Mighty was the magic of the Great Sage,
> Awful the monster's power.
> One of them wielded an iron cudgel;
> The other, a sword of tempered steel.
> When the sword was raised it shone with a bright aura;
> The parrying cudgel was wreathed in cloud.
> They leapt to and fro protecting their heads,
> Turning and somersaulting over and over.
> One of them changed his face with every breeze,
> The other stood still and shook his body.
> One glared with fiery eyes as he stretched out his simian
>   arm,
> The other flashed his golden pupils as he twisted his
>   tigerish waist.
> They were locked in mortal combat
> As sword and cudgel struck without mercy.
> The Monkey King wielded his iron club according to the
>   martial classic,
> And the monster's swordplay followed the ancient
>   manuals.
> One was a demon king experienced in the black arts,
> The other used magical powers to protect the Tang
>   Priest.
> The ferocious Monkey King became fiercer than ever,
> The heroic monster grew an even greater hero.
> They fought in space, ignoring death,
> All because the Tang Priest went to see the Buddha.

They had fought fifty or sixty rounds without issue when
Monkey thought, "That bloody monster's sword is as good as
my cudgel. I'll pretend to give him an opening and see if he

can tell it's a trick." The Monkey King raised his cudgel and did a "Reaching Up to a Tall Horse" movement. The monster, not realizing that this was a trick, and imagining that he saw a real opening, took a tremendous swipe at Monkey with his sword. Monkey at once did a high swing to avoid the blow, then struck at the monster's head with a "Stealing a Peach from under the Leaves" movement and knocked him so hard he vanished without a trace. Monkey put his cudgel away and looked for him but without success. "Wow," exclaimed Monkey in astonishment, "I didn't just hit him — I knocked him out of existence. But if I really killed him there ought at least to be some blood and pus, and there's no sign of any. Perhaps he got away." He leapt up on a cloud to look around, but nothing was moving. "My eyes can see anything at a glance," he thought, "so how can he have got away so mysteriously? Now I see. He said he seemed to recognize me, so he can't be an ordinary monster. He must be some spirit from Heaven."

This was too much for Monkey, who lost his temper and somersaulted up to the Southern Gate of Heaven with his cudgel in his hands. The startled Heavenly Generals Pang, Liu, Gou, Bi, Zhang, Tao, Deng, and Xin bowed low on either side of the gateway, not daring to block his way. They let him fight his way through the gates and straight on to the Hall of Universal Brightness, where the four great Heavenly Teachers Zhang, Ge, Xu and Qiu asked, "What have you come for, Great Sage?" "As I was escorting the Tang Priest to Elephantia an evil monster abducted a princess and harmed the master. I had to fight him, and in the middle of our battle he disappeared. I thought that he couldn't be an ordinary monster and was probably a spirit from Heaven, so I've come to check up if any wicked deities have left their posts." On hearing this the Heavenly Teachers went and reported it to the Jade Emperor in the Hall of Miraculous Mist. He ordered an investigation. They found that nobody was missing among the Nine Bright Shiners, the Gods of the Twelve Branches, the five Dippers of North, South, East, West and Centre, the hosts of the Milky Way, the Five Peaks, the Four Rivers, and all the other gods.

of Heaven. Then they investigated outside the Palace of the Dipper and the Bull, and found that one of the Twenty-eight Constellations, the Strider, was missing.

"Strider, the Wooden, Wolf, has gone down to Earth," they reported to the throne. "How long has he been away from Heaven?" the Jade Emperor asked. "He has missed four roll-calls," they replied, "and with one roll-call every three days that makes thirteen days." "Thirteen days in Heaven would be thirteen years down on Earth," said the emperor, and he ordered the Strider's fellow stars to go down and bring him back to Heaven.

On receiving this edict the twenty-seven other constellations went out through the gates of Heaven and startled the Strider as each chanted his own spell. Do you know where he had been hiding? He had been one of the heavenly generals who was beaten when Monkey had sacked the Heavenly Palace, and he had lain low in a mountain stream that masked his demonic cloud and kept him out of sight. Only when he heard the other constellations shouting their spells did he dare to emerge from the water and go back to Heaven with them. The Great Sage was blocking the gates of Heaven and would have killed him but for the pleas of the other constellations, who saved him and escorted him to see the Jade Emperor. The monster now produced his golden tablet of office from his belt and kowtowed on the floor of the palace, admitting his guilt. "Strider the Wooden Wolf," said the Jade Emperor, "why did you go off by yourself instead of being content with the infinite beauty of Heaven?" "I deserve to die, Your Majesty," the Strider replied. "That daughter of the king of Elephantia was no ordinary mortal. She was a Jade Maiden in the Hall of Incense who wanted to have an affair with me. As we did not want to defile the Heavenly Palace she decided to become a mortal first and was reborn in a king's palace. Then I became an evil monster and occupied a mountain in order not to let her down. I carried her off to my cave, and we were man and wife for thirteen years. 'Every bite and every sip is pre-ordained,' as the saying goes, and now the Great Sage has succeeded in bringing me here."

The Jade Emperor withdrew his tablet of office and degraded him to be a menial helping Lord Lao Zi stoke his fires in the Tushita Palace while retaining his old pay. If he did well he would be restored to his previous post; if not, his sentence would be made heavier. Monkey was delighted to see how the Jade Emperor dealt with him, and chanting a "re-e-er" of respect he said to the assembled gods, "Gentlemen, I'm off." "That monkey is as ill-mannered as ever," chuckled the Heavenly Teachers, "just chanting a 're-e-er' and going without thanking Your Majesty for your celestial kindness in catching the monster for him." "We can consider ourselves fortunate," said the Jade Emperor, "if he leaves without disturbing the peace of Heaven."

The Great Sage brought his shining cloud straight down to the Moon Waters Cave on Bowl Mountain, found the princess, and told her off for becoming a mortal and marrying a fiend. As he was doing this he heard Pig and Friar Sand shouting in mid-air, "Leave us a few demons to polish off, brother." "I've already wiped them out," Monkey replied. "Doesn't matter," said Friar Sand. "Let's take the princess back to the palace. Don't open your eyes, brothers. We'll travel by distance-shortening magic."

The princess heard a rush of wind in her ears, and in a moment she was back in the city. The three disciples took her to the throne hall, where she bowed to her royal parents and met her sisters again. All the officials came to bow to greet her. Then she reported, "We are indebted to the infinite powers of the venerable Monkey for the defeat of the Yellow-robed Monster and my rescue." "What type of monster was he?" the king asked. "Your Majesty's son-in-law," Monkey replied, "is the Strider constellation from Heaven, and your daughter was a Jade Maiden who held the incense until she decided to become a mortal and came down to this world. This marriage was predestined. When I went up to the Heavenly Palace and submitted a memorial to him, the Jade Emperor found that the monster had missed four roll-calls and had been away from heaven for thirteen days, which is thirteen years down here on earth. The emperor sent his fellow stars down to fetch him, then banished him to the Tushita Heaven, where he is to redeem his sins. That's how I rescued your daughter and brought her here." The king thanked Monkey and told him to go and see his master.

The three disciples left the throne hall and went with all the courtiers to the antechamber, where the iron cage was carried in and the false tiger unchained. Monkey was the only one who could see that he was human; all the others thought he was really a tiger. As Sanzang was under the demon's spell he could not move, and although he was clear in his mind, he was unable to open his mouth or his eyes. "What a fine monk you are, Master," said Monkey, "getting yourself into this revolting shape. You accused me of being a murderer and sent me home for it, but you wouldn't be such an awful sight if your heart had been set on goodness." "Save him, brother, don't tell him off," said Pig. "It was you who put him up to it all," said Monkey. "You were his favourite disciple. Why didn't you save him instead of sending for me? Besides, I told you that I'd go back when I'd defeated the monster and avenged that insult." Friar Sand went over and knelt down before him. "As the old saying goes," he pleaded, " 'If you won't do it for the monk's sake, do it for the Buddha's sake.' I beg you to save him now that you're here. I wouldn't have gone all that way to ask you to come if we'd been able to save him ourselves." "I couldn't bear not to save him," replied Monkey, raising Friar Sand to his feet. "Bring me some water." Pig flew back to the hostel, fetched the horse and luggage, took the golden begging bowl from it, half-filled it with water, and handed it to Monkey. Monkey took the water in his hand, said the words of a spell, and spurted it at the tiger's head. The evil magic was dissolved, and the tiger-aura was dispersed.

Sanzang was seen in his true form once more. Once he had gathered himself together and opened his eyes he saw Monkey, took hold of him, and said, "Monkey, where have you come from?" Friar Sand, who was standing in attendance, told him all about how Monkey had been asked back, defeated the monster, rescued the princess, dispersed the tiger-aura, and come back to the palace. "Worthy disciple," said Sanzang, full of gratitude, "thank you, thank you. When we return to the East from our journey to the West I shall report to the Tang Emperor that you have won the greatest distinction." "Don't mention it," said a smiling Monkey, "don't mention it. The best way you can show your gratitude is by not saying that spell." When the king heard about all this he thanked the four of them and gave a great vegetarian banquet for them in the eastern wing. After this expression of the king's kindness master and disciples took their leave of him and set out for the West. The king and his courtiers came a long way to see them off, after which

> *The monarch returned to the palace to rule his country,*
> *The monk went on to Thunder Monastery to see the Buddha.*

If you don't know what happened next or when they reached the Western Heaven, listen to the explanation in the next instalment.

图书在版编目(CIP)数据

西游记 第一卷:英文/(明)吴承恩著.—
北京:外文出版社,1995
ISBN 7 – 119 – 00653 – 3

Ⅰ.西… Ⅱ.吴… Ⅲ.古典小说:章回小说—中国
—古代—英文 Ⅳ.I242.4

中国版本图书馆 CIP 数据核字 (95) 第 08464 号

西游记
(一)

吴承恩 著

*

©外文出版社

外文出版社出版

(中国北京百万庄路 24 号)

邮政编码 100037

北京外文印刷厂印刷

中国国际图书贸易总公司发行

(中国北京车公庄西路 35 号)

北京邮政信箱第 399 号 邮政编码 100044

1982 年(28 开)第一版

1995 年第二版二次印刷

(英)

ISBN 7 – 119 – 00653 – 3 /I·84(外)

03480

10 – E – 1610SA